The Broadview Anthology of SHORT FICTION

THE BROADVIEW ANTHOLOGY OF SHORT FICTION

second edition

EDITED BY
JULIA GAUNCE,
SUZETTE MAYR,
DON LEPAN,
MARJORIE MATHER, &
BRYANNE MILLER

broadview press

Library and Archives Canada Cataloguing in Publication

The Broadview anthology of short fiction / edited by Julia Gaunce ... [et al.]. — 2nd ed.

Includes bibliographical references.
ISBN 978-1-55481-076-5

1. Short stories, English. 2. Short stories, American.
I. Gaunce, Julia, 1965- II. Title: Anthology of short fiction.

PS648.S5B76 2012 823'.0108 C2012-903786-9

Broadview Press is an independent, international publishing house, incorporated in 1985.

We welcome comments and suggestions regarding any aspect of our publications—please feel free to contact us at the addresses below or at broadview@broadviewpress.com.

North America
PO Box 1243, Peterborough, Ontario, Canada K9J 7H5
2215 Kenmore Ave., Buffalo, New York, USA 14207
Tel: (705) 743-8990; Fax: (705) 743-8353
email: customerservice@broadviewpress.com

UK, Europe, Central Asia, Middle East, Africa, India, and Southeast Asia
Eurospan Group, 3 Henrietta St., London WC2E 8LU, United Kingdom
Tel: 44 (0) 1767 604972; Fax: 44 (0) 1767 601640
email: eurospan@turpin-distribution.com

Australia and New Zealand
NewSouth Books
c/o TL Distribution, 15-23 Helles Ave., Moorebank, NSW, Australia 2170
Tel: (02) 8778 9999; Fax: (02) 8778 9944
email: orders@tldistribution.com.au

www.broadviewpress.com

Broadview Press acknowledges the financial support of the Government of Canada through the Canada Book Fund for our publishing activities.

PRINTED IN CANADA

CONTENTS

For website selections, please visit
<http://sites.broadviewpress.com/shortfictionstudent>.

PREFACE

The Broadview Anthology of Short Fiction has been forged from competing desires: the desire for a truly concise and reasonably priced anthology, and the desire for a genuinely wide-ranging selection of excellent writing. The volume has been designed with the demands of one-semester courses very much in mind; we have aimed for manageable proportions and broad genre representation. The thirty-nine stories range from the nineteenth to the twenty-first centuries. The selection includes examples of a broad spectrum of narrative styles—and the stories depict a broad spectrum of human experiences. The one quality we feel all the stories have in common is literary excellence.

Stories are organized chronologically by authors' birth dates, are lightly annotated for the undergraduate reader, and are prefaced by short introductions. Also included is a glossary of basic critical terms, with examples drawn in many cases from the stories included in the volume.

For the second edition we have expanded the number of stories included, not only to make space for recently published fiction but also to expand in two other areas. The first edition excluded translations entirely; this time around we were persuaded by the arguments of a number of academics that De Maupassant and Chekhov are such frequent and vitally important reference points whenever short fiction is taught that we should find a way to make space for them. Several instructors also suggested to us the inclusion of two or more stories by some authors, so that at least some writers can be studied in greater depth. That piece of advice we have also taken; the bound book anthology now includes two stories each by Poe, Joyce, Mansfield, and Munro. A second Hawthorne story and a third story by Joyce and by Poe are among the stories included on a new companion website[1] (where we have also posted some of the stories included in the first edition that we were unable to find space for this time).

1 See <http://sites.broadviewpress.com/shortfictionstudent>.

Neither Julia Gaunce nor Suzette Mayr was able to work on the second edition—but a great deal of the fine work they did for the first edition remains. As with the first edition, the selection of stories has been a collaborative venture, this time involving Marjorie Mather, Bryanne Miller, and me, in consultation with a number of others. Nora Ruddock contributed very significantly to the drafting of introductions to the authors new to this volume, and Tim Patterson assisted with research. We would also like to thank the academics who provided valuable comments and suggestions towards the shaping of the second edition, among them Deborah Burnham, Stephen Cain, Adrienne Eastwood, Danine Farquharson, Theresa Flowers, Roberta Jackson, Jasmine Kitses, Carrie Nartker, Claudia Ricci, Morgan Rooney, Roger Schlobin, Deanna Smid, Judy R. Smith, Karen Stein, Elizabeth Templeman, Andrea Westcott, and Erin Wunker.

We would like to acknowledge others who contributed to the first edition, including Allyson Foster, Lesley Jeannotte, Craig Lawson, Jennifer McCue, Kathleen Renne, Tammy Roberts, and Tania Therien.

If you have comments about either the selections or the presentation of this anthology, we encourage you to write to us at broadview@broadviewpress.com.

Don LePan

NATHANIEL HAWTHORNE

Among Nathaniel Hawthorne's paternal ancestors was one of the judges who participated in the 1692 Salem witch trials; on his mother's side, rumours of incest and public shaming that occurred generations before circulated in the family. Thomas E. Connolly has suggested that a "deep family guilt settled upon [Hawthorne], and this guilt undoubtedly prompted him to critical attacks in his literary works on the rigours of Puritanism." Whether or not it was Hawthorne's "family guilt" that drove him to write what he did, a number of his works are concerned with exposing the hypocrisy of Puritan culture—among them, the short stories "Young Goodman Brown" and "The Minister's Black Veil," and his best-known novel, *The Scarlet Letter* (1850).

Hawthorne was born in 1804 in Salem, Massachusetts. His sea captain father died of yellow fever while in Suriname when Hawthorne was only four years old. His mother then moved him and his two sisters to her family home, where he was raised among his eight unmarried aunts and uncles, and where he had a large library at his disposal. At the age of nine, an injury to his foot required him to stop attending school; he spent much of the three years it took him to recuperate reading his favourite authors—among them Edmund Spenser and William Shakespeare. From 1821 to 1825, Hawthorne attended Bowdoin College, where he counted Franklin Pierce and Henry Wadsworth Longfellow among his colleagues. He was not a brilliant student—he came in eighteenth in a class of thirty-eight and was once fined for playing cards.

Hawthorne returned home to Salem after graduation to live with his mother and devote himself to his writing. During this time he wrote work that was often rejected (he burned the manuscript for one short story collection in frustration). In 1828 he privately published anonymously and at his own expense *Fanshawe*, a work he would later refuse to acknowledge or reprint. He published stories anonymously in various periodicals, and in 1837 his friend Horatio Bridge secretly gave a publisher $250 to publish Hawthorne's *Twice-Told Tales*, a collection of short stories. This collection was not widely noticed, though it received favourable reviews from Longfellow and from Edgar Allan Poe.

Hawthorne married Sophia Peabody in 1842, and they moved to a house once inhabited by the famous American writer Ralph Waldo Emerson in Concord called the Old Manse. It was here that he published a volume of short pieces entitled *Mosses from an Old Manse* in 1846. When Sophia gave birth to their two children in rapid succession, the Hawthornes struggled to meet the financial demands of their new family. During this time of financial hardship, Hawthorne concentrated his efforts on writing *The Scarlet Letter*, the book that would make his literary reputation. His novel *The House of Seven Gables* followed in 1851. He died in 1864 and was buried at Sleepy Hollow Cemetery in Concord, Massachusetts.

A story from *Twice Told Tales*, "The Minister's Black Veil" takes place in a town in Puritan New England. When the town Reverend appears one day wearing a black veil, a darkness sets in on the congregation as those within it are forced to grapple with the guilt, hypocrisy, and questions of morality that hover behind their own unseen veils.

The Minister's Black Veil *A Parable*

NATHANIEL HAWTHORNE

THE SEXTON[1] stood in the porch of Milford meeting-house, pulling busily at the bell-rope. The old people of the village came stooping along the street. Children, with bright faces, tripped merrily beside their parents, or mimicked a graver gait, in the conscious dignity of their Sunday clothes. Spruce bachelors looked sidelong at the pretty maidens, and fancied that the Sabbath sunshine made them prettier than on week days. When the throng had mostly streamed into the porch, the sexton began to toll the bell, keeping his eye on the Reverend Mr. Hooper's door. The first glimpse of the clergyman's figure was the signal for the bell to cease its summons.

"But what has good Parson Hooper got upon his face?" cried the sexton in astonishment.

All within hearing immediately turned about, and beheld the semblance of Mr. Hooper, pacing slowly his meditative way towards the meeting-house. With

1 An officer responsible for maintaining a church.

one accord they started, expressing more wonder than if some strange minister were coming to dust the cushions of Mr. Hooper's pulpit.

"Are you sure it is our parson?" inquired Goodman Gray of the sexton.

"Of a certainty it is good Mr. Hooper," replied the sexton. "He was to have exchanged pulpits with Parson Shute, of Westbury; but Parson Shute sent to excuse himself yesterday, being to preach a funeral sermon."

The cause of so much amazement may appear sufficiently slight. Mr. Hooper, a gentlemanly person, of about thirty, though still a bachelor, was dressed with due clerical neatness, as if a careful wife had starched his band, and brushed the weekly dust from his Sunday's garb. There was but one thing remarkable in his appearance. Swathed about his forehead, and hanging down over his face, so low as to be shaken by his breath, Mr. Hooper had on a black veil. On a nearer view it seemed to consist of two folds of crape, which entirely concealed his features, except the mouth and chin, but probably did not intercept his sight, further than to give a darkened aspect to all living and inanimate things. With this gloomy shade before him, good Mr. Hooper walked onward, at a slow and quiet pace, stooping somewhat, and looking on the ground, as is customary with abstracted men, yet nodding kindly to those of his parishioners who still waited on the meeting-house steps. But so wonder-struck were they that his greeting hardly met with a return.

"I can't really feel as if good Mr. Hooper's face was behind that piece of crape," said the sexton.

"I don't like it," muttered an old woman, as she hobbled into the meeting-house. "He has changed himself into something awful, only by hiding his face."

"Our parson has gone mad!" cried Goodman Gray, following him across the threshold.

A rumor of some unaccountable phenomenon had preceded Mr. Hooper into the meeting-house, and set all the congregation astir. Few could refrain from twisting their heads towards the door; many stood upright, and turned directly about; while several little boys clambered upon the seats, and came down again with a terrible racket. There was a general bustle, a rustling of the women's gowns and shuffling of the men's feet, greatly at variance with that hushed repose which should attend the entrance of the minister. But Mr. Hooper appeared not to notice the perturbation of his people. He entered with an almost noiseless step, bent his head mildly to the pews on each side, and bowed as he passed his oldest parishioner, a white-haired great-grandsire, who occupied an arm-chair in the centre of the aisle. It was strange to observe how slowly this venerable man became conscious of something singular in the appearance of his pastor. He seemed not fully to partake of the prevailing wonder, till Mr. Hooper had ascended the stairs, and showed himself in the pulpit, face to face with his congregation, except for the black veil. That mysterious emblem was never once withdrawn. It shook with his measured breath, as he gave out the psalm; it threw its obscurity between him and the holy page, as he read the Scriptures; and while he prayed, the veil lay heavily on his uplifted countenance. Did he seek to hide it from the dread Being whom he was addressing?

Such was the effect of this simple piece of crape, that more than one woman of delicate nerves was forced to leave the meeting-house. Yet perhaps the pale-faced congregation was almost as fearful a sight to the minister, as his black veil to them.

Mr. Hooper had the reputation of a good preacher, but not an energetic one: he strove to win his people heavenward by mild, persuasive influences, rather than to drive them thither by the thunders of the Word. The sermon which he now delivered was marked by the same characteristics of style and manner as the general series of his pulpit oratory. But there was something, either in the sentiment of the discourse itself, or in the imagination of the auditors, which made it greatly the most powerful effort that they had ever heard from their pastor's lips. It was tinged, rather more darkly than usual, with the gentle gloom of Mr. Hooper's temperament. The subject had reference to secret sin, and those sad mysteries which we hide from our nearest and dearest, and would fain conceal from our own consciousness, even forgetting that the Omniscient can detect them. A subtle power was breathed into his words. Each member of the congregation, the most innocent girl, and the man of hardened breast, felt as if the preacher had crept upon them, behind his awful veil, and discovered their hoarded iniquity of deed or thought. Many spread their clasped hands on their bosoms. There was nothing terrible in what Mr. Hooper said, at least, no violence; and yet, with every tremor of his melancholy voice, the hearers quaked. An unsought pathos came hand in hand with awe. So sensible were the audience of some unwonted attribute in their minister, that they longed for a breath of wind to blow aside the veil, almost believing that a stranger's visage would be discovered, though the form, gesture, and voice were those of Mr. Hooper.

At the close of the services, the people hurried out with indecorous confusion, eager to communicate their pent-up amazement, and conscious of lighter spirits the moment they lost sight of the black veil. Some gathered in little circles, huddled closely together, with their mouths all whispering in the centre; some went homeward alone, wrapt in silent meditation; some talked loudly, and profaned the Sabbath day with ostentatious laughter. A few shook their sagacious heads, intimating that they could penetrate the mystery; while one or two affirmed that there was no mystery at all, but only that Mr. Hooper's eyes were so weakened by the midnight lamp, as to require a shade. After a brief interval, forth came good Mr. Hooper also, in the rear of his flock. Turning his veiled face from one group to another, he paid due reverence to the hoary heads, saluted the middle aged with kind dignity as their friend and spiritual guide, greeted the young with mingled authority and love, and laid his hands on the little children's heads to bless them. Such was always his custom on the Sabbath day. Strange and bewildered looks repaid him for his courtesy. None, as on former occasions, aspired to the honor of walking by their pastor's side. Old Squire Saunders, doubtless by an accidental lapse of memory, neglected to invite Mr. Hooper to his table, where the good clergyman had been wont to bless the food, almost every Sunday since his settlement. He returned, therefore, to the parsonage, and, at the moment of closing the door, was observed to look back upon the people, all of whom had their eyes fixed upon the minister. A sad smile gleamed faintly from beneath the black veil, and flickered about his mouth, glimmering as he disappeared.

"How strange," said a lady, "that a simple black veil, such as any woman might wear on her bonnet, should become such a terrible thing on Mr. Hooper's face!"

"Something must surely be amiss with Mr. Hooper's intellects," observed her husband, the physician of the village. "But the strangest part of the affair is the effect of this vagary, even on a sober-minded man like myself. The black veil, though it covers only our pastor's face, throws its influence over his whole person, and makes him ghostlike from head to foot. Do you not feel it so?"

"Truly do I," replied the lady; "and I would not be alone with him for the world. I wonder he is not afraid to be alone with himself!"

"Men sometimes are so," said her husband.

The afternoon service was attended with similar circumstances. At its conclusion, the bell tolled for the funeral of a young lady. The relatives and friends were assembled in the house, and the more distant acquaintances stood about the door, speaking of the good qualities of the deceased, when their talk was interrupted by the appearance of Mr. Hooper, still covered with his black veil. It was now an appropriate emblem. The clergyman stepped into the room where the corpse was laid, and bent over the coffin, to take a last farewell of his deceased parishioner. As he stooped, the veil hung straight down from his forehead, so that, if her eyelids had not been closed forever, the dead maiden might have seen his face. Could Mr. Hooper be fearful of her glance, that he so hastily caught back the black veil? A person who watched the interview between the dead and living, scrupled not to affirm, that, at the instant when the clergyman's features were disclosed, the corpse had slightly shuddered, rustling the shroud and muslin cap, though the countenance retained the composure of death. A superstitious old woman was the only witness of this prodigy. From the coffin Mr. Hooper passed into the chamber of the mourners, and thence to the head of the staircase, to make the funeral prayer. It was a tender and heart-dissolving prayer, full of sorrow, yet so imbued with celestial hopes, that the music of a heavenly harp, swept by the fingers of the dead, seemed faintly to be heard among the saddest accents of the minister. The people trembled, though they but darkly understood him when he prayed that they, and himself, and all of mortal race, might be ready, as he trusted this young maiden had been, for the dreadful hour that should snatch the veil from their faces. The bearers went heavily forth, and the mourners followed, saddening all the street, with the dead before them, and Mr. Hooper in his black veil behind.

"Why do you look back?" said one in the procession to his partner.

"I had a fancy," replied she, "that the minister and the maiden's spirit were walking hand in hand."

"And so had I, at the same moment," said the other.

That night, the handsomest couple in Milford village were to be joined in wedlock. Though reckoned a melancholy man, Mr. Hooper had a placid cheerfulness for such occasions, which often excited a sympathetic smile where livelier merriment would have been thrown away. There was no quality of his disposition which made him more beloved than this. The company at the wedding awaited his arrival with impatience, trusting that the strange awe, which had gathered over him throughout the day, would now be dispelled. But such was not the result. When Mr. Hooper came, the first thing that their eyes rested on was the same horrible black veil, which had added deeper gloom to the funeral, and could portend nothing but evil to the wedding. Such was its immediate effect on the guests that a cloud seemed to have rolled duskily from beneath the black crape, and dimmed the light of the candles. The bridal pair stood up before the minister. But the bride's cold fingers quivered in the tremulous hand of the bridegroom, and her deathlike paleness caused a whisper that the maiden who had been buried a few hours before was come from her grave to be married. If ever another wedding were so dismal, it was that famous one where they tolled the wedding knell. After performing the ceremony, Mr. Hooper raised a glass of wine to his lips, wishing happiness to the new-married couple in a strain of mild pleasantry that ought to have brightened the features of the guests, like a cheerful gleam from the hearth. At that instant, catching a glimpse of his figure in the looking-glass, the black veil involved his own spirit in the horror with which it overwhelmed all others. His frame shuddered, his lips grew white, he spilt the untasted wine upon the carpet, and rushed forth into the darkness. For the Earth, too, had on her Black Veil.

The next day, the whole village of Milford talked of little else than Parson Hooper's black veil. That, and the mystery concealed behind it, supplied a topic for discussion between acquaintances meeting in the street, and good women gossiping at their open windows. It was the first item of news that the tavern-keeper told to his guests. The children babbled of it on their way to school. One imitative little imp covered his face with an old black handkerchief, thereby so affrighting his playmates that the panic seized himself, and he well-nigh lost his wits by his own waggery.

It was remarkable that of all the busybodies and impertinent people in the parish, not one ventured to put the plain question to Mr. Hooper, wherefore he did this thing. Hitherto, whenever there appeared the slightest call for such interference, he had never lacked advisers, nor shown himself averse to be guided by their judgment. If he erred at all, it was by so painful a degree of self-distrust, that even the mildest censure would lead him to consider an indifferent action as a crime. Yet, though so well acquainted with this amiable weakness, no individual among his parishioners chose to make the black veil a subject of friendly remonstrance. There was a feeling of dread, neither plainly confessed nor carefully concealed, which caused each to shift the responsibility upon another, till at length it was found expedient to send a deputation to the church, in order to deal with Mr. Hooper about the mystery, before it should grow into a scandal. Never did an embassy so ill discharge its duties. The minister received them with friendly courtesy, but became silent, after they were seated, leaving to his visitors, the whole burden of introducing their important business. The topic, it might be supposed, was obvious enough. There was the black veil swathed round Mr. Hooper's forehead, and concealing every feature above his placid mouth, on which, at times, they could perceive the glimmering of a melancholy smile. But that piece of crape, to their imagination, seemed to hang down before his heart, the symbol of a fearful secret between him and them. Were the veil but cast aside, they might speak freely of it, but not till then. Thus they sat a considerable time, speechless, confused, and shrinking uneasily from Mr. Hooper's eye, which they felt to be fixed upon them with an invisible glance. Finally, the deputies returned abashed to their constituents, pronouncing the matter too weighty to be handled, except by a council of the churches, if, indeed, it might not require a general synod.

But there was one person in the village unappalled by the awe with which the black veil had impressed all beside herself. When the deputies returned without an explanation, or even venturing to demand one, she, with the calm energy of her character, determined to chase away the strange cloud that appeared to be settling round Mr. Hooper, every moment more darkly than before. As his plighted wife, it should be her privilege to know what the black veil concealed. At the minister's first visit, therefore, she entered upon the subject with a direct simplicity, which made the task easier both for him and her. After he had seated himself, she fixed her eyes steadfastly upon the veil, but could discern nothing of the dreadful gloom that had so overawed the multitude: it was but a double fold of crape, hanging down from his forehead to his mouth, and slightly stirring with his breath.

"No," she said aloud, and smiling, "there is nothing terrible in this piece of crape, except that it hides a face which I am always glad to look upon. Come, good sir, let the sun shine from behind the cloud. First lay aside your black veil: then tell me why you put it on."

Mr. Hooper's smile glimmered faintly.

"There is an hour to come," said he, "when all of us shall cast aside our veils. Take it not amiss, beloved friend, if I wear this piece of crape till then."

"Your words are a mystery, too," returned the young lady. "Take away the veil from them, at least."

"Elizabeth, I will," said he, "so far as my vow may suffer me. Know, then, this veil is a type and a symbol, and I am bound to wear it ever, both in light and darkness, in solitude and before the gaze of multitudes, and as with strangers, so with my familiar friends. No mortal eye will see it withdrawn. This dismal shade must separate me from the world: even you, Elizabeth, can never come behind it!"

"What grievous affliction hath befallen you," she earnestly inquired, "that you should thus darken your eyes forever?"

"If it be a sign of mourning," replied Mr. Hooper, "I, perhaps, like most other mortals, have sorrows dark enough to be typified by a black veil."

"But what if the world will not believe that it is the type of an innocent sorrow?" urged Elizabeth. "Beloved and respected as you are, there may be whispers that you hide your face under the consciousness of secret sin. For the sake of your holy office, do away this scandal!"

The color rose into her cheeks as she intimated the nature of the rumors that were already abroad in the village. But Mr. Hooper's mildness did not forsake him. He even smiled again—that same sad smile, which always appeared like a faint glimmering of light, proceeding from the obscurity beneath the veil.

"If I hide my face for sorrow, there is cause enough," he merely replied; "and if I cover it for secret sin, what mortal might not do the same?"

And with this gentle, but unconquerable obstinacy did he resist all her entreaties. At length Elizabeth sat silent. For a few moments she appeared lost in thought, considering, probably, what new methods might be tried to withdraw her lover from so dark a fantasy, which, if it had no other meaning, was perhaps a symptom of mental disease. Though of a firmer character than his own, the tears rolled down her cheeks. But, in an instant, as it were, a new feeling took the place of sorrow: her eyes were fixed insensibly on the black veil, when, like a sudden twilight in the air, its terrors fell around her. She arose, and stood trembling before him.

"And do you feel it then, at last?" said he mournfully.

She made no reply, but covered her eyes with her hand, and turned to leave the room. He rushed forward and caught her arm.

"Have patience with me, Elizabeth!" cried he, passionately. "Do not desert me, though this veil must be between us here on earth. Be mine, and hereafter there shall be no veil over my face, no darkness between our souls! It is but a mortal veil—it is not for eternity! O! you know not how lonely I am, and how frightened, to be alone behind my black veil. Do not leave me in this miserable obscurity forever!"

"Lift the veil but once, and look me in the face," said she.

"Never! It cannot be!" replied Mr. Hooper.

"Then farewell!" said Elizabeth.

She withdrew her arm from his grasp, and slowly departed, pausing at the door, to give one long shuddering gaze, that seemed almost to penetrate the mystery of the black veil. But, even amid his grief, Mr. Hooper smiled to think that only a material emblem had separated him from happiness, though the horrors, which it shadowed forth, must be drawn darkly between the fondest of lovers.

From that time no attempts were made to remove Mr. Hooper's black veil, or, by a direct appeal, to discover the secret which it was supposed to hide. By persons who claimed a superiority to popular prejudice, it was reckoned merely an eccentric whim, such as often mingles with the sober actions of men otherwise rational, and tinges them all with its own semblance of insanity. But with the multitude, good Mr. Hooper was irreparably a bugbear.[2] He could not walk the street with any peace of mind, so conscious was he that the gentle and timid would turn aside to avoid him, and that others would make it a point of hardihood to throw themselves in his way. The impertinence of the latter class compelled him to give up his customary walk at sunset to the burial ground; for when he leaned pensively over the gate, there would always be faces behind the gravestones, peeping at his black veil. A fable went the rounds that the stare of the dead people drove him thence. It grieved him, to the very depth of his kind heart, to observe how the children fled from his approach, breaking up their merriest sports, while his melancholy figure was yet afar off. Their instinctive dread caused him to feel more strongly than aught else, that a preternatural horror was interwoven with the threads of the black crape. In truth, his own antipathy to the veil was known to be so great, that he never willingly passed before a mirror, nor stooped to drink at a still fountain, lest, in its peaceful bosom, he should be affrighted by himself. This was what gave plausibility to the whispers,

2 A creature that causes great fear or anxiety.

that Mr. Hooper's conscience tortured him for some great crime too horrible to be entirely concealed, or otherwise than so obscurely intimated. Thus, from beneath the black veil, there rolled a cloud into the sunshine, an ambiguity of sin or sorrow, which enveloped the poor minister, so that love or sympathy could never reach him. It was said that ghost and fiend consorted with him there. With self-shudderings and outward terrors, he walked continually in its shadow, groping darkly within his own soul, or gazing through a medium that saddened the whole world. Even the lawless wind, it was believed, respected his dreadful secret, and never blew aside the veil. But still good Mr. Hooper sadly smiled at the pale visages of the worldly throng as he passed by.

Among all its bad influences, the black veil had one desirable effect, of making its wearer a very efficient clergyman. By the aid of his mysterious emblem—for there was no other apparent cause—he became a man of awful power over souls that were in agony for sin. His converts always regarded him with a dread peculiar to themselves, affirming, though but figuratively, that, before he brought them to celestial light, they had been with him behind the black veil. Its gloom, indeed, enabled him to sympathize with all dark affections. Dying sinners cried aloud for Mr. Hooper, and would not yield their breath till he appeared; though ever, as he stooped to whisper consolation, they shuddered at the veiled face so near their own. Such were the terrors of the black veil, even when Death had bared his visage! Strangers came long distances to attend service at his church, with the mere idle purpose of gazing at his figure, because it was forbidden them to behold his face. But many were made to quake ere they departed! Once, during Governor Belcher's administration,[3] Mr. Hooper was appointed to preach the election sermon. Covered with his black veil, he stood before the chief magistrate, the council, and the representatives, and wrought so deep an impression, that the legislative measures of that year were characterized by all the gloom and piety of our earliest ancestral sway.

In this manner Mr. Hooper spent a long life, irreproachable in outward act, yet shrouded in dismal suspicions; kind and loving, though unloved, and dimly feared; a man apart from men, shunned in their health and joy, but ever summoned to their aid in mortal anguish. As years wore on, shedding their snows above his sable veil, he acquired a name throughout the New England churches, and they called him Father Hooper. Nearly all his parishioners, who were of mature age when he was settled, had been borne away by many a funeral: he had one congregation in the church, and a more crowded one in the churchyard; and

---

3 Jonathan Belcher was governor of the British colonies of Massachusetts, New Hampshire, and New Jersey from 1730 to 1741.

having wrought so late into the evening, and done his work so well, it was now good Father Hooper's turn to rest.

Several persons were visible by the shaded candle-light, in the death chamber of the old clergyman. Natural connections he had none. But there was the decorously grave, though unmoved physician, seeking only to mitigate the last pangs of the patient whom he could not save. There were the deacons, and other eminently pious members of his church. There, also, was the Reverend Mr. Clark, of Westbury, a young and zealous divine, who had ridden in haste to pray by the bedside of the expiring minister. There was the nurse, no hired handmaiden of death, but one whose calm affection had endured thus long in secrecy, in solitude, amid the chill of age, and would not perish, even at the dying hour. Who, but Elizabeth! And there lay the hoary head of good Father Hooper upon the death pillow, with the black veil still swathed about his brow, and reaching down over his face, so that each more difficult gasp of his faint breath caused it to stir. All through life that piece of crape had hung between him and the world: it had separated him from cheerful brotherhood and woman's love, and kept him in that saddest of all prisons, his own heart; and still it lay upon his face, as if to deepen the gloom of his darksome chamber, and shade him from the sunshine of eternity.

For some time previous, his mind had been confused, wavering doubtfully between the past and the present, and hovering forward, as it were, at intervals, into the indistinctness of the world to come. There had been feverish turns, which tossed him from side to side, and wore away what little strength he had. But in his most convulsive struggles, and in the wildest vagaries of his intellect, when no other thought retained its sober influence, he still showed an awful solicitude lest the black veil should slip aside. Even if his bewildered soul could have forgotten, there was a faithful woman at his pillow, who, with averted eyes, would have covered that aged face, which she had last beheld in the comeliness of manhood. At length the death-stricken old man lay quietly in the torpor of mental and bodily exhaustion, with an imperceptible pulse, and breath that grew fainter and fainter, except when a long, deep, and irregular inspiration seemed to prelude the flight of his spirit.

The minister of Westbury approached the bedside.

"Venerable Father Hooper," said he, "the moment of your release is at hand. Are you ready for the lifting of the veil that shuts in time from eternity?"

Father Hooper at first replied merely by a feeble motion of his head; then, apprehensive, perhaps, that his meaning might be doubtful, he exerted himself to speak.

"Yea," said he, in faint accents, "my soul hath a patient weariness until that veil be lifted."

"And is it fitting," resumed the Reverend Mr. Clark, "that a man so given to prayer, of such a blameless example, holy in deed and thought, so far as mortal judgment may pronounce; is it fitting that a father in the church should leave a shadow on his memory, that may seem to blacken a life so pure? I pray you, my venerable brother, let not this thing be! Suffer us to be gladdened by your triumphant aspect as you go to your reward. Before the veil of eternity be lifted, let me cast aside this black veil from your face!"

And thus speaking, the Reverend Mr. Clark bent forward to reveal the mystery of so many years. But, exerting a sudden energy, that made all the beholders stand aghast, Father Hooper snatched both his hands from beneath the bedclothes, and pressed them strongly on the black veil, resolute to struggle, if the minister of Westbury would contend with a dying man.

"Never!" cried the veiled clergyman. "On earth, never!"

"Dark old man!" exclaimed the affrighted minister, "with what horrible crime upon your soul are you now passing to the judgment?"

Father Hooper's breath heaved; it rattled in his throat; but, with a mighty effort, grasping forward with his hands, he caught hold of life, and held it back till he should speak. He even raised himself in bed; and there he sat, shivering with the arms of death around him, while the black veil hung down, awful, at that last moment, in the gathered terrors of a lifetime. And yet the faint, sad smile, so often there, now seemed to glimmer from its obscurity, and linger on Father Hooper's lips.

"Why do you tremble at me alone?" cried he, turning his veiled face round the circle of pale spectators. "Tremble also at each other! Have men avoided me, and women shown no pity, and children screamed and fled, only for my black veil? What, but the mystery which it obscurely typifies, has made this piece of crape so awful? When the friend shows his inmost heart to his friend; the lover to his best beloved; when man does not vainly shrink from the eye of his Creator, loathsomely treasuring up the secret of his sin; then deem me a monster for the symbol beneath which I have lived, and die! I look around me, and lo! on every visage a Black Veil!"

While his auditors shrank from one another, in mutual affright, Father Hooper fell back upon his pillow, a veiled corpse, with a faint smile lingering on his lips. Still veiled, they laid him in his coffin, and a veiled corpse they bore him to the grave. The grass of many years has sprung up and withered on that grave; the burial stone is moss-grown, and good Mr. Hooper's face is dust; but awful is still the thought that it mouldered beneath the Black Veil!

—1836

EDGAR ALLAN POE

Edgar Allan Poe was born in 1809 in Boston, Massachusetts, the son of itinerant stage actors David Poe and Elizabeth Arnold Poe. David Poe disappeared when Poe was two, and his mother, although a popular performer, struggled with poverty as she tried to raise her three young children. She died of tuberculosis when Poe was only four years old, and he and his brother and sister were split up and sent to live with three different families. By all accounts Poe was a happy child, but in adolescence he began having conflicts with his foster father, a well-to-do tobacco and dry goods merchant. His university education at the University of Virginia was terminated after he incurred huge gambling debts, at which point he ran away to Boston and published his first collection of poems, *Tamerlane and Other Poems* (1827), under the pseudonym "a Bostonian." Poe enlisted in the army in 1827 using a false name to hide himself from his creditors. He managed to publish a second collection of poems, entitled *Al Aaraaf, Tamerlane, and Minor Poems*, in 1829. In 1830 he was accepted into the US Military Academy at West Point, but he was expelled for carousing and irresponsible behaviour.

Having been cast out by his foster family, Poe continued to struggle financially, often taking on substandard writing jobs in order to pay the bills. He achieved some level of comfort by taking on editorial work for various publications, but his drinking and subsequent unreliability made him unable to maintain a job for long. Throughout this time, he wrote numerous short stories and poems that were published in periodicals and that occasionally appeared collected in book form, including *Tales of the Grotesque and Arabesque* (1840) and *The Raven and Other Poems* (1845).

In 1836, Poe married his cousin, Virginia Clemm. In spite of recurring bouts of grinding poverty, the marriage was reported to be a happy one. In 1845, Virginia died of tuberculosis. In 1849 Poe became engaged to Sarah Elmira Royster, a widow who had been a childhood love. In October 1849, Poe was returning to his home in New York from Richmond, Virginia, when he was found delirious on the street in Baltimore, Maryland and taken to a charity hospital, where he later died. There has been much speculation about the cause of Poe's death, but no medical records survive, and his death remains a mystery.

During his lifetime, Poe was well known, but his work did not sell widely. With the exception of one novel written at the urging of a publisher, *The Narrative of Arthur Gordon Pym of Nantucket* (1838), his works were all oriented towards periodical publication. He mastered the form of the short story, and, in the words of Alberto Manguel, "set out the laws that govern a tale of horror." Published in 1843 and 1846 respectively, "The Black Cat" and the "The Cask of Amontillado" are perfect examples of Poe's brilliance as a skilled practitioner of horror fiction.

The Black Cat

EDGAR ALLAN POE

FOR THE most wild, yet most homely narrative which I am about to pen, I neither expect nor solicit belief. Mad indeed would I be to expect it, in a case where my very senses reject their own evidence. Yet, mad am I not—and very surely do I not dream. But to-morrow I die, and to-day I would unburthen my soul. My immediate purpose is to place before the world, plainly, succinctly, and without comment, a series of mere household events. In their consequences, these events have terrified—have tortured—have destroyed me. Yet I will not attempt to expound them. To me, they have presented little but Horror—to many they will seem less terrible than *barroques*.[1] Hereafter, perhaps, some intellect may be found which will reduce my phantasm[2] to the common-place—some intellect more calm, more logical, and far less excitable than my own, which will perceive, in the circumstances I detail with awe, nothing more than an ordinary succession of very natural causes and effects.

From my infancy I was noted for the docility and humanity of my disposition. My tenderness of heart was even so conspicuous as to make me the jest of my companions. I was especially fond of animals, and was indulged by my parents with a great variety of pets. With these I spent most of my time, and never was so happy as when feeding and caressing them. This peculiarity of character grew with my growth, and in my manhood, I derived from it one of my principal sources of pleasure. To those who have cherished an affection for

---

1 Grotesque or strangely irregular.

2 Delusion or imagined reality.

a faithful and sagacious dog, I need hardly be at the trouble of explaining the nature or the intensity of the gratification thus derivable. There is something in the unselfish and self-sacrificing love of a brute, which goes directly to the heart of him who has had frequent occasion to test the paltry friendship and gossamer fidelity of mere *Man*.

I married early, and was happy to find in my wife a disposition not uncongenial with my own. Observing my partiality for domestic pets, she lost no opportunity of procuring those of the most agreeable kind. We had birds, gold-fish, a fine dog, rabbits, a small monkey, and *a cat*.

This latter was a remarkably large and beautiful animal, entirely black, and sagacious to an astonishing degree. In speaking of his intelligence, my wife, who at heart was not a little tinctured with superstition, made frequent allusion to the ancient popular notion, which regarded all black cats as witches in disguise. Not that she was ever *serious* upon this point—and I mention the matter at all for no better reason than that it happens, just now, to be remembered.

Pluto—this was the cat's name—was my favorite pet and playmate. I alone fed him, and he attended me wherever I went about the house. It was even with difficulty that I could prevent him from following me through the streets.

Our friendship lasted, in this manner, for several years, during which my general temperament and character—through the instrumentality of the Fiend Intemperance[3]—had (I blush to confess it) experienced a radical alteration for the worse. I grew, day by day, more moody, more irritable, more regardless of the feelings of others. I suffered myself to use intemperate language to my wife. At length, I even offered her personal violence. My pets, of course, were made to feel the change in my disposition. I not only neglected, but ill-used them. For Pluto, however, I still retained sufficient regard to restrain me from maltreating him, as I made no scruple of maltreating the rabbits, the monkey, or even the dog, when by accident, or through affection, they came in my way. But my disease grew upon me—for what disease is like Alcohol!—and at length even Pluto, who was now becoming old, and consequently somewhat peevish—even Pluto began to experience the effects of my ill temper.

One night, returning home, much intoxicated, from one of my haunts about town, I fancied that the cat avoided my presence. I seized him; when, in his fright at my violence, he inflicted a slight wound upon my hand with his teeth. The fury of a demon instantly possessed me. I knew myself no longer. My original soul seemed, at once, to take its flight from my body and a more than fiendish malevolence, gin-nurtured, thrilled every fibre of my frame. I took from my waistcoat-pocket a pen-knife, opened it, grasped the poor beast by the throat,

3 Excessive consumption of alcohol.

and deliberately cut one of its eyes from the socket! I blush, I burn, I shudder, while I pen the damnable atrocity.

When reason returned with the morning—when I had slept off the fumes of the night's debauch—I experienced a sentiment half of horror, half of remorse, for the crime of which I had been guilty; but it was, at best, a feeble and equivocal feeling, and the soul remained untouched. I again plunged into excess, and soon drowned in wine all memory of the deed.

In the meantime the cat slowly recovered. The socket of the lost eye presented, it is true, a frightful appearance, but he no longer appeared to suffer any pain. He went about the house as usual, but, as might be expected, fled in extreme terror at my approach. I had so much of my old heart left, as to be at first grieved by this evident dislike on the part of a creature which had once so loved me. But this feeling soon gave place to irritation. And then came, as if to my final and irrevocable overthrow, the spirit of PERVERSENESS. Of this spirit philosophy takes no account. Yet I am not more sure that my soul lives, than I am that perverseness is one of the primitive impulses of the human heart—one of the indivisible primary faculties, or sentiments, which give direction to the character of Man. Who has not, a hundred times, found himself committing a vile or a silly action, for no other reason than because he knows he should not? Have we not a perpetual inclination, in the teeth of our best judgment, to violate that which is *Law*, merely because we understand it to be such? This spirit of perverseness, I say, came to my final overthrow. It was this unfathomable longing of the soul *to vex itself*—to offer violence to its own nature—to do wrong for the wrong's sake only—that urged me to continue and finally to consummate the injury I had inflicted upon the unoffending brute. One morning, in cool blood, I slipped a noose about its neck and hung it to the limb of a tree;—hung it with the tears streaming from my eyes, and with the bitterest remorse at my heart;—hung it *because* I knew that it had loved me, and *because* I felt it had given me no reason of offence;—hung it *because* I knew that in so doing I was committing a sin—a deadly sin that would so jeopardize my immortal soul as to place it—if such a thing were possible—even beyond the reach of the infinite mercy of the Most Merciful and Most Terrible God.

On the night of the day on which this cruel deed was done, I was aroused from sleep by the cry of fire. The curtains of my bed were in flames. The whole house was blazing. It was with great difficulty that my wife, a servant, and myself, made our escape from the conflagration.[4] The destruction was complete. My entire worldly wealth was swallowed up, and I resigned myself thenceforward to despair.

---

4 Destructive fire.

I am above the weakness of seeking to establish a sequence of cause and effect, between the disaster and the atrocity. But I am detailing a chain of facts—and wish not to leave even a possible link imperfect. On the day succeeding the fire, I visited the ruins. The walls, with one exception, had fallen in. This exception was found in a compartment wall, not very thick, which stood about the middle of the house, and against which had rested the head of my bed. The plastering had here, in great measure, resisted the action of the fire—a fact which I attributed to its having been recently spread. About this wall a dense crowd were collected, and many persons seemed to be examining a particular portion of it with very minute and eager attention. The words "strange!" "singular!" and other similar expressions, excited my curiosity. I approached and saw, as if graven in *bas relief*[5] upon the white surface, the figure of a gigantic *cat*. The impression was given with an accuracy truly marvellous. There was a rope about the animal's neck.

When I first beheld this apparition—for I could scarcely regard it as less—my wonder and my terror were extreme. But at length reflection came to my aid. The cat, I remembered, had been hung in a garden adjacent to the house. Upon the alarm of fire, this garden had been immediately filled by the crowd—by some one of whom the animal must have been cut from the tree and thrown, through an open window, into my chamber. This had probably been done with the view of arousing me from sleep. The falling of other walls had compressed the victim of my cruelty into the substance of the freshly-spread plaster; the lime of which, with the flames, and the *ammonia* from the carcass, had then accomplished the portraiture as I saw it.

Although I thus readily accounted to my reason, if not altogether to my conscience, for the startling fact just detailed, it did not the less fail to make a deep impression upon my fancy. For months I could not rid myself of the phantasm of the cat; and, during this period, there came back into my spirit a half-sentiment that seemed, but was not, remorse. I went so far as to regret the loss of the animal, and to look about me, among the vile haunts which I now habitually frequented, for another pet of the same species, and of somewhat similar appearance, with which to supply its place.

One night as I sat, half stupified, in a den of more than infamy, my attention was suddenly drawn to some black object, reposing upon the head of one of the immense hogsheads[6] of Gin, or of Rum, which constituted the chief furniture of the apartment. I had been looking steadily at the top of this hogshead for some minutes, and what now caused me surprise was the fact that I had not sooner

5 Relief sculpture characterized by slightly raised features that project from the background.
6 Large flask.

perceived the object thereupon. I approached it, and touched it with my hand. It was a black cat—a very large one—fully as large as Pluto, and closely resembling him in every respect but one. Pluto had not a white hair upon any portion of his body; but this cat had a large, although indefinite splotch of white, covering nearly the whole region of the breast. Upon my touching him, he immediately arose, purred loudly, rubbed against my hand, and appeared delighted with my notice. This, then, was the very creature of which I was in search. I at once offered to purchase it of the landlord; but this person made no claim to it—knew nothing of it—had never seen it before.

I continued my caresses, and, when I prepared to go home, the animal evinced a disposition to accompany me. I permitted it to do so; occasionally stooping and patting it as I proceeded. When it reached the house it domesticated itself at once, and became immediately a great favorite with my wife.

For my own part, I soon found a dislike to it arising within me. This was just the reverse of what I had anticipated; but—I know not how or why it was—its evident fondness for myself rather disgusted and annoyed. By slow degrees, these feelings of disgust and annoyance rose into the bitterness of hatred. I avoided the creature; a certain sense of shame, and the remembrance of my former deed of cruelty, preventing me from physically abusing it. I did not, for some weeks, strike, or otherwise violently ill use it; but gradually—very gradually—I came to look upon it with unutterable loathing, and to flee silently from its odious presence, as from the breath of a pestilence.

What added, no doubt, to my hatred of the beast, was the discovery, on the morning after I brought it home, that, like Pluto, it also had been deprived of one of its eyes. This circumstance, however, only endeared it to my wife, who, as I have already said, possessed, in a high degree, that humanity of feeling which had once been my distinguishing trait, and the source of many of my simplest and purest pleasures.

With my aversion to this cat, however, its partiality for myself seemed to increase. It followed my footsteps with a pertinacity which it would be difficult to make the reader comprehend. Whenever I sat, it would crouch beneath my chair, or spring upon my knees, covering me with its loathsome caresses. If I arose to walk it would get between my feet and thus nearly throw me down, or, fastening its long and sharp claws in my dress, clamber, in this manner, to my breast. At such times, although I longed to destroy it with a blow, I was yet withheld from so doing, partly by a memory of my former crime, but chiefly—let me confess it at once—by absolute dread of the beast.

This dread was not exactly a dread of physical evil—and yet I should be at a loss how otherwise to define it. I am almost ashamed to own—yes, even in this felon's cell, I am almost ashamed to own—that the terror and horror with which the animal inspired me, had been heightened by one of the merest chimaeras[7] it would be possible to conceive. My wife had called my attention, more than once, to the character of the mark of white hair, of which I have spoken, and which constituted the sole visible difference between the strange beast and the one I had destroyed. The reader will remember that this mark, although large, had been originally very indefinite; but, by slow degrees—degrees nearly imperceptible, and which for a long time my Reason struggled to reject as fanciful—it had, at length, assumed a rigorous distinctness of outline. It was now the representation of an object that I shudder to name—and for this, above all, I loathed, and dreaded, and would have rid myself of the monster *had I dared*—it was now, I say, the image of a hideous—of a ghastly thing—of the GALLOWS!—oh, mournful and terrible engine of Horror and of Crime—of Agony and of Death!

And now was I indeed wretched beyond the wretchedness of mere Humanity. And a brute beast—whose fellow I had contemptuously destroyed—*a brute beast* to work out for *me*—for me a man, fashioned in the image of the High God—so much of insufferable woe! Alas! neither by day nor by night knew I the blessing of Rest any more! During the former the creature left me no moment alone; and, in the latter, I started, hourly, from dreams of unutterable fear, to find the hot breath of *the thing* upon my face, and its vast weight—an incarnate Night-Mare that I had no power to shake off—incumbent eternally upon my *heart!*

Beneath the pressure of torments such as these, the feeble remnant of the good within me succumbed. Evil thoughts became my sole intimates—the darkest and most evil of thoughts. The moodiness of my usual temper increased to hatred of all things and of all mankind; while, from the sudden, frequent, and ungovernable outbursts of a fury to which I now blindly abandoned myself, my uncomplaining wife, alas! was the most usual and the most patient of sufferers.

One day she accompanied me, upon some household errand, into the cellar of the old building which our poverty compelled us to inhabit. The cat followed me down the steep stairs, and, nearly throwing me headlong, exasperated me to madness. Uplifting an axe, and forgetting, in my wrath, the childish dread which had hitherto stayed my hand, I aimed a blow at the animal which, of course, would have proved instantly fatal had it descended as I wished. But this blow was arrested by the hand of my wife. Goaded,[8] by the interference, into a

7 A wild creation of the imagination.

8 Provoked.

rage more than demoniacal, I withdrew my arm from her grasp and buried the axe in her brain. She fell dead upon the spot, without a groan.

This hideous murder accomplished, I set myself forthwith, and with entire deliberation, to the task of concealing the body. I knew that I could not remove it from the house, either by day or by night, without the risk of being observed by the neighbors. Many projects entered my mind. At one period I thought of cutting the corpse into minute fragments, and destroying them by fire. At another, I resolved to dig a grave for it in the floor of the cellar. Again, I deliberated about casting it in the well in the yard—about packing it in a box, as if merchandize, with the usual arrangements, and so getting a porter to take it from the house. Finally I hit upon what I considered a far better expedient than either of these. I determined to wall it up in the cellar—as the monks of the middle ages are recorded to have walled up their victims.

For a purpose such as this the cellar was well adapted. Its walls were loosely constructed, and had lately been plastered throughout with a rough plaster, which the dampness of the atmosphere had prevented from hardening. Moreover, in one of the walls was a projection, caused by a false chimney, or fireplace, that had been filled up, and made to resemble the red of the cellar. I made no doubt that I could readily displace the bricks at this point, insert the corpse, and wall the whole up as before, so that no eye could detect any thing suspicious. And in this calculation I was not deceived. By means of a crow-bar I easily dislodged the bricks, and, having carefully deposited the body against the inner wall, I propped it in that position, while, with little trouble, I re-laid the whole structure as it originally stood. Having procured mortar, sand, and hair, with every possible precaution, I prepared a plaster which could not be distinguished from the old, and with this I very carefully went over the new brickwork. When I had finished, I felt satisfied that all was right. The wall did not present the slightest appearance of having been disturbed. The rubbish on the floor was picked up with the minutest care. I looked around triumphantly, and said to myself—"Here at least, then, my labor has not been in vain."

My next step was to look for the beast which had been the cause of so much wretchedness; for I had, at length, firmly resolved to put it to death. Had I been able to meet with it, at the moment, there could have been no doubt of its fate; but it appeared that the crafty animal had been alarmed at the violence of my previous anger, and forebore to present itself in my present mood. It is impossible to describe, or to imagine, the deep, the blissful sense of relief which the absence of the detested creature occasioned in my bosom. It did not make its appearance during the night—and thus for one night at least, since its introduction into the house, I soundly and tranquilly slept; aye, slept even with the burden of murder upon my soul!

The second and the third day passed, and still my tormentor came not. Once again I breathed as a freeman. The monster, in terror, had fled the premises forever! I should behold it no more! My happiness was supreme! The guilt of my dark deed disturbed me but little. Some few inquiries had been made, but these had been readily answered. Even a search had been instituted—but of course nothing was to be discovered. I looked upon my future felicity as secured.

Upon the fourth day of the assassination, a party of the police came, very unexpectedly, into the house, and proceeded again to make rigorous investigation of the premises. Secure, however, in the inscrutability of my place of concealment, I felt no embarrassment whatever. The officers bade me accompany them in their search. They left no nook or corner unexplored. At length, for the third or fourth time, they descended into the cellar. I quivered not in a muscle. My heart beat calmly as that of one who slumbers in innocence. I walked the cellar from end to end. I folded my arms upon my bosom, and roamed easily to and fro. The police were thoroughly satisfied and prepared to depart. The glee at my heart was too strong to be restrained. I burned to say if but one word, by way of triumph, and to render doubly sure their assurance of my guiltlessness.

"Gentlemen," I said at last, as the party ascended the steps, "I delight to have allayed your suspicions. I wish you all health, and a little more courtesy. By the bye, gentlemen, this—this is a very well constructed house." [In the rabid desire to say something easily, I scarcely knew what I uttered at all.]—"I may say an *excellently* well constructed house. These walls—are you going, gentlemen?—these walls are solidly put together;" and here, through the mere phrenzy of bravado, I rapped heavily, with a cane which I held in my hand, upon that very portion of the brick-work behind which stood the corpse of the wife of my bosom.

But may God shield and deliver me from the fangs of the Arch-Fiend! No sooner had the reverberation of my blows sunk into silence, than I was answered by a voice from within the tomb!—by a cry, at first muffled and broken, like the sobbing of a child, and then quickly swelling into one long, loud, and continuous scream, utterly anomalous and inhuman—a howl—a wailing shriek, half of horror and half of triumph, such as might have arisen only out of hell, conjointly from the throats of the damned in their agony and of the demons that exult in the damnation.

Of my own thoughts it is folly to speak. Swooning, I staggered to the opposite wall. For one instant the party upon the stairs remained motionless, through extremity of terror and of awe. In the next, a dozen stout arms were toiling at the wall. It fell bodily. The corpse, already greatly decayed and clotted with gore, stood erect before the eyes of the spectators. Upon its head, with red extended mouth and solitary eye of fire, sat the hideous beast whose craft had seduced me into murder, and whose informing voice had consigned me to the hangman. I had walled the monster up within the tomb!

—1843

The Cask of Amontillado

EDGAR ALLAN POE

THE THOUSAND injuries of Fortunato I had borne as I best could, but when he ventured upon insult I vowed revenge. You, who so well know the nature of my soul, will not suppose, however, that I gave utterance to a threat. *At length* I would be avenged; this was a point definitely settled—but the very definitiveness with which it was resolved precluded the idea of risk. I must not only punish but punish with impunity. A wrong is unredressed when retribution overtakes its redresser. It is equally unredressed when the avenger fails to make himself felt as such to him who has done the wrong.

It must be understood that neither by word nor deed had I given Fortunato cause to doubt my good will. I continued, as was my wont, to smile in his face, and he did not perceive that my smile *now* was at the thought of his immolation.

He had a weak point—this Fortunato—although in other regards he was a man to be respected and even feared. He prided himself on his connoisseurship in wine. Few Italians have the true virtuoso spirit. For the most part their enthusiasm is adopted to suit the time and opportunity, to practise imposture upon the British and Austrian millionaires. In painting and gemmary, Fortunato, like his countrymen, was a quack, but in the matter of old wines he was sincere. In this respect I did not differ from him materially;—I was skilful in the Italian vintages myself, and bought largely whenever I could.

It was about dusk, one evening during the supreme madness of the carnival season, that I encountered my friend. He accosted me with excessive warmth, for he had been drinking much. The man wore motley. He had on a tight-fitting parti-striped dress, and his head was surmounted by the conical cap and bells. I was so pleased to see him that I thought I should never have done wringing his hand.

I said to him—"My dear Fortunato, you are luckily met. How remarkably well you are looking today. But I have received a pipe of what passes for Amontillado, and I have my doubts."

"How?" said he. "Amontillado? A pipe? Impossible! And in the middle of the carnival!"

"I have my doubts," I replied; "and I was silly enough to pay the full Amontillado price without consulting you in the matter. You were not to be found, and I was fearful of losing a bargain."

"Amontillado!"

"I have my doubts."

"Amontillado!"

"And I must satisfy them."

"Amontillado!"

"As you are engaged, I am on my way to Luchresi. If any one has a critical turn it is he. He will tell me—"

"Luchresi cannot tell Amontillado from Sherry."

"And yet some fools will have it that his taste is a match for your own."

"Come, let us go."

"Whither?"

"To your vaults."

"My friend, no; I will not impose upon your good nature. I perceive you have an engagement. Luchresi—"

"I have no engagement;—come."

"My friend, no. It is not the engagement, but the severe cold with which I perceive you are afflicted. The vaults are insufferably damp. They are encrusted with nitre."

"Let us go, nevertheless. The cold is merely nothing. Amontillado! You have been imposed upon. And as for Luchresi, he cannot distinguish Sherry from Amontillado."

Thus speaking, Fortunato possessed himself of my arm; and putting on a mask of black silk and drawing a *roquelaire*[1] closely about my person, I suffered him to hurry me to my palazzo.

There were no attendants at home; they had absconded to make merry in honour of the time. I had told them that I should not return until the morning, and had given them explicit orders not to stir from the house. These orders were sufficient, I well knew, to insure their immediate disappearance, one and all, as soon as my back was turned.

I took from their sconces two flambeaux, and giving one to Fortunato, bowed him through several suites of rooms to the archway that led into the vaults. I passed down a long and winding staircase, requesting him to be cautious as he

1 A knee-length cloak.

followed. We came at length to the foot of the descent, and stood together upon the damp ground of the catacombs of the Montresors.

The gait of my friend was unsteady, and the bells upon his cap jingled as he strode.

"The pipe," he said.

"It is farther on," said I; "but observe the white web-work which gleams from these cavern walls."

He turned towards me, and looked into my eyes with two filmy orbs that distilled the rheum of intoxication.

"Nitre?" he asked, at length.

"Nitre," I replied. "How long have you had that cough?"

"Ugh! ugh! ugh!—ugh! ugh! ugh!—ugh! ugh! ugh!—ugh! ugh! ugh!—ugh! ugh! ugh!"

My poor friend found it impossible to reply for many minutes.

"It is nothing," he said, at last.

"Come," I said, with decision, "we will go back; your health is precious. You are rich, respected, admired, beloved; you are happy, as once I was. You are a man to be missed. For me it is no matter. We will go back; you will be ill, and I cannot be responsible. Besides, there is Luchresi—"

"Enough," he said; "the cough is a mere nothing; it will not kill me. I shall not die of a cough."

"True—true," I replied; "and, indeed, I had no intention of alarming you unnecessarily—but you should use all proper caution. A draught of this Medoc will defend us from the damps."

Here I knocked off the neck of a bottle which I drew from a long row of its fellows that lay upon the mould.

"Drink," I said, presenting him the wine.

He raised it to his lips with a leer. He paused and nodded to me familiarly, while his bells jingled.

"I drink," he said, "to the buried that repose around us."

"And I to your long life."

He again took my arm, and we proceeded.

"These vaults," he said, "are extensive."

"The Montresors," I replied, "were a great and numerous family."

"I forget your arms."

"A huge human foot d'or, in a field azure;[2] the foot crushes a serpent rampant whose fangs are imbedded in the heel."

"And the motto?"

---

2 A golden foot upon a blue background.

"*Nemo me impune lacessit.*"[3]

"Good!" he said.

The wine sparkled in his eyes and the bells jingled. My own fancy grew with the Medoc. We had passed through long walls of piled skeletons, with casks and puncheons intermingling, into the inmost recesses of the catacombs. I paused again, and this time I made bold to seize Fortunato by an arm above the elbow.

"The nitre!" I said; "see, it increases. It hangs like moss upon the vaults. We are below the river's bed. The drops of moisture trickle among the bones. Come, we will go back ere it is too late. Your cough—"

"It is nothing," he said; "let us go on. But first, another draught of the Medoc."

I broke and reached him a flagon of De Grave. He emptied it at a breath. His eyes flashed with a fierce light. He laughed and threw the bottle upwards with a gesticulation I did not understand.

I looked at him in surprise. He repeated the movement—a grotesque one.

"You do not comprehend?" he said.

"Not I," I replied.

"Then you are not of the brotherhood."

"How?"

"You are not of the masons."

"Yes, yes," I said; "yes, yes."

"You? Impossible! A mason?"

"A mason," I replied.

"A sign," he said, "a sign."

"It is this," I answered, producing from beneath the folds of my *roquelaire* a trowel.

"You jest," he exclaimed, recoiling a few paces. "But let us proceed to the Amontillado."

"Be it so," I said, replacing the tool beneath the cloak and again offering him my arm. He leaned upon it heavily. We continued our route in search of the Amontillado. We passed through a range of low arches, descended, passed on, and descending again, arrived at a deep crypt, in which the foulness of the air caused our flambeaux rather to glow than flame.

At the most remote end of the crypt there appeared another less spacious. Its walls had been lined with human remains, piled to the vault overhead, in the fashion of the great catacombs of Paris. Three sides of this interior crypt were still ornamented in this manner. From the fourth side the bones had been thrown down, and lay promiscuously upon the earth, forming at one point

---

3 Latin: "No one may insult me without being punished."

a mound of some size. Within the wall thus exposed by the displacing of the bones, we perceived a still interior crypt or recess, in depth about four feet, in width three, in height six or seven. It seemed to have been constructed for no especial use within itself, but formed merely the interval between two of the colossal supports of the roof of the catacombs, and was backed by one of their circumscribing walls of solid granite.

It was in vain that Fortunato, uplifting his dull torch, endeavoured to pry into the depth of the recess. Its termination the feeble light did not enable us to see.

"Proceed," I said; "herein is the Amontillado. As for Luchresi—"

"He is an ignoramus," interrupted my friend, as he stepped unsteadily forward, while I followed immediately at his heels. In an instant he had reached the extremity of the niche, and finding his progress arrested by the rock, stood stupidly bewildered. A moment more and I had fettered him to the granite. In its surface were two iron staples, distant from each other about two feet, horizontally. From one of these depended a short chain, from the other a padlock. Throwing the links about his waist, it was but the work of a few seconds to secure it. He was too much astounded to resist. Withdrawing the key I stepped back from the recess.

"Pass your hand," I said, "over the wall; you cannot help feeling the nitre. Indeed, it is *very* damp. Once more let me *implore* you to return. No? Then I must positively leave you. But I must first render you all the little attentions in my power."

"The Amontillado!" ejaculated my friend, not yet recovered from his astonishment.

"True," I replied; "the Amontillado."

As I said these words I busied myself among the pile of bones of which I have before spoken. Throwing them aside, I soon uncovered a quantity of building stone and mortar. With these materials and with the aid of my trowel, I began vigorously to wall up the entrance of the niche.

I had scarcely laid the first tier of the masonry when I discovered that the intoxication of Fortunato had in a great measure worn off. The earliest indication I had of this was a low moaning cry from the depth of the recess. It was *not* the cry of a drunken man. There was then a long and obstinate silence. I laid the second tier, and the third, and the fourth; and then I heard the furious vibrations of the chain. The noise lasted for several minutes, during which, that I might hearken to it with the more satisfaction, I ceased my labours and sat down upon the bones. When at last the clanking subsided, I resumed the trowel, and finished without interruption the fifth, the sixth, and the seventh tier. The wall was now nearly upon a level with my breast. I again paused, and holding the flambeaux over the mason-work, threw a few feeble rays upon the figure within.

A succession of loud and shrill screams, bursting suddenly from the throat of the chained form, seemed to thrust me violently back. For a brief moment I hesitated, I trembled. Unsheathing my rapier, I began to grope with it about the recess; but the thought of an instant reassured me. I placed my hand upon the solid fabric of the catacombs, and felt satisfied. I reapproached the wall; I replied to the yells of him who clamoured. I re-echoed, I aided, I surpassed them in volume and in strength. I did this, and the clamourer grew still.

It was now midnight, and my task was drawing to a close. I had completed the eighth, the ninth and the tenth tier. I had finished a portion of the last and the eleventh; there remained but a single stone to be fitted and plastered in. I struggled with its weight; I placed it partially in its destined position. But now there came from out the niche a low laugh that erected the hairs upon my head. It was succeeded by a sad voice, which I had difficulty in recognizing as that of the noble Fortunato. The voice said—

"Ha! ha! ha!—he! he! he!—a very good joke, indeed—an excellent jest. We will have many a rich laugh about it at the palazzo—he! he! he!—over our wine—he! he! he!"

"The Amontillado!" I said.

"He! he! he!—he! he! he!—yes, the Amontillado. But is it not getting late? Will not they be awaiting us at the palazzo, the Lady Fortunato and the rest? Let us be gone."

"Yes," I said, "let us be gone."

"*For the love of God, Montresor!*"

"Yes," I said, "for the love of God!"

But to these words I hearkened in vain for a reply. I grew impatient. I called aloud—

"Fortunato!"

No answer. I called again—

"Fortunato!"

No answer still. I thrust a torch through the remaining aperture and let it fall within. There came forth in return only a jingling of the bells. My heart grew sick; it was the dampness of the catacombs that made it so. I hastened to make an end of my labour. I forced the last stone into its position; I plastered it up. Against the new masonry I re-erected the old rampart of bones. For the half of a century no mortal has disturbed them. *In pace requiescat!*[4]

—1846

4 Latin: "Rest in peace!"

THOMAS HARDY

Although Thomas Hardy once said that he considered poetry a more serious genre than fiction (and calculated that he spent more years writing the former than the latter), it is as the author of novels such as *Tess of the D'Urbervilles* (1891) and *Jude the Obscure* (1896) that he is best known. Hardy was born in 1840, the son of a stonemason and his wife who lived in Higher Bockhampton in Dorset, near Dorchester. From an early age he was made aware of the hierarchy of the rich and poor, and of the more subtle divisions between different strata of the working class—an awareness that would later inform his work as a writer.

As a young man, Hardy articled with John Hicks, a Dorchester architect, and for some years he worked as an architect, specializing in the restoration of old churches in his home region and in London. He worked simultaneously on his writing, and in 1868 he submitted for publication to several publishers the manuscript for his first novel, *The Poor Man and the Lady*. According to the publishers, the novel showed much promise, but was not good enough for publication. In 1870, during one of his assignments in church restoration, Hardy met his future wife, Emma Lavinia Gifford, the sister-in-law of a church rector. During the long engagement, Hardy managed to publish several works, including his first novel, *Desperate Remedies* (1871). The serializing of his fourth novel, *Far from the Madding Crowd*, in *Cornhill Magazine* (1874) and its subsequent publication in book form established Hardy as a serious writer. The couple settled in London. Hardy gave up architecture in order to write full time; he became recognized as a major figure in the literary world.

In 1885, Hardy and his wife moved to Dorchester and into a house Hardy had designed himself, called Max Gate. The Hardys travelled little, and, although solid, their marriage was disturbed by the conflict between Emma Lavinia's strong evangelical faith and Hardy's agnosticism.

The publication of *Jude the Obscure* in 1896 served as a major turning point in Hardy's literary career. Some of the reviews were vicious (one reviewer re-titled the novel, "Jude the Obscene"), and Hardy soon gave up novel writing to concentrate on his poetry. By this time, however, Hardy's reputation as one of the foremost novelists of the nineteenth century had already been well established. After his first wife's death in 1912, Hardy married Florence Emily Dugdale in 1914; interestingly, when Hardy died in 1928, his heart was buried with Emma Lavinia in Stinsford churchyard while his ashes were interred at Westminster Abbey.

"The Son's Veto" was first published in *The Illustrated London News* in 1891 and then included in the short story collection *Life's Little Ironies* (1894). This story—which Hardy said was his favourite—covers a familiar theme in Hardy's work: class based division. In this case the conflict is not (as is often the case in Hardy's work) between lovers divided and defeated by their social stations, but between a mother and the social prejudices of her son.

The Son's Veto

THOMAS HARDY

I

TO THE EYES of a man viewing it from behind, the nut-brown hair was a wonder and a mystery. Under the black beaver hat, surmounted by its tuft of black feathers, the long locks, braided and twisted and coiled like the rushes of a basket, composed a rare, if somewhat barbaric, example of ingenious art. One could understand such weavings and coilings being wrought to last intact for a year, or even a calendar month; but that they should be all demolished regularly at bedtime, after a single day of permanence, seemed a reckless waste of successful fabrication.

And she had done it all herself, poor thing. She had no maid, and it was almost the only accomplishment she could boast of. Hence the unstinted pains.

She was a young invalid lady—not so very much of an invalid—sitting in a wheeled chair, which had been pulled up in the front part of a green enclosure, close to a band-stand, where a concert was going on, during a warm June afternoon. It had place in one of the minor parks or private gardens that are to be found in the suburbs of London, and was the effort of a local association to raise money for some charity. There are worlds within worlds in the great city, and though nobody outside the immediate district had ever heard of the charity, or the band, or the garden, the enclosure was filled with an interested audience sufficiently informed on all these.

As the strains proceeded many of the listeners observed the chaired lady, whose back hair, by reason of her prominent position, so challenged inspection.

Her face was not easily discernible, but the aforesaid cunning tress-weavings, the white ear and poll, and the curve of a cheek which was neither flaccid nor sallow, were signals that led to the expectation of good beauty in front. Such expectations are not infrequently disappointed as soon as the disclosure comes; and in the present case, when the lady, by a turn of the head, at length revealed herself, she was not so handsome as the people behind her had supposed, and even hoped—they did not know why.

For one thing (alas! the commonness of this complaint), she was less young than they had fancied her to be. Yet attractive her face unquestionably was, and not at all sickly. The revelation of its details came each time she turned to talk to a boy of twelve or thirteen who stood beside her, and the shape of whose hat and jacket implied that he belonged to a well-known public school. The immediate by-standers could hear that he called her "Mother."

When the end of the programme was reached, and the audience withdrew, many chose to find their way out by passing at her elbow. Almost all turned their heads to take a full and near look at the interesting woman, who remained stationary in the chair till the way should be clear enough for her to be wheeled out without obstruction. As if she expected their glances, and did not mind gratifying their curiosity, she met the eyes of several of her observers by lifting her own, showing these to be soft, brown, and affectionate orbs, a little plaintive in their regard.

She was conducted out of the garden, and passed along the pavement till she disappeared from view, the school-boy walking beside her. To inquiries made by some persons who watched her away, the answer came that she was the second wife of the incumbent of a neighboring parish, and that she was lame. She was generally believed to be a woman with a story—an innocent one, but a story of some sort or other.

In conversing with her on their way home the boy who walked at her elbow said that he hoped his father had not missed them.

"He have been so comfortable these last few hours that I am sure he cannot have missed us," she replied.

"*Has*, dear mother—not *have*!" exclaimed the public-school boy, with an impatient fastidiousness that was almost harsh. "Surely you know that by this time!"

His mother hastily adopted the correction, and did not resent his making it, or retaliate, as she might well have done, by bidding him to wipe that crumby mouth of his, whose condition had been caused by surreptitious attempts to eat a piece of cake without taking it out of the pocket wherein it lay concealed. After this the pretty woman and the boy went onward in silence.

That question of grammar bore upon her history, and she fell into reverie, of a somewhat sad kind to all appearance. It might have been assumed that she was wondering if she had done wisely in shaping her life as she had shaped it, to bring out such a result as this.

In a remote nook in North Wessex, forty miles from London, near the thriving county-town of Aldbrickham, there stood a pretty village with its church and parsonage, which she knew well enough, but her son had never seen. It was her native village, Gaymead, and the first event bearing upon her present situation had occurred at that place when she was only a girl of nineteen.

How well she remembered it, that first act in her little tragi-comedy, the death of her reverend husband's first wife. It happened on a spring evening, and she who now and for many years had filled that first wife's place was then parlor-maid in the parson's house.

When everything had been done that could be done, and the death was announced, she had gone out in the dusk to visit her parents, who were living in the same village, to tell them the sad news. As she opened the white swing-gate and looked towards the trees which rose westward, shutting out the pale light of the evening sky, she discerned, without much surprise, the figure of a man standing in the hedge, though she roguishly exclaimed, as a matter of form, "Oh, Sam, how you frightened me!"

He was a young gardener of her acquaintance. She told him the particulars of the late event, and they stood silent, these two young people, in that elevated, calmly philosophic mind which is engendered when a tragedy has happened close at hand, and has not happened to the philosophers themselves. But it had its bearings upon their relations.

"And will you stay on now at the Vicarage, just the same?" asked he.

She had hardly thought of that. "Oh yes—I suppose," she said. "Everything will be just as usual, I imagine."

He walked beside her towards her mother's. Presently his arm stole round her waist. She gently removed it; but he placed it there again, and she yielded the point. "You see, dear Sophy, you don't know that you'll stay on; you may want a home; and I shall be ready to offer one some day, though I may not be ready just yet."

"Why, Sam, how can you be so fast? I've never even said I liked 'ee; and it is all your own doing, coming after me."

"Still, it is nonsense to say I am not to have a try at you, like the rest." He stooped to kiss her a farewell, for they had reached her mother's door.

"No, Sam; you sha'n't!" she cried, putting her hand over his mouth. "You ought to be more serious on such a night as this." And she bade him adieu without allowing him to kiss her or to come indoors.

The vicar just left a widower was at this time a man about forty years of age, of good family, and childless. He had led a secluded existence in this college living, partly because there were no resident landowners; and his loss now intensified his habit of withdrawal from outward observation. He was still less seen than heretofore, kept himself still less in time with the rhythm and racket of the movements called progress in the world without. For many months after his wife's decease the economy of his household remained as before; the cook, the house-maid, the parlor-maid, and the man out-of-doors performed their duties or left them undone, just as nature prompted them—the vicar knew not which. It was then represented to him that his servants seemed to have nothing to do in his small family of one. He was struck with the truth of this representation, and decided to cut down his establishment. But he was forestalled by Sophy, the parlor-maid, who said one evening that she wished to leave him.

"And why?" said the parson.

"Sam Hobson has asked me to marry him, sir."

"Well—do you want to marry?"

"Not much. But it would be a home for me. And we have heard that one of us will have to leave."

A day or two after she said: "I don't want to leave just yet, sir, if you don't wish it. Sam and I have quarrelled."

He looked at her. He had hardly ever observed her before, though he had been frequently conscious of her soft presence in the room. What a kitten-like, flexuous, tender creature she was! She was the only one of the servants with whom he came into immediate and continuous relation. What should he do if Sophy were gone?

Sophy did not go, but one of the others did, and things proceeded quietly again.

When Mr. Twycott, the vicar, was ill, Sophy brought up his meals to him, and she had no sooner left the room one day than he heard a noise on the stairs. She had slipped down with the tray, and so twisted her foot that she could not stand. The village surgeon was called in; the vicar got better, but Sophy was incapacitated for a long time; and she was informed that she must never again walk much or engage in any occupation which required her to stand long on her feet. As soon as she was comparatively well she spoke to him alone. Since she was forbidden to walk and bustle about, and, indeed, could not do so, it became her duty to leave. She could very well work at something sitting down, and she had an aunt a seamstress.

The parson had been very greatly moved by what she had suffered on his account, and he exclaimed, "No, Sophy; lame or not lame, I cannot let you go. You must never leave me again."

He came close to her, and, though she could never exactly tell how it happened, she became conscious of his lips upon her cheek. He then asked her to marry him. Sophy did not exactly love him, but she had a respect for him which almost amounted to veneration. Even if she had wished to get away from him she hardly dared refuse a personage so reverend and august in her eyes, and she assented forthwith to be his wife.

Thus it happened that one fine morning, when the doors of the church were naturally open for ventilation, and the singing birds fluttered in and alighted on the tie-beams of the roof, there was a marriage-service at the communion rails which hardly a soul knew of. The parson and a neighboring curate had entered at one door, and Sophy at another, followed by two necessary persons, whereupon in a short time there emerged a newly-made husband and wife.

Mr. Twycott knew perfectly well that he had committed social suicide by this step, despite Sophy's spotless character, and he had taken his measures accordingly. An exchange of livings had been arranged with an acquaintance who was incumbent of a church in the south of London, and as soon as possible the couple removed thither, abandoning their pretty country home with trees and shrubs and glebe[1] for a narrow, dusty house in a long, straight street, and their fine peal of bells for the wretchedest one-tongue clangor that ever tortured mortal ears. It was all on her account. They were, however, away from every one who had known her former position, and also under less observation from without than they would have had to put up with in any country parish.

Sophy the woman was as charming a partner as a man could possess, though Sophy the lady had her deficiencies. She showed a natural aptitude for little domestic refinements, so far as related to things and manners; but in what is called culture she was less intuitive. She had now been married more than fourteen years, and her husband had taken much trouble with her education; but she still held confused ideas on the use of "was" and "were," which did not beget a respect for her among the few acquaintances she made. Her great grief in this relation was that her only child, on whose education no expense had been or would be spared, was now old enough to perceive these deficiencies in his mother, and not only to see them but to feel irritated at their existence.

Thus she lived on in the city, and wasted hours in braiding her beautiful hair, till her once apple cheeks waned to pink of the very faintest. Her foot had never regained its natural strength after the accident, and she was mostly obliged to avoid walking altogether. Her husband had grown to like London for its freedom and its domestic privacy; but he was twenty years his Sophy's senior, and had latterly been seized with a serious illness. On this day, however, he had seemed to be well enough to justify her accompanying her son Randolph to the concert.

1 Land granted to a clergyman.

II

THE NEXT time we get a glimpse of her is when she appears in the mournful attire of a widow.

Mr. Twycott had never rallied, and now lay in a well-packed cemetery to the south of the great city, where, if all the dead it contained had stood erect and alive, not one would have known him or recognized his name. The boy had dutifully followed him to the grave, and was now again at school.

Throughout these changes Sophy had been treated like the child she was in nature though not in years. She was left with no control over anything that had been her husband's beyond her modest personal income. In his anxiety lest her inexperience should be overreached he had safeguarded with trustees all he possibly could. The completion of the boy's course at the public school, to be followed in due time by Oxford and ordination, had been all previsioned and arranged, and she really had nothing to occupy her in the world but to eat and drink, and make a business of indolence, and go on weaving and coiling the nut-brown hair, merely keeping a home open for the son whenever he came to her during vacations.

Foreseeing his probable decease long years before her, her husband in his lifetime had purchased for her use a semi-detached villa in the same long, straight road whereon the church and parsonage faced, which was to be hers as long as she chose to live in it. Here she now resided, looking out upon the fragment of lawn in front, and through the railings at the ever-flowing traffic; or, bending forward over the window-sill on the first floor, stretching her eyes far up and down the vista of sooty trees, hazy air, and drab house façades, along which echoed the noises common to a suburban main thoroughfare.

Somehow, her boy, with his aristocratic school-knowledge, his grammars, and his aversions, was losing those wide infantine sympathies, extending as far as to the sun and moon themselves, with which he, like other children, had been born, and which his mother, a child of nature herself, had loved in him; he was reducing their compass to a population of a few thousand wealthy and titled people, the mere veneer of a thousand million or so of others who did not interest him at all. He drifted further and further away from her. Sophy's *milieu* being a suburb of minor tradesmen and under-clerks, and her almost only companions the two servants of her own house, it was not surprising that after her husband's death she soon lost the little artificial tastes she had acquired from him, and became—in her son's eyes—a mother whose mistakes and origin it was his painful lot as a gentleman to blush for. As yet he was far from being man enough—if he ever would be—to rate these sins of hers at their true infinitesimal value beside the yearning fondness that welled up and remained penned in her heart till it should be more fully accepted by him, or by some other person or thing. If he had lived at home with her he would have had all of it; but he seemed to require so very little in present circumstances, and it remained stored.

Her life became insupportably dreary; she could not take walks, and had no interest in going for drives, or, indeed, in travelling anywhere. Nearly two years passed without an event, and still she looked on that suburban road, thinking of the village in which she had been born, and whither she would have gone back—oh, how gladly!—even to work in the fields.

Taking no exercise, she often could not sleep, and would rise in the night or early morning and look out upon the then vacant thoroughfare, where the lamps stood like sentinels waiting for some procession to go by. An approximation to such a procession was indeed made every early morning about one o'clock, when the country vehicles passed up with loads of vegetables for Covent Garden market. She often saw them creeping along at this silent and dusky hour—wagon after wagon, bearing green bastions of cabbages nodding to their fall, yet never falling; walls of baskets enclosing masses of beans and pease; pyramids of snow-white turnips, swaying howdahs[2] of mixed produce—creeping along behind aged night-horses, who seemed ever patiently wondering between their hollow coughs why they had always to work at that still hour when all other sentient creatures were privileged to rest. Wrapped in a cloak, it was soothing to watch and sympathize with them when depression and nervousness hindered sleep, and to see how the fresh green-stuff brightened to life as it came opposite the lamp, and how the sweating animals steamed and shone with their miles of travel.

They had an interest, almost a charm, for Sophy, these semi-rural people and vehicles moving in an urban atmosphere, leading a life quite distinct from that of the daytime toilers on the same road. One morning a man who accompanied a wagon-load of potatoes gazed rather hard at the house fronts as he passed, and with a curious emotion she thought his form was familiar to her. She looked out for him again. His being an old-fashioned conveyance with a yellow front, it was easily recognizable, and on the third night after she saw it a second time. The man alongside was, as she had fancied, Sam Hobson, formerly gardener at Gaymead, who would at one time have married her.

She had occasionally thought of him, and wondered if life in a cottage with him would not have been a happier lot than the life she had accepted. She had not thought of him passionately, but her now dismal situation lent an interest to his resurrection—a tender interest which it is impossible to exaggerate. She went back to bed, and began thinking. When did these market-gardeners, who travelled up to town so regularly at one or two in the morning, come back?

2 Platforms placed on the backs of work horses.

She dimly recollected seeing their empty wagons, hardly noticeable among the ordinary day-traffic, passing down at some hour before noon.

It was only April, but that morning, after breakfast, she had the window opened, and sat looking out, the feeble sun shining full upon her. She affected to sew, but her eyes never left the street. Between ten and eleven the desired wagon, now unladen, reappeared on its return journey. But Sam was not looking round him then, and drove on in a reverie.

"Sam!" cried she.

Turning with a start, his face lighted up. He called to him a little boy to hold the horse, alighted, and came and stood under her window.

"I can't come down easily, Sam, or I would!" she said. "Did you know I lived here?"

"Well, Mrs. Twycott, I knew you lived along here somewhere. I have often looked out for 'ee."

He briefly explained his own presence on the scene. He had long since given up his gardening in the village near Aldbrickham, and was now manager at a market-gardener's on the south side of London, it being part of his duty to go up to Covent Garden with wagon-loads of produce two or three times a week. In answer to her curious inquiry, he admitted that he had come to this particular district because he had seen in the Aldbrickham paper a year or two before the announcement of the death in South London of the aforetime vicar of Gaymead, which had revived an interest in her dwelling-place that he could not extinguish, leading him to hover about the locality till his present post had been secured.

They spoke of their native village in dear old North Wessex, the spots in which they had played together as children. She tried to feel that she was a dignified personage now, that she must not be too confidential with Sam. But she could not keep it up, and the tears hanging in her eyes were indicated in her voice.

"You are not happy, Mrs. Twycott, I'm afraid," he said.

"Oh, of course not! I lost my husband only the year before last."

"Ah! I meant in another way. You'd like to be home again?"

"This is my home—for life. The house belongs to me. But I understand"—She let it out then. "Yes, Sam. I long for home—*our* home! I *should* like to be there, and never leave it, and die there." But she remembered herself. "That's only a momentary feeling. I have a son, you know, a dear boy. He's at school now."

"Somewhere handy, I suppose? I see there's lots of 'em along this road."

"Oh no! Not in one of these wretched holes! At a public school—one of the most distinguished in England."

"Chok it all! of course! I forgot, ma'am, that you've been a lady for so many years."

"No, I am not a lady," she said, sadly. "I never shall be. But he's a gentleman, and that—makes it—oh, how difficult for me!"

III

THE ACQUAINTANCE thus oddly reopened proceeded apace. She often looked out to get a few words with him, by night or by day. Her sorrow was that she could not accompany her one old friend on foot a little way, and talk more freely than she could do while he paused before the house. One night, at the beginning of June, when she was again on the watch after an absence of some days from the window, he entered the gate and said, softly, "Now, wouldn't some air do you good? I've only half a load this morning. Why not ride up to Covent Garden with me? There's a nice seat on the cabbages, where I've spread a sack. You can be home again in a cab before anybody is up."

She refused at first, and then, trembling with excitement, hastily finished her dressing, and wrapped herself up in cloak and veil, afterwards sidling downstairs by the aid of the handrail, in a way she could adopt on an emergency. When she had opened the door she found Sam on the step, and he lifted her bodily on his strong arm across the little forecourt into his vehicle. Not a soul was visible or audible in the infinite length of the straight, flat highway, with its ever-waiting lamps converging to points in each direction. The air was fresh as country air at this hour, and the stars shone, except to the north-eastward; where there was a whitish light—the dawn. Sam carefully placed her in the seat and drove on.

They talked as they had talked in old days, Sam pulling himself up now and then, when he thought himself too familiar. More than once she said with misgiving that she wondered if she ought to have indulged in the freak. "But I am so lonely in my house," she added, "and this makes me so happy!"

"You must come again, dear Mrs. Twycott. There is no time o' day for taking the air like this."

It grew lighter and lighter. The sparrows became busy in the streets, and the city waxed denser around them. When they approached the river it was day, and on the bridge they beheld the full blaze of morning sunlight in the direction of St. Paul's, the river glistening towards it, and not a craft stirring.

Near Covent Garden he put her into a cab, and they parted, looking into each other's faces like the very old friends they were. She reached home without adventure, limped to the door, and let herself in with her latch key unseen.

The air and Sam's presence had revived her; her cheeks were quite pink—almost beautiful. She had something to live for in addition to her son. A woman of pure instincts, she knew there had been nothing really wrong in the journey, but supposed it conventionally to be very wrong indeed.

Soon, however, she gave way to the temptation of going with him again, and on this occasion their conversation was distinctly tender, and Sam said he never should forget her, notwithstanding that she had served him rather badly at one time. After much hesitation he told her of a plan it was in his power to carry out, and one he should like to take in hand, since he did not care for London work; it was to set up as a master greengrocer down at Aldbrickham, the county-town of their native place. He knew of an opening—a shop kept by aged people who wished to retire.

"And why don't you do it, then, Sam?" she asked, with a slight heart-sinking.

"Because I'm not sure if—you'd join me. I know you wouldn't—couldn't! Such a lady as ye've been so long, you couldn't be a wife to a man like me."

"I hardly suppose I could!" she assented, also frightened at the idea.

"If you could," he said, eagerly, "you'd on'y have to sit in the back parlor and look through the glass partition when I was away sometimes—just to keep an eye on things. The lameness wouldn't hinder that. I'd keep you as genteel as ever I could, dear Sophy—if I might think of it," he pleaded.

"Sam, I'll be frank," she said, putting her hand on his. "If it were only myself I would do it, and gladly, though everything I possess would be lost to me by marrying again."

"I don't mind that. It's more independent."

"That's good of you, dear, dear Sam. But there's something else. I have a son. I almost fancy when I am miserable sometimes that he is not really mine, but one I hold in trust for my late husband. He seems to belong so little to me personally, so entirely to his dead father. He is so much educated and I so little that I do not feel dignified enough to be his mother. Well, he would have to be told."

"Yes. Unquestionably." Sam saw her thought and her fear. "Still, you can do as you like, Sophy—Mrs. Twycott," he added. "It is not you who are the child, but he."

"Ah, you don't know! Sam, if I could, I would marry you, some day. But you must wait awhile, and let me think."

It was enough for him, and he was blithe at their parting. Not so she. To tell Randolph seemed impossible. She could wait till he had gone up to Oxford, when what she did would affect his life but little. But would he ever tolerate the idea? And if not, could she defy him?

She had not told him a word when the yearly cricket-match came on at Lord's between the public schools, though Sam had already gone back to Aldbrickham. Mrs. Twycott felt stronger than usual. She went to the match with Randolph, and was able to leave her chair and walk about occasionally. The bright idea occurred to her that she could casually broach the subject while moving round among the spectators, when the boy's spirits were high with interest in the game, and he would weigh domestic matters as feathers in the scale beside the day's victory. They promenaded under the lurid July sun, this pair, so wide apart, yet so near, and Sophy saw the large proportion of boys like her own, in their broad white collars and dwarf hats, and all around the rows of great coaches under which was jumbled the debris of luxurious luncheons—bones, pie-crusts, champagne-bottles, glasses, plates, napkins, and the family silver; while on the coaches sat the proud fathers and mothers; but never a poor mother like her. If Randolph had not appertained to these, had not centred all his interests in them, had not cared exclusively for the class they belonged to, how happy would things have been! A great huzza at some small performance with the bat burst from the multitude of relatives, and Randolph jumped wildly into the air to see what had happened. Sophy fetched up the sentence that had been already shaped; but she could not get it out. The occasion was, perhaps, an inopportune one. The contrast between her story and the display of fashion to which Randolph had grown to regard himself as akin would be fatal. She awaited a better time.

It was on an evening when they were alone in their plain suburban residence, where life was not blue but brown, that she ultimately broke silence, qualifying her announcement of a probable second marriage by assuring him that it would not take place for a long time to come, when he would be living quite independently of her.

The boy thought the idea a very reasonable one, and asked if she had chosen anybody. She hesitated; and he seemed to have a misgiving. He hoped his stepfather would be a gentleman, he said.

"Not what you call a gentleman," she answered, timidly. "He'll be much as I was before I knew your father;" and by degrees she acquainted him with the whole. The youth's face remained fixed for a moment; then he flushed, leaned on the table, and burst into passionate tears.

His mother went up to him, kissed all of his face that she could get at, and patted his back as if he were still the baby he once had been, crying herself the while. When he had somewhat recovered from his paroxysm he went hastily to his own room and fastened the door.

Parleyings were attempted through the key-hole, outside which she waited and listened. It was long before he would reply, and when he did it was to say sternly at her from within: "I am ashamed of you! It will ruin me! A miserable boor! a churl! a clown! It will degrade me in the eyes of all the gentlemen of England!"

"Say no more—perhaps I am wrong! I will struggle against it!" she cried, miserably.

Before Randolph left her that summer a letter arrived from Sam to inform her that he had been unexpectedly fortunate in obtaining the shop. He was in possession; it was the largest in the town, combining fruit with vegetables, and he thought it would form a home worthy even of her some day. Might he not run up to town to see her?

She met him by stealth, and said he must still wait for her final answer. The autumn dragged on, and when Randolph was home at Christmas for the holidays she broached the matter again. But the young gentleman was inexorable.

It was dropped for months; renewed again; abandoned under his repugnance; again attempted, and thus the gentle creature reasoned and pleaded till four or five long years had passed. Then the faithful Sam revived his suit with some peremptoriness. Sophy's son, now an undergraduate, was down from Oxford one Easter, when she again opened the subject. As soon as he was ordained, she argued, he would have a home of his own, wherein she, with her bad grammar and her ignorance, would be an encumbrance to him. Better obliterate her as much as possible.

He showed a more manly anger now, but would not agree. She on her side was more persistent, and he had doubts whether she could be trusted in his absence. But by indignation and contempt for her taste he completely maintained his ascendency; and finally taking her before a little cross and shrine that he had erected in his bedroom for his private devotions, there bade her kneel, and swear that she would not wed Samuel Hobson without his consent. "I owe this to my father!" he said.

The poor woman swore, thinking he would soften as soon as he was ordained and in full swing of clerical work. But he did not. His education had by this time sufficiently ousted his humanity to keep him quite firm; though his mother might have led an idyllic life with her faithful fruiterer and green-grocer, and nobody have been anything the worse in the world.

Her lameness became more confirmed as time went on, and she seldom or never left the house in the long southern thoroughfare, where she seemed to be pining her heart away. "Why mayn't I say to Sam that I'll marry him? Why mayn't I?" she would murmur plaintively to herself when nobody was near.

Some four years after this date a middle-aged man was standing at the door of the largest fruiterer's shop in Aldbrickham. He was the proprietor, but to-day, instead of his usual business attire, he wore a neat suit of black; and his window was partly shuttered. From the railway station a funeral procession was seen approaching; it passed his door and went out of the town towards the village of Gaymead. The man, whose eyes were wet, held his hat in his hand as the vehicles moved by; while from the mourning coach a young smooth-shaven priest in a high waistcoat looked black as a cloud at the shopkeeper standing there.

—*1891*

KATE CHOPIN

Katherine Chopin was born in St. Louis, Missouri, in 1850. She was one of three children and the only child to reach adulthood in a family presided over by an Irish immigrant father and a mother who belonged to an aristocratic Creole family. Her father died in a train wreck in 1855 and Kate, with her mother, went to live with her widowed maternal grandmother and great-grandmother. She graduated in 1868 from the Catholic St. Louis Academy of the Sacred Heart, and in 1870 made her debut into St. Louis society. During a trip to New Orleans, she met Oscar Chopin, a cotton trader and plantation owner; they were married in 1871. The couple moved to Cloutierville, Louisiana, where Oscar owned several plantations. By all accounts their marriage was a happy one, and, while married to Oscar, Kate Chopin gave birth to six children. Her marriage was cut short, however, by Oscar's death from swamp fever in 1883. She ran the plantations for a time, but returned to St. Louis in 1884 after conducting a scandalous affair with a married neighbour.

From her teenage years and onward, Chopin read and wrote with avid interest, but it was not until after the death of her husband that she began writing in earnest. In 1889, she published her first story, and in 1890, her first novel, *At Fault*. Publishers rejected her second novel and she destroyed it. In 1894 her short stories began appearing in important periodicals such as *Vogue* and *The Atlantic Monthly*. Not long after, her first collection of short stories, *Bayou Folk* (1894), was published, followed by a second collection entitled *A Night in Acadie* (1897). Her work until this point garnered favourable reviews and was classified as part of the literary genre known as "local colour," a kind of fiction popular in the United States in the late nineteenth century that was expressive of regional flavour (Mark Twain's depiction of life in the American west and Mary Wilkins Freeman's New England writings are also examples of "local colour").

Chopin's third novel, *The Awakening*, (1899) tells the story of a married woman in an uninspiring marriage who "wakens" to her own eroticism and sensuality through amorous relations with other men. The novel received mixed reviews and was banned from St. Louis libraries. The negative reviews affected Chopin very deeply; her ill fortune was compounded when her publisher also refused to publish her fourth novel, *A Vocation and a Voice*. She published very little thereafter, and died in 1904 of a cerebral hemorrhage. Her writing was largely ignored until the 1950s and '60s, when scholars began to recognize the value of her work—and to treat *The Awakening* as a literary classic.

"The Story of an Hour" first appeared in *Vogue* in 1894, under the title "The Dream of an Hour." The story prefigures *The Awakening* in its challenge to the institution of marriage. Mrs. Mallard's epiphany on hearing of her husband's death runs contrary to all the assumptions of the time as to a wife's proper role. Although the story is short, it explores in some depth not only the hour that contains the story, but also the full span of Mrs. Mallard's married life.

The Story of an Hour

KATE CHOPIN

KNOWING that Mrs. Mallard was afflicted with a heart trouble, great care was taken to break to her as gently as possible the news of her husband's death.

It was her sister Josephine who told her, in broken sentences; veiled hints that revealed in half concealing. Her husband's friend Richards was there, too, near her. It was he who had been in the newspaper office when intelligence of the railroad disaster was received, with Brently Mallard's name leading the list of "killed." He had only taken the time to assure himself of its truth by a second telegram, and had hastened to forestall any less careful, less tender friend in bearing the sad message.

She did not hear the story as many women have heard the same, with a paralyzed inability to accept its significance. She wept at once, with sudden, wild abandonment, in her sister's arms. When the storm of grief had spent itself she went away to her room alone. She would have no one follow her.

There stood, facing the open window, a comfortable, roomy armchair. Into this she sank, pressed down by a physical exhaustion that haunted her body and seemed to reach into her soul.

She could see in the open square before her house the tops of trees that were all aquiver with the new spring life. The delicious breath of rain was in the air. In the street below a peddler was crying his wares. The notes of a distant song which some one was singing reached her faintly, and countless sparrows were twittering in the eaves.

There were patches of blue sky showing here and there through the clouds that had met and piled one above the other in the west facing her window.

She sat with her head thrown back upon the cushion of the chair, quite motionless, except when a sob came up into her throat and shook her, as a child who has cried itself to sleep continues to sob in its dreams.

She was young, with a fair, calm face, whose lines bespoke repression and even a certain strength. But now there was a dull stare in her eyes, whose gaze was fixed away off yonder on one of those patches of blue sky. It was not a glance of reflection, but rather indicated a suspension of intelligent thought.

There was something coming to her and she was waiting for it, fearfully. What was it? She did not know; it was too subtle and elusive to name. But she felt it, creeping out of the sky, reaching toward her through the sounds, the scents, the color that filled the air.

Now her bosom rose and fell tumultuously. She was beginning to recognize this thing that was approaching to possess her, and she was striving to beat it back with her will—as powerless as her two white slender hands would have been.

When she abandoned herself a little whispered word escaped her slightly parted lips. She said it over and over under her breath: "free, free, free!" The vacant stare and the look of terror that had followed it went from her eyes. They stayed keen and bright. Her pulses beat fast, and the coursing blood warmed and relaxed every inch of her body.

She did not stop to ask if it were or were not a monstrous joy that held her. A clear and exalted perception enabled her to dismiss the suggestion as trivial.

She knew that she would weep again when she saw the kind, tender hands folded in death; the face that had never looked save with love upon her, fixed and gray and dead. But she saw beyond that bitter moment a long procession of years to come that would belong to her absolutely. And she opened and spread her arms out to them in welcome.

There would be no one to live for her during those coming years; she would live for herself. There would be no powerful will bending hers in that blind persistence with which men and women believe they have a right to impose a private will upon a fellow-creature. A kind intention or a cruel intention made the act seem no less a crime as she looked upon it in that brief moment of illumination.

And yet she had loved him—sometimes. Often she had not. What did it matter! What could love, the unsolved mystery, count for in face of this possession of self-assertion which she suddenly recognized as the strongest impulse of her being!

"Free! Body and soul free!" she kept whispering.

Josephine was kneeling before the closed door with her lips to the keyhold, imploring for admission. "Louise, open the door! I beg; open the door—you will make yourself ill. What are you doing, Louise? For heaven's sake open the door."

"Go away. I am not making myself ill." No; she was drinking in a very elixir of life through that open window.

Her fancy was running riot along those days ahead of her. Spring days, and summer days, and all sorts of days that would be her own. She breathed a quick prayer that life might be long. It was only yesterday she had thought with a shudder that life might be long.

She arose at length and opened the door to her sister's importunities. There was a feverish triumph in her eyes, and she carried herself unwittingly like a goddess of Victory. She clasped her sister's waist, and together they descended the stairs. Richards stood waiting for them at the bottom.

Some one was opening the front door with a latchkey. It was Brently Mallard who entered, a little travel-stained, composedly carrying his grip-sack and umbrella. He had been far from the scene of accident, and did not even know there had been one. He stood amazed at Josephine's piercing cry; at Richards' quick motion to screen him from the view of his wife.

But Richards was too late.

When the doctors came they said she had died of heart disease—of joy that kills.

—1894

GUY DE MAUPASSANT

Guy de Maupassant was a French short-story writer and novelist; he is considered one of the nineteenth-century masters of short fiction. He was born in Normandy in 1850 and raised by his mother, a kind and cultured woman to whom he was devoted. He first studied law, then served in the Franco-Prussian war, and finally settled in Paris, where he worked in the civil service until his writing provided him with a living wage.

After 1880 and the publication of *Boule-de-Suif,* Maupassant achieved great success and wealth; he moved in high social circles and had numerous love affairs. Although his stories vary widely in form, theme, and genre, they focus on revealing the too-often petty and selfish motives behind human interactions. His characters are drawn from all walks of life, from aristocrats to prostitutes, though most often they are middle class, either country people or urban civil servants. Like other nineteenth-century Naturalist writers, Maupassant often depicted characters unable to control their destiny in a world governed by biological forces and harsh social conditions. The novelist Gustave Flaubert was a key influence; it was he who helped Maupassant develop his subtle and highly-crafted prose style.

Maupassant seemed to his contemporaries to be an open, spirited, and healthy man; he loved exercise and spent much of his free time rowing on the Seine. When he was eighteen, he rescued the English poet Algernon Swinburne from drowning off the coast of Normandy. But the successful young writer suffered from dark preoccupations. He had contracted syphilis; the disease spread and gradually debilitated him, physically and mentally. He died at age 42 in an asylum, a year after attempting suicide.

Emile Zola, a friend of Maupassant's and key proponent of literary Naturalism, said of Maupassant: "We leave his pages looking at ourselves, with the same moral and physical joy that we gain from a walk in the plain light of day." Maupassant's stories, seeking as they do to lay bare our delusions, continue to be influential. The clarity of his plots, his deceptively simple style, and his detached narrative voice have all been formative in the development of the short story.

In "The Necklace," Madame Loisel has recently married a "small clerk." A pretty and charming girl, she feels unhappy with her marriage and with middle-class life; she longs for riches and for the attention of elegant men. Her husband is kind and loving to her, but she is blind to the true worth of anything in her life, seeing only its material deficiencies: "She had no pretty gowns, no jewels, nothing—and yet she cared for nothing else." Maupassant's stylistic mastery, care for detail, and sure hand with plot create a memorable commentary on human vanity and human folly.

The Necklace[1] *(La Parure)*

GUY DE MAUPASSANT

SHE WAS one of those pretty and charming girls who, by some freak of destiny, are born into families that have always held subordinate appointments. Possessing neither dowry nor expectations, she had no hope of meeting some man of wealth and distinction, who would understand her, fall in love with her, and wed her. So she consented to marry a small clerk in the Ministry of Public Instruction.

She dressed plainly, because she could not afford to be elegant, but she felt as unhappy as if she had married beneath her. Women are dependent on neither caste nor ancestry. With them, beauty, grace, and charm take the place of birth and breeding. In their case, natural delicacy, instinctive refinement, and adaptability constitute their claims to aristocracy and raise girls of the lower classes to an equality with the greatest of great ladies. She was eternally restive under the conviction that she had been born to enjoy every refinement and luxury. Depressed by her humble surroundings, the sordid walls of her dwelling, its worn furniture and shabby fabrics were a torment to her. Details which another woman of her class would scarcely have noticed, tortured her and filled her with resentment. The sight of her little Breton[2] maid-of-all-work roused in her forlorn repinings and frantic yearnings. She pictured to herself silent antechambers, upholstered with oriental tapestry, lighted by great bronze standard lamps, where two tall footmen in knee-breeches slumbered in huge arm-chairs, overcome by the oppressive heat from the stove. She dreamed of spacious

1 Translated by Albert M.C. McMaster, A.E. Henderson, and Louise Charlotte Garstin Quesada.

2 From Brittany, a region of northwestern France.

drawing-rooms with hangings of antique silk, and beautiful tables laden with priceless ornaments: of fragrant and coquettish boudoirs, exquisitely adapted for afternoon chats with intimate friends, men of note and distinction, whose attentions are coveted by every woman.

She would sit down to dinner at the round table, its cloth already three days old, while her husband, seated opposite to her, removed the lid from the soup tureen and exclaimed, "*Pot-au-feu!*[3] How splendid! My favourite soup!" But her own thoughts were dallying with the idea of exquisite dinners and shining silver, in rooms whose tapestried walls were gay with antique figures and grotesque birds in fairy forests. She would dream of delicious dishes served on wonderful plate, of soft, whispered nothings, which evoke a sphinx-like smile, while one trifles with the pink flesh of a trout or the wing of a plump pullet.

She had no pretty gowns, no jewels, nothing—and yet she cared for nothing else. She felt that it was for such things as these that she had been born. What joy it would have given her to attract, to charm, to be envied by women, courted by men! She had a wealthy friend, who had been at school at the same convent, but after a time she refused to go and see her, because she suffered so acutely after each visit. She spent whole days in tears of grief, regret, despair, and misery.

One evening her husband returned home in triumph with a large envelope in his hand.

"Here is something for you," he cried.

Hastily she tore open the envelope and drew out a printed card with the following inscription:

"The Minister of Public Instruction and Madame Georges Ramponneau have the honour to request the company of Monsieur and Madame Loisel at an At Home at the Education Office on Monday, 18th January."

Instead of being delighted as her husband had hoped, she flung the invitation irritably on the table, exclaiming:

"What good is that to me?"

"Why, my dear, I thought you would be pleased. You never go anywhere, and this is a really splendid chance for you. I had no end of trouble in getting it. Everybody is trying to get an invitation. It's very select, and only a few invitations are issued to the clerks. You will see all the officials there."

She looked at him in exasperation, and exclaimed petulantly:

"What do you expect me to wear at a reception like that?"

He had not considered the matter, but he replied hesitatingly:

"Why, that dress you always wear to the theatre seems to me very nice indeed ..."

---

3 A French beef stew; literally, "pot on the fire."

He broke off. To his horror and consternation he saw that his wife was in tears. Two large drops were rolling slowly down her cheeks.

"What on earth is the matter?" he gasped.

With a violent effort she controlled her emotion, and drying her wet cheeks said in a calm voice:

"Nothing. Only I haven't a frock, and so I can't go to the reception. Give your invitation to some friend in your office, whose wife is better dressed than I am."

He was greatly distressed.

"Let us talk it over, Mathilde. How much do you think a proper frock would cost, something quite simple that would come in useful for other occasions afterwards?"

She considered the matter for a few moments, busy with her calculations, and wondering how large a sum she might venture to name without shocking the little clerk's instincts of economy and provoking a prompt refusal.

"I hardly know," she said at last, doubtfully, "but I think I could manage with four hundred francs."

He turned a little pale. She had named the exact sum that he had saved for buying a gun and treating himself to some Sunday shooting parties the following summer with some friends, who were going to shoot larks in the plain of Nanterre.[4]

But he replied:

"Very well, I'll give you four hundred francs. But mind you buy a really handsome gown."

○ ○ ○

The day of the party drew near. But although her gown was finished Madame Loisel seemed depressed and dissatisfied.

"What is the matter?" asked her husband one evening. "You haven't been at all yourself the last three days."

She answered: "It vexes me to think that I haven't any jewellery to wear, not even a brooch. I shall feel like a perfect pauper. I would almost rather not go to the party."

"You can wear some fresh flowers. They are very fashionable this year. For ten francs you can get two or three splendid roses."

She was not convinced.

"No, there is nothing more humiliating than to have an air of poverty among a crowd of rich women."

---

4 An area west of Paris.

"How silly you are!" exclaimed her husband. "Why don't you ask your friend, Madame Forestier, to lend you some jewellery. You know her quite well enough for that."

She uttered a cry of joy.

"Yes, of course, it never occurred to me."

The next day she paid her friend a visit and explained her predicament.

Madame Forestier went to her wardrobe, took out a large jewel case and placed it open before her friend.

"Help yourself, my dear," she said.

Madame Loisel saw some bracelets, a pearl necklace, a Venetian cross exquisitely worked in gold and jewels. She tried on these ornaments in front of the mirror and hesitated, reluctant to take them off and give them back.

"Have you nothing else?" she kept asking.

"Oh, yes, look for yourself. I don't know what you would prefer."

At length, she discovered a black satin case containing a superb diamond necklace, and her heart began to beat with frantic desire. With trembling hands she took it out, fastened it over her high-necked gown, and stood gazing at herself in rapture.

Then, in an agony of doubt, she said:

"Will you lend me this? I shouldn't want anything else."

"Yes, certainly."

She threw her arms round her friend's neck, kissed her effusively, and then fled with her treasure.

° ° °

It was the night of the reception. Madame Loisel's triumph was complete. All smiles and graciousness, in her exquisite gown, she was the prettiest woman in the room. Her head was in a whirl of joy. All the men stared at her and inquired her name and begged for an introduction; all the junior staff asked her for waltzes. She even attracted the attention of the minister himself.

Carried away by her enjoyment, glorying in her beauty and her success, she threw herself ecstatically into the dance. She moved as in a beatific dream, wherein were mingled all the homage and admiration she had evoked, all the desires she had kindled, all that complete and perfect triumph, so dear to a woman's heart.

It was close on four before she could tear herself away. Ever since midnight her husband had been dozing in a little, deserted drawing-room together with three other men whose wives were enjoying themselves immensely.

He threw her outdoor wraps round her shoulders, unpretentious, every-day garments, whose shabbiness contrasted strangely with the elegance of her ball dress. Conscious of the incongruity, she was eager to be gone, in order to escape the notice of the other women in their luxurious furs. Loisel tried to restrain her.

"Wait here while I fetch a cab. You will catch cold outside."

But she would not listen to him and hurried down the staircase. They went out into the street, but there was no cab to be seen. They continued their search, vainly hailing drivers whom they caught sight of in the distance. Shivering with cold and in desperation they made their way towards the Seine. At last, on the quay, they found one of those old vehicles which are only seen in Paris after nightfall, as if ashamed to display their shabbiness by daylight.

The cab took them to their door in the Rue des Martyrs and they gloomily climbed the stairs to their dwelling. All was over for her. As for him, he was thinking that he would have to be in the office by ten o'clock.

She took off her wraps in front of the mirror, for the sake of one last glance at herself in all her glory. But suddenly she uttered a cry. The diamonds were no longer round her neck.

"What is the matter?" asked her husband, who was already half undressed.

She turned to him in horror. "I ... I've ... lost Madame Forestier's necklace."

He started in dismay. "What? Lost the necklace? Impossible!"

They searched the pleats of the gown, the folds of the cloak, and all the pockets, but in vain.

"You are sure you had it on when you came away from the ball?"

"Yes, I remember feeling it in the lobby at the Education Office."

"But if you had lost it in the street we should have heard it drop. It must be in the cab."

"Yes. I expect it is. Did you take the number?"

"No. Did you?"

"No."

They gazed at each other, utterly appalled. In the end Loisel put on his clothes again.

"I will go over the ground that we covered on foot and see if I cannot find it."

He left the house. Lacking the strength to go to bed, unable to think, she collapsed into a chair and remained there in her evening gown, without a fire.

About seven o'clock her husband returned. He had not found the diamonds.

He applied to the police, advertised a reward in the newspapers, made inquiries of all the hackney cab offices; he visited every place that seemed to hold out a vestige of hope.

His wife waited all day long in the same distracted condition, overwhelmed by this appalling calamity.

Loisel returned home in the evening, pale and hollow-cheeked. His efforts had been in vain.

"You must write to your friend," he said, "and tell her that you have broken the catch of the necklace and that you are having it mended. That will give us time to think things over."

She wrote a letter to his dictation.

° ° °

After a week had elapsed, they gave up all hope. Loisel, who looked five years older, said:

"We must take steps to replace the diamonds."

On the following day they took the empty case to the jeweller whose name was inside the lid. He consulted his books.

"The necklace was not bought here, madam; I can only have supplied the case."

They went from jeweller to jeweller, in an endeavour to find a necklace exactly like the one they had lost, comparing their recollections. Both of them were ill with grief and despair.

At last in a shop in the Palais-Royal they found a diamond necklace, which seemed to them exactly like the other. Its price was forty thousand francs. The jeweller agreed to sell it to them for thirty-six. They begged him not to dispose of it for three days, and they stipulated for the right to sell it back for thirty-four thousand francs, if the original necklace was found before the end of February.

Loisel had eighteen thousand francs left to him by his father. The balance of the sum he proposed to borrow. He raised loans in all quarters, a thousand francs from one man, five hundred from another, five louis here, three louis there. He gave promissory notes, agreed to exorbitant terms, had dealings with usurers, and with all the money-lending hordes. He compromised his whole future, and had to risk his signature, hardly knowing if he would be able to honour it. Overwhelmed by the prospect of future suffering, the black misery which was about to come upon him, the physical privations and moral torments, he went to fetch the new necklace, and laid his thirty-six thousand francs down on the jeweller's counter.

When Madame Loisel brought back the necklace, Madame Forestier said reproachfully:

"You ought to have returned it sooner; I might have wanted to wear it."

To Madame Loisel's relief she did not open the case. Supposing she had noticed the exchange, what would she have thought? What would she have said? Perhaps she would have taken her for a thief.

° ° °

Madame Loisel now became acquainted with the horrors of extreme poverty. She made up her mind to it, and played her part heroically. This appalling debt had to be paid, and pay it she would. The maid was dismissed; the flat was given up, and they moved to a garret. She undertook all the rough household work and the odious duties of the kitchen. She washed up after meals and ruined her pink finger-nails scrubbing greasy dishes and saucepans. She washed the linen, the shirts, and the dusters, and hung them out on the line to dry. Every morning she carried down the sweepings to the street, and brought up the water, pausing for breath at each landing. Dressed like a working woman, she went with her basket on her arm to the greengrocer, the grocer, and the butcher, bargaining, wrangling, and fighting for every farthing.

Each month some of the promissory notes had to be redeemed, and others renewed, in order to gain time.

Her husband spent his evenings working at some tradesman's accounts, and at night he would often copy papers at five sous a page.

This existence went on for ten years.

At the end of that time they had paid off everything to the last penny, including the usurious rates and the accumulations of interest.

Madame Loisel now looked an old woman. She had become the typical poor man's wife, rough, coarse, hardbitten. Her hair was neglected, her skirts hung awry, and her hands were red. Her voice was no longer gentle, and she washed down the floors vigorously. But now and then, when her husband was at the office, she would sit by the window and her thoughts would wander back to that far-away evening, the evening of her beauty and her triumph.

What would have been the end of it if she had not lost the necklace? Who could say? Who could say? How strange, how variable are the chances of life! How small a thing can serve to save or ruin you!

One Sunday she went for a stroll in the Champs-Élysées,[5] for the sake of relaxation after the week's work, and she caught sight of a lady with a child. She recognized Madame Forestier, who looked as young, as pretty and as attractive as ever. Madame Loisel felt a thrill of emotion. Should she speak to her? Why not? Now that the debt was paid, why should she not tell her the whole story? She went up to her.

"Good morning, Jeanne."

Her friend did not recognize her and was surprised at being addressed so familiarly by this homely person.

5 A street in Paris famous for its fashionable shops and restaurants.

"I am afraid I do not know you—you must have made a mistake," she said hesitatingly.

"No. I am Mathilde Loisel."

Her friend uttered a cry.

"Oh, my poor, dear Mathilde how you have changed!"

"Yes, I have been through a very hard time since I saw you last, no end of trouble, and all through you."

"Through me? What do you mean?"

"You remember the diamond necklace you lent me to wear at the reception at the Education Office?"

"Yes. Well?"

"Well, I lost it."

"I don't understand; you brought it back to me."

"What I brought you back was another one, exactly like it. And for the last ten years we have been paying for it. You will understand that it was not an easy matter for people like us, who hadn't a penny. However, it's all over now. I can't tell you what a relief it is."

Madame Forestier stopped dead.

"You mean to say that you bought a diamond necklace to replace mine?"

"Yes. And you never noticed it? They were certainly very much alike."

She smiled with ingenuous pride and satisfaction.

Madame Forestier seized both her hands in great distress.

"Oh, my poor, dear Mathilde! Why, mine was only imitation. At the most it was worth five hundred francs!"

—1884

ANTON CHEKHOV

Anton Chekhov was born in Taganrog, a small seaport in southern Russia. He is one of the most influential and respected writers in Western literature; his innovative techniques of narration and characterization have shaped the short story genre, and his work has also been formative in the development of modern drama. Both his stories and his plays have proved to be enduringly popular.

Chekhov was the third of six children, the son of a grocer. His father's bankruptcy in 1875 broke up the family; after watching his mother lose their house and all their possessions, he was left alone in Taganrog. He supported himself by publishing pieces in humour journals between 1880 and 1885, thus paying his way through medical school at Moscow University. He graduated in 1884 and began practicing in country hospitals. In a letter to a friend in 1888, he said: "Medicine is my lawful wife and literature is my mistress. When I get tired of one I spend the night with the other."

In 1885, Chekhov began publishing more serious stories. He outlined his approach in a letter to his brother, Aleksandr: "1. Absence of lengthy verbiage of political-social-economic nature; 2. total objectivity; 3. truthful descriptions of persons and objects; 4. extreme brevity; 5. audacity and originality: flee the stereotype; 6. compassion." He experimented extensively with narrative voice; in the typical Chekhov story the governing narrative voice is objective and aloof, but the narrative may frequently adopt the point of view of one or more of the characters. (This technique, which has come to be known as free indirect discourse, anticipates the more extended "stream of consciousness" narrative techniques adopted by Dorothy Richardson, James Joyce, and other modernist writers.) His stories eschew conventional plot structures, often concluding with one of Chekhov's "zero" endings, in which nothing is clearly resolved.

Late in 1884, Chekhov began to suffer from tuberculosis. As a doctor he must have recognized the disease, but he ignored it and continued to work. He settled on his own estate at Melikhovo, where he stayed until 1898, continuing to write and practice medicine, and often travelling for miles to visit the sick. He ran a free clinic for peasants and organized relief during cholera and famine outbreaks. He also had affairs with various women, but soon tired of each—a pattern that finally ended when he fell in love with the actress Olga Knipper in the late 1890s.

Chekhov's last years were spent in Nice and Yalta, as he sought a better climate to help his worsening illness. During this period he wrote some of his greatest short stories, among them "The Little Trilogy" (1898), "The Lady with a Dog" (1899), "In the Ravine" (1900), and "The Bishop" (1902). In 1904 Chekhov went to Badenweiler, Germany with his wife Olga, where he died on July 15. Famously, he announced he was dying, took a sip of champagne, and then promptly passed away.

"An Upheaval" (1886) tells the story of a young governess accused by the lady of the house of stealing an expensive brooch. An educated woman, the governess is insulted—but must reconcile her own guilt for hiding excess food in her room with the larger sense of injustice she feels at the false accusation.

An Upheaval[1]

ANTON CHEKHOV

MASHENKA PAVLETSKY, a young girl who had only just finished her studies at a boarding school, returning from a walk to the house of the Kushkins, with whom she was living as a governess, found the household in a terrible turmoil. Mihailo, the porter who opened the door to her, was excited and red as a crab.

Loud voices were heard from upstairs.

"Madame Kushkin is in a fit, most likely, or else she has quarreled with her husband," thought Mashenka.

In the hall and in the corridor she met maid-servants. One of them was crying. Then Mashenka saw, running out of her room, the master of the house himself, Nikolay Sergeitch, a little man with a flabby face and a bald head, though he was not old. He was red in the face and twitching all over. He passed the governess without noticing her, and throwing up his arms, exclaimed:

"Oh, how horrible it is! How tactless! How stupid! How barbarous! Abominable!"

Mashenka went into her room, and then, for the first time in her life, it was her lot to experience in all its acuteness the feeling that is so familiar to persons

1 Translated by Constance Garnett.

in dependent positions, who eat the bread of the rich and powerful, and cannot speak their minds. There was a search going on in her room. The lady of the house, Fedosya Vassilyevna, a stout, broad-shouldered, uncouth woman with thick black eyebrows, a faintly perceptible moustache, and red hands, who was exactly like a plain, illiterate cook in face and manners, was standing, without her cap on, at the table, putting back into Mashenka's workbag balls of wool, scraps of materials, and bits of paper.... Evidently the governess's arrival took her by surprise, since, on looking round and seeing the girl's pale and astonished face, she was a little taken aback, and muttered:

"*Pardon*. I ... I upset it accidentally.... My sleeve caught in it ..."

And saying something more, Madame Kushkin rustled her long skirts and went out. Mashenka looked round her room with wondering eyes, and, unable to understand it, not knowing what to think, shrugged her shoulders, and turned cold with dismay. What had Fedosya Vassilyevna been looking for in her work-bag? If she really had, as she said, caught her sleeve in it and upset everything, why had Nikolay Sergeitch dashed out of her room so excited and red in the face? Why was one drawer of the table pulled out a little way? The money-box, in which the governess put away ten kopeck pieces and old stamps, was open. They had opened it, but did not know how to shut it, though they had scratched the lock all over. The whatnot with her books on it, the things on the table, the bed—all bore fresh traces of a search. Her linen-basket, too. The linen had been carefully folded, but it was not in the same order as Mashenka had left it when she went out. So the search had been thorough, most thorough. But what was it for? Why? What had happened? Mashenka remembered the excited porter, the general turmoil which was still going on, the weeping servant-girl; had it not all some connection with the search that had just been made in her room? Was not she mixed up in something dreadful? Mashenka turned pale, and feeling cold all over, sank on to her linen-basket.

A maid-servant came into the room.

"Liza, you don't know why they have been rummaging in my room?" the governess asked her.

"Mistress has lost a brooch worth two thousand," said Liza.

"Yes, but why have they been rummaging in my room?"

"They've been searching every one, miss. They've searched all my things, too. They stripped us all naked and searched us.... God knows, miss, I never went near her toilet-table, let alone touching the brooch. I shall say the same at the police-station."

"But ... why have they been rummaging here?" the governess still wondered.

"A brooch has been stolen, I tell you. The mistress has been rummaging in everything with her own hands. She even searched Mihailo, the porter, herself.

It's a perfect disgrace! Nikolay Sergeitch simply looks on and cackles like a hen. But you've no need to tremble like that, miss. They found nothing here. You've nothing to be afraid of if you didn't take the brooch."

"But, Liza, it's vile ... it's insulting," said Mashenka, breathless with indignation. "It's so mean, so low! What right had she to suspect me and to rummage in my things?"

"You are living with strangers, miss," sighed Liza. "Though you are a young lady, still you are ... as it were ... a servant.... It's not like living with your papa and mamma."

Mashenka threw herself on the bed and sobbed bitterly. Never in her life had she been subjected to such an outrage, never had she been so deeply insulted.... She, well-educated, refined, the daughter of a teacher, was suspected of theft; she had been searched like a street-walker! She could not imagine a greater insult. And to this feeling of resentment was added an oppressive dread of what would come next. All sorts of absurd ideas came into her mind. If they could suspect her of theft, then they might arrest her, strip her naked, and search her, then lead her through the street with an escort of soldiers, cast her into a cold, dark cell with mice and woodlice, exactly like the dungeon in which Princess Tarakanov[2] was imprisoned. Who would stand up for her? Her parents lived far away in the provinces; they had not the money to come to her. In the capital she was as solitary as in a desert, without friends or kindred. They could do what they liked with her.

"I will go to all the courts and all the lawyers," Mashenka thought, trembling. "I will explain to them, I will take an oath.... They will believe that I could not be a thief!"

Mashenka remembered that under the sheets in her basket she had some sweetmeats, which, following the habits of her schooldays, she had put in her pocket at dinner and carried off to her room. She felt hot all over, and was ashamed at the thought that her little secret was known to the lady of the house; and all this terror, shame, resentment, brought on an attack of palpitation of the heart, which set up a throbbing in her temples, in her heart, and deep down in her stomach.

"Dinner is ready," the servant summoned Mashenka.

"Shall I go, or not?"

Mashenka brushed her hair, wiped her face with a wet towel, and went into the dining-room. There they had already begun dinner. At one end of the table sat Fedosya Vassilyevna with a stupid, solemn, serious face; at the other end

---

2 Yelizaveta Alekseyevna (1753–75), an impostor who claimed to be a Russian princess. She was captured in 1775, and died of tuberculosis while in prison.

Nikolay Sergeitch. At the sides there were the visitors and the children. The dishes were handed by two footmen in swallowtails and white gloves. Every one knew that there was an upset in the house, that Madame Kushkin was in trouble, and every one was silent. Nothing was heard but the sound of munching and the rattle of spoons on the plates.

The lady of the house, herself, was the first to speak.

"What is the third course?" she asked the footman in a weary, injured voice.

"*Esturgeon à la russe*,"[3] answered the footman.

"I ordered that, Fenya," Nikolay Sergeitch hastened to observe. "I wanted some fish. If you don't like it, *ma chère*,[4] don't let them serve it. I just ordered it...."

Fedosya Vassilyevna did not like dishes that she had not ordered herself, and now her eyes filled with tears.

"Come, don't let us agitate ourselves," Mamikov, her household doctor, observed in a honeyed voice, just touching her arm, with a smile as honeyed. "We are nervous enough as it is. Let us forget the brooch! Health is worth more than two thousand roubles!"

"It's not the two thousand I regret," answered the lady, and a big tear rolled down her cheek. "It's the fact itself that revolts me! I cannot put up with thieves in my house. I don't regret it—I regret nothing; but to steal from me is such ingratitude! That's how they repay me for my kindness...."

They all looked into their plates, but Mashenka fancied after the lady's words that every one was looking at her. A lump rose in her throat; she began crying and put her handkerchief to her lips.

"*Pardon*," she muttered. "I can't help it. My head aches. I'll go away."

And she got up from the table, scraping her chair awkwardly, and went out quickly, still more overcome with confusion.

"It's beyond everything!" said Nikolay Sergeitch, frowning. "What need was there to search her room? How out of place it was!"

"I don't say she took the brooch," said Fedosya Vassilyevna, "but can you answer for her? To tell the truth, I haven't much confidence in these learned paupers."

"It really was unsuitable, Fenya.... Excuse me, Fenya, but you've no kind of legal right to make a search."

"I know nothing about your laws. All I know is that I've lost my brooch. And I will find the brooch!" She brought her fork down on the plate with a clatter,

3 A French preparation of sturgeon, a large, freshwater fish ("à la russe" translates literally as "in the Russian style").

4 French: "my dear."

and her eyes flashed angrily. "And you eat your dinner, and don't interfere in what doesn't concern you!"

Nikolay Sergeitch dropped his eyes mildly and sighed. Meanwhile Mashenka, reaching her room, flung herself on her bed. She felt now neither alarm nor shame, but she felt an intense longing to go and slap the cheeks of this hard, arrogant, dull-witted, prosperous woman.

Lying on her bed she breathed into her pillow and dreamed of how nice it would be to go and buy the most expensive brooch and fling it into the face of this bullying woman. If only it were God's will that Fedosya Vassilyevna should come to ruin and wander about begging, and should taste all the horrors of poverty and dependence, and that Mashenka, whom she had insulted, might give her alms! Oh, if only she could come in for a big fortune, could buy a carriage, and could drive noisily past the windows so as to be envied by that woman!

But all these were only dreams, in reality there was only one thing left to do—to get away as quickly as possible, not to stay another hour in this place. It was true it was terrible to lose her place, to go back to her parents, who had nothing; but what could she do? Mashenka could not bear the sight of the lady of the house nor of her little room; she felt stifled and wretched here. She was so disgusted with Fedosya Vassilyevna, who was so obsessed by her illnesses and her supposed aristocratic rank, that everything in the world seemed to have become coarse and unattractive because this woman was living in it. Mashenka jumped up from the bed and began packing.

"May I come in?" asked Nikolay Sergeitch at the door; he had come up noiselessly to the door, and spoke in a soft, subdued voice. "May I?"

"Come in."

He came in and stood still near the door. His eyes looked dim and his red little nose was shiny. After dinner he used to drink beer, and the fact was perceptible in his walk, in his feeble, flabby hands.

"What's this?" he asked, pointing to the basket.

"I am packing. Forgive me, Nikolay Sergeitch, but I cannot remain in your house. I feel deeply insulted by this search!"

"I understand.... Only you are wrong to go. Why should you? They've searched your things, but you ... what does it matter to you? You will be none the worse for it."

Mashenka was silent and went on packing. Nikolay Sergeitch pinched his moustache, as though wondering what he should say next, and went on in an ingratiating voice:

"I understand, of course, but you must make allowances. You know my wife is nervous, headstrong; you mustn't judge her too harshly."

Mashenka did not speak.

"If you are so offended," Nikolay Sergeitch went on, "well, if you like, I'm ready to apologise. I ask your pardon."

Mashenka made no answer, but only bent lower over her box. This exhausted, irresolute man was of absolutely no significance in the household. He stood in the pitiful position of a dependent and hanger-on, even with the servants, and his apology meant nothing either.

"H'm! … You say nothing! That's not enough for you. In that case, I will apologise for my wife. In my wife's name.… She behaved tactlessly, I admit it as a gentleman.…"

Nikolay Sergeitch walked about the room, heaved a sigh, and went on: "Then you want me to have it rankling here, under my heart.… You want my conscience to torment me.…"

"I know it's not your fault, Nikolay Sergeitch," said Mashenka, looking him full in the face with her big tear-stained eyes. "Why should you worry yourself?"

"Of course, no.… But still, don't you … go away. I entreat you."

Mashenka shook her head. Nikolay Sergeitch stopped at the window and drummed on the pane with his finger-tips.

"Such misunderstandings are simply torture to me," he said. "Why, do you want me to go down on my knees to you, or what? Your pride is wounded, and here you've been crying and packing up to go; but I have pride, too, and you do not spare it! Or do you want me to tell you what I would not tell as Confession? Do you? Listen; you want me to tell you what I won't tell the priest on my deathbed?"

Mashenka made no answer.

"I took my wife's brooch," Nikolay Sergeitch said quickly. "Is that enough now? Are you satisfied? Yes, I … took it.… But, of course, I count on your discretion.… For God's sake, not a word, not half a hint to any one!"

Mashenka, amazed and frightened, went on packing; she snatched her things, crumpled them up, and thrust them anyhow into the box and the basket. Now, after this candid avowal on the part of Nikolay Sergeitch, she could not remain another minute, and could not understand how she could have gone on living in the house before.

"And it's nothing to wonder at," Nikolay Sergeitch went on after a pause. "It's an everyday story! I need money, and she … won't give it to me. It was my father's money that bought this house and everything, you know! It's all mine, and the brooch belonged to my mother, and … it's all mine! And she took it, took possession of everything.… I can't go to law with her, you'll admit.… I beg you most earnestly, overlook it … stay on. *Tout comprendre, tout pardonner*.[5] Will you stay?"

---

5 A French aphorism: "To understand all is to forgive all."

"No!" said Mashenka resolutely, beginning to tremble. "Let me alone, I entreat you!"

"Well, God bless you!" sighed Nikolay Sergeitch, sitting down on the stool near the box. "I must own I like people who still can feel resentment, contempt, and so on. I could sit here forever and look at your indignant face.... So you won't stay, then? I understand.... It's bound to be so ... Yes, of course.... It's all right for you, but for me—wo-o-o-o! ... I can't stir a step out of this cellar. I'd go off to one of our estates, but in every one of them there are some of my wife's rascals ... stewards, experts, damn them all! They mortgage and remortgage.... You mustn't catch fish, must keep off the grass, mustn't break the trees."

"Nikolay Sergeitch!" his wife's voice called from the drawing-room. "Agnia, call your master!"

"Then you won't stay?" asked Nikolay Sergeitch, getting up quickly and going towards the door. "You might as well stay, really. In the evenings I could come and have a talk with you. Eh? Stay! If you go, there won't be a human face left in the house. It's awful!"

Nikolay Sergeitch's pale, exhausted face besought her, but Mashenka shook her head, and with a wave of his hand he went out.

Half an hour later she was on her way.

—1886

CHARLOTTE PERKINS GILMAN

Born in 1860 in Hartford, Connecticut, Charlotte Perkins grew up in poverty and domestic instability after her father abandoned the family. When she turned eighteen, Gilman went against her mother's wishes and enrolled in the Rhode Island School of Design to study art and painting, where she met a fellow artist, Charles Walter Stetson. Gilman married Stetson in 1884 and gave up her formerly vigorous intellectual life—a move that sparked a descent into depression. Her depression deepened when she gave birth to her daughter Katharine in 1885, and, after an ill-fated attempt at Philadelphia neurologist S. Weir Mitchell's famous "rest-cure" (a medical prescription that involved complete inactivity and little to no intellectual stimulation), she left her husband and moved with Katharine to California. She later divorced Stetson and gave him custody of their daughter, an incident that led to the charge that she was an "unnatural mother."

For the remainder of her life, Gilman lectured widely. She published seven novels (including the feminist utopian novel *Herland*), several collections of poetry, her monthly magazine *The Forerunner*, and numerous essays on topics relevant to feminism and socialism. In 1900 she married her first cousin George Houghton Gilman after an extended courtship. The marriage was regarded as a relatively happy one—this time Perkins Gilman did not give up her career plans or her sense of independence—but George Gilman died in 1934 of a cerebral hemorrhage. In 1935, three years after learning that she had breast cancer, Gilman committed suicide; her belief—as stated in her posthumously published autobiography *The Living of Charlotte Perkins Gilman*—was that it is "the simplest of human rights to choose a quick and easy death in place of a slow and horrible one."

Although during her lifetime Gilman was best-known for her book *Women and Economics: A Study of the Economic Relation Between Men and Women* (1898), modern interest in her work has centred on *Herland* and on the short story "The Yellow Wallpaper." First published in 1892 in *The New England Magazine*, the story draws on Gilman's experiences with the "rest-cure" that nearly drove her insane. Horace P. Scudder, the publisher she initially submitted it to, rejected the story, saying "I should never forgive myself if I made other people as miserable as reading your story has made me." The story's reception was mixed, and editor William Dean Howells believed that the story was "unpopular because ... it 'struck too deeply and effectively at traditional ways of seeing the world and woman's place in it.'" Although it was anthologized regularly in the decades after its publication, it was not until the explosion of American feminism in the 1970s that it began to be thought of as a classic. Gilman's uncanny ability to convey the narrator's descent into madness via the wallpaper in her sickroom resembles a horror story but without the characteristic, easily dismissible trappings of horror literature. The "horror" comes from the reader's witnessing of a sane woman's descent into madness through unrelenting, "rational" intervention.

The Yellow Wallpaper

CHARLOTTE PERKINS GILMAN

IT IS VERY seldom that mere ordinary people like John and myself secure ancestral halls for the summer.

A colonial mansion, a hereditary estate, I would say a haunted house and reach the height of romantic felicity—but that would be asking too much of fate!

Still I will proudly declare that there is something queer about it.

Else, why should it be let so cheaply? And why have stood so long untenanted?

John laughs at me, of course, but one expects that.

John is practical in the extreme. He has no patience with faith, an intense horror of superstition, and he scoffs openly at any talk of things not to be felt and seen and put down in figures.

John is a physician, and *perhaps*—(I would not say it to a living soul, of course, but this is dead paper and a great relief to my mind)—*perhaps* that is one reason I do not get well faster.

You see, he does not believe I am sick! And what can one do?

If a physician of high standing, and one's own husband, assures friends and relatives that there is really nothing the matter with one but temporary nervous depression—a slight hysterical tendency—what is one to do?

My brother is also a physician, and also of high standing, and he says the same thing.

So I take phosphates or phosphites—whichever it is—and tonics, and air and exercise, and journeys, and am absolutely forbidden to "work" until I am well again.

Personally, I disagree with their ideas.

Personally, I believe that congenial work, with excitement and change, would do me good.

But what is one to do?

I did write for a while in spite of them, but it *does* exhaust me a good deal—having to be so sly about it, or else meet with heavy opposition.

I sometimes fancy that in my condition, if I had less opposition and more society and stimulus—but John says the very worst thing I can do is to think about my condition, and I confess it always makes me feel bad.

So I will let it alone and talk about the house.

The most beautiful place! It is quite alone, standing well back from the road, quite three miles from the village. It makes me think of English places that you read about, for there are hedges and walls and gates that lock, and lots of separate little houses for the gardeners and people.

There is a *delicious* garden! I never saw such a garden—large and shady, full of box-bordered paths, and lined with long grape-covered arbors with seats under them.

There were greenhouses, but they are all broken now.

There was some legal trouble, I believe, something about the heirs and coheirs; anyhow, the place has been empty for years.

That spoils my ghostliness, I am afraid, but I don't care—there is something strange about the house—I can feel it.

I even said so to John one moonlight evening, but he said what I felt was a draught, and shut the window.

I get unreasonably angry with John sometimes. I'm sure I never used to be so sensitive. I think it is due to this nervous condition.

But John says if I feel so, I shall neglect proper self-control; so I take pains to control myself—before him, at least, and that makes me very tired.

I don't like our room a bit. I wanted one downstairs that opened on the piazza and had roses all over the window, and such pretty old-fashioned chintz hangings! But John would not hear of it.

He said there was only one window and not room for two beds, and no near room for him if he took another.

He is very careful and loving, and hardly lets me stir without special direction.

I have a schedule prescription for each hour in the day; he takes all care from me, and so I feel basely ungrateful not to value it more.

He said we came here solely on my account, that I was to have perfect rest and all the air I could get. "Your exercise depends on your strength, my dear," said he, "and your food somewhat on your appetite; but air you can absorb all the time." So we took the nursery at the top of the house.

It is a big, airy room, the whole floor nearly, with windows that look all ways, and air and sunshine galore. It was nursery first and then playroom and gymnasium, I should judge; for the windows are barred for little children, and there are rings and things in the walls.

The paint and paper look as if a boys' school had used it. It is stripped off—the paper—in great patches all around the head of my bed, about as far as I can reach, and in a great place on the other side of the room low down. I never saw a worse paper in my life. One of those sprawling flamboyant patterns committing every artistic sin.

It is dull enough to confuse the eye in following, pronounced enough to constantly irritate and provoke study, and when you follow the lame uncertain curves for a little distance they suddenly commit suicide—plunge off at outrageous angles, destroy themselves in unheard-of contradictions.

The color is repellent, almost revolting; a smouldering unclean yellow, strangely faded by the slow-turning sunlight. It is a dull yet lurid orange in some places, a sickly sulphur tint in others.

No wonder the children hated it! I should hate it myself if I had to live in this room long.

There comes John, and I must put this away—he hates to have me write a word.

o o o

We have been here two weeks, and I haven't felt like writing before, since that first day.

I am sitting by the window now, up in this atrocious nursery, and there is nothing to hinder my writing as much as I please, save lack of strength.

John is away all day, and even some nights when his cases are serious.

I am glad my case is not serious!

But these nervous troubles are dreadfully depressing.

John does not know how much I really suffer. He knows there is no reason to suffer, and that satisfies him.

Of course it is only nervousness. It does weigh on me so not to do my duty in any way!

I mean to be such a help to John, such a real rest and comfort, and here I am a comparative burden already!

Nobody would believe what an effort it is to do what little I am able—to dress and entertain, and order things.

It is fortunate Mary is so good with the baby. Such a dear baby!

And yet I *cannot* be with him, it makes me so nervous.

I suppose John never was nervous in his life. He laughs at me so about this wallpaper!

At first he meant to repaper the room, but afterwards he said that I was letting it get the better of me, and that nothing was worse for a nervous patient than to give way to such fancies.

He said that after the wallpaper was changed it would be the heavy bedstead, and then the barred windows, and then that gate at the head of the stairs, and so on.

"You know the place is doing you good," he said, "and really, dear, I don't care to renovate the house just for a three months' rental."

"Then do let us go downstairs," I said. "There are such pretty rooms there."

Then he took me in his arms and called me a blessed little goose, and said he would go down cellar, if I wished, and have it whitewashed into the bargain.

But he is right enough about the beds and windows and things.

It is as airy and comfortable a room as anyone need wish, and, of course, I would not be so silly as to make him uncomfortable just for a whim.

I'm really getting quite fond of the big room, all but that horrid paper.

Out of one window I can see the garden—those mysterious deep-shaded arbors, the riotous old-fashioned flowers, and bushes and gnarly trees.

Out of another I get a lovely view of the bay and a little private wharf belonging to the estate. There is a beautiful shaded lane that runs down there from the house. I always fancy I see people walking in these numerous paths and arbors, but John has cautioned me not to give way to fancy in the least. He says that with my imaginative power and habit of story-making, a nervous weakness like mine is sure to lead to all manner of excited fancies, and that I ought to use my will and good sense to check the tendency. So I try.

I think sometimes that if I were only well enough to write a little it would relieve the press of ideas and rest me.

But I find I get pretty tired when I try.

It is so discouraging not to have any advice and companionship about my work. When I get really well, John says we will ask Cousin Henry and Julia down for a long visit; but he says he would as soon put fireworks in my pillow-case as to let me have those stimulating people about now.

I wish I could get well faster.

But I must not think about that. This paper looks to me as if it *knew* what a vicious influence it had!

There is a recurrent spot where the pattern lolls like a broken neck and two bulbous eyes stare at you upside down.

I get positively angry with the impertinence of it and the everlastingness. Up and down and sideways they crawl, and those absurd unblinking eyes are everywhere. There is one place where two breadths didn't match, and the eyes go all up and down the line, one a little higher than the other.

I never saw so much expression in an inanimate thing before, and we all know how much expression they have! I used to lie awake as a child and get more entertainment and terror out of blank walls and plain furniture than most children could find in a toy-store.

I remember what a kindly wink the knobs of our big old bureau used to have, and there was one chair that always seemed like a strong friend.

I used to feel that if any of the other things looked too fierce I could always hop into that chair and be safe.

The furniture in this room is no worse than inharmonious, however, for we had to bring it all from downstairs. I suppose when this was used as a playroom they had to take the nursery things out, and no wonder! I never saw such ravages as the children have made here.

The wallpaper, as I said before, is torn off in spots, and it sticketh closer than a brother—they must have had perseverance as well as hatred.

Then the floor is scratched and gouged and splintered, the plaster itself is dug out here and there, and this great heavy bed which is all we found in the room, looks as if it had been through the wars.

But I don't mind it a bit—only the paper.

There comes John's sister. Such a dear girl as she is, and so careful of me! I must not let her find me writing.

She is a perfect and enthusiastic housekeeper, and hopes for no better profession. I verily believe she thinks it is the writing which made me sick!

But I can write when she is out, and see her a long way off from these windows.

There is one that commands the road, a lovely shaded winding road, and one that just looks off over the country. A lovely country, too, full of great elms and velvet meadows.

This wallpaper has a kind of sub-pattern in a different shade, a particularly irritating one, for you can only see it in certain lights, and not clearly then.

But in the places where it isn't faded and where the sun is just so—I can see a strange, provoking, formless sort of figure that seems to skulk about behind that silly and conspicuous front design.

There's sister on the stairs!

o o o

Well, the Fourth of July is over! The people are all gone, and I am tired out. John thought it might do me good to see a little company, so we just had Mother and Nellie and the children down for a week.

Of course I didn't do a thing. Jennie sees to everything now.

But it tired me all the same.

John says if I don't pick up faster he shall send me to Weir Mitchell in the fall.

But I don't want to go there at all. I had a friend who was in his hands once, and she says he is just like John and my brother, only more so!

Besides, it is such an undertaking to go so far.

I don't feel as if it was worthwhile to turn my hand over for anything, and I'm getting dreadfully fretful and querulous.

I cry at nothing, and cry most of the time.

Of course I don't when John is here, or anybody else, but when I am alone.

And I am alone a good deal just now. John is kept in town very often by serious cases, and Jennie is good and lets me alone when I want her to.

So I walk a little in the garden or down that lovely lane, sit on the porch under the roses, and lie down up here a good deal.

I'm getting really fond of the room in spite of the wallpaper. Perhaps because of the wallpaper.

It dwells in my mind so!

I lie here on this great immovable bed—it is nailed down, I believe—and follow that pattern about by the hour. It is as good as gymnastics, I assure you. I start, we'll say, at the bottom, down in the corner over there where it has not been touched, and I determine for the thousandth time that I *will* follow that pointless pattern to some sort of conclusion.

I know a little of the principle of design, and I know this thing was not arranged on any laws of radiation, or alternation, or repetition, or symmetry, or anything else that I ever heard of.

It is repeated, of course, by the breadths, but not otherwise.

Looked at in one way, each breadth stands alone; the bloated curves and flourishes—a kind of "debased Romanesque"[1] with delirium tremens—go waddling up and down in isolated columns of fatuity.

But, on the other hand, they connect diagonally, and the sprawling outlines run off in great slanting waves of optic horror, like a lot of wallowing sea-weeds in full chase.

The whole thing goes horizontally, too, at least it seems so, and I exhaust myself trying to distinguish the order of its going in that direction.

They have used a horizontal breadth for a frieze, and that adds wonderfully to the confusion.

There is one end of the room where it is almost intact, and there, when the crosslights fade and the low sun shines directly upon it, I can almost fancy radiation after all—the interminable grotesque seems to form around a common center and rush off in headlong plunges of equal distraction.

It makes me tired to follow it. I will take a nap, I guess.

1 "Romanesque" is a style of architecture originating in the eleventh and twelfth centuries.

○ ○ ○

I don't know why I should write this.

I don't want to.

I don't feel able.

And I know John would think it absurd. But I *must* say what I feel and think in some way—it is such a relief!

But the effort is getting to be greater than the relief.

Half the time now I am awfully lazy, and lie down ever so much.

John says I mustn't lose my strength, and has me take cod liver oil and lots of tonics and things, to say nothing of the ale and wine and rare meat.

Dear John! He loves me very dearly, and hates to have me sick. I tried to have a real earnest reasonable talk with him the other day, and tell him how I wish he would let me go and make a visit to Cousin Henry and Julia.

But he said I wasn't able to go, nor able to stand it after I got there; and I did not make out a very good case for myself, for I was crying before I had finished.

It is getting to be a great effort for me to think straight. Just this nervous weakness, I suppose.

And dear John gathered me up in his arms, and just carried me upstairs and laid me on the bed, and sat by me and read to me till it tired my head.

He said I was his darling and his comfort and all he had, and that I must take care of myself for his sake, and keep well.

He says no one but myself can help me out of it, that I must use my will and self-control and not let any silly fancies run away with me.

There's one comfort—the baby is well and happy, and does not have to occupy this nursery with the horrid wallpaper.

If we had not used it, that blessed child would have! What a fortunate escape! Why, I wouldn't have a child of mine, an impressionable little thing, live in such a room for worlds.

I never thought of it before, but it is lucky that John kept me here after all, I can stand it so much easier than a baby, you see.

Of course I never mention it to them any more—I am too wise—but I keep watch for it all the same.

There are things in that paper that nobody knows about but me, or ever will.

Behind that outside pattern the dim shapes get clearer every day.

It is always the same shape, only very numerous.

And it is like a woman stooping down and creeping about behind that pattern. I don't like it a bit. I wonder—I begin to think—I wish John would take me away from here!

○ ○ ○

It is so hard to talk with John about my case, because he is so wise, and because he loves me so.

But I tried it last night.

It was moonlight. The moon shines in all around just as the sun does.

I hate to see it sometimes, it creeps so slowly, and always comes in by one window or another.

John was asleep and I hated to waken him, so I kept still and watched the moonlight on that undulating wallpaper till I felt creepy.

The faint figure behind seemed to shake the pattern, just as if she wanted to get out.

I got up softly and went to feel and see if the paper *did* move, and when I came back John was awake.

"What is it, little girl?" he said. "Don't go walking about like that—you'll get cold."

I thought it was a good time to talk, so I told him that I really was not gaining here, and that I wished he would take me away.

"Why, darling!" said he. "Our lease will be up in three weeks, and I can't see how to leave before."

"The repairs are not done at home, and I cannot possibly leave town just now. Of course if you were in any danger, I could and would, but you really are better, dear, whether you can see it or not. I am a doctor, dear, and I know. You are gaining flesh and color, your appetite is better, I feel really much easier about you."

"I don't weigh a bit more," said I, "nor as much; and my appetite may be better in the evening when you are here but it is worse in the morning when you are away!"

"Bless her little heart!" said he with a big hug. "She shall be as sick as she pleases! But now let's improve the shining hours by going to sleep, and talk about it in the morning!"

"And you won't go away?" I asked gloomily.

"Why, how can I, dear? It is only three weeks more and then we will take a nice little trip of a few days while Jennie is getting the house ready. Really, dear, you are better!"

"Better in body perhaps—" I began, and stopped short, for he sat up straight and looked at me with such a stern, reproachful look that I could not say another word.

"My darling," said he, "I beg of you, for my sake and for our child's sake, as well as your own, that you will never for one instant let that idea enter your mind! There is nothing so dangerous, so fascinating, to a temperament like yours. It is a false and foolish fancy. Can you not trust me as a physician when I tell you so?"

So of course I said no more on that score, and we went to sleep before long. He thought I was asleep first, but I wasn't, and lay there for hours trying to decide whether that front pattern and the back pattern really did move together or separately.

o o o

On a pattern like this, by daylight, there is a lack of sequence, a defiance of law, that is a constant irritant to a normal mind.

The color is hideous enough, and unreliable enough, and infuriating enough, but the pattern is torturing.

You think you have mastered it, but just as you get well under way in following, it turns a back-somersault and there you are. It slaps you in the face, knocks you down, and tramples upon you. It is like a bad dream.

The outside pattern is a florid arabesque, reminding one of a fungus. If you can imagine a toadstool in joints, an interminable string of toadstools, budding and sprouting in endless convolutions—why, that is something like it.

That is, sometimes!

There is one marked peculiarity about this paper, a thing nobody seems to notice but myself, and that is that it changes as the light changes.

When the sun shoots in through the east window—I always watch for that first long, straight ray—it changes so quickly that I never can quite believe it.

That is why I watch it always.

By moonlight—the moon shines in all night when there is a moon—I wouldn't know it was the same paper.

At night in any kind of light, in twilight, candlelight, lamplight, and worst of all by moonlight, it becomes bars! The outside pattern, I mean, and the woman behind it is as plain as can be.

I didn't realize for a long time what the thing was that showed behind, that dim sub-pattern, but now I am quite sure it is a woman.

By daylight she is subdued, quiet. I fancy it is the pattern that keeps her so still. It is so puzzling. It keeps me quiet by the hour.

I lie down ever so much now. John says it is good for me, and to sleep all I can.

Indeed he started the habit by making me lie down for an hour after each meal.

It is a very bad habit I am convinced, for you see, I don't sleep.

And that cultivates deceit, for I don't tell them I'm awake—O no!

The fact is I am getting a little afraid of John.

He seems very queer sometimes, and even Jennie has an inexplicable look.

It strikes me occasionally, just as a scientific hypothesis, that perhaps it is the paper!

I have watched John when he did not know I was looking, and come into the room suddenly on the most innocent excuses, and I've caught him several times *looking at the paper*! And Jennie too. I caught Jennie with her hand on it once.

She didn't know I was in the room, and when I asked her in a quiet, a very quiet voice, with the most restrained manner possible, what she was doing with the paper—she turned around as if she had been caught stealing, and looked quite angry—asked me why I should frighten her so!

Then she said that the paper stained everything it touched, that she had found yellow smooches on all my clothes and John's, and she wished we would be more careful!

Did not that sound innocent? But I know she was studying that pattern, and I am determined that nobody shall find it out but myself!

° ° °

Life is very much more exciting now than it used to be. You see I have something more to expect, to look forward to, to watch. I really do eat better, and am more quiet than I was.

John is so pleased to see me improve! He laughed a little the other day, and said I seemed to be flourishing in spite of my wallpaper.

I turned it off with a laugh. I had no intention of telling him it was *because* of the wallpaper—he would make fun of me. He might even want to take me away.

I don't want to leave now until I have found it out. There is a week more, and I think that will be enough.

° ° °

I'm feeling so much better!

I don't sleep much at night, for it is so interesting to watch developments; but I sleep a good deal during the daytime.

In the daytime it is tiresome and perplexing.

There are always new shoots on the fungus, and new shades of yellow all over it. I cannot keep count of them, though I have tried conscientiously.

It is the strangest yellow, that wallpaper! It makes me think of all the yellow things I ever saw—not beautiful ones like buttercups, but old, foul, bad yellow things.

But there is something else about that paper—the smell! I noticed it the moment we came into the room, but with so much air and sun it was not bad. Now we have had a week of fog and rain, and whether the windows are open or not, the smell is here.

It creeps all over the house.

I find it hovering in the dining-room, skulking in the parlor, hiding in the hall, lying in wait for me on the stairs.

It gets into my hair.

Even when I go to ride, if I turn my head suddenly and surprise it—there is that smell!

Such a peculiar odor, too! I have spent hours in trying to analyze it, to find what it smelled like.

It is not bad—at first—and very gentle, but quite the subtlest, most enduring odor I ever met.

In this damp weather it is awful, I wake up in the night and find it hanging over me.

It used to disturb me at first. I thought seriously of burning the house—to reach the smell.

But now I am used to it. The only thing I can think of that it is like is the *color* of the paper! A yellow smell.

There is a very funny mark on this wall, low down, near the mopboard. A streak that runs round the room. It goes behind every piece of furniture, except the bed, a long, straight, even *smooch*, as if it had been rubbed over and over.

I wonder how it was done and who did it, and what they did it for. Round and round and round—round and round and round—it makes me dizzy!

° ° °

I really have discovered something at last.

Through watching so much at night, when it changes so, I have finally found out.

The front pattern *does* move—and no wonder! The woman behind shakes it!

Sometimes I think there are a great many women behind, and sometimes only one, and she crawls around fast, and her crawling shakes it all over.

Then in the very bright spots she keeps still, and in the very shady spots she just takes hold of the bars and shakes them hard.

And she is all the time trying to climb through. But nobody could climb through that pattern—it strangles so; I think that is why it has so many heads.

They get through, and then the pattern strangles them off and turns them upside down, and makes their eyes white!

If those heads were covered or taken off it would not be half so bad.

° ° °

I think that woman gets out in the daytime!

And I'll tell you why—privately—I've seen her!

I can see her out of every one of my windows!

It is the same woman, I know, for she is always creeping, and most women do not creep by daylight.

I see her in that long shaded lane, creeping up and down. I see her in those dark grape arbors, creeping all around the garden.

I see her on that long road under the trees, creeping along, and when a carriage comes she hides under the blackberry vines.

I don't blame her a bit. It must be very humiliating to be caught creeping by daylight!

I always lock the door when I creep by daylight. I can't do it at night, for I know John would suspect something at once.

And John is so queer now that I don't want to irritate him. I wish he would take another room! Besides, I don't want anybody to get that woman out at night but myself.

I often wonder if I could see her out of all the windows at once.

But, turn as fast as I can, I can only see out of one at one time.

And though I always see her, she *may* be able to creep faster than I can turn! I have watched her sometimes away off in the open country, creeping as fast as a cloud shadow in a wind.

o o o

If only that top pattern could be gotten off from the under one! I mean to try it, little by little.

I have found out another funny thing, but I shan't tell it this time! It does not do to trust people too much.

There are only two more days to get this paper off, and I believe John is beginning to notice. I don't like the look in his eyes.

And I heard him ask Jennie a lot of professional questions about me. She had a very good report to give.

She said I slept a good deal in the daytime.

John knows I don't sleep very well at night, for all I'm so quiet!

He asked me all sorts of questions, too, and pretended to be very loving and kind.

As if I couldn't see through him!

Still, I don't wonder he acts so, sleeping under this paper for three months.

It only interests me, but I feel sure John and Jennie are affected by it.

o o o

Hurrah! This is the last day, but it is enough. John is to stay in town over night, and won't be out until this evening.

Jennie wanted to sleep with me—the sly thing; but I told her I should undoubtedly rest better for a night all alone.

That was clever, for really I wasn't alone a bit! As soon as it was moonlight and that poor thing began to crawl and shake the pattern, I got up and ran to help her.

I pulled and she shook, I shook and she pulled, and before morning we had peeled off yards of that paper.

A strip about as high as my head and half around the room.

And then when the sun came and that awful pattern began to laugh at me, I declared I would finish it today!

We go away tomorrow, and they are moving all my furniture down again to leave things as they were before.

Jennie looked at the wall in amazement, but I told her merrily that I did it out of pure spite at the vicious thing.

She laughed and said she wouldn't mind doing it herself, but I must not get tired.

How she betrayed herself that time!

But I am here, and no person touches this paper but Me—not *alive*!

She tried to get me out of the room—it was too patent! But I said it was so quiet and empty and clean now that I believed I would lie down again and sleep all I could; and not to wake me even for dinner—I would call when I woke.

So now she is gone, and the servants are gone, and the things are gone, and there is nothing left but that great bedstead nailed down, with the canvas mattress we found on it.

We shall sleep downstairs tonight, and take the boat home tomorrow.

I quite enjoy the room, now it is bare again.

How those children did tear about here!

This bedstead is fairly gnawed!

But I must get to work.

I have locked the door and thrown the key down into the front path.

I don't want to go out, and I don't want to have anybody come in, till John comes.

I want to astonish him.

I've got a rope up here that even Jennie did not find. If that woman does get out, and tries to get away, I can tie her!

But I forgot I could not reach far without anything to stand on!

This bed will *not* move!

I tried to lift and push it until I was lame, and then I got so angry I bit off a little piece at one corner—but it hurt my teeth.

Then I peeled off all the paper I could reach standing on the floor. It sticks horribly and the pattern just enjoys it! All those strangled heads and bulbous eyes and waddling fungus growths just shriek with derision!

I am getting angry enough to do something desperate. To jump out of the window would be admirable exercise, but the bars are too strong even to try.

Besides I wouldn't do it. Of course not. I know well enough that a step like that is improper and might be misconstrued.

I don't like to *look* out of the windows even—there are so many of those creeping women, and they creep so fast.

I wonder if they all come out of that wallpaper as I did?

But I am securely fastened now by my well-hidden rope—you don't get me out in the road there!

I suppose I shall have to get back behind the pattern when it comes night, and that is hard!

It is so pleasant to be out in this great room and creep around as I please!

I don't want to go outside. I won't, even if Jennie asks me to.

For outside you have to creep on the ground, and everything is green instead of yellow.

But here I can creep smoothly on the floor, and my shoulder just fits in that long smooch around the wall, so I cannot lose my way.

Why there's John at the door!

It is no use, young man, you can't open it!

How he does call and pound!

Now he's crying to Jennie for an axe.

It would be a shame to break down that beautiful door!

"John dear!" said I in the gentlest voice. "The key is down by the front steps, under a plantain leaf!"

That silenced him for a few moments.

Then he said—very quietly indeed, "Open the door, my darling!"

"I can't," said I. "The key is down by the front door under a plantain leaf!"

And then I said it again, several times, very gently and slowly, and said it so often that he had to go and see, and he got it of course, and came in. He stopped short by the door.

"What is the matter?" he cried. "For God's sake, what are you doing!"

I kept on creeping just the same, but I looked at him over my shoulder.

"I've got out at last," said I, "in spite of you and Jane! And I've pulled off most of the paper, so you can't put me back!"

Now why should that man have fainted? But he did, and right across my path by the wall, so that I had to creep over him every time!

—1892

STEPHEN CRANE

Stephen Crane was the youngest of fourteen children of a Methodist minister who wrote about the evils of drinking and dance, and a mother who lobbied on behalf of the New Jersey Women's Christian Temperance Union. Born in 1871 in Newark, New Jersey, Crane lived only to the age of twenty-eight, but produced a substantial body of work. Best known for the novels *Maggie: A Girl of the Streets* (1893) and *The Red Badge of Courage: An Episode of the American Civil War* (1895), he also wrote numerous other novels, books of poetry, short story collections, sketches, and articles.

Crane's father died of heart failure when Stephen was eight years old, and his mother supported the family by lecturing and writing about religious events and doing good works. Between 1888 and 1891, Crane attended four post-secondary institutions (including Syracuse University and Claverack College), but he never finished his schooling at any of them, stating at one point that he "preferred base-ball."

Crane moved to New York City to work as a freelance newspaper reporter and lived in poverty in the Lower East Side, fraternizing with prostitutes, homeless people, and struggling visual artists, experiences he drew upon both in *Maggie* and in *George's Mother* (1896). *Maggie* attracted the attention of writers Hamlin Garland and William Dean Howells when it appeared; the publication of *The Red Badge of Courage* (when Crane was only 23) made him an overnight sensation in both the United States and Britain.

Crane became a travelling correspondent and worked all over the world, including reporting on the Greco-Turkish and Spanish-American Wars. In 1898, he moved to England and lived with his lover and companion, Cora Taylor (the former madam of a Jacksonville brothel called House de Dream) while attempting to evade his creditors and unwelcome guests. During this period Crane and Taylor made friends with writers such as H.G. Wells, Joseph Conrad, and Henry James.

Crane never achieved the same level of success with his other writings that he had with *The Red Badge of Courage.* Never completely healthy, Crane contracted tuberculosis and sought treatment at a sanatorium in southern Germany, where he died on June 5, 1900.

The short story "The Open Boat" first appeared in *Scribner's Magazine* in 1897. It is based on a factual account Crane published shortly after he survived the shipwreck of a freighter named the *Commodore* off the coast of Florida. The story's apparent simplicity—four men rowing for their lives in a dinghy—belies the complexity of its investigation into the nature of interpretation and belief. Early in his life Crane rejected religion as a means of making sense of the universe, coming to believe, rather, in uncertainty as the primary ordering structure. This concept is movingly reflected in the story's first line, "None of them knew the color of the sky."

The Open Boat

STEPHEN CRANE

A Tale Intended to Be after the Fact: Being the Experience of Four Men from the Sunk Steamer COMMODORE

I

NONE OF THEM knew the color of the sky. Their eyes glanced level and were fastened upon the waves that swept toward them. These waves were of the hue of slate, save for the tops, which were of foaming white, and all of the men knew the colors of the sea. The horizon narrowed and widened, and dipped and rose, and at all times its edge was jagged with waves that seemed thrust up in points like rocks.

Many a man ought to have a bathtub larger than the boat which here rode upon the sea. These waves were most wrongfully and barbarously abrupt and tall, and each froth-top was a problem in small-boat navigation.

The cook squatted in the bottom, and looked with both eyes at the six inches of gunwale which separated him from the ocean. His sleeves were rolled over his fat forearms, and the two flaps of his unbuttoned vest dangled as he bent to bail out the boat. Often he said, "Gawd! that was a narrow clip." As he remarked it he invariably gazed eastward over the broken sea.

The oiler, steering with one of the two oars in the boat, sometimes raised himself suddenly to keep clear of water that swirled in over the stern. It was a thin little oar, and it seemed often ready to snap.

The correspondent, pulling at the other oar, watched the waves and wondered why he was there.

The injured captain, lying in the bow, was at this time buried in that profound dejection and indifference which comes, temporarily at least, to even the bravest and most enduring when, willy-nilly, the firm fails, the army loses, the ship goes down. The mind of the master of a vessel is rooted deep in the timbers of her, though he command for a day or a decade; and this captain had on him the stern impression of a scene in the grays of dawn of seven turned faces, and later a stump of a topmast with a white ball on it, that slashed to and fro at the waves, went low and lower, and down. Thereafter there was something strange in his voice. Although steady, it was deep with mourning, and of a quality beyond oration or tears.

"Keep'er a little more south, Billie," said he.

"A little more south, sir," said the oiler in the stern.

A seat in his boat was not unlike a seat upon a bucking broncho, and by the same token a broncho is not much smaller. The craft pranced and reared and plunged like an animal. As each wave came, and she rose for it, she seemed like a horse making at a fence outrageously high. The manner of her scramble over these walls of water is a mystic thing, and, moreover, at the top of them were ordinarily these problems in white water, the foam racing down from the summit of each wave requiring a new leap, and a leap from the air. Then, after scornfully bumping a crest, she would slide and race and splash down a long incline, and arrive bobbing and nodding in front of the next menace.

A singular disadvantage of the sea lies in the fact that after successfully surmounting one wave you discover that there is another behind it just as important and just as nervously anxious to do something effective in the way of swamping boats. In a ten-foot dinghy one can get an idea of the resources of the sea in the line of waves that is not probable to the average experience, which is never at sea in a dinghy. As each slaty wall of water approached, it shut all else from the view of the men in the boat, and it was not difficult to imagine that this particular wave was the final outburst of the ocean, the last effort of the grim water. There was a terrible grace in the move of the waves, and they came in silence, save for the snarling of the crests.

In the wan light the faces of the men must have been gray. Their eyes must have glinted in strange ways as they gazed steadily astern. Viewed from a balcony, the whole thing would, doubtless, have been weirdly picturesque. But the men in the boat had no time to see it, and if they had had leisure, there were other things to occupy their minds. The sun swung steadily up the sky, and they knew it was broad day because the color of the sea changed from slate to emerald-green streaked with amber lights, and the foam was like tumbling snow. The process of the breaking day was unknown to them. They were aware only of this effect upon the color of the waves that rolled toward them.

In disjointed sentences the cook and the correspondent argued as to the difference between a life-saving station and a house of refuge. The cook had said:

"There's a house of refuge just north of the Mosquito Inlet Light, and as soon as they see us they'll come off in their boat and pick us up."

"As soon as who see us?" said the correspondent.

"The crew," said the cook.

"Houses of refuge don't have crews," said the correspondent. "As I understand them, they are only places where clothes and grub are stored for the benefit of shipwrecked people. They don't carry crews."

"Oh, yes, they do," said the cook.

"No, they don't," said the correspondent.

"Well, we're not there yet, anyhow," said the oiler, in the stern.

"Well," said the cook, "perhaps it's not a house of refuge that I'm thinking of as being near Mosquito Inlet Light; perhaps it's a life-saving station."

"We're not there yet," said the oiler in the stern.

II

AS THE BOAT bounced from the top of each wave the wind tore through the hair of the hatless men, and as the craft plopped her stern down again the spray slashed past them. The crest of each of these waves was a hill, from the top of which the men surveyed for a moment a broad tumultuous expanse, shining and wind-riven. It was probably splendid, it was probably glorious, this play of the free sea, wild with lights of emerald and white and amber.

"Bully good thing it's an on-shore wind," said the cook. "If not, where would we be? Wouldn't have a show."

"That's right," said the correspondent.

The busy oiler nodded his assent.

Then the captain, in the bow, chuckled in a way that expressed humor, contempt, tragedy, all in one. "Do you think we've got much of a show now, boys?" said he.

Whereupon the three were silent, save for a trifle of hemming and hawing. To express any particular optimism at this time they felt to be childish and stupid, but they all doubtless possessed this sense of the situation in their minds. A young man thinks doggedly at such times. On the other hand, the ethics of their condition was decidedly against any open suggestion of hopelessness. So they were silent.

"Oh, well," said the captain, soothing his children, "we'll get ashore all right."

But there was that in his tone which made them think; so the oiler quoth, "Yes! if this wind holds."

The cook was bailing. "Yes! if we don't catch hell in the surf."

Canton-flannel gulls flew near and far. Sometimes they sat down on the sea, near patches of brown seaweed that rolled over the waves with a movement like carpets on a line in a gale. The birds sat comfortably in groups, and they were envied by some in the dinghy, for the wrath of the sea was no more to them than it was to a covey of prairie chickens a thousand miles inland. Often they came very close and stared at the men with black bead-like eyes. At these times they were uncanny and sinister in their unblinking scrutiny, and the men hooted angrily at them, telling them to be gone. One came, and evidently decided to alight on the top of the captain's head. The bird flew parallel to the boat and did not circle, but made short sidelong jumps in the air in chicken fashion. His black eyes were wistfully fixed upon the captain's head. "Ugly brute," said the oiler to the bird. "You look as if you were made with a jackknife." The cook and the correspondent swore darkly at the creature. The captain naturally wished to knock it away with the end of the heavy painter, but he did not dare do it, because anything resembling an emphatic gesture would have capsized this freighted boat; and so, with his open hand, the captain gently and carefully waved the gull away. After it had been discouraged from the pursuit the captain breathed easier on account of his hair, and others breathed easier because the bird struck their minds at this time as being somehow gruesome and ominous.

In the meantime the oiler and the correspondent rowed; and also they rowed. They sat together in the same seat, and each rowed an oar. Then the oiler took both oars; then the correspondent took both oars, then the oiler; then the correspondent. They rowed and they rowed. The very ticklish part of the business was when the time came for the reclining one in the stern to take his turn at the oars. By the very last star of truth, it is easier to steal eggs from under a hen than it was to change seats in the dinghy. First the man in the stern slid his hand along the thwart and moved with care, as if he were of Sèvres. Then the man in the rowing-seat slid his hand along the other thwart. It was all done with the most extraordinary care. As the two sidled past each other, the whole party kept watchful eyes on the coming wave, and the captain cried: "Look out, now! Steady, there!"

The brown mats of seaweed that appeared from time to time were like islands, bits of earth. They were travelling, apparently, neither one way nor the other. They were, to all intents, stationary. They informed the men in the boat that it was making progress slowly toward the land.

The captain, rearing cautiously in the bow after the dinghy soared on a great swell, said that he had seen the lighthouse at Mosquito Inlet. Presently the cook remarked that he had seen it. The correspondent was at the oars then, and for some reason he too wished to look at the lighthouse; but his back was toward the far shore, and the waves were important, and for some time he could not seize an opportunity to turn his head. But at last there came a wave more gentle than the others, and when at the crest of it he swiftly scoured the western horizon.

"See it?" said the captain.

"No," said the correspondent, slowly; "I didn't see anything."

"Look again," said the captain. He pointed. "It's exactly in that direction."

At the top of another wave the correspondent did as he was bid, and this time his eyes chanced on a small, still thing on the edge of the swaying horizon. It was precisely like the point of a pin. It took an anxious eye to find a lighthouse so tiny.

"Think we'll make it, Captain?"

"If this wind holds and the boat don't swamp, we can't do much else," said the captain.

The little boat, lifted by each towering sea and splashed viciously by the crests, made progress that in the absence of seaweed was not apparent to those in her. She seemed just a wee thing wallowing, miraculously top up, at the mercy of five oceans. Occasionally a great spread of water, like white flames, swarmed into her.

"Bail her, cook," said the captain, serenely.

"All right, Captain," said the cheerful cook.

III

IT WOULD be difficult to describe the subtle brotherhood of men that was here established on the seas. No one said that it was so. No one mentioned it. But it dwelt in the boat, and each man felt it warm him. They were a captain, an oiler, a cook, and a correspondent, and they were friends—friends in a more curiously iron-bound degree than may be common. The hurt captain, lying against the water jar in the bow, spoke always in a low voice and calmly; but he could never command a more ready and swiftly obedient crew than the motley three of the dinghy. It was more than a mere recognition of what was best for the common safety. There was surely in it a quality that was personal and heart-felt. And after this devotion to the commander of the boat, there was this comradeship, that the correspondent, for instance, who had been taught to be cynical of men, knew even at the time was the best experience of his life. But no one said that it was so. No one mentioned it.

"I wish we had a sail," remarked the captain. "We might try my overcoat on the end of an oar, and give you two boys a chance to rest." So the cook and the correspondent held the mast and spread wide the overcoat; the oiler steered; and the little boat made good way with her new rig. Sometimes the oiler had to scull sharply to keep a sea from breaking into the boat, but otherwise sailing was a success.

Meanwhile the lighthouse had been growing slowly larger. It had now almost assumed color, and appeared like a little gray shadow on the sky. The man at the oars could not be prevented from turning his head rather often to try for a glimpse of this little gray shadow.

At last, from the top of each wave, the men in the tossing boat could see land. Even as the lighthouse was an upright shadow on the sky, this land seemed but a long black shadow on the sea. It certainly was thinner than paper. "We must be about opposite New Smyrna," said the cook, who had coasted this shore often in schooners. "Captain, by the way, I believe they abandoned that life-saving station there about a year ago."

"Did they?" said the captain.

The wind slowly died away. The cook and the correspondent were not now obliged to slave in order to hold high the oar. But the waves continued their old impetuous swooping at the dinghy, and the little craft, no longer underway, struggled woundily over them. The oiler or the correspondent took the oars again.

Shipwrecks are *apropos* of nothing. If men could only train for them and have them occur when the men had reached pink condition, there would be less drowning at sea. Of the four in the dinghy none had slept any time worth mentioning for two days and two nights previous to embarking in the dinghy, and in the excitement of clambering about the deck of a foundering ship they had also forgotten to eat heartily.

For these reasons, and for others, neither the oiler nor the correspondent was fond of rowing at this time. The correspondent wondered ingenuously how in the name of all that was sane could there be people who thought it amusing to row a boat. It was not an amusement; it was a diabolical punishment, and even a genius of mental aberrations could never conclude that it was anything but a horror to the muscles and a crime against the back. He mentioned to the boat in general how the amusement of rowing struck him, and the weary-faced oiler smiled in full sympathy. Previously to the foundering, by the way, the oiler had worked a double watch in the engine-room of the ship.

"Take her easy, now, boys," said the captain. "Don't spend yourselves. If we have to run a surf you'll need all your strength, because we'll sure have to swim for it. Take your time."

Slowly the land arose from the sea. From a black line it became a line of black and a line of white—trees and sand. Finally the captain said that he could make out a house on the shore. "That's the house of refuge, sure," said the cook. "They'll see us before long, and come out after us."

The distant lighthouse reared high. "The keeper ought to be able to make us out now, if he's looking through a glass," said the captain. "He'll notify the life-saving people."

"None of those other boats could have got ashore to give word of the wreck," said the oiler, in a low voice, "else the life-boat would be out hunting us."

Slowly and beautifully the land loomed out of the sea. The wind came again. It had veered from the northeast to the southeast. Finally a new sound struck the ears of the men in the boat. It was the low thunder of the surf on the shore. "We'll never be able to make the lighthouse now," said the captain. "Swing her head a little more north Billie."

"A little more north, sir," said the oiler.

Whereupon the little boat turned her nose once more down the wind, and all but the oarsman watched the shore grow. Under the influence of this expansion doubt and direful apprehension were leaving the minds of the men. The management of the boat was still most absorbing, but it could not prevent a quiet cheerfulness. In an hour, perhaps, they would be ashore.

Their backbones had become thoroughly used to balancing in the boat, and they now rode this wild colt of a dinghy like circus men. The correspondent thought that he had been drenched to the skin, but happening to feel in the top pocket of his coat, he found therein eight cigars. Four of them were soaked with sea-water; four were perfectly scatheless. After a search, somebody produced three dry matches; and thereupon the four waifs rode impudently in their little boat and, with an assurance of an impending rescue shining in their eyes, puffed at the big cigars, and judged well and ill of all men. Everybody took a drink of water.

IV

"COOK," remarked the captain, "there don't seem to be any signs of life about your house of refuge."

"No," replied the cook. "Funny they don't see us!"

A broad stretch of lowly coast lay before the eyes of the men. It was of low dunes topped with dark vegetation. The roar of the surf was plain, and sometimes they could see the white lip of a wave as it spun up the beach. A tiny house was blocked out black upon the sky. Southward, the slim lighthouse lifted its little gray length.

Tide, wind, and waves were swinging the dinghy northward. "Funny they don't see us," said the men.

The surf's roar was here dulled, but its tone was nevertheless thunderous and mighty. As the boat swam over the great rollers the men sat listening to this roar. "We'll swamp sure," said everybody.

It is fair to say here that there was not a life-saving station within twenty miles in either direction; but the men did not know this fact, and in consequence they made dark and opprobrious remarks concerning the eyesight of the nation's life-savers. Four scowling men sat in the dinghy and surpassed records in the invention of epithets.

"Funny they don't see us."

The light-heartedness of a former time had completely faded. To their sharpened minds it was easy to conjure pictures of all kinds of incompetency and blindness and, indeed, cowardice. There was the shore of the populous land, and it was bitter and bitter to them that from it came no sign.

"Well," said the captain, ultimately, "I suppose we'll have to make a try for ourselves. If we stay out here too long, we'll none of us have strength left to swim after the boat swamps."

And so the oiler, who was at the oars, turned the boat straight for the shore. There was a sudden tightening of muscles. There was some thinking.

"If we don't all get ashore," said the captain—"if we don't all get ashore, I suppose you fellows know where to send news of my finish?"

They then briefly exchanged some addresses and admonitions. As for the reflections of the men, there was a great deal of rage in them. Perchance they might be formulated thus: "If I am going to be drowned—if I am going to be drowned—if I am going to be drowned, why, in the name of the seven mad gods who rule the sea, was I allowed to come thus far and contemplate sand and trees? Was I brought here merely to have my nose dragged away as I was about to nibble the sacred cheese of life? It is preposterous. If this old ninny-woman, Fate, cannot do better than this, she should be deprived of the management of men's fortunes. She is an old hen who knows not her intention. If she has decided to drown me, why did she not do it in the beginning and save me all this trouble? The whole affair is absurd.... But no; she cannot mean to drown me. She dare not drown me. She cannot drown me. Not after all this work." Afterward the man might have had an impulse to shake his fist at the clouds. "Just you drown me, now, and then hear what I call you!"

The billows that came at this time were more formidable. They seemed always just about to break and roll over the little boat in a turmoil of foam. There was a preparatory and long growl in the speech of them. No mind unused to the sea would have concluded that the dinghy could ascend these sheer heights in time. The shore was still afar. The oiler was a wily surfman. "Boys," he said, swiftly, "she won't live three minutes more, and we're too far out to swim. Shall I take her to sea again, Captain?"

"Yes, go ahead!" said the captain.

This oiler, by a series of quick miracles and fast and steady oarsmanship, turned the boat in the middle of the surf and took her safely to sea again.

There was a considerable silence as the boat bumped over the furrowed sea to deeper water. Then somebody in gloom spoke: "Well, anyhow, they must have seen us from the shore by now."

The gulls went in slanting flight up the wind toward the gray, desolate east. A squall, marked by dingy clouds and clouds brick-red, like smoke from a burning building, appeared from the southeast.

"What do you think of those life-saving people? Ain't they peaches?"

"Funny they haven't seen us."

"Maybe they think we're out here for sport! Maybe they think we're fishin'. Maybe they think we're damned fools."

It was a long afternoon. A changed tide tried to force them southward, but wind and wave said northward. Far ahead, where coast-line, sea, and sky formed their mighty angle, there were little dots which seemed to indicate a city on the shore.

"St. Augustine?"

The captain shook his head. "Too near Mosquito Inlet."

And the oiler rowed, and then the correspondent rowed; then the oiler rowed. It was a weary business. The human back can become the seat of more aches and pains than are registered in books for the composite anatomy of a regiment. It is a limited area, but it can become the theatre of innumerable muscular conflicts, tangles, wrenches, knots, and other comforts.

"Did you ever like to row, Billie?" asked the correspondent.

"No," said the oiler; "hang it!"

When one exchanged the rowing-seat for a place in the bottom of the boat, he suffered a bodily depression that caused him to be careless of everything save an obligation to wiggle one finger. There was cold seawater swashing to and fro in the boat, and he lay in it. His head, pillowed on a thwart, was within an inch of the swirl of a wave-crest, and sometimes a particularly obstreperous sea came inboard and drenched him once more. But these matters did not annoy him. It is almost certain that if the boat had capsized he would have tumbled comfortably out upon the ocean as if he felt sure that it was a great soft mattress.

"Look! There's a man on the shore!"

"Where?"

"There? See 'im? See 'im?"

"Yes, sure! He's walking along."

"Now he's stopped. Look! He's facing us!"

"He's waving at us!"

"So he is! By thunder!"

"Ah, now we're all right! Now we're all right! There'll be a boat out here for us in half an hour."

"He's going on. He's running. He's going up to that house there."

The remote beach seemed lower than the sea, and it required a searching glance to discern the little black figure. The captain saw a floating stick, and they rowed to it. A bath towel was by some weird chance in the boat, and, tying this on the stick, the captain waved it. The oarsman did not dare turn his head, so he was obliged to ask questions.

"What's he doing now?"

"He's standing still again. He's looking, I think.... There he goes again—toward the house.... Now he's stopped again."

"Is he waving at us?"

"No, not now; he was, though."

"Look! There comes another man!"

"He's running."

"Look at him go, would you!"

"Why, he's on a bicycle. Now he's met the other man. They're both waving at us. Look!"

"There comes something up the beach."

"What the devil is that thing?"

"Why, it looks like a boat."

"Why, certainly, it's a boat."

"No, it's on wheels."

"Yes, so it is. Well, that must be the life-boat. They drag them along shore on a wagon."

"That's the life-boat, sure."

"No, by God, it's—it's an omnibus."

"I tell you it's a life-boat."

"It is not! It's an omnibus. I can see it plain. See? One of these big hotel omnibuses."

"By thunder, you're right. It's an omnibus, sure as fate. What do you suppose they are doing with an omnibus? Maybe they are going around collecting the life-crew, hey?"

"That's it, likely. Look! There's a fellow waving a little black flag. He's standing on the steps of the omnibus. There come those other two fellows. Now they're all talking together. Look at the fellow with the flag. Maybe he ain't waving it!"

"That ain't a flag, is it? That's his coat. Why, certainly, that's his coat."

"So it is; it's his coat. He's taken it off and is waving it around his head. But would you look at him swing it!"

"Oh, say, there isn't any life-saving station there. That's just a winter-resort hotel omnibus that has brought over some of the boarders to see us drown."

"What's that idiot with the coat mean? What's he signaling, anyhow?"

"It looks as if he were trying to tell us to go north. There must be a life-saving station up there."

"No; he thinks we're fishing. Just giving us a merry hand. See? Ah, there, Willie!"

"Well, I wish I could make something out of those signals. What do you suppose he means?"

"He don't mean anything; he's just playing."

"Well, if he'd just signal us to try the surf again, or to go to sea and wait, or go north, or go south, or go to hell, there would be some reason in it. But look at him! He just stands there and keeps his coat revolving like a wheel. The ass!"

"There come more people."

"Now there's quite a mob. Look! Isn't that a boat?"

"Where? Oh, I see where you mean. No, that's no boat."

"That fellow is still waving his coat."

"He must think we like to see him do that. Why don't he quit it? It don't mean anything."

"I don't know. I think he is trying to make us go north. It must be that there's a life-saving station there somewhere."

"Say, he ain't tired yet. Look at 'im wave!"

"Wonder how long he can keep that up. He's been revolving his coat ever since he caught sight of us. He's an idiot. Why aren't they getting men to bring a boat out? A fishing boat—one of those big yawls—could come out here all right. Why don't he do something?"

"Oh, it's all right now."

"They'll have a boat out here for us in less than no time, now that they've seen us."

A faint yellow tone came into the sky over the low land. The shadows on the sea slowly deepened. The wind bore coldness with it, and the men began to shiver.

"Holy smoke!" said one, allowing his voice to express his impious mood, "if we keep on monkeying out here! If we've got to flounder out here all night!"

"Oh, we'll never have to stay here all night! Don't you worry. They've seen us now, and it won't be long before they'll come chasing out after us."

The shore grew dusky. The man waving a coat blended gradually into this gloom, and it swallowed in the same manner the omnibus and the group of people. The spray, when it dashed uproariously over the side, made the voyagers shrink and swear like men who were being branded.

"I'd like to catch the chump who waved the coat. I feel like socking him one, just for luck."

"Why? What did he do?"

"Oh, nothing, but then he seemed so damned cheerful."

In the meantime the oiler rowed, and then the correspondent rowed, and then the oiler rowed. Gray-faced and bowed forward, they mechanically, turn by turn, plied the leaden oars. The form of the lighthouse had vanished from the southern horizon, but finally a pale star appeared, just lifting from the sea. The streaked saffron in the west passed before the all-merging darkness, and the sea to the east was black. The land had vanished, and was expressed only by the low and drear thunder of the surf.

"If I am going to be drowned—if I am going to be drowned—if I am going to be drowned, why, in the name of the seven mad gods who rule the sea, was I allowed to come thus far and contemplate sand and trees? Was I brought here merely to have my nose dragged away as I was about to nibble the sacred cheese of life?"

The patient captain, drooped over the water-jar, was sometimes obliged to speak to the oarsman.

"Keep her head up! Keep her head up!"

"Keep her head up, sir." The voices were weary and low.

This was surely a quiet evening. All save the oarsman lay heavily and listlessly in the boat's bottom. As for him, his eyes were just capable of noting the tall black waves that swept forward in a most sinister silence, save for an occasional subdued growl of a crest.

The cook's head was on a thwart, and he looked without interest at the water under his nose. He was deep in other scenes. Finally he spoke. "Billie," he murmured, dreamfully, "what kind of pie do you like best?"

V

"PIE!" said the oiler and the correspondent, agitatedly. "Don't talk about those things, blast you!"

"Well," said the cook, "I was just thinking about ham sandwiches, and—"

A night on the sea in an open boat is a long night. As darkness settled finally, the shine of the light, lifting from the sea in the south, changed to full gold. On the northern horizon a new light appeared, a small bluish gleam on the edge of the waters. These two lights were the furniture of the world. Otherwise there was nothing but waves.

Two men huddled in the stern, and distances were so magnificent in the dinghy that the rower was enabled to keep his feet partly warm by thrusting them under his companions. Their legs indeed extended far under the rowing-seat until they touched the feet of the captain forward. Sometimes, despite the efforts of the tired oarsman, a wave came piling into the boat, an icy wave of the night, and the chilling water soaked them anew. They would twist their bodies for a moment and groan, and sleep the dead sleep once more, while the water in the boat gurgled about them as the craft rocked.

The plan of the oiler and the correspondent was for one to row until he lost the ability, and then arouse the other from his sea-water couch in the bottom of the boat.

The oiler plied the oars until his head drooped forward and the overpowering sleep blinded him; and he rowed yet afterward. Then he touched a man in the bottom of the boat, and called his name. "Will you spell me for a little while?" he said meekly.

"Sure, Billie," said the correspondent, awaking and dragging himself to a sitting position. They exchanged places carefully, and the oiler, cuddling down in the sea-water at the cook's side, seemed to go to sleep instantly.

The particular violence of the sea had ceased. The waves came without snarling. The obligation of the man at the oars was to keep the boat headed so that the tilt of the rollers would not capsize her, and to preserve her from filling when the crests rushed past. The black waves were silent and hard to be seen in the darkness. Often one was almost upon the boat before the oarsman was aware.

In a low voice the correspondent addressed the captain. He was not sure that the captain was awake, although this iron man seemed to be always awake. "Captain, shall I keep her making for that light north, sir?"

The same steady voice answered him. "Yes. Keep it about two points off the port bow."

The cook had tied a life-belt around himself in order to get even the warmth which this clumsy cork contrivance could donate, and he seemed almost stove-like when a rower, whose teeth invariably chattered wildly as soon as he ceased his labor, dropped down to sleep.

The correspondent, as he rowed, looked down at the two men sleeping underfoot. The cook's arm was around the oiler's shoulders, and, with their fragmentary clothing and haggard faces, they were the babes of the sea—a grotesque rendering of the old babes in the wood.

Later he must have grown stupid at his work, for suddenly there was a growling of water, and a crest came with a roar and a swash into the boat, and it was a wonder that it did not set the cook afloat in his life-belt. The cook continued to sleep, but the oiler sat up, blinking his eyes and shaking with the new cold.

"Oh, I'm awful sorry, Billie," said the correspondent, contritely.

"That's all right, old boy," said the oiler, and lay down again and was asleep.

Presently it seemed that even the captain dozed, and the correspondent thought that he was the one man afloat on all the ocean. The wind had a voice as it came over the waves, and it was sadder than the end.

There was a long, loud swishing astern of the boat, and a gleaming trail of phosphorescence, like blue flame, was furrowed on the black waters. It might have been made by a monstrous knife.

Then there came a stillness, while the correspondent breathed with open mouth and looked at the sea.

Suddenly there was another swish and another long flash of bluish light, and this time it was alongside the boat, and might almost have been reached with an oar. The correspondent saw an enormous fin speed like a shadow through the water, hurling the crystalline spray and leaving the long glowing trail.

The correspondent looked over his shoulder at the captain. His face was hidden, and he seemed to be asleep. He looked at the babes of the sea. They certainly were asleep. So, being bereft of sympathy, he leaned a little way to one side and swore softly into the sea.

But the thing did not then leave the vicinity of the boat. Ahead or astern, on one side or the other, at intervals long or short, fled the long sparkling streak, and there was to be heard the *whirroo* of the dark fin. The speed and power of the thing was greatly to be admired. It cut the water like a gigantic and keen projectile.

The presence of this biding thing did not affect the man with the same horror that it would if he had been a picnicker. He simply looked at the sea dully and swore in an undertone.

Nevertheless, it is true that he did not wish to be alone with the thing. He wished one of his companions to awake by chance and keep him company with it. But the captain hung motionless over the water-jar and the oiler and the cook in the bottom of the boat were plunged in slumber.

VI

"IF I AM going to be drowned—if I am going to be drowned—if I am going to be drowned, why, in the name of the seven mad gods who rule the sea, was I allowed to come thus far and contemplate sand and trees?"

During this dismal night, it may be remarked that a man would conclude that it was really the intention of the seven mad gods to drown him, despite the abominable injustice of it. For it was certainly an abominable injustice to drown a man who had worked so hard, so hard. The man felt it would be a crime most unnatural. Other people had drowned at sea since galleys swarmed with painted sails, but still—

When it occurs to a man that nature does not regard him as important, and that she feels she would not maim the universe by disposing of him, he at first wishes to throw bricks at the temple, and he hates deeply the fact that there are no bricks and no temples. Any visible expression of nature would surely be pelleted with his jeers.

Then, if there be no tangible thing to hoot, he feels, perhaps, the desire to confront a personification and indulge in pleas, bowed to one knee, and with hands supplicant, saying, "Yes, but I love myself."

A high cold star on a winter's night is the word he feels that she says to him. Thereafter he knows the pathos of his situation.

The men in the dinghy had not discussed these matters, but each had, no doubt, reflected upon them in silence and according to his mind. There was seldom any expression upon their faces save the general one of complete weariness. Speech was devoted to the business of the boat.

To chime the notes of his emotions, a verse mysteriously entered the correspondent's head. He had even forgotten that he had forgotten this verse, but it suddenly was in his mind.

> A soldier of the Legion lay dying in Algiers;
> There was lack of woman's nursing,
> there was dearth of woman's tears;
> But a comrade stood beside him,
> and he took the comrade's hand,
> And he said, "I never more shall see
> my own, my native land."[1]

In his childhood the correspondent had been made acquainted with the fact that a soldier of the Legion lay dying in Algiers, but he had never regarded it as important. Myriads of his schoolfellows had informed him of the soldier's plight, but the dinning had naturally ended by making him perfectly indifferent. He had never considered it his affair that a soldier of the Legion lay dying in Algiers, nor had it appeared to him as a matter for sorrow. It was less to him than the breaking of a pencil's point.

Now, however, it quaintly came to him as a human, living thing. It was no longer merely a picture of a few throes in the breast of a poet, meanwhile drinking tea and warming his feet at the grate; it was an actuality—stern, mournful, and fine.

The correspondent plainly saw the soldier. He lay on the sand with his feet out straight and still. While his pale left hand was upon his chest in an attempt to thwart the going of his life, the blood came between his fingers. In the far Algerian distance, a city of low square forms was set against a sky that was faint with the last sunset hues. The correspondent, plying the oars and dreaming of the slow and slower movements of the lips of the soldier, was moved by a profound and perfectly impersonal comprehension. He was sorry for the soldier of the Legion who lay dying in Algiers.

The thing which had followed the boat and waited had evidently grown bored at the delay. There was no longer to be heard the slash of the cutwater, and there was no longer the flame of the long trail. The light in the north still glimmered, but it was apparently no nearer to the boat. Sometimes the boom of the surf rang in the correspondent's ears, and he turned the craft seaward then and rowed harder. Southward, some one had evidently built a watch-fire on the

---

1 From Caroline E.S. Norton's poem, "Bingen on the Rhine" (1883).

beach. It was too low and too far to be seen, but it made a shimmering, roseate reflection upon the bluff in back of it, and this could be discerned from the boat. The wind came stronger, and sometimes a wave suddenly raged out like a mountain-cat, and there was to be seen the sheen and sparkle of a broken crest.

The captain, in the bow, moved on his water-jar and sat erect. "Pretty long night," he observed to the correspondent. He looked at the shore. "Those life-saving people take their time."

"Did you see that shark playing around?"

"Yes, I saw him. He was a big fellow, all right."

"Wish I had known you were awake."

Later the correspondent spoke into the bottom of the boat. "Billie!" There was a slow and gradual disentanglement. "Billie, will you spell me?"

"Sure," said the oiler.

As soon as the correspondent touched the cold, comfortable seawater in the bottom of the boat and had huddled close to the cook's life-belt he was deep in sleep, despite the fact that his teeth played all the popular airs. This sleep was so good to him that it was but a moment before he heard a voice call his name in a tone that demonstrated the last stages of exhaustion. "Will you spell me?"

"Sure, Billie."

The light in the north had mysteriously vanished, but the correspondent took his course from the wide-awake captain.

Later in the night, they took the boat farther out to sea, and the captain directed the cook to take one oar at the stern and keep the boat facing the seas. He was to call out if he should hear the thunder of the surf. This plan enabled the oiler and the correspondent to get respite together. "We'll give those boys a chance to get into shape again," said the captain. They curled down and, after a few preliminary chatterings and trembles, slept once more the dead sleep. Neither knew they had bequeathed to the cook the company of another shark, or perhaps the same shark.

As the boat caroused on the waves, spray occasionally bumped over the side and gave them a fresh soaking, but this had no power to break their repose. The ominous slash of the wind and the water affected them as it would have affected mummies.

"Boys," said the cook, with the notes of every reluctance in his voice, "she's drifted in pretty close. I guess one of you had better take her to sea again." The correspondent, aroused, heard the crash of the toppled crests.

As he was rowing, the captain gave him some whiskey-and-water, and this steadied the chills out of him. "If I ever get ashore and anybody shows me even a photograph of an oar—"

At last there was a short conversation.

"Billie! ... Billie, will you spell me?"

"Sure," said the other.

VII

WHEN THE correspondent again opened his eyes, the sea and the sky were each of the gray hue of the dawning. Later, carmine and gold was painted upon the waters. The morning appeared finally, in its splendor, with a sky of pure blue, and the sunlight flamed on the tips of the waves.

On the distant dunes were set many little black cottages, and a tall white windmill reared above them. No man, nor dog, nor bicycle appeared on the beach. The cottages might have formed a deserted village.

The voyagers scanned the shore. A conference was held in the boat. "Well," said the captain, "if no help is coming, we might better try a run through the surf right away. If we stay out here much longer we will be too weak to do anything for ourselves at all." The others silently acquiesced in this reasoning. The boat was headed for the beach. The correspondent wondered if none ever ascended the tall wind-tower, and if then they never looked seaward. This tower was a giant, standing with its back to the plight of the ants. It represented in a degree, to the correspondent, the serenity of nature amid the struggles of the individual—nature in the wind, and nature in the vision of men. She did not seem cruel to him then, nor beneficent, nor treacherous, nor wise. But she was indifferent, flatly indifferent. It is, perhaps, plausible that a man in this situation, impressed with the unconcern of the universe, should see the innumerable flaws of his life, and have them taste wickedly in his mind, and wish for another chance. A distinction between right and wrong seems absurdly clear to him, then, in this new ignorance of the grave-edge, and he understands that if he were given another opportunity he would mend his conduct and his words, and be better and brighter during an introduction or at a tea.

"Now, boys," said the captain, "she is going to swamp sure. All we can do is to work her in as far as possible, and then when she swamps, pile out and scramble for the beach. Keep cool now, and don't jump until she swamps sure."

The oiler took the oars. Over his shoulder he scanned the surf. "Captain," he said, "I think I'd better bring her about and keep her head-on to the seas and back her in."

"All right, Billie," said the captain. "Back her in." The oiler swung the boat then, and, seated in the stern, the cook and the correspondent were obliged to look over their shoulders to contemplate the lonely and indifferent shore.

The monstrous inshore rollers heaved the boat high until the men were again enabled to see the white sheets of water scudding up the slanted beach. "We won't get in very close," said the captain. Each time a man could wrest his attention from the rollers, he turned his glance toward the shore, and in the expression of the eyes during this contemplation there was a singular quality. The correspondent, observing the others, knew that they were not afraid, but the full meaning of their glances was shrouded.

As for himself, he was too tired to grapple fundamentally with the fact. He tried to coerce his mind into thinking of it, but the mind was dominated at this time by the muscles, and the muscles said they did not care. It merely occurred to him that if he should drown it would be a shame.

There were no hurried words, no pallor, no plain agitation. The men simply looked at the shore. "Now, remember to get well clear of the boat when you jump," said the captain.

Seaward the crest of a roller suddenly fell with a thunderous crash, and the long white comber came roaring down upon the boat.

"Steady now," said the captain. The men were silent. They turned their eyes from the shore to the comber and waited. The boat slid up the incline, leaped at the furious top, bounced over it, and swung down the long back of the wave. Some water had been shipped, and the cook bailed it out.

But the next crest crashed also. The tumbling, boiling flood of white water caught the boat and whirled it almost perpendicular. Water swarmed in from all sides. The correspondent had his hands on the gunwale at this time, and when the water entered at that place he swiftly withdrew his fingers, as if he objected to wetting them.

The little boat, drunken with this weight of water, reeled and snuggled deeper into the sea.

"Bail her out, cook! Bail her out!" said the captain.

"All right, Captain," said the cook.

"Now, boys, the next one will do for us sure," said the oiler. "Mind to jump clear of the boat."

The third wave moved forward, huge, furious, implacable. It fairly swallowed the dinghy and almost simultaneously the men tumbled into the sea. A piece of life-belt had lain in the bottom of the boat, and as the correspondent went overboard he held this to his chest with his left hand.

The January water was icy, and he reflected immediately that it was colder than he had expected to find it off the coast of Florida. This appeared to his dazed mind as a fact important enough to be noted at the time. The coldness of the water was sad; it was tragic. This fact was somehow mixed and confused with his opinion of his own situation, so that it seemed almost a proper reason for tears. The water was cold.

When he came to the surface he was conscious of little but the noisy water. Afterward he saw his companions in the sea. The oiler was ahead in the race. He was swimming strongly and rapidly. Off to the correspondent's left, the cook's great white and corked back bulged out of the water, and in the rear the captain was hanging with his one good hand to the keel of the overturned dinghy.

There is a certain immovable quality to a shore, and the correspondent wondered at it amid the confusion of the sea.

It seemed also very attractive; but the correspondent knew that it was a long journey, and he paddled leisurely. The piece of life-preserver lay under him, and sometimes he whirled down the incline of a wave as if he were on a hand-sled.

But finally he arrived at a place in the sea where travel was beset with difficulty. He did not pause swimming to inquire what manner of current had caught him, but there his progress ceased. The shore was set before him like a bit of scenery on a stage, and he looked at it and understood with his eyes each detail of it.

As the cook passed, much farther to the left, the captain was calling to him, "Turn over on your back, cook! Turn over on your back and use the oar."

"All right, sir." The cook turned on his back, and, paddling with an oar, went ahead as if he were a canoe.

Presently the boat also passed to the left of the correspondent, with the captain clinging with one hand to the keel. He would have appeared like a man raising himself to look over a board fence if it were not for the extraordinary gymnastics of the boat. The correspondent marvelled that the captain could still hold to it.

They passed on nearer to shore—the oiler, the cook, the captain—and following them went the water-jar, bouncing gaily over the seas.

The correspondent remained in the grip of this strange new enemy, a current. The shore, with its white slope of sand and its green bluff topped with little silent cottages, was spread like a picture before him. It was very near to him then, but he was impressed as one who, in a gallery, looks at a scene from Brittany or Algiers.

He thought: "I am going to drown? Can it be possible? Can it be possible? Can it be possible?" Perhaps an individual must consider his own death to be the final phenomenon of nature.

But later a wave perhaps whirled him out of this small deadly current, for he found suddenly that he could again make progress toward the shore. Later still he was aware that the captain, clinging with one hand to the keel of the dinghy had his face turned away from the shore and toward him, and was calling his name. "Come to the boat! Come to the boat!"

In his struggle to reach the captain and the boat, he reflected that when one gets properly wearied drowning must really be a comfortable arrangement—a cessation of hostilities accompanied by a large degree of relief; and he was glad of it, for the main thing in his mind for some moments had been horror of the temporary agony; he did not wish to be hurt.

Presently he saw a man running along the shore. He was undressing with most remarkable speed. Coat, trousers, shirt, everything flew magically off him.

"Come to the boat!" called the captain.

"All right, Captain." As the correspondent paddled, he saw the captain let himself down to bottom and leave the boat. Then the correspondent performed his one little marvel of the voyage. A large wave caught him and flung him with ease and supreme speed completely over the boat and far beyond it. It struck him even then as an event in gymnastics and a true miracle of the sea. An overturned boat in the surf is not a plaything to a swimming man.

The correspondent arrived in water that reached only to his waist, but his condition did not enable him to stand for more than a moment. Each wave knocked him into a heap, and the undertow pulled at him.

Then he saw the man who had been running and undressing, and undressing and running, come bounding into the water. He dragged ashore the cook, and then waded toward the captain; but the captain waved him away and sent him to the correspondent. He was naked—naked as a tree in winter; but a halo was about his head, and he shone like a saint. He gave a strong pull, and a long drag, and a bully heave at the correspondent's hand. The correspondent, schooled in the minor formulae, said, "Thanks, old man." But suddenly the man cried, "What's that?" He pointed a swift finger. The correspondent said, "Go."

In the shallows, face downward, lay the oiler. His forehead touched sand that was periodically, between each wave, clear of the sea.

The correspondent did not know all that transpired afterward. When he achieved safe ground he fell, striking the sand with each particular part of his body. It was as if he had dropped from a roof, but the thud was grateful to him.

It seems that instantly the beach was populated with men with blankets, clothes, and flasks, and women with coffee-pots and all the remedies sacred to their minds. The welcome of the land to the men from the sea was warm and generous; but a still and dripping shape was carried slowly up the beach, and the land's welcome for it could only be the different and sinister hospitality of the grave.

When it came night, the white waves paced to and fro in the moonlight, and the wind brought the sound of the great sea's voice to the men on the shore, and they felt that they could then be interpreters.

—1897

SOMERSET MAUGHAM

Said to be the British Maupassant of the twentieth century, William Somerset Maugham wrote close to one hundred short stories, dozens of plays, and twenty or so novels over the course of his long and intriguing life. Though Maugham never compared himself to the French short story writer, he readily admitted having "a great admiration for Guy de Maupassant ... who had so great a gift for telling a story so clearly, straightforwardly and effectively." Maugham affected to think much less highly of his own writing, classifying himself "in the very front row of the second rate."

Maugham was born at the British Embassy in France in 1874 to Robert Ormond Maugham, a lawyer, and Edith Mary, a well-to-do socialite. With his parents both dead by the time he was ten, Maugham went to live at his uncle's vicarage, where he was often treated unkindly; he took refuge among the books in his uncle's impressive library. Maugham attended the prestigious King's School of Canterbury. He began writing in his late teens, and wrote his first book, a biography, after leaving King's School to study in Germany. Following his return to England, he began studying medicine in London. His dealings with death and illness as a medical student and his glimpse of London's underbelly during this time shaped his second book, *Liza of Lambeth* (1897) and later, his most famous novel, the loosely autobiographical *Of Human Bondage* (1915). The success of these and other works enabled Maugham to live his life as a man of letters.

Maugham was a quiet and withdrawn person and an astute judge of character. He worked for the British Red Cross in the First World War, and was later recruited as a member of the British Secret Intelligence Service. For most of World War II Maugham lived in America, a cultural experience that informed his last major novel, *The Razor's Edge* (1944). The novel was an instant success and was made into a film shortly after its publication. He spent the remainder of his years on the French Riviera, writing, travelling, and keeping company with the likes of Winston Churchill and Lord Beaverbrook. In 1965, he died one of the wealthiest and most prolific writers of his time.

Maugham's role in the Secret Service and his interests as a writer led him to travel a good deal during the 1920s and '30s, including to India, China, and the South Pacific. Many of his stories are set in some colonial outpost—in these decades the sun had not yet set on the British empire—and they often depict a markedly British way of life. Maugham's fiction often explores troubling themes, but he typically maintains a level, even an understated, tone regardless of how sensational his story material may be.

"The Lotus Eater," first published in 1935, is set in Capri, a Mediterranean island that had become a popular resort. Recounted by a peripheral narrator, the story describes the unusual situation of Thomas Wilson, a bank manager who gives up his career for an island life of leisure. Wilson is thought to be based on a real-life friend of Maugham's—"a lazy, amiable, self-centered man." It is an extraordinary tale, but one that connects to fundamental decisions made by ordinary humans of all sorts—whether to lead "the lives that circumstances thrust upon" us, or to try to control our own destiny.

The Lotus Eater

SOMERSET MAUGHAM

MOST PEOPLE, the vast majority in fact, lead the lives that circumstances have thrust upon them, and though some repine, looking upon themselves as round pegs in square holes, and think that if things had been different they might have made a much better showing, the greater part accept their lot, if not with serenity, at all events with resignation. They are like tram-cars travelling for ever on the selfsame rails. They go backwards and forwards, backwards and forwards, inevitably, till they can go no longer and then are sold as scrap-iron. It is not often that you find a man who has boldly taken the course of his life into his own hands. When you do, it is worth while having a good look at him.

That was why I was curious to meet Thomas Wilson. It was an interesting and a bold thing he had done. Of course the end was not yet and until the experiment was concluded it was impossible to call it successful. But from what I had heard it seemed he must be an odd sort of fellow and I thought I should like to know him. I had been told he was reserved, but I had a notion that with patience and tact I could persuade him to confide in me. I wanted to hear the facts from his own lips. People exaggerate, they love to romanticize, and I was quite prepared to discover that his story was not nearly so singular as I had been led to believe.

And this impression was confirmed when at last I made his acquaintance. It was on the Piazza in Capri, where I was spending the month of August at a friend's villa, and a little before sunset, when most of the inhabitants, native and foreign, gather together to chat with their friends in the cool of the evening. There is a terrace that overlooks the Bay of Naples, and when the sun sinks slowly into the sea the island of Ischia is silhouetted against a blaze of splendour. It is one of the most lovely sights in the world. I was standing there with my friend and host watching it, when suddenly he said:

"Look, there's Wilson."

"Where?"

"The man sitting on the parapet,[1] with his back to us. He's got a blue shirt on."

I saw an undistinguished back and a small head of grey hair, short and rather thin.

"I wish he'd turn round," I said.

"He will presently."

"Ask him to come and have a drink with us at Morgano's."

"All right."

The instant of overwhelming beauty had passed and the sun, like the top of an orange, was dipping into a wine-red sea. We turned round and leaning our backs against the parapet looked at the people who were sauntering to and fro. They were all talking their heads off and the cheerful noise was exhilarating. Then the church bell, rather cracked, but with a fine resonant note, began to ring. The Piazza at Capri, with its clock tower over the footpath that leads up from the harbour, with the church up a flight of steps, is a perfect setting for an opera by Donizetti,[2] and you felt that the voluble crowd might at any moment break out into a rattling chorus. It was charming and unreal.

I was so intent on the scene that I had not noticed Wilson get off the parapet and come towards us. As he passed us my friend stopped him.

"Hullo, Wilson, I haven't seen you bathing the last few days."

"I've been bathing on the other side for a change."

My friend then introduced me. Wilson shook hands with me politely, but with indifference; a great many strangers come to Capri for a few days, or a few weeks, and I had no doubt he was constantly meeting people who came and went; and then my friend asked him to come along and have a drink with us.

"I was just going back to supper," he said.

"Can't it wait?" I asked.

"I suppose it can," he smiled.

---

1 A low wall or railing.

2 Domenico Gaetano Maria Donizetti (1797–1848) was a prolific Italian composer.

Though his teeth were not very good his smile was attractive. It was gentle and kindly. He was dressed in a blue cotton shirt and a pair of grey trousers, much creased and none too clean, of a thin canvas, and on his feet he wore a pair of very old espadrilles. The get-up was picturesque, and very suitable to the place and the weather, but it did not at all go with his face. It was a lined, long face, deeply sunburned, thin-lipped, with small grey eyes rather close together and tight, neat features. The grey hair was carefully brushed. It was not a plain face, indeed in his youth Wilson might have been good-looking, but a prim one. He wore the blue shirt, open at the neck, and the grey canvas trousers, not as though they belonged to him, but as though, shipwrecked in his pyjamas, he had been fitted out with odd garments by compassionate strangers. Notwithstanding this careless attire he looked like the manager of a branch office in an insurance company, who should by rights be wearing a black coat with pepper-and-salt trousers, a white collar, and an unobjectionable tie. I could very well see myself going to him to claim the insurance money when I had lost a watch, and being rather disconcerted while I answered the questions he put to me by his obvious impression, for all his politeness, that people who made such claims were either fools or knaves.

Moving off, we strolled across the Piazza and down the street till we came to Morgano's. We sat in the garden. Around us people were talking in Russian, German, Italian, and English. We ordered drinks. Donna Lucia, the host's wife, waddled up and in her low, sweet voice passed the time of day with us. Though middle-aged now and portly, she had still traces of the wonderful beauty that thirty years before had driven artists to paint so many bad portraits of her. Her eyes, large and liquid, were the eyes of Hera[3] and her smile was affectionate and gracious. We three gossiped for a while, for there is always a scandal of one sort or another in Capri to make a topic of conversation, but nothing was said of particular interest and in a little while Wilson got up and left us. Soon afterwards we strolled up to my friend's villa to dine. On the way he asked me what I had thought of Wilson.

"Nothing," I said. "I don't believe there's a word of truth in your story."

"Why not?"

"He isn't the sort of man to do that sort of thing."

"How does anyone know what anyone is capable of?"

"I should put him down as an absolutely normal man of business who's retired on a comfortable income from gilt-edged securities. I think your story's just the ordinary Capri tittle-tattle."

"Have it your own way," said my friend.

---

3 Greek mythology: Hera was the wife of Zeus, and the goddess of women and marriage.

We were in the habit of bathing at a beach called the Baths of Tiberius.[4] We took a fly down the road to a certain point and then wandered through lemon groves and vineyards, noisy with cicadas[5] and heavy with the hot smell of the sun, till we came to the top of the cliff down which a steep winding path led to the sea. A day or two later, just before we got down my friend said:

"Oh, there's Wilson back again."

We scrunched over the beach, the only drawback to the bathing-place being that it was shingle and not sand, and as we came along Wilson saw us and waved. He was standing up, a pipe in his mouth, and he wore nothing but a pair of trunks. His body was dark brown, thin, but not emaciated, and, considering his wrinkled face and grey hair, youthful. Hot from our walk, we undressed quickly and plunged at once into the water. Six feet from the shore it was thirty feet deep, but so clear that you could see the bottom. It was warm, yet invigorating.

When I got out Wilson was lying on his belly, with a towel under him reading a book. I lit a cigarette and went and sat down beside him.

"Had a nice swim?" he asked.

He put his pipe inside his book to mark the place and closing it put it down on the pebbles beside him. He was evidently willing to talk.

"Lovely," I said. "It's the best bathing in the world."

"Of course people think those were the Baths of Tiberius." He waved his hand towards a shapeless mass of masonry that stood half in the water and half out. "But that's all rot. It was just one of his villas, you know."

I did. But it is just as well to let people tell you things when they want to. It disposes them kindly towards you if you suffer them to impart information. Wilson gave a chuckle.

"Funny old fellow, Tiberius. Pity they're saying now there's not a word of truth in all those stories about him."

He began to tell me all about Tiberius. Well, I had read my Suetonius[6] too and I had read histories of the Early Roman Empire, so there was nothing very new to me in what he said. But I observed that he was not ill-read. I remarked on it.

"Oh, well, when I settled down here I was naturally interested, and I have plenty of time for reading. When you live in a place like this, with all its associa-

---

4 Tiberius Julius Caesar Augustus (14 BCE–37 CE) was the second emperor of the Roman Empire; the baths are likely the remains of one of the twelve villas he constructed on the island during his rule.

5 A large, grasshopper-like insect.

6 Gaius Suetonius Tranquillus (c. 69/75–130 CE) was a Roman historian and biographer of twelve of the Roman rulers; the biographies were compiled in his work *De Vita Caesarum*.

tions, it seems to make history so actual. You might almost be living in historical times yourself."

I should remark here that this was in 1913. The world was an easy, comfortable place and no one could have imagined that anything might happen seriously to disturb the serenity of existence.

"How long have you been here?" I asked.

"Fifteen years." He gave the blue and placid sea a glance, and a strangely tender smile hovered on his thin lips. "I fell in love with the place at first sight. You've heard, I daresay, of the mythical German who came here on the Naples boat just for lunch and a look at the Blue Grotto and stayed forty years; well, I can't say I exactly did that, but it's come to the same thing in the end. Only it won't be forty years in my case. Twenty-five. Still, that's better than a poke in the eye with a sharp stick."

I waited for him to go on. For what he had just said looked indeed as though there might be something after all in the singular story I had heard. But at that moment my friend came dripping out of the water very proud of himself because he had swum a mile, and the conversation turned to other things.

After that I met Wilson several times, either in the Piazza or on the beach. He was amiable and polite. He was always pleased to have a talk and I found out that he not only knew every inch of the island but also the adjacent mainland. He had read a great deal on all sorts of subjects, but his speciality was the history of Rome and on this he was very well informed. He seemed to have little imagination and to be of no more than average intelligence. He laughed a good deal, but with restraint, and his sense of humour was tickled by simple jokes. A commonplace man. I did not forget the odd remark he had made during the first short chat we had had by ourselves, but he never so much as approached the topic again. One day on our return from the beach, dismissing the cab at the Piazza, my friend and I told the driver to be ready to take us up to Anacapri[7] at five. We were going to climb Monte Solaro, dine at a tavern we favoured, and walk down in the moonlight. For it was full moon and the views by night were lovely. Wilson was standing by while we gave the cabman instructions, for we had given him a lift to save him the hot dusty walk, and more from politeness than for any other reason I asked him if he would care to join us.

"It's my party," I said.

"I'll come with pleasure," he answered.

But when the time came to set out my friend was not feeling well, he thought he had stayed too long in the water, and would not face the long and tiring walk. So I went alone with Wilson. We climbed the mountain, admired the spacious

---

7 A township on a high plateau above Capri town.

view, and got back to the inn as night was falling, hot, hungry, and thirsty. We had ordered our dinner beforehand. The food was good, for Antonio was an excellent cook, and the wine came from his own vineyard. It was so light that you felt you could drink it like water and we finished the first bottle with our macaroni. By the time we had finished the second we felt that there was nothing much wrong with life. We sat in a little garden under a great vine laden with grapes. The air was exquisitely soft. The night was still and we were alone. The maid brought us *bel paese* cheese[8] and a plate of figs. I ordered coffee and strega, which is the best liqueur they make in Italy. Wilson would not have a cigar, but lit his pipe.

"We've got plenty of time before we need start," he said, "the moon won't be over the hill for another hour."

"Moon or no moon," I said briskly, "of course we've got plenty of time. That's one of the delights of Capri, that there's never any hurry."

"Leisure," he said. "If people only knew! It's the most priceless thing a man can have and they're such fools they don't even know it's something to aim at. Work? They work for work's sake. They haven't got the brains to realize that the only object of work is to obtain leisure."

Wine has the effect on some people of making them indulge in general reflections. These remarks were true, but no one could have claimed that they were original. I did not say anything, but struck a match to light my cigar.

"It was full moon the first time I came to Capri," he went on reflectively. "It might be the same moon as tonight."

"It was, you know," I smiled.

He grinned. The only light in the garden was what came from an oil lamp that hung over our heads. It had been scanty to eat by, but it was good now for confidences.

"I didn't mean that. I mean, it might be yesterday. Fifteen years it is, and when I look back it seems like a month. I'd never been to Italy before. I came for my summer holiday. I went to Naples by boat from Marseilles and I had a look round, Pompeii, you know, and Paestum[9] and one or two places like that; then I came here for a week. I liked the look of the place right away, from the sea, I mean, as I watched it come closer and closer; and then when we got into the little boats from the steamer and landed at the quay, with all that crowd of jabbering people who wanted to take your luggage, and the hotel touts, and the tumbledown houses on the Marina and the walk up to the hotel, and dining on

---

8 A mild-tasting, semi-soft Italian cheese; *bel paese* Italian: beautiful country.

9 Marseilles is a city in the south of France; Pompeii is a historic city close to Naples; Paestum is a coastal town southeast of Naples.

the terrace—well, it just got me. That's the truth. I didn't know if I was standing on my head or my heels. I'd never drunk Capri wine before, but I'd heard of it; I think I must have got a bit tight. I sat on that terrace after they'd all gone to bed and watched the moon over the sea, and there was Vesuvius[10] with a great red plume of smoke rising up from it. Of course I know now that wine I drank was ink, Capri wine my eye, but I thought it all right then. But it wasn't the wine that made me drunk, it was the shape of the island and those jabbering people, the moon and the sea and the oleander in the hotel garden. I'd never seen an oleander before."

It was a long speech and it had made him thirsty. He took up his glass, but it was empty. I asked him if he would have another strega.

"It's sickly stuff. Let's have a bottle of wine. That's sound, that is, pure juice of the grape and can't hurt anyone."

I ordered more wine, and when it came filled the glasses. He took a long drink and after a sigh of pleasure went on.

"Next day I found my way to the bathing-place we go to. Not bad bathing, I thought. Then I wandered about the island. As luck would have it, there was a *festa*[11] up at the Punta di Timberio[12] and I ran straight into the middle of it. An image of the Virgin and priests, acolytes[13] swinging censers, and a whole crowd of jolly, laughing, excited people, a lot of them all dressed up. I ran across an Englishman there and asked him what it was all about. "Oh, it's the feast of the Assumption," he said, "at least that's what the Catholic Church says it is, but that's just their hanky-panky. It's the festival of Venus. Pagan, you know. Aphrodite rising from the sea and all that."[14] It gave me quite a funny feeling to hear him. It seemed to take one a long way back, if you know what I mean. After that I went down one night to have a look at the Faraglioni[15] by moonlight. If the fates had wanted me to go on being a bank manager they oughtn't to have let me take that walk."

"You were a bank manager, were you?" I asked.

I had been wrong about him, but not far wrong.

---

10 Mount Vesuvius is an active volcano east of Naples.

11 Christian celebration; *festa* Italian: feast day.

12 Likely a reference to the Villa Jovis, a villa constructed by the Emperor Tiberius (14 BCE–37 CE) on the top of Mount Tiberius; *Punta di Timberio* Italian: Point of Tiberius.

13 One who performs religious ceremonial duties.

14 Greek mythology: Aphrodite was the goddess of love and beauty; she was said to have been born out of the sea.

15 Rock formations in the sea, located in the Bay of Naples.

"Yes. I was manager of the Crawford Street branch of the York and City. It was convenient for me because I lived up Hendon way. I could get from door to door in thirty-seven minutes."

He puffed at his pipe and relit it.

"That was my last night, that was. I'd got to be back at the bank on Monday morning. When I looked at those two great rocks sticking out of the water, with the moon above them, and all the little lights of the fishermen in their boats catching cuttlefish, all so peaceful and beautiful, I said to myself, well, after all, why should I go back? It wasn't as if I had anyone dependent on me. My wife had died of bronchial pneumonia four years before and the kid went to live with her grandmother, my wife's mother. She was an old fool, she didn't look after the kid properly and she got blood-poisoning, they amputated her leg, but they couldn't save her and she died, poor little thing."

"How terrible," I said.

"Yes, I was cut up at the time, though of course not so much as if the kid had been living with me, but I dare say it was a mercy. Not much chance for a girl with only one leg. I was sorry about my wife too. We got on very well together. Though I don't know if it would have continued. She was the sort of woman who was always bothering about what other people'd think. She didn't like travelling. Eastbourne[16] was her idea of a holiday. D'you know, I'd never crossed the Channel till after her death."

"But I suppose you've got other relations, haven't you?"

"None. I was an only child. My father had a brother, but he went to Australia before I was born. I don't think anyone could easily be more alone in the world than I am. There wasn't any reason I could see why I shouldn't do exactly what I wanted. I was thirty-four at that time."

He had told me he had been on the island for fifteen years. That would make him forty-nine. Just about the age I should have given him.

"I'd been working since I was seventeen. All I had to look forward to was doing the same old thing day after day till I retired on my pension. I said to myself, is it worth it? What's wrong with chucking it all up and spending the rest of my life down here? It was the most beautiful place I'd ever seen. But I'd had a business training, I was cautious by nature. 'No,' I said, 'I won't be carried away like this, I'll go tomorrow like I said I would and think it over. Perhaps when I get back to London I'll think quite differently.' Damned fool, wasn't I? I lost a whole year that way."

"You didn't change your mind, then?"

---

16 A resort town on the southeast coast of England.

"You bet I didn't. All the time I was working I kept thinking of the bathing here and the vineyards and the walks over the hills and the moon and the sea, and the Piazza in the evening when everyone walks about for a bit of a chat after the day's work is over. There was only one thing that bothered me: I wasn't sure if I was justified in not working like everybody else did. Then I read a sort of history book, by a man called Marion Crawford[17] it was, and there was a story about Sybaris and Crotona.[18] There were two cities; and in Sybaris they just enjoyed life and had a good time, and in Crotona they were hardy and industrious and all that. And one day the men of Crotona came over and wiped Sybaris out, and then after a while a lot of other fellows came over from somewhere else and wiped Crotona out. Nothing remains of Sybaris, not a stone, and all that's left of Crotona is just one column. That settled the matter for me."

"Oh?"

"It came to the same in the end, didn't it? And when you look back now, who were the mugs?"

I did not reply and he went on.

"The money was rather a bother. The bank didn't pension one off till after thirty years' service, but if you retired before that they gave you a gratuity. With that and what I'd got for the sale of my house and the little I'd managed to save, I just hadn't enough to buy an annuity to last the rest of my life. It would have been silly to sacrifice everything so as to lead a pleasant life and not have a sufficient income to make it pleasant. I wanted to have a little place of my own, a servant to look after me, enough to buy tobacco, decent food, books now and then, and something over for emergencies. I knew pretty well how much I needed. I found I had just enough to buy an annuity for twenty-five years."

"You were thirty-five at the time?"

"Yes. It would carry me on till I was sixty. After all, no one can be certain of living longer than that, a lot of men die in their fifties, and by the time a man's sixty he's had the best of life."

"On the other hand no one can be sure of dying at sixty," I said.

"Well, I don't know. It depends on himself, doesn't it?"

"In your place I should have stayed on at the bank till I was entitled to my pension."

"I should have been forty-seven then. I shouldn't have been too old to enjoy my life here, I'm older than that now and I enjoy it as much as I ever did, but I should have been too old to experience the particular pleasure of a young man.

---

17 Francis Marion Crawford (1854–1909) was an American fiction writer.

18 The cities of Sybaris and Crotona were part of ancient Greek colonies located in the south of Italy.

You know, you can have just as good a time at fifty as you can at thirty, but it's not the same sort of good time. I wanted to live the perfect life while I still had the energy and the spirit to make the most of it. Twenty-five years seemed a long time to me, and twenty-five years of happiness seemed worth paying something pretty substantial for. I'd made up my mind to wait a year and I waited a year. Then I sent in my resignation and as soon as they paid me my gratuity I bought the annuity and came on here."

"An annuity for twenty-five years?"

"That's right."

"Have you never regretted?"

"Never. I've had my money's worth already. And I've got ten years more. Don't you think after twenty-five years of perfect happiness one ought to be satisfied to call it a day?"

"Perhaps."

He did not say in so many words what he would do then, but his intention was clear. It was pretty much the story my friend had told me, but it sounded different when I heard it from his own lips. I stole a glance at him. There was nothing about him that was not ordinary. No one, looking at that neat, prim face, could have thought him capable of an unconventional action. I did not blame him. It was his own life that he had arranged in this strange manner, and I did not see why he should not do what he liked with it. Still, I could not prevent the little shiver that ran down my spine.

"Getting chilly?" he smiled. "We might as well start walking down. The moon'll be up by now."

Before we parted Wilson asked me if I would like to go and see his house one day; and two or three days later, finding out where he lived, I strolled up to see him. It was a peasant's cottage, well away from the town, in a vineyard, with a view of the sea. By the side of the door grew a great oleander in full flower. There were only two small rooms, a tiny kitchen, and a lean-to in which firewood could be kept. The bedroom was furnished like a monk's cell, but the sitting-room, smelling agreeably of tobacco, was comfortable enough, with two large arm-chairs that he had brought from England, a large roll-top desk, a cottage piano, and crowded bookshelves. On the walls were framed engravings of pictures by G.F. Watts and Lord Leighton.[19] Wilson told me that the house belonged to the owner of the vineyard who lived in another cottage higher up the hill, and his wife came in every day to do the rooms and the cooking. He had found the place on his first visit to Capri, and taking it on his return for good

19 George Frederic Watts (1817–1904) and Frederic Leighton (1830–96) were highly successful English artists in the late nineteenth century.

had been there ever since. Seeing the piano and music open on it, I asked him if he would play.

"I'm no good, you know, but I've always been fond of music and I get a lot of fun out of strumming."

He sat down at the piano and played one of the movements from a Beethoven sonata. He did not play very well. I looked at his music, Schumann and Schubert, Beethoven, Bach, and Chopin. On the table on which he had his meals was a greasy pack of cards. I asked him if he played patience.

"A lot."

From what I saw of him then and from what I heard from other people I made for myself what I think must have been a fairly accurate picture of the life he had led for the last fifteen years. It was certainly a very harmless one. He bathed; he walked a great deal, and he seemed never to lose his sense of the beauty of the island which he knew so intimately; he played the piano and he played patience; he read. When he was asked to a party he went and, though a trifle dull, was agreeable. He was not affronted if he was neglected. He liked people, but with an aloofness that prevented intimacy. He lived thriftily, but with sufficient comfort. He never owed a penny. I imagine he had never been a man whom sex had greatly troubled, and if in his younger days he had had now and then a passing affair with a visitor to the island whose head was turned by the atmosphere, his emotion, while it lasted, remained, I am pretty sure, well under his control. I think he was determined that nothing should interfere with his independence of spirit. His only passion was for the beauty of nature, and he sought felicity in the simple and natural things that life offers to everyone. You may say that it was a grossly selfish existence. It was. He was of no use to anybody, but on the other hand he did nobody any harm. His only object was his own happiness, and it looked as though he had attained it. Very few people know where to look for happiness; fewer still find it. I don't know whether he was a fool or a wise man. He was certainly a man who knew his own mind. The odd thing about him to me was that he was so immensely commonplace. I should never have given him a second thought but for what I knew, that on a certain day, ten years from then, unless a chance illness cut the thread before, he must deliberately take leave of the world he loved so well. I wondered whether it was the thought of this, never quite absent from his mind, that gave him the peculiar zest with which he enjoyed every moment of the day.

I should do him an injustice if I omitted to state that he was not at all in the habit of talking about himself. I think the friend I was staying with was the only person in whom he had confided. I believe he only told me the story because he suspected I already knew it, and on the evening on which he told it me he had drunk a good deal of wine.

My visit drew to a close and I left the island. The year after, war broke out. A number of things happened to me, so that the course of my life was greatly altered, and it was thirteen years before I went to Capri again. My friend had been back some time, but he was no longer so well off, and had moved into a house that had no room for me; so I was putting up at the hotel. He came to meet me at the boat and we dined together. During dinner I asked him where exactly his house was.

"You know it," he answered. "It's the little place Wilson had. I've built on a room and made it quite nice."

With so many other things to occupy my mind I had not given Wilson a thought for years; but now, with a little shock, I remembered. The ten years he had before him when I made his acquaintance must have elapsed long ago.

"Did he commit suicide as he said he would?"

"It's rather a grim story."

Wilson's plan was all right. There was only one flaw in it and this, I suppose, he could not have foreseen. It had never occurred to him that after twenty-five years of complete happiness, in this quiet backwater, with nothing in the world to disturb his serenity, his character would gradually lose its strength. The will needs obstacles in order to exercise its power; when it is never thwarted, when no effort is needed to achieve one's desires, because one has placed one's desires only in the things that can be obtained by stretching out one's hand, the will grows impotent. If you walk on a level all the time the muscles you need to climb a mountain will atrophy. These observations are trite, but there they are. When Wilson's annuity expired he had no longer the resolution to make the end which was the price he had agreed to pay for that long period of happy tranquillity. I do not think, as far as I could gather, both from what my friend told me and afterwards from others, that he wanted courage. It was just that he couldn't make up his mind. He put it off from day to day.

He had lived on the island for so long and had always settled his accounts so punctually that it was easy for him to get credit; never having borrowed money before, he found a number of people who were willing to lend him small sums when now he asked for them. He had paid his rent regularly for so many years that his landlord, whose wife Assunta still acted as his servant, was content to let things slide for several months. Everyone believed him when he said that a relative had died and that he was temporarily embarrassed because owing to legal formalities he could not for some time get the money that was due to him. He managed to hang on after this fashion for something over a year. Then he could get no more credit from the local tradesmen, and there was no one to lend him any more money. His landlord gave him notice to leave the house unless he paid up arrears of rent before a certain date.

The day before this he went into his tiny bedroom, closed the door and the window, drew the curtain, and lit a brazier of charcoal. Next morning when Assunta came to make his breakfast she found him insensible but still alive. The room was draughty, and though he had done this and that to keep out the fresh air he had not done it very thoroughly. It almost looked as though at the last moment, and desperate though his situation was, he had suffered from a certain infirmity of purpose. Wilson was taken to the hospital, and though very ill for some time he at last recovered. But as a result either of the charcoal poisoning or of the shock he was no longer in complete possession of his faculties. He was not insane, at all events not insane enough to be put in an asylum, but he was quite obviously no longer in his right mind.

"I went to see him," said my friend. "I tried to get him to talk, but he kept looking at me in a funny sort of way, as though he couldn't quite make out where he'd seen me before. He looked rather awful lying there in bed, with a week's growth of grey beard on his chin; but except for that funny look in his eyes he seemed quite normal."

"What funny look in his eyes?"

"I don't know exactly how to describe it. Puzzled. It's an absurd comparison, but suppose you threw a stone up into the air and it didn't come down but just stayed there ..."

"It would be rather bewildering," I smiled.

"Well, that's the sort of look he had."

It was difficult to know what to do with him. He had no money and no means of getting any. His effects were sold, but for too little to pay what he owed. He was English, and the Italian authorities did not wish to make themselves responsible for him. The British Consul in Naples had no funds to deal with the case. He could of course be sent back to England, but no one seemed to know what could be done with him when he got there. Then Assunta, the servant, said that he had been a good master and a good tenant, and as long as he had the money had paid his way; he could sleep in the woodshed in the cottage in which she and her husband lived, and he could share their meals. This was suggested to him. It was difficult to know whether he understood or not. When Assunta came to take him from the hospital he went with her without remark. He seemed to have no longer a will of his own. She had been keeping him now for two years.

"It's not very comfortable, you know," said my friend. "They've rigged him up a ramshackle bed and given him a couple of blankets, but there's no window, and it's icy cold in winter and like an oven in summer. And the food's pretty rough. You know how these peasants eat: macaroni on Sundays and meat once in a blue moon."

"What does he do with himself all the time?"

"He wanders about the hills. I've tried to see him two or three times, but it's no good; when he sees you coming he runs like a hare. Assunta comes down to have a chat with me now and then and I give her a bit of money so that she can buy him tobacco, but God knows if he ever gets it."

"Do they treat him all right?" I asked.

"I'm sure Assunta's kind enough. She treats him like a child. I'm afraid her husband's not very nice to him. He grudges the cost of his keep. I don't believe he's cruel or anything like that, but I think he's a bit sharp with him. He makes him fetch water and clean the cow-shed and that sort of thing."

"It sounds pretty rotten," I said.

"He brought it on himself. After all, he's only got what he deserved."

"I think on the whole we all get what we deserve," I said. "But that doesn't prevent its being rather horrible."

Two or three days later my friend and I were taking a walk. We were strolling along a narrow path through an olive grove.

"There's Wilson," said my friend suddenly. "Don't look, you'll only frighten him. Go straight on."

I walked with my eyes on the path, but out of the corners of them I saw a man hiding behind an olive tree. He did not move as we approached, but I felt that he was watching us. As soon as we had passed I heard a scamper. Wilson, like a hunted animal, had made for safety. That was the last I ever saw of him.

He died last year. He had endured that life for six years. He was found one morning on the mountainside lying quite peacefully as though he had died in his sleep. From where he lay he had been able to see those two great rocks called the Faraglioni which stand out of the sea. It was full moon and he must have gone to see them by moonlight. Perhaps he died of the beauty of that night.

—1935

JAMES JOYCE

James Joyce was born in a south Dublin suburb in 1882. The second of ten children, he was educated at various Jesuit-run schools in and around Dublin, where he excelled in his studies. In 1898, Joyce enrolled at University College, Dublin, and began writing reviews, a play inspired by Henrik Ibsen (he later destroyed it), and essays that marked him as a unique, if iconoclastic, talent. After a brief attempt to study medicine in Paris, he returned home to Dublin, where he met Nora Barnacle, a woman from Galway who would become his lifelong companion and the mother of his two children (they would marry in 1931). Joyce suffered from severe eye problems, including glaucoma, and endured over ten operations to treat his ailments over the course of his life.

Joyce and his family led something of a nomadic existence, their moves motivated variously by Joyce's flight from creditors, by his search for work, and by the dangers of war. Though several of his stories had been published in the periodical *Irish Homestead*, his breakthrough came in 1914. In that year his book of short stories *Dubliners* was published, and excerpts from his semi-autobiographical novel *A Portrait of the Artist as a Young Man* (1916) were serialized in Ezra Pound's periodical *The Egoist*.

Joyce suffered a major blow in 1922 when the US Post Office confiscated copies of the magazine *Little Review* that contained excerpts from his novel in progress, *Ulysses*; the publisher was charged with publishing pornography. *Ulysses* was finally published by American expatriate Sylvia Beach's bookstore press, Shakespeare and Co., in Paris; Joyce was soon hailed as a genius by writers such as T.S. Eliot and Ernest Hemingway. In the meantime, Joyce had begun work on his novel *Finnegans Wake*—his most ambitious text and one that would take him almost seventeen years to write. When it was finally published in 1939, the novel's innovative form and structure provoked new controversy. Joyce died in 1941 after an operation for a perforated ulcer.

Dubliners was not published in its entirety until June 15, 1914. Joyce had submitted and resubmitted the collection to various publishers, but their squeamishness over the subject matter prevented the collection from being published for almost ten years. Even the collection's eventual publisher worried that the negative portrayal of Dublin and its inhabitants in the collection would provoke charges of libel. In a letter to his publisher, Joyce states his reason for leaving the stories as he originally wrote them:

> My intention was to write a chapter of the moral history of my country and I chose Dublin for the scene because the city seemed to me the centre of paralysis.... I have written it for the most part in a style of scrupulous meanness and with the conviction that he is a very bold man who dares to alter in the presentment, still more to deform, whatever he has seen and heard. I cannot do any more than this.

"Araby," the third story in the collection and one of the few recounted in the first person, examines a young boy's romantic fantasies and longing for adventure. The story "Eveline" also engages the idea of escape; the central character must choose between the dysfunctional yet familiar nature of her current reality and the promise of a better life.

Araby

JAMES JOYCE

NORTH Richmond Street, being blind,[1] was a quiet street except at the hour when the Christian Brothers' School set the boys free. An uninhabited house of two storeys stood at the blind end, detached from its neighbours in a square ground. The other houses of the street, conscious of decent lives within them, gazed at one another with brown imperturbable faces.

The former tenant of our house, a priest, had died in the back drawing-room. Air, musty from having been long enclosed, hung in all the rooms, and the waste room behind the kitchen was littered with old useless papers. Among these I found a few paper-covered books, the pages of which were curled and damp: *The Abbot*,[2] by Walter Scott, *The Devout Communicant*[3] and *The Memoirs of Vidocq*.[4] I liked the last best because its leaves were yellow. The wild garden behind the house contained a central apple-tree and a few straggling bushes

1 A dead-end street.

2 An 1820 historical novel by Sir Walter Scott about Mary, Queen of Scots.

3 Several nineteenth-century religious tracts have this title.

4 The popular autobiography of François Vidocq, a nineteenth-century Parisian criminal turned police detective.

under one of which I found the late tenant's rusty bicycle-pump. He had been a very charitable priest; in his will he had left all his money to institutions and the furniture of his house to his sister.

When the short days of winter came dusk fell before we had well eaten our dinners. When we met in the street the houses had grown sombre. The space of sky above us was the colour of ever-changing violet and towards it the lamps of the street lifted their feeble lanterns. The cold air stung us and we played till our bodies glowed. Our shouts echoed in the silent street. The career of our play brought us through the dark muddy lanes behind the houses where we ran the gantlet of the rough tribes from the cottages, to the back doors of the dark dripping gardens where odours arose from the ash-pits, to the dark odorous stables where a coachman smoothed and combed the horse or shook music from the buckled harness. When we returned to the street light from the kitchen windows had filled the areas. If my uncle was seen turning the corner we hid in the shadow until we had seen him safely housed. Or if Mangan's sister came out on the doorstep to call her brother in to his tea we watched her from our shadow peer up and down the street. We waited to see whether she would remain or go in and, if she remained, we left our shadow and walked up to Mangan's steps resignedly. She was waiting for us, her figure defined by the light from the half-opened door. Her brother always teased her before he obeyed and I stood by the railings looking at her. Her dress swung as she moved her body and the soft rope of her hair tossed from side to side.

Every morning I lay on the floor in the front parlour watching her door. The blind was pulled down to within an inch of the sash so that I could not be seen. When she came out on the doorstep my heart leaped. I ran to the hall, seized my books and followed her. I kept her brown figure always in my eye and, when we came near the point at which our ways diverged, I quickened my pace and passed her. This happened morning after morning. I had never spoken to her, except for a few casual words, and yet her name was like a summons to all my foolish blood.

Her image accompanied me even in places the most hostile to romance. On Saturday evenings when my aunt went marketing I had to go to carry some of the parcels. We walked through the flaring streets, jostled by drunken men and bargaining women, amid the curses of labourers, the shrill litanies of shop boys who stood on guard by the barrels of pigs' cheeks, the nasal chanting of street-singers, who sang a *come-all-you* about O'Donovan Rossa,[5] or a ballad about the troubles in our native land. These noises converged in a single sensation of life for me: I imagined that I bore my chalice safely through a throng of foes.

---

5 Jeremiah O'Donovan Rossa (1831-1915), an activist for Irish independence.

Her name sprang to my lips at moments in strange prayers and praises which I myself did not understand. My eyes were often full of tears (I could not tell why) and at times a flood from my heart seemed to pour itself out into my bosom. I thought little of the future. I did not know whether I would ever speak to her or not or, if I spoke to her, how I could tell her of my confused adoration. But my body was like a harp and her words and gestures were like fingers running upon the wires.

One evening I went into the back drawing-room in which the priest had died. It was a dark rainy evening and there was no sound in the house. Through one of the broken panes I heard the rain impinge upon the earth, the fine incessant needles of water playing in the sodden beds. Some distant lamp or lighted window gleamed below me. I was thankful that I could see so little. All my senses seemed to desire to veil themselves and, feeling that I was about to slip from them, I pressed the palms of my hands together until they trembled, murmuring: *O love! O love!* many times.

At last she spoke to me. When she addressed the first words to me I was so confused that I did not know what to answer. She asked me was I going to *Araby*. I forget whether I answered yes or no. It would be a splendid bazaar, she said; she would love to go.

—And why can't you? I asked.

While she spoke she turned a silver bracelet round and round her wrist. She could not go, she said, because there would be a retreat that week in her convent. Her brother and two other boys were fighting for their caps and I was alone at the railings. She held one of the spikes, bowing her head towards me. The light from the lamp opposite our door caught the white curve of her neck, lit up her hair that rested there and, falling, lit up the hand upon the railing. It fell over one side of her dress and caught the white border of a petticoat, just visible as she stood at ease.

—It's well for you, she said.

—If I go, I said, I will bring you something.

What innumerable follies laid waste my waking and sleeping thoughts after that evening! I wished to annihilate the tedious intervening days. I chafed against the work of school. At night in my bedroom and by day in the classroom her image came between me and the page I strove to read. The syllables of the word *Araby* were called to me through the silence in which my soul luxuriated and cast an Eastern enchantment over me. I asked for leave to go to the bazaar on Saturday night. My aunt was surprised and hoped it was not some Freemason[6] affair. I answered few questions in class. I watched my master's face pass

6 The Freemasons are a secret society, believed by many in Ireland to be anti-Catholic.

from amiability to sternness; he hoped I was not beginning to idle. I could not call my wandering thoughts together. I had hardly any patience with the serious work of life which, now that it stood between me and my desire, seemed to me child's play, ugly monotonous child's play.

On Saturday morning I reminded my uncle that I wished to go to the bazaar in the evening. He was fussing at the hallstand, looking for the hat-brush, and answered me curtly:

—Yes, boy, I know.

As he was in the hall I could not go into the front parlour and lie at the window. I left the house in bad humour and walked slowly towards the school. The air was pitilessly raw and already my heart misgave me.

When I came home to dinner my uncle had not yet been home. Still it was early. I sat staring at the clock for some time and, when its ticking began to irritate me, I left the room. I mounted the staircase and gained the upper part of the house. The high cold empty gloomy rooms liberated me and I went from room to room singing. From the front window I saw my companions playing below in the street. Their cries reached me weakened and indistinct and, leaning my forehead against the cool glass, I looked over at the dark house where she lived. I may have stood there for an hour, seeing nothing but the brown-clad figure cast by my imagination, touched discreetly by the lamplight at the curved neck, at the hand upon the railings and at the border below the dress.

When I came downstairs again I found Mrs Mercer sitting at the fire. She was an old garrulous woman, a pawnbroker's widow, who collected used stamps for some pious purpose. I had to endure the gossip of the tea-table. The meal was prolonged beyond an hour and still my uncle did not come. Mrs Mercer stood up to go: she was sorry she couldn't wait any longer, but it was after eight o'clock and she did not like to be out late, as the night air was bad for her. When she had gone I began to walk up and down the room, clenching my fists. My aunt said:

—I'm afraid you may put off your bazaar for this night of Our Lord.

At nine o'clock I heard my uncle's latchkey in the halldoor. I heard him talking to himself and heard the hallstand rocking when it had received the weight of his overcoat. I could interpret these signs. When he was midway through his dinner I asked him to give me the money to go to the bazaar. He had forgotten.

—The people are in bed and after their first sleep now, he said.

I did not smile. My aunt said to him energetically:

—Can't you give him the money and let him go? You've kept him late enough as it is.

My uncle said he was very sorry he had forgotten. He said he believed in the old saying: *All work and no play makes Jack a dull boy.* He asked where I was going and, when I had told him a second time he asked me did I know *The Arab's*

Farewell to his Steed.[7] When I left the kitchen he was about to recite the opening lines of the piece to my aunt.

I held a florin tightly in my hand as I strode down Buckingham Street towards the station. The sight of the streets thronged with buyers and glaring with gas recalled to me the purpose of my journey. I took my seat in a third-class carriage of a deserted train. After an intolerable delay the train moved out of the station slowly. It crept onward among ruinous houses and over the twinkling river. At Westland Row Station a crowd of people pressed to the carriage doors; but the porters moved them back, saying that it was a special train for the bazaar. I remained alone in the bare carriage. In a few minutes the train drew up beside an improvised wooden platform. I passed out on to the road and saw by the lighted dial of a clock that it was ten minutes to ten. In front of me was a large building which displayed the magical name.

I could not find any sixpenny entrance and, fearing that the bazaar would be closed, I passed in quickly through a turnstile, handing a shilling to a weary-looking man. I found myself in a big hall girdled at half its height by a gallery. Nearly all the stalls were closed and the greater part of the hall was in darkness. I recognized a silence like that which pervades a church after a service. I walked into the centre of the bazaar timidly. A few people were gathered about the stalls which were still open. Before a curtain, over which the words *Café Chantant* were written in coloured lamps, two men were counting money on a salver. I listened to the fall of the coins.

Remembering with difficulty why I had come I went over to one of the stalls and examined porcelain vases and flowered tea-sets. At the door of the stall a young lady was talking and laughing with two young gentlemen. I remarked their English accents and listened vaguely to their conversation.

—Oh, I never said such a thing!

—O, but you did!

—O, but I didn't!

—Didn't she say that?

—Yes. I heard her.

—O, there's a ... fib!

Observing me the young lady came over and asked me did I wish to buy anything. The tone of her voice was not encouraging; she seemed to have spoken to me out of a sense of duty. I looked humbly at the great jars that stood like eastern guards at either side of the dark entrance to the stall and murmured:

—No, thank you.

---

7 Popular Romantic poem by Caroline Norton (1808-77).

The young lady changed the position of one of the vases and went back to the two young men. They began to talk of the same subject. Once or twice the young lady glanced at me over her shoulder.

I lingered before her stall, though I knew my stay was useless, to make my interest in her wares seem the more real. Then I turned away slowly and walked down the middle of the bazaar. I allowed the two pennies to fall against the sixpence in my pocket. I heard a voice call from one end of the gallery that the light was out. The upper part of the hall was now completely dark.

Gazing up into the darkness I saw myself as a creature driven and derided by vanity; and my eyes burned with anguish and anger.

—1914

Eveline

JAMES JOYCE

SHE SAT at the window watching the evening invade the avenue. Her head was leaned against the window curtains and in her nostrils was the odour of dusty cretonne.[1] She was tired.

Few people passed. The man out of the last house passed on his way home; she heard his footsteps clacking along the concrete pavement and afterwards crunching on the cinder path before the new red houses. One time there used to be a field there in which they used to play every evening with other people's children. Then a man from Belfast bought the field and built houses in it—not like their little brown houses but bright brick houses with shining roofs. The children of the avenue used to play together in that field—the Devines, the Waters, the Dunns, little Keogh the cripple, she and her brothers and sisters. Ernest, however, never played: he was too grown up. Her father used often to hunt them in out of the field with his blackthorn stick; but usually little Keogh used to keep *nix* and call out when he saw her father coming. Still they seemed to have been rather happy then. Her father was not so bad then; and besides, her mother was alive. That was a long time ago; she and her brothers and sisters were all grown up; her mother was dead. Tizzie Dunn was dead, too, and the Waters had gone back to England. Everything changes. Now she was going to go away like the others, to leave her home.

Home! She looked round the room, reviewing all its familiar objects which she had dusted once a week for so many years, wondering where on earth all the

1 Cotton fabric.

dust came from. Perhaps she would never see again those familiar objects from which she had never dreamed of being divided. And yet during all those years she had never found out the name of the priest whose yellowing photograph hung on the wall above the broken harmonium[2] beside the coloured print of the promises made to Blessed Margaret Mary Alacoque.[3] He had been a school friend of her father. Whenever he showed the photograph to a visitor her father used to pass it with a casual word:

—He is in Melbourne now.

She had consented to go away, to leave her home. Was that wise? She tried to weigh each side of the question. In her home anyway she had shelter and food; she had those whom she had known all her life about her. Of course she had to work hard both in the house and at business. What would they say of her in the Stores when they found out that she had run away with a fellow? Say she was a fool, perhaps; and her place would be filled up by advertisement. Miss Gavan would be glad. She had always had an edge on her, especially whenever there were people listening.

—Miss Hill, don't you see these ladies are waiting?

—Look lively, Miss Hill, please.

She would not cry many tears at leaving the Stores.

But in her new home, in a distant unknown country, it would not be like that. Then she would be married—she, Eveline. People would treat her with respect then. She would not be treated as her mother had been. Even now, though she was over nineteen, she sometimes felt herself in danger of her father's violence. She knew it was that that had given her the palpitations. When they were growing up he had never gone for her, like he used to go for Harry and Ernest, because she was a girl; but latterly he had begun to threaten her and say what he would do to her only for her dead mother's sake. And now she had nobody to protect her. Ernest was dead and Harry, who was in the church decorating business, was nearly always down somewhere in the country. Besides, the invariable squabble for money on Saturday nights had begun to weary her unspeakably. She always gave her entire wages—seven shillings—and Harry always sent up what he could but the trouble was to get any money from her father. He said she used to squander the money, that she had no head, that he wasn't going to give her his hard-earned money to throw about the streets, and much more, for he was usually fairly bad of a Saturday night. In the end he would give her the money and ask her had she any intention of buying Sunday's dinner. Then she had to rush out as quickly as she could and do her marketing, holding her black

---

2 A reed instrument similar to an organ.

3 Marguerite Marie Alacoque (1647-90), a French Catholic nun and religious mystic.

leather purse tightly in her hand as she elbowed her way through the crowds and returning home late under her load of provisions. She had hard work to keep the house together and to see that the two young children who had been left to her charge went to school regularly and got their meals regularly. It was hard work—a hard life—but now that she was about to leave it she did not find it a wholly undesirable life.

She was about to explore another life with Frank. Frank was very kind, manly, open-hearted. She was to go away with him by the night-boat to be his wife and to live with him in Buenos Ayres where he had a home waiting for her. How well she remembered the first time she had seen him; he was lodging in a house on the main road where she used to visit. It seemed a few weeks ago. He was standing at the gate, his peaked cap pushed back on his head and his hair tumbled forward over a face of bronze. Then they had come to know each other. He used to meet her outside the Stores every evening and see her home. He took her to see *The Bohemian Girl*[4] and she felt elated as she sat in an unaccustomed part of the theatre with him. He was awfully fond of music and sang a little. People knew that they were courting and, when he sang about the lass that loves a sailor, she always felt pleasantly confused. He used to call her Poppens out of fun. First of all it had been an excitement for her to have a fellow and then she had begun to like him. He had tales of distant countries. He had started as a deck boy at a pound a month on a ship of the Allan Line[5] going out to Canada. He told her the names of the ships he had been on and the names of the different services. He had sailed through the Straits of Magellan and he told her stories of the terrible Patagonians. He had fallen on his feet in Buenos Ayres, he said, and had come over to the old country just for a holiday. Of course, her father had found out the affair and had forbidden her to have anything to say to him.

—I know these sailor chaps, he said.

One day he had quarrelled with Frank and after that she had to meet her lover secretly.

The evening deepened in the avenue. The white of two letters in her lap grew indistinct. One was to Harry; the other was to her father. Ernest had been her favourite but she liked Harry too. Her father was becoming old lately, she noticed; he would miss her. Sometimes he could be very nice. Not long before, when she had been laid up for a day, he had read her out a ghost story and made toast for her at the fire. Another day, when their mother was alive, they had all

4 An 1843 opera by Irish composer Michael Balfe.

5 A steamship company that made weekly sailings between Liverpool and western Canada via South America.

gone for a picnic to the Hill of Howth.[6] She remembered her father putting on her mother's bonnet to make the children laugh.

Her time was running out but she continued to sit by the window, leaning her head against the window curtain, inhaling the odour of dusty cretonne. Down far in the avenue she could hear a street organ playing. She knew the air. Strange that it should come that very night to remind her of the promise to her mother, her promise to keep the home together as long as she could. She remembered the last night of her mother's illness; she was again in the close dark room at the other side of the hall and outside she heard a melancholy air of Italy. The organ-player had been ordered to go away and given sixpence. She remembered her father strutting back into the sickroom saying:

—Damned Italians! coming over here!

As she mused the pitiful vision of her mother's life laid its spell on the very quick of her being—that life of commonplace sacrifices closing in final craziness. She trembled as she heard again her mother's voice saying constantly with foolish insistence:

—Derevaun Seraun! Derevaun Seraun![7]

She stood up in a sudden impulse of terror. Escape! She must escape! Frank would save her. He would give her life, perhaps love, too. But she wanted to live. Why should she be unhappy? She had a right to happiness. Frank would take her in his arms, fold her in his arms. He would save her.

She stood among the swaying crowd in the station at the North Wall. He held her hand and she knew that he was speaking to her, saying something about the passage over and over again. The station was full of soldiers with brown baggages. Through the wide doors of the sheds she caught a glimpse of the black mass of the boat, lying in beside the quay wall, with illumined portholes. She answered nothing. She felt her cheek pale and cold and, out of a maze of distress, she prayed to God to direct her, to show her what was her duty. The boat blew a long mournful whistle into the mist. If she went, to-morrow she would be on the sea with Frank, steaming towards Buenos Ayres. Their passage had been booked. Could she still draw back after all he had done for her? Her distress awoke a nausea in her body and she kept moving her lips in silent fervent prayer.

A bell clanged upon her heart. She felt him seize her hand:

—Come!

All the seas of the world tumbled about her heart. He was drawing her into them: he would drown her. She gripped with both hands at the iron railing.

---

6 A hill located northeast of Dublin.

7 The meaning of this phrase is uncertain; it may be garbled Irish or simply gibberish.

—Come!

No! No! No! It was impossible. Her hands clutched the iron in frenzy. Amid the seas she sent a cry of anguish!

—Eveline! Evvy!

He rushed beyond the barrier and called to her to follow. He was shouted at to go on but he still called to her. She set her white face to him, passive, like a helpless animal. Her eyes gave him no sign of love or farewell or recognition.

—1914

KATHERINE MANSFIELD

Katherine Mansfield was the daughter of a businessman who later became the affluent director of the Bank of New Zealand. She was born in 1888 in Wellington, New Zealand, the setting for a large part of her fiction. At fifteen, she travelled with her family to England, where she studied music for three years at Queen's College. There she met Ida Baker (later known as Leslie Moore or L.M.) with whom she would form a lifelong relationship.

Upon completing her education, Mansfield made London her home. Over the course of ten years, Mansfield had numerous affairs with men (one of whom she married) and continued to maintain her connection with L.M. (her mother committed her to "cold water therapy" in a small Bavarian town in order to "cure" her of her lesbian affection for L.M.). In 1911 she met John Middleton Murry, an Oxford undergraduate and literary editor of the new review, *Rhythm*, when he visited her in order to discuss a story she had sent to his review; soon afterward they became lovers, and they married in 1918, after her divorce from her first husband was completed.

Two of Mansfield's most important friendships were with the writers D.H. Lawrence and Virginia Woolf. Although she occasionally criticized Mansfield's bohemian behaviour and attitudes, Woolf was a great admirer of Mansfield and once wrote that Mansfield was the only writer of whom she felt jealous. Mansfield's friendship with Lawrence was less stable, and Lawrence may have drawn on aspects of Mansfield's life and personality in his sometimes unflattering fictional portrait of Gudrun Brangwen in the novel *Women in Love* (1920). During World War I, Mansfield's only brother Leslie was killed in a training accident. Mansfield wrote *Prelude* (1918) and *At the Bay* (1921) in response to the tragedy and as a means of reconstructing the childhood she had shared with her brother.

In the final years of her life, Mansfield suffered from a number of illnesses—the most serious of which was tuberculosis—but she still managed to produce critically well-received works such as *Bliss and Other Stories* (1920) and *The Garden Party and Other Stories* (1922). Throughout this time she was faithfully attended by L.M. She died of a hemorrhage in 1923.

Murry collected her loose papers and notebooks together after her death, and published them under the titles *The Journal of Katherine Mansfield* (1927) and *The Scrapbook of Katherine Mansfield* (1939). Also published posthumously were two collections of fiction, *The Dove's Nest* (1923) and *Something Childish* (1924). Mansfield was a fervent admirer of Anton Chekhov's writing, and numerous literary scholars have noted the similarities between the two writers' works. Published in *The Garden Party and Other Stories* (1922), "The Doll's House" shows Mansfield's satirical eye turned to Wellington's "middle class and its rather smudged carbon copy of how the English do things." From the same collection, "The Garden Party" also deals with classist assumptions; both stories turn on petty divisions of a sort often found in the higher echelons of society.

The Doll's House

KATHERINE MANSFIELD

WHEN dear old Mrs. Hay went back to town after staying with the Burnells she sent the children a doll's house. It was so big that the carter and Pat carried it into the courtyard, and there it stayed, propped up on two wooden boxes beside the feed-room door. No harm could come to it; it was summer. And perhaps the smell of paint would have gone off by the time it had to be taken in. For, really, the smell of paint coming from that doll's house ('Sweet of old Mrs. Hay, of course; most sweet and generous!')—but the smell of paint was quite enough to make anyone seriously ill, in Aunt Beryl's opinion. Even before the sacking was taken off. And when it was ...

There stood the Doll's house, a dark, oily, spinach green, picked out with bright yellow. Its two solid little chimneys, glued on to the roof, were painted red and white, and the door, gleaming with yellow varnish, was like a little slab of toffee. Four windows, real windows, were divided into panes by a broad streak of green. There was actually a tiny porch, too, painted yellow, with big lumps of congealed paint hanging along the edge.

But perfect, perfect little house! Who could possibly mind the smell. It was part of the joy, part of the newness.

"Open it quickly, someone!"

The hook at the side was stuck fast. Pat prized it open with his penknife, and the whole house front swung back, and—there you were, gazing at one and the same moment into the drawing-room and dining-room, the kitchen and two bedrooms. That is the way for a house to open! Why don't all houses open like that? How much more exciting than peering through the slit of a door into a mean little hall with a hat-stand and two umbrellas! That is—isn't it?—what you long to know about a house when you put your hand on the knocker. Perhaps it is the way God opens houses at the dead of night when He is taking a quiet turn with an angel ...

"O-oh!" The Burnell children sounded as though they were in despair. It was too marvellous; it was too much for them. They had never seen anything like it in their lives. All the rooms were papered. There were pictures on the walls, painted on the paper, with gold frames complete. Red carpet covered all the floors except the kitchen; red plush chairs in the drawing-room, green in the dining-room; tables, beds with real bedclothes, a cradle, a stove, a dresser with tiny plates and one big jug. But what Kezia liked more than anything, what she liked frightfully, was the lamp. It stood in the middle of the dining-room table, an exquisite little amber lamp with a white globe. It was even filled all ready for lighting, though, of course, you couldn't light it. But there was something inside that looked like oil and moved when you shook it.

The father and mother dolls, who sprawled very stiff as though they had fainted in the drawing-room, and their two little children asleep upstairs, were really too big for the doll's house. They didn't look as though they belonged. But the lamp was perfect. It seemed to smile at Kezia, to say, "I live here." The lamp was real.

The Burnell children could hardly walk to school fast enough the next morning. They burned to tell everybody, to describe, to—well—to boast about their doll's house before the school-bell rang.

"I'm to tell," said Isabel, "because I'm the eldest. And you two can join in after. But I'm to tell first."

There was nothing to answer. Isabel was bossy, but she was always right, and Lottie and Kezia knew too well the powers that went with being eldest. They brushed through the thick buttercups at the road edge and said nothing.

"And I'm to choose who's to come and see it first. Mother said I might."

For it had been arranged that while the doll's house stood in the courtyard they might ask the girls at school, two at a time, to come and look. Not to stay to tea, of course, or to come traipsing through the house. But just to stand quietly in the courtyard while Isabel pointed out the beauties, and Lottie and Kezia looked pleased ...

But hurry as they might, by the time they had reached the tarred palings of the boys' playground the bell had begun to jangle. They only just had time to whip off their hats and fall into line before the roll was called. Never mind. Isabel tried to make up for it by looking very important and mysterious and by whispering behind her hand to the girls near her, "Got something to tell you at playtime."

Playtime came and Isabel was surrounded. The girls of her class nearly fought to put their arms round her, to walk away with her, to beam flatteringly, to be her special friend. She held quite a court under the huge pine trees at the side of the playground. Nudging, giggling together, the little girls pressed up close. And the only two who stayed outside the ring were the two who were always outside, the little Kelveys. They knew better than to come anywhere near the Burnells.

For the fact was, the school the Burnell children went to was not at all the kind of place their parents would have chosen if there had been any choice. But there was none. It was the only school for miles. And the consequence was all the children of the neighbourhood, the Judge's little girls, the doctor's daughters, the store-keeper's children, the milkman's, were forced to mix together. Not to speak of there being an equal number of rude, rough little boys as well. But the line had to be drawn somewhere. It was drawn at the Kelveys. Many of the children, including the Burnells, were not allowed even to speak to them. They walked past the Kelveys with their heads in the air, and as they set the fashion in all matters of behaviour, the Kelveys were shunned by everybody. Even the teacher had a special voice for them, and a special smile for the other children when Lil Kelvey came up to her desk with a bunch of dreadfully common-looking flowers.

They were the daughters of a spry, hard-working little washerwoman, who went about from house to house by the day. This was awful enough. But where was Mr. Kelvey? Nobody knew for certain. But everybody said he was in prison. So they were the daughters of a washerwoman and a gaolbird. Very nice company for other people's children! And they looked it. Why Mrs. Kelvey made them so conspicuous was hard to understand. The truth was they were dressed in "bits" given to her by the people for whom she worked. Lil, for instance, who was a stout, plain child, with big freckles, came to school in a dress made from a green art-serge table-cloth of the Burnells', with red plush sleeves from the Logans' curtains. Her hat, perched on top of her high forehead, was a grown-up woman's hat, once the property of Miss Lecky, the postmistress. It was turned up at the back and trimmed with a large scarlet quill. What a little guy she looked! It was impossible not to laugh. And her little sister, our Else, wore a long white dress, rather like a nightgown, and a pair of little boy's boots. But whatever our Else wore she would have looked strange. She was a tiny wishbone of a child, with cropped hair and enormous solemn eyes—a little white owl. Nobody had ever seen her smile; she scarcely ever spoke. She went through life holding on to Lil, with a piece of Lil's skirt screwed up in her hand. Where Lil went, our Else followed. In the playground, on the road going to and from school, there was Lil marching in front and our Else holding on behind. Only when she wanted anything, or when she was out of breath, our Else gave Lil a tug, a twitch, and Lil stopped and turned round. The Kelveys never failed to understand each other.

Now they hovered at the edge; you couldn't stop them listening. When the little girls turned round and sneered, Lil, as usual, gave her silly, shamefaced smile, but our Else only looked.

And Isabel's voice, so very proud, went on telling. The carpet made a great sensation, but so did the beds with real bedclothes, and the stove with an oven door.

When she finished Kezia broke in. "You've forgotten the lamp, Isabel."

"Oh, yes," said Isabel, "and there's a teeny little lamp, all made of yellow glass, with a white globe that stands on the dining-room table. You couldn't tell it from a real one."

"The lamp's best of all," cried Kezia. She thought Isabel wasn't making half enough of the little lamp. But nobody paid any attention. Isabel was choosing the two who were to come back with them that afternoon and see it. She chose Emmie Cole and Lena Logan. But when the others knew they were all to have a chance, they couldn't be nice enough to Isabel. One by one they put their arms round Isabel's waist and walked her off. They had something to whisper to her, a secret. "Isabel's *my* friend."

Only the little Kelveys moved away forgotten; there was nothing more for them to hear.

Days passed, and as more children saw the doll's house, the fame of it spread. It became the one subject, the rage. The one question was, "Have you seen Burnells' doll's house? Oh, ain't it lovely!" "Haven't you seen it? Oh, I say!"

Even the dinner hour was given up to talking about it. The little girls sat under the pines eating their thick mutton sandwiches and big slabs of johnny cake spread with butter. While always, as near as they could get, sat the Kelveys, our Else holding on to Lil, listening too, while they chewed their jam sandwiches out of a newspaper soaked with large red blobs.

"Mother," said Kezia, "can't I ask the Kelveys just once?"

"Certainly not, Kezia."

"But why not?"

"Run away, Kezia; you know quite well why not."

At last everybody had seen it except them. On that day the subject rather flagged. It was the dinner hour. The children stood together under the pine trees, and suddenly, as they looked at the Kelveys eating out of their paper, always by themselves, always listening, they wanted to be horrid to them. Emmie Cole started the whisper.

"Lil Kelvey's going to be a servant when she grows up."

"O-oh, how awful!" said Isabel Burnell, and she made eyes at Emmie.

Emmie swallowed in a very meaning way and nodded to Isabel as she'd seen her mother do on those occasions.

"It's true—it's true—it's true," she said.

Then Lena Logan's little eyes snapped. "Shall I ask her?" she whispered.

"Bet you don't," said Jessie May.

"Pooh, I'm not frightened," said Lena. Suddenly she gave a little squeal and danced in front of the other girls. "Watch! Watch me! Watch me now!" said Lena. And sliding, gliding, dragging one foot, giggling behind her hand, Lena went over to the Kelveys.

Lil looked up from her dinner. She wrapped the rest quickly away. Our Else stopped chewing. What was coming now?

"Is it true you're going to be a servant when you grow up, Lil Kelvey?" shrilled Lena.

Dead silence. But instead of answering, Lil only gave her silly, shamefaced smile. She didn't seem to mind the question at all. What a sell for Lena! The girls began to titter.

Lena couldn't stand that. She put her hands on her hips; she shot forward. "Yah, yer father's in prison!" she hissed, spitefully.

This was such a marvellous thing to have said that the little girls rushed away in a body, deeply, deeply excited, wild with joy. Someone found a long rope, and they began skipping. And never did they skip so high, run in and out so fast, or do such daring things as on that morning.

In the afternoon Pat called for the Burnell children with the buggy and they drove home. There were visitors. Isabel and Lottie, who liked visitors, went upstairs to change their pinafores. But Kezia thieved out at the back. Nobody was about; she began to swing on the big white gates of the courtyard. Presently, looking along the road, she saw two little dots. They grew bigger, they were coming towards her. Now she could see that one was in front and one close behind. Now she could see that they were the Kelveys. Kezia stopped swinging. She slipped off the gate as if she was going to run away. Then she hesitated. The Kelveys came nearer, and beside them walked their shadows, very long, stretching right across the road with their heads in the buttercups. Kezia clambered back on the gate; she had made up her mind; she swung out

"Hullo," she said to the passing Kelveys.

They were so astounded that they stopped. Lil gave her silly smile. Our Else stared.

"You can come and see our doll's house if you want to," said Kezia, and she dragged one toe on the ground. But at that Lil turned red and shook her head quickly.

"Why not?" asked Kezia.

Lil gasped, then she said, "Your ma told our ma you wasn't to speak to us."

"Oh, well," said Kezia. She didn't know what to reply. "It doesn't matter. You can come and see our doll's house all the same. Come on. Nobody's looking."

But Lil shook her head still harder.

"Don't you want to?" asked Kezia.

Suddenly there was a twitch, a tug at Lil's skirt. She turned round. Our Else was looking at her with big, imploring eyes; she was frowning; she wanted to go. For a moment Lil looked at Else very doubtfully. But then our Else twitched her skirt again. She started forward. Kezia led the way. Like two little stray cats they followed across the courtyard to where the doll's house stood.

"There it is," said Kezia.

There was a pause. Lil breathed loudly, almost snorted; our Else was still as stone.

"I'll open it for you," said Kezia kindly. She undid the hook and they looked inside.

"There's the drawing-room and the dining-room, and that's the—"

"Kezia!"

Oh, what a start they gave!

"Kezia!"

It was Aunt Beryl's voice. They turned round. At the back door stood Aunt Beryl, staring as if she couldn't believe what she saw.

"How dare you ask the little Kelveys into the courtyard?" said her cold, furious voice. "You know as well as I do, you're not allowed to talk to them. Run away, children, run away at once. And don't come back again," said Aunt Beryl. And she stepped into the yard and shooed them out as if they were chickens.

"Off you go immediately!" she called, cold and proud.

They did not need telling twice. Burning with shame, shrinking together, Lil huddling along like her mother, our Else dazed, somehow they crossed the big courtyard and squeezed through the white gate.

"Wicked, disobedient little girl!" said Aunt Beryl bitterly to Kezia, and she slammed the doll's house to.

The afternoon had been awful. A letter had come from Willie Brent, a terrifying, threatening letter, saying if she did not meet him that evening in Pulman's Bush, he'd come to the front door and ask the reason why! But now that she had frightened those little rats of Kelveys and given Kezia a good scolding, her heart felt lighter. That ghastly pressure was gone. She went back to the house humming.

When the Kelveys were well out of sight of Burnells', they sat down to rest on a big red drainpipe by the side of the road. Lil's cheeks were still burning; she took off the hat with the quill and held it on her knee. Dreamily they looked over the hay paddocks, past the creek, to the group of wattles where Logan's cows stood waiting to be milked. What were their thoughts?

Presently our Else nudged up close to her sister. But now she had forgotten the cross lady. She put out a finger and stroked her sister's quill; she smiled her rare smile.

"I seen the little lamp," she said, softly.

Then both were silent once more.

—1922

The Garden Party

KATHERINE MANSFIELD

AND AFTER all the weather was ideal. They could not have had a more perfect day for a garden party if they had ordered it. Windless, warm, the sky without a cloud. Only the blue was veiled with a haze of light gold, as it is sometimes in early summer. The gardener had been up since dawn, mowing the lawns and sweeping them, until the grass and the dark flat rosettes where the daisy plants had been seemed to shine. As for the roses, you could not help feeling they understood that roses are the only flowers that impress people at garden parties; the only flowers that everybody is certain of knowing. Hundreds, yes, literally hundreds, had come out in a single night; the green bushes bowed down as though they had been visited by archangels.

Breakfast was not yet over before the men came to put up the marquee.

"Where do you want the marquee put, mother?"

"My dear child, it's no use asking me. I'm determined to leave everything to you children this year. Forget I am your mother. Treat me as an honoured guest."

But Meg could not possibly go and supervise the men. She had washed her hair before breakfast, and she sat drinking her coffee in a green turban, with a dark wet curl stamped on each cheek. Jose, the butterfly, always came down in a silk petticoat and a kimono jacket.

"You'll have to go, Laura, you're the artistic one."

Away Laura flew, still holding her piece of bread-and-butter. It's so delicious to have an excuse for eating out of doors and, besides, she loved having to arrange things; she always felt she could do it so much better than anybody else.

Four men in their shirt-sleeves stood grouped together on the garden path. They carried staves covered with rolls of canvas, and they had big tool-bags slung on their backs. They looked impressive. Laura wished now that she was not holding that piece of bread-and-butter, but there was nowhere to put it, and she couldn't possibly throw it away. She blushed and tried to look severe and even a little bit short-sighted as she came up to them.

"Good morning," she said, copying her mother's voice. But that sounded so fearfully affected that she was ashamed, and stammered like a little girl, "Oh—er—have you come—is it about the marquee?"

"That's right, miss," said the tallest of the men, a lanky, freckled fellow, and he shifted his tool-bag, knocked back his straw hat, and smiled down at her. "That's about it."

His smile was so easy, so friendly, that Laura recovered. What nice eyes he had, small, but such a dark blue! And now she looked at the others, they were smiling too. "Cheer up, we won't bite," their smile seemed to say. How very nice workmen were! And what a beautiful morning! She mustn't mention the morning; she must be businesslike. The marquee.

"Well, what about the lily-lawn? Would that do?"

And she pointed to the lily-lawn with the hand that didn't hold the bread-and-butter. They turned, they stared in the direction. A little fat chap thrust out his underlip, and the tall fellow frowned.

"I don't fancy it," said he. "Not conspicuous enough. You see, with a thing like a marquee," and he turned to Laura in his easy way, "you want to put it somewhere where it'll give you a bang slap in the eye, if you follow me."

Laura's upbringing made her wonder for a moment whether it was quite respectful of a workman to talk to her of bangs slap in the eye. But she did quite follow him.

"A corner of the tennis court," she suggested. "But the band's going to be in one corner."

"H'm, going to have a band, are you?" said another of the workmen. He was pale. He had a haggard look as his dark eyes scanned the tennis court. What was he thinking?

"Only a very small band," said Laura gently. Perhaps he wouldn't mind so much if the band was quite small. But the tall fellow interrupted.

"Look here, miss, that's the place. Against those trees. Over there. That'll do fine."

Against the karakas. Then the karaka trees would be hidden. And they were so lovely, with their broad, gleaming leaves, and their clusters of yellow fruit. They were like trees you imagined growing up on a desert island, proud, solitary, lifting their leaves and fruits to the sun in a kind of silent splendour. Must they be hidden by a marquee?

They must. Already the men had shouldered their staves and were making for the place. Only the tall fellow was left. He bent down, pinched a sprig of lavender, put his thumb and forefinger to his nose and snuffed up the smell. When Laura saw that gesture she forgot all about the karakas in her wonder at him caring for things like that—caring for the smell of lavender. How many men that she knew would have done such a thing. *Oh, how extraordinarily nice workmen were*, she thought. Why couldn't she have workmen for friends rather than the silly boys she danced with and who came to Sunday night supper? She would get on much better with men like these.

It's all the fault, she decided, as the tall fellow drew something on the back of an envelope, something that was to be looped up or left to hang, of these absurd class distinctions. Well, for her part, she didn't feel them. Not a bit, not an atom.... And now there came the chock-chock of wooden hammers. Someone whistled, someone sang out, "Are you right there, matey?" "Matey!" The friendliness of it, the—the—Just to prove how happy she was, just to show the tall fellow how at home she felt, and how she despised stupid conventions, Laura took a big bite of her bread-and-butter as she stared at the little drawing. She felt just like a work-girl.

"Laura, Laura, where are you? Telephone, Laura!" a voice cried from the house.

"Coming!" Away she skimmed, over the lawn, up the path, up the steps, across the veranda, and into the porch. In the hall her father and Laurie were brushing their hats ready to go to the office.

"I say, Laura," said Laurie very fast, "you might just give a squiz[1] at my coat before this afternoon. See if it wants pressing."

"I will," said she. Suddenly she couldn't stop herself. She ran at Laurie and gave him a small, quick squeeze. "Oh, I do love parties, don't you?" gasped Laura.

"Ra-ther," said Laurie's warm, boyish voice, and he squeezed his sister too, and gave her a gentle push. "Dash off to the telephone, old girl."

The telephone. "Yes, yes; oh yes. Kitty? Good morning, dear. Come to lunch? Do, dear. Delighted of course. It will only be a very scratch meal—just the sandwich crusts and broken meringue-shells and what's left over. Yes, isn't it a perfect morning? Your white? Oh, I certainly should. One moment—hold the line. Mother's calling." And Laura sat back. "What, mother? Can't hear."

Mrs Sheridan's voice floated down the stairs. "Tell her to wear that sweet hat she had on last Sunday."

"Mother says you're to wear that *sweet* hat you had on last Sunday. Good. One o'clock. Bye-bye."

Laura put back the receiver, flung her arms over her head, took a deep breath, stretched, and let them fall. "Huh," she sighed, and the moment after the sigh

1 New Zealand slang for "a quick, close look."

she sat up quickly. She was still, listening. All the doors in the house seemed to be open. The house was alive with soft, quick steps and running voices. The green baize door[2] that led to the kitchen regions swung open and shut with a muffled thud. And now there came a long, chuckling absurd sound. It was the heavy piano being moved on its stiff castors. But the air! If you stopped to notice, was the air always like this? Little faint winds were playing chase in at the tops of the windows, out at the doors. And there were two tiny spots of sun, one on the inkpot, one on a silver photograph frame, playing too. Darling little spots. Especially the one on the inkpot lid. It was quite warm. A warm little silver star. She could have kissed it.

The front door bell pealed, and there sounded the rustle of Sadie's print skirt on the stairs. A man's voice murmured; Sadie answered, careless, "I'm sure I don't know. Wait. I'll ask Mrs Sheridan."

"What is it, Sadie?" Laura came into the hall.

"It's the florist, Miss Laura."

It was, indeed. There, just inside the door, stood a wide, shallow tray full of pots of pink lilies. No other kind. Nothing but lilies—canna lilies, big pink flowers, wide open, radiant, almost frighteningly alive on bright crimson stems.

"O-oh, Sadie!" said Laura, and the sound was like a little moan. She crouched down as if to warm herself at that blaze of lilies; she felt they were in her fingers, on her lips, growing in her breast.

"It's some mistake," she said faintly. "Nobody ever ordered so many. Sadie, go and find mother."

But at that moment Mrs Sheridan joined them.

"It's quite right," she said calmly. "Yes, I ordered them. Aren't they lovely?" She pressed Laura's arm. "I was passing the shop yesterday, and I saw them in the window, and I suddenly thought for once in my life I shall have enough canna lilies. The garden party will be a good excuse."

"But I thought you said you didn't mean to interfere," said Laura. Sadie had gone. The florist's man was still outside at his van. She put her arm round her mother's neck and gently, very gently, she bit her mother's ear.

"My darling child, you wouldn't like a logical mother, would you? Don't do that. Here's the man."

He carried more lilies still, another whole tray.

"Bank them up, just inside the door, on both sides of the porch, please," said Mrs Sheridan. "Don't you agree, Laura?"

"Oh, I *do*, mother."

---

2 A swinging door that separated the servants' quarters from the rest of the house. Baize, a felt-like fabric, was often tacked to the inside of doors to insulate against noise.

In the drawing room Meg, Jose, and good little Hans had at last succeeded in moving the piano.

"Now, if we put this chesterfield against the wall and move everything out of the room except the chairs, don't you think?"

"Quite."

"Hans, move these tables into the smoking room, and bring a sweeper to take these marks off the carpet and—one moment, Hans—" Jose loved giving orders to the servants, and they loved obeying her. She always made them feel they were taking part in some drama. "Tell Mother and Miss Laura to come here at once."

"Very good, Miss Jose."

She turned to Meg. "I want to hear what the piano sounds like, just in case I'm asked to sing this afternoon. Let's try over 'This Life is Weary.'"

Pom! Ta-ta-ta *Tee*-ta! The piano burst out so passionately that Jose's face changed. She clasped her hands. She looked mournfully and enigmatically at her mother and Laura as they came in.

This Life is *Wee*-ary,
A Tear—a Sigh.
A Love that *Chan*-ges,
  This Life is *Wee*-ary,
A Tear—a Sigh.
A Love that *Chan*-ges,
And then ... Good-bye!

But at the word "Good-bye", and although the piano sounded more desperate than ever, her face broke into a brilliant, dreadfully unsympathetic smile.

"Aren't I in good voice, mummy?" she beamed.

This Life is *Wee*-ary,
Hope comes to Die,
A Dream—a *Wa*-kening.

But now Sadie interrupted them. "What is it, Sadie?"

"If you please, m'm, cook says have you got the flags for the sandwiches?"

"The flags for the sandwiches, Sadie?" echoed Mrs Sheridan dreamily. And the children knew by her face that she hadn't got them. "Let me see." And she said to Sadie firmly, "Tell cook I'll let her have them in ten minutes."

Sadie went.

"Now, Laura," said her mother quickly, "come with me into the smoking room. I've got the names somewhere on the back of an envelope. You'll have to write them out for me. Meg, go upstairs this minute and take that wet thing off your head. Jose, run and finish dressing this instant. Do you hear me, children, or shall I have to tell your father when he comes home tonight? And—and, Jose, pacify cook if you do go into the kitchen, will you? I'm terrified of her this morning."

The envelope was found at last behind the dining-room clock, though how it had got there Mrs Sheridan could not imagine.

"One of you children must have stolen it out of my bag, because I remember vividly—cream-cheese and lemon-curd. Have you done that?"

"Yes."

"Egg and—" Mrs Sheridan held the envelope away from her. "It looks like mice. It can't be mice, can it?"

"Olive, pet," said Laura, looking over her shoulder.

"Yes, of course, olive. What a horrible combination it sounds. Egg and olive."

They were finished at last, and Laura took them off to the kitchen. She found Jose there pacifying the cook, who did not look at all terrifying.

"I have never seen such exquisite sandwiches," said Jose's rapturous voice. "How many kinds did you say there were, cook? Fifteen?"

"Fifteen, Miss Jose."

"Well, cook, I congratulate you."

Cook swept up crusts with the long sandwich knife, and smiled broadly.

"Godber's has come," announced Sadie, issuing out of the pantry. She had seen the man pass the window.

That meant that cream puffs had come. Godber's were famous for their cream puffs. Nobody ever thought of making them at home.

"Bring them in and put them on the table, my girl," ordered cook.

Sadie brought them in and went back to the door. Of course Laura and Jose were far too grown-up to really care about such things. All the same, they couldn't help agreeing that the puffs looked very attractive. Very. Cook began arranging them, shaking off the extra icing sugar.

"Don't they carry one back to all one's parties?" said Laura.

"I suppose they do," said practical Jose, who never liked to be carried back. "They look beautifully light and feathery, I must say."

"Have one each, my dears," said cook in her comfortable voice. "Yer ma won't know."

Oh, impossible. Fancy cream puffs so soon after breakfast. The very idea made one shudder. All the same, two minutes later Jose and Laura were licking their fingers with that absorbed inward look that only comes from whipped cream.

"Let's go into the garden, out by the back way," suggested Laura. "I want to see how the men are getting on with the marquee. They're such awfully nice men."

But the back door was blocked by cook, Sadie, Godber's man and Hans. Something had happened.

"Tuk-tuk-tuk," clucked cook like an agitated hen. Sadie had her hand clapped to her cheek as though she had a toothache. Hans's face was screwed up in the effort to understand. Only Godber's man seemed to be enjoying himself; it was his story.

"What's the matter? What happened?"

"There's been a horrible accident," said cook. "A man killed."

"A man killed! Where? How? When?"

But Godber's man wasn't going to have his story snatched from under his very nose.

"Know those little cottages just below here, miss?" Know them? Of course, she knew them. "Well, there's a young chap living there, name of *Scott*, a carter.[3] His horse shied at a traction-engine, corner of Hawke Street this morning, and he was thrown out on the back of his head. Killed."

"Dead!" Laura stared at Godber's man.

"Dead when they picked him up," said Godber's man with relish. "They were taking the body home as I come up here." And he said to the cook, "He's left a wife and five little ones."

"Jose, come here." Laura caught hold of her sister's sleeve and dragged her through the kitchen to the other side of the green baize door. There she paused and leaned against it. "Jose!" she said, horrified, "however are we going to stop everything?"

"Stop everything, Laura!" cried Jose in astonishment. "What do you mean?"

"Stop the garden party, of course." Why did Jose pretend?

But Jose was still more amazed. "Stop the garden party? My dear Laura, don't be so absurd. Of course we can't do anything of the kind. Nobody expects us to. Don't be so extravagant."

"But we can't possibly have a garden party with a man dead just outside the front gate."

That really was extravagant, for the little cottages were in a lane to themselves at the very bottom of a steep rise that led up to the house. A broad road ran between. True, they were far too near. They were the greatest possible eyesore and they had no right to be in that neighbourhood at all. They were little mean dwellings painted a chocolate brown. In the garden patches there was nothing but cabbage stalks, sick hens and tomato cans. The very smoke coming out of their chimneys was poverty-stricken. Little rags and shreds of smoke, so unlike the great silvery plumes that uncurled from the Sheridans'

3 One who drives a horse-drawn vehicle used to transport goods or farming materials.

chimneys. Washerwomen lived in the lane and sweeps and a cobbler and a man whose house-front was studded all over with minute bird-cages. Children swarmed. When the Sheridans were little they were forbidden to set foot there because of the revolting language and of what they might catch. But since they were grown up, Laura and Laurie on their prowls sometimes walked through. It was disgusting and sordid. They came out with a shudder. But still one must go everywhere; one must see everything. So through they went.

"And just think of what the band would sound like to that poor woman," said Laura.

"Oh, Laura!" Jose began to be seriously annoyed. "If you're going to stop a band playing every time someone has an accident, you'll lead a very strenuous life. I'm every bit as sorry about it as you. I feel just as sympathetic." Her eyes hardened. She looked at her sister just as she used to when they were little and fighting together. "You won't bring a drunken workman back to life by being sentimental," she said softly.

"Drunk! Who said he was drunk?" Laura turned furiously on Jose. She said just as they had used to say on those occasions, "I'm going straight up to tell mother."

"Do, dear," cooed Jose.

"Mother, can I come into your room?" Laura turned the big glass doorknob.

"Of course, child. Why, what's the matter? What's given you such a colour?" And Mrs Sheridan turned round from her dressing-table. She was trying on a new hat.

"Mother, a man's been killed," began Laura.

"*Not* in the garden?" interrupted her mother.

"No, no!"

"Oh, what a fright you gave me!" Mrs Sheridan sighed with relief, and took off the big hat and held it on her knees.

"But listen, mother," said Laura. Breathless, half-choking, she told the dreadful story. "Of course, we can't have our party, can we?" she pleaded. "The band and everybody arriving. They'd hear us, mother; they're nearly neighbours!"

To Laura's astonishment her mother behaved just like Jose; it was harder to bear because she seemed amused. She refused to take Laura seriously.

"But, my dear child, use your common sense. It's only by accident we've heard of it. If someone had died there normally—and I can't understand how they keep alive in those poky[4] little holes—we should still be having our party, shouldn't we?"

---

4 Small or cramped.

Laura had to say "yes" to that, but she felt it was all wrong. She sat down on her mother's sofa and pinched the cushion frill.

"Mother, isn't it really terribly heartless of us?" she asked.

"Darling!" Mrs Sheridan got up and came over to her, carrying the hat. Before Laura could stop her she had popped it on. "My child!" said her mother, "the hat is yours. It's made for you. It's much too young for me. I have never seen you look such a picture. Look at yourself!" And she held up her hand-mirror.

"But, mother," Laura began again. She couldn't look at herself; she turned aside.

This time Mrs Sheridan lost patience just as Jose had done.

"You are being very absurd, Laura," she said coldly. "People like that don't expect sacrifices from us. And it's not very sympathetic to spoil everybody's enjoyment as you're doing now."

"I don't understand," said Laura, and she walked quickly out of the room into her own bedroom. There, quite by chance, the first thing she saw was this charming girl in the mirror, in her black hat trimmed with gold daisies and a long black velvet ribbon. Never had she imagined she could look like that. Is mother right? she thought. And now she hoped her mother was right. Am I being extravagant? Perhaps it was extravagant. Just for a moment she had another glimpse of that poor woman and those little children, and the body being carried into the house. But it all seemed blurred, unreal, like a picture in the newspaper. I'll remember it again after the party's over, she decided. And somehow that seemed quite the best plan....

Lunch was over by half-past one. By half-past two they were all ready for the fray. The green-coated band had arrived and was established in a corner of the tennis court.

"My dear!" trilled Kitty Maitland, "aren't they too like frogs for words? You ought to have arranged them round the pond with the conductor in the middle on a leaf."

Laurie arrived and hailed them on his way to dress. At the sight of him Laura remembered the accident again. She wanted to tell him. If Laurie agreed with the others, then it was bound to be all right. And she followed him into the hall.

"Laurie!"

"Hallo!" He was halfway upstairs, but when he turned round and saw Laura he suddenly puffed out his cheeks and goggled his eyes at her. "My word, Laura! You do look stunning," said Laurie. "What an absolutely topping hat!"

Laura said faintly "Is it?" and smiled up at Laurie, and didn't tell him after all.

Soon after that people began coming in streams. The band struck up; the hired waiters ran from the house to the marquee. Wherever you looked there were couples strolling, bending to the flowers, greeting, moving on over the lawn. They were like bright birds that had alighted in the Sheridans' garden for this one afternoon, on their way to—where? Ah, what happiness it is to be with people who all are happy, to press hands, press cheeks, smile into eyes.

"Darling Laura, how well you look!"

"What a becoming hat, child!"

"Laura, you look quite Spanish. I've never seen you look so striking."

And Laura, glowing, answered softly, "Have you had tea? Won't you have an ice? The passion-fruit ices really are rather special." She ran to her father and begged him: "Daddy darling, can't the band have something to drink?"

And the perfect afternoon slowly ripened, slowly faded, slowly its petals closed.

"Never a more delightful garden party ..." "The greatest success ..." "Quite the most ..."

Laura helped her mother with the good-byes. They stood side by side on the porch till it was all over.

"All over, all over, thank heaven," said Mrs Sheridan. "Round up the others, Laura. Let's go and have some fresh coffee. I'm exhausted. Yes, it's been very successful. But oh, these parties, these parties! Why will you children insist on giving parties!" And they all of them sat down in the deserted marquee.

"Have a sandwich, daddy dear. I wrote the flag."

"Thanks." Mr Sheridan took a bite and the sandwich was gone. He took another. "I suppose you didn't hear of a beastly accident that happened today?" he said.

"My dear," said Mrs Sheridan, holding up her hand, "we did. It nearly ruined the party. Laura insisted we should put it off."

"Oh, mother!" Laura didn't want to be teased about it.

"It was a horrible affair all the same," said Mr Sheridan. "The chap was married too. Lived just below in the lane, and leaves a wife and half a dozen kiddies, so they say."

An awkward little silence fell. Mrs Sheridan fidgeted with her cup. Really, it was very tactless of father....

Suddenly she looked up. There on the table were all those sandwiches, cakes, puffs, all uneaten, all going to be wasted. She had one of her brilliant ideas.

"I know," she said. "Let's make up a basket. Let's send that poor creature some of this perfectly good food. At any rate, it will be the greatest treat for the children. Don't you agree? And she's sure to have neighbours calling in and so on. What a point to have it all ready prepared. Laura!" She jumped up. "Get me the big basket out of the stairs cupboard."

"But, mother, do you really think it's a good idea?" said Laura.

Again, how curious, she seemed to be different from them all. To take scraps from their party. Would the poor woman really like that?

"Of course! What's the matter with you today? An hour or two ago you were insisting on us being sympathetic."

Oh well! Laura ran for the basket. It was filled, it was now heaped by her mother.

"Take it yourself, darling," said she. "Run down just as you are. No, wait, take the arum lilies too. People of that class are so impressed by arum lilies."

"The stems will ruin her lace frock," said practical Jose.

So they would. Just in time. "Only the basket, then. And, Laura!"—her mother followed her out of the marquee—"don't on any account—"

"What, mother?"

No, better not put such ideas into the child's head! "Nothing! Run along."

It was just growing dusky as Laura shut their garden gates. A big dog ran by like a shadow. The road gleamed white, and down below in the hollow the little cottages were in deep shade. How quiet it seemed after the afternoon. Here she was going down the hill to somewhere where a man lay dead, and she couldn't realize it. Why couldn't she? She stopped a minute. And it seemed to her that kisses, voices, tinkling spoons, laughter, the smell of crushed grass were somehow inside her. She had no room for anything else. How strange! She looked up at the pale sky, and all she thought was, "Yes, it was the most successful party."

Now the broad road was crossed. The lane began, smoky and dark. Women in shawls and men's tweed caps hurried by. Men hung over the palings; the children played in the doorways. A low hum came from the mean little cottages. In some of them there was a flicker of light, and a shadow, crab-like, moved across the window. Laura bent her head and hurried on. She wished now she had put on a coat. How her frock shone! And the big hat with the velvet streamer—if only it was another hat! Were the people looking at her? They must be. It was a mistake to have come; she knew all along it was a mistake. Should she go back even now?

No, too late. This was the house. It must be. A dark knot of people stood outside. Beside the gate an old, old woman with a crutch sat in a chair, watching. She had her feet on a newspaper. The voices stopped as Laura drew near. The group parted. It was as though she was expected, as though they had known she was coming here.

Laura was terribly nervous. Tossing the velvet ribbon over her shoulder, she said to a woman standing by, "Is this Mrs Scott's house?" and the woman, smiling queerly, said, "It is, my lass."

Oh, to be away from this! She actually said, "Help me, God," as she walked up the tiny path and knocked. To be away from those staring eyes, or to be covered up in anything, one of those women's shawls even. I'll just leave the basket and go, she decided. I shan't even wait for it to be emptied.

Then the door opened. A little woman in black showed in the gloom.

Laura said, "Are you Mrs Scott?" But to her horror the woman answered, "Walk in, please, miss," and she was shut in the passage.

"No," said Laura, "I don't want to come in. I only want to leave this basket. Mother sent—"

The little woman in the gloomy passage seemed not to have heard her. "Step this way, please, miss," she said in an oily voice, and Laura followed her.

She found herself in a wretched little low kitchen, lighted by a smoky lamp. There was a woman sitting before the fire.

"Em," said the little creature who had let her in. "Em! It's a young lady." She turned to Laura. She said meaningly, "I'm 'er sister, miss. You'll excuse 'er, won't you?"

"Oh, but of course!" said Laura. "Please, please don't disturb her. I—I only want to leave—"

But at that moment the woman at the fire turned round. Her face, puffed up, red, with swollen eyes and swollen lips, looked terrible. She seemed as though she couldn't understand why Laura was there. What did it mean? Why was this stranger standing in the kitchen with a basket? What was it all about? And the poor face puckered up again.

"All right, my dear," said the other. "I'll thenk the young lady."

And again she began, "You'll excuse her, miss, I'm sure," and her face, swollen too, tried an oily smile.

Laura only wanted to get out, to get away. She was back in the passage. The door opened. She walked straight through into the bedroom where the dead man was lying.

"You'd like a look at 'im, wouldn't you?" said Em's sister, and she brushed past Laura over to the bed. "Don't be afraid, my lass,"—and now her voice sounded fond and sly, and fondly she drew down the sheet—"'e looks a picture. There's nothing to show. Come along, my dear."

Laura came.

There lay a young man, fast asleep—sleeping so soundly, so deeply, that he was far, far away from them both. Oh, so remote, so peaceful. He was dreaming. Never wake him up again. His head was sunk in the pillows, his eyes were closed; they were blind under the closed eyelids. He was given up to his dream. What did garden parties and baskets and lace frocks matter to him? He was far from all those things. He was wonderful, beautiful. While they were laughing and while the band was playing, this marvel had come to the lane. Happy ... happy.... All is well, said that sleeping face. This is just as it should be. I am content.

But all the same you had to cry, and she couldn't go out of the room without saying something to him. Laura gave a loud childish sob.

"Forgive my hat," she said.

And this time she didn't wait for Em's sister. She found her way out of the door, down the path, past all those dark people. At the corner of the lane she met Laurie.

He stepped out of the shadow. "Is that you, Laura?"

"Yes."

"Mother was getting anxious. Was it all right?"

"Yes, quite. Oh, Laurie!" She took his arm, she pressed up against him.

"I say, you're not crying, are you?" asked her brother.

Laura shook her head. She was.

Laurie put his arm round her shoulder. "Don't cry," he said in his warm, loving voice. "Was it awful?"

"No," sobbed Laura. "It was simply marvellous. But, Laurie—" She stopped, she looked at her brother. "Isn't life," she stammered, "isn't life—" But what life was she couldn't explain. No matter. He quite understood.

"*Isn't* it, darling?" said Laurie.

—1922

WILLIAM FAULKNER

William Faulkner (original spelling "Falkner") is most famous for his novels and short stories set in the fictional Yoknapatawpha County, a county that corresponds to Lafayette County, Mississippi, where Faulkner grew up. More than ten of his novels and numerous short stories take place in Yoknapatawpha, including *The Sound and the Fury* (1929), *Go Down Moses* (1942), and the short story, "A Rose for Emily."

The descendant of a Confederate Colonel, William Faulkner was born in 1897 in New Albany, Mississippi. Although he was a prolific reader, Faulkner did not do well in school and dropped out in the eleventh grade; he enlisted for pilot training during the First World War, but the war ended before his training did. He then enrolled at the University of Mississippi for a short time and worked at the university post office, among other odd jobs.

Faulkner had written poetry since he was a child and published a collection of poetry, *The Marble Faun*, at his own expense in 1924. In 1927, he published his first novel, *Mosquitoes*. Two years later, Faulkner married Estelle Oldham—a match arranged by their families, and a marriage that would be troubled by both partners' periodic bouts of alcoholism.

Faulkner continued to write novels and short stories for literary periodicals; to supplement this income and support his family, he found work in Hollywood as a screenwriter. Faulkner collaborated with director Howard Hawks on several well-known films—among them *To Have and Have Not* (1945) and *The Big Sleep* (1946)—but he resented having to write for Hollywood. By 1944, most of his books were out of print, his marriage to Estelle had ended in divorce, and his drinking was at an unprecedented level of excess. In France, however, his fiction was being read enthusiastically by writers such as Jean-Paul Sartre and Albert Camus, whose admiration for his work would later contribute to the resurrection of his literary career.

In 1946, Faulkner's literary profile took a major turn for the better when American poet and literary critic Malcolm Cowley brought out *The Portable Faulkner* and reawakened American interest in the writer's work. Praise and critical accolades were unreserved in the period following: Faulkner was awarded the Nobel Prize for Literature in 1949; he was made a member of the French Legion of Honour; and he won two Pulitzer Prizes, among other awards, for his books *A Fable* (1954) and *The Reivers* (1962). In 1954 he was made an ambassador for the US State Department, and in 1957 was writer-in-residence at the University of Virginia. He died in 1962 of heart failure.

"A Rose for Emily" was originally published in a 1930 issue of *Forum*. The story's enduring appeal lies in the enigma that is Miss Emily as she denies the passage of time and clings to the traditions of the old South as embodied by the late Colonel Sartoris and his generation. She both exploits these traditions and is exploited by them—an exchange made apparent in the story's startling ending.

A Rose for Emily

WILLIAM FAULKNER

I

WHEN Miss Emily Grierson died, our whole town went to her funeral: the men through a sort of respectful affection for a fallen monument, the women mostly out of curiosity to see the inside of her house, which no one save an old manservant—a combined gardener and cook—had seen in at least ten years.

It was a big, squarish frame house that had once been white, decorated with cupolas and spires and scrolled balconies in the heavily lightsome style of the seventies, set on what had once been our most select street. But garages and cotton gins had encroached and obliterated even the august names of that neighborhood; only Miss Emily's house was left, lifting its stubborn and coquettish decay above the cotton wagons and the gasoline pumps—an eyesore among eyesores. And now Miss Emily had gone to join the representatives of those august names where they lay in the cedar-bemused cemetery among the ranked and anonymous graves of Union and Confederate soldiers who fell at the battle of Jefferson.

Alive, Miss Emily had been a tradition, a duty, and a care; a sort of hereditary obligation upon the town, dating from that day in 1894 when Colonel Sartoris, the mayor—he who fathered the edict that no Negro woman should appear on the streets without an apron—remitted her taxes, the dispensation dating from the death of her father on into perpetuity. Not that Miss Emily would have accepted charity. Colonel Sartoris invented an involved tale to the effect that Miss Emily's father had loaned money to the town, which the town, as a matter of business, preferred this way of repaying. Only a man of Colonel Sartoris' generation and thought could have invented it, and only a woman could have believed it.

When the next generation, with its more modern ideas, became mayors and aldermen, this arrangement created some little dissatisfaction. On the first of the year they mailed her a tax notice. February came, and there was no reply. They wrote her a formal letter, asking her to call at the sheriff's office at her convenience. A week later the mayor wrote her himself, offering to call or to send his car for her, and received in reply a note on paper of an archaic shape, in a thin, flowing calligraphy in faded ink, to the effect that she no longer went out at all. The tax notice was also enclosed, without comment.

They called a special meeting of the Board of Aldermen. A deputation waited upon her, knocked at the door through which no visitor had passed since she ceased giving china-painting lessons eight or ten years earlier. They were admitted by the old Negro into a dim hall from which a stairway mounted into still more shadow. It smelled of dust and disuse—a close, dank smell. The Negro led them into the parlor. It was furnished in heavy, leather-covered furniture. When the Negro opened the blinds of one window, a faint dust rose sluggishly about their thighs, spinning with slow motes in the single sun-ray. On a tarnished gilt easel before the fireplace stood a crayon portrait of Miss Emily's father.

They rose when she entered—a small, fat woman in black, with a thin gold chain descending to her waist and vanishing into her belt, leaning on an ebony cane with a tarnished gold head. Her skeleton was small and spare; perhaps that was why what would have been merely plumpness in another was obesity in her. She looked bloated, like a body long submerged in motionless water, and of that pallid hue. Her eyes, lost in the fatty ridges of her face, looked like two small pieces of coal pressed into a lump of dough as they moved from one face to another while the visitors stated their errand.

She did not ask them to sit. She just stood in the door and listened quietly until the spokesman came to a stumbling halt. Then they could hear the invisible watch ticking at the end of the gold chain.

Her voice was dry and cold. "I have no taxes in Jefferson. Colonel Sartoris explained it to me. Perhaps one of you can gain access to the city records and satisfy yourselves."

"But we have. We are the city authorities, Miss Emily. Didn't you get a notice from the sheriff, signed by him?"

"I received a paper, yes," Miss Emily said. "Perhaps he considers himself the sheriff.... I have no taxes in Jefferson."

"But there is nothing on the books to show that, you see. We must go by the—"

"See Colonel Sartoris. I have no taxes in Jefferson."

"But Miss Emily—"

"See Colonel Sartoris." (Colonel Sartoris had been dead almost ten years.) "I have no taxes in Jefferson. Tobe!" The Negro appeared. "Show these gentlemen out."

II

SO SHE vanquished them, horse and foot, just as she had vanquished their fathers thirty years before about the smell. That was two years after her father's death and a short time after her sweetheart—the one we believed would marry her—had deserted her. After her father's death she went out very little; after her sweetheart went away, people hardly saw her at all. A few of the ladies had the temerity to call, but were not received, and the only sign of life about the place was the Negro man—a young man then—going in and out with a market basket.

"Just as if a man—any man—could keep a kitchen properly," the ladies said; so they were not surprised when the smell developed. It was another link between the gross, teeming world and the high and mighty Griersons.

A neighbor, a woman, complained to the mayor, Judge Stevens, eighty years old.

"But what will you have me do about it, madam?" he said.

"Why, send her word to stop it," the woman said. "Isn't there a law?"

"I'm sure that won't be necessary," Judge Stevens said. "It's probably just a snake or a rat that nigger[1] of hers killed in the yard. I'll speak to him about it."

The next day he received two more complaints, one from a man who came in diffident deprecation. "We really must do something about it, Judge. I'd be the last one in the world to bother Miss Emily, but we've got to do something." That night the Board of Aldermen met—three gray-beards and one younger man, a member of the rising generation.

"It's simple enough," he said. "Send her word to have her place cleaned up. Give her a certain time to do it in, and if she don't ..."

"Dammit, sir," Judge Stevens said, "will you accuse a lady to her face of smelling bad?"

So the next night, after midnight, four men crossed Miss Emily's lawn and slunk about the house like burglars, sniffing along the base of the brickwork and at the cellar openings while one of them performed a regular sowing motion with his hand out of a sack slung from his shoulder. They broke open the cellar door and sprinkled lime there, and in all the outbuildings. As they recrossed the lawn, a window that had been dark was lighted and Miss Emily sat in it, the light behind her, and her upright torso motionless as that of an idol. They crept

---

1 This pejorative term remained in frequent use by many white Americans in the South until well into the 1960s.

quietly across the lawn and into the shadow of the locusts that lined the street. After a week or two the smell went away.

That was when people had begun to feel really sorry for her. People in our town, remembering how old lady Wyatt, her great-aunt, had gone completely crazy at last, believed that the Griersons held themselves a little too high for what they really were. None of the young men were quite good enough for Miss Emily and such. We had long thought of them as a tableau; Miss Emily a slender figure in white in the background, her father a spraddled silhouette in the foreground, his back to her and clutching a horsewhip, the two of them framed by the backflung front door. So when she got to be thirty and was still single, we were not pleased exactly, but vindicated; even with insanity in the family she wouldn't have turned down all of her chances if they had really materialized.

When her father died, it got about that the house was all that was left to her; and in a way, people were glad. At last they could pity Miss Emily. Being left alone, and a pauper, she had become humanized. Now she too would know the old thrill and the old despair of a penny more or less.

The day after his death all the ladies prepared to call at the house and offer condolence and aid, as is our custom. Miss Emily met them at the door, dressed as usual and with no trace of grief on her face. She told them that her father was not dead. She did that for three days, with the ministers calling on her, and the doctors, trying to persuade her to let them dispose of the body. Just as they were about to resort to law and force, she broke down, and they buried her father quickly.

We did not say she was crazy then. We believed she had to do that. We remembered all the young men her father had driven away, and we knew that with nothing left, she would have to cling to that which had robbed her, as people will.

III

SHE WAS sick for a long time. When we saw her again, her hair was cut short, making her look like a girl, with a vague resemblance to those angels in colored church windows—sort of tragic and serene.

The town had just let the contracts for paving the sidewalks, and in the summer after her father's death they began to work. The construction company came with niggers and mules and machinery, and a foreman named Homer Barron, a Yankee—a big, dark, ready man, with a big voice and eyes lighter than his face. The little boys would follow in groups to hear him cuss the niggers, and the niggers singing in time to the rise and fall of picks. Pretty soon he knew everybody in town. Whenever you heard a lot of laughing anywhere about the square, Homer Barron would be in the center of the group. Presently we began to see him and Miss Emily on Sunday afternoons driving in the yellow-wheeled buggy and the matched team of bays from the livery stable.

At first we were glad that Miss Emily would have an interest, because the ladies all said, "Of course a Grierson would not think seriously of a Northerner, a day laborer." But there were still others, older people, who said that even grief could not cause a real lady to forget *noblesse oblige*[2]—without calling it *noblesse oblige*. They just said, "Poor Emily. Her kinsfolk should come to her." She had some kin in Alabama; but years ago her father had fallen out with them over the estate of old lady Wyatt, the crazy woman, and there was no communication between the two families. They had not even been represented at the funeral.

And as soon as the old people said, "Poor Emily," the whispering began. "Do you suppose it's really so?" they said to one another. "Of course it is. What else could ..." This behind their hands; rustling of craned silk and satin behind jalousies closed upon the sun of Sunday afternoon as the thin, swift clop-clop-clop of the matched team passed: "Poor Emily."

She carried her head high enough—even when we believed that she was fallen. It was as if she demanded more than ever the recognition of her dignity as the last Grierson; as if it had wanted that touch of earthiness to reaffirm her imperviousness. Like when she bought the rat poison, the arsenic. That was over a year after they had begun to say "Poor Emily," and while the two female cousins were visiting her.

"I want some poison," she said to the druggist. She was over thirty then, still a slight woman, though thinner than usual, with cold, haughty black eyes in a face the flesh of which was strained across the temples and about the eyesockets as you imagine a lighthouse-keeper's face ought to look. "I want some poison," she said.

"Yes, Miss Emily. What kind? For rats and such? I'd recom—"

"I want the best you have. I don't care what kind."

The druggist named several. "They'll kill anything up to an elephant. But what you want is—"

"Arsenic," Miss Emily said. "Is that a good one?"

"Is ... arsenic? Yes, ma'am. But what you want—"

"I want arsenic."

The druggist looked down at her. She looked back at him, erect, her face like a strained flag. "Why, of course," the druggist said. "If that's what you want. But the law requires you to tell what you are going to use it for."

Miss Emily just stared at him, her head tilted back in order to look him eye for eye, until he looked away and went and got the arsenic and wrapped it up. The Negro delivery boy brought her the package; the druggist didn't come back.

---

2 In this case, the supposed obligation of the nobility to be morally upright.

When she opened the package at home there was written on the box, under the skull and bones: "For rats."

IV

SO THE NEXT day we all said, "She will kill herself"; and we said it would be the best thing. When she had first begun to be seen with Homer Barron, we had said, "She will marry him." Then we said, "She will persuade him yet," because Homer himself had remarked—he liked men, and it was known that he drank with the younger men in the Elk's Club—that he was not a marrying man. Later we said, "Poor Emily," behind the jalousies as they passed on Sunday afternoon in the glittering buggy, Miss Emily with her head high and Homer Barron with his hat cocked and a cigar in his teeth, reins and whip in a yellow glove.

Then some of the ladies began to say that it was a disgrace to the town and a bad example to the young people. The men did not want to interfere, but at last the ladies forced the Baptist minister—Miss Emily's people were Episcopal—to call upon her. He would never divulge what happened during that interview, but he refused to go back again. The next Sunday they again drove about the streets, and the following day the minister's wife wrote to Miss Emily's relations in Alabama.

So she had blood-kin under her roof again and we sat back to watch developments. At first nothing happened. Then we were sure that they were to be married. We learned that Miss Emily had been to the jeweler's and ordered a man's toilet set in silver, with the letters H.B. on each piece. Two days later we learned that she had bought a complete outfit of men's clothing, including a nightshirt, and we said, "They are married." We were really glad. We were glad because the two female cousins were even more Grierson than Miss Emily had ever been.

So we were not surprised when Homer Barron—the streets had been finished some time since—was gone. We were a little disappointed that there was not a public blowing-off, but we believed that he had gone on to prepare for Miss Emily's coming, or to give her a chance to get rid of the cousins. (By that time it was a cabal, and we were all Miss Emily's allies to help circumvent the cousins.) Sure enough, after another week they departed. And, as we had expected all along, within three days Homer Barron was back in town. A neighbor saw the Negro man admit him at the kitchen door at dusk one evening.

And that was the last we saw of Homer Barron. And of Miss Emily for some time. The Negro man went in and out with the market basket, but the front door remained closed. Now and then we would see her at a window for a moment, as the men did that night when they sprinkled the lime, but for almost six months she did not appear on the streets. Then we knew that this was to be expected too: as if that quality of her father which had thwarted her woman's life so many times had been too virulent and too furious to die.

When we next saw Miss Emily, she had grown fat and her hair was turning gray. During the next few years it grew grayer and grayer until it attained an even pepper-and-salt iron-gray, when it ceased turning. Up to the day of her death at seventy-four it was still that vigorous iron-gray, like the hair of an active man.

From that time on her front door remained closed, save for a period of six or seven years, when she was about forty, during which she gave lessons in china-painting. She fitted up a studio in one of the downstairs rooms, where the daughters and grand-daughters of Colonel Sartoris' contemporaries were sent to her with the same regularity and in the same spirit that they were sent on Sundays with a twenty-five cent piece for the collection plate. Meanwhile her taxes had been remitted.

Then the newer generation became the backbone and the spirit of the town, and the painting pupils grew up and fell away and did not send their children to her with boxes of color and tedious brushes and pictures cut from the ladies' magazines. The front door closed upon the last one and remained closed for good. When the town got free postal delivery Miss Emily alone refused to let them fasten the metal numbers above her door and attach a mailbox to it. She would not listen to them.

Daily, monthly, yearly we watched the Negro grow grayer and more stooped, going in and out with the market basket. Each December we sent her a tax notice, which would be returned by the post office a week later, unclaimed. Now and then we would see her in one of the downstairs windows—she had evidently shut up the top floor of the house—like the carven torso of an idol in a niche, looking or not looking at us, we could never tell which. Thus she passed from generation to generation—dear, inescapable, impervious, tranquil, and perverse.

And so she died. Fell ill in the house filled with dust and shadows, with only a doddering Negro man to wait on her. We did not even know she was sick; we had long since given up trying to get any information from the Negro. He talked to no one, probably not even to her, for his voice had grown harsh and rusty, as if from disuse.

She died in one of the downstairs rooms, in a heavy walnut bed with a curtain, her gray head propped on a pillow yellow and moldy with age and lack of sunlight.

V

THE NEGRO met the first of the ladies at the front door and let them in, with their hushed, sibilant voices and their quick, curious glances, and then he disappeared. He walked right through the house and out the back and was not seen again.

The two female cousins came at once. They held the funeral on the second day, with the town coming to look at Miss Emily beneath a mass of bought flowers, with the crayon face of her father musing profoundly above the bier and the ladies sibilant and macabre; and the very old men—some in their brushed Confederate uniforms—on the porch and the lawn, talking of Miss Emily as if she had been a contemporary of theirs, believing that they had danced with her and courted her perhaps, confusing time with its mathematical progression, as the old do, to whom all the past is not a diminishing road, but, instead, a huge meadow which no winter ever quite touches, divided from them now by the narrow bottleneck of the most recent decade of years.

Already we knew that there was one room in that region above stairs which no one had seen in forty years, and which would have to be forced. They waited until Miss Emily was decently in the ground before they opened it.

The violence of breaking down the door seemed to fill this room with pervading dust. A thin, acrid pall as of the tomb seemed to lie everywhere upon this room decked and furnished as for a bridal: upon the valance curtains of faded rose color, upon the rose-shaded lights, upon the dressing table, upon the delicate array of crystal and the man's toilet things backed with tarnished silver, silver so tarnished that the monogram was obscured. Among them lay a collar and tie, as if they had just been removed, which, lifted, left upon the surface a pale crescent in the dust. Upon a chair hung the suit, carefully folded; beneath it the two mute shoes and the discarded socks.

The man himself lay in the bed.

For a long while we just stood there, looking down at the profound and fleshless grin. The body had apparently once lain in the attitude of an embrace, but now the long sleep that outlasts love, that conquers even the grimace of love, had cuckolded him. What was left of him, rotted beneath what was left of the nightshirt, had become inextricable from the bed in which he lay; and upon him and upon the pillow beside him lay that even coating of the patient and biding dust.

Then we noticed that in the second pillow was the indentation of a head. One of us lifted something from it, and leaning forward, that faint and invisible dust dry and acrid in the nostrils, we saw a long strand of iron-gray hair.

—1931

ERNEST HEMINGWAY

Ernest Miller Hemingway lived such a varied and spectacular life that often his reputation as a Pulitzer and Nobel Prize-winning author is overshadowed by the details of his biography. His work includes the novels *The Sun Also Rises* (1926), *A Farewell to Arms* (1929), and *The Old Man and the Sea* (1952); several collections of short stories; and non-fiction such as the memoir *A Moveable Feast* (1964). His writing style is noted for its extremely spare, journalistic qualities.

Born in 1899 in Oak Park, Illinois, Hemingway began honing his writing skills by writing for his high school newspaper; he later worked for a short time as a cub reporter for the *Kansas City Star*. In 1918 he enlisted as an ambulance driver for the Red Cross and was sent to serve on the Italian front. At the very end of his first week at the front, Hemingway was hit by fragments of mortar shell, and while he was dragging a wounded soldier to shelter, machine-gun bullets hit him in the knee. He spent a year recuperating in a Red Cross hospital in Milan, where he had a love affair with a nurse, Agnes von Kurowski. This time during the war and his recuperation would serve as the raw material for *A Farewell to Arms*.

The rest of Hemingway's life was equally dramatic. He was married four times; lived in Paris, Spain, Cuba, and Florida; served as a war correspondent and reporter for newspapers such as the *Toronto Star*; fraternized with literary greats Gertrude Stein and Ezra Pound, among many others; and indulged in big game hunting, fishing, skiing, boxing, bull-fighting—all while producing a body of work that permanently altered the face of contemporary fiction written in English.

By the late 1950s Hemingway's reputation as a writer was sliding, as was his health; he suffered from recurring depression, hypertension, and a rare disease called hemochromatosis. He also sustained severe internal tissue damage and a serious concussion as a result of a plane crash during which he used his head to butt open the jammed door of the burning airplane. He died in 1961 of a self-inflicted shotgun wound.

During his lifetime, Hemingway wrote nine novels and more than fifty short stories. He wrote "Hills Like White Elephants" while he was based in Paris; he had just divorced his first wife, Hadley Richardson, and was preparing to marry Pauline Pfeiffer. The story is part of the 1927 short story collection *Men Without Women*. One review by Dorothy Parker in the *New Yorker* refers to the collection as "a truly magnificent work" and describes "Hills Like White Elephants" as "delicate and tragic." In spite of Parker's praise, Ernest Hemingway once complained to Max Perkins that "not one damn critic thought *anything* of [the story] when it came out." Hemingway's writing is at its most spare here. The story is largely taken up with dialogue between the American and his lover Jig, but for the reader what they say is not important; the narrative revolves around what they resolutely refuse to say.

Hills Like White Elephants

ERNEST HEMINGWAY

THE HILLS across the valley of the Ebro[1] were long and white. On this side there was no shade and no trees and the station was between two lines of rails in the sun. Close against the side of the station there was the warm shadow of the building and a curtain, made of strings of bamboo beads, hung across the open door into the bar, to keep out flies. The American and the girl with him sat at a table in the shade, outside the building. It was very hot and the express from Barcelona would come in forty minutes. It stopped at this junction for two minutes and went on to Madrid.

"What should we drink?" the girl asked. She had taken off her hat and put it on the table.

"It's pretty hot," the man said.

"Let's drink beer."

"Dos cervezas," the man said into the curtain.

"Big ones?" a woman asked from the doorway.

"Yes. Two big ones."

The woman brought two glasses of beer and two felt pads. She put the felt pads and the beer glasses on the table and looked at the man and the girl. The girl was looking off at the line of hills. They were white in the sun and the country was brown and dry.

---

1 The second largest river in Spain, rising in the Cantabrian Mountains and flowing to the Mediterranean Sea.

"They look like white elephants," she said.

"I've never seen one," the man drank his beer.

"No, you wouldn't have."

"I might have," the man said. "Just because you say I wouldn't have doesn't prove anything."

The girl looked at the bead curtain. "They've painted something on it," she said. "What does it say?"

"Anis del Toro. It's a drink."

"Could we try it?"

The man called "Listen" through the curtain. The woman came out from the bar.

"Four reales."

"We want two Anis del Toro."

"With water?"

"Do you want it with water?"

"I don't know," the girl said. "Is it good with water?"

"It's all right."

"You want them with water?" asked the woman.

"Yes, with water."

"It tastes like licorice," the girl said and put the glass down.

"That's the way with everything."

"Yes," said the girl. "Everything tastes of licorice. Especially all the things you've waited so long for, like absinthe."

"Oh, cut it out."

"You started it," the girl said. "I was being amused. I was having a fine time."

"Well, let's try and have a fine time."

"All right. I was trying. I said the mountains looked like white elephants. Wasn't that bright?"

"That was bright."

"I wanted to try this new drink. That's all we do, isn't it—look at things and try new drinks?"

"I guess so."

The girl looked across at the hills.

"They're lovely hills," she said. "They don't really look like white elephants. I just meant the coloring of their skin through the trees."

"Should we have another drink?"

"All right."

The warm wind blew the bead curtain against the table.

"The beer's nice and cool," the man said.

"It's lovely," the girl said.

"It's really an awfully simple operation, Jig," the man said. "It's not really an operation at all."

The girl looked at the ground the table legs rested on.

"I know you wouldn't mind it, Jig. It's really not anything. It's just to let the air in."

The girl did not say anything.

"I'll go with you and I'll stay with you all the time. They just let the air in and then it's all perfectly natural."

"Then what will we do afterward?"

"We'll be fine afterward. Just like we were before."

"What makes you think so?"

"That's the only thing that bothers us. It's the only thing that's made us unhappy."

The girl looked at the bead curtain, put her hand out and took hold of two of the strings of beads.

"And you think then we'll be all right and be happy."

"I know we will. You don't have to be afraid. I've known lots of people that have done it."

"So have I," said the girl. "And afterwards they were all so happy."

"Well," the man said, "if you don't want to you don't have to. I wouldn't have you do it if you didn't want to. But I know it's perfectly simple."

"And you really want to?"

"I think it's the best thing to do. But I don't want you to do it if you don't really want to."

"And if I do it you'll be happy and things will be like they were and you'll love me?"

"I love you now. You know I love you."

"I know. But if I do it, then it will be nice again if I say things are like white elephants, and you'll like it?"

"I'll love it. I love it now but I just can't think about it. You know how I get when I worry."

"If I do it you won't ever worry?"

"I won't worry about that because it's perfectly simple."

"Then I'll do it. Because I don't care about me."

"What do you mean?"

"I don't care about me."

"Well, I care about you."

"Oh, yes. But I don't care about me. And I'll do it and then everything will be fine."

"I don't want you to do it if you feel that way."

The girl stood up and walked to the end of the station. Across, on the other side, were fields of grain and trees along the banks of the Ebro. Far away, beyond the river, were mountains. The shadow of a cloud moved across the field of grain and she saw the river through the trees.

"And we could have all this," she said. "And we could have everything and every day we make it more impossible."

"What did you say?"

"I said we could have everything."

"We can have everything."

"No, we can't."

"We can have the whole world."

"No, we can't."

"We can go everywhere."

"No, we can't. It isn't ours any more."

"It's ours."

"No, it isn't. And once they take it away, you never get it back."

"But they haven't taken it away."

"We'll wait and see."

"Come on back in the shade," he said. "You mustn't feel that way."

"I don't feel any way," the girl said. "I just know things."

"I don't want you to do anything that you don't want to do—"

"Nor that isn't good for me," she said. "I know. Could we have another beer?"

"All right. But you've got to realize—"

"I realize," the girl said. "Can't we maybe stop talking?"

They sat down at the table and the girl looked across at the hills on the dry side of the valley and the man looked at her and at the table.

"You've got to realize," he said, "that I don't want you to do it if you don't want to. I'm perfectly willing to go through with it if it means anything to you."

"Doesn't it mean anything to you? We could get along."

"Of course it does. But I don't want anybody but you. I don't want any one else. And I know it's perfectly simple."

"Yes, you know it's perfectly simple."

"It's all right for you to say that, but I do know it."

"Would you do something for me now?"

"I'd do anything for you."

"Would you please please please please please please please stop talking?"

He did not say anything but looked at the bags against the wall of the station. There were labels on them from all the hotels where they had spent nights.

"But I don't want you to," he said, "I don't care anything about it."

"I'll scream," the girl said.

The woman came out through the curtains with two glasses of beer and put them down on the damp felt pads. "The train comes in five minutes," she said.

"What did she say?" asked the girl.

"That the train is coming in five minutes."

The girl smiled brightly at the woman, to thank her.

"I'd better take the bags over to the other side of the station," the man said. She smiled at him.

"All right. Then come back and we'll finish the beer."

He picked up the two heavy bags and carried them around the station to the other tracks. He looked up the tracks but could not see the train. Coming back, he walked through the barroom, where people waiting for the train were drinking. He drank an Anis at the bar and looked at the people. They were all waiting reasonably for the train. He went out through the bead curtain. She was sitting at the table and smiled at him.

"Do you feel better?" he asked.

"I feel fine," she said. "There's nothing wrong with me. I feel fine."

—1927

HISAYE YAMAMOTO

Hisaye Yamamoto's life as a second-generation Japanese American (or *nisei*) was unequivocally altered by the 1942 American Japanese Relocation Act that forced the relocation and detention of over 100,000 Japanese nationals and Americans of Japanese heritage who lived on the west coast of the United States. Along with her family, she was forced to move from Redondo Beach, California, where she was born in 1921, to live in internment camps in Poston, Arizona. Yamamoto had begun writing as a teenager, and, in spite of the hardship, she continued writing and submitting her work for publication. Her first publication in 1942, a mystery entitled "Death Rides the Rails to Poston," appeared in the internment camp newspaper, the *Poston Chronicle*.

After World War II ended and the camps were dissolved, Yamamoto moved to Los Angeles, where she worked from 1945–48 as a columnist for the *Los Angeles Tribune*, an African American weekly newspaper and the only newspaper in Los Angeles that would hire Japanese people. In 1948, she sold her first story, "The High-Heeled Shoes," to *Partisan Review*; in 1950 she was awarded a John Hay Whitney Foundation Opportunity Fellowship. The fellowship allowed her to write for a year without worrying about money, and she turned to writing full-time. From 1953–55 she volunteered at a Catholic Worker rehabilitation farm in Staten Island, New York.

In 1955, she married, returned to Los Angeles, and began having children; her life became so involved in raising her family for a time that she listed her profession as "housewife." She continued writing short stories, however, which were published in periodicals such as *Harper's Bazaar*, *Kenyon Review*, and *Arizona Quarterly*. Several of her stories were also included in anthologies; by 1980 her work had been included in at least twenty anthologies. As her stories accumulated, they received more and more critical attention, resulting in accolades such as an American Book Award for Lifetime Achievement from the Before Columbus Foundation in 1986. Her stories were eventually collected in *Seventeen Syllables: 5 Stories of Japanese American Life* (published in Japan in 1985), and *Seventeen Syllables and Other Stories*, published in 1988. Yamamoto died in 2011 at the age of 89, a year after receiving the 2010 Asian American Writers Workshop's Lifetime Achievement Award.

Written in 1949, "Seventeen Syllables" is one of Yamamoto's most well-known and frequently anthologized stories. A coming of age story about the teenaged protagonist Rosie, it explores the generational, cultural, and gender constraints that threaten to prevent Rosie from making her own choices as she approaches adulthood.

Seventeen Syllables

HISAYE YAMAMOTO

THE FIRST Rosie knew that her mother had taken to writing poems was one evening when she finished one and read it aloud for her daughter's approval. It was about cats, and Rosie pretended to understand it thoroughly and appreciate it no end, partly because she hesitated to disillusion her mother about the quantity and quality of Japanese she had learned in all the years now that she had been going to Japanese school every Saturday (and Wednesday, too, in the summer). Even so, her mother must have been skeptical about the depth of Rosie's understanding, because she explained afterwards about the kind of poem she was trying to write.

See, Rosie, she said, it was a *haiku*, a poem in which she must pack all her meaning into seventeen syllables only, which were divided into three lines of five, seven, and five syllables. In the one she had just read, she had tried to capture the charm of a kitten, as well as comment on the superstition that owning a cat of three colors meant good luck.

"Yes, yes, I understand. How utterly lovely," Rosie said, and her mother, either satisfied or seeing through the deception and resigned, went back to composing.

The truth was that Rosie was lazy; English lay ready on the tongue but Japanese had to be searched for and examined, and even then put forth tentatively (probably to meet with laughter). It was so much easier to say yes, yes, even when one meant no, no. Besides, this was what was in her mind to say: I was looking through one of your magazines from Japan last night, Mother, and towards the back I found some *haiku* in English that delighted me. There was one that made me giggle off and on until I fell asleep—

It is morning, and lo!
I lie awake, comme il faut,
sighing for some dough.

Now, how to reach her mother, how to communicate the melancholy song? Rosie knew formal Japanese by fits and starts, her mother had even less English, no French. It was much more possible to say yes, yes.

It developed that her mother was writing the *haiku* for a daily newspaper, the *Mainichi Shimbun*, that was published in San Francisco. Los Angeles, to be sure, was closer to the farming community in which the Hayashi family lived and several Japanese vernaculars were printed there, but Rosie's parents said they preferred the tone of the northern paper. Once a week, the *Mainichi* would have a section devoted to *haiku*, and her mother became an extravagant contributor, taking for herself the blossoming pen name, Ume Hanazono.

So Rosie and her father lived for awhile with two women, her mother and Ume Hanazono. Her mother (Tome Hayashi by name) kept house, cooked, washed, and along with her husband and the Carrascos, the Mexican family hired for the harvest, did her ample share of picking tomatoes out in the sweltering fields and boxing them in tidy strata in the cool packing shed. Ume Hanazono, who came to life after the dinner dishes were done, was an earnest, muttering stranger who often neglected speaking when spoken to and stayed busy at the parlor table as late as midnight scribbling with pencil on scratch paper or carefully copying characters on good paper with her fat, pale green Parker.

The new interest had some repercussions on the household routine. Before, Rosie had been accustomed to her parents and herself taking their hot baths early and going to bed almost immediately afterwards, unless her parents challenged each other to a game of flower cards or unless company dropped in. Now if her father wanted to play cards, he had to resort to solitaire (at which he always cheated fearlessly), and if a group of friends came over, it was bound to contain someone who was also writing *haiku*, and the small assemblage would be split in two, her father entertaining the nonliterary members and her mother comparing ecstatic notes with the visiting poet.

If they went out, it was more of the same thing. But Ume Hanazono's life span, even for a poet's, was very brief—perhaps three months at most.

One night they went over to see the Hayano family in the neighboring town to the west, an adventure both painful and attractive to Rosie. It was attractive because there were four Hayano girls, all lovely and each one named after a season of the year (Haru, Natsu, Aki, Fuyu), painful because something had been wrong with Mrs. Hayano ever since the birth of her first child. Rosie would sometimes watch Mrs. Hayano, reputed to have been the belle of her native village, making her way about a room, stooped, slowly shuffling, violently trembling (*always* trembling), and she would be reminded that this woman, in this same condition, had carried and given issue to three babies. She would look wonderingly at Mr. Hayano, handsome, tall, and strong, and she would look at her four pretty friends. But it was not a matter she could come to any decision about.

On this visit, however, Mrs. Hayano sat all evening in the rocker, as motionless and unobtrusive as it was possible for her to be, and Rosie found the greater part of the evening practically anesthetic. Too, Rosie spent most of it in the girls' room, because Haru, the garrulous one, said almost as soon as the bows and other greetings were over, "Oh, you must see my new coat!"

It was a pale plaid of grey, sand, and blue, with an enormous collar, and Rosie, seeing nothing special in it, said, "Gee, how nice."

"Nice?" said Haru, indignantly. "Is that all you can say about it? It's gorgeous! And so cheap, too. Only seventeen-ninety eight, because it was a sale. The saleslady said it was twenty-five dollars regular."

"Gee," said Rosie. Natsu, who never said much and when she said anything said it shyly, fingered the coat covetously and Haru pulled it away.

"Mine," she said, putting it on. She minced in the aisle between the two large beds and smiled happily. "Let's see how your mother likes it."

She broke into the front room and the adult conversation and went to stand in front of Rosie's mother, while the rest watched from the door. Rosie's mother was properly envious. "May I inherit it when you're through with it?"

Haru, pleased, giggled and said yes, she could, but Natsu reminded gravely from the door, "You promised me, Haru."

Everyone laughed but Natsu, who shamefacedly retreated into the bedroom. Haru came in laughing, taking off the coat. "We were only kidding, Natsu," she said. "Here, you try it on now."

After Natsu buttoned herself into the coat, inspected herself solemnly in the bureau mirror, and reluctantly shed it, Rosie, Aki, and Fuyu got their turns, and Fuyu, who was eight, drowned in it while her sisters and Rosie doubled up in amusement. They all went into the front room later, because Haru's mother quaveringly called to her to fix the tea and rice cakes and open a can of sliced peaches for everybody. Rosie noticed that her mother and Mr. Hayano were talking together at the little table—they were discussing a *haiku* that Mr. Hayano was planning to send to the *Mainichi*, while her father was sitting at one end of the sofa looking through a copy of *Life*, the new picture magazine. Occasionally, her father would comment on a photograph, holding it toward Mrs. Hayano and speaking to her as he always did—loudly, as though he thought someone such as she must surely be at least a trifle deaf also.

The five girls had their refreshments at the kitchen table, and it was while Rosie was showing the sisters her trick of swallowing peach slices without chewing (she chased each slippery crescent down with a swig of tea) that her father brought his empty teacup and untouched saucer to the sink and said, "Come on, Rosie, we're going home now."

"Already?" asked Rosie.

"Work tomorrow," he said.

He sounded irritated, and Rosie, puzzled, gulped one last yellow slice and stood up to go, while the sisters began protesting, as was their wont.

"We have to get up at five-thirty," he told them, going into the front room quickly, so that they did not have their usual chance to hang onto his hands and plead for an extension of time.

Rosie, following, saw that her mother and Mr. Hayano were sipping tea and still talking together, while Mrs. Hayano concentrated, quivering, on raising the handleless Japanese cup to her lips with both her hands and lowering it back to her lap. Her father, saying nothing, went out the door, onto the bright porch, and down the steps. Her mother looked up and asked, "Where is he going?"

"Where is he going?" Rosie said. "He said we were going home now."

"Going home?" Her mother looked with embarrassment at Mr. Hayano and his absorbed wife and then forced a smile. "He must be tired," she said.

Haru was not giving up yet. "May Rosie stay overnight?" she asked, and Natsu, Aki, and Fuyu came to reinforce their sister's plea by helping her make a circle around Rosie's mother. Rosie, for once having no desire to stay was relieved when her mother, apologizing to the perturbed Mr. and Mrs. Hayano for her father's abruptness at the same time, managed to shake her head no at the quartet, kindly but adamant, so that they broke their circle and let her go.

Rosie's father looked ahead into the windshield as the two joined him. "I'm sorry," her mother said. "You must be tired." Her father, stepping on the starter, said nothing. "You know how I get when it's *haiku*," she continued, "I forget what time it is." He only grunted.

As they rode homeward silently, Rosie, sitting between, felt a rush of hate for both—for her mother for begging, for her father for denying her mother. I wish this old Ford would crash, right now, she thought, then immediately, no, no, I wish my father would laugh, but it was too late: already the vision had passed through her mind of the green pick-up crumpled in the dark against one of the mighty eucalyptus trees they were just riding past, of the three contorted, bleeding bodies, one of them hers.

Rosie ran between two patches of tomatoes, her heart working more rambunctiously than she had ever known it to. How lucky it was that Aunt Taka and Uncle Gimpachi had come tonight, though, how very lucky. Otherwise she might not have really kept her half-promise to meet Jesus Carrasco. Jesus was going to be a senior in September at the same school she went to, and his parents were the ones helping with the tomatoes this year. She and Jesus, who hardly remembered seeing each other at Cleveland High where there were so many other people and two whole grades between them, had become great friends this summer—he always had a joke for her when he periodically drove the loaded pick-up up from the fields to the shed where she was usually sorting while her mother and father did the packing, and they laughed a great deal together over infinitesimal repartee during the afternoon break for chilled watermelon or ice cream in the shade of the shed.

What she enjoyed most was racing him to see who could finish picking a double row first. He, who could work faster, would tease her by slowing down until she thought she would surely pass him this time, then speeding up furiously to leave her several sprawling vines behind. Once he had made her screech hideously by crossing over, while her back was turned, to place atop the tomatoes in her green-stained bucket a truly monstrous, pale green worm (it had looked more like an infant snake). And it was when they had finished a contest this morning, after she had pantingly pointed a green finger at the immature tomatoes evident in the lugs at the end of his row and he had returned the accusation (with justice), that he had startlingly brought up the matter of their possibly meeting outside the range of both their parents' dubious eyes.

"What for?" she had asked.

"I've got a secret I want to tell you," he said.

"Tell me now," she demanded.

"It won't be ready till tonight," he said.

She laughed. "Tell me tomorrow then."

"It'll be gone tomorrow," he threatened.

"Well, for seven hakes, what is it?" she had asked, more than twice, and when he had suggested that the packing shed would be an appropriate place to find out, she had cautiously answered maybe. She had not been certain she was going to keep the appointment until the arrival of mother's sister and her husband. Their coming seemed a sort of signal of permission, of grace, and she had definitely made up her mind to lie and leave as she was bowing them welcome.

So as soon as everyone appeared settled back for the evening, she announced loudly that she was going to the privy outside, "I'm going to the *benjo*!" and slipped out the door. And now that she was actually on her way, her heart pumped in such an undisciplined way that she could hear it with her ears. It's because I'm running, she told herself, slowing to a walk. The shed was up ahead, one more patch away, in the middle of the fields. Its bulk, looming in the dimness, took on a sinisterness that was funny when Rosie reminded herself that it was only a wooden frame with a canvas roof and three canvas walls that made a slapping noise on breezy days.

Jesus was sitting on the narrow plank that was the sorting platform and she went around to the other side and jumped backwards to seat herself on the rim of a packing stand. "Well, tell me," she said without greeting, thinking her voice sounded reassuringly familiar.

"I saw you coming out the door," Jesus said. "I heard you running part of the way, too."

"Uh-huh," Rosie said. "Now tell me the secret."

"I was afraid you wouldn't come," he said.

Rosie delved around the chicken-wire bottom of the stall for number two tomatoes, ripe, which she was sitting beside, and came up with a left-over that felt edible. She bit into it and began sucking out the pulp and seeds. "I'm here," she pointed out.

"Rosie, are you sorry you came?"

"Sorry? What for?" she said. "You said you were going to tell me something."

"I will, I will," Jesus said, but his voice contained disappointment, and Rosie fleetingly felt the older of the two, realizing a brand-new power which vanished without category under her recognition.

"I have to go back in a minute," she said. "My aunt and uncle are here from Wintersburg. I told them I was going to the privy."

Jesus laughed. "You funny thing," he said. "You slay me!"

"Just because you have a bathroom *inside*," Rosie said. "Come on, tell me."

Chuckling, Jesus came around to lean on the stand facing her. They still could not see each other very clearly, but Rosie noticed that Jesus became very sober again as he took the hollow tomato from her hand and dropped it back into the stall. When he took hold of her empty hand, she could find no words to protest; her vocabulary had become distressingly constricted and she thought desperately that all that remained intact now was yes and no and oh, and even these few sounds would not easily out. Thus, kissed by Jesus, Rosie fell for the first time entirely victim to a helplessness delectable beyond speech. But the terrible, beautiful sensation lasted no more than a second, and the reality of Jesus' lips and tongue and teeth and hands made her pull away with such strength that she nearly tumbled.

Rosie stopped running as she approached the lights from the windows of home. How long since she had left? She could not guess, but gasping yet, she went to the privy in back and locked herself in. Her own breathing deafened her in the dark, close space, and she sat and waited until she could hear at last the nightly calling of the frogs and crickets. Even then, all she could think to say was oh, my, and the pressure of Jesus' face against her face would not leave.

No one had missed her in the parlor, however, and Rosie walked in and through quickly, announcing that she was next going to take a bath. "Your father's in the bathhouse," her mother said, and Rosie, in her room, recalled that she had not seen him when she entered. There had been only Aunt Taka and Uncle Gimpachi with her mother at the table, drinking tea. She got her robe and straw sandals and crossed the parlor again to go outside. Her mother was telling them about the *haiku* competition in the *Mainichi* and the poem she had entered.

Rosie met her father coming out of the bathhouse. "Are you through, Father?" she asked. "I was going to ask you to scrub my back."

"Scrub your own back," he said shortly, going toward the main house.

"What have I done now?" she yelled after him. She suddenly felt like doing a lot of yelling. But he did not answer, and she went into the bathhouse. Turning on the dangling light, she removed her denims and T-shirt and threw them in the big carton for dirty clothes standing next to the washing machine. Her other things she took with her into the bath compartment to wash after her bath. After she had scooped a basin of hot water from the square wooden tub, she sat on the grey cement of the floor and soaped herself at exaggerated leisure, singing "Red Sails in the Sunset" at the top of her voice and using da-da-da where she suspected her words. Then, standing up, still singing, for she was possessed by the notion that any attempt now to analyze would result in spoilage and she believed that the larger her volume the less she would be able to hear herself think, she obtained more hot water and poured it on until she was free of lather. Only then did she allow herself to step into the steaming vat, one leg first, then the remainder of her body inch by inch until the water no longer stung and she could move around at will.

She took a long time soaking, afterwards remembering to go around outside to stoke the embers of the tin-lined fireplace beneath the tub and to throw on a few more sticks so that the water might keep its heat for her mother, and when she finally returned to the parlor, she found her mother still talking *haiku* with her aunt and uncle, the three of them on another round of tea. Her father was nowhere in sight.

At Japanese school the next day (Wednesday, it was), Rosie was grave and giddy by turns. Preoccupied at her desk in the row for students on Book Eight, she made up for it at recess by performing wild mimicry for the benefit of her friend Chizuko. She held her nose and whined a witticism or two in what she considered was the manner of Fred Allen; she assumed intoxication and a British accent to go over the climax of the Rudy Vallee recording of the pub conversation about William Ewart Gladstone; she was the child Shirley Temple piping, "On the Good Ship Lollipop"; she was the gentleman soprano of the Four Inkspots trilling, "If I Didn't Care."[1] And she felt reasonably satisfied when Chizuko wept and gasped, "Oh, Rosie, you ought to be in the movies!"

Her father came after her at noon, bringing her sandwiches of minced ham and two nectarines to eat while she rode, so that she could pitch right into the sorting when they got home. The lugs were piling up, he said, and the ripe tomatoes in them would probably have to be taken to the cannery tomorrow if they were not ready for the produce haulers tonight. "This heat's not doing them any good. And we've got no time for a break today."

It *was* hot, probably the hottest day of the year, and Rosie's blouse stuck damply to her back even under the protection of the canvas. But she worked as efficiently as a flawless machine and kept the stalls heaped, with one part of her mind listening in to the parental murmuring about the heat and the tomatoes and with another part planning the exact words she would say to Jesus when he drove up with the first load of the afternoon. But when at last she saw that the pick-up was coming, her hands went berserk and the tomatoes started falling in the wrong stalls, and her father said, "Hey, hey! Rosie, watch what you're doing!"

"Well, I have to go to the *benjo*," she said, hiding panic.

"Go in the weeds over there," he said, only half-joking.

"Oh, Father!" she protested.

"Oh, go on home," her mother said. "We'll make out for awhile."

In the privy Rosie peered through a knothole toward the fields, watching as much as she could of Jesus. Happily she thought she saw him look in the direction of the house from time to time before he finished unloading and went back toward the patch where his mother and father worked. As she was heading for the shed, a very presentable black car purred up the dirt driveway to the house and its driver motioned to her. Was this the Hayashi home, he wanted to know. She nodded. Was she a Hayashi? Yes, she said, thinking that he was a good-looking man. He got out of the car with a huge, flat package and she saw that he warmly wore a business suit. "I have something here for your mother then," he said, in a more elegant Japanese than she was used to.

She told him where her mother was and he came along with her, patting his face with an immaculate white handkerchief and saying something

1 Fred Allen (1894–1956) was a popular radio comedian; Rudy Vallee (1901–86) was a popular singer in the 1920s; William E. Gladstone (1809–98) led the Liberal Party in Britain and was Prime Minister for many years; Shirley Temple (b.1928) was a famous Hollywood child actor; The Ink Spots were a vocal quartet popular in the 1930s and '40s.

about the coolness of San Francisco. To her surprised mother and father, he bowed and introduced himself as, among other things, the *haiku* editor of the *Mainichi Shimbun*, saying that since he had been coming as far as Los Angeles anyway, he had decided to bring her the first prize she had won in the recent contest.

"First prize?" her mother echoed, believing and not believing, pleased and overwhelmed. Handed the package with a bow, she bobbed her head up and down numerous times to express her utter gratitude.

"It is nothing much," he added, "but I hope it will serve as a token of our great appreciation for your contributions and our great admiration of your considerable talent."

"I am not worthy," she said, falling easily into his style. "It is I who should make some sign of my humble thanks for being permitted to contribute."

"No, no, to the contrary," he said, bowing again.

But Rosie's mother insisted, and then saying that she knew she was being unorthodox, she asked if she might open the package because her curiosity was so great. Certainly she might. In fact, he would like her reaction to it, for personally, it was one of his favorite *Hiroshiges*.[2]

Rosie thought it was a pleasant picture, which looked to have been sketched with delicate quickness. There were pink clouds, containing some graceful calligraphy, and a sea that was a pale blue except at the edges, containing four sampans[3] with indications of people in them. Pines edged the water and on the far-off beach there was a cluster of thatched huts towered over by pine-dotted mountains of grey and blue. The frame was scalloped and gilt.

After Rosie's mother pronounced it without peer and somewhat prodded her father into nodding agreement, she said Mr. Kuroda must at least have a cup of tea after coming all this way, and although Mr. Kuroda did not want to impose, he soon agreed that a cup of tea would be refreshing and went along with her to the house, carrying the picture for her.

"Ha, your mother's crazy!" Rosie's father said, and Rosie laughed uneasily as she resumed judgment on the tomatoes. She had emptied six lugs when he broke into an imaginary conversation with Jesus to tell her to go and remind her mother of the tomatoes, and she went slowly.

Mr. Kuroda was in his shirtsleeves expounding some *haiku* theory as he munched a rice cake, and her mother was rapt. Abashed in the great man's presence, Rosie stood next to her mother's chair until her mother looked up

2 Japanese artist Ando Hiroshige (1797–1858) is perhaps best-known for his colour woodblock prints of landscapes.

3 A type of small boat propelled by oars or a sail.

inquiringly, and then she started to whisper the message, but her mother pushed her gently away and reproached, "You are not being very polite to our guest."

"Father says the tomatoes ..." Rosie said aloud, smiling foolishly.

"Tell him I shall only be a minute," her mother said, speaking the language of Mr. Kuroda.

When Rosie carried the reply to her father, he did not seem to hear and she said again, "Mother says she'll be back in a minute."

"All right, all right," he nodded, and they worked again in silence. But suddenly, her father uttered an incredible noise, exactly like the cork of a bottle popping, and the next Rosie knew, he was stalking angrily toward the house, almost running in fact, and she chased after him crying, "Father! Father! What are you going to do?"

He stopped long enough to order her back to the shed. "Never mind!" he shouted. "Get on with the sorting!"

And from the place in the fields where she stood, frightened and vacillating, Rosie saw her father enter the house. Soon Mr. Kuroda came out alone, putting on his coat. Mr. Kuroda got into his car and backed out down the driveway onto the highway. Next her father emerged, also alone, something in his arms (it was the picture, she realized), and, going over to the bathhouse woodpile, he threw the picture on the ground and picked up the axe. Smashing the picture, glass and all (she heard the explosion faintly), he reached over for the kerosene that was used to encourage the bath fire and poured it over the wreckage. I am dreaming, Rosie said to herself, I am dreaming, but her father, having made sure that his act of cremation was irrevocable, was even then returning to the fields.

Rosie ran past him and toward the house. What had become of her mother? She burst into the parlor and found her mother at the back window watching the dying fire. They watched together until there remained only a feeble smoke under the blazing sun. Her mother was very calm.

"Do you know why I married your father?" she said without turning.

"No," said Rosie. It was the most frightening question she had ever been called upon to answer. Don't tell me now, she wanted to say, tell me tomorrow, tell me next week, don't tell me today. But she knew she would be told now, that the telling would combine with the other violence of the hot afternoon to level her life, her world to the very ground.

It was like a story out of the magazines illustrated in sepia, which she had consumed so greedily for a period until the information had somehow reached her that those wretchedly unhappy autobiographies, offered to her as the testimonials of living men and women, were largely inventions: Her mother, at nineteen, had come to America and married her father as an alternative to suicide.

At eighteen she had been in love with the first son of one of the well-to-do families in her village. The two had met whenever and wherever they could, secretly, because it would not have done for his family to see him favor her—her father had no money; he was a drunkard and a gambler besides. She had learned she was with child; an excellent match had already been arranged for her lover. Despised by her family, she had given premature birth to a stillborn son, who would be seventeen now. Her family did not turn her out, but she could no longer project herself in any direction without refreshing in them the memory of her indiscretion. She wrote to Aunt Taka, her favorite sister in America, threatening to kill herself if Aunt Taka would not send for her. Aunt Taka hastily arranged a marriage with a young man of whom she knew, but lately arrived from Japan, a young man of simple mind, it was said, but of kindly heart. The young man was never told why his unseen betrothed was so eager to hasten the day of meeting.

The story was told perfectly, with neither groping for words nor untoward passion. It was as though her mother had memorized it by heart, reciting it to herself so many times over that its nagging vileness had long since gone.

"I had a brother then?" Rosie asked, for this was what seemed to matter now; she would think about the other later, she assured herself, pushing back the illumination which threatened all that darkness that had hitherto been merely mysterious or even glamorous. "A half-brother?"

"Yes."

"I would have liked a brother," she said.

Suddenly, her mother knelt on the floor and took her by the wrists. "Rosie," she said urgently, "Promise me you will never marry!" Shocked more by the request than the revelation, Rosie stared at her mother's face. Jesus, Jesus, she called silently, not certain whether she was invoking the help of the son of Carrascos or of God, until there returned sweetly the memory of Jesus' hand, how it had touched her and where. Still her mother waited for an answer, holding her wrists so tightly that her hands were going numb. She tried to pull free. Promise, her mother whispered fiercely, promise. Yes, yes, I promise, Rosie said. But for an instant she turned away, and her mother, hearing the familiar glib agreement, released her. Oh, you, you, you, her eyes and twisted mouth said, you fool. Rosie, covering her face, began at last to cry, and the embrace and consoling hand came much later than she expected.

—1949

JAMES BALDWIN

James Baldwin had a varied, controversial career as a writer and as a prominent spokesperson for African Americans during the 1950s and '60s American civil rights movement. Born in New York City in 1924, Baldwin was the eldest child in a family of nine children. Typical of most families in Harlem during the Depression, Baldwin's family suffered from severe poverty, and Baldwin took on a huge portion of the responsibility for the care of his siblings. From junior high school and on, Baldwin was writing, contributing to student publications, and fervently reading and re-reading Harriet Beecher Stowe's *Uncle Tom's Cabin* and works by Charles Dickens.

Upon graduating from high school, Baldwin moved to Greenwich Village in 1943, and for five years worked during the day and wrote at night. In 1948, he published his first short story, "Previous Condition," and, on the strength of his writing, won a Rosenwald Fellowship. In 1948, in the face of oppressive racism towards blacks in the United States and with a dawning awareness of his own homosexuality, Baldwin moved to Paris—with "holes in his socks and $40 in his pocket."

Baldwin never returned to live permanently in America again, but visited often—in his own words, as a "commuter"—for the rest of his life. Baldwin quickly fell in with Parisian culture and attitudes, and became part of the expatriate black Paris community known as "la Rive Noire." His first book, *Go Tell It on the Mountain* (1953), was a critical success but not a financial one, and he worked as a journalist in order to support himself. In 1957, he returned to the United States to report on the American South. His essays and journalistic pieces catapulted him to national prominence; he lectured and was present at major civil rights events, including the March on Washington and the drive to register voters in Selma, Alabama. He came in contact with major civil rights figures such as Martin Luther King, Jr., and later Malcolm X, Angela Davis, and Huey Newton, and for a time was regarded as one of the most important spokespersons for the civil rights movement.

Baldwin's political presence and literary career reached an all time high in 1963 with the publication of his novel *The Fire Next Time*, which provided him with financial stability for the first time. His work continued to explore the uneasy complexities of racial oppression and the subject of homosexuality in a time of widespread intolerance. As the '60s progressed, however, he fell out of favour, in part because of the perception that he had "sold out" to white America. Baldwin lived the remainder of his life primarily in Turkey and France, where in 1986 he received the French Legion of Honour. In 1987, in St. Paul de Vence, France, he died of cancer.

"Sonny's Blues" first appeared in 1957 in *Partisan Review*; it was reprinted in 1965 in the short story collection *Going to Meet the Man*. The story examines the complicated relationship between the narrator and his younger brother, Sonny. It is literally only through Sonny's "blues" that the brothers can approach a connection that explains their fraternal interaction; the narrator comes closest to Sonny through Sonny's music.

Sonny's Blues

JAMES BALDWIN

I READ about it in the paper, in the subway, on my way to work. I read it, and I couldn't believe it, and I read it again. Then perhaps I just stared at it, at the newsprint spelling out his name, spelling out the story. I stared at it in the swinging lights of the subway car, and in the faces and bodies of the people, and in my own face, trapped in the darkness which roared outside.

It was not to be believed and I kept telling myself that, as I walked from the subway station to the high school. And at the same time I couldn't doubt it. I was scared, scared for Sonny. He became real to me again. A great block of ice got settled in my belly and kept melting there slowly all day long, while I taught my classes algebra. It was a special kind of ice. It kept melting, sending trickles of ice water all up and down my veins, but it never got less. Sometimes it hardened and seemed to expand until I felt my guts were going to come spilling out or that I was going to choke or scream. This would always be at a moment when I was remembering some specific thing Sonny had once said or done.

When he was about as old as the boys in my classes his face had been bright and open, there was a lot of copper in it; and he'd had wonderfully direct brown eyes, and great gentleness and privacy. I wondered what he looked like now. He had been picked up, the evening before, in a raid on an apartment downtown, for peddling and using heroin.

I couldn't believe it but what I mean by that is that I couldn't find any room for it anywhere inside me, I had kept it outside me for a long time. I hadn't wanted to know. I had had suspicions, but I didn't name them. I kept putting them away. I told myself that Sonny was wild, but he wasn't crazy. And he'd always been a good boy, he hadn't ever turned hard or evil or disrespectful, the way kids can, so quick, so quick, especially in Harlem. I didn't want to believe that I'd ever see my brother going down, coming to nothing, all that light in his face gone out, in the condition I'd already seen so many others. Yet it had happened and here I was, talking about algebra to a lot of boys who might, every one of them for all I knew, be popping off needles every time they went to the head. Maybe it did more for them than algebra could.

I was sure that the first time Sonny had ever had horse, he couldn't have been much older than these boys were now. These boys, now, were living as we'd been living then, they were growing up with a rush and their heads bumped abruptly against the low ceiling of their actual possibilities. They were filled with rage. All they really knew were two darknesses, the darkness of their lives, which was now closing in on them, and the darkness of the movies, which had blinded them to that other darkness, and in which they now, vindictively, dreamed, at once more together than they were at any other time, and more alone.

When the last bell rang, the last class ended, I let out my breath. It seemed I'd been holding it for all that time. My clothes were wet—I may have looked as though I'd been sitting in a steam bath, all dressed up, all afternoon. I sat alone in the classroom a long time. I listened to the boys outside, downstairs, shouting and cursing and laughing. Their laughter struck me for perhaps the first time. It was not the joyous laughter which—God knows why—one associates with children. It was mocking and insular, its intent was to denigrate. It was disenchanted, and in this, also, lay the authority of their curses. Perhaps I was listening to them because I was thinking about my brother and in them I heard my brother. And myself.

One boy was whistling a tune, at once very complicated and very simple, it seemed to be pouring out of him as though he were a bird, and it sounded very cool and moving through all that harsh, bright air, only just holding its own through all those other sounds.

I stood up and walked over to the window and looked down into the courtyard. It was the beginning of the spring and the sap was rising in the boys. A teacher passed through them every now and again, quickly, as though he or she couldn't wait to get out of that courtyard, to get those boys out of their sight and off their minds. I started collecting my stuff. I thought I'd better get home and talk to Isabel.

The courtyard was almost deserted by the time I got downstairs. I saw this boy standing in the shadow of a doorway looking just like Sonny. I almost called his name. Then I saw that it wasn't Sonny, but somebody we used to know, a boy from around our block. He'd been Sonny's friend. He'd never been mine, having been too young for me, and, anyway, I'd never liked him. And now, even though he was a grown-up man, he still hung around that block, still spent hours on the street corners, was always high and raggy. I used to run into him from time to time and he'd often work around to asking me for a quarter or fifty cents. He always had some real good excuse, too, and I always gave it to him. I don't know why.

But now, abruptly, I hated him. I couldn't stand the way he looked at me, partly like a dog, partly like a cunning child. I wanted to ask him what the hell he was doing in the school courtyard.

He sort of shuffled over to me, and he said, "I see you got the papers. So you already know about it."

"You mean about Sonny? Yes, I already know about it. How come they didn't get you?"

He grinned. It made him repulsive and it also brought to mind what he'd looked like as a kid. "I wasn't there. I stay away from them people."

"Good for you." I offered him a cigarette and I watched him through the smoke. "You come all the way down here just to tell me about Sonny?"

"That's right." He was sort of shaking his head and his eyes looked strange, as though they were about to cross. The bright sun deadened his damp dark brown skin and it made his eyes look yellow and showed up the dirt in his kinked hair. He smelled funky. I moved a little away from him and I said, "Well, thanks. But I already know about it and I got to get home."

"I'll walk you a little ways," he said. We started walking. There were a couple of kids still loitering in the courtyard and one of them said goodnight to me and looked strangely at the boy beside me.

"What're you going to do?" he asked me. "I mean, about Sonny?"

"Look. I haven't seen Sonny for over a year, I'm not sure I'm going to do anything. Anyway, what the hell *can* I do?"

"That's right," he said quickly, "ain't nothing you can do. Can't much help old Sonny no more, I guess."

It was what I was thinking and so it seemed to me he had no right to say it.

"I'm surprised at Sonny, though," he went on—he had a funny way of talking, he looked straight ahead as though he were talking to himself—"I thought Sonny was a smart boy. I thought he was too smart to get hung."

"I guess he thought so too," I said sharply, "and that's how he got hung. And how about you? You're pretty goddamn smart, I bet."

Then he looked directly at me, just for a minute. "I ain't smart," he said. "If I was smart, I'd have reached for a pistol a long time ago."

"Look. Don't tell *me* your sad story, if it was up to me, I'd give you one." Then I felt guilty—guilty, probably, for never having supposed that the poor bastard *had* a story of his own, much less a sad one, and I asked, quickly, "What's going to happen to him now?"

He didn't answer this. He was off by himself some place.

"Funny thing," he said, and from his tone we might have been discussing the quickest way to get to Brooklyn, "when I saw the papers this morning, the first thing I asked myself was if I had anything to do with it. I felt sort of responsible."

I began to listen more carefully. The subway station was on the corner, just before us, and I stopped. He stopped, too. We were in front of a bar and he ducked slightly, peering in, but whoever he was looking for didn't seem to be there. The juke box was blasting away with something black and bouncy and I half watched the barmaid as she danced her way from the juke box to her place behind the bar. And I watched her face as she laughingly responded to something someone said to her, still keeping time to the music. When she smiled one saw the little girl, one sensed the doomed, still-struggling woman beneath the battered face of the semi-whore.

"I never *give* Sonny nothing," the boy said finally, "but a long time ago I come to school high and Sonny asked me how it felt." He paused, I couldn't bear to watch him, I watched the barmaid, and I listened to the music which seemed to be causing the pavement to shake. "I told him it felt great." The music stopped, the barmaid paused and watched the juke box until the music began again. "It did."

All this was carrying me some place I didn't want to go. I certainly didn't want to know how it felt. It filled everything, the people, the houses, the music, the dark quicksilver barmaid, with menace; and this menace was their reality.

"What's going to happen to him now?" I asked again.

"They'll send him away some place and they'll try to cure him." He shook his head. "Maybe he'll even think he's kicked the habit. Then they'll let him loose"—he gestured, throwing his cigarette into the gutter. "That's all."

"What do you mean, that's *all*?"

But I knew what he meant.

"I *mean*, that's *all*." He turned his head and looked at me, pulling down the corners of his mouth. "Don't you know what I mean?" he asked, softly.

"How the hell *would* I know what you mean?" I almost whispered it, I don't know why.

"That's right," he said to the air, "how would *he* know what I mean?" He turned toward me again, patient and calm, and yet I somehow felt him shaking, shaking as though he were going to fall apart. I felt that ice in my guts again, the dread I'd felt all afternoon; and again I watched the barmaid, moving about the bar, washing glasses, and singing. "Listen. They'll let him out and then it'll just start all over again. That's what I mean."

"You mean—they'll let him out. And then he'll just start working his way back in again. You mean he'll never kick the habit. Is that what you mean?"

"That's right," he said, cheerfully. "*You* see what I mean."

"Tell me," I said at last, "why does he want to die? He must want to die, he's killing himself, why does he want to die?"

He looked at me in surprise. He licked his lips. "He don't want to die. He wants to live. Don't nobody want to die, ever."

Then I wanted to ask him—too many things. He could not have answered, or if he had, I could not have borne the answers. I started walking. "Well, I guess it's none of my business."

"It's going to be rough on old Sonny," he said. We reached the subway station. "This is your station?" he asked. I nodded. I took one step down. "Damn!" he said, suddenly. I looked up at him. He grinned again. "Damn it if I didn't leave all my money home. You ain't got a dollar on you, have you? Just for a couple of days, is all."

All at once something inside gave and threatened to come pouring out of me. I didn't hate him any more. I felt that in another moment I'd start crying like a child.

"Sure," I said. "Don't sweat." I looked in my wallet and didn't have a dollar, I only had a five. "Here," I said. "That hold you?"

He didn't look at it—he didn't want to look at it. A terrible, closed look came over his face, as though he were keeping the number on the bill a secret from him and me. "Thanks," he said, and now he was dying to see me go. "Don't worry about Sonny. Maybe I'll write him or something."

"Sure," I said. "You do that. So long."

"Be seeing you," he said. I went on down the steps.

And I didn't write Sonny or send him anything for a long time. When I finally did, it was just after my little girl died, and he wrote me back a letter which made me feel like a bastard.

Here's what he said:

Dear brother,

You don't know how much I needed to hear from you. I wanted to write you many a time but I dug how much I must have hurt you and so I didn't write. But now I feel like a man who's been trying to climb up out of some deep, real deep and funky hole and just saw the sun up there, outside. I got to get outside.

I can't tell you much about how I got here. I mean I don't know how to tell you. I guess I was afraid of something or I was trying to escape from something and you know I have never been very strong in the head (smile). I'm glad Mama and Daddy are dead and can't see what's happened to their son and I swear if I'd known what I was doing I would never have hurt you so, you and a lot of other fine people who were nice to me and who believed in me.

I don't want you to think it had anything to do with me being a musician. It's more than that. Or maybe less than that. I can't get anything straight in my head down here and I try not to think about what's going to happen to me when I get outside again. Sometime I think I'm going to flip and *never* get outside and sometime I think I'll come straight back. I tell you one thing, though, I'd rather blow my brains out than go through this again. But that's what they all say, so they tell me. If I tell you when I'm coming to New York and if you could meet me, I sure would appreciate it. Give my love to Isabel and the kids and I was sure sorry to hear about little Gracie. I wish I could be like Mama and say the Lord's will be done, but I don't know it seems to me that trouble is the one thing that never does get stopped and I don't know what good it does to blame it on the Lord. But maybe it does some good if you believe it.

Your brother,
Sonny

Then I kept in constant touch with him and I sent him whatever I could and I went to meet him when he came back to New York. When I saw him many things I thought I had forgotten came flooding back to me. This was because I had begun, finally, to wonder about Sonny, about the life that Sonny lived inside. This life, whatever it was, had made him older and thinner and it had deepened the distant stillness in which he had always moved. He looked very unlike my baby brother. Yet, when he smiled, when we shook hands, the baby brother I'd never known looked out from the depths of his private life, like an animal waiting to be coaxed into the light.

"How you been keeping?" he asked me.

"All right. And you?"

"Just fine." He was smiling all over his face. "It's good to see you again."

"It's good to see you."

The seven years' difference in our ages lay between us like a chasm: I wondered if these years would ever operate between us as a bridge. I was remembering, and it made it hard to catch my breath, that I had been there when he was born; and I had heard the first words he had ever spoken. When he started to walk, he walked from our mother straight to me. I caught him just before he fell when he took the first steps he ever took in this world.

"How's Isabel?"

"Just fine. She's dying to see you."

"And the boys?"

"They're fine, too. They're anxious to see their uncle."

"Oh, come on. You know they don't remember me."

"Are you kidding? Of course they remember you."

He grinned again. We got into a taxi. We had a lot to say to each other, far too much to know how to begin.

As the taxi began to move, I asked, "You still want to go to India?"

He laughed. "You still remember that. Hell, no. This place is Indian enough for me."

"It used to belong to them," I said.

And he laughed again. "They damn sure knew what they were doing when they got rid of it."

Years ago, when he was around fourteen, he'd been all hipped on the idea of going to India. He read books about people sitting on rocks, naked, in all kinds of weather, but mostly bad, naturally, and walking barefoot through hot coals and arriving at wisdom. I used to say that it sounded to me as though they were getting away from wisdom as fast as they could. I think he sort of looked down on me for that.

"Do you mind," he asked, "if we have the driver drive alongside the park? On the west side—I haven't seen the city in so long."

"Of course not," I said. I was afraid that I might sound as though I were humoring him, but I hoped he wouldn't take it that way.

So we drove along, between the green of the park and the stony, lifeless elegance of hotels and apartment buildings, toward the vivid, killing streets of our childhood. These streets hadn't changed, though housing projects jutted up out of them now like rocks in the middle of a boiling sea. Most of the houses in which we had grown up had vanished, as had the stores from which we had stolen, the basements in which we had first tried sex, the rooftops from which we had hurled tin cans and bricks. But houses exactly like the houses of our past yet dominated the landscape, boys exactly like the boys we once had been found themselves smothering in these houses, came down into the streets for light and air and found themselves encircled by disaster. Some escaped the trap, most didn't. Those who got out always left something of themselves behind, as some animals amputate a leg and leave it in the trap. It might be said, perhaps, that I had escaped, after all, I was a school teacher; or that Sonny had, he hadn't lived in Harlem for years. Yet, as the cab moved uptown through streets which seemed, with a rush, to darken with dark people, and as I covertly studied Sonny's face, it came to me that what we both were seeking through our separate cab windows was that part of ourselves which had been left behind. It's always at the hour of trouble and confrontation that the missing member aches.

We hit 110th Street and started rolling up Lenox Avenue. And I'd known this avenue all my life, but it seemed to me again, as it had seemed on the day I'd first heard about Sonny's trouble, filled with a hidden menace which was its very breath of life.

"We almost there," said Sonny.

"Almost." We were both too nervous to say anything more.

We live in a housing project. It hasn't been up long. A few days after it was up it seemed uninhabitably new, now, of course, it's already rundown. It looks like a parody of the good, clean, faceless life—God knows the people who live in it do their best to make it a parody. The beat-looking grass lying around isn't enough to make their lives green, the hedges will never hold out the streets, and they know it. The big windows fool no one, they aren't big enough to make space out of no space. They don't bother with the windows, they watch the TV screen instead. The playground is most popular with the children who don't play at jacks, or skip rope, or roller skate, or swing, and they can be found in it after dark. We moved in partly because it's not too far from where I teach, and partly for the kids; but it's really just like the houses in which Sonny and I grew up. The same things happen, they'll have the same things to remember. The moment Sonny and I started into the house I had the feeling that I was simply bringing him back into the danger he had almost died trying to escape.

Sonny had never been talkative. So I don't know why I was sure he'd be dying to talk to me when supper was over the first night. Everything went fine, the oldest boy remembered him, and the youngest boy liked him, and Sonny had remembered to bring something for each of them; and Isabel, who is really much nicer than I am, more open and giving, had gone to a lot of trouble about dinner and was genuinely glad to see him. And she's always been able to tease Sonny in a way that I haven't. It was nice to see her face so vivid again and to hear her laugh and watch her make Sonny laugh. She wasn't, or, anyway, she didn't seem to be, at all uneasy or embarrassed. She chatted as though there were no subject which had to be avoided and she got Sonny past his first, faint stiffness. And thank God she was there, for I was filled with that icy dread again. Everything I did seemed awkward to me, and everything I said sounded freighted with hidden meaning. I was trying to remember everything I'd heard about dope addiction and I couldn't help watching Sonny for signs. I wasn't doing it out of malice. I was trying to find out something about my brother. I was dying to hear him tell me he was safe.

"Safe!" my father grunted, whenever Mama suggested trying to move to a neighborhood which might be safer for children. "Safe, hell! Ain't no place safe for kids, nor nobody."

He always went on like this, but he wasn't, ever, really as bad as he sounded, not even on weekends, when he got drunk. As a matter of fact, he was always on the lookout for "something a little better," but he died before he found it. He died suddenly during a drunken weekend in the middle of the war, when Sonny was fifteen. He and Sonny hadn't ever got on too well. And this was partly because Sonny was the apple of his father's eye. It was because he loved Sonny so much and was frightened for him, that he was always fighting with him. It doesn't do any good to fight with Sonny. Sonny just moves back, inside himself, where he can't be reached. But the principal reason that they never hit it off is that they were so much alike. Daddy was big and rough and loud-talking, just the opposite of Sonny, but they both had—that same privacy.

Mama tried to tell me something about this, just after Daddy died. I was home on leave from the army.

This was the last time I ever saw my mother alive. Just the same, this picture gets all mixed up in my mind with pictures I had of her when she was younger. The way I always see her is the way she used to be on a Sunday afternoon, say, when the old folks were talking after the big Sunday dinner. I always see her wearing pale blue. She'd be sitting on the sofa. And my father would be sitting in the easy chair, not far from her. And the living room would be full of church folks and relatives. There they sit, in chairs all around the living room, and the night is creeping up outside, but nobody knows it yet. You can see the darkness growing against the windowpanes and you hear the street noises every now and again, or maybe the jangling beat of a tambourine from one of the churches close by, but it's real quiet in the room. For a moment nobody's talking, but every face looks darkening, like the sky outside. And my mother rocks a little from the waist, and my father's eyes are closed. Everyone is looking at something a child can't see. For a minute they've forgotten the children. Maybe a kid is lying on the rug, half asleep. Maybe somebody's got a kid in his lap and is absent-mindedly stroking the kid's head. Maybe there's a kid, quiet and big-eyed, curled up in a big chair in the corner. The silence, the darkness coming, and the darkness in the faces frighten the child obscurely. He hopes that the hand which strokes his forehead will never stop—will never die. He hopes that there will never come a time when the old folks won't be sitting around the living room, talking about where they've come from, and what they've seen, and what's happened to them and their kinfolk.

But something deep and watchful in the child knows that this is bound to end, is already ending. In a moment someone will get up and turn on the light. Then the old folks will remember the children and they won't talk any more that day. And when light fills the room, the child is filled with darkness. He knows that every time this happens he's moved just a little closer to that darkness outside. The darkness outside is what the old folks have been talking about. It's what they've come from. It's what they endure. The child knows that they won't talk any more because if he knows too much about what's happened to *them*, he'll know too much too soon, about what's going to happen to *him*.

The last time I talked to my mother, I remember I was restless. I wanted to get out and see Isabel. We weren't married then and we had a lot to straighten out between us.

There Mama sat, in black, by the window. She was humming an old church song, *Lord, you brought me from a long ways off*. Sonny was out somewhere. Mama kept watching the streets.

"I don't know," she said, "if I'll ever see you again, after you go off from here. But I hope you'll remember the things I tried to teach you."

"Don't talk like that," I said, and smiled. "You'll be here a long time yet."

She smiled, too, but she said nothing. She was quiet for a long time. And I said, "Mama, don't you worry about nothing. I'll be writing all the time, and you be getting the checks ..."

"I want to talk to you about your brother," she said, suddenly. "If anything happens to me he ain't going to have nobody to look out for him."

"Mama," I said, "ain't nothing going to happen to you *or* Sonny. Sonny's all right. He's a good boy and he's got good sense."

"It ain't a question of his being a good boy," Mama said, "nor of his having good sense. It ain't only the bad ones, nor yet the dumb ones that gets sucked under." She stopped, looking at me. "Your Daddy once had a brother," she said, and she smiled in a way that made me feel she was in pain. "You didn't never know that, did you?"

"No," I said, "I never knew that," and I watched her face.

"Oh, yes," she said, "your Daddy had a brother." She looked out of the window again. "I know you never saw your Daddy cry. But *I* did—many a time, through all these years."

I asked her, "What happened to his brother? How come nobody's ever talked about him?"

This was the first time I ever saw my mother look old.

"His brother got killed," she said, "when he was just a little younger than you are now. I knew him. He was a fine boy. He was maybe a little full of the devil, but he didn't mean nobody no harm."

Then she stopped and the room was silent, exactly as it had sometimes been on those Sunday afternoons. Mama kept looking out into the streets.

"He used to have a job in the mill," she said, "and, like all young folks, he just liked to perform on Saturday nights. Saturday nights, him and your father would drift around to different places, go to dances and things like that, or just sit around with people they knew, and your father's brother would sing, he had a fine voice, and play along with himself on his guitar. Well, this particular Saturday night, him and your father was coming home from some place, and they were both a little drunk and there was a moon that night, it was bright like day. Your father's brother was feeling kind of good, and he was whistling to himself, and he had his guitar slung over his shoulder. They was coming down a hill and beneath them was a road that turned off from the highway. Well, your father's brother, being always kind of frisky, decided to run down this hill, and he did, with that guitar banging and clanging behind him, and he ran across the road, and he was making water behind a tree. And your father was sort of amused at him and he was still coming down the hill, kind of slow. Then he heard a car motor and that same minute his brother stepped from behind the tree, into the road, in the moonlight. And he started to cross the road. And your father started to run down the hill, he says he don't know why. This car was full of white men. They was all drunk, and when they seen your father's brother they let out a great whoop and holler and they aimed the car straight at him. They was having fun, they just wanted to scare him, the way they do sometimes, you know. But they was drunk. And I guess the boy being drunk, too, and scared, kind of lost his head. By the time he jumped it was too late. Your father says he heard his brother scream when the car rolled over him, and he heard the wood of that guitar when it give, and he heard them strings go flying, and he heard them white men shouting, and the car kept on a-going and it ain't stopped till this day. And, time your father got down the hill, his brother weren't nothing but blood and pulp."

Tears were gleaming on my mother's face. There wasn't anything I could say.

"He never mentioned it," she said, "because I never let him mention it before you children. Your Daddy was like a crazy man that night and for many a night thereafter. He says he never in his life seen anything as dark as that road after the lights of that car had gone away. Weren't nothing, weren't nobody on that road, just your Daddy and his brother and that busted guitar. Oh, yes. Your Daddy never did really get right again. Till the day he died he weren't sure but that every white man he saw was the man that killed his brother."

She stopped and took out her handkerchief and dried her eyes and looked at me.

"I ain't telling you all this," she said, "to make you scared or bitter or to make you hate nobody. I'm telling you this because you got a brother. And the world ain't changed."

I guess I didn't want to believe this. I guess she saw this in my face. She turned away from me, toward the window again, searching those streets.

"But I praise my Redeemer," she said at last, "that He called your Daddy home before me. I ain't saying it to throw no flowers at myself, but, I declare, it keeps me from feeling too cast down to know I helped your father get safely through this world. Your father always acted like he was the roughest, strongest man on earth. And everybody took him to be like that. But if he hadn't had me there—to see his tears!"

She was crying again. Still, I couldn't move. I said, "Lord, Lord, Mama, I didn't know it was like that."

"Oh, honey," she said, "there's a lot that you don't know. But you are going to find out." She stood up from the window and came over to me. "You got to hold on to your brother," she said, "and don't let him fall, no matter what it looks like is happening to him and no matter how evil you gets with him. You going to be evil with him many a time. But don't you forget what I told you, you hear?"

"I won't forget," I said. "Don't you worry, I won't forget. I won't let nothing happen to Sonny."

My mother smiled as though she was amused at something she saw in my face. Then, "You may not be able to stop nothing from happening. But you got to let him know you's *there*."

Two days later I was married, and then I was gone. And I had a lot of things on my mind and I pretty well forgot my promise to Mama until I got shipped home on a special furlough for her funeral.

And, after the funeral, with just Sonny and me alone in the empty kitchen, I tried to find out something about him.

"What do you want to do?" I asked him.

"I'm going to be a musician," he said.

For he had graduated, in the time I had been away, from dancing to the juke box to finding out who was playing what, and what they were doing with it, and he had bought himself a set of drums.

"You mean, you want to be a drummer?" I somehow had the feeling that being a drummer might be all right for other people but not for my brother Sonny.

"I don't think," he said, looking at me very gravely, "that I'll ever be a good drummer. But I think I can play a piano."

I frowned. I'd never played the role of the oldest brother quite so seriously before, had scarcely ever, in fact, *asked* Sonny a damn thing. I sensed myself in the presence of something I didn't really know how to handle, didn't understand. So I made my frown a little deeper as I asked: "What kind of musician do you want to be?"

He grinned. "How many kinds do you think there are?"

"Be *serious*," I said.

He laughed, throwing his head back, and then looked at me. "I *am* serious."

"Well, then, for Christ's sake, stop kidding around and answer a serious question. I mean, do you want to be a concert pianist, you want to play classical music and all that, or—or what?" Long before I finished he was laughing again. "For Christ's *sake*, Sonny!"

He sobered, but with difficulty. "I'm sorry. But you sound so—*scared*!" and he was off again.

"Well, you may think it's funny now, baby, but it's not going to be so funny when you have to make your living at it, let me tell you *that*." I was furious because I knew he was laughing at me and I didn't know why.

"No," he said, very sober now, and afraid, perhaps, that he'd hurt me, "I don't want to be a classical pianist. That isn't what interests me. I mean"—he paused, looking hard at me, as though his eyes would help me to understand, and then gestured helplessly, as though perhaps his hand would help—"I mean, I'll have a lot of studying to do, and I'll have to study *everything*, but, I mean, I want to play *with*—jazz musicians." He stopped. "I want to play jazz," he said.

Well, the word had never before sounded as heavy, as real, as it sounded that afternoon in Sonny's mouth. I just looked at him and I was probably frowning a real frown by this time. I simply couldn't see why on earth he'd want to spend his time hanging around nightclubs, clowning around on bandstands, while people pushed each other around a dance floor. It seemed—beneath him, somehow. I had never thought about it before, had never been forced to, but I suppose I had always put jazz musicians in a class with what Daddy called "good-time people."

"Are you *serious*?"

"Hell, *yes*, I'm serious."

He looked more helpless than ever, and annoyed, and deeply hurt.

I suggested, helpfully: "You mean—like Louis Armstrong?"

His face closed as though I'd struck him. "No. I'm not talking about none of that old-time, down home crap."

"Well, look, Sonny, I'm sorry, don't get mad. I just don't altogether get it, that's all. Name somebody—you know, a jazz musician you admire."

"Bird."

"Who?"

"Bird! Charlie Parker! Don't they teach you nothing in the goddamn army?"

I lit a cigarette. I was surprised and then a little amused to discover that I was trembling. "I've been out of touch," I said. "You'll have to be patient with me. Now. Who's this Parker character?"

"He's just one of the greatest jazz musicians alive," said Sonny, sullenly, his hands in his pockets, his back to me. "Maybe *the* greatest," he added, bitterly, "that's probably why *you* never heard of him."

"All right," I said. "I'm ignorant. I'm sorry. I'll go out and buy all the cat's records right away, all right?"

"It don't," said Sonny, with dignity, "make any difference to me. I don't care what you listen to. Don't do me no favors."

I was beginning to realize that I'd never seen him so upset before. With another part of my mind I was thinking that this would probably turn out to be one of those things kids go through and that I shouldn't make it seem important by pushing it too hard. Still, I didn't think it would do any harm to ask: "Doesn't all this take a lot of time? Can you make a living at it?"

He turned back to me and half leaned, half sat, on the kitchen table. "Everything takes time," he said, "and—well, yes, sure, I can make a living at it. But what I don't seem to be able to make you understand is that it's the only thing I want to do."

"Well, Sonny," I said gently, "you know people can't always do exactly what they *want* to do—"

"*No*, I don't know that," said Sonny, surprising me. "I think people *ought* to do what they want to do, what else are they alive for?"

"You getting to be a big boy," I said desperately, "it's time you started thinking about your future."

"I'm thinking about my future," said Sonny, grimly. "I think about it all the time."

I gave up. I decided, if he didn't change his mind, that we could always talk about it later. "In the meantime," I said, "you got to finish school." We had already decided that he'd have to move in with Isabel and her folks. I knew this wasn't the ideal arrangement because Isabel's folks are inclined to be dicty[1] and they hadn't especially wanted Isabel to marry me. But I didn't know what else to do. "And we have to get you fixed up at Isabel's."

There was a long silence. He moved from the kitchen table to the window. "That's a terrible idea. You know it yourself."

"Do you have a *better* idea?"

He just walked up and down the kitchen for a minute. He was as tall as I was. He had started to shave. I suddenly had the feeling that I didn't know him at all.

He stopped at the kitchen table and picked up my cigarettes. Looking at me with a kind of mocking, amused defiance, he put one between his lips. "You mind?"

"You smoking already?"

He lit the cigarette and nodded, watching me through the smoke. "I just wanted to see if I'd have the courage to smoke in front of you." He grinned and blew a great cloud of smoke to the ceiling. "It was easy." He looked at my face. "Come on, now. I bet you was smoking at my age, tell the truth."

---

1 Bossy or snobbish.

I didn't say anything but the truth was on my face, and he laughed. But now there was something very strained in his laugh. "Sure. And I bet that ain't all you was doing."

He was frightening me a little. "Cut the crap," I said. "We already decided that you was going to go and live at Isabel's. Now what's got into you all of a sudden?"

"*You* decided it," he pointed out. "*I* didn't decide nothing." He stopped in front of me, leaning against the stove, arms loosely folded. "Look, brother, I don't want to stay in Harlem no more, I really don't." He was very earnest. He looked at me, then over toward the kitchen window. There was something in his eyes I'd never seen before, some thoughtfulness, some worry all his own. He rubbed the muscle of one arm. "It's time I was getting out of here."

"Where do you want to *go*, Sonny?"

"I want to join the army. Or the navy, I don't care. If I say I'm old enough, they'll believe me."

Then I got mad. It was because I was so scared. "You must be crazy. You goddamn fool, what the hell do you want to go and join the *army* for?"

"I just told you. To get out of Harlem."

"Sonny, you haven't even finished *school*. And if you really want to be a musician, how do you expect to study if you're in the *army*?"

He looked at me, trapped, and in anguish. "There's ways. I might be able to work out some kind of deal. Anyway, I'll have the G.I. Bill when I come out."

"*If* you come out." We stared at each other. "Sonny, please. Be reasonable. I know the setup is far from perfect. But we got to do the best we can."

"I ain't learning nothing in school," he said. "Even when I go." He turned away from me and opened the window and threw his cigarette out into the narrow alley. I watched his back. "At least, I ain't learning nothing you'd want me to learn." He slammed the window so hard I thought the glass would fly out, and turned back to me. "And I'm sick of the stink of these garbage cans!"

"Sonny," I said, "I know how you feel. But if you don't finish school now, you're going to be sorry later that you didn't." I grabbed him by the shoulders. "And you only got another year. It ain't so bad. And I'll come back and I swear I'll help you do *whatever* you want to do. Just try to put up with it till I come back. Will you please do that? For me?"

He didn't answer and he wouldn't look at me.

"Sonny. You hear me?"

He pulled away. "I hear you. But you never hear anything *I* say."

I didn't know what to say to that. He looked out the window and then back at me. "OK," he said, and sighed. "I'll try."

Then I said, trying to cheer him up a little, "They got a piano at Isabel's. You can practice on it."

And as a matter of fact, it did cheer him up for a minute. "That's right," he said to himself. "I forgot that." His face relaxed a little. But the worry, the thoughtfulness, played on it still, the way shadows play on a face which is staring into the fire.

But I thought I'd never hear the end of that piano. At first, Isabel would write me, saying how nice it was that Sonny was so serious about his music and how, as soon as he came in from school, or wherever he had been when he was supposed to be at school, he went straight to that piano and stayed there until suppertime. And, after supper, he went back to that piano and stayed there until everybody went to bed. He was at the piano all day Saturday and all day Sunday. Then he bought a record player and started playing records. He'd play one record over and over again, all day long sometimes, and he'd improvise along with it on the piano. Or he'd play one section of the record, one chord, one change, one progression, then he'd do it on the piano. Then back to the record. Then back to the piano.

Well, I really don't know how they stood it. Isabel finally confessed that it wasn't like living with a person at all, it was like living with sound. And the sound didn't make any sense to her, didn't make any sense to any of them—naturally. They began, in a way, to be afflicted by this presence that was living in their home. It was as though Sonny were some sort of god, or monster. He moved in an atmosphere which wasn't like theirs at all. They fed him and he ate, he washed himself, he walked in and out of their door; he certainly wasn't nasty or unpleasant or rude. Sonny isn't any of those things; but it was as though he were all wrapped up in some cloud, some fire, some vision all his own; and there wasn't any way to reach him.

At the same time, he wasn't really a man yet, he was still a child, and they had to watch out for him in all kinds of ways. They certainly couldn't throw him out. Neither did they dare to make a great scene about that piano because even they dimly sensed, as I sensed, from so many thousands of miles away, that Sonny was at that piano playing for his life.

But he hadn't been going to school. One day a letter came from the school board and Isabel's mother got it—there had, apparently, been other letters but Sonny had torn them up. This day, when Sonny came in, Isabel's mother showed him the letter and asked where he'd been spending his time. And she finally got it out of him that he'd been down in Greenwich Village, with musicians and other characters, in a white girl's apartment. And this scared her and she started to scream at him and what came up, once she began—though she denies it to this day—was what sacrifices they were making to give Sonny a decent home and how little he appreciated it.

Sonny didn't play the piano that day. By evening, Isabel's mother had calmed down but then there was the old man to deal with, and Isabel herself. Isabel says she did her best to be calm but she broke down and started crying. She says she just watched Sonny's face. She could tell, by watching him, what was happening with him. And what was happening was that they penetrated his cloud, they had reached him. Even if their fingers had been a thousand times more gentle than human fingers ever are, he could hardly help feeling that they had stripped him naked and were spitting on that nakedness. For he also had to see that his presence, that music, which was life or death to him, had been torture for them and that they had endured it, not at all for his sake, but only for mine. And Sonny couldn't take that. He can take it a little better today than he could then but he's still not very good at it and, frankly, I don't know anybody who is.

The silence of the next few days must have been louder than the sound of all the music ever played since time began. One morning, before she went to work, Isabel was in his room for something and she suddenly realized that all of his records were gone. And she knew for certain that he was gone. And he was. He went as far as the navy would carry him. He finally sent me a postcard from some place in Greece and that was the first I knew that Sonny was still alive. I didn't see him any more until we were both back in New York and the war had long been over.

He was a man by then, of course, but I wasn't willing to see it. He came by the house from time to time, but we fought almost every time we met. I didn't like the way he carried himself, loose and dreamlike all the time, and I didn't like his friends, and his music seemed to be merely an excuse for the life he led. It sounded just that weird and disordered.

Then we had a fight, a pretty awful fight, and I didn't see him for months. By and by I looked him up, where he was living, in a furnished room in the Village, and I tried to make it up. But there were lots of other people in the room and Sonny just lay on his bed, and he wouldn't come downstairs with me, and he treated these other people as though they were his family and I weren't. So I got mad and then he got mad, and then I told him that he might just as well be dead as live the way he was living. Then he stood up and he told me not to worry about him any more in life, that he *was* dead as far as I was concerned. Then he pushed me to the door and the other people looked on as though nothing were happening, and he slammed the door behind me. I stood in the hallway, staring at the door. I heard somebody laugh in the room and then the tears came to my eyes. I started down the steps, whistling to keep from crying, I kept whistling to myself, *You going to need me, baby, one of these cold, rainy days.*

I read about Sonny's trouble in the spring. Little Grace died in the fall. She was a beautiful little girl. But she only lived a little over two years. She died of polio and she suffered. She had a slight fever for a couple of days, but it didn't seem like anything and we just kept her in bed. And we would certainly have called the doctor, but the fever dropped, she seemed to be all right. So we thought it had just been a cold. Then, one day she was up, playing, Isabel was in the kitchen fixing lunch for the two boys when they'd come in from school, and she heard Grace fall down in the living room. When you have a lot of children you don't always start running when one of them falls, unless they start screaming or something. And, this time, Gracie was quiet. Yet, Isabel says that when she heard that *thump* and then that silence, something happened to her to make her afraid. And she ran to the living room and there was little Grace on the floor, all twisted up, and the reason she hadn't screamed was that she couldn't get her breath. And when she did scream, it was the worst sound, Isabel says, that she'd ever heard in all her life, and she still hears it sometimes in her dreams. Isabel will sometimes wake me up with a low, moaning, strangling sound and I have to be quick to awaken her and hold her to me and where Isabel is weeping against me seems a mortal wound.

I think I may have written Sonny the very day that little Grace was buried. I was sitting in the living room in the dark, by myself, and I suddenly thought of Sonny. My trouble made his real.

One Saturday afternoon, when Sonny had been living with us, or anyway, been in our house, for nearly two weeks, I found myself wandering aimlessly about the living room, drinking from a can of beer, and trying to work up courage to search Sonny's room. He was out, he was usually out whenever I was home, and Isabel had taken the children to see their grandparents. Suddenly I was standing still in front of the living room window, watching Seventh Avenue. The idea of searching Sonny's room made me still. I scarcely dared to admit to myself what I'd be searching for. I didn't know what I'd do if I found it. Or if I didn't.

On the sidewalk across from me, near the entrance to a barbecue joint, some people were holding an old-fashioned revival meeting. The barbecue cook, wearing a dirty white apron, his conked hair reddish and metallic in the pale sun, and a cigarette between his lips, stood in the doorway, watching them. Kids and older people paused in their errands and stood there, along with some older men and a couple of very tough-looking women who watched everything that happened on the avenue, as though they owned it, or were maybe owned by it. Well, they were watching this, too. The revival was being carried on by three sisters in black, and a brother. All they had were their voices and their Bibles and a tambourine. The brother was testifying and while he testified two of the sisters stood together, seeming to say amen, and the third sister walked around with the tambourine outstretched and a couple of people dropped coins into it.

Then the brother's testimony ended and the sister who had been taking up the collection dumped the coins into her palm and transferred them to the pocket of her long black robe. Then she raised both hands, striking the tambourine against the air, and then against one hand, and she started to sing. And the two other sisters and the brother joined in.

It was strange, suddenly, to watch, though I had been seeing these meetings all my life. So, of course, had everybody else down there. Yet, they paused and watched and listened and I stood still at the window. "*'Tis the old ship of Zion,*" they sang, and the sister with the tambourine kept a steady, jangling beat, "*it has rescued many a thousand!*" Not a soul under the sound of their voices was hearing this song for the first time, not one of them had been rescued. Nor had they seen much in the way of rescue work being done around them. Neither did they especially believe in the holiness of the three sisters and the brother, they knew too much about them, knew where they lived, and how. The woman with the tambourine, whose voice dominated the air, whose face was bright with joy, was divided by very little from the woman who stood watching her, a cigarette between her heavy, chapped lips, her hair a cuckoo's nest, her face scarred and swollen from many beatings, and her black eyes glittering like coal. Perhaps they both knew this, which was why, when, as rarely, they addressed each other, they addressed each other as Sister. As the singing filled the air the watching, listening faces underwent a change; the eyes focusing on something within; the music seemed to soothe a poison out of them; and time seemed, nearly, to fall away from the sullen, belligerent, battered faces, as though they were fleeing back to their first condition, while dreaming of their last. The barbecue cook half shook his head and smiled, and dropped his cigarette and disappeared into his joint. A man fumbled in his pockets for change and stood holding it in his hand impatiently, as though he had just remembered a pressing appointment further up the avenue. He looked furious. Then I saw Sonny, standing on the edge of the crowd. He was carrying a wide, flat notebook, with a green cover, and it made him look, from where I was standing, almost like a schoolboy. The coppery sun brought out the copper in his skin, he was very faintly smiling, standing very still. Then the singing stopped, the tambourine turned into a collection plate again. The furious man dropped in his coins and vanished, so did a couple of the women, and Sonny dropped some change in the plate, looking directly at the woman with a little smile. He started across the avenue, toward the house. He has a slow, loping walk, something like the way Harlem hipsters walk, only he's imposed on this his own half-beat. I had never really noticed it before.

I stayed at the window, both relieved and apprehensive. As Sonny disappeared from my sight, they began singing again. And they were still singing when his key turned in the lock.

"Hey," he said.

"Hey, yourself. You want some beer?"

"No. Well maybe." But he came up to the window and stood beside me, looking out. "What a warm voice," he said.

They were singing *If I could only hear my mother pray again!*

"Yes," I said, "and she can sure beat that tambourine."

"But what a terrible song," he said, and laughed. He dropped his notebook on the sofa and disappeared into the kitchen. "Where's Isabel and the kids?"

"I think they went to see their grandparents. You hungry?"

"No." He came back into the living room with his can of beer. "You want to come some place with me tonight?"

I sensed, I don't know how, that I couldn't possibly say no. "Sure. Where?"

He sat down on the sofa and picked up his notebook and started leafing through it. "I'm going to sit in with some fellows in a joint in the Village."

"You mean, you're going to play, tonight?"

"That's right." He took a swallow of his beer and moved back to the window. He gave me a sidelong look. "If you can stand it."

"I'll try," I said.

He smiled to himself and we both watched as the meeting across the way broke up. The three sisters and the brother, heads bowed, were singing *God be with you till we meet again*. The faces around them were very quiet. Then the song ended. The small crowd dispersed. We watched the three women and the lone man walk slowly up the avenue.

"When she was singing before," said Sonny, abruptly, "her voice reminded me for a minute of what heroin feels like sometimes—when it's in your veins. It makes you feel sort of warm and cool at the same time. And distant. And—and sure." He sipped his beer, very deliberately not looking at me. I watched his face. "It makes you feel—in control. Sometimes you've got to have that feeling."

"Do you?" I sat down slowly in the easy chair.

"Sometimes." He went to the sofa and picked up his notebook again. "Some people do."

"In order," I asked, "to play?" And my voice was very ugly, full of contempt and anger.

"Well"—he looked at me with great, troubled eyes, as though, in fact, he hoped his eyes would tell me things he could never otherwise say—"they *think* so. And *if* they think so—!"

"And what do *you* think?" I asked.

He sat on the sofa and put his can of beer on the floor. "I don't know," he said, and I couldn't be sure if he were answering my question or pursuing his thoughts. His face didn't tell me. "It's not so much to *play*. It's to *stand* it, to be able to make it at all. On any level." He frowned and smiled: "In order to keep from shaking to pieces."

"But these friends of yours," I said, "they seem to shake themselves to pieces pretty goddamn fast."

"Maybe." He played with the notebook. And something told me that I should curb my tongue, that Sonny was doing his best to talk, that I should listen. "But of course you only know the ones that've gone to pieces. Some don't—or at least they haven't *yet* and that's just about all *any* of us can say." He paused. "And then there are some who just live, really, in hell, and they know it and they see what's happening and they go right on. I don't know." He sighed, dropped the notebook, folded his arms. "Some guys, you can tell from the way they play they on something *all* the time. And you can see that, well, it makes something real for them. But of course," he picked up his beer from the floor and sipped it and put the can down again, "they *want* to, too, you've got to see that. Even some of them that say they don't—*some*, not all."

"And what about you?" I asked—I couldn't help it. "What about you? Do *you* want to?"

He stood up and walked to the window and I remained silent for a long time. Then he sighed. "Me," he said. Then: "While I was downstairs before, on my way here, listening to that woman sing, it struck me all of a sudden how much suffering she must have had to go through—to sing like that. It's *repulsive* to think you have to suffer that much."

I said: "But there's no way not to suffer—is there, Sonny?"

"I believe not," he said and smiled, "but that's never stopped anyone from trying." He looked at me. "Has it?" I realized, with this mocking look, that there stood between us, forever, beyond the power of time or forgiveness, the fact that I had held silence—so long!—when he had needed human speech to help him. He turned back to the window. "No, there's no way not to suffer. But you try all kinds of ways to keep from drowning in it, to keep on top of it, and to make it seem—well, like *you*. Like you did something, all right, and now you're suffering for it. You know?" I said nothing. "Well, you know," he said, impatiently, "why *do* people suffer? Maybe it's better to do something to give it a reason, *any* reason."

"But we just agreed," I said, "that there's no way not to suffer. Isn't it better, then, just to—take it?"

"But nobody just takes it," Sonny cried, "that's what I'm telling you! *Everybody* tries not to. You're just hung up on the *way* some people try—it's not *your* way!"

The hair on my face began to itch, my face felt wet. "That's not true," I said, "that's not true. I don't give a damn what other people do, I don't even care how they suffer. I just care how *you* suffer." And he looked at me. "Please believe me," I said, "I don't want to see you—die—trying not to suffer."

"I won't," he said flatly, "die trying not to suffer. At least, not any faster than anybody else."

"But there's no need," I said, trying to laugh, "is there? in killing yourself."

I wanted to say more, but I couldn't. I wanted to talk about will power and how life could be—well, beautiful. I wanted to say that it was all within; but was it? or, rather, wasn't that exactly the trouble? And I wanted to promise that I would never fail him again. But it would all have sounded—empty words and lies.

So I made the promise to myself and prayed that I would keep it.

"It's terrible sometimes, inside," he said, "that's what's the trouble. You walk these streets, black and funky and cold, and there's not really a living ass to talk to, and there's nothing shaking, and there's no way of getting it out—that storm inside. You can't talk it and you can't make love with it, and when you finally try to get with it and play it, you realize *nobody's* listening. So *you've* got to listen. You got to find a way to listen."

And then he walked away from the window and sat on the sofa again, as though all the wind had suddenly been knocked out of him. "Sometimes you'll do *anything* to play, even cut your mother's throat." He laughed and looked at me. "Or your brother's." Then he sobered. "Or your own." Then: "Don't worry. I'm all right now and I think I'll *be* all right. But I can't forget—where I've been. I don't mean just the physical place I've been, I mean where I've *been*. And *what* I've been."

"What have you been, Sonny?" I asked.

He smiled—but sat sideways on the sofa, his elbow resting on the back, his fingers playing with his mouth and chin, not looking at me. "I've been something I didn't recognize, didn't know I could be. Didn't know anybody could be." He stopped, looking inward, looking helplessly young, looking old. "I'm not talking about it now because I feel *guilty* or anything like that—maybe it would be better if I did, I don't know. Anyway, I can't really talk about it. Not to you, not to anybody," and now he turned and faced me. "Sometimes, you know, and it was actually when I was most *out* of the world, I felt that I was in it, that I was *with* it, really, and I could play or I didn't really have to *play*, it just came out of me, it was there. And I don't know how I played, thinking about it now, but I know I did awful things, those times, sometimes to people. Or it wasn't that I *did* anything to them—it was that they weren't real." He picked up the beer can; it was empty; he rolled it between his palms: "And other times—well, I needed a fix, I needed to find a place to lean. I needed to clear a space to *listen*—and I couldn't find it, and I went *crazy*. I did terrible things to *me*, I was terrible *for* me." He began pressing the beer can between his hands, I watched the metal begin to give. It glittered, as he played with it like a knife, and I was afraid he would cut himself, but I said nothing. "Oh well. I can never tell you. I was all by myself at the bottom of something, stinking and sweating and crying and shaking, and I smelled it, you know? *my* stink, and I thought I'd die if I couldn't get away from it and yet, all the same, I knew that everything I was doing was just locking me in with it. And I didn't know," he paused, still flattening the beer can, "I didn't know, I still *don't* know, something kept telling me that maybe it was good to smell your own stink, but I didn't think that *that* was what I'd been trying to do—and—who can stand it?" and he abruptly dropped the ruined beer can, looking at me with a small, still smile, and then rose, walking to the window as though it were the lodestone rock. I watched his face, he watched the avenue. "I couldn't tell you when Mama died—but the reason I wanted to leave Harlem so bad was to get away from drugs. And then, when I ran away, that's what I was running from—really. When I came back, nothing had changed, *I* hadn't changed, I was just—older." And he stopped, drumming with his fingers on the windowpane. The sun had vanished, soon darkness would fall. I watched his face. "It can come again," he said, almost as though speaking to himself. Then he turned to me. "It can come again," he repeated. "I just want you to know that."

"All right," I said, at last. "So it can come again. All right."

He smiled, but the smile was sorrowful. "I had to try to tell you," he said.

"Yes," I said. "I understand that."

"You're my brother," he said, looking straight at me, and not smiling at all.

"Yes," I repeated, "yes, I understand that."

He turned back to the window, looking out. "All that hatred down there," he said, "all that hatred and misery and love. It's a wonder it doesn't blow the avenue apart."

We went to the only nightclub on a short, dark street, downtown. We squeezed through the narrow, chattering, jampacked bar to the entrance of the big room, where the bandstand was. And we stood there for a moment, for the lights were very dim in this room and we couldn't see. Then, "Hello, boy," said the voice and an enormous black man, much older than Sonny or myself, erupted out of all that atmospheric lighting and put an arm around Sonny's shoulder. "I been sitting right here," he said, "waiting for you."

He had a big voice, too, and heads in the darkness turned toward us.

Sonny grinned and pulled a little away, and said, "Creole, this is my brother. I told you about him."

Creole shook my hand. "I'm glad to meet you, son," he said, and it was clear that he was glad to meet me *there*, for Sonny's sake. And he smiled, "You got a real musician in *your* family," and he took his arm from Sonny's shoulder and slapped him, lightly, affectionately, with the back of his hand.

"Well. Now I've heard it all," said a voice behind us. This was another musician, and a friend of Sonny's, a coal-black, cheerful-looking man, built close to the ground. He immediately began confiding to me, at the top of his lungs, the most terrible things about Sonny his teeth gleaming like a lighthouse and his laugh coming up out of him like the beginning of an earthquake. And it turned out that everyone at the bar knew Sonny, or almost everyone, some were musicians, working there, or nearby, or not working, some were simply hangers-on, and some were there to hear Sonny play. I was introduced to all of them and they were all very polite to me. Yet, it was clear that, for them, I was only Sonny's brother. Here, I was in Sonny's world. Or, rather, his kingdom. Here, it was not even a question that his veins bore royal blood.

They were going to play soon and Creole installed me, by myself, at a table in a dark corner. Then I watched them, Creole, and the little black man, and Sonny, and the others, while they horsed around, standing just below the bandstand. The light from the bandstand spilled just a little short of them and, watching them laughing and gesturing and moving about, I had the feeling that they, nevertheless, were being most careful not to step into that circle of light too suddenly; that if they moved into the light too suddenly without thinking, they would perish in flame. Then, while I watched, one of them, the small black man, moved into the light and crossed the bandstand and started fooling around with his drums. Then—being funny and being, also, extremely ceremonious—Creole took Sonny by the arm and led him to the piano. A woman's voice called Sonny's name and a few hands started clapping. And Sonny, also being funny and being ceremonious, and so touched, I think, that he could have cried, but neither hiding it nor showing it, riding it like a man, grinned, and put both hands to his heart and bowed from the waist.

Creole then went to the bass fiddle and a lean, very bright-skinned brown man jumped up on the bandstand and picked up his horn. So there they were, and the atmosphere on the bandstand and in the room began to change and tighten. Someone stepped up to the microphone and announced them. Then there were all kinds of murmurs. Some people at the bar shushed others. The waitress ran around, frantically getting in the last orders, guys and chicks got closer to each other, and the lights on the bandstand, on the quartet, turned to a kind of indigo. Then they all looked different there. Creole looked about him for the last time, as though he were making certain that all his chickens were in the coop, and then he—jumped and struck the fiddle. And there they were.

All I know about music is that not many people ever really hear it. And even then, on the rare occasions when something opens within, and the music enters, what we mainly hear, or hear corroborated, are personal, private, vanishing evocations. But the man who creates the music is hearing something else, is dealing with the roar rising from the void and imposing order on it as it hits the air. What is evoked in him, then, is of another order, more terrible because it has no words, and triumphant, too, for that same reason. And his triumph, when he triumphs, is ours. I just watched Sonny's face. His face was troubled, he was working hard, but he wasn't with it. And I had the feeling that, in a way, everyone on the bandstand was waiting for him, both waiting for him and pushing him along. But as I began to watch Creole, I realized that it was Creole who held them all back. He had them on a short rein. Up there, keeping the beat with his whole body, waiting on the fiddle, with his eyes half closed, he was listening to everything, but he was listening to Sonny. He was having a dialogue with Sonny. He wanted Sonny to leave the shoreline and strike out for the deep water. He was Sonny's witness that deep water and drowning were not the same thing—he had been there, and he knew. And he wanted Sonny to know. He was waiting for Sonny to do the things on the keys which would let Creole know that Sonny was in the water.

And, while Creole listened, Sonny moved, deep within, exactly like someone in torment. I had never before thought of how awful the relationship must be between the musician and his instrument. He has to fill it, this instrument, with the breath of life, his own. He has to make it do what he wants it to do. And a piano is just a piano. It's made out of so much wood and wires and little hammers and big ones, and ivory. While there's only so much you can do with it, the only way to find this out is to try: to try and make it do everything.

And Sonny hadn't been near a piano for over a year. And he wasn't on much better terms with his life, not the life that stretched before him now. He and the piano stammered, started one way, got scared, stopped; started another way, panicked, marked time, started again; then seemed to have found a direction, panicked again, got stuck. And the face I saw on Sonny I'd never seen before. Everything had been burned out of it, and, at the same time, things usually hidden were being burned in, by the fire and fury of the battle which was occurring in him up there.

Yet, watching Creole's face as they neared the end of the first set, I had the feeling that something had happened, something I hadn't heard. Then they finished, there was scattered applause, and then, without an instant's warning, Creole started into something else, it was almost sardonic, it was *Am I Blue*. And, as though he commanded, Sonny began to play. Something began to happen. And Creole let out the reins. The dry, low, black man said something awful on the drums. Creole answered, and the drums talked back. Then the horn insisted, sweet and high, slightly detached perhaps, and Creole listened, commenting now and then, dry and driving, beautiful and calm and old. Then they all came together again, and Sonny was part of the family again. I could tell this from his face. He seemed to have found, right there beneath his fingers, a damn brand-new piano. It seemed that he couldn't get over it. Then, for a while, just being happy with Sonny, they seemed to be agreeing with him that brand-new pianos certainly were a gas.

Then Creole stepped forward to remind them that what they were playing was the blues. He hit something in all of them, he hit something in me, myself, and the music tightened and deepened, apprehension began to beat the air. Creole began to tell us what the blues were all about. They were not about anything very new. He and his boys up there were keeping it new, at the risk of ruin, destruction, madness, and death, in order to find new ways to make us listen. For, while the tale of how we suffer, and how we are delighted, and how we may triumph is never new, it always must be heard. There isn't any other tale to tell, it's the only light we've got in all this darkness.

And this tale, according to that face, that body, those strong hands on those strings, has another aspect in every country, and a new depth in every generation. Listen, Creole seemed to be saying, listen. Now these are Sonny's blues. He made the little black man on the drums know it, and the bright, brown man on the horn. Creole wasn't trying any longer to get Sonny in the water. He was wishing him Godspeed. Then he stepped back, very slowly, filling the air with the immense suggestion that Sonny speak for himself.

Then they all gathered around Sonny and Sonny played. Every now and again one of them seemed to say amen. Sonny's fingers filled the air with life, his life. But that life contained so many others. And Sonny went all the way back, he really began with the spare, flat statement of the opening phrase of the song. Then he began to make it his. It was very beautiful because it wasn't hurried and it was no longer a lament. I seemed to hear with what burning he had made it his, and what burning we had yet to make it ours, how we could cease lamenting. Freedom lurked around us and I understood, at last, that he could help us to be free if we would listen, that he would never be free until we did. Yet, there was no battle in his face now, I heard what he had gone through, and would continue to go through until he came to rest in earth. He had made it his: that long line, of which we knew only Mama and Daddy. And he was giving it back, as everything must be given back, so that, passing through death, it can live forever. I saw my mother's face again, and felt, for the first time, how the stones of the road she had walked on must have bruised her feet. I saw the moonlit road where my father's brother died. And it brought something else back to me, and carried me past it, I saw my little girl again and felt Isabel's tears again, and I felt my own tears begin to rise. And I was yet aware that this was only a moment, that the world waited outside, as hungry as a tiger, and that trouble stretched above us, longer than the sky.

Then it was over. Creole and Sonny let out their breath, both soaking wet, and grinning. There was a lot of applause and some of it was real. In the dark, the girl came by and I asked her to take drinks to the bandstand. There was a long pause, while they talked up there in the indigo light and after awhile I saw the girl put a Scotch and milk on top of the piano for Sonny. He didn't seem to notice it, but just before they started playing again, he sipped from it and looked toward me, and nodded. Then he put it back on top of the piano. For me, then, as they began to play again, it glowed and shook above my brother's head like the very cup of trembling.

—1957

FLANNERY O'CONNOR

Mary Flannery O'Connor was born in 1925 in Savannah, Georgia, the only child of Regina and Edward Francis O'Connor. Her father was afflicted with lupus for several years and in 1941 he succumbed to the disease that would later affect his daughter. After O'Connor graduated from high school, she attended Georgia State College for Women with the intention of completing an English degree; partway through she changed her major to Social Science, and received her Bachelor's degree in 1945.

A teacher at Georgia State submitted one of the stories O'Connor had published in the college literary quarterly to the prestigious Writers' Workshop at the State University of Iowa. O'Connor was awarded a Rinehart Fellowship from the university and embarked on a graduate degree in writing. O'Connor flourished at the Writers' Workshop, which she attended from 1945 to 1948. During that time, she sold "The Geranium," her first short story and one of the stories that would compose her MFA thesis, to *Accent* magazine. After receiving her MFA, O'Connor was invited to spend the winter of 1948 at Yaddo, the famous American writers' colony in Saratoga Springs, New York. Later, she moved to Connecticut and lived with writers Sally and Robert Fitzgerald while she worked on her novel, *Wise Blood.*

O'Connor probably would have stayed in the northern United States had she not been struck in 1950 by lupus. Weakened by the disease and the debilitating cortisone treatments, she went to live with her mother on her farm in Milledgeville, Georgia, where she continued to write for the remainder of her life.

Wise Blood was published in 1952, and in the following year O'Connor was awarded a *Kenyon Review* Fellowship. She published the short story collection *A Good Man Is Hard to Find* in 1955, and in 1957 received the O. Henry prize for short fiction. She also travelled when her health permitted and gave lectures at various universities, colleges, and high schools. Using the financial support from a Ford Foundation grant, O'Connor completed her second novel, *The Violent Bear It Away* (1960), and finished the manuscript for her second short story collection, *Everything that Rises Must*

Converge (published posthumously in 1965). In 1963, O'Connor's health began to deteriorate seriously; she was diagnosed with acute anemia, and abdominal surgery to remove a benign tumour reactivated her lupus. She died in Milledgeville on August 3, 1964.

Flannery O'Connor's fiction is distinctive for its mingling of horror and humour, and for the ways in which it problematizes the "Southern grotesque" from the perspective of O'Connor's intensely deep Catholic faith. Indeed, she writes that "the meaning of life is centered in our Redemption by Christ and what I see in the world I see in its relation to that." These combinations result in provocative writing that is startling and enlightening. The short story "A Good Man Is Hard to Find" is the first story in the collection of the same name. The character of the Misfit is a prime example of the sort of "grotesque" that features in much of O'Connor's fiction. He is not so different from the "lady-like" grandmother, however, and his peculiar distortion of her values and beliefs is borne out in the story's shocking conclusion.

A Good Man Is Hard to Find

FLANNERY O'CONNOR

THE GRANDMOTHER didn't want to go to Florida. She wanted to visit some of her connections in east Tennessee and she was seizing at every chance to change Bailey's mind. Bailey was the son she lived with, her only boy. He was sitting on the edge of his chair at the table, bent over the orange sports section of the *Journal*. "Now look here, Bailey," she said, "see here, read this," and she stood with one hand on her thin hip and the other rattling the newspaper at his bald head. "Here this fellow that calls himself The Misfit is aloose from the Federal Pen and headed toward Florida and you read here what it says he did to these people. Just you read it. I wouldn't take my children in any direction with a criminal like that aloose in it. I couldn't answer to my conscience if I did."

Bailey didn't look up from his reading so she wheeled around then and faced the children's mother, a young woman in slacks, whose face was as broad and innocent as a cabbage and was tied around with a green head-kerchief that had two points on the top like rabbit's ears. She was sitting on the sofa, feeding the baby his apricots out of a jar. "The children have been to Florida before," the old lady said. "You all ought to take them somewhere else for a change so they would see different parts of the world and be broad. They never have been to east Tennessee."

The children's mother didn't seem to hear her but the eight-year-old boy, John Wesley, a stocky child with glasses, said, "If you don't want to go to Florida, why dontcha stay at home?" He and the little girl, June Star, were reading the funny papers on the floor.

"She wouldn't stay at home to be queen for a day," June Star said without raising her yellow head.

"Yes and what would you do if this fellow, The Misfit, caught you?" the grandmother asked.

"I'd smack his face," John Wesley said.

"She wouldn't stay at home for a million bucks," June Star said. "Afraid she'd miss something. She has to go everywhere we go."

"All right, Miss," the grandmother said. "Just remember that the next time you want me to curl your hair."

June Star said her hair was naturally curly.

The next morning the grandmother was the first one in the car, ready to go. She had her big black valise that looked like the head of a hippopotamus in one corner, and underneath it she was hiding a basket with Pitty Sing, the cat, in it. She didn't intend for the cat to be left alone in the house for three days because he would miss her too much and she was afraid he might brush against one of the gas burners and accidentally asphyxiate himself. Her son, Bailey, didn't like to arrive at a motel with a cat.

She sat in the middle of the back seat with John Wesley and June Star on either side of her. Bailey and the children's mother and the baby sat in front and they left Atlanta at eight forty-five with the mileage on the car at 55890. The grandmother wrote this down because she thought it would be interesting to say how many miles they had been when they got back. It took them twenty minutes to reach the outskirts of the city.

The old lady settled herself comfortably, removing her white cotton gloves and putting them up with her purse on the shelf in front of the back window. The children's mother still had on slacks and still had her head tied up in a green kerchief, but the grandmother had on a navy blue straw sailor hat with a bunch of white violets on the brim and a navy blue dress with a small white dot in the print. Her collars and cuffs were white organdy trimmed with lace and at her neckline she had pinned a purple spray of cloth violets containing a sachet. In case of an accident, anyone seeing her dead on the highway would know at once that she was a lady.

She said she thought it was going to be a good day for driving, neither too hot nor too cold, and she cautioned Bailey that the speed limit was fifty-five miles an hour and that the patrolmen hid themselves behind billboards and small clumps of trees and sped out after you before you had a chance to slow down. She pointed out interesting details of the scenery: Stone Mountain; the blue granite that in some places came up to both sides of the highway; the brilliant red clay banks slightly streaked with purple; and the various crops that made rows of green lace-work on the ground. The trees were full of silver-white sunlight and the meanest of them sparkled. The children were reading comic magazines and their mother had gone back to sleep.

"Let's go through Georgia fast so we won't have to look at it much," John Wesley said.

"If I were a little boy," said the grandmother, "I wouldn't talk about my native state that way. Tennessee has the mountains and Georgia has the hills."

"Tennessee is just a hillbilly dumping ground," John Wesley said, "and Georgia is a lousy state too."

"You said it," June Star said.

"In my time," said the grandmother, folding her thin veined fingers, "children were more respectful of their native states and their parents and everything else. People did right then. Oh look at the cute little pickaninny!"[1] she said and pointed to a Negro child standing in the door of a shack. "Wouldn't that make a picture, now?" she asked and they all turned and looked at the little Negro out of the back window. He waved.

"He didn't have any britches on," June Star said.

"He probably didn't have any," the grandmother explained. "Little niggers[2] in the country don't have things like we do. If I could paint, I'd paint that picture," she said.

The children exchanged comic books.

The grandmother offered to hold the baby and the children's mother passed him over the front seat to her. She set him on her knee and bounced him and told him about the things they were passing. She rolled her eyes and screwed up her mouth and stuck her leathery thin face into his smooth bland one. Occasionally he gave her a faraway smile. They passed a large cotton field with five or six graves fenced in the middle of it, like a small island. "Look at the graveyard!" the grandmother said, pointing it out. "That was the old family burying ground. That belonged to the plantation."

"Where's the plantation?" John Wesley asked.

"Gone With the Wind," said the grandmother. "Ha. Ha."

When the children finished all the comic books they had brought, they opened the lunch and ate it. The grandmother ate a peanut butter sandwich and

---

1 Derogatory term for an African American child.

2 This pejorative term remained in frequent use by many white Americans in the South until well into the 1960s.

an olive and would not let the children throw the box and the paper napkins out the window. When there was nothing else to do they played a game by choosing a cloud and making the other two guess what shape it suggested. John Wesley took one the shape of a cow and June Star guessed a cow and John Wesley said, no, an automobile, and June Star said he didn't play fair, and they began to slap each other over the grandmother.

The grandmother said she would tell them a story if they would keep quiet. When she told a story, she rolled her eyes and waved her head and was very dramatic. She said once when she was a maiden lady she had been courted by a Mr. Edgar Atkins Teagarden from Jasper, Georgia. She said he was a very good-looking man and a gentleman and that he brought her a watermelon every Saturday afternoon with his initials cut in it, E.A.T. Well, one Saturday, she said, Mr. Teagarden brought the watermelon and there was nobody at home and he left it on the front porch and returned in his buggy to Jasper, but she never got the watermelon, she said, because a nigger boy ate it when he saw the initials, E.A.T.! This story tickled John Wesley's funny bone and he giggled and giggled but June Star didn't think it was any good. She said she wouldn't marry a man that just brought her a watermelon on Saturday. The grandmother said she would have done well to marry Mr. Teagarden because he was a gentleman and had bought Coca-Cola stock when it first came out and that he had died only a few years ago, a very wealthy man.

They stopped at The Tower for barbecued sandwiches. The Tower was a part stucco and part wood filling station and dance hall set in a clearing outside of Timothy. A fat man named Red Sammy Butts ran it and there were signs stuck here and there on the building and for miles up and down the highway saying, TRY RED SAMMY'S FAMOUS BARBECUE. NONE LIKE FAMOUS RED SAMMY'S! RED SAM! THE FAT BOY WITH THE HAPPY LAUGH. A VETERAN! RED SAMMY'S YOUR MAN!

Red Sammy was lying on the bare ground outside The Tower with his head under a truck while a gray monkey about a foot high, chained to a small chinaberry tree, chattered nearby. The monkey sprang back into the tree and got on the highest limb as soon as he saw the children jump out of the car and run toward him.

Inside, The Tower was a long dark room with a counter at one end and tables at the other and dancing space in the middle. They all sat down at a board table next to the nickelodeon and Red Sam's wife, a tall burnt-brown woman with hair and eyes lighter than her skin, came and took their order. The children's mother put a dime in the machine and played "The Tennessee Waltz," and the grandmother said that tune always made her want to dance. She asked Bailey if he would like to dance but he only glared at her. He didn't have a naturally sunny disposition like she did and trips made him nervous. The grandmother's brown eyes were very bright. She swayed her head from side to side and pretended she was dancing in her chair. June Star said play something she could tap to so the children's mother put in another dime and played a fast number and June Star stepped out onto the dance floor and did her tap routine.

"Ain't she cute?" Red Sam's wife said, leaning over the counter. "Would you like to come be my little girl?"

"No I certainly wouldn't," June Star said. "I wouldn't live in a broken-down place like this for a million bucks!" and she ran back to the table.

"Ain't she cute?" the woman repeated, stretching her mouth politely.

"Ain't you ashamed?" hissed the grandmother.

Red Sam came in and told his wife to quit lounging on the counter and hurry up with these people's order. His khaki trousers reached just to his hip bones and his stomach hung over them like a sack of meal swaying under his shirt. He came over and sat down at a table nearby and let out a combination sigh and yodel. "You can't win," he said. "You can't win," and he wiped his sweating red face off with a gray handkerchief. "These days you don't know who to trust," he said. "Ain't that the truth?"

"People are certainly not nice like they used to be," said the grandmother.

"Two fellers come in here last week," Red Sammy said, "driving a Chrysler. It was a old beat-up car but it was a good one and these boys looked all right to me. Said they worked at the mill and you know I let them fellers charge the gas they bought? Now why did I do that?"

"Because you're a good man!" the grandmother said at once.

"Yes'm, I suppose so," Red Sam said as if he were struck with this answer.

His wife brought the orders, carrying the five plates all at once without a tray, two in each hand and one balanced on her arm. "It isn't a soul in this green world of God's that you can trust," she said. "And I don't count nobody out of that, not nobody," she repeated, looking at Red Sammy.

"Did you read about that criminal, The Misfit, that's escaped?" asked the grandmother.

"I wouldn't be a bit surprised if he didn't attact this place right here," said the woman. "If he hears about it being here, I wouldn't be none surprised to see him. If he hears it's two cent in the cash register, I wouldn't be a tall surprised if he ..."

"That'll do," Red Sam said. "Go bring these people their Co'-Colas," and the woman went off to get the rest of the order.

"A good man is hard to find," Red Sammy said. "Everything is getting terrible. I remember the day you could go off and leave your screen door unlatched. Not no more."

He and the grandmother discussed better times. The old lady said that in her opinion Europe was entirely to blame for the way things were now. She said the way Europe acted you would think we were made of money and Red Sam said it was no use talking about it, she was exactly right. The children ran outside into the white sunlight and looked at the monkey in the lacy chinaberry tree. He was busy catching fleas on himself and biting each one carefully between his teeth as if it were a delicacy.

They drove off again into the hot afternoon. The grandmother took cat naps and woke up every few minutes with her own snoring. Outside of Toombsboro she woke up and recalled an old plantation that she had visited in this neighborhood once when she was a young lady. She said the house had six white columns across the front and that there was an avenue of oaks leading up to it and two little wooden trellis arbors on either side in front where you sat down with your suitor after a stroll in the garden. She recalled exactly which road to turn off to get to it. She knew that Bailey would not be willing to lose any time looking at an old house, but the more she talked about it, the more she wanted to see it once again and find out if the little twin arbors were still standing. "There was a secret panel in this house," she said craftily, not telling the truth but wishing that she were, "and the story went that all the family silver was hidden in it when Sherman[3] came through but it was never found ..."

"Hey!" John Wesley said. "Let's go see it! We'll find it! We'll poke all the woodwork and find it! Who lives there? Where do you turn off at? Hey Pop, can't we turn off there?"

"We never have seen a house with a secret panel!" June Star shrieked. "Let's go to the house with the secret panel! Hey, Pop, can't we go see the house with the secret panel!"

"It's not far from here, I know," the grandmother said. "It wouldn't take over twenty minutes."

Bailey was looking straight ahead. His jaw was as rigid as a horseshoe. "No," he said.

The children began to yell and scream that they wanted to see the house with the secret panel. John Wesley kicked the back of the front seat and June Star hung over her mother's shoulder and whined desperately into her ear that they never had any fun even on their vacation, that they could never do what THEY wanted to do. The baby began to scream and John Wesley kicked the back of the seat so hard that his father could feel the blows in his kidney.

---

3 American Union commander William Tecumseh Sherman marched his troops through Georgia to Atlanta in 1864 during the American Civil War.

"All right!" he shouted and drew the car to a stop at the side of the road. "Will you all shut up? Will you all just shut up for one second? If you don't shut up, we won't go anywhere."

"It would be very educational for them," the grandmother murmured.

"All right," Bailey said, "but get this: this is the only time we're going to stop for anything like this. This is the one and only time."

"The dirt road that you have to turn down is about a mile back," the grandmother directed. "I marked it when we passed."

"A dirt road," Bailey groaned.

After they had turned around and were headed toward the dirt road, the grandmother recalled other points about the house, the beautiful glass over the front doorway and the candle-lamp in the hall. John Wesley said that the secret panel was probably in the fireplace.

"You can't go inside this house," Bailey said. "You don't know who lives there."

"While you all talk to the people in front, I'll run around behind and get in a window," John Wesley suggested.

"We'll all stay in the car," his mother said.

They turned onto the dirt road and the car raced roughly along in a swirl of pink dust. The grandmother recalled the times when there were no paved roads and thirty miles was a day's journey. The dirt road was hilly and there were sudden washes in it and sharp curves on dangerous embankments. All at once they would be on a hill, looking down over the blue tops of trees for miles around, then the next minute, they would be in a red depression with the dust-coated trees looking down on them.

"This place had better turn up in a minute," Bailey said, "or I'm going to turn around."

The road looked as if no one had traveled on it in months.

"It's not much farther," the grandmother said and just as she said it, a horrible thought came to her. The thought was so embarrassing that she turned red in the face and her eyes dilated and her feet jumped up, upsetting her valise in the corner. The instant the valise moved, the newspaper top she had over the basket under it rose with a snarl and Pitty Sing, the cat, sprang onto Bailey's shoulder.

The children were thrown to the floor and their mother, clutching the baby, was thrown out the door onto the ground; the old lady was thrown into the front seat. The car turned over once and landed right-side-up in a gulch off the side of the road. Bailey remained in the driver's seat with the cat—gray-striped with a broad white face and an orange nose—clinging to his neck like a caterpillar.

As soon as the children saw they could move their arms and legs, they scrambled out of the car, shouting, "We've had an ACCIDENT!" The grandmother was curled up under the dashboard, hoping she was injured so that Bailey's wrath would not come down on her all at once. The horrible thought she had had before the accident was that the house she had remembered so vividly was not in Georgia but in Tennessee.

Bailey removed the cat from his neck with both hands and flung it out the window against the side of a pine tree. Then he got out of the car and started looking for the children's mother. She was sitting against the side of the red gutted ditch, holding the screaming baby, but she only had a cut down her face and a broken shoulder. "We've had an ACCIDENT!" the children screamed in a frenzy of delight.

"But nobody's killed," June Star said with disappointment as the grandmother limped out of the car, her hat still pinned to her head but the broken front brim standing up at a jaunty angle and the violet spray hanging off the side. They all sat down in the ditch, except the children, to recover from the shock. They were all shaking.

"Maybe a car will come along," said the children's mother hoarsely.

"I believe I have injured an organ," said the grandmother, pressing her side, but no one answered her. Bailey's teeth were clattering. He had on a yellow sport shirt with bright blue parrots designed in it and his face was as yellow as the shirt. The grandmother decided that she would not mention that the house was in Tennessee.

The road was about ten feet above and they could see only the tops of the trees on the other side of it. Behind the ditch they were sitting in there were more woods, tall and dark and deep. In a few minutes they saw a car some distance away on top of a hill, coming slowly as if the occupants were watching them. The grandmother stood up and waved both arms dramatically to attract their attention. The car continued to come on slowly, disappeared around a bend and appeared again, moving even slower, on top of the hill they had gone over. It was a big black battered hearse-like automobile. There were three men in it.

It came to a stop just over them and for some minutes, the driver looked down with a steady expressionless gaze to where they were sitting, and didn't speak. Then he turned his head and muttered something to the other two and they got out. One was a fat boy in black trousers and a red sweat shirt with a silver stallion embossed on the front of it. He moved around on the right side of them and stood staring, his mouth partly open in a kind of loose grin. The other had on khaki pants and a blue striped coat and a gray hat pulled down very low, hiding most of his face. He came around slowly on the left side. Neither spoke.

The driver got out of the car and stood by the side of it, looking down at them. He was an older man than the other two. His hair was just beginning to gray and he wore silver-rimmed spectacles that gave him a scholarly look. He had a long creased face and didn't have on any shirt or undershirt. He had on blue jeans that were too tight for him and was holding a black hat and a gun. The two boys also had guns.

"We've had an ACCIDENT!" the children screamed.

The grandmother had the peculiar feeling that the bespectacled man was someone she knew. His face was as familiar to her as if she had known him all her life but she could not recall who he was. He moved away from the car and began to come down the embankment, placing his feet carefully so that he wouldn't slip. He had on tan and white shoes and no socks, and his ankles were red and thin. "Good afternoon," he said. "I see you all had you a little spill."

"We turned over twice!" said the grandmother.

"Oncet," he corrected. "We seen it happen. Try their car and see will it run, Hiram," he said quietly to the boy with the gray hat.

"What you got that gun for?" John Wesley asked. "Whatcha gonna do with that gun?"

"Lady," the man said to the children's mother, "would you mind calling them children to sit down by you? Children make me nervous. I want all you all to sit down right together there where you're at."

"What are you telling US what to do for?" June Star asked.

Behind them the line of woods gaped like a dark open mouth. "Come here," said their mother.

"Look here now," Bailey began suddenly, "we're in a predicament! We're in ..."

The grandmother shrieked. She scrambled to her feet and stood staring. "You're The Misfit!" she said. "I recognized you at once!"

"Yes'm," the man said, smiling slightly as if he were pleased in spite of himself to be known, "but it would have been better for all of you, lady, if you hadn't of reckernized me."

Bailey turned his head sharply and said something to his mother that shocked even the children. The old lady began to cry and The Misfit reddened.

"Lady," he said, "don't you get upset. Sometimes a man says things he don't mean. I don't reckon he meant to talk to you thataway."

"You wouldn't shoot a lady, would you?" the grandmother said and removed a clean handkerchief from her cuff and began to slap at her eyes with it.

The Misfit pointed the toe of his shoe into the ground and made a little hole and then covered it up again. "I would hate to have to," he said.

"Listen," the grandmother almost screamed, "I know you're a good man. You don't look a bit like you have common blood. I know you must come from nice people!"

"Yes mam," he said, "finest people in the world." When he smiled he showed a row of strong white teeth. "God never made a finer woman than my mother and my daddy's heart was pure gold," he said. The boy with the red sweat shirt had come around behind them and was standing with his gun at his hip. The Misfit squatted down on the ground. "Watch them children, Bobby Lee," he said. "You know they make me nervous." He looked at the six of them huddled together in front of him and he seemed to be embarrassed as if he couldn't think of anything to say. "Ain't a cloud in the sky," he remarked, looking up at it. "Don't see no sun but don't see no cloud neither."

"Yes, it's a beautiful day," said the grandmother. "Listen," she said, "you shouldn't call yourself The Misfit because I know you're a good man at heart. I can just look at you and tell."

"Hush!" Bailey yelled. "Hush! Everybody shut up and let me handle this!" He was squatting in the position of a runner about to sprint forward but he didn't move.

"I pre-chate that, lady," The Misfit said and drew a little circle in the ground with the butt of his gun.

"It'll take a half a hour to fix this here car," Hiram called, looking over the raised hood of it.

"Well, first you and Bobby Lee get him and that little boy to step over yonder with you," The Misfit said, pointing to Bailey and John Wesley. "The boys want to ast you something," he said to Bailey. "Would you mind stepping back in them woods there with them?"

"Listen," Bailey began, "we're in a terrible predicament! Nobody realizes what this is," and his voice cracked. His eyes were as blue and intense as the parrots in his shirt and he remained perfectly still.

The grandmother reached up to adjust her hat brim as if she were going to the woods with him but it came off in her hand. She stood staring at it and after a second she let it fall on the ground. Hiram pulled Bailey up by the arm as if he were assisting an old man. John Wesley caught hold of his father's hand and Bobby Lee followed. They went off toward the woods and just as they reached the dark edge, Bailey turned and supporting himself against a gray naked pine trunk, he shouted, "I'll be back in a minute, Mamma, wait on me!"

"Come back this instant!" his mother shrilled but they all disappeared into the woods.

"Bailey Boy!" the grandmother called in a tragic voice but she found she was looking at The Misfit squatting on the ground in front of her. "I just know you're a good man," she said desperately. "You're not a bit common!"

"Nome, I ain't a good man," The Misfit said after a second as if he had considered her statement carefully, "but I ain't the worst in the world neither. My daddy said I was a different breed of dog from my brothers and sisters. 'You know,' Daddy said, 'it's some that can live their whole life out without asking about it and it's others has to know why it is, and this boy is one of the latters. He's going to be into everything!'" He put on his black hat and looked up suddenly and then away deep into the woods as if he were embarrassed again. "I'm sorry I don't have on a shirt before you ladies," he said, hunching his shoulders slightly. "We buried our clothes that we had on when we escaped and we're just making do until we can get better. We borrowed these from some folks we met," he explained.

"That's perfectly all right," the grandmother said. "Maybe Bailey has an extra shirt in his suitcase."

"I'll look and see terrectly," The Misfit said.

"Where are they taking him?" the children's mother screamed.

"Daddy was a card himself," The Misfit said. "You couldn't put anything over on him. He never got in trouble with the Authorities though. Just had the knack of handling them."

"You could be honest too if you'd only try," said the grandmother. "Think how wonderful it would be to settle down and live a comfortable life and not have to think about somebody chasing you all the time."

The Misfit kept scratching in the ground with the butt of his gun as if he were thinking about it. "Yes'm, somebody is always after you," he murmured.

The grandmother noticed how thin his shoulder blades were just behind his hat because she was standing up looking down on him. "Do you ever pray?" she asked.

He shook his head. All she saw was the black hat wiggle between his shoulder blades. "Nome," he said.

There was a pistol shot from the woods, followed closely by another. Then silence. The old lady's head jerked around. She could hear the wind move through the tree tops like a long satisfied insuck of breath. "Bailey Boy!" she called.

"I was a gospel singer for a while," The Misfit said. "I been most everything. Been in the arm service, both land and sea, at home and abroad, been twict married, been an undertaker, been with the railroads, plowed Mother Earth, been in a tornado, seen a man burnt alive oncet," and he looked up at the children's mother and the little girl who were sitting close together, their faces white and their eyes glassy; "I even seen a woman flogged," he said.

"Pray, pray," the grandmother began, "pray, pray ..."

"I never was a bad boy that I remember of," The Misfit said in an almost dreamy voice, "but somewheres along the line I done something wrong and got sent to the penitentiary. I was buried alive," and he looked up and held her attention to him by a steady stare.

"That's when you should have started to pray," she said. "What did you do to get sent to the penitentiary that first time?"

"Turn to the right, it was a wall," The Misfit said, looking up again at the cloudless sky. "Turn to the left, it was a wall. Look up it was a ceiling, look down it was a floor. I forget what I done, lady. I set there and set there, trying to remember what it was I done and I ain't recalled it to this day. Oncet in a while, I would think it was coming to me, but it never come."

"Maybe they put you in by mistake," the old lady said vaguely.

"Nome," he said. "It wasn't no mistake. They had the papers on me."

"You must have stolen something," she said.

The Misfit sneered slightly. "Nobody had nothing I wanted," he said. "It was a head-doctor at the penitentiary said what I had done was kill my daddy but I known that for a lie. My daddy died in nineteen ought nineteen of the epidemic flu and I never had a thing to do with it. He was buried in the Mount Hopewell Baptist churchyard and you can go there and see for yourself."

"If you would pray," the old lady said, "Jesus would help you."

"That's right," The Misfit said.

"Well then, why don't you pray?" she asked trembling with delight suddenly.

"I don't want no hep," he said. "I'm doing all right by myself."

Bobby Lee and Hiram came ambling back from the woods. Bobby Lee was dragging a yellow shirt with bright blue parrots in it.

"Thow me that shirt, Bobby Lee," The Misfit said. The shirt came flying at him and landed on his shoulder and he put it on. The grandmother couldn't name what the shirt reminded her of. "No, lady," The Misfit said while he was buttoning it up, "I found out the crime don't matter. You can do one thing or you can do another, kill a man or take a tire off his car, because sooner or later you're going to forget what it was you done and just be punished for it."

The children's mother had begun to make heaving noises as if she couldn't get her breath. "Lady," he asked, "would you and that little girl like to step off yonder with Bobby Lee and Hiram and join your husband?"

"Yes, thank you," the mother said faintly. Her left arm dangled helplessly and she was holding the baby, who had gone to sleep, in the other. "Hep that lady up, Hiram," The Misfit said as she struggled to climb out of the ditch, "and Bobby Lee, you hold onto that little girl's hand."

"I don't want to hold hands with him," June Star said. "He reminds me of a pig."

The fat boy blushed and laughed and caught her by the arm and pulled her into the woods after Hiram and her mother.

Alone with The Misfit, the grandmother found that she had lost her voice. There was not a cloud in the sky nor any sun. There was nothing around her but woods. She wanted to tell him that he must pray. She opened and closed her mouth several times before anything came out. Finally she found herself saying,

"Jesus. Jesus," meaning, Jesus will help you, but the way she was saying it, it sounded as if she might be cursing.

"Yes'm," The Misfit said as if he agreed. "Jesus thown everything off balance. It was the same case with Him as with me except He hadn't committed any crime and they could prove I had committed one because they had the papers on me. Of course," he said, "they never shown me my papers. That's why I sign myself now. I said long ago, you get you a signature and sign everything you do and keep a copy of it. Then you'll know what you done and you can hold up the crime to the punishment and see do they match and in the end you'll have something to prove you ain't been treated right. I call myself The Misfit," he said, "because I can't make what all I done wrong fit what all I gone through in punishment."

There was a piercing scream from the woods, followed closely by a pistol report. "Does it seem right to you, lady, that one is punished a heap and another ain't punished at all?"

"Jesus!" the old lady cried. "You've got good blood! I know you wouldn't shoot a lady! I know you come from nice people! Pray! Jesus, you ought not to shoot a lady. I'll give you all the money I've got!"

"Lady," The Misfit said, looking beyond her far into the woods, "there never was a body that give the undertaker a tip."

There were two more pistol reports and the grandmother raised her head like a parched old turkey hen crying for water and called, "Bailey Boy, Bailey Boy!" as if her heart would break.

"Jesus was the only One that ever raised the dead," The Misfit continued, "and He shouldn't have done it. He thown everything off balance. If He did what He said, then it's nothing for you to do but thow away everything and follow Him, and if He didn't, then it's nothing for you to do but enjoy the few minutes you got left the best way you can—by killing somebody or burning down his house or doing some other meanness to him. No pleasure but meanness," he said and his voice had become almost a snarl.

"Maybe He didn't raise the dead," the old lady mumbled, not knowing what she was saying and feeling so dizzy that she sank down in the ditch with her legs twisted under her.

"I wasn't there so I can't say He didn't," The Misfit said. "I wisht I had of been there," he said, hitting the ground with his fist. "It ain't right I wasn't there because if I had of been there I would of known. Listen lady," he said in a high voice, "if I had of been there I would of known and I wouldn't be like I am now." His voice seemed about to crack and the grandmother's head cleared for an instant. She saw the man's face twisted close to her own as if he were going to cry and she murmured, "Why you're one of my babies. You're one of my own children!" She reached out and touched him on the shoulder. The Misfit sprang back as if a snake had bitten him and shot her three times through the chest. Then he put his gun down on the ground and took off his glasses and began to clean them.

Hiram and Bobby Lee returned from the woods and stood over the ditch, looking down at the grandmother who half sat and half lay in a puddle of blood with her legs crossed under her like a child's and her face smiling up at the cloudless sky.

Without his glasses, The Misfit's eyes were red-rimmed and pale and defenseless-looking. "Take her off and thow her where you thown the others," he said, picking up the cat that was rubbing itself against his leg.

"She was a talker, wasn't she?" Bobby Lee said, sliding down the ditch with a yodel.

"She would of been a good woman," The Misfit said, "if it had been somebody there to shoot her every minute of her life."

"Some fun!" Bobby Lee said.

"Shut up, Bobby Lee," The Misfit said. "It's no real pleasure in life."

—1953

URSULA K. LE GUIN

Ursula K. Le Guin was born in 1929 in Berkeley, California to the cultural anthropologist Alfred Kroeber and the anthropologist and writer Theodora Kroeber. Le Guin studied at Radcliffe College and did graduate work at Columbia University. In addition to her twenty-two novels, she has published seven books of poetry, seven volumes of short stories, twelve books for children, and four works in translation, including a translation of Lao Tzu's *Tao Te Ching*.

Le Guin writes in many genres, but is best known for her pioneering work in science fiction and fantasy. Despite the lack of critical respect accorded these genres early in her career, she has achieved both popularity and acclaim; among her many honours are five Hugo Awards, five Nebula awards, and a National Book Award. Of her entry into science fiction, Le Guin has said: "Literature [had] been categorized as 'realism,' and if you weren't writing realism, you weren't respectable. I had to ignore that and say to myself that I could do things in science fiction that I could never do in realism."

Le Guin has created a number of vividly imagined fictional worlds in her speculative fiction. The most famous of these are the archipelago Earthsea, the setting of her six-part Books of Earthsea series, and the Hainish universe, a complex planetary system in which many of her works, beginning with *Rocannon's World* in 1966, are set. When "world-making," her focus is very largely on geography (she begins the creation of any new world by drawing a map) and on the details of everyday life.

Since the late 1960s, social justice and gender issues have been central concerns in Le Guin's writing. *The Left Hand of Darkness*, a 1969 novel, is set on a planet whose citizens are androgynous, and recent stories and novels in the Earthsea series have undermined the traditional science fiction model (often found in Le Guin's own early work, she admits) of the solitary male hero. Le Guin is also notable for deliberately writing protagonists that are people of colour, but not emphasizing their race in the story; she has called this a "sneaky approach" to making readers empathize with characters of colour.

"The Ones Who Walk Away from Omelas" was first published in *New Dimensions*, a science fiction anthology, in 1973. In her introduction to the story in her collection *The Wind's Twelve Quarters* (1975), Le Guin writes that she was inspired in part by a road sign ("Salem, Oregon" read backwards) and in part by a quotation from the philosopher William James, in which he writes of the "specifical and independent sort of emotion" that would make us resist perfect happiness for millions if it depended on the terrible suffering of one person.

The Ones Who Walk Away from Omelas

URSULA K. LE GUIN

WITH A clamor of bells that set the swallows soaring, the Festival of Summer came to the city. Omelas, bright-towered by the sea. The rigging of the boats in harbor sparkled with flags. In the streets between houses with red roofs and painted walls, between old moss-grown gardens and under avenues of trees, past great parks and public buildings, processions moved. Some were decorous: old people in long stiff robes of mauve and grey, grave master workmen, quiet, merry women carrying their babies and chatting as they walked. In other streets the music beat faster, a shimmering of gong and tambourine, and the people went dancing, the procession was a dance. Children dodged in and out, their high calls rising like the swallows' crossing flights over the music and the singing. All the processions wound towards the north side of the city, where on the great water-meadow called the Green Fields boys and girls, naked in the bright air, with mud-stained feet and ankles and long, lithe arms, exercised their restive horses before the race. The horses wore no gear at all but a halter without bit. Their manes were braided with streamers of silver, gold, and green. They flared their nostrils and pranced and boasted to one another; they were vastly excited, the horse being the only animal who has adopted our ceremonies as his own. Far off to the north and west the mountains stood up half encircling Omelas on her bay. The air of morning was so clear that the snow still crowning the Eighteen Peaks burned with white-gold fire across the miles of sunlit air, under the dark blue of the sky. There was just enough wind to make the banners that marked the racecourse snap and flutter now and then. In the silence of the broad green meadows one could hear the music winding through the city streets, farther and nearer and ever approaching, a cheerful faint sweetness of the air that from time to time trembled and gathered together and broke out into the great joyous clanging of the bells.

Joyous! How is one to tell about joy? How describe the citizens of Omelas?

They were not simple folk, you see, though they were happy. But we do not say the words of cheer much any more. All smiles have become archaic.[1] Given a description such as this one tends to make certain assumptions. Given a description such as this one tends to look next for the King, mounted on a splendid stallion and surrounded by his noble knights, or perhaps in a golden litter borne by great-muscled slaves. But there was no king. They did not use swords, or keep slaves. They were not barbarians. I do not know the rules and laws of their society, but I suspect that they were singularly few. As they did without monarchy and slavery, so they also got on without the stock exchange, the advertisement, the secret police, and the bomb. Yet I repeat that these were not simple folk, not dulcet shepherds, noble savages, bland utopians. They were not less complex than us. The trouble is that we have a bad habit, encouraged by pedants and sophisticates, of considering happiness as something rather stupid. Only pain is intellectual, only evil interesting. This is the treason of the artist: a refusal to admit the banality of evil and the terrible boredom of pain. If you can't lick 'em, join 'em. If it hurts, repeat it. But to praise despair is to condemn delight, to embrace violence is to lose hold of everything else. We have almost lost hold; we can no longer describe a happy man, nor make any celebration of joy. How can I tell you about the people of Omelas? They were not naive and happy children—though their children were, in fact, happy. They were mature, intelligent, passionate adults whose lives were not wretched. O miracle! but I wish I could describe it better. I wish I could convince you. Omelas sounds in my words like a city in a fairy tale, long ago and far away, once upon a time. Perhaps it would be best if you imagined it as your own fancy bids, assuming it will rise to the occasion, for certainly I cannot suit you all. For instance, how about technology? I think that there would be no cars or helicopters in and above the streets; this follows from the fact that the people of Omelas are happy people. Happiness is based on a just discrimination of what is necessary, what is neither necessary nor destructive, and what is destructive. In the middle category, however—that of the unnecessary but undestructive, that of comfort, luxury, exuberance, etc.—they could perfectly well have central heating, subway trains, washing machines, and all kinds of marvelous devices not yet invented here, floating light-sources, fuelless power, a cure for the common cold. Or they could have none of that: it doesn't matter. As you like it. I incline to think that people from towns up and down the coast have been coming in to Omelas during the last days before the Festival on very fast little trains and double-decked

1 A reference to the "archaic smile," an expression found on the faces of many sculpted figures from Ancient Greece.

trains and that the train station of Omelas is actually the handsomest building in town, though plainer than the magnificent Farmers' Market. But even granted trains, I fear that Omelas so far strikes some of you as goody-goody. Smiles, bells, parades, horses, bleh. If so, please add an orgy. If an orgy would help, don't hesitate. Let us not, however, have temples from which issue beautiful nude priests and priestesses already half in ecstasy and ready to copulate with any man or woman, lover or stranger, who desires union with the deep godhead of the blood, although that was my first idea. But really it would be better not to have any temples in Omelas—at least, not manned temples. Religion yes, clergy no. Surely the beautiful nudes can just wander about, offering themselves like divine soufflés to the hunger of the needy and the rapture of the flesh. Let them join the processions. Let tambourines be struck above the copulations, and the glory of desire be proclaimed upon the gongs, and (a not unimportant point) let the offspring of these delightful rituals be beloved and looked after by all. One thing I know there is none of in Omelas is guilt. But what else should there be? I thought at first there were no drugs, but that is puritanical. For those who like it, the faint insistent sweetness of *drooz* may perfume the ways of the city, *drooz* which first brings a great lightness and brilliance to the mind and limbs, and then after some hours a dreamy languor, and wonderful visions at last of the very arcana and inmost secrets of the Universe, as well as exciting the pleasure of sex beyond all belief; and it is not habit-forming. For more modest tastes I think there ought to be beer. What else, what else belongs in the joyous city? The sense of victory, surely, the celebration of courage. But as we did without clergy, let us do without soldiers. The joy built upon successful slaughter is not the right kind of joy; it will not do; it is fearful and it is trivial. A boundless and generous contentment, a magnanimous triumph felt not against some outer enemy but in communion with the finest and fairest in the souls of all men everywhere and the splendor of the world's summer: this is what swells the hearts of the people of Omelas, and the victory they celebrate is that of life. I really don't think many of them need to take *drooz*.

Most of the processions have reached the Green Fields by now. A marvelous smell of cooking goes forth from the red and blue tents of the provisioners. The faces of small children are amiably sticky; in the benign grey beard of a man a couple of crumbs of rich pastry are entangled. The youths and girls have mounted their horses and are beginning to group around the starting line of the course. An old woman, small, fat, and laughing, is passing out flowers from a basket, and tall young men wear her flowers in their shining hair. A child of nine or ten sits at the edge of the crowd, alone, playing on a wooden flute. People pause to listen, and they smile, but they do not speak to him, for he never ceases playing and never sees them, his dark eyes wholly rapt in the sweet, thin magic of the tune.

He finishes, and slowly lowers his hands holding the wooden flute.

As if that little private silence were the signal, all at once a trumpet sounds from the pavillion near the starting line: imperious, melancholy, piercing. The horses rear on their slender legs, and some of them neigh in answer. Sober-faced, the young riders stroke the horses' necks and soothe them, whispering, "Quiet, quiet, there my beauty, my hope...." They begin to form in rank along the starting line. The crowds along the racecourse are like a field of grass and flowers in the wind. The Festival of Summer has begun.

Do you believe? Do you accept the festival, the city, the joy? No? Then let me describe one more thing.

In a basement under one of the beautiful public buildings of Omelas, or perhaps in the cellar of one of its spacious private homes, there is a room. It has one locked door, and no window. A little light seeps in dustily between cracks in the boards, secondhand from a cobwebbed window somewhere across the cellar. In one corner of the little room a couple of mops, with stiff, clotted, foul-smelling heads, stand near a rusty bucket. The floor is dirt, a little damp to the touch, as cellar dirt usually is. The room is about three paces long and two wide: a mere broom closet or disused tool room. In the room a child is sitting. It could be a boy or a girl. It looks about six, but actually is nearly ten. It is feeble-minded. Perhaps it was born defective, or perhaps it has become imbecile through fear, malnutrition, and neglect. It picks its nose and occasionally fumbles vaguely with its toes or genitals, as it sits hunched in the corner farthest from the bucket and the two mops. It is afraid of the mops. It finds them horrible. It shuts its eyes, but it knows the mops are still standing there; and the door is locked; and nobody will come. The door is always locked; and nobody ever comes, except that sometimes—the child has no understanding of time or interval—sometimes the door rattles terribly and opens, and a person, or several people, are there. One of them may come in and kick the child to make it stand up. The others never come close, but peer in at it with frightened, disgusted eyes. The food bowl and the water jug are hastily filled, the door is locked, the eyes disappear. The people at the door never say anything, but the child, who has not always lived in the tool room, and can remember sunlight and its mother's voice, sometimes speaks. "I will be good," it says. "Please let me out. I will be good!" They never answer. The child used to scream for help at night, and cry a good deal, but now it only makes a kind of whining, "eh-haa, eh-haa," and it speaks less and less often. It is so thin there are no calves to its legs; its belly protrudes; it lives on a half-bowl of corn meal and grease a day. It is naked. Its buttocks and thighs are a mass of festered sores, as it sits in its own excrement continually.

They all know it is there, all the people of Omelas. Some of them have come to see it, others are content merely to know it is there. They all know that it has to be there. Some of them understand why, and some do not, but they all understand that their happiness, the beauty of their city, the tenderness of their friendships, the health of their children, the wisdom of their scholars, the skill of their makers, even the abundance of their harvest and the kindly weathers of their skies, depend wholly on this child's abominable misery.

This is usually explained to children when they are between eight and twelve, whenever they seem capable of understanding; and most of those who come to see the child are young people, though often enough an adult comes, or comes back, to see the child. No matter how well the matter has been explained to them, these young spectators are always shocked and sickened at the sight. They feel disgust, which they had thought themselves superior to. They feel anger, outrage, impotence, despite all the explanations. They would like to do something for the child. But there is nothing they can do. If the child were brought up into the sunlight out of that vile place, if it were cleaned and fed and comforted, that would be a good thing, indeed; but if it were done, in that day and hour all the prosperity and beauty and delight of Omelas would wither and be destroyed. Those are the terms. To exchange all the goodness and grace of every life in Omelas for that single, small improvement: to throw away the happiness of thousands for the chance of the happiness of one: that would be to let guilt within the walls indeed.

The terms are strict and absolute; there may not even be a kind word spoken to the child.

Often the young people go home in tears, or in a tearless rage, when they have seen the child and faced this terrible paradox. They may brood over it for weeks or years. But as time goes on they begin to realize that even if the child could be released, it would not get much good of its freedom: a little vague pleasure of warmth and food, no doubt, but little more. It is too degraded and imbecile to know any real joy. It has been afraid too long ever to be free of fear. Its habits are too uncouth for it to respond to humane treatment. Indeed, after so long it would probably be wretched without walls about it to protect it, and darkness for its eyes, and its own excrement to sit in. Their tears at the bitter injustice dry when they begin to perceive the terrible justice of reality and to accept it. Yet it is their tears and anger, the trying of their generosity and the acceptance of their helplessness, which are perhaps the true source of the splendor of their lives. Theirs is no vapid, irresponsible happiness. They know that they, like the child, are not free. They know compassion. It is the existence of the child, and their knowledge of its existence, that makes possible the nobility of their architecture, the poignancy of their music, the profundity of their science. It is because of the child that they are so gentle with children. They know that if the wretched one were not there snivelling in the dark, the other one, the flute-player, could make no joyful music as the young riders line up in their beauty for the race in the sunlight of the first morning of summer.

Now do you believe in them? Are they not more credible? But there is one more thing to tell, and this is quite incredible.

At times one of the adolescent girls or boys who go to see the child does not go home to weep or rage, does not, in fact, go home at all. Sometimes also a man or woman much older falls silent for a day or two, and then leaves home. These people go out into the street, and walk down the street alone. They keep walking, and walk straight out of the city of Omelas, through the beautiful gates. They keep walking across the farmlands of Omelas. Each one goes alone, youth or girl, man or woman. Night falls; the traveler must pass down village streets, between the houses with yellow-lit windows, and on out into the darkness of the fields. Each alone, they go west or north, towards the mountains. They go on. They leave Omelas, they walk ahead into the darkness, and they do not come back. The place they go towards is a place even less imaginable to most of us than the city of happiness. I cannot describe it at all. It is possible that it does not exist. But they seem to know where they are going, the ones who walk away from Omelas.

—1973

CHINUA ACHEBE

Albert Chinualumogu Achebe was born in 1930 in Ogidi, Igboland, in eastern Nigeria. Achebe's novels occupy a central place in the tradition of African literature; in content and form they trace African history from precolonialism through to decolonization and postcolonialism. He has been awarded numerous international literary prizes, including, in 2007, the Man Booker International Prize, which honours a living author for an entire body of work.

Achebe was born thirty years before Nigeria declared its independence from British colonial rule. As a boy he went to the Church Mission Society School, yet was simultaneously immersed in Igbo culture and tradition. In 1948 he began attending University College, Ibadan, initially to study medicine. He decided to quit medicine and take a degree in literature: "I was abandoning the realm of stories and they would not let me go."

Achebe's degree focused on the English canon, in which the only depiction of his own people was found in the narratives and language of colonizers—works such as Joyce Cary's *Mister Johnson* and Joseph Conrad's *Heart of Darkness*. Convinced of the power of stories to change history, Achebe became determined to re-tell the stories of Nigeria in order "to help my society regain belief in itself and put away the complexes of the years of denigration and self-abasement." *Things Fall Apart* (1958), Achebe's first novel, was followed by *No Longer At Ease* in 1960. Both are historical novels that begin in the precolonial period and trace the destructive legacy of colonialism through several generations. Though Achebe wrote in English, he forged a unique prose style that attempted to give voice to Nigerian experience in its own terms, weaving Igbo proverbs, terms, speech patterns, and images into the language of the colonizer.

In *Arrow of God* (1964) and *A Man of the People* (1966) Achebe continued to develop the themes of his earlier novels, but in these novels, set in the early years of Nigerian independence, he is also critical of the corruption and violence that were overtaking Nigerian politics. Achebe's work approaches experience and conflict from several perspectives, presenting them with intelligence and compassion: "Whatever you are is never enough; you must find a way to accept something however small from the other to make you whole."

In 1966 the Nigerian government was overthrown, and the country fell into chaos and civil war. Achebe joined the struggle to establish an independent Republic for the Igbo people, who were under threat of genocide. The Igbo Republic, Biafra, capitulated in 1970, after over a million civilians had starved to death as a result of an economic blockade. Achebe began writing poetry and short stories after this conflict; *Girls at War and Other Stories* was published in 1973. A car accident in Nigeria in 1990 left Achebe paralyzed from the waist down; he moved to the United States for treatment, and has lived there since.

"Dead Men's Path" is a story about Michael Obi, the young, idealistic headmaster of Ndume Central School. He and his wife intend to transform and beautify a school that had been considered behind the times. An ancestral path cuts across the school's organized garden, and the new headmaster refuses to allow the villagers to pass. The chaos and destruction that follow prompt many questions.

Dead Men's Path

CHINUA ACHEBE

MICHAEL OBI'S hopes were fulfilled much earlier than he had expected. He was appointed headmaster of Ndume Central School in January 1949. It had always been an unprogressive school, so the Mission authorities[1] decided to send a young and energetic man to run it. Obi accepted this responsibility with enthusiasm. He had many wonderful ideas and this was an opportunity to put them into practice. He had had sound secondary school education which designated him a "pivotal teacher" in the official records and set him apart from the other headmasters in the mission field. He was outspoken in his condemnation of the narrow views of these older and often less-educated ones.

"We shall make a good job of it, shan't we?" he asked his young wife when they first heard the joyful news of his promotion.

"We shall do our best," she replied. "We shall have such beautiful gardens and everything will be just *modern* and delightful...." In their two years of married life she had become completely infected by his passion for "modern methods" and his denigration of "these old and superannuated people in the teaching field

---

1 Many schools in African countries formerly colonized by the British were run by Christian missionary organizations.

who would be better employed as traders in the Onitsha[2] market." She began to see herself already as the admired wife of the young headmaster, the queen of the school.

The wives of the other teachers would envy her position. She would set the fashion in everything.... Then, suddenly, it occurred to her that there might not be other wives. Wavering between hope and fear, she asked her husband, looking anxiously at him.

"All our colleagues are young and unmarried," he said with enthusiasm which for once she did not share. "Which is a good thing," he continued.

"Why?"

"Why? They will give all their time and energy to the school."

Nancy was downcast. For a few minutes she became skeptical about the new school; but it was only for a few minutes. Her little personal misfortune could not blind her to her husband's happy prospects. She looked at him as he sat folded up in a chair. He was stoop-shouldered and looked frail. But he sometimes surprised people with sudden bursts of physical energy. In his present posture, however, all his bodily strength seemed to have retired behind his deep-set eyes, giving them an extraordinary power of penetration. He was only twenty-six, but looked thirty or more. On the whole, he was not unhandsome.

"A penny for your thoughts, Mike," said Nancy after a while, imitating the woman's magazine she read.

"I was thinking what a grand opportunity we've got at last to show these people how a school should be run."

Ndume School was backward in every sense of the word. Mr. Obi put his whole life into the work, and his wife hers too. He had two aims. A high standard of teaching was insisted upon, and the school compound was to be turned into a place of beauty. Nancy's dream-gardens came to life with the coming of the rains, and blossomed. Beautiful hibiscus and allamanda hedges in brilliant red and yellow marked out the carefully tended school compound from the rank neighborhood bushes.

One evening as Obi was admiring his work he was scandalized to see an old woman from the village hobble right across the compound, through a marigold flower-bed and the hedges. On going up there he found faint signs of an almost disused path from the village across the school compound to the bush on the other side.

---

2 A city in southeastern Nigeria.

"It amazes me," said Obi to one of his teachers who had been three years in the school, "that you people allowed the villagers to make use of this footpath. It is simply incredible." He shook his head.

"The path," said the teacher apologetically, "appears to be very important to them. Although it is hardly used, it connects the village shrine with their place of burial."

"And what has that got to do with the school?" asked the headmaster.

"Well, I don't know," replied the other with a shrug of the shoulders. "But I remember there was a big row some time ago when we attempted to close it."

"That was some time ago. But it will not be used now," said Obi as he walked away. "What will the Government Education Officer think of this when he comes to inspect the school next week? The villagers might, for all I know, decide to use the schoolroom for a pagan ritual during the inspection."

Heavy sticks were planted closely across the path at the two places where it entered and left the school premises. These were further strengthened with barbed wire.

Three days later the village priest of *Ani*[3] called on the headmaster. He was an old man and walked with a slight stoop. He carried a stout walking-stick which he usually tapped on the floor, by way of emphasis, each time he made a new point in his argument.

"I have heard," he said after the usual exchange of cordialities, "that our ancestral footpath has recently been closed...."

"Yes," replied Mr. Obi. "We cannot allow people to make a highway of our school compound."

"Look here, my son," said the priest bringing down his walking-stick, "this path was here before you were born and before your father was born. The whole life of this village depends on it. Our dead relatives depart by it and our ancestors visit us by it. But most important, it is the path of children coming in to be born...."

Mr. Obi listened with a satisfied smile on his face.

"The whole purpose of our school," he said finally, "is to eradicate just such beliefs as that. Dead men do not require footpaths. The whole idea is just fantastic. Our duty is to teach your children to laugh at such ideas."

"What you say may be true," replied the priest, "but we follow the practices of our fathers. If you reopen the path we shall have nothing to quarrel about. What I always say is: let the hawk perch and let the eagle perch." He rose to go.

---

3 The traditional belief system of the Igbo people of Nigeria, often called Odinani.

"I am sorry," said the young headmaster. "But the school compound cannot be a thoroughfare. It is against our regulations. I would suggest your constructing another path, skirting our premises. We can even get our boys to help in building it. I don't suppose the ancestors will find the little detour too burdensome."

"I have no more words to say," said the old priest, already outside.

Two days later a young woman in the village died in childbed. A diviner was immediately consulted and he prescribed heavy sacrifices to propitiate ancestors insulted by the fence.

Obi woke up next morning among the ruins of his work. The beautiful hedges were torn up not just near the path but right round the school, the flowers trampled to death and one of the school buildings pulled down ... That day, the white Supervisor came to inspect the school and wrote a nasty report on the state of the premises but more seriously about the "tribal-war situation developing between the school and the village, arising in part from the misguided zeal of the new headmaster."

—1953

ALICE MUNRO

Jonathan Franzen has written in *The New York Times* that Alice Munro "has a strong claim to being the best fiction writer now working in North America." Her short story collections have received three Governor General's Awards, two Giller Prizes, the Man Booker International Prize, and the Canada Council Molson Prize for her "outstanding lifetime contribution to the cultural and intellectual life of Canada." In 2010 she was honoured as Knight of the Order of Arts and Letters for her literary contributions. In 2013 she received the Nobel Prize in Literature.

Munro was born in 1931 in Wingham, Huron County, Ontario. Her mother was an ex-elementary school teacher and her father a fox farmer who later turned to turkey farming. Munro left Wingham in 1949 to study journalism at the University of Western Ontario as a scholarship student. In her second year, she switched her major to English, and her first short stories appeared in the university publication *Folio*. In 1951, her scholarship money ran out; she dropped out of university and married James Munro. The Munros moved to the West Coast where she sold her first short story, "A Basket of Strawberries," to *Mayfair* in 1953, and continued to write while raising two daughters. Shortly after the birth of her third daughter in 1966, she published her first collection of short stories, *Dance of the Happy Shades* (1968), which won Canada's Governor General's Award for Fiction; this collection was followed by a collection of linked short stories entitled *Lives of Girls and Women*, which won the 1971 Canadian Bookseller's Award.

The demands of motherhood affected Munro's writing in significant ways. She put it this way in a 1973 interview with Graeme Gibson: "in twenty years I've never had a day when I didn't have to think about somebody else's needs. And this means the writing has to be fitted in around it.... I think it's a miracle that I've produced anything." In 1973, Alice and James Munro divorced and she moved back to Ontario. She remarried in 1976 and returned to Ontario's Huron County area. In recent years she has divided her time between Clinton, Ontario and Comox, British Columbia. Her 2009 collection *Too Much Happiness* was preceded by *Runaway* (2004), *Carried Away* (2006), and *The View from Castle Rock* (2006).

Though Munro has set her stories in a wide variety of locations—from Scotland to Illinois to British Columbia—her use of Huron County as the setting for much of her fiction has led to the redefining of the area by national and international Munro readers and scholars as "Alice Munro country." Writing from the southern United States by authors such as Flannery O'Connor was influential for Munro, because, as she explains, she "felt there a country being depicted that was like my own ... the part of the country I come from is absolutely Gothic." The "Ontario Gothic" in Munro's work touches on the complexity that underlies the domestic—what the main character Del Jordan in *Lives of Girls and Women* describes as "dull, simple, amazing and unfathomable—deep caves paved with kitchen linoleum." "Miles City, Montana" (from the 1986 collection *The Progress of Love*) explores the image of linoleum-lined "caves" and the Gothic nature of a small-town Ontario childhood—a daughter's temporary misadventure leads the female narrator to reflect on the porous boundary that separates the apparently innocent world of the child from the world of the adult. Twenty-five years later, Munro considers this same boundary in her 2011 story "Gravel," when a young girl's slow reaction to a tragic situation creates a burden of guilt that she carries with her into adulthood.

Miles City, Montana

ALICE MUNRO

MY FATHER came across the field carrying the body of the boy who had been drowned. There were several men together, returning from the search, but he was the one carrying the body. The men were muddy and exhausted, and walked with their heads down, as if they were ashamed. Even the dogs were dispirited, dripping from the cold river. When they all set out, hours before, the dogs were nervy and yelping, the men tense and determined, and there was a constrained, unspeakable excitement about the whole scene. It was understood that they might find something horrible.

The boy's name was Steve Gauley. He was eight years old. His hair and clothes were mud-coloured now and carried some bits of dead leaves, twigs, and grass. He was like a heap of refuse that had been left out all winter. His face was turned in to my father's chest, but I could see a nostril, an ear, plugged up with greenish mud.

I don't think so. I don't think I really saw all this. Perhaps I saw my father carrying him, and the other men following along, and the dogs, but I would not have been allowed to get close enough to see something like mud in his nostril. I must have heard someone talking about that and imagined that I saw it. I see his face unaltered except for the mud—Steve Gauley's familiar, sharp-honed, sneaky-looking face—and it wouldn't have been like that; it would have been bloated and changed and perhaps muddied all over after so many hours in the water.

To have to bring back such news, such evidence, to a waiting family, particularly a mother, would have made searchers move heavily, but what was happening here was worse. It seemed a worse shame (to hear people talk) that there was no mother, no woman at all—no grandmother or aunt, or even a sister—to receive Steve Gauley and give him his due of grief. His father was a hired man, a drinker but not a drunk, an erratic man without being entertaining, not friendly but not exactly a troublemaker. His fatherhood seemed accidental, and the fact that the child had been left with him when the mother went away, and that they continued living together, seemed accidental. They lived in a steep-roofed, grey-shingled hillbilly sort of house and that was just a bit better than a shack—the father fixed the roof and put supports under the porch, just enough and just in time—and their life was held together in a similar manner; that is, just well enough to keep the Children's Aid at bay. They didn't eat meals together or cook for each other, but there was food. Sometimes the father would give Steve money to buy food at the store, and Steve was seen to buy quite sensible things, such as pancake mix and macaroni dinner.

I had known Steve Gauley fairly well. I had not liked him more often than I had liked him. He was two years older than I was. He would hang around our place on Saturdays, scornful of whatever I was doing but unable to leave me alone. I couldn't be on the swing without him wanting to try it, and if I wouldn't give it up he came and pushed me so that I went crooked. He teased the dog. He got me into trouble—deliberately and maliciously, it seemed to me afterward—by daring me to do things I wouldn't have thought of on my own: digging up the potatoes to see how big they were when they were still only the size of marbles, and pushing over the stacked firewood to make a pile we could jump off. At school, we never spoke to each other. He was solitary, though not tormented. But on Saturday mornings, when I saw his thin, self-possessed figure sliding through the cedar hedge, I knew I was in for something and he would decide what. Sometimes it was all right. We pretended we were cowboys who had come to tame wild horses. We played in the pasture by the river, not far from the place where Steve drowned. We were horses and riders both, screaming and neighing and bucking and waving whips of tree branches beside a little nameless river that flows into the Saugeen in southern Ontario.

The funeral was held in our house. There was not enough room at Steve's father's place for the large crowd that was expected because of the circumstances.

I have a memory of the crowded room but no picture of Steve in his coffin, or of the minister, or of wreaths of flowers. I remember that I was holding one flower, a white narcissus, which must have come from a pot somebody forced indoors, because it was too early for even the forsythia bush or the trilliums and march marigolds in the woods. I stood in a row of children, each of us holding a narcissus. We sang a children's hymn, which somebody played on our piano: "When He Cometh, When He Cometh, to Make Up His Jewels." I was wearing white ribbed stockings, which were disgustingly itchy, and wrinkled at the knees and ankles. The feeling of these stockings on my legs is mixed up with another feeling in my memory. It is hard to describe. It had to do with my parents. Adults in general but my parents in particular. My father, who had carried Steve's body from the river, and my mother, who must have done most of the arranging of this funeral. My father in his dark-blue suit and my mother in her brown velvet dress with the creamy satin collar. They stood side by side opening and closing their mouths for the hymn, and I stood removed from them, in the row of children, watching. I felt a furious and sickening disgust. Children sometimes have an access of disgust concerning adults. The size, the lumpy shapes, the bloated power. The breath, the coarseness, the hairiness, the horrid secretions. But this was more. And the accompanying anger had nothing sharp and self-respecting about it. There was no release, as when I would finally bend and pick up a stone and throw it at Steve Gauley. It could not be understood or expressed, though it died down after a while into a heaviness, then just a taste, an occasional taste—a thin, familiar misgiving.

o o o

Twenty years or so later, in 1961, my husband, Andrew, and I got a brand-new car, our first—that is, our first brand-new. It was a Morris Oxford, oyster-coloured (the dealer had some fancier name for the colour)—a big small car, with plenty of room for us and our two children. Cynthia was six and Meg three and a half.

Andrew took a picture of me standing beside the ear. I was wearing white pants, a black turtleneck, and sunglasses. I lounged against the car door, canting my hips to make myself look slim.

"Wonderful," Andrew said. "Great. You look like Jackie Kennedy." All over this continent probably, dark-haired, reasonably slender young women were told, when they were stylishly dressed or getting their pictures taken, that they looked like Jackie Kennedy.

Andrew took a lot of pictures of me, and of the children, our house, our garden, our excursions and possessions. He got copies made, labelled them carefully, and sent them back to his mother and his aunt and uncle in Ontario.

He got copies for me to send to my father, who also lived in Ontario, and I did so, but less regularly than he sent his. When he saw pictures he thought I had already sent lying around the house, Andrew was perplexed and annoyed. He liked to have this record go forth.

That summer, we were presenting ourselves, not pictures. We were driving back from Vancouver, where we lived, to Ontario, which we still called "home," in our new car. Five days to get there, ten days there, five days back. For the first time, Andrew had three weeks' holiday. He worked in the legal department at BC Hydro.

On a Saturday morning, we loaded suitcases, two thermos bottles—one filled with coffee and one with lemonade—some fruit and sandwiches, picture books and colouring books, crayons, drawing pads, insect repellent, sweaters (in case it got cold in the mountains), and our two children into the car. Andrew locked the house, and Cynthia said ceremoniously, "Goodbye, house."

Meg said, "Goodbye, house." Then she said, "Where will we live now?"

"It's not goodbye forever," said Cynthia. "We're coming back. Mother! Meg thought we weren't ever coming back!"

"I did not," said Meg, kicking the back of my seat.

Andrew and I put on our sunglasses, and we drove away, over the Lions Gate Bridge and through the main part of Vancouver. We shed our house, the neighbourhood, the city, and—at the crossing point between Washington and British Columbia—our country. We were driving east across the United States, taking the most northerly route, and would cross into Canada again at Sarnia, Ontario. I don't know if we chose this route because the Trans-Canada Highway was not completely finished at the time or if we just wanted the feeling of driving through a foreign, a very slightly foreign, country—that extra bit of interest and adventure.

We were both in high spirits. Andrew congratulated the car several times. He said he felt so much better driving it than our old car, a 1951 Austin that slowed down dismally on the hills and had a fussy-old-lady image. So Andrew said now.

"What kind of image does this one have?" said Cynthia. She listened to us carefully and liked to try out new words such as "image." Usually she got them right.

"Lively," I said. "Slightly sporty. It's not show-off."

"It's sensible, but it has class," Andrew said. "Like my image."

Cynthia thought that over and said with cautious pride, "That means like you think you want to be, Daddy?"

As for me, I was happy because of the shedding. I loved taking off. In my own house, I seemed to be more often looking for a place to hide—sometimes from the children but more often from the jobs to be done and the phone ringing and the sociability of the neighbourhood. I wanted to hide so that I could get busy at my real work, which was a sort of wooing of distant parts of myself. I lived in a state of siege, always losing just what I wanted to hold on to. But on trips there was no difficulty. I could be talking to Andrew, talking to the children and looking at whatever they wanted me to look at—a pig on a sign, a pony in a field, a Volkswagen on a revolving stand—and pouring lemonade into plastic cups, and all the time those bits and pieces would be flying together inside me. The essential composition would be achieved. This made me hopeful and lighthearted. It was being a watcher that did it. A watcher, not a keeper.

We turned east at Everett and climbed into the Cascades. I showed Cynthia our route on the map. First I showed her the map of the whole United States, which showed also the bottom part of Canada. Then I turned to the separate maps of each of the states we were going to pass through. Washington, Idaho, Montana, North Dakota, Minnesota, Wisconsin. I showed her the dotted line across Lake Michigan, which was the route of the ferry we would take. Then we would drive across Michigan to the bridge that linked the United States and Canada at Sarnia, Ontario. Home.

Meg wanted to see, too.

"You won't understand," said Cynthia. But she took the road atlas into the back seat.

"Sit back," she said to Meg. "Sit still. I'll show you."

I could hear her tracing the route for Meg, very accurately, just as I had done it for her. She looked up all the states' maps, knowing how to find them in alphabetical order.

"You know what that line is?" she said. "It's the road. That line is the road we're driving on. We're going right along this line."

Meg did not say anything.

"Mother, show me where we are right this minute," said Cynthia.

I took the atlas and pointed out the road through the mountains, and she took it back and showed it to Meg. "See where the road is all wiggly?" she said. "It's wiggly because there are so many turns in it. The wiggles are the turns." She flipped some pages and waited a moment. "Now," she said, "show me where we are." Then she called to me, "Mother, she understands! She pointed to it! Meg understands maps!"

It seems to me now that we invented characters for our children. We had them firmly set to play their parts. Cynthia was bright and diligent, sensitive, courteous, watchful. Sometimes we teased her for being too conscientious, too eager to be what we in fact depended on her to be. Any reproach or failure, any rebuff, went terribly deep with her. She was fair-haired, fair-skinned, easily showing the effects of the sun, raw winds, pride, or humiliation. Meg was more solidly built, more reticent—not rebellious but stubborn sometimes, mysterious. Her silences seemed to us to show her strength of character, and her negatives were taken as signs of imperturbable independence. Her hair was brown, and we cut it in straight bangs. Her eyes were a light hazel, clear and dazzling.

We were entirely pleased with these characters, enjoying the contradictions as well as the confirmations of them. We disliked the heavy, the uninventive, approach to being parents. I had a dread of turning into a certain kind of mother—the kind whose body sagged, who moved in woolly-smelling, milky-smelling fog, solemn with trivial burdens. I believed that all the attention these mothers paid, their need to be burdened, was the cause of colic, bed-wetting, asthma. I favoured another approach—the mock desperation, the inflated irony of the professional mothers who wrote for magazines. In those magazine pieces, the children were splendidly self-willed, hard-edged, perverse, indomitable. So were the mothers, through their wit, indomitable. The real-life mothers I warmed to were the sort who would phone up and say, "Is my embryo Hitler by any chance over at your house?" They cackled clear above the milky fog.

We saw a dead deer strapped across the front of a pickup truck.

"Somebody shot it," Cynthia said. "Hunters shoot the deer."

"It's not hunting season yet," Andrew said. "They may have hit it on the road. See the sign for deer crossing?"

"I would cry if we hit one," Cynthia said sternly.

I had made peanut-butter-and-marmalade sandwiches for the children and salmon-and-mayonnaise for us. But I had not put any lettuce in, and Andrew was disappointed.

"I didn't have any," I said.

"Couldn't you have got some?"

"I'd have had to buy a whole head of lettuce just to get enough for the sandwiches, and I decided it wasn't worth it."

This was a lie. I had forgotten.

"They're a lot better with lettuce."

"I didn't think it made that much difference." After a silence, I said, "Don't be mad."

"I'm not mad. I like lettuce on sandwiches."

"I just didn't think it mattered that much."

"How would it be if I didn't bother to fill up the gas tank?"

"That's not the same thing."

"Sing a song," said Cynthia. She started to sing:

> Five little ducks went out one day,
> Over the hills and far away.

One little duck went
"Quack-quack-quack."
Four little ducks came swimming back.

Andrew squeezed my hand and said, "Let's not fight."

"You're right. I should have got lettuce."

"It doesn't matter that much."

I wish that I could get my feelings about Andrew to come together into a serviceable and dependable feeling. I had even tried writing two lists, one of things I liked about him, one of things I disliked—in the cauldron of intimate life, things I loved and things I hated—as if I hoped by this to prove something, to come to a conclusion one way or the other. But I gave it up when I saw that all it proved was what I already knew—that I had violent contradictions. Sometimes the very sound of his footsteps seemed to me tyrannical, the set of his mouth smug and mean, his hard, straight body a barrier interposed—quite consciously, even dutifully, and with a nasty pleasure in its masculine authority—between me and whatever joy or lightness I could get in life. Then, with not much warning, he became my good friend and most essential companion. I felt the sweetness of his light bones and serious ideas, the vulnerability of his love, which I imagined to be much purer and more straightforward than my own. I could be greatly moved by an inflexibility, a harsh propriety, that at other times I scorned. I would think how humble he was, really, taking on such a ready-made role of husband, father, breadwinner, and how I myself in comparison was really a secret monster of egotism. Not so secret, either—not from him.

At the bottom of our fights, we served up what we thought were the ugliest truths. "I know there is something basically selfish and basically untrustworthy about you," Andrew once said. "I've always known it. I also know that that is why I fell in love with you."

"Yes," I said, feeling sorrowful but complacent.

"I know that I'd be better off without you."

"Yes. You would."

"You'd be happier without me."

"Yes."

And finally—finally—racked and purged, we clasped hands and laughed, laughed at those two benighted people, ourselves. Their grudges, their grievances, their self-justification. We leap-frogged over them. We declared them liars. We would have wine with dinner, or decide to give a party.

I haven't seen Andrew for years, don't know if he is still thin, has gone completely grey, insists on lettuce, tells the truth, or is hearty and disappointed.

We stayed the night in Wenatchee, Washington, where it hadn't rained for weeks. We ate dinner in a restaurant built about a tree—not a sapling in a tub but a tall, sturdy cottonwood. In the early-morning light, we climbed out of the irrigated valley, up dry, rocky, very steep hillsides that would seem to lead to more hills, and there on the top was a wide plateau, cut by the great Spokane and Columbia rivers. Grainland and grassland, mile after mile. There were straight roads here, and little farming towns with grain elevators. In fact, there was a sign announcing that this county we were going through, Douglas County, had the second-highest wheat yield of any county in the United States. The towns had planted shade trees. At least, I thought they had been planted, because there were no such big trees in the countryside.

All this was marvellously welcome to me. "Why do I love it so much?" I said to Andrew. "Is it because it isn't scenery?"

"It reminds you of home," said Andrew. "A bout of severe nostalgia." But he said this kindly.

When we said "home" and meant Ontario, we had very different places in mind. My home was a turkey farm, where my father lived as a widower, and though it was the same house my mother had lived in, had papered, painted, cleaned, furnished, it showed the effects now of neglect and of some wild sociability. A life went on in it that my mother could not have predicted or condoned. There were parties for the turkey crew, the gutters and pluckers, and sometimes one or two of the young men would be living there temporarily, inviting their own friends and having their own impromptu parties. This life, I thought, was better for my father than being lonely, and I did not disapprove, had certainly no right to disapprove; Andrew did not like to go there, naturally enough, because he was not the sort who could sit around the kitchen table with the turkey crew, telling jokes. They were intimidated by him and contemptuous of him, and it seemed to me that my father, when they were around, had to be on their side. And it wasn't only Andrew who had trouble. I could manage those jokes, but it was an effort.

I wished for the days when I was little, before we had the turkeys. We had cows, and sold the milk to the cheese factory. A turkey farm is nothing like as pretty as a dairy farm or a sheep farm. You can see that the turkeys are on a straight path to becoming frozen carcasses and table meat. They don't have the pretence of a life of their own, a browsing idyll, that cattle have, or pigs in the dappled orchard. Turkey barns are long, efficient buildings—tin sheds. No beams or hay or warm stables. Even the smell of guano seems thinner and more offensive than the usual smell of stable manure. No hints there of hay coils and rail fences and songbirds and the flowering hawthorn. The turkeys were all let out into one long field, which they picked clean. They didn't look like great birds there but like fluttering laundry.

Once, shortly after my mother died, and after I was married—in fact, I was packing to join Andrew in Vancouver—I was at home alone for a couple of days with my father. There was a freakishly heavy rain all night. In the early light, we saw that the turkey field was flooded. At least, the low-lying parts of it were flooded—it was like a lake with many islands. The turkeys were huddled on these islands. Turkeys are very stupid. (My father would say, "You know a chicken? You know how stupid a chicken is? Well, a chicken is an Einstein compared with a turkey.") But they had managed to crowd to higher ground and avoid drowning. Now they might push each other off, suffocate each other, get cold and die. We couldn't wait for the water to go down. We went out in the old rowboat we had. I rowed and my father pulled the heavy, wet turkeys into the boat and we took them to the barn. It was still raining a little. The job was difficult and absurd and very uncomfortable. We were laughing. I was happy to be working with my father. I felt close to all hard, repetitive, appalling work, in which the body is finally worn out, the mind sunk (though sometimes the spirit can stay marvellously light), and I was homesick in advance for this life and this place. I thought that if Andrew could see me there in the rain, red-handed, muddy, trying to hold on to turkey legs and row the boat at the same time, he would only want to get me out of there and make me forget about it. The raw life angered him. My attachment to it angered him. I thought that I shouldn't have married him. But who else? One of the turkey crew?

And I didn't want to stay there. I might feel bad about leaving, but I would feel worse if somebody made me stay.

Andrew's mother lived in Toronto, in an apartment building looking out on Muir Park. When Andrew and his sister were both at home, his mother slept in the living room. Her husband, a doctor, had died when the children were still too young to go to school. She took a secretarial course and sold her house at Depression prices, moved to this apartment, managed to raise her children, with some help from relatives—her sister Caroline, her brother-in-law Roger. Andrew and his sister went to private schools and to camp in the summer.

"I suppose that was courtesy of the Fresh Air fund?" I said once, scornful of his claim that he had been poor. To my mind, Andrew's urban life had been sheltered and fussy. His mother came home with a headache from working all day in the noise, the harsh light of the department store office, but it did not occur to me that hers was a hard or admirable life. I don't think she herself believed that she was admirable—only unlucky. She worried about her work in the office, her clothes, her cooking, her children. She worried most of all about what Roger and Caroline would think.

Caroline and Roger lived on the east side of the park, in a handsome stone house. Roger was a tall man with a bald, freckled head, a fat, firm stomach. Some operation on his throat had deprived him of his voice—he spoke in a rough whisper. But everybody paid attention. At dinner once in the stone house—where all the dining-room furniture was enormous, darkly glowing, palatial—I asked him a question. I think it had to do with Whittaker Chambers, whose story was then appearing in the *Saturday Evening Post*. The question was mild in tone, but he guessed its subversive intent and took to calling me Mrs. Gromyko, referring to what he alleged to be my "sympathies." Perhaps he really craved an adversary, and could not find one. At that dinner, I saw Andrew's hand tremble as he lit his mother's cigarette. His Uncle Roger had paid for Andrew's education, and was on the board of directors of several companies.

"He is just an opinionated old man," Andrew said to me later. "What is the point of arguing with him?"

Before we left Vancouver, Andrew's mother had written, "Roger seems quite intrigued by the idea of your buying a small car!" Her exclamation mark showed apprehension. At that time, particularly in Ontario, the choice of a small European car over a large American car could be seen as some sort of declaration—a declaration of tendencies Roger had been sniffing after all along.

"It isn't that small a car," said Andrew huffily.

"That's not the point," I said. "The point is, it isn't any of his business!"

We spent the second night in Missoula. We had been told in Spokane, at a gas station, that there was a lot of repair work going on along Highway 2, and that we were in for a very hot, dusty drive, with long waits, so we turned on to the interstate and drove through Coeur d'Alene and Kellogg into Montana. After Missoula, we turned south toward Butte, but detoured to see Helena, the state capital. In the car, we played Who Am I?

Cynthia was somebody dead, and an American, and a girl. Possibly a lady. She was not in a story. She had not been seen on television. Cynthia had not read about her in a book. She was not anybody who had come to the kindergarten, or a relative of any of Cynthia's friends.

"Is she human?" said Andrew, with a sudden shrewdness.

"No! That's what you forgot to ask!"

"An animal," I said reflectively.

"Is that a question? Sixteen questions!"

"No, it is not a question. I'm thinking. A dead animal."

"It's the deer," said Meg, who hadn't been playing.

"That's not fair!" said Cynthia. "She's not playing!"

"What deer?" said Andrew.

I said, "Yesterday."

"The day before," said Cynthia. "Meg wasn't playing. Nobody got it."

"The deer on the truck," said Andrew.

"It was a lady deer, because it didn't have antlers, and it was an American and it was dead," Cynthia said.

Andrew said, "I think it's kind of morbid, being a dead deer."

"I got it," said Meg.

Cynthia said, "I think I know what morbid is. It's depressing."

Helena, an old silver-mining town, looked forlorn to us even in the morning sunlight. Then Bozeman and Billings, not forlorn in the slightest—energetic, strung-out towns, with miles of blinding tinsel fluttering over used-car lots. We got too tired and hot even to play Who Am I? These busy, prosaic cities reminded me of similar places in Ontario, and I thought about what was really waiting there—the great tombstone furniture of Roger and Caroline's dining-room, the dinners for which I must iron the children's dresses and warn them about forks, and then the other table a hundred miles away, the jokes of my father's crew. The pleasures I had been thinking of—looking at the countryside or drinking a Coke in an old-fashioned drugstore with fans and a high, pressed-tin ceiling—would have to be snatched in between.

"Meg's asleep," Cynthia said. "She's so hot. She makes me hot in the same seat with her."

"I hope she isn't feverish," I said, not turning around.

What are we doing this for, I thought, and the answer came—to show off. To give Andrew's mother and my father the pleasure of seeing their grandchildren. That was our duty. But beyond that we wanted to show them something. What strenuous children we were, Andrew and I, what relentless seekers of approbation. It was as if at some point we had received an unforgettable, indigestible message—that we were far from satisfactory, and that the most commonplace success in life was probably beyond us. Roger dealt out such messages, of course—that was his style—but Andrew's mother, my own mother and father couldn't have meant to do so. All they meant to tell us was "Watch out. Get along." My father, when I was in high school, teased me that I was getting to think I was so smart I would never find a boyfriend. He would have forgotten that in a week. I never forgot it. Andrew and I didn't forget things. We took umbrage.

"I wish there was a beach," said Cynthia.

"There probably is one," Andrew said. "Right around the next curve."

"There isn't a curve," she said, sounding insulted.

"That's what I mean."

"I wish there was some more lemonade."

"I will just wave my magic wand and produce some," I said. "Okay, Cynthia? Would you rather have grape juice? Will I do a beach while I'm at it?"

She was silent, and soon I felt repentant. "Maybe in the next town there might be a pool," I said. I looked at the map. "In Miles City. Anyway, there'll be something cool to drink."

"How far is it?" Andrew said.

"Not so far," I said. "Thirty miles, about."

"In Miles City," said Cynthia, in the tones of an incantation, "there is a beautiful blue swimming pool for children, and a park with lovely trees."

Andrew said to me, "You could have started something."

But there was a pool. There was a park, too, though not quite the oasis of Cynthia's fantasy. Prairie trees with thin leaves—cottonwood and poplars—worn grass, and a high wire fence around the pool. Within this fence, a wall, not yet completed, of cement blocks. There were no shouts or splashes; over the entrance I saw a sign that said the pool was closed every day from noon until two o'clock. It was then twenty-five after twelve.

Nevertheless I called out, "Is anybody there?" I thought somebody must be around, because there was a small truck parked near the entrance. On the side of the truck were these words: "We have Brains, to fix your Drains. (We have Roto-Rooter too.)"

A girl came out, wearing a red lifeguard's shirt over her bathing suit. "Sorry, we're closed."

"We were just driving through," I said.

"We close every day from twelve until two. It's on the sign." She was eating a sandwich.

"I saw the sign," I said. "But this is the first water we've seen for so long, and the children are awfully hot, and I wondered if they could just dip in and out—just five minutes. We'd watch them."

A boy came into sight behind her. He was wearing jeans and a T-shirt with the words "Roto-Rooter" on it.

I was going to say that we were driving from British Columbia to Ontario, but I remembered that Canadian place names usually meant nothing to Americans. "We're driving right across the country," I said. "We haven't time to wait for the pool to open. We were just hoping the children could get cooled off."

Cynthia came running up barefoot behind me. "Mother, Mother, where is my bathing suit?" Then she stopped, sensing the serious adult negotiations. Meg was climbing out of the car—just wakened, and her top pulled up and her shorts pulled down, showing her pink stomach.

"Is it just those two?" the girl said.

"Just the two. We'll watch them."

"I can't let any adults in. If it's just the two, I guess I could watch them. I'm having my lunch." She said to Cynthia, "Do you want to come in the pool?"

"Yes, please," said Cynthia firmly.

Meg looked at the ground.

"Just a short time, because the pool is really closed," I said. "We appreciate this very much," I said to the girl.

"Well, I can eat my lunch out there, if it's just the two of them." She looked toward the car as if she thought I might try to spring some more children on her.

When I found Cynthia's bathing suit, she took it into the changing room. She would not permit anybody, even Meg, to see her naked. I changed Meg, who stood on the front seat of the car. She had a pink cotton bathing suit with straps that crossed and buttoned. There were ruffles across the bottom.

"She *is* hot," I said. "But I don't think she's feverish."

I loved helping Meg to dress or undress, because her body still had the solid unself-consciousness, the sweet indifference, something of the milky smell, of a baby's body. Cynthia's body had long ago been pared down, shaped and altered, into Cynthia. We all liked to hug Meg, press and nuzzle her. Sometimes she would scowl and beat us off, and this forthright independence, this ferocious bashfulness, simply made her more appealing, more apt to be tormented and tickled in the way of family love.

Andrew and I sat in the car with the windows open. I could hear a radio playing, and thought it must belong to the girl or her boyfriend. I was thirsty, and got out of the car to look for a concession stand, or perhaps a soft-drink machine, somewhere in the park. I was wearing shorts, and the backs of my legs were slick with sweat. I saw a drinking fountain at the other side of the park and was walking toward it in a roundabout way, keeping to the shade of the trees. No place became real till you got out of the car. Dazed with the heat, with the sun on the blistered houses, the pavement, the burned grass, I walked slowly. I paid attention to a squashed leaf, ground a Popsicle stick under the heel of my sandal, squinted at a trash can strapped to a tree. This is the way you look at the poorest details of the world resurfaced, after you've been driving for a long time—you feel their singleness and precise location and the forlorn coincidence of your being there to see them.

Where are the children?

I turned around and moved quickly, not quite running, to a part of the fence beyond which the cement wall was not completed. I could see some of the pool. I saw Cynthia, standing about waist-deep in the water, fluttering her hands on the surface and discreetly watching something at the end of the pool, which I could not see. I thought by her pose, her discretion, the look on her face, that she must be watching some byplay between the lifeguard and her boyfriend. I couldn't see Meg. But I thought she must be playing in the shallow water—both the shallow and deep ends of the pool were out of my sight.

"Cynthia!" I had to call twice before she knew where my voice was coming from. "Cynthia! Where's Meg?"

It always seems to me, when I recall this scene, that Cynthia turns very gracefully toward me, then turns all around in the water—making me think of a ballerina on point—and spreads her arms in a gesture of the stage. "Dis-ap-peared!"

Cynthia was naturally graceful, and she did take dancing lessons, so these movements may have been as I have described. She did say "Disappeared" after looking all around the pool, but the strangely artificial style of speech and gesture, the lack of urgency is more likely my invention. The fear I felt instantly when I couldn't see Meg—even while I was telling myself she must be in the shallower water—must have made Cynthia's movements seem unbearably slow and inappropriate to me, and the tone in which she could say "Disappeared" before the implications struck her (or was she covering, at once, some ever-ready guilt?) was heard by me as quite exquisitely, monstrously self-possessed.

I cried out for Andrew, and the lifeguard came into view. She was pointing toward the deep end of the pool, saying, "What's that?"

There, just within my view, a cluster of pink ruffles appeared, a bouquet, beneath the surface of the water. Why would a lifeguard stop and point, why would she ask what that was, why didn't she just dive into the water and swim to it? She didn't swim; she ran all the way around the edge of the pool. But by that time Andrew was over the fence. So many things seemed not quite plausible—Cynthia's behaviour, then the lifeguard's—and now I had the impression that Andrew jumped with one bound over this fence, which seemed about seven feet high. He must have climbed it very quickly, getting a grip on the wire.

I could not jump or climb it, so I ran to the entrance, where there was a sort of lattice gate, locked. It was not very high, and I did pull myself over it. I ran through the cement corridors, through the disinfectant pool for your feet, and came out on the edge of the pool.

The drama was over.

Andrew had got to Meg first, and had pulled her out of the water. He just had to reach over and grab her, because she was swimming somehow, with her head underwater—she was moving toward the edge of the pool. He was carrying her now, and the lifeguard was trotting along behind. Cynthia had climbed out of the water and was running to meet them. The only person aloof from the situation was the boyfriend, who had stayed on the bench at the shallow end, drinking a milkshake. He smiled at me, and I thought that unfeeling of him, even though the danger was past. He may have meant it kindly. I noticed that he had not turned the radio off, just down.

Meg had not swallowed any water. She hadn't even scared herself. Her hair was plastered to her head and her eyes were wide open, golden with amazement.

"I was getting the comb," she said. "I didn't know it was deep."

Andrew said, "She was swimming! She was swimming by herself. I saw her bathing suit in the water and then I saw her swimming."

"She nearly drowned," Cynthia said. "Didn't she? Meg nearly drowned."

"I don't know how it could have happened," said the lifeguard. "One moment she was there, and the next she wasn't."

What had happened was that Meg had climbed out of the water at the shallow end and run along the edge of the pool toward the deep end. She saw a comb that somebody had dropped lying on the bottom. She crouched down and reached in to pick it up, quite deceived about the depth of the water. She went over the edge and slipped into the pool, making such a light splash that nobody heard—not the lifeguard, who was kissing her boyfriend, or Cynthia, who was watching them. That must have been the moment under the trees when I thought, Where are the children? It must have been the same moment. At that moment, Meg was slipping, surprised, into the treacherously clear blue water.

"It's okay," I said to the lifeguard, who was nearly crying. "She can move pretty fast." (Though that wasn't what we usually said about Meg at all. We said she thought everything over and took her time.)

"You swam, Meg," said Cynthia, in a congratulatory way. (She told us about the kissing later.)

"I didn't know it was deep," Meg said. "I didn't drown."

° ° °

We had lunch at a take-out place, eating hamburgers and fries at a picnic table not far from the highway. In my excitement, I forgot to get Meg a plain hamburger, and had to scrape off the relish and mustard with plastic spoons, then wipe the meat with a paper napkin, before she would eat it. I took advantage of the trash can there to clean out the car. Then we resumed driving east, with the car windows open in front. Cynthia and Meg fell asleep in the back seat.

Andrew and I talked quietly about what had happened. Suppose I hadn't had the impulse just at that moment to check on the children? Suppose we had gone uptown to get drinks, as we had thought of doing? How had Andrew got over the fence? Did he jump or climb? (He couldn't remember.) How had he reached Meg so quickly? And think of the lifeguard not watching. And Cynthia, taken up with the kissing. Not seeing anything else. Not seeing Meg drop over the edge.

Disappeared.

But she swam. She held her breath and came up swimming.

What a chain of lucky links.

That was all we spoke about—luck. But I was compelled to picture the opposite. At this moment, we could have been filling out forms. Meg removed from us, Meg's body being prepared for shipment. To Vancouver—where we had never noticed such a thing as a graveyard—or to Ontario? The scribbled drawings she had made this morning would still be in the back seat of the car. How could this be borne all at once, how did people bear it? The plump, sweet shoulders and hands and feet, the fine brown hair, the rather satisfied, secretive expression—all exactly the same as when she had been alive. The most ordinary tragedy. A child drowned in a swimming pool at noon on a sunny day. Things tidied up quickly. The pool opens as usual at two o'clock. The lifeguard is a bit shaken up and gets the afternoon off. She drives away with her boyfriend in the Roto-Rooter truck. The body sealed away in some kind of shipping coffin. Sedatives, phone calls, arrangements. Such a sudden vacancy, a blind sinking and shifting. Waking up groggy from the pills, thinking for a moment it wasn't true. Thinking if only we hadn't stopped, if only we hadn't taken this route, if only they hadn't let us use the pool. Probably no one would ever have known about the comb.

There's something trashy about this kind of imagining, isn't there? Something shameful. Laying your finger on the wire to get the safe shock, feeling a bit of what it's like, then pulling back. I believed that Andrew was more scrupulous than I about such things, and that at this moment he was really trying to think about something else.

When I stood apart from my parents at Steve Gauley's funeral and watched them, and had this new, unpleasant feeling about them, I thought that I was understanding something about them for the first time. It was a deadly serious thing. I was understanding that they were implicated. Their big, stiff, dressed-up bodies did not stand between me and sudden death, or any kind of death. They gave consent. So it seemed. They gave consent to the death of children and to my death not by anything they said or thought but by the very fact that they had made children—they had made me. They had made me, and for that reason my death—however grieved they were, however they carried on—would seem to them anything but impossible or unnatural. This was a fact, and even then I knew they were not to blame.

But I did blame them. I charged them with effrontery, hypocrisy. On Steve Gauley's behalf, and on behalf of all children, who knew that by rights they should have sprung up free, to live a new, superior kind of life, not to be caught in the snares of vanquished grown-ups, with their sex and funerals.

Steve Gauley drowned, people said, because he was next thing to an orphan and was let run free. If he had been warned enough and given chores to do and kept in check, he wouldn't have fallen from an untrustworthy tree branch into a spring pond, a full gravel pit near the river—he wouldn't have drowned. He was neglected, he was free, so he drowned. And his father took it as an accident, such as might happen to a dog. He didn't have a good suit for the funeral, and he didn't bow his head for the prayers. But he was the only grown-up that I let off the hook. He was the only one I didn't see giving consent. He couldn't prevent anything, but he wasn't implicated in anything, either—not like the others, saying the Lord's Prayer in their unnaturally weighted voices, oozing religion and dishonour.

At Glendive, not far from the North Dakota border, we had a choice—either to continue on the interstate or head north-east, toward Williston, taking Route 16, then some secondary roads that would get us back to Highway 2.

We agreed that the interstate would be faster, and that it was important to us not to spend too much time—that is, money—on the road. Nevertheless we decided to cut back to Highway 2.

"I just like the idea of it better," I said.

Andrew said, "That's because it's what we planned to do in the beginning."

"We missed seeing Kalispell and Havre. And Wolf Point. I like the name."

"We'll see them on the way back."

Andrew's saying "on the way back" was a surprising pleasure to me. Of course, I had believed that we would be coming back, with our car and our lives and our family intact, having covered all that distance, having dealt somehow with those loyalties and problems, held ourselves up for inspection in such a foolhardy way. But it was a relief to hear him say it.

"What I can't get over," said Andrew, "is how you got the signal. It's got to be some kind of extra sense that mothers have."

Partly I wanted to believe that, to bask in my extra sense. Partly I wanted to warn him—to warn everybody—never to count on it.

"What I can't understand," I said, "is how you got over the fence."

"Neither can I."

So we went on, with the two in the back seat trusting us, because of no choice, and we ourselves trusting to be forgiven, in time, for everything that had first to be seen and condemned by those children: whatever was flippant, arbitrary, careless, callous—all our natural, and particular, mistakes.

—1986

Gravel

ALICE MUNRO

AT THAT TIME we were living beside a gravel pit. Not a large one, hollowed out by monster machinery, just a minor pit that a farmer must have made some money from years before. In fact, the pit was shallow enough to lead you to think that there might have been some other intention for it—foundations for a house, maybe, that never made it any further.

My mother was the one who insisted on calling attention to it. "We live by the old gravel pit out the service-station road," she'd tell people, and laugh, because she was so happy to have shed everything connected with the house, the street—the husband—with the life she'd had before.

I barely remember that life. That is, I remember some parts of it clearly, but without the links you need to form a proper picture. All that I retain in my head of the house in town is the wallpaper with Teddy bears in my old room. In this new house, which was really a trailer, my sister, Caro, and I had narrow cots, stacked one above the other. When we first moved there, Caro talked to me a lot about our old house, trying to get me to remember this or that. It was when we were in bed that she talked like this, and generally the conversation ended with me failing to remember and her getting cross. Sometimes I thought I did remember, but out of contrariness or fear of getting things wrong I pretended not to.

It was summer when we moved to the trailer. We had our dog with us. Blitzee. "Blitzee loves it here," my mother said, and it was true. What dog wouldn't love to exchange a town street, even one with spacious lawns and big houses, for the wide-open countryside? She took to barking at every car that went past, as if she owned the road, and now and then she brought home a squirrel or a groundhog she'd killed. At first Caro was quite upset by this, and Neal would have a talk with her, explaining about a dog's nature and the chain of life in which some things had to eat other things.

"She gets her dog food," Caro argued, but Neal said, "Suppose she didn't? Suppose someday we all disappeared and she had to fend for herself?"

"I'm not going to," Caro said. "I'm not going to disappear, and I'm always going to look after her."

"You think so?" Neal said, and our mother stepped in to deflect him. Neal was always ready to get on the subject of the Americans and the atomic bomb, and our mother didn't think we were ready for that yet. She didn't know that when he brought it up I thought he was talking about an atomic bun. I knew that there was something wrong with this interpretation, but I wasn't about to ask questions and get laughed at.

Neal was an actor. In town there was a professional summer theatre, a new thing at the time, which some people were enthusiastic about and others worried about, fearing that it would bring in riffraff. My mother and father had been among those in favor, my mother more actively so, because she had more time. My father was an insurance agent and travelled a lot. My mother had got busy with various fund-raising schemes for the theatre and donated her services as an usher. She was good-looking and young enough to be mistaken for an actress. She'd begun to dress like an actress, too, in shawls and long skirts and dangling necklaces. She'd left her hair wild and stopped wearing makeup. Of course, I had not understood or even particularly noticed these changes at the time. My mother was my mother. But no doubt Caro had. And my father. Though, from all that I know of his nature and his feelings for my mother, I think he may have been proud to see how good she looked in these liberating styles and how well she fit in with the theatre people. When he spoke about this time later on, he said that he had always approved of the arts. I can imagine now how embarrassed my mother would have been, cringing and laughing to cover up her cringing, if he'd made this declaration in front of her theatre friends.

Well, then came a development that could have been foreseen and probably was, but not by my father. I don't know if it happened to any of the other volunteers. I do know, though I don't remember it, that my father wept and for a whole day followed my mother around the house, not letting her out of his sight and refusing to believe her. And, instead of telling him anything to make him feel better, she told him something that made him feel worse.

She told him that the baby was Neal's.

Was she sure?

Absolutely. She had been keeping track.

What happened then?

My father gave up weeping. He had to get back to work. My mother packed up our things and took us to live with Neal in the trailer he had found, out in the country. She said afterward that she had wept, too. But she said also that she had felt alive. Maybe for the first time in her life, truly alive. She felt as if she had been given a chance; she had started her life all over again. She'd walked out on her silver and her china and her decorating scheme and her flower garden and even on the books in her bookcase. She would live now, not read. She'd left her clothes hanging in the closet and her high-heeled shoes in their shoe trees. Her diamond ring and her wedding ring on the dresser. Her silk nightdresses in their drawer. She meant to go around naked at least some of the time in the country, as long as the weather stayed warm.

That didn't work out, because when she tried it Caro went and hid in her cot and even Neal said he wasn't crazy about the idea.

What did he think of all this? Neal. His philosophy, as he put it later, was to welcome whatever happened. Everything is a gift. We give and we take.

I am suspicious of people who talk like this, but I can't say that I have a right to be.

He was not really an actor. He had got into acting, he said, as an experiment. To see what he could find out about himself. In college, before he dropped out, he had performed as part of the chorus in "Oedipus Rex."[1] He had liked that—the giving yourself over, blending with others. Then one day, on the street in Toronto, he ran into a friend who was on his way to try out for a summer job with a new small-town theatre company. He went along, having nothing better to do, and ended up getting the job, while the other fellow didn't. He would play Banquo.[2] Sometimes they make Banquo's ghost visible, sometimes not. This time they wanted a visible version and Neal was the right size. An excellent size. A solid ghost.

He had been thinking of wintering in our town anyway, before my mother sprang her surprise. He had already spotted the trailer. He had enough carpentry experience to pick up work renovating the theatre, which would see him through till spring. That was as far ahead as he liked to think.

Caro didn't even have to change schools. She was picked up by the school bus at the end of the short lane that ran alongside the gravel pit. She had to make friends with the country children, and perhaps explain some things to the town children who had been her friends the year before, but if she had any difficulty with that I never heard about it.

Blitzee was always waiting by the road for her to come home.

I didn't go to kindergarten, because my mother didn't have a car. But I didn't mind doing without other children. Caro, when she got home, was enough for me. And my mother was often in a playful mood. As soon as it snowed that winter she and I built a snowman and she asked, "Shall we call it Neal?" I said O.K., and we stuck various things on it to make it funny. Then we decided that I would run out of the house when his car came and say, "Here's Neal, here's Neal!" but be pointing up at the snowman. Which I did, but Neal got out of the car mad and yelled that he could have run me over.

That was one of the few times that I saw him act like a father.

Those short winter days must have seemed strange to me—in town, the lights came on at dusk. But children get used to changes. Sometimes I wondered about

---

1 *Oedipus the King* (c. 429 BCE): a Greek tragedy written by Sophocles. A chorus of Theban Elders advise Oedipus throughout the play.

2 From *Macbeth* (1606), a tragedy by William Shakespeare: Macbeth has Banquo murdered when he perceives him as a threat to his rise to power. Banquo's ghost appears before Macbeth later in the play.

our other house. I didn't exactly miss it or want to live there again—I just wondered where it had gone.

My mother's good times with Neal went on into the night. If I woke up and had to go to the bathroom, I'd call for her. She would come happily but not in any hurry, with some piece of cloth or a scarf wrapped around her—also a smell that I associated with candlelight and music. And love.

Something did happen that was not so reassuring, but I didn't try to make much sense of it at the time. Blitzee, our dog, was not very big, but she didn't seem small enough to fit under Caro's coat. I don't know how Caro managed to do it. Not once but twice. She hid the dog under her coat on the school bus, and then, instead of going straight to school, she took Blitzee back to our old house in town, which was less than a block away. That was where my father found the dog, on the winter porch, which was not locked, when he came home for his solitary lunch. There was great surprise that she had got there, found her way home like a dog in a story. Caro made the biggest fuss, and claimed not to have seen the dog at all that morning. But then she made the mistake of trying it again, maybe a week later, and this time, though nobody on the bus or at school suspected her, our mother did.

I can't remember if our father brought Blitzee back to us. I can't imagine him in the trailer or at the door of the trailer or even on the road to it. Maybe Neal went to the house in town and picked her up. Not that that's any easier to imagine.

If I've made it sound as though Caro was unhappy or scheming all the time, that isn't the truth. As I've said, she did try to make me talk about things, at night in bed, but she wasn't constantly airing grievances. It wasn't her nature to be sulky. She was far too keen on making a good impression. She liked people to like her; she liked to stir up the air in a room with the promise of something you could even call merriment. She thought more about that than I did.

She was the one who most took after our mother, I think now.

There must have been some probing about what she'd done with the dog. I think I can remember some of it.

"I did it for a trick."

"Do you want to go and live with your father?"

I believe that was asked, and I believe she said no.

I didn't ask her anything. What she had done didn't seem strange to me. That's probably how it is with younger children—nothing that the strangely powerful older child does seems out of the ordinary.

Our mail was deposited in a tin box on a post, down by the road. My mother and I would walk there every day, unless it was particularly stormy, to see what had been left for us. We did this after I got up from my nap. Sometimes it was the only time we went outside all day. In the morning, we watched children's television shows—or she read while I watched. (She had not given up reading for very long.) We heated up some canned soup for lunch, then I went down for my nap while she read some more. She was quite big with the baby now and it stirred around in her stomach, so that I could feel it. Its name was going to be Brandy—already was Brandy—whether it was a boy or a girl.

One day when we were going down the lane for the mail, and were in fact not far from the box, my mother stopped and stood quite still.

"Quiet," she said to me, though I hadn't said a word or even played the shuffling game with my boots in the snow.

"I was being quiet," I said.

"Shush. Turn around."

"But we didn't get the mail."

"Never mind. Just walk."

Then I noticed that Blitzee, who was always with us, just behind or ahead of us, wasn't there anymore. Another dog was, on the opposite side of the road, a few feet from the mailbox.

My mother phoned the theatre as soon as we got home and let in Blitzee, who was waiting for us. Nobody answered. She phoned the school and asked someone to tell the bus driver to drive Caro up to the door. It turned out that the driver couldn't do that, because it had snowed since Neal last plowed the lane, but he did watch until she got to the house. There was no wolf to be seen by that time.

Neal was of the opinion that there never had been one. And if there had been, he said, it would have been no danger to us, weak as it was probably from hibernation.

Caro said that wolves did not hibernate. "We learned about them in school."

Our mother wanted Neal to get a gun.

"You think I'm going to get a gun and go and shoot a goddam poor mother wolf who has probably got a bunch of babies back in the bush and is just trying to protect them, the way you're trying to protect yours?" he said quietly.

Caro said, "Only two. They only have two at a time."

"O.K. O.K. I'm talking to your mother."

"You don't know that," my mother said. "You don't know if it's got hungry cubs or anything."

I had never thought she'd talk to him like that.

He said, "Easy. Easy. Let's just think a bit. Guns are a terrible thing. If I went and got a gun, then what would I be saying? That Vietnam[3] was O.K.? That I might as well have gone to Vietnam?"

3 The Vietnam War (1955–75) was between communist North Vietnam and the anti-communist South Vietnam; America's role as an ally of South Vietnam was (and still is) a source of much controversy.

"You're not an American."

"You're not going to rile me."

This is more or less what they said, and it ended up with Neal not having to get a gun. We never saw the wolf again, if it was a wolf. I think my mother stopped going to get the mail, but she may have become too big to be comfortable doing that anyway.

The snow dwindled magically. The trees were still bare of leaves and my mother made Caro wear her coat in the mornings, but she came home after school dragging it behind her.

My mother said that the baby had got to be twins, but the doctor said it wasn't.

"Great. Great," Neal said, all in favor of the twins idea. "What do doctors know."

The gravel pit had filled to its brim with melted snow and rain, so that Caro had to edge around it on her way to catch the school bus. It was a little lake, still and dazzling under the clear sky. Caro asked with not much hope if we could play in it.

Our mother said not to be crazy. "It must be twenty feet deep," she said.

Neal said, "Maybe ten."

Caro said, "Right around the edge it wouldn't be."

Our mother said yes it was. "It just drops off," she said. "It's not like going in at the beach, for fuck's sake. Just stay away from it."

She had started saying "fuck" quite a lot, perhaps more than Neal did, and in a more exasperated tone of voice.

"Should we keep the dog away from it, too?" she asked him.

Neal said that that wasn't a problem. "Dogs can swim."

A Saturday. Caro watched "The Friendly Giant"[4] with me and made comments that spoiled it. Neal was lying on the couch, which unfolded into his and my mother's bed. He was smoking his kind of cigarettes, which could not be smoked at work so had to be made the most of on weekends. Caro sometimes bothered him, asking to try one. Once he had let her, but told her not to tell our mother.

I was there, though, so I told.

There was alarm, though not quite a row.

"You know he'd have those kids out of here like a shot," our mother said. "Never again."

"Never again," Neal said agreeably. "So what if he feeds them poison Rice Krispies crap?"

---

4 A popular Canadian television show for children that aired from 1958 to 1985.

In the beginning, we hadn't seen our father at all. Then, after Christmas, a plan had been worked out for Saturdays. Our mother always asked afterward if we had had a good time. I always said yes, and meant it, because I thought that if you went to a movie or to look at Lake Huron or ate in a restaurant, that meant that you had had a good time. Caro said yes, too, but in a tone of voice that suggested that it was none of our mother's business. Then my father went on a winter holiday to Cuba (my mother remarked on this with some surprise and maybe approval) and came back with a lingering sort of flu that caused the visits to lapse. They were supposed to resume in the spring, but so far they hadn't.

After the television was turned off, Caro and I were sent outside to run around, as our mother said, and get some fresh air. We took the dog with us.

When we got outside, the first thing we did was loosen and let trail the scarves our mother had wrapped around our necks. (The fact was, though we may not have put the two things together, the deeper she got into her pregnancy the more she slipped back into behaving like an ordinary mother, at least when it was a matter of scarves we didn't need or regular meals. There was not so much championing of wild ways as there had been in the fall.) Caro asked me what I wanted to do, and I said I didn't know. This was a formality on her part but the honest truth on mine. We let the dog lead us, anyway, and Blitzee's idea was to go and look at the gravel pit. The wind was whipping the water up into little waves, and very soon we got cold, so we wound our scarves back around our necks.

I don't know how much time we spent just wandering around the water's edge, knowing that we couldn't be seen from the trailer. After a while, I realized that I was being given instructions.

I was to go back to the trailer and tell Neal and our mother something.

That the dog had fallen into the water.

The dog had fallen into the water and Caro was afraid she'd be drowned.

Blitzee. Drownded.

Drowned.

But Blitzee wasn't in the water.

She could be. And Caro could jump in to save her.

I believe I still put up some argument, along the lines of she hasn't, you haven't, it could happen but it hasn't. I also remembered that Neal had said dogs didn't drown.

Caro instructed me to do as I was told.

Why?

I may have said that, or I may have just stood there not obeying and trying to work up another argument.

In my mind I can see her picking up Blitzee and tossing her, though Blitzee was trying to hang on to her coat. Then backing up, Caro backing up to take a run at the water. Running, jumping, all of a sudden hurling herself at the water. But I can't recall the sound of the splashes as they, one after the other, hit the water. Not a little splash or a big one. Perhaps I had turned toward the trailer by then—I must have done so.

When I dream of this, I am always running. And in my dreams I am running not toward the trailer but back toward the gravel pit. I can see Blitzee floundering around and Caro swimming toward her, swimming strongly, on the way to rescue her. I see her light-brown checked coat and her plaid scarf and her proud successful face and reddish hair darkened at the end of its curls by the water. All I have to do is watch and be happy—nothing required of me, after all.

What I really did was make my way up the little incline toward the trailer. And when I got there I sat down. Just as if there had been a porch or a bench, though in fact the trailer had neither of these things. I sat down and waited for the next thing to happen.

I know this because it's a fact. I don't know, however, what my plan was or what I was thinking. I was waiting, maybe, for the next act in Caro's drama. Or in the dog's.

I don't know if I sat there for five minutes. More? Less? It wasn't too cold.

I went to see a professional person about this once and she convinced me—for a time, she convinced me—that I must have tried the door of the trailer and found it locked. Locked because my mother and Neal were having sex and had locked it against interruptions. If I'd banged on the door they would have been angry. The counsellor was satisfied to bring me to this conclusion, and I was satisfied, too. For a while. But I no longer think that was true. I don't think they would have locked the door, because I know that once they didn't and Caro walked in and they laughed at the look on her face.

Maybe I remembered that Neal had said that dogs did not drown, which meant that Caro's rescue of Blitzee would not be necessary. Therefore she herself wouldn't be able to carry out her game. So many games, with Caro.

Did I think she could swim? At nine, many children can. And in fact it turned out that she'd had one lesson the summer before, but then we had moved to the trailer and she hadn't taken any more. She may have thought she could manage well enough. And I may indeed have thought that she could do anything she wanted to.

The counsellor did not suggest that I might have been sick of carrying out Caro's orders, but the thought did occur to me. It doesn't quite seem right, though. If I'd been older, maybe. At the time, I still expected her to fill my world.

How long did I sit there? Likely not long. And it's possible that I did knock. After a while. After a minute or two. In any case, my mother did, at some point, open the door, for no reason. A presentiment.

Next thing, I am inside. My mother is yelling at Neal and trying to make him understand something. He is getting to his feet and standing there speaking to her, touching her, with such mildness and gentleness and consolation. But that is not what my mother wants at all and she tears herself away from him and runs out the door. He shakes his head and looks down at his bare feet. His big helpless-looking toes.

I think he says something to me with a singsong sadness in his voice. Strange. Beyond that I have no details.

My mother didn't throw herself into the water. She didn't go into labor from the shock. My brother, Brent, was not born until a week or ten days after the funeral, and he was a full-term infant. Where she was while she waited for the birth to happen I do not know. Perhaps she was kept in the hospital and sedated as much as possible under the circumstances.

I remember the day of the funeral quite well. A very pleasant and comfortable woman I didn't know—her name was Josie—took me on an expedition. We visited some swings and a sort of doll's house that was large enough for me to go inside, and we ate a lunch of my favorite treats, but not enough to make me sick. Josie was somebody I got to know very well later on. She was a friend my father had made in Cuba, and after the divorce she became my stepmother, his second wife.

My mother recovered. She had to. There was Brent to look after and, most of the time, me. I believe I stayed with my father and Josie while she got settled in the house that she planned to live in for the rest of her life. I don't remember being there with Brent until he was big enough to sit up in his high chair.

My mother went back to her old duties at the theatre. At first she may have worked as she had before, as a volunteer usher, but by the time I was in school she had a real job, with pay, and year-round responsibilities. She was the business manager. The theatre survived, through various ups and downs, and is still going now.

Neal didn't believe in funerals, so he didn't attend Caro's. He never saw Brent. He wrote a letter—I found this out much later—saying that since he did not intend to act as a father it would be better for him to bow out at the start. I never mentioned him to Brent, because I thought it would upset my mother. Also because Brent showed so little sign of being like him—like Neal—and seemed, in fact, so much more like my father that I really wondered about what was going on around the time he was conceived. My father has never said anything about this and never would. He treats Brent just as he treats me, but he is the kind of man who would do that anyway.

He and Josie have not had any children of their own, but I don't think that bothers them. Josie is the only person who ever talks about Caro, and even she doesn't do it often. She does say that my father doesn't hold my mother responsible. He has also said that he must have been sort of a stick-in-the-mud when my mother wanted more excitement in her life. He needed a shaking-up, and he got one. There's no use being sorry about it. Without the shaking-up, he would never have found Josie and the two of them would not have been so happy now.

"Which two?" I might say, just to derail him, and he would staunchly say, "Josie. Josie, of course."

My mother cannot be made to recall any of those times, and I don't bother her with them. I know that she has driven down the lane we lived on, and found it quite changed, with the sort of trendy houses you see now, put up on unproductive land. She mentioned this with the slight scorn that such houses evoke in her. I went down the lane myself but did not tell anyone. All the eviscerating that is done in families these days strikes me as a mistake.

Even where the gravel pit was a house now stands, the ground beneath it levelled.

I have a partner, Ruthann, who is younger than I am but, I think, somewhat wiser. Or at least more optimistic about what she calls routing out my demons. I would never have got in touch with Neal if it had not been for her urging. Of course, for a long time I had no way, just as I had no thought, of getting in touch. It was he who finally wrote to me. A brief note of congratulations, he said, after seeing my picture in the *Alumni Gazette.* What he was doing looking through the *Alumni Gazette* I have no idea. I had received one of those academic honors that mean something in a restricted circle and little anywhere else.

He was living hardly fifty miles away from where I teach, which also happens to be where I went to college. I wondered if he had been there at that time. So close. Had he become a scholar?

At first I had no intention of replying to the note, but I told Ruthann and she said that I should think about writing back. So the upshot was that I sent him an e-mail, and arrangements were made. I was to meet him in his town, in the unthreatening surroundings of a university cafeteria. I told myself that if he looked unbearable—I did not quite know what I meant by this—I could just walk on through.

He was shorter than he used to be, as adults we remember from childhood usually are. His hair was thin, and trimmed close to his head. He got me a cup of tea. He was drinking tea himself.

What did he do for a living?

He said that he tutored students in preparation for exams. Also, he helped them write their essays. Sometimes, you might say, he wrote those essays. Of course, he charged.

"It's no way to get to be a millionaire, I can tell you."

He lived in a dump. Or a semi-respectable dump. He liked it. He looked for clothes at the Sally Ann. That was O.K., too.

"Suits my principles."

I did not congratulate him on any of this, but, to tell the truth, I doubt that he expected me to.

"Anyway, I don't think my life style is so interesting. I think you might want to know how it happened."

I could not figure out how to speak.

"I was stoned," he said. "And, furthermore, I'm not a swimmer. Not many swimming pools around where I grew up. I'd have drowned, too. Is that what you wanted to know?"

I said that he was not really the one that I was wondering about.

Then he became the third person I'd asked, "What do you think Caro had in mind?"

The counsellor had said that we couldn't know. "Likely she herself didn't know what she wanted. Attention? I don't think she meant to drown herself. Attention to how bad she was feeling?"

Ruthann had said, "To make your mother do what she wanted? Make her smarten up and see that she had to go back to your father?"

Neal said, "It doesn't matter. Maybe she thought she could paddle better than she could. Maybe she didn't know how heavy winter clothes can get. Or that there wasn't anybody in a position to help her."

He said to me, "Don't waste your time. You're not thinking what if you had hurried up and told, are you? Not trying to get in on the guilt?"

I said that I had considered what he was saying, but no.

"The thing is to be happy," he said. "No matter what. Just try that. You can. It gets to be easier and easier. It's nothing to do with circumstances. You wouldn't believe how good it is. Accept everything and then tragedy disappears. Or tragedy lightens, anyway, and you're just there, going along easy in the world."

Now, goodbye.

I see what he meant. It really is the right thing to do. But, in my mind, Caro keeps running at the water and throwing herself, as if in triumph, and I'm still caught, waiting for her to explain to me, waiting for the splash.

—2011

ALISTAIR MacLEOD

Alistair MacLeod is a Canadian short-story writer and novelist, born in North Battleford, Saskatchewan in 1936. He is internationally renowned for his short stories and for his novel, *No Great Mischief* (1999), which won the International IMPAC Dublin Literary Award in 2001. He has written only sixteen stories and one novel, but the power and quality of the work place it among the best Canadian writing of the twentieth century.

MacLeod lived on the prairies until he was 10, when his parents, both natives of Cape Breton Island, moved the family back home to Inverness. After finishing high school, he attended St. Francis Xavier University, graduating with a B.A. and B.Ed. in 1960. He then went on to receive a M.A. in 1961 from the University of New Brunswick, and a Ph.D. in 1968 from Notre Dame, specializing in early nineteenth century British literature. His own work has strong affinities with the fiction of that period, particularly in its focus on local landscape, rural life, folk traditions, and the changes imposed by industrialism and urbanization on small communities.

MacLeod began publishing short stories in journals in the 1960s and 1970s, with early international recognition following the publication of "The Boat" in the *Massachusetts Review* in 1968. This story was published again in the annual volume of *Best American Short Stories* of 1969. His first collection, *The Last Salt Gift of Blood*, was published in 1976 to high critical acclaim. He accepted a post at the University of Windsor in 1969, where he taught literature and creative writing. Each summer, he and his family would return to Inverness, where he would write his stories. He retired in 2000.

His fiction depicts the psychological, physical, and emotional experience of the mining and fishing communities of Nova Scotia, set against the natural cycles of the seasons, of the sea, and of life and death. He often uses first-person present-tense narration, bringing immediacy to his subjects and themes, and foregrounding the experience of memory. Joyce Carol Oates has written that the "single underlying motive" for the stories "is the urge to memorialize, the urge to sanctify." This elegiac tone is reminiscent of the

Scottish and English traditions of oral literature, and the lyrical power of MacLeod's prose underscores this association, as does the natural ease of the storytelling.

From *The Last Salt Gift of Blood*, "In the Fall" is a coming of age story set in Nova Scotia, on a family farm "between the ocean and the coal-mining town." The teenage narrator tells the story of Scott, his father's horse, who has lived with the family since before the boy could remember. The exigencies of survival in a harsh climate drive the adults in the story to make a wrenching decision. This story traces the child's first, transformative, experience of the loss that so often follows love.

In the Fall

ALISTAIR MACLEOD

"WE'LL JUST have to sell him," I remember my mother saying with finality. "It will be a long winter and I will be alone here with only these children to help me. Besides, he eats too much and we will not have enough feed for the cattle as it is."

It is the second Saturday of November and already the sun seems to have vanished for the year. Each day dawns duller and more glowering and the waves of the grey Atlantic are sullen and almost yellow at their peaks as they pound relentlessly against the round smooth boulders that lie scattered as if by a careless giant at the base of the ever-resisting cliffs. At night, when we lie in our beds, we can hear the waves rolling in and smashing, rolling in and smashing, so relentless and regular that it is possible to count rhythmically between the thunder of each: one, two, three, four; one, two, three, four.

It is hard to realize that this is the same ocean that is the crystal blue of summer when only the thin oil-slicks left by the fishing boats or the startling whiteness of the riding seagulls mar its azure sameness. Now it is roiled and angry, and almost anguished; hurling up the brown dirty balls of scudding foam, the sticks of pulpwood from some lonely freighter, the caps of unknown men, buoys from mangled fishing nets and the inevitable bottles that contain no messages. And always also the shreds of blackened and stringy seaweed that it has ripped and torn from its own lower regions, as if this is the season for self-mutilation—the puffing out of the secret, private, unseen hair.

We are in the kitchen of our house and my mother is speaking as she energetically pokes at the wood and coal within her stove. The smoke escapes, billows upward and flattens itself out against the ceiling. Whenever she speaks she does something with her hands. It is as if the private voice within her can only be liberated by some kind of physical action. She is tall and dark with high cheekbones and brown eyes. Her hair, which is very long and very black, is pulled back severely and coiled in a bun at the base of her neck, where it is kept in place by combs of coral.

My father is standing with his back toward us and is looking out the window to where the ocean pounds against the cliffs. His hands are clasped behind his back. He must be squeezing them together very tightly because they are almost white—especially the left. My father's left hand is larger than his right and his left arm is about three inches longer than normal. That is because he holds his stevedore's hook in his left hand when he works upon the waterfront in Halifax. His complexion is lighter than my mother's and his eyes are grey, which is also the predominant colour of his thinning hair.

We have always lived on the small farm between the ocean and the coal mining town. My father has always worked on his land in the summer and at one time he would spend his winters working within the caverns of the coal mine. Later when he could bear the underground no longer he had spent the time from November to April as an independent coal-hauler, or working in his woodlot where he cut timbers for the mine roof's support. But it must have been a long time ago, for I can scarcely remember a time when the mine worked steadily or a winter when he has been with us, and I am almost fourteen. Now each winter he goes to Halifax but he is often a long time in going. He will stand as he does now, before the window, for perhaps a week or more and then he will be gone and we will see him only at Christmas and on the odd weekend; for he will be over two hundred miles away and the winter storms will make travelling difficult and uncertain. Once, two years ago, he came home for a weekend and the blizzard came so savagely and with such intensity that he could not return until Thursday. My mother told him he was a fool to make such a journey and that he had lost a week's wages for nothing—a week's wages that she and six children could certainly use. After that he did not come again until it was almost spring.

"It wouldn't hurt to keep him another winter," he says now, still looking out the window. "We've kept him through all of them before. He doesn't eat much now since his teeth have gone bad."

"He was of some use before," says my mother shortly and rattling the lids of her stove. "When you were home you used him in the woods or to haul coal—not that it ever got us much. These last years he's been worthless. It would be cheaper to rent a horse for the summer or perhaps even hire a tractor. We don't need a horse any more, not even a young one, let alone one that will probably die in March after we've fed him all that time." She replaces the stove-lids—all in their proper places.

They are talking about our old horse Scott, who has been with us all of my life. My father had been his driver for two winters in the underground and they had become fond of one another and in the time of the second spring, when he left the mine forever, the man had purchased the horse from the Company so that they might both come out together to see the sun and walk upon the grass. And that the horse might be saved from the blindness that would inevitably come if he remained within the deeps; the darkness that would make him like itself.

At one time he had even looked like coal, when his coat was black and shiny strong, relieved by only a single white star in the centre of his forehead; but that too was a long time ago and now he is very grey about the eyes, and his legs are stiff when he first begins to walk.

"Oh, he won't die in March," says my father, "he'll be okay. You said the same thing last fall and he came through okay. Once he was on the grass again he was like a two-year-old."

For the past three or four years Scott has had heaves. I guess heaves come to horses from living too near the ocean and its dampness; like asthma comes to people, making them cough and sweat and struggle for breath. Or perhaps from eating dry and dusty hay for too many winters in the prison of a narrow stall. Perhaps from old age too. Perhaps from all of them. I don't know. Someone told my little brother David who is ten that dampening the hay would help, and last winter from early January when Scott began to cough really bad, David would take a dipper of water and sprinkle it on the hay after we'd put it in the manger. Then David would say the coughing was much better and I would say so too.

"He's not a two-year-old," says my mother shortly and begins to put on her coat before going out to feed her chickens. "He's old and useless and we're not running a rest home for retired horses. I am alone here with six children and I have plenty to do."

Long ago when my father was a coal-hauler and before he was married he would sometimes become drunk, perhaps because of his loneliness, and during a short February day and a long February night he had drunk and talked and slept inside the bootlegger's, oblivious to the frozen world without, until in the next morning's dehydrated despair he had staggered to the door and seen both horse and sleigh where he had left them and where there was no reason for them to be. The coal was glowing black on the sleigh beneath the fine powdered snow that seems to come even when it is coldest, seeming more to form like dew than fall like rain, and the horse was standing like a grey ghostly form in the early morning's darkness. His own black coat was covered with the hoar frost that had formed of yesterday's sweat, and tiny icicles hung from his nose.

My father could not believe that the horse had waited for him throughout the night of bitter cold, untied and unnecessary, shifting his feet on the squeaking snow, and flickering his muscles beneath the frozen harness. Before that night he had never been waited for by any living thing and he had buried his face in the hoar-frost mane and stood there quietly for a long, long time, his face in the heavy black hair and the ice beading on his cheeks.

He has told us this story many times, even though it bores my mother. When he tells it David sits on his lap and says that he would have waited too, no matter how long and no matter how cold. My mother says she hopes David would have more sense.

"Well, I have called MacRae and he is to come for him today," my mother says as she puts on her coat and prepares to feed her chickens. "I wanted to get it over with while you were still here. The next thing I know you'll be gone and we'll be stuck with him for another winter. Grab the pail, James," she says to me, "come and help me feed the chickens. At least there's some point in feeding them."

"Just a minute," he says, "just a goddamn minute." He turns quickly from the window and I see his hands turn into fists and his knuckles white and cold. My mother points to the younger children and shakes her head. He is temporarily stymied because she has so often told him he must not swear before them and while he hesitates we take our pails and escape.

As we go to where the chickens are kept, the ocean waves are even higher, and the wind has risen so that we have to use our bodies to shield the pails that we carry. If we do not, their contents will be scooped out and scattered wildly to the skies. It is beginning to rain and the drops are so driven by the fierceness of the wind that they ping against the galvanized sides of the pails and sting and then burn upon our cheeks.

Inside the chicken-house it is warm and acrid as the chickens press around us. They are really not chickens any more but full grown capons[1] which my mother has been raising all summer and will soon sell on the Christmas market. Each spring she gets day-old chicks and we feed them ground-up hardboiled eggs and chick-starter. Later we put them into outside pens and then in the fall into this house where they are fattened. They are Light Sussex which is the breed my mother favours because they are hardy and good weight-producers. They are very, very white now with red combs and black and gold glittering eyes and with a ring of startling black at the base of their white, shining necks. It is as if a white fluid had been poured over their heads and cascaded down their necks to where it suddenly and magically changed to black after exposure to the air. The opposite in colour but the same in lustre. Like piano keys.

My mother moves about them with ease and they are accustomed to her and jostle about her as she fills their troughs with mash and the warm water we have

1 Castrated roosters.

brought. Sometimes I like them and sometimes I do not. The worst part seems to be that it doesn't really matter. Before Christmas they will all be killed and dressed and then in the spring there will be another group and they will always look and act and end in the same way. It is hard to really like what you are planning to kill and almost as hard to feel dislike, and when there are many instead of one they begin to seem almost as the blueberries and strawberries we pick in summer. Just a whole lot of them to be alive in their way for a little while and then to be picked and eaten, except it seems the berries would be there anyway but the capons we are responsible for and encourage them to eat a great deal, and try our best to make them warm and healthy and strong so that we may kill them in the end. My father is always uncomfortable around them and avoids them as much as possible. My friend Henry Van Dyken says that my father feels that way because he is Scottish, and that Scotsmen are never any good at raising poultry or flowers because they think such tasks are for women and that they make a man ashamed. Henry's father is very good at raising both.

As we move about the closeness of the chicken-house the door bangs open and David is almost blown in upon us by the force of the wind and the rain. "There's a man with a big truck that's got an old bull on it," he says, "he just went in the house."

When we enter the kitchen MacRae is standing beside the table, just inside the door. My father is still at the window although now with his back to it. It does not seem that they have said anything.

MacRae, the drover, is in his fifties. He is short and heavy-set with a red face and a cigar in the corner of his mouth. His eyes are small and bloodshot. He wears Wellington boots with his trousers tucked inside them, a broad western-style belt, and a brown suede jacket over a flannel shirt which is open at the neck exposing his reddish chest-hair. He carries a heavy stock whip in his hand and taps it against the side of his boot. Because of his short walk in the wind-driven rain, his clothes are wet and now in the warmth of the kitchen they give off a steamy, strong odour that mingles uncomfortably with that of his cigar. An odour that comes of his jostling and shoving the countless frightened animals that have been carried on the back of his truck, an odour of manure and sweat and fear.

"I hear you've got an old knacker," he says now around the corner of his cigar. "Might get rid of him for mink-feed if I'm lucky. The price is twenty dollars."

My father says nothing, but his eyes, which seem the grey of the ocean behind him, remind me of a time when the log which Scott was hauling seemed to ricochet wildly off some half-submerged obstacle, catching the man's legs beneath its onrushing force and dragging and grinding him beneath it until it smashed into a protruding stump, almost uprooting it and knocking Scott back upon his haunches. And his eyes then in their greyness had reflected fear and pain and almost a mute wonder at finding himself so painfully trapped by what seemed all too familiar.

And it seemed now that we had, all of us, conspired against him, his wife and six children and the cigar-smoking MacRae, and that we had almost brought him to bay with his back against the ocean-scarred window so pounded by the driving rain and with all of us ringed before him. But still he says nothing, although I think his mind is racing down all the possible avenues of argument, and rejecting them all because he knows the devastating truth that awaits him at the end of each: "There is no need of postponing it; the truck is here and there will never be a better opportunity; you will soon be gone; he will never be any younger; the price will never be any higher; he may die this winter and we will get nothing at all; we are not running a rest home for retired horses; I am alone here with six children and I have more than enough to do; the money for his feed could be spent on your children; don't your children mean more to you than a horse; it is unfair to go and leave us here with him to care for."

Then with a nod he moves from the window and starts toward the door. "You're not ..." begins David, but he is immediately silenced by his mother. "Be quiet," she says, "go and finish feeding the chickens," and then, as if she cannot help it, "at least there is some point in feeding them." Almost before my father stops, I know she is sorry about the last part. That she fears that she has reached for too much and perhaps even now has lost all she had before. It is like when you attempt to climb one of the almost vertical sea-washed cliffs, edging upward slowly and groping with blue-tipped fingers from one tiny crevice to the next and then seeing the tantalizing twig which you cannot resist seizing, although even as you do, you know it can be grounded in nothing, for there is no vegetation there nor soil to support it and the twig is but a reject tossed up there by the sea, and even then you are tensing yourself for the painful, bruising slide that must inevitably follow. But this time for my mother, it does not. He only stops and looks at her for a moment before forcing open the door and going out into the wind. David does not move.

"I think he's going to the barn," says my mother then with surprising softness in her voice, and telling me with her eyes that I should go with him. By the time MacRae and I are outside he is already halfway to the barn; he has no hat nor coat and is walking sideways and leaning and knifing himself into the wind which blows his trousers taut against the outlines of his legs.

As MacRae and I pass the truck I cannot help but look at the bull. He is huge and old and is an Ayrshire.[2] He is mostly white except for the almost cherry-red markings of his massive shoulders and on his neck and jowls. His heavy head

---

2 Breed of dairy cattle, originally from Ayrshire, Scotland.

is forced down almost to the truck's floor by a reinforced chain halter and by a rope that has been doubled through his nose ring and fastened to an iron bar bolted to the floor. He has tried to turn his back into the lashing wind and rain, and his bulk is pressed against the truck's slatted side at an unnatural angle to his grotesquely fastened head. The floor of the truck is greasy and slippery with a mixture of the rain and his own excrement, and each time he attempts to move, his feet slide and threaten to slip from under him. He is trembling with the strain, and the muscles in his shoulders give involuntary little twitches and his eyes roll upward in their sockets. The rain mingles with his sweat and courses down his flanks in rivulets of grey.

"How'd you like to have a pecker on you like that fella?" shouts MacRae into the wind. "Bet he's had his share and driven it into them little heifers a good many times. Boy, you get hung like that, you'll have all them horny little girls squealin' for you to take 'em behind the bushes. No time like it with them little girls, just when the juice starts runnin' in em and they're findin' out what it's for." He runs his tongue over his lips appreciatively and thwacks his whip against the sodden wetness of his boot.

Inside the barn it is still and sheltered from the storm. Scott is in the first stall and then there is a vacant one and then those of the cattle. My father has gone up beside Scott and is stroking his nose but saying nothing. Scott rubs his head up and down against my father's chest. Although he is old he is still strong and the force of his neck as he rubs almost lifts my father off his feet and pushes him against the wall.

"Well, no time like the present," says MacRae, as he unzips his fly and begins to urinate in the alleyway behind the stalls.

The barn is warm and close and silent, and the odour from the animals and from the hay is almost sweet. Only the sound of MacRae's urine and the faint steam that rises from it disturb the silence and the scene. "Ah, sweet relief," he says, rezipping his trousers and giving his knees a little bend for adjustment as he turns toward us. "Now let's see what we've got here."

He puts his back against Scott's haunches and almost heaves him across the stall before walking up beside him to where my father stands. The inspection does not take long; I suppose because not much is expected of future mink-feed. "You've got a good halter on him there," says MacRae, "I'll throw in a dollar for it, you won't be needin' it anyway." My father looks at him for what seems a very long time and then almost imperceptibly nods his head. "Okay," says MacRae, "twenty-one dollars, a deal's a deal." My father takes the money, still without saying anything, opens the barn door and without looking backward walks through the rain toward his house. And I follow him because I do not know what else to do.

Within the house it is almost soundless. My mother goes to the stove and begins rinsing her teapot and moving her kettle about. Outside we hear MacRae starting the engine of his truck and we know he is going to back it against the little hill beside the barn. It will be easier to load his purchase from there. Then it is silent again, except for the hissing of the kettle which is now too hot and which someone should move to the back of the stove; but nobody does.

And then all of us are drawn with a strange fascination to the window, and, yes, the truck is backed against the little hill as we knew and MacRae is going into the barn with his whip still in his hand. In a moment he reappears, leading Scott behind him.

As he steps out of the barn the horse almost stumbles but regains his balance quickly. Then the two ascend the little hill, both of them turning their faces from the driving rain. Scott stands quietly while MacRae lets down the tailgate of his truck. When the tailgate is lowered it forms a little ramp from the hill to the truck and MacRae climbs it with the halter-shank in his hand, tugging it impatiently. Scott places one foot on the ramp and we can almost hear, or perhaps I just imagine it, the hollow thump of his hoof upon the wet planking; but then he hesitates, withdraws his foot and stops. MacRae tugs at the rope but it has no effect. He tugs again. He comes halfway down the little ramp, reaches out his hand, grasps the halter itself and pulls; we can see his lips moving and he is either coaxing or cursing or both; he is facing directly into the rain now and it is streaming down his face. Scott does not move. MacRae comes down from the truck and leads Scott in a wide circle through the wet grass. He goes faster and faster, building up speed and soon both man and horse are almost running. Through the greyness of the blurring, slanting rain they look almost like a black-and-white movie that is badly out of focus. Suddenly without changing speed, MacRae hurries up the ramp of the truck and the almost-trotting horse follows him, until his hoof strikes the tailboard. Then he stops suddenly. As the rope jerks taut, MacRae, who is now in the truck and has been carried forward by his own momentum, is snapped backward; he bounces off the side of the bull, loses his footing on the slimy planking and falls into the wet filth of the truck box's floor. Almost before we can wonder if he is hurt, he is back upon his feet; his face is livid and his clothes are smeared with manure and running brown rivulets; he brings the whip, which he has somehow never relinquished even in his fall, down savagely between the eyes of Scott, who is still standing rigidly at the tailgate. Scott shakes his head as if dazed and backs off into the wet grass trailing the rope behind him.

It has all happened so rapidly that we in the window do not really know what to do, and are strangely embarrassed by finding ourselves where we are. It is almost as if we have caught ourselves and each other doing something that is shameful. Then David breaks the spell. "He is not going to go," he says, and then almost shouts, "he is just not going to go—ever. Good for him. Now that he's hit him, it's for sure. He'll never go and he'll have to stay." He rushes toward my father and throws his arms around his legs.

And then the door is jerked open and MacRae is standing there angrily with his whip still in his hand. His clothes are still soggy from his fall and the water trails from them in brown drops upon my mother's floor. His face is almost purple as he says, "Unless I get that fuckin' horse on the truck in the next five minutes, the deal's off and you'll be a goddamn long time tryin' to get anybody else to pay that kinda money for the useless old cocksucker."

It is as if all of the worst things one imagines happening suddenly have. But it is not at all as you expected. And I think I begin to understand for the first time how difficult and perhaps how fearful it is to be an adult and I am suddenly and selfishly afraid not only for myself now but for what it seems I am to be. For I had somehow always thought that if one talked like that before women or small children or perhaps even certain men, the earth would open up or lightning would strike or that at least many people would scream and clap their hands over their ears in horror or that the offender, if not turned to stone, would certainly be beaten by a noble, clean-limbed hero. But it does not happen that way at all. All that happens is the deepening of the thundercloud greyness in my father's eyes and the heightening of the colour in my mother's cheeks. And I realize also with a sort of shock that in spite of Scott's refusal to go on the truck, nothing has really changed. I mean not really; and that all of the facts remain awfully and simply the same: that Scott is old and that we are poor and that my father must soon go away and that he must leave us either with Scott or without him. And that it is somehow like my mother's shielding her children from "swearing" for so many years, only to find one day that it too is there in its awful reality, in spite of everything that she had wished and wanted. And even as I am thinking this, my father goes by MacRae, who is still standing in the ever-widening puddles of brown, seeming like some huge growth that is nourished by the foul-smelling waters that he himself has brought.

David, who had released my father's legs with the entrance of MacRae, makes a sort of flying tackle for them now, but I intercept him and find myself saying as if from a great distance my mother's phrases in something that sounds almost like her voice, "Let's go and finish feeding the chickens." I tighten my grip on his arm and we almost have to squeeze past MacRae whose bulk is blocking the doorway and who has not yet made a motion to leave.

Out of doors my father is striding directly into the slashing rain to where Scott is standing in something like puzzlement with his back to the rain and his halter-shank dangling before him. When he sees my father approach he cocks his ears and nickers in recognition. My father who looks surprisingly slight with his wet clothes plastered to his body takes the rope in his hand and moves off with the huge horse following him eagerly. Their movement seems almost that of the small tug docking the huge ocean freighter, except that they are so individually and collectively alive. As they approach the truck's ramp, it is my father who hesitates and seems to flinch, and it is his foot which seems to recoil as it touches the planking; but on the part of Scott there is no hesitation at all; his hooves echo firmly and confidently on the strong wet wood and his head is almost pressed into the small of my father's back; he is so eager to get to wherever they are going.

He follows him as I have remembered them all of my life and imagined them even before. Following wildly through the darkened caverns of the mine in its dryness as his shoes flashed sparks from the tracks and the stone; and in its wetness with both of them up to their knees in water, feeling rather than seeing the landing of their splashing feet and with the coal cars thundering behind them with such momentum that were the horse to stumble, the very cars he had set in motion would roll over him, leaving him mangled and grisly to be hauled above ground only as carrion for the wheeling gulls. And on the surface, following, in the summer's heat with the jolting haywagon and the sweat churned to froth between his legs and beneath his collar, fluttering white on the blackness of his glistening coat. And in the winter, following, over the semi-frozen swamps as the snapping, whistling logs snaked behind him, grunting as he broke through the shimmering crystal ice which slashed his fetlocks and caused a scarlet trail of bloodied perforations on the whiteness of the snow. And in the winter, too, with the ton of coal upon the sleigh, following, even over the snowless stretches, driven bare by the wind, leaning low with his underside parallel and almost touching the ground, grunting, and swinging with violent jolts to the right and then to the left, moving the sleigh forward only by moving it sideways, which he had learned was the only way it would move at all.

Even as my father is knotting the rope, MacRae is hurrying past us and slamming shut the tailgate and dropping down the iron bolts that will hold it in its place. My father climbs over the side of the box and down as MacRae steps onto the running-board and up into the cab. The motor roars and the truck lurches forward. It leaves two broad wet tracks in the grass like the trails of two slimy giant slugs and the smell of its exhaust hangs heavy on the air. As it takes the turn at the bottom of the lane Scott tries to turn his head and look back but the rope has been tied very short and he is unable to do so. The sheets of rain come down like so many slanted, beaded curtains, making it impossible to see what we know is there, and then there is only the receding sound of the motor, the wet trails on the grass and the exhaust fumes in the air.

It is only then that I realize that David is no longer with me, but even as the question comes to the surface so also does its answer and I run toward the squawking of the chicken-house.

Within the building it is difficult to see and difficult to breathe and difficult to believe that so small a boy could wreak such havoc in so short a time. The air is thick with myriad dust particles from the disturbed floor, and bits of straw and tiny white scarlet-flecked feathers eddy and dip and swirl. The frightened capons, many of them already bloodied and mangled, attempt short and ungainly flights, often colliding with each other in midair. Their overfed bodies are too heavy for their weak and unused wings and they are barely able to get off the floor and flounder for a few feet before thumping down to dusty crippled landings. They are screaming with terror and their screams seem as unnatural as their flights, as if they had been terribly miscast in the most unsuitable of roles. Many of them are already lifeless and crumpled and dustied and bloodied on the floor, like sad, grey wadded newspapers that have been used to wipe up blood. The sheen of their feathers forever gone.

In the midst of it all David moves like a small blood-spattered dervish, swinging his axe in all directions and almost unknowingly as if he were blindfolded. Dust has settled on the dampness of his face and the tears make tiny trails through its greyness, like lonely little rivers that have really nothing to water. A single tiny feather is plastered to his forehead and he is coughing and sobbing, both at the same time.

When my father appears beside me in the doorway he seems to notice for the first time that he is not alone. With a final exhausted heave he throws the axe at my father. "Cocksucker," he says in some kind of small, sad parody of MacRae, and bolts past us through the door, almost colliding with my mother, who now comes from out of the rain. He has had very little strength with which to throw the axe and it clatters uselessly off the wall and comes to rest against my father's boot, wet and bloodied, with feathers and bits of flesh still clinging to its blade.

I am tremendously sorry for the capons, now so ruined and so useless, and for my mother and for all the time and work she has put into them for all of us. But I do not know what to do and I know not what to say.

As we leave the melancholy little building the wind cuts in from the ocean with renewed fury. It threatens to lift you off your feet and blow you to the skies and your crotch is numb and cold as your clothes are flattened hard against the front of your body, even as they tug and snap at your back in insistent, billowing balloons. Unless you turn or lower your head it is impossible to breathe, for the air is blown back almost immediately into your lungs, and your throat convulses and heaves. The rain is now a stinging sleet which is rapidly becoming the winter's first snow. It is impossible to see into it, and the ocean off which it rushes is lost in the swirling whiteness, although it thunders and roars in its invisible nearness like the heavy bass blending with the shrieking tenor of the wind. You hear so much that you can hardly hear at all. And you are almost immobile and breathless and blind and deaf. Almost but not quite. For by turning and leaning your body and your head, you can move and breathe and see and hear a little at a time. You do not gain much but you can hang on to what little you have and your toes curl almost instinctively within your shoes as if they are trying to grasp the earth.

I stop and turn my face from the wind and look back the way I have come. My parents are there, blown together behind me. They are not moving, either, only trying to hold their place. They have turned sideways to the wind and are facing and leaning into each other with their shoulders touching, like the end-timbers of a gabled roof. My father puts his arms around my mother's waist and she does not remove them as I have always seen her do. Instead she reaches up and removes the combs of coral from the heaviness of her hair. I have never seen her hair in all its length before and it stretches out now almost parallel to the earth, its shining blackness whipped by the wind and glistening like the snow that settles and melts upon it. It surrounds and engulfs my father's head and he buries his face within its heavy darkness, and draws my mother closer toward him. I think they will stand there for a long, long time, leaning into each other and into the wind-whipped snow and with the ice freezing to their cheeks. It seems that perhaps they should be left alone, so I turn and take one step and then another and move forward a little at a time. I think I will try to find David, that perhaps he may understand.

—1976

RAYMOND CARVER

The son of a hard-drinking, sawmill-worker father, Raymond Carver was born in Clatskanie, Oregon, in 1938, but grew up in Yakima, Washington, after his family moved there in 1941. After graduating from high school, Carver joined his father as a labourer at the sawmill, married Maryann Burk at the age of nineteen, and had two children in less than two years. Debt-ridden, Carver and his family moved in 1958 to California, where he enrolled part-time at Chico State College and received encouragement from writer John Gardner. To support himself and his family financially, Carver worked at what he called "crap jobs," including gas station attendant and hospital janitor, while his wife worked as a waitress and door-to-door salesperson. In 1960, he transferred to Humboldt State College, where he graduated with a B.A. in 1963; during this time he began to publish stories and poems in small periodicals. He also began to struggle with frequent moves, a lack of money, and alcoholism.

In 1970, Carver was fired from his editing job at Science Research Associates, but he won the National Endowment for the Arts Discovery Award for Poetry: this enabled him to complete his first short story collection, *Will You Please Be Quiet, Please* (published in 1976 and a National Book Award nominee), and the poetry book, *Winter Insomnia* (1970). His growing success as a writer was accompanied by growing alcoholism. In the early 1970s he worked in a number of teaching jobs, but his alcoholism made working difficult, and he and his wife separated in 1977.

Although he is best known as a short story writer, Carver's first two book-length publications were poetry collections. His work has appeared in many important anthologies, including *Best American Short Stories* and *Best Little Magazine Fiction*. Carver quit drinking in 1977 and the last decade of his life saw a variety of successes, including nominations for *Cathedral* for the Pulitzer Prize and the National Book Critics Circle Award. In 1983, he received the prestigious Mildred and Harold Strauss Living Award and was awarded a Doctorate of Letters from Hartford University. In 1988 he married long-time partner and poet Tess Gallagher and was elected to the

American Academy and Institute of Arts and Letters. He died of lung cancer in the same year.

Together with Alice Munro, Raymond Carver is often credited with rejuvenating the genre of the short story in the last quarter of the twentieth century. Some literary scholars have named him as second only to Ernest Hemingway in terms of his stylistic influence on the contemporary short story. Carver scholar Kirk Nesset has described the characters that populate his world:

> From the earliest story to the last, Carver's characters are unhappily estranged, out of work, disillusioned by meaningless jobs and meaningless marriages; they suffer in various degrees from alcoholism as well as bad luck and bad timing, battered by a world which typically leaves them inert and speechless in the wake of longings and fears they cannot begin to identify.

The main character in "Cathedral" (published in the collection *Cathedral*, in 1983) starts out very much in this mould. But in this case something positive begins to happen; the character Robert's physical blindness allows the insecure main character to "see" past his own prejudices.

Cathedral

RAYMOND CARVER

THIS BLIND man, an old friend of my wife's, he was on his way to spend the night. His wife had died. So he was visiting the dead wife's relatives in Connecticut. He called my wife from his in-laws'. Arrangements were made. He would come by train, a five-hour trip, and my wife would meet him at the station. She hadn't seen him since she worked for him one summer in Seattle ten years ago. But she and the blind man had kept in touch. They made tapes and mailed them back and forth. I wasn't enthusiastic about his visit. He was no one I knew. And his being blind bothered me. My idea of blindness came from the movies. In the movies, the blind moved slowly and never laughed. Sometimes they were led by seeing-eye dogs. A blind man in my house was not something I looked forward to.

That summer in Seattle she had needed a job. She didn't have any money. The man she was going to marry at the end of the summer was in officers' training school. He didn't have any money, either. But she was in love with the guy, and he was in love with her, etc. She'd seen something in the paper: HELP

WANTED—*Reading to Blind Man*, and a telephone number. She phoned and went over, was hired on the spot. She'd worked with this blind man all summer. She read stuff to him, case studies, reports, that sort of thing. She helped him organize his little office in the county social-service department. They'd become good friends, my wife and the blind man. How do I know these things? She told me. And she told me something else. On her last day in the office, the blind man asked if he could touch her face. She agreed to this. She told me he touched his fingers to every part of her face, her nose—even her neck! She never forgot it. She even tried to write a poem about it. She was always trying to write a poem. She wrote a poem or two every year, usually after something really important had happened to her.

When we first started going out together, she showed me the poem. In the poem, she recalled his fingers and the way they had moved around over her face. In the poem, she talked about what she had felt at the time, about what went through her mind when the blind man touched her nose and lips. I can remember I didn't think much of the poem. Of course, I didn't tell her that. Maybe I just don't understand poetry. I admit it's not the first thing I reach for when I pick up something to read.

Anyway, this man who'd first enjoyed her favors, the officer-to-be, he'd been her childhood sweetheart. So okay. I'm saying that at the end of the summer she let the blind man run his hands over her face, said goodbye to him, married her childhood etc., who was now a commissioned officer, and she moved away from Seattle. But they'd kept in touch, she and the blind man. She made the first contact after a year or so. She called him up one night from an Air Force base in Alabama. She wanted to talk. They talked. He asked her to send him a tape and tell him about her life. She did this. She sent the tape. On the tape, she told the blind man about her husband and about their life together in the military. She told the blind man she loved her husband but she didn't like it where they lived and she didn't like it that he was a part of the military-industrial thing. She told the blind man she'd written a poem about what it was like to be an Air Force officer's wife. The poem wasn't finished yet. She was still writing it. The blind man made a tape. He sent her the tape. She made a tape. This went on for years. My wife's officer was posted to one base and then another. She sent tapes from Moody AFB, McGuire, McConnell, and finally Travis, near Sacramento, where one night she got to feeling lonely and cut off from people she kept losing in that moving-around life. She got to feeling she couldn't go it another step. She went in and swallowed all the pills and capsules in the medicine chest and washed them down with a bottle of gin. Then she got into a hot bath and passed out.

But instead of dying, she got sick. She threw up. Her officer—why should he have a name? he was the childhood sweetheart, and what more does he want?—came home from somewhere, found her, and called the ambulance. In time, she put it all on a tape and sent the tape to the blind man. Over the years, she put all kinds of stuff on tapes and sent the tapes off lickety-split. Next to writing a poem every year, I think it was her chief means of recreation. On one tape, she told the blind man she'd decided to live away from her officer for a time. On another tape, she told him about her divorce. She and I began going out, and of course she told her blind man about it. She told him everything, or so it seemed to me. Once she asked me if I'd like to hear the latest tape from the blind man. This was a year ago. I was on the tape, she said. So I said okay, I'd listen to it. I got us drinks and we settled down in the living room. We made ready to listen. First she inserted the tape into the player and adjusted a couple of dials. Then she pushed a lever. The tape squeaked and someone began to talk in this loud voice. She lowered the volume. After a few minutes of harmless chitchat, I heard my own name in the mouth of this stranger, this blind man I didn't even know! And then this: "From all you've said about him, I can only conclude—" But we were interrupted, a knock at the door, something, and we didn't ever get back to the tape. Maybe it was just as well. I'd heard all I wanted to.

Now this same blind man was coming to sleep in my house.

"Maybe I could take him bowling," I said to my wife. She was at the draining board doing scalloped potatoes. She put down the knife she was using and turned around.

"If you love me," she said, "you can do this for me. If you don't love me, okay. But if you had a friend, any friend, and the friend came to visit, I'd make him feel comfortable." She wiped her hands with the dish towel.

"I don't have any blind friends," I said.

"You don't have *any* friends," she said. "Period. Besides," she said, "goddamn it, his wife's just died! Don't you understand that? The man's lost his wife!"

I didn't answer. She'd told me a little about the blind man's wife. Her name was Beulah. Beulah! That's a name for a colored woman.

"Was his wife a Negro?" I asked.

"Are you crazy?" my wife said. "Have you just flipped or something?" She picked up a potato. I saw it hit the floor, then roll under the stove. "What's wrong with you?" she said. "Are you drunk?"

"I'm just asking," I said.

Right then my wife filled me in with more detail than I cared to know. I made a drink and sat at the kitchen table to listen. Pieces of the story began to fall into place.

Beulah had gone to work for the blind man the summer after my wife had stopped working for him. Pretty soon Beulah and the blind man had themselves a church wedding. It was a little wedding—who'd want to go to such a wedding in the first place?—just the two of them, plus the minister and the minister's wife. But it was a church wedding just the same. It was what Beulah had wanted, he'd said. But even then Beulah must have been carrying the cancer in her glands. After they had been inseparable for eight years—my wife's word, *inseparable*—Beulah's health went into a rapid decline. She died in a Seattle hospital room, the blind man sitting beside the bed and holding on to her hand. They'd married, lived and worked together, slept together—had sex, sure—and then the blind man had to bury her. All this without his having ever seen what the goddamned woman looked like. It was beyond my understanding. Hearing this, I felt sorry for the blind man for a little bit. And then I found myself thinking what a pitiful life this woman must have led. Imagine a woman who could never see herself as she was seen in the eyes of her loved one. A woman who could go on day after day and never receive the smallest compliment from her beloved. A woman whose husband could never read the expression on her face, be it misery or something better. Someone who could wear makeup or not—what difference to him? She could, if she wanted, wear green eye-shadow around one eye, a straight pin in her nostril, yellow slacks and purple shoes, no matter. And then to slip off into death, the blind man's hand on her hand, his blind eyes streaming tears—I'm imagining now—her last thought maybe this: that he never even knew what she looked like, and she on an express to the grave. Robert was left with a small insurance policy and half of a twenty-peso Mexican coin. The other half of the coin went into the box with her. Pathetic.

So when the time rolled around, my wife went to the depot to pick him up. With nothing to do but wait—sure, I blamed him for that—I was having a drink and watching the TV when I heard the car pull into the drive. I got up from the sofa with my drink and went to the window to have a look.

I saw my wife laughing as she parked the car. I saw her get out of the car and shut the door. She was still wearing a smile. Just amazing. She went around to the other side to where the blind man was already starting to get out. This blind man, feature this, he was wearing a full beard! A beard on a blind man! Too much, I say. The blind man reached into the back seat and dragged out a suitcase. My wife took his arm, shut the car door, and, talking all the way, moved him down the drive and then up the steps to the front porch. I turned off the TV. I finished my drink, rinsed the glass, dried my hands. Then I went to the door.

My wife said, "I want you to meet Robert. Robert, this is my husband. I've told you all about him." She was beaming. She had this blind man by his coat sleeve.

The blind man let go of his suitcase and up came his hand.

I took it. He squeezed hard, held my hand, and then he let it go.

"I feel like we've already met," he boomed.

"Likewise," I said. I didn't know what else to say. Then I said, "Welcome. I've heard a lot about you." We began to move then, a little group, from the porch into the living room, my wife guiding him by the arm. The blind man was carrying his suitcase in his other hand. My wife said things like, "To your left here, Robert. That's right. Now watch it, there's a chair. That's it. Sit down right here. This is the sofa. We just bought this sofa two weeks ago."

I started to say something about the old sofa. I'd liked that old sofa. But I didn't say anything. Then I wanted to say something else, small-talk, about the scenic ride along the Hudson. How going *to* New York, you should sit on the right-hand side of the train, and coming *from* New York, the left-hand side.

"Did you have a good train ride?" I said. "Which side of the train did you sit on, by the way?"

"What a question, which side!" my wife said. "What's it matter which side?" she said.

"I just asked," I said.

"Right side," the blind man said. "I hadn't been on a train in nearly forty years. Not since I was a kid. With my folks. That's been a long time. I'd nearly forgotten the sensation. I have winter in my beard now," he said. "So I've been told, anyway. Do I look distinguished, my dear?" the blind man said to my wife.

"You look distinguished, Robert," she said. "Robert," she said. "Robert, it's just so good to see you."

My wife finally took her eyes off the blind man and looked at me. I had the feeling she didn't like what she saw. I shrugged.

I've never met, or personally known, anyone who was blind. This blind man was late forties, a heavy-set, balding man with stooped shoulders, as if he carried a great weight there. He wore brown slacks, brown shoes, a light-brown shirt, a tie, a sports coat. Spiffy. He also had this full beard. But he didn't use a cane and he didn't wear dark glasses. I'd always thought dark glasses were a must for the blind. Fact was, I wished he had a pair. At first glance, his eyes looked like anyone else's eyes. But if you looked close, there was something different about them. Too much white in the iris, for one thing, and the pupils seemed to move around in the sockets without his knowing it or being able to stop it. Creepy. As I stared at his face, I saw the left pupil turn in toward his nose while the other made an effort to keep in one place. But it was only an effort, for that eye was on the roam without his knowing it or wanting it to be.

I said, "Let me get you a drink. What's your pleasure? We have a little of everything. It's one of our pastimes."

"Bub, I'm a Scotch man myself," he said fast enough in this big voice.

"Right," I said. Bub! "Sure you are. I knew it."

He let his fingers touch his suitcase, which was sitting alongside the sofa. He was taking his bearings. I didn't blame him for that.

"I'll move that up to your room," my wife said.

"No, that's fine," the blind man said loudly. "It can go up when I go up."

"A little water with the Scotch?" I said.

"Very little," he said.

"I knew it," I said.

He said, "Just a tad. The Irish actor, Barry Fitzgerald? I'm like that fellow. When I drink water, Fitzgerald said, I drink water. When I drink whiskey, I drink whiskey." My wife laughed. The blind man brought his hand up under his beard. He lifted his beard slowly and let it drop.

I did the drinks, three big glasses of Scotch with a splash of water in each. Then we made ourselves comfortable and talked about Robert's travels. First the long flight from the West Coast to Connecticut, we covered that. Then from Connecticut up here by train. We had another drink concerning that leg of the trip.

I remembered having read somewhere that the blind didn't smoke because, as speculation had it, they couldn't see the smoke they exhaled. I thought I knew that much and that much only about blind people. But this blind man smoked his cigarette down to the nubbin and then lit another one. This blind man filled his ashtray and my wife emptied it.

When we sat down at the table for dinner, we had another drink. My wife heaped Robert's plate with cube steak, scalloped potatoes, green beans. I buttered him up two slices of bread. I said, "Here's bread and butter for you." I swallowed some of my drink. "Now let us pray," I said, and the blind man lowered his head. My wife looked at me, her mouth agape. "Pray the phone won't ring and the food doesn't get cold," I said.

We dug in. We ate everything there was to eat on the table. We ate like there was no tomorrow. We didn't talk. We ate. We scarfed. We grazed that table. We were into serious eating. The blind man had right away located his foods, he knew just where everything was on his plate. I watched with admiration as he used his knife and fork on the meat. He'd cut two pieces of meat, fork the meat into his mouth, and then go all out for the scalloped potatoes, the beans next, and then he'd tear off a hunk of buttered bread and eat that. He'd follow this up with a big drink of milk. It didn't seem to bother him to use his fingers once in a while, either.

We finished everything, including half a strawberry pie. For a few moments, we sat as if stunned. Sweat beaded on our faces. Finally, we got up from the table and left the dirty plates. We didn't look back. We took ourselves into the living room and sank into our places again. Robert and my wife sat on the sofa. I took the big chair. We had us two or three more drinks while they talked about the major things that had come to pass for them in the past ten years. For the most part, I just listened. Now and then I joined in. I didn't want him to think I'd left the room, and I didn't want her to think I was feeling left out. They talked of things that had happened to them—to them!—these past ten years. I waited in vain to hear my name on my wife's sweet lips: "And then my dear husband came into my life"—something like that. But I heard nothing of the sort. More talk of Robert. Robert had done a little of everything, it seemed, a regular blind jack-of-all-trades. But most recently he and his wife had had an Amway distributorship, from which, I gathered, they'd earned their living, such as it was. The blind man was also a ham radio operator. He talked in his loud voice about conversations he'd had with fellow operators in Guam, in the Philippines, in Alaska, and even in Tahiti. He said he'd have a lot of friends there if he ever wanted to go visit those places. From time to time, he'd turn his blind face toward me, put his hand under his beard, ask me something. How long had I been in my present position? (Three years.) Did I like my work? (I didn't.) Was I going to stay with it? (What were the options?) Finally, when I thought he was beginning to run down, I got up and turned on the TV.

My wife looked at me with irritation. She was heading toward a boil. Then she looked at the blind man and said, "Robert, do you have a TV?"

The blind man said, "My dear, I have two TVs. I have a color set and a black-and-white thing, an old relic. It's funny, but if I turn the TV on, and I'm always turning it on, I turn on the color set. It's funny, don't you think?"

I didn't know what to say to that. I had absolutely nothing to say to that. No opinion. So I watched the news program and tried to listen to what the announcer was saying.

"This is a color TV," the blind man said. "Don't ask me how, but I can tell."

"We traded up a while ago." I said.

The blind man had another taste of his drink. He lifted his beard, sniffed it, and let it fall. He leaned forward on the sofa. He positioned his ashtray on the coffee table, then put the lighter to his cigarette. He leaned back on the sofa and crossed his legs at the ankles.

My wife covered her mouth, and then she yawned. She stretched. She said, "I think I'll go upstairs and put on my robe. I think I'll change into something else. Robert, you make yourself comfortable," she said.

"I'm comfortable," the blind man said.

"I want you to feel comfortable in this house," she said.

"I am comfortable," the blind man said.

After she'd left the room, he and I listened to the weather report and then to the sports roundup. By that time, she'd been gone so long I didn't know if she was going to come back. I thought she might have gone to bed. I wished she'd come back downstairs. I didn't want to be left alone with a blind man. I asked him if he wanted to smoke some dope with me. I said I'd just rolled a number. I hadn't, but I planned to do so in about two shakes.

"I'll try some with you," he said.

"Damn right," I said. "That's the stuff."

I got our drinks and sat down on the sofa with him. Then I rolled us two fat numbers. I lit one and passed it. I brought it to his fingers. He took it and inhaled.

"Hold it as long as you can," I said. I could tell he didn't know the first thing.

My wife came back downstairs wearing her pink robe and her pink slippers.

"What do I smell?" she said.

"We thought we'd have us some cannabis," I said.

My wife gave me a savage look. Then she looked at the blind man and said, "Robert, I didn't know you smoked."

He said, "I do now, my dear. There's a first time for everything. But I don't feel anything yet."

"This stuff is pretty mellow," I said. "This stuff is mild. It's dope you can reason with," I said. "It doesn't mess you up."

"Not much it doesn't bub," he said, and laughed.

My wife sat on the sofa between the blind man and me. I passed her the number. She took it and toked and then passed it back to me. "Which way is this going?" she said. Then she said, "I shouldn't be smoking this. I can hardly keep my eyes open as it is. That dinner did me in. I shouldn't have eaten so much."

"It was the strawberry pie," the blind man said. "That's what did it," he said, and he laughed his big laugh. Then he shook his head.

"There's more strawberry pie," I said.

"Do you want some more, Robert?" my wife said.

"Maybe in a little while," he said.

We gave our attention to the TV. My wife yawned again. She said, "Your bed is made up when you feel like going to bed, Robert. I know you must have had a long day. When you're ready to go to bed, say so." She pulled his arm. "Robert?"

He came to and said, "I've had a real nice time. This beats tapes, doesn't it?"

I said, "Coming at you," and I put the number between his fingers. He inhaled, held the smoke, and then let it go. It was like he'd been doing it since he was nine years old.

"Thanks, bub," he said. "But I think this is all for me. I think I'm beginning to feel it," he said. He held the burning roach out for my wife.

"Same here," she said. "Ditto. Me, too." She took the roach and passed it to me. "I may just sit here for a while between you two guys with my eyes closed.

But don't let me bother you, okay? Either one of you. If it bothers you, say so. Otherwise, I may just sit here with my eyes closed until you're ready to go to bed," she said. "Your bed's made up, Robert, when you're ready. It's right next to our room at the top of the stairs. We'll show you up when you're ready. You wake me up now, you guys, if I fall asleep." She said that and then she closed her eyes and went to sleep.

The news program ended. I got up and changed the channel. I sat back down on the sofa. I wished my wife hadn't pooped out. Her head lay across the back of the sofa, her mouth open. She'd turned so that her robe had slipped away from her legs, exposing a juicy thigh. I reached to draw her robe back over her, and it was then that I glanced at the blind man. What the hell! I flipped the robe open again.

"You say when you want some strawberry pie," I said.

"I will," he said.

I said, "Are you tired? Do you want me to take you up to your bed? Are you ready to hit the hay?"

"Not yet," he said. "No, I'll stay up with you, bub. If that's all right. I'll stay up until you're ready to turn in. We haven't had a chance to talk. Know what I mean? I feel like me and her monopolized the evening." He lifted his beard and he let it fall. He picked up his cigarettes and lighter.

"That's all right," I said. Then I said, "I'm glad for the company."

And I guess I was. Every night I smoked dope and stayed up as long as I could before I fell asleep. My wife and I hardly ever went to bed at the same time. When I did go to sleep, I had these dreams. Sometimes I'd wake up from one of them, my heart going crazy.

Something about the church and the Middle Ages was on the TV. Not your run-of-the-mill TV fare. I wanted to watch something else. I turned to the other channels. But there was nothing on them, either. So I turned back to the first channel and apologized.

"Bub, it's all right," the blind man said. "It's fine with me. Whatever you want to watch is okay. I'm always learning something. Learning never ends. It won't hurt me to learn something tonight. I got ears," he said.

We didn't say anything for a time. He was leaning forward with his head turned at me, his right ear aimed in the direction of the set. Very disconcerting. Now and then his eyelids dropped and then they snapped open again. Now and then he put his fingers into his beard and tugged, like he was thinking about something he was hearing on the television.

On the screen, a group of men wearing cowls was being set upon and tormented by men dressed in skeleton costumes and men dressed as devils. The men dressed as devils wore devil masks, horns, and long tails. This pageant was part of a procession. The Englishman who was narrating the thing said it took place in Spain once a year. I tried to explain to the blind man what was happening.

"Skeletons," he said. "I know about skeletons," he said and he nodded.

The TV showed this one cathedral. Then there was a long, slow look at another one. Finally, the picture switched to the famous one in Paris, with its flying buttresses and its spires reaching up to the clouds. The camera pulled away to show the whole of the cathedral rising above the skyline.

There were times when the Englishman who was telling the thing would shut up, would simply let the camera move around over the cathedrals. Or else the camera would tour the countryside, men in fields walking behind oxen. I waited as long as I could. Then I felt I had to say something. I said, "They're showing the outside of this cathedral now. Gargoyles. Little statues carved to look like monsters. Now I guess they're in Italy. Yeah, they're in Italy. There's paintings on the walls of this one church."

"Are those fresco paintings, bub?" he asked, and he sipped from his drink.

I reached for my glass. But it was empty. I tried to remember what I could remember. "You're asking me are those frescoes?" I said. "That's a good question. I don't know."

The camera moved to a cathedral outside Lisbon. The differences in the Portuguese cathedral compared with the French and Italian were not that great. But they were there. Mostly the interior stuff. Then something occurred to me, and I said, "Something has occurred to me. Do you have any idea what a cathedral is? What they look like, that is? Do you follow me? If somebody says cathedral to you, do you have any notion what they're talking about? Do you know the difference between that and a Baptist church, say?"

He let the smoke dribble from his mouth. "I know they took hundreds of workers fifty or a hundred years to build," he said. "I just heard the man say that, of course. I know generations of the same families worked on a cathedral. I heard him say that, too. The men who began their life's work on them, they never lived to see the completion of their work. In that wise, bub, they're no different from the rest of us, right?" He laughed. Then his eyelids drooped again. His head nodded. He seemed to be snoozing. Maybe he was imagining himself in Portugal. The TV was showing another cathedral now. This one was in Germany. The Englishman's voice droned on. "Cathedrals," the blind man said. He sat up and rolled his head back and forth. "If you want the truth, bub, that's about all I know. What I just said. What I heard him say. But maybe you could describe one to me? I wish you'd do it. I'd like that. If you want to know, I really don't have a good idea."

I stared hard at the shot of the cathedral on the TV. How could I even begin to describe it? But say my life depended on it. Say my life was being threatened by an insane guy who said I had to do it or else.

I stared some more at the cathedral before the picture flipped off into the countryside. There was no use. I turned to the blind man and said, "To begin with, they're very tall." I was looking around the room for clues. "They reach way up. Up and up. Toward the sky. They're so big, some of them, they have to have these supports. To help hold them up, so to speak. These supports are called buttresses. They remind me of viaducts, for some reason. But maybe you don't know viaducts, either? Sometimes the cathedrals have devils and such carved into the front. Sometimes lords and ladies. Don't ask me why this is," I said.

He was nodding. The whole upper part of his body seemed to be moving back and forth.

"I'm not doing so good, am I?" I said.

He stopped nodding and leaned forward on the edge of the sofa. As he listened to me, he was running his fingers through his beard. I wasn't getting through to him, I could see that. But he waited for me to go on just the same. He nodded, like he was trying to encourage me. I tried to think what else to say. "They're really big," I said. "They're massive. They're built of stone. Marble, too, sometimes. In those olden days, when they built cathedrals, men wanted to be close to God. In those olden days, God was an important part of everyone's life. You could tell this from their cathedral-building. I'm sorry," I said, "but it looks like that's the best I can do for you. I'm just no good at it."

"That's all right, bub," the blind man said. "Hey, listen, I hope you don't mind my asking you. Can I ask you something? Let me ask you a simple question, yes or no. I'm just curious and there's no offense. You're my host. But let me ask if you are in any way religious? You don't mind my asking?"

I shook my head. He couldn't see that, though. A wink is the same as a nod to a blind man. "I guess I don't believe in it. In anything. Sometimes it's hard. You know what I'm saying?"

"Sure, I do," he said.

"Right," I said.

The Englishman was still holding forth. My wife sighed in her sleep. She drew a long breath and went on with her sleeping.

"You'll have to forgive me," I said. "But I can't tell you what a cathedral looks like. It just isn't in me to do it. I can't do any more than I've done."

The blind man sat very still, his head down, as he listened to me.

I said, "The truth is, cathedrals don't mean anything special to me. Nothing. Cathedrals. They're something to look at on late-night TV. That's all they are."

It was then that the blind man cleared his throat. He brought something up. He took a handkerchief from his back pocket. Then he said, "I get it, bub. It's okay. It happens. Don't worry about it," he said. "Hey, listen to me. Will you do me a favor? I got an idea. Why don't you find us some heavy paper? And a pen. We'll do something. We'll draw one together. Get us a pen and some heavy paper. Go on, bub, get the stuff," he said.

So I went upstairs. My legs felt like they didn't have any strength in them. They felt like they did after I'd done some running. In my wife's room, I looked around. I found some ballpoints in a little basket on her table. And then I tried to think where to look for the kind of paper he was talking about.

Downstairs, in the kitchen, I found a shopping bag with onion skins at the bottom of the bag. I emptied the bag and shook it. I brought it into the living room and sat down with it near his legs. I moved some things, smoothed the wrinkles from the bag, spread it out on the coffee table.

The blind man got down from the sofa and sat next to me on the carpet.

He ran his fingers over the paper. He went up and down the sides of the paper. The edges, even the edges. He fingered the corners.

"All right," he said. "All right, let's do her."

He found my hand, the hand with the pen. He closed his hand over my hand. "Go ahead, bub, draw," he said. "Draw. You'll see. I'll follow along with you. It'll be okay. Just begin now like I'm telling you. You'll see. Draw," the blind man said.

So I began. First I drew a box that looked like a house. It could have been the house I lived in. Then I put a roof on it. At either end of the roof, I drew spires. Crazy.

"Swell," he said. "Terrific. You're doing fine," he said. "Never thought anything like this could happen in your lifetime, did you, bub? Well, it's a strange life, we all know that. Go on now. Keep it up."

I put in windows with arches. I drew flying buttresses. I hung great doors. I couldn't stop. The TV station went off the air. I put down the pen and closed and opened my fingers. The blind man felt around over the paper. He moved the tips of his fingers over the paper, all over what I had drawn, and he nodded.

"Doing fine," the blind man said.

I took up the pen again, and he found my hand. I kept at it. I'm no artist. But I kept drawing just the same.

My wife opened up her eyes and gazed at us. She sat up on the sofa, her robe hanging open. She said, "What are you doing? Tell me, I want to know."

I didn't answer her.

The blind man said, "We're drawing a cathedral. Me and him are working on it. Press hard," he said to me. "That's right. That's good," he said. "Sure. You got it, bub. I can tell. You didn't think you could. But you can, can't you? You're cooking with gas now. You know what I'm saying? We're going to really have us something here in a minute. How's the old arm?" he said. "Put some people in there now. What's a cathedral without people?"

My wife said, "What's going on? Robert, what are you doing? What's going on?"

"It's all right," he said to her. "Close your eyes now," the blind man said to me.

I did it. I closed them just like he said.

"Are they closed?" he said. "Don't fudge."

"They're closed," I said.

"Keep them that way," he said. He said, "Don't stop now. Draw."

So we kept on with it. His fingers rode my fingers as my hand went over the paper. It was like nothing else in my life up to now.

Then he said, "I think that's it. I think you got it," he said. "Take a look. What do you think?"

But I had my eyes closed. I thought I'd keep them that way for a little longer. I thought it was something I ought to do.

"Well?" he said. "Are you looking?"

My eyes were still closed. I was in my house. I knew that. But I didn't feel like I was inside anything.

"It's really something," I said.

—1983

MARGARET ATWOOD

Canada's best-known writer, Margaret Atwood is the author of over fifty works, in genres as diverse as fiction, poetry, the critical essay, opera, and political comic strips. She is part of the literary generation that came of age in the explosion of Canadian nationalism in the 1960s and '70s and that pushed Canadian writing and writers to the forefront of Canadian culture. She graduated from Victoria College, University of Toronto in 1961, and completed her M.A. in 1962 at Radcliffe College, where she studied Victorian literature and early American literature. She worked toward a Ph.D. at Harvard, but returned to Canada in 1963. For a year she worked as a market researcher, an experience she later mined to write her first novel, *The Edible Woman* (1969). In 1966 she won a Governor General's Award for her first poetry collection, *The Circle Game* (1964).

Atwood has continued to publish acclaimed works of poetry, but she is best known for her fiction. Her major novels include works of speculative fiction such as *The Handmaid's Tale* (1986), *Oryx and Crake* (2003), and *The Year of the Flood* (2009); works of contemporary social satire such as *The Robber Bride* (1993); and historical novels such as *Alias Grace* (1996) and *The Blind Assassin* (winner of the prestigious Man Booker Prize in 2000).

Atwood intended her first book of literary criticism to be a general reader's guide and introduction to Canadian literature, but *Survival: A Thematic Guide to Canadian Literature* (1972) became a landmark in Canadian literary criticism, and sparked a charged debate about marginalized figures in Canadian writing. Atwood's career has also been notable for her literary and political activism; she is a co-founder and past president of the Writers' Union of Canada, and has been president of PEN-International's Canadian English-speaking branch and vice-president of PEN-International. Political issues are close to the surface in much of her fiction—as well as in *Payback: Debt and the Shadow Side of Wealth* (2008), which became a non-fiction bestseller.

Born in Ottawa in 1939, Atwood spent her childhood living with her family in Ottawa in the winters and spending the remaining parts of the year in Northern Quebec and Ontario while her entomologist father conducted his research on bees, spruce budworms, and tent caterpillars. In an interview with Eleanor Wachtel, Atwood has described the wild landscape of her childhood:

> [I]f you are watching a figure in that landscape, one minute you see it and the next minute you don't. It disappears among the trees, it goes around the corner, people dive. There is a constant metamorphosis going on between human figures, foliage and water surfaces in that sort of landscape.... it's easy to get lost and there is always the possibility that something may come out of the woods.

Living in Toronto with her partner, novelist Graeme Gibson, Atwood continues to be active in the Canadian arts and culture scene. Not long after her novel *The Year of the Flood* was published in 2009, she was commissioned to write a chamber opera about author Pauline Johnson.

"Death by Landscape," which was published in the Trillium Award-winning collection *Wilderness Tips* (1991), is a story informed by Atwood's early intimate knowledge of the Ontario bush. The story ventures into familiar Atwoodian territory in its concentration on the danger that exists below the most benign of surfaces.

Death by Landscape

MARGARET ATWOOD

NOW THAT the boys are grown up and Rob is dead, Lois has moved to a condominium apartment in one of the newer waterfront developments. She is relieved not to have to worry about the lawn, or about the ivy pushing its muscular little suckers into the brickwork, or the squirrels gnawing their way into the attic and eating the insulation off the wiring, or about strange noises. This building has a security system, and the only plant life is in pots in the solarium.

Lois is glad she's been able to find an apartment big enough for her pictures. They are more crowded together than they were in the house, but this arrangement gives the walls a European look: blocks of pictures, above and beside one another, rather than one over the chesterfield, one over the fireplace, one in the front hall, in the old acceptable manner of sprinkling art around so it does not get too intrusive. This way has more of an impact. You know it's not supposed to be furniture.

None of the pictures is very large, which doesn't mean they aren't valuable. They are paintings, or sketches and drawings, by artists who were not nearly as well known when Lois began to buy them as they are now. Their work later turned up on stamps, or as silk-screen reproductions hung in the principals' offices of high schools, or as jigsaw puzzles, or on beautifully printed calendars sent out by corporations as Christmas gifts, to their less important clients. These artists painted mostly in the twenties and thirties and forties; they painted landscapes. Lois has two Tom Thomsons, three A.Y. Jacksons, a Lawren Harris. She has an Arthur Lismer, she has a J.E.H. MacDonald. She has a David Milne. They are pictures of convoluted tree trunks on an island of pink wave-smoothed stone, with more islands behind; of a lake with rough, bright, sparsely wooded cliffs; of a vivid river shore with a tangle of bush and two beached canoes, one red, one grey; of a yellow autumn woods with the ice-blue gleam of a pond half-seen through the interlaced branches.

It was Lois who'd chosen them. Rob had no interest in art, although he could see the necessity of having something on the walls. He left all the decorating decisions to her, while providing the money, of course. Because of this collection of hers, Lois's friends—especially the men—have given her the reputation of having a good nose for art investments.

But this is not why she bought the pictures, way back then. She bought them because she wanted them. She wanted something that was in them, although she could not have said at the time what it was. It was not peace: she does not find them peaceful in the least. Looking at them fills her with a wordless unease. Despite the fact that there are no people in them or even animals, it's as if there is something, or someone, looking back out.

When she was thirteen, Lois went on a canoe trip. She'd only been on overnights before. This was to be a long one, into the trackless wilderness, as Cappie put it. It was Lois's first canoe trip, and her last.

Cappie was the head of the summer camp to which Lois had been sent ever since she was nine. Camp Manitou, it was called; it was one of the better ones, for girls, though not the best. Girls of her age whose parents could afford it were routinely packed off to such camps, which bore a generic resemblance to one another. They favoured Indian names and had hearty, energetic leaders, who were called Cappie or Skip or Scottie. At these camps you learned to swim well and sail, and paddle a canoe, and perhaps ride a horse or play tennis. When you weren't doing these things you could do Arts and Crafts and turn out dingy, lumpish clay ashtrays for your mother—mothers smoked more, then—or bracelets made of coloured braided string.

Cheerfulness was required at all times, even at breakfast. Loud shouting and the banging of spoons on the tables were allowed, and even encouraged, at ritual intervals. Chocolate bars were rationed, to control tooth decay and pimples.

At night, after supper, in the dining hall or outside around a mosquito-infested campfire ring for special treats, there were singsongs. Lois can still remember all the words to "My Darling Clementine," and to "My Bonnie Lies Over the Ocean," with acting-out gestures; a rippling of the hands for "the ocean," two hands together under the cheek for "lies." She will never be able to forget them, which is a sad thought.

Lois thinks she can recognize women who went to these camps, and were good at it. They have a hardness to their handshakes, even now; a way of standing, legs planted firmly and farther apart than usual; a way of sizing you up, to see if you'd be any good in a canoe—the front, not the back. They themselves would be in the back. They would call it the stern.

She knows that such camps still exist, although Camp Manitou does not. They are one of the few things that haven't changed much. They now offer copper enamelling and functionless pieces of stained glass baked in electric ovens, though judging from the production of her friends' grandchildren the artistic standards have not improved.

To Lois, encountering it in the first year after the war, Camp Manitou seemed ancient. Its log-sided buildings with the white cement in between the half-logs, its flagpole ringed with whitewashed stones, its weathered grey dock jutting out into Lake Prospect, with its woven rope bumpers and its rusty rings for tying up, its prim round flowerbed of petunias near the office door, must surely have been there always. In truth it dated only from the first decade of the century; it had been founded by Cappie's parents, who'd thought of camping as bracing to the character, like cold showers, and had been passed along to her as an inheritance, and an obligation.

Lois realized, later, that it must have been a struggle for Cappie to keep Camp Manitou going, during the Depression and then the war, when money did not flow freely. If it had been a camp for the very rich, instead of the merely well off, there would have been fewer problems. But there must have been enough Old Girls, ones with daughters, to keep the thing in operation, though not entirely shipshape: furniture was battered, painted trim was peeling, roofs leaked. There were dim photographs of these Old Girls dotted around the dining hall, wearing ample woollen bathing suits and showing their fat, dimpled legs, or standing, arms twined, in odd tennis outfits with baggy skirts.

In the dining hall, over the stone fireplace that was never used, there was a huge moulting stuffed moose head, which looked somehow carnivorous. It was a sort of mascot; its name was Monty Manitou. The older campers spread the story that it was haunted, and came to life in the dark, when the feeble and undependable lights had been turned off or, due to yet another generator failure, had gone out. Lois was afraid of it at first, but not after she got used to it.

Cappie was the same: you had to get used to her. Possibly she was forty, or thirty-five, or fifty. She had fawn-coloured hair that looked as if it was cut with a bowl. Her head jutted forward, jiggling like a chicken's as she strode around the camp, clutching notebooks and checking things off in them. She was like their minister in church: both of them smiled a lot and were anxious because they wanted things to go well; they both had the same overwashed skins and stringy necks. But all this disappeared when Cappie was leading a singsong, or otherwise leading. Then she was happy, sure of herself, her plain face almost luminous. She wanted to cause joy. At these times she was loved, at others merely trusted.

There were many things Lois didn't like about Camp Manitou, at first. She hated the noisy chaos and spoon-banging of the dining hall, the rowdy singsongs at which you were expected to yell in order to show that you were enjoying yourself. Hers was not a household that encouraged yelling. She hated the necessity of having to write dutiful letters to her parents claiming she was having fun. She could not complain, because camp cost so much money.

She didn't much like having to undress in a roomful of other girls, even in the dim light, although nobody paid any attention, or sleeping in a cabin with seven other girls, some of whom snored because they had adenoids or colds, some of whom had nightmares, or wet their beds and cried about it. Bottom bunks made her feel closed in, and she was afraid of falling out of top ones; she was afraid of heights. She got homesick, and suspected her parents of having a better time when she wasn't there than when she was, although her mother wrote to her every week saying how much they missed her. All this was when she was nine. By the time she was thirteen she liked it. She was an old hand by then.

Lucy was her best friend at camp. Lois had other friends in winter, when there was school and itchy woollen clothing and darkness in the afternoons, but Lucy was her summer friend.

She turned up the second year, when Lois was ten, and a Bluejay. (Chickadees, Bluejays, Ravens, and Kingfishers—these were the names Camp Manitou assigned to the different age groups, a sort of totemic clan system. In those days, thinks Lois, it was birds for girls, animals for boys: wolves, and so forth. Though some animals and birds were suitable and some were not. Never vultures, for instance; never skunks, or rats.)

Lois helped Lucy to unpack her tin trunk and place the folded clothes on the wooden shelves, and to make up her bed. She put her in the top bunk right above her, where she could keep an eye on her. Already she knew that Lucy was an exception, to a good many rules; already she felt proprietorial.

Lucy was from the United States, where the comic books came from, and the movies. She wasn't from New York or Hollywood or Buffalo, the only American cities Lois knew the names of, but from Chicago. Her house was on the lake shore and had gates to it, and grounds. They had a maid, all of the time. Lois's family only had a cleaning lady twice a week.

The only reason Lucy was being sent to *this* camp (she cast a look of minor scorn around the cabin, diminishing it and also offending Lois, while at the same time daunting her) was that her mother had been a camper here. Her mother had been a Canadian once, but had married her father, who had a patch over one eye, like a pirate. She showed Lois the picture of him in her wallet. He got the patch in the war. "Shrapnel," said Lucy. Lois, who was unsure about shrapnel, was so impressed she could only grunt. Her own two-eyed, unwounded father was tame by comparison.

"My father plays golf," she ventured at last.

"*Everyone* plays golf," said Lucy. "My *mother* plays golf."

Lois's mother did not. Lois took Lucy to see the outhouses and the swimming dock and the dining hall with Monty Manitou's baleful head, knowing in advance they would not measure up.

This was a bad beginning; but Lucy was good-natured, and accepted Camp Manitou with the same casual shrug with which she seemed to accept everything. She would make the best of it, without letting Lois forget that this was what she was doing.

However, there were things Lois knew that Lucy did not. Lucy scratched the tops off all her mosquito bites and had to be taken to the infirmary to be daubed with Ozonol. She took her T-shirt off while sailing, and although the counsellor spotted her after a while and made her put it back on, she burnt spectacularly bright red, with the X of her bathing-suit straps standing out in alarming white; she let Lois peel the sheets of whispery-thin burned skin off her shoulders. When they sang "Alouette" around the campfire, she did not know any of the French words. The difference was that Lucy did not care about the things she didn't know, whereas Lois did.

During the next winter, and subsequent winters, Lucy and Lois wrote to each other. They were both only children, at a time when this was thought to be a disadvantage, so in their letters they pretended to be sisters, or even twins. Lois had to strain a little over this, because Lucy was so blonde, with translucent skin and large blue eyes like a doll's, and Lois was nothing out of the ordinary—just a tallish, thinnish, brownish person with freckles. They signed their letters LL, with the Ls entwined together like the monograms on a towel. (Lois and Lucy thinks Lois. How our names date us. Lois Lane, Superman's girlfriend, enterprising female reporter; "I Love Lucy." Now we are obsolete, and it's little Jennifers, and little Emilys, little Alexandras and Carolines and Tiffanys.)

They were more effusive in their letters than they ever were in person. They bordered their pages with X's and O's, but when they met again in the summers it was always a shock. They had changed so much, or Lucy had. It was like watching someone grow up in jolts. At first it would be hard to think up things to say.

But Lucy always had a surprise or two, something to show, some marvel to reveal. The first year she had a picture of herself in a tutu, her hair in a ballerina's knot on the top of her head; she pirouetted around the swimming dock, to show Lois how it was done, and almost fell off. The next year she had given that up and was taking horseback riding. (Camp Manitou did not have horses.) The next year her mother and father had been divorced, and she had a new stepfather, one with both eyes, and a new house, although the maid was the same. The next year, when they had graduated from Bluejays and entered Ravens, she got her period, right in the first week of camp. The two of them snitched some matches from their counsellor, who smoked illegally, and made a small fire out behind the farthest outhouse, at dusk, using their flashlights. They could set all kinds of fires by now; they had learned how in Campcraft. On this fire they burned one of Lucy's used sanitary napkins. Lois is not sure why they did this, or whose idea it was. But she can remember the feeling of deep satisfaction it gave her as the white fluff singed and the blood sizzled, as if some wordless ritual had been fulfilled.

They did not get caught, but then they rarely got caught at any of their camp transgressions. Lucy had such large eyes, and was such an accomplished liar.

This year Lucy is different again: slower, more languorous. She is no longer interested in sneaking around after dark, purloining cigarettes from the counsellor, dealing in black-market candy bars. She is pensive, and hard to wake in the mornings. She doesn't like her stepfather, but she doesn't want to live with her real father either, who has a new wife. She thinks her mother may be having a love affair with a doctor; she doesn't know for sure, but she's seen them smooching in his car, out on the driveway, when her stepfather wasn't there. It serves him right. She hates her private school. She has a boyfriend, who is sixteen and works as a gardener's assistant. This is how she met him: in the garden. She describes to Lois what it is like when he kisses her—rubbery at first, but then your knees go limp. She has been forbidden to see him, and threatened with boarding school. She wants to run away from home.

Lois has little to offer in return. Her own life is placid and satisfactory, but there is nothing much that can be said about happiness. "You're so lucky," Lucy tells her, a little smugly. She might as well say *boring* because this is how it makes Lois feel.

Lucy is apathetic about the canoe trip, so Lois has to disguise her own excitement. The evening before they are to leave, she slouches into the campfire ring as if coerced, and sits down with a sigh of endurance, just as Lucy does.

Every canoe trip that went out of camp was given a special send-off by Cappie and the section leader and counsellors, with the whole section in attendance. Cappie painted three streaks of red across each of her cheeks with a lipstick. They looked like three-fingered claw marks. She put a blue circle on her forehead with fountain-pen ink, and tied a twisted bandanna around her head and stuck a row of frazzle-ended feathers around it, and wrapped herself in a red-and-black Hudson's Bay blanket. The counsellors, also in blankets but with only two streaks of red, beat on tom-toms made of round wooden cheese boxes with leather stretched over the top and nailed in place. Cappie was Chief Cappeosota. They all had to say "How!" when she walked into the circle and stood there with one hand raised.

Looking back on this, Lois finds it disquieting. She knows too much about Indians this is why. She knows, for instance, that they should not even be called Indians, and that they have enough worries without other people taking their names and dressing up as them. It has all been a form of stealing.

But she remembers, too, that she was once ignorant of this. Once she loved the campfire, the flickering of light on the ring of faces, the sound of the fake tom-toms, heavy and fast like a scared heartbeat; she loved Cappie in a red blanket and feathers, solemn, as a chief should be, raising her hand and saying, "Greetings, my Ravens." It was not funny, it was not making fun. She wanted to be an Indian. She wanted to be adventurous and pure, and aboriginal.

"You go on big water," says Cappie. This is her idea—all their ideas—of how Indians talk. "You go where no man has ever trod. You go many moons." This is not true. They are only going for a week, not many moons. The canoe route is clearly marked, they have gone over it on a map, and there are prepared campsites with names which are used year after year. But when Cappie says this—and despite the way Lucy rolls up her eyes—Lois can feel the water stretching out, with the shores twisting away on either side, immense and a little frightening.

"You bring back much wampum," says Cappie. "Do good in war, my braves, and capture many scalps." This is another of her pretences: that they are boys, and blood-thirsty. But such a game cannot be played by substituting the word "squaw." It would not work at all.

Each of them has to stand up and step forward and have a red line drawn across her cheeks by Cappie. She tells them they must follow in the paths of their ancestors (who most certainly thinks Lois, looking out the window of her apartment and remembering the family stash of daguerreotypes and sepia-coloured portraits on her mother's dressing table, the stiff-shirted, black-coated, grim-faced men and the beflounced women with their severe hair and their corseted respectability, would never have considered heading off onto an open lake, in a canoe, just for fun).

At the end of the ceremony they all stood and held hands around the circle, and sang taps. This did not sound very Indian, thinks Lois. It sounded like a bugle call at a military post, in a movie. But Cappie was never one to be much concerned with consistency, or with archaeology.

After breakfast the next morning they set out from the main dock, in four canoes, three in each. The lipstick stripes have not come off completely, and still show faintly pink, like healing burns. They wear their white denim sailing hats, because of the sun, and thin-striped T-shirts, and pale baggy shorts with the cuffs rolled up. The middle one kneels, propping her rear end against the rolled sleeping bags. The counsellors going with them are Pat and Kip. Kip is no-nonsense; Pat is easier to wheedle, or fool.

There are white puffy clouds and a small breeze. Glints come from the little waves. Lois is in the bow of Kip's canoe. She still can't do a J-stroke very well, and she will have to be in the bow or the middle for the whole trip. Lucy is behind her; her own J-stroke is even worse. She splashes Lois with her paddle, quite a big splash.

"I'll get you back," says Lois.

"There was a stable fly on your shoulder," Lucy says.

Lois turns to look at her, to see if she's grinning. They're in the habit of splashing each other. Back there, the camp has vanished behind the first long point of rock and rough trees. Lois feels as if an invisible rope has broken. They're floating free, on their own, cut loose. Beneath the canoe the lake goes down, deeper and colder than it was a minute before.

"No horsing around in the canoe," says Kip. She's rolled her T-shirt sleeves up to the shoulder; her arms are brown and sinewy, her jaw determined, her stroke perfect. She looks as if she knows exactly what she is doing.

The four canoes keep close together. They sing, raucously and with defiance; they sing "The Quartermaster's Store," and "Clementine," and "Alouette." It is more like bellowing than singing.

After that the wind grows stronger, blowing slantwise against the bows, and they have to put all their energy into shoving themselves through the water.

Was there anything important, anything that would provide some sort of reason or clue to what happened next? Lois can remember everything, every detail; but it does her no good.

They stopped at noon for a swim and lunch, and went on in the afternoon. At last they reached Little Birch, which was the first campsite for overnight.

Lois and Lucy made the fire, while the others pitched the heavy canvas tents. The fireplace was already there, flat stones piled into a U. A burned tin can and a beer bottle had been left in it. Their fire went out, and they had to restart it. "Hustle your bustle," said Kip. "We're starving."

The sun went down, and in the pink sunset light they brushed their teeth and spat the toothpaste froth into the lake. Kip and Pat put all the food that wasn't in cans into a packsack and slung it into a tree, in case of bears.

Lois and Lucy weren't sleeping in a tent. They'd begged to be allowed to sleep out; that way they could talk without the others hearing. If it rained, they told Kip, they promised not to crawl dripping into the tent over everyone's legs; they would get under the canoes. So they were out on the point.

Lois tried to get comfortable inside her sleeping bag, which smelled of musty storage and of earlier campers, a stale salty sweetness. She curled herself up, with her sweater rolled up under her head for a pillow and her flashlight inside her sleeping bag so it wouldn't roll away. The muscles of her sore arms were making small pings, like rubber bands breaking.

Beside her Lucy was rustling around. Lois could see the glimmering oval of her white face.

"I've got a rock poking into my back," said Lucy.

"So do I," said Lois. "You want to go into the tent?" She herself didn't, but it was right to ask.

"No," said Lucy. She subsided into her sleeping bag. After a moment she said, "It would be nice not to go back."

"To camp?" said Lois.

"To Chicago," said Lucy. "I hate it there."

"What about your boyfriend?" said Lois. Lucy didn't answer. She was either asleep or pretending to be.

There was a moon, and a movement of the trees. In the sky there were stars, layers of stars that went down and down. Kip said that when the stars were bright like that instead of hazy it meant bad weather later on. Out on the lake there were two loons, calling to each other in their insane, mournful voices. At the time it did not sound like grief. It was just background.

The lake in the morning was flat calm. They skimmed along over the glassy surface, leaving V-shaped trails behind them; it felt like flying. As the sun rose higher it got hot, almost too hot. There were stable flies in the canoes, landing on a bare arm or leg for a quick sting. Lois hoped for wind.

They stopped for lunch at the next of the named campsites, Lookout Point. It was called this because, although the site itself was down near the water on a flat shelf of rock, there was a sheer cliff nearby and a trail that led up to the top. The top was the lookout, although what you were supposed to see from there was not clear. Kip said it was just a view.

Lois and Lucy decided to make the climb anyway. They didn't want to hang around waiting for lunch. It wasn't their turn to cook, though they hadn't avoided much by not doing it, because cooking lunch was no big deal, it was just unwrapping the cheese and getting out the bread and peanut butter, but Pat and Kip always had to do their woodsy act and boil up a billy tin for their own tea.

They told Kip where they were going. You had to tell Kip where you were going, even if it was only a little way into the woods to get dry twigs for kindling. You could never go anywhere without a buddy.

"Sure," said Kip, who was crouching over the fire, feeding driftwood into it. "Fifteen minutes to lunch."

"Where are they off to?" said Pat. She was bringing their billy tin of water from the lake.

"Lookout," said Kip.

"Be careful," said Pat. She said it as an afterthought, because it was what she always said.

"They're old hands," Kip said.

Lois looks at her watch: it's ten to twelve. She is the watchminder; Lucy is careless of time. They walk up the path, which is dry earth and rocks, big rounded pinky-grey boulders or split-open ones with jagged edges. Spindly balsam and spruce trees grow to either side, the lake is blue fragments to the left. The sun is right overhead; there are no shadows anywhere. The heat comes up at them as well as down. The forest is dry and crackly.

It isn't far, but it's a steep climb and they're sweating when they reach the top. They wipe their faces with their bare arms, sit gingerly down on a scorching-hot rock, five feet from the edge but too close for Lois. It's a lookout all right, a sheer drop to the lake and a long view over the water, back the way they've come. It's amazing to Lois that they've travelled so far, over all that water, with nothing to propel them but their own arms. It makes her feel strong. There are all kinds of things she is capable of doing.

"It would be quite a dive off here," says Lucy.

"You'd have to be nuts," says Lois.

"Why?" says Lucy. "It's really deep. It goes straight down." She stands up and takes a step nearer the edge. Lois gets a stab in her midriff, the kind she gets when a car goes too fast over a bump. "Don't," she says.

"Don't what?" says Lucy, glancing around at her mischievously. She knows how Lois feels about heights. But she turns back. "I really have to pee," she says.

"You have toilet paper?" says Lois, who is never without it. She digs in her shorts pocket.

"Thanks," says Lucy.

They are both adept at peeing in the woods: doing it fast so the mosquitoes don't get you, the underwear pulled up between the knees, the squat with the feet apart so you don't wet your legs, facing downhill. The exposed feeling of your bum, as if someone is looking at you from behind. The etiquette when you're with someone else is not to look. Lois stands up and starts to walk back down the path, to be out of sight.

"Wait for me?" says Lucy.

Lois climbed down, over and around the boulders, until she could not see Lucy; she waited. She could hear the voices of the others, talking and laughing, down near the shore. One voice was yelling, "Ants! Ants!" Someone must have sat on an ant hill. Off to the side, in the woods, a raven was croaking, a hoarse single note.

She looked at her watch: it was noon. This is when she heard the shout.

She has gone over and over in her mind since, so many times that the first, real shout has been obliterated, like a footprint trampled by other footprints. But she is sure (she is almost positive, she is nearly certain) that it was not a shout of fear. Not a scream. More like a cry of surprise, cut off too soon. Short, like a dog's bark.

"Lucy?" Lois said. Then she called "Lucy!" By now she was clambering back up, over the stones of the path. Lucy was not up there. Or she was not in sight.

"Stop fooling around," Lois said. "It's lunch-time." But Lucy did not rise from behind a rock or step out, smiling, from behind a tree. The sunlight was all around; the rocks looked white. "This isn't funny!" Lois said, and it wasn't, panic was rising in her, the panic of a small child who does not know where the bigger ones are hidden. She could hear her own heart. She looked quickly around; she lay down on the ground and looked over the edge of the cliff. It made her feel cold. There was nothing.

She went back down the path, stumbling; she was breathing too quickly; she was too frightened to cry. She felt terrible—guilty and dismayed, as if she had done something very bad, by mistake. Something that could never be repaired. "Lucy's gone," she told Kip.

Kip looked up from her fire, annoyed. The water in the billy can was boiling. "What do you mean, gone?" she said. "Where did she go?"

"I don't know," said Lois. "She's just gone."

No one had heard the shout, but then no one had heard Lois calling, either. They had been talking among themselves, by the water.

Kip and Pat went up to the lookout and searched and called, and blew their whistles. Nothing answered.

Then they came back down, and Lois had to tell exactly what had happened. The other girls all sat in a circle and listened to her. Nobody said anything. They all looked frightened, especially Pat and Kip. They were the leaders. You did not just lose a camper like this, for no reason at all.

"Why did you leave her alone?" said Kip.

"I was just down the path," said Lois. "I told you. She had to go to the bathroom." She did not say *pee* in front of people older than herself.

Kip looked disgusted.

"Maybe she just walked off into the woods and got turned around," said one of the girls.

"Maybe she's doing it on purpose," said another.

Nobody believed either of these theories.

They took the canoes and searched around the base of the cliff, and peered down into the water. But there had been no sound of falling rock; there had been no splash. There was no clue, nothing at all. Lucy had simple vanished.

That was the end of the canoe trip. It took them the same two days to go back that it had taken coming in, even though they were short a paddler. They did not sing.

After that, the police went in a motorboat, with dogs; they were the Mounties and the dogs were German shepherds, trained to follow trails in the woods. But it had rained since, and they could find nothing.

Lois is sitting in Cappie's office. Her face is bloated with crying, she's seen that in the mirror. By now she feels numbed; she feels as if she has drowned. She can't stay here. It has been too much of a shock. Tomorrow her parents are coming to take her away. Several of the other girls who were on the canoe trip are also being collected. The others will have to stay, because their parents are in Europe, or cannot be reached.

Cappie is grim. They've tried to hush it up, but of course everyone in camp knows. Soon the papers will know too. You can't keep it quiet, but what can be said? What can be said that makes any sense? "Girl vanishes in broad daylight, without a trace." It can't be believed. Other things, worse things, will be suspected. Negligence, at the very least. But they have always taken such care. Bad luck will gather around Camp Manitou like a fog; parents will avoid it, in favour of other, luckier places. Lois can see Cappie thinking all this, even through her numbness. It's what anyone would think.

Lois sits on the hard wooden chair in Cappie's office, beside the old wooden desk, over which hangs the thumb-tacked bulletin board of normal camp routine, and gazes at Cappie through her puffy eyelids. Cappie is now smiling what is supposed to be a reassuring smile. Her manner is too casual: she's after something. Lois has seen this look on Cappie's face when she's been sniffing out contraband chocolate bars, hunting down those rumoured to have snuck out of their cabins at night.

"Tell me again," says Cappie, "from the beginning."

Lois has told her story so many times by now, to Pat and Kip, to Cappie, to the police, that she knows it word for word. She knows it, but she no longer believes it. It has become a story. "I told you," she said. "She wanted to go to the bathroom. I gave her my toilet paper. I went down the path, I waited for her. I heard this kind of shout ..."

"Yes," says Cappie, smiling confidingly, "but before that. What did you say to one another?"

Lois thinks. Nobody has asked her this before. "She said you could dive off there. She said it went straight down."

"And what did you say?"

"I said you'd have to be nuts."

"Were you mad at Lucy?" says Cappie, in an encouraging voice.

"No," says Lois. "Why would I be mad at Lucy? I wasn't ever mad at Lucy." She feels like crying again. The times when she has in fact been mad at Lucy have been erased already. Lucy was always perfect.

"Sometimes we're angry when we don't know we're angry," says Cappie, as if to herself. "Sometimes we get really mad and we don't even know it. Sometimes we might do a thing without meaning to, or without knowing what will happen. We lose our tempers."

Lois is only thirteen, but it doesn't take her long to figure out that Cappie is not including herself in any of this. By *we* she means Lois. She is accusing Lois of pushing Lucy off the cliff. The unfairness of this hits her like a slap.

"I didn't!" she says.

"Didn't what?" says Cappie softly. "Didn't what, Lois?"

Lois does the worst thing, she begins to cry. Cappie gives her a look like a pounce. She's got what she wanted.

Later, when she was grown up, Lois was able to understand what this interview had been about. She could see Cappie's desperation, her need for a story, a real story with a reason in it; anything but the senseless vacancy Lucy had left for her to deal with. Cappie wanted Lois to supply the reason, to be the reason. It wasn't even for the newspapers or the parents, because she could never make such an accusation without proof. It was for herself: something to explain the loss of Camp Manitou and of all she had worked for, the years of entertaining spoiled children and buttering up parents and making a fool of herself with feathers stuck in her hair. Camp Manitou was in fact lost. It did not survive.

Lois worked all this out, twenty years later. But it was far too late. It was too late even ten minutes afterwards, when she'd left Cappie's office and was walking slowly back to her cabin to pack. Lucy's clothes were still there, folded on the shelves, as if waiting. She felt the other girls in the cabin watching her with speculation in their eyes. *Could she have done it? She must have done it.* For the rest of her life, she has caught people watching her in this way.

Maybe they weren't thinking this. Maybe they were merely sorry for her. But she felt she had been tried and sentenced, and this is what has stayed with her: the knowledge that she had been singled out, condemned for something that was not her fault.

Lois sits in the living room of her apartment, drinking a cup of tea. Through the knee-to-ceiling window she has a wide view of Lake Ontario, with its skin of wrinkled blue-grey light, and of the willows of Centre Island shaken by a wind, which is silent at this distance, and on this side of the glass. When there isn't too much pollution she can see the far shore, the foreign shore; though today it is obscured.

Possibly she could go out, go downstairs, do some shopping; there isn't much in the refrigerator. The boys say she doesn't get out enough. But she isn't hungry and moving, stirring from this space, is increasingly an effort.

She can hardly remember, now, having her two boys in the hospital, nursing them as babies; she can hardly remember getting married, or what Rob looked like. Even at the time she never felt she was paying full attention. She was tired a lot, as if she was living not one life but two: her own, and another, shadowy life that hovered around her and would not let itself be realized—the life of what would have happened if Lucy had not stepped sideways, and disappeared from time.

She would never go up north, to Rob's family cottage or to any place with wild lakes and wild trees and the calls of loons. She would never go anywhere near. Still, it was as if she was always listening for another voice, the voice of a person who should have been there but was not. An echo.

While Rob was alive, while the boys were growing up, she could pretend she didn't hear it, this empty space in sound. But now there is nothing much left to distract her.

She turns away from the window and looks at her pictures. There is the pinkish island, in the lake, with the intertwisted trees. It's the same landscape they paddled through, that distant summer. She's seen travelogues of this country, aerial photographs; it looks different from above, bigger, more hopeless: lake after lake, random blue puddles in dark green bush, the trees like bristles.

How could you ever find anything there, once it was lost? Maybe if they cut it all down, drained it all away, they might find Lucy's bones, some time, wherever they are hidden. A few bones, some buttons, the buckle from her shorts.

But a dead person is a body; a body occupies space, it exists somewhere. You can see it; you put it in a box and bury it in the ground, and then it's in a box in the ground. But Lucy is not in a box, or in the ground. Because she is nowhere definite, she could be anywhere.

And these paintings are not landscape paintings. Because there aren't any landscapes up there, not in the old, tidy European sense, with a gentle hill, a curving river, a cottage, a mountain in the background, a golden evening sky. Instead there's a tangle, a receding maze, in which you can become lost almost as soon as you step off the path. There are no backgrounds in any of these paintings, no vistas; only a great deal of foreground that goes back and back, endlessly, involving you in its twists and turns of tree and branch and rock. No matter how far back in you go, there will be more. And the trees themselves are hardly trees; they are currents of energy, charged with violent colour.

Who knows how many trees there were on the cliff just before Lucy disappeared? Who counted? Maybe there was one more, afterwards.

Lois sits in her chair and does not move. Her hand with the cup is raised halfway to her mouth. She hears something, almost hears it: a shout of recognition, or of joy.

She looks at the paintings, she looks into them. Every one of them is a picture of Lucy. You can't see her exactly, but she's there, in behind the pink stone island or the one behind that. In the picture of the cliff she is hidden by the clutch of fallen rocks towards the bottom, in the one of the river shore she is crouching beneath the overturned canoe. In the yellow autumn woods she's behind the tree that cannot be seen because of the other trees, over beside the blue sliver of pond; but if you walked into the picture and found the tree, it would be the wrong one, because the right one would be further on.

Everyone has to be somewhere, and this is where Lucy is. She is in Lois's apartment, in the holes that open inwards on the wall, not like windows but like doors. She is here. She is entirely alive.

—1991

RICHARD FORD

Born in Jackson, Mississippi, in 1944, Richard Ford has lived in many parts of the United States, in Mexico, and in France. In an interview with Don Lee of *Ploughshares* magazine, he addressed earlier reviewers' tendency to try to categorize him with other writers from the southern United States such as William Faulkner: "I'm a Southerner, God knows," says Ford, "but I always wanted my books to exist outside the limits of so-called Southern writing." He is perhaps best known for his break-out novel *The Sportswriter* (1986) and its sequel, *Independence Day* (1995), which was the first book to win both the Pulitzer Prize and the PEN/Faulkner Award for Fiction.

Ford's writing career had many false starts before he settled into writing as a full-time vocation. As a result of his father's heart problems, from the age of eight Ford lived both in Jackson with his father and in Little Rock, Arkansas, with his grandfather. Ford's father died of heart failure when he was sixteen, and by the time Ford graduated from high school he had resolved to follow in his grandfather's footsteps and become a hotel manager. He enrolled in the Hotel Science school at Michigan State University; on a whim, he later changed his major to literature. During this time he experimented with writing fiction but never treated it as a serious option.

Upon graduation, Ford worked at a number of jobs, including junior high school teacher and assistant science editor for *American Druggist*; he also enrolled in law school for one semester. On the advice of a former teacher, he eventually applied to the M.F.A. program at the University of California at Irvine, from which he graduated in 1970. Unable to find publishers for his short fiction, he began working on the novel *A Piece of My Heart*, which was published in 1976 and was nominated for the Ernest Hemingway Award for Best First Novel. The novel *The Ultimate Good Luck* followed in 1981. Ford took on various creative writing teaching jobs at the University of Michigan, Williams College, and Princeton but became dissatisfied with teaching and with his writing career, and was ready to quit writing fiction altogether. In 1981 he took a job as a sportswriter for the New York magazine *Inside Sports*. The magazine folded a year later and Ford was left without work; in his time without a job he wrote the novel *The Sportswriter*, which brought him national recognition when it was nominated for the PEN/Faulkner Award for Fiction. *The Sportswriter* and *Independence Day* have been followed by the novels *The Lay of the Land* (2006), and *Canada* (2012). Ford has also published the short story collections *Rock Springs* (1987) and *A Multitude of Sins* (2001), three novellas collected under the title *Women with Men* (1997), essays, a play, a screenplay, and several short story anthologies.

"Under the Radar" is from the collection *A Multitude of Sins.* Like other stories in the collection, it explores the themes of marital discontent and infidelity. In this case infidelity reveals fissures in a marriage that the characters have desperately tried to deny.

Under the Radar

RICHARD FORD

ON THE drive over to the Nicholsons' for dinner—their first in some time—Marjorie Reeves told her husband, Steven Reeves, that she had had an affair with George Nicholson (their host) a year ago, but that it was all over with now and she hoped he—Steven—would not be mad about it and could go on with life.

At this point they were driving along Quaker Bridge Road where it leaves the Perkins Great Woods Road and begins to border the Shenipsit Reservoir, dark and shadowy and calmly mirrored in the late spring twilight. On the right was dense young timber, beech and alder saplings in pale leaf, the ground damp and cakey. Peepers were calling out from the watery lows. Their turn onto Apple Orchard Lane was still a mile on.

Steven, on hearing this news, began gradually and very carefully to steer their car a tan Mercedes wagon with hooded yellow headlights—off of Quaker Bridge Road and onto the damp grassy shoulder so he could organize this information properly before going on.

They were extremely young. Steven Reeves was twenty-eight. Marjorie Reeves a year younger. They weren't rich, but they'd been lucky. Steven's job at Packard-Wells was to stay on top of a small segment of a larger segment of a rather small prefabrication intersection that serviced the automobile industry, and where any sudden alteration, or even the rumor of an alteration in certain polymer-bonding formulas could tip crucial down-the-line demand patterns, and in that way affect the betting lines and comfort zones of a good many meaningful client positions. His job meant poring over dense and esoteric petrochemical-industry journals, attending technical seminars, flying to vendor conventions, then writing up detailed status reports and all the while keeping an eye on the market for the benefit of his higher-ups. He'd been a scholarship boy at Bates, studied chemistry, was the only son of a hard-put but upright lobstering family in Pemaquid, Maine, and had done well. His bosses at Packard-Wells liked him, saw themselves in him, and also in him saw character qualities they'd never quite owned—blond and slender callowness tending to gullibility, but backed by caution, ingenuity and a thorough-going, compact toughness. He was sharp. It was his seventh year with the company—his first job. He and Marjorie had been married two years. They had no children. The car had been his bonus two Christmases ago.

When the station wagon eased to a stop, Steven sat for a minute with the motor running, the salmon colored dash lights illuminating his face. The radio had been playing softly—the last of the news, then an interlude for French horns. Responding to no particular signal, he pressed off the radio and in the same movement switched off the ignition, which left the headlights shining on the empty, countrified road. The windows were down to attract the fresh spring air, and when the engine noise ceased the evening's ambient sounds were waiting. The peepers. A sound of thrush wings fluttering in the brush only a few yards away. The noise of something falling from a small distance and hitting an invisible water surface. Beyond the stand of saplings was the West, and through the darkened trunks, the sky was still pale yellow with the day's light, though here on Quaker Bridge Road it was nearly dark.

When Marjorie said what she had just said, she'd been looking straight ahead to where the headlights made a bright path in the dark. Perhaps she'd looked at Steven once, but having said what she'd said, she kept her hands in her lap and continued looking ahead. She was a pretty, blond, convictionless girl with small demure features—small nose, small ears, small chin, though with a surprisingly full-lipped smile which she practiced on everyone. She was fond of getting a little tipsy at parties and lowering her voice and sitting on a flowered ottoman or a burl table top with a glass of something and showing too much of her legs or inappropriate amounts of her small breasts. She had grown up in Indiana, studied art at Purdue. Steven had met her in New York at a party while she was working for a firm that did child-focused advertising for a large toymaker. He'd liked her bobbed hair, her fragile, wispy features, translucent skin and the slightly husky voice that made her seem more sophisticated than she was, but somehow convinced her she was, too. In their community, east of Hartford, the women who knew Marjorie Reeves thought of her as a bimbo who would not stay married to sweet Steven Reeves for very long. His second wife would be the right wife for him. Marjorie was just a starter.

Marjorie, however, did not think of herself that way, only that she liked men and felt happy and confident around them and assumed Steven thought this was fine and that in the long run it would help his career to have a pretty, spirited wife no one could pigeonhole. To set herself apart and to take an interest in the community she'd gone to work as a volunteer at a grieving-children's center in Hartford, which meant all black. And it was in Hartford that she'd had the chance to encounter George Nicholson and fuck him at a Red Roof Inn until they'd both gotten tired of it. It would never happen again, was her view, since in a year it hadn't happened again.

For the two or possibly five minutes now that they had sat on the side of Quaker Bridge Road in the still airish evening, with the noises of spring floating in and out of the open window, Marjorie had said nothing and Steven had also said nothing, though he realized that he was saying nothing because he was at a loss for words. A loss for words, he realized, meant that nothing which comes to mind seems very interesting to say as a next thing to what has just been said. He knew he was a callow man—a boy in some ways, still—but he was not stupid. At Bates, he had taken Dr. Sudofsky's class on *Ulysses*,[1] and come away with a sense of irony and humor and the assurance that true knowledge was a spiritual process, a quest, not a storage of dry facts—a thing like freedom which you only fully experienced in practice. He'd also played hockey, and knew that knowledge and aggressiveness were a subtle and surprising and uncommon combination. He had sought to practice both at Packard-Wells.

But for a brief and terrifying instant in the cool padded semi-darkness, just when he began experiencing his loss for words, he entered or at least nearly slipped into a softened fugue-like state in which he began to fear that he perhaps *could* not say another word; that something (work fatigue, shock, disappointment over what Marjorie had admitted) was at that moment causing him to detach from reality and to slide away from the present, and in fact to begin to lose his mind and go crazy to the extent that he was in jeopardy of beginning to gibber like a chimp, or just to slowly slump sideways against the upholstered door and not speak for a long, long time—months—and then only with the aid of drugs be able merely to speak in simple utterances that would seem cryptic, so that eventually he would have to be looked after by his mother's family in Damariscotta. A terrible thought.

And so to avoid that—to save his life and sanity—he abruptly just said a word, any word that he could say into the perfumed twilight inhabiting the car, where his wife was obviously anticipating his reply to her unhappy confession.

And for some reason the word—phrase, really—that he uttered was "ground clutter." Something he'd heard on the TV weather report as they were dressing for dinner.

---

1 Novel published in 1922 by Irish writer James Joyce and considered revolutionary in its treatment of novel form and structure. The novel follows the wanderings of Leopold Bloom through Dublin in a single day.

"Hm?" Marjorie said. "What was it?" She turned her pretty small-featured face toward him so that her pearl earrings caught light from some unknown source. She was wearing a tiny green cocktail dress and green satin shoes that showed off her incredibly thin ankles and slender bare, brown calves. She had two tiny matching green bows in her hair. She smelled sweet. "I know this wasn't what you wanted to hear, Steven," she said, "but I felt I should tell you before we got to George's. The Nicholsons', I mean. It's all over. It'll never happen again. I promise you. No one will ever mention it. I just lost my bearings last year with the move. I'm sorry." She had made a little steeple of her fingertips, as if she'd been concentrating very hard as she spoke these words. But now she put her hands again calmly in her minty green lap. She had bought her dress especially for this night at the Nicholsons'. She'd thought George would like it and Steven, too. She turned her face away and exhaled a small but detectable sigh in the car. It was then that the headlights went off automatically.

George Nicholson was a big squash-playing, thick-chested, hairy-armed Yale lawyer who sailed his own Hinckley-61 out of Essex and had started backing off from his high-priced Hartford plaintiffs' practice at fifty to devote more time to competitive racket sports and senior skiing. George was a college roommate of one of Steven's firm's senior partners and had "adopted" the Reeves when they moved into the community following their wedding. Marjorie had volunteered Saturdays with George's wife, Patsy, at the Episcopal Thrift Shop during their first six months in Connecticut. To Steven, George Nicholson had recounted a memorable, seasoning summer spent hauling deep-water lobster traps with some tough old sea dogs out of Matinicus, Maine. Later, he'd been a Marine, and sported a faded anchor, ball and chain tattooed on his forearm. Later yet he'd fucked Steven's wife.

Having said something, even something that made no sense, Steven felt a sense of glum and deflated relief as he sat in the silent car beside Marjorie, who was still facing forward. Two thoughts had begun to compete in his reviving awareness. One was clearly occasioned by his conception of George Nicholson. He thought of George Nicholson as a gasbag, but also a forceful man who'd made his pile by letting very little stand in his way. When he thought about George he always remembered the story about Matinicus, which then put into his mind a mental picture of his own father and himself hauling traps somewhere out toward Monhegan. The reek of the bait, the toss of the ocean in late spring, the consoling monotony of the solid, tree-lined shore barely visible through the mists. Thinking through that circuitry always made him vaguely admire George Nicholson, and oddly made him think he liked George even now, in spite of everything.

The other competing thought was that part of Marjorie's character had always been to confess upsetting things that turned out, he believed, not to be true:

being a hooker for a summer up in Saugatuck; topless dancing while she was an undergraduate; heroin experimentation; taking part in armed robberies with her high school boyfriend in Goshen, Indiana, where she was from. When she told these far-fetched stories she would grow distracted and shake her head, as though they were true. And now, while he didn't particularly think any of these stories was a bit truer, he did realize that he didn't really know his wife at all; and that in fact the entire conception of knowing another person—of trust, of closeness, of marriage itself—while not exactly a lie since it existed *someplace* if only as an idea (in his parents' life, at least marginally) was still completely out-of-date, defunct, was something typifying another era, now unfortunately gone. Meeting a girl, falling in love, marrying her, moving to Connecticut, buying a fucking house, starting a life with her and thinking you really knew anything about her—the last part was a complete fiction, which made all the rest a joke. Marjorie might as well have *been* a hooker or held up 7-11s and shot people, for all he really knew about her. And what was more, if he'd said any of this to her, sitting next to him thinking he would never know what, she either would not have understood a word of it or simply would've said, "Well, okay, that's fine." When people talked about the bottom line, Steven Reeves thought, they weren't talking about money, they were talking about what *this* meant, *this* kind of fatal ignorance. Money—losing it, gaining it, spending it, hoarding it—all that was only an emblem, though a good one, for what was happening here right now.

At this moment a pair of car lights rounded a curve somewhere out ahead of where the two of them sat in their station wagon. The lights found both their white faces staring forward in silence. The lights also found a raccoon just crossing the road from the reservoir shore, headed for the woods that was beside them. The car was going faster than might've been evident. The raccoon paused to peer up into the approaching beams, then continued on into the safe, opposite lane. But only then did it look up and notice Steven and Marjorie's car stopped on the verge of the road, silent in the murky evening. And because of that notice it must've decided that where it had been was much better than where it was going, and so turned to scamper back across Quaker Bridge Road toward the cool waters of the reservoir, which was what caused the car—actually it was a beat-up Ford pick-up—to rumble over it, pitching and spinning it off to the side and then motionlessness near the opposite shoulder. "Yaaaa-haaaa-yipeeee!" a man's shrill voice shouted from inside the dark cab of the pick-up, followed by another man's laughter.

And then it became very silent again. The raccoon lay on the road twenty yards in front of the Reeves's car. It didn't struggle. It was merely there.

"Gross," Marjorie said.

Steven said nothing, though he felt less at a loss for words now. His eyes, indeed, felt relieved to fix on the still corpse of the raccoon.

"Do we do something?" Marjorie said. She had leaned forward a few inches as if to study the raccoon through the windshield. Light was dying away behind the slender, young beech trees to the west of them.

"No," Steven said. These were his first words—except for the words he took no responsibility for—since Marjorie had said what she'd importantly said and their car was still moving toward dinner.

It was then that he hit her. He hit her before he knew he'd hit her, but not before he knew he wanted to. He hit her with the back of his open hand without even looking at her, hit her straight in the front of her face, straight in the nose. And hard. In a way, it was more a gesture than a blow; though it was, he understood, a blow. He felt the soft tip of her nose, and then the knuckly cartilage against the hard bones of the backs of his fingers. He had never hit a woman before, and he had never even thought of hitting Marjorie, always imagining he *couldn't* hit her when he'd read newspaper accounts of such things happening in the sad, lives of others. He'd hit other people, been hit by other people, plenty of times—tough Maine boys on the ice rinks. Girls were out, though. His father always made that clear. His mother, too.

"Oh, my goodness," was all that Marjorie said when she received the blow. She put her hand over her nose immediately, but then sat silently in the car while neither of them said anything. His heart was not beating hard. The back of his hand hurt a little. This was all new ground. Steven had a small rosy birthmark just where his left side-burn ended and his shaved face began. It resembled the shape of the state of West Virginia. He thought he could feel this birthmark now. His skin tingled there.

And the truth was he felt even more relieved, and didn't feel at all sorry for Marjorie, sitting there stoically making a little tent of her hand to cover her nose and staring ahead as if nothing had happened. He thought she would cry, certainly. She was a girl who cried—when she was unhappy, when he said something insensitive, when she was approaching her period. Crying was natural. Clearly, though, it was a new experience for her to be hit. And so it called upon something new, and if not new then some strength, resilience, self-mastery normally reserved for other experiences.

"I can't go to the Nicholsons' now," Marjorie said almost patiently. She removed her hand and viewed her palm as if her palm had her nose in it. Of course it was blood she was thinking about. He heard her breathe in through what sounded like a congested nose, then the breath was completed out through her mouth. She was not crying yet. And for that moment he felt not even sure he *had* smacked her—if it hadn't just been just a thought he'd entertained, a gesture somehow uncommissioned.

What he wanted to do, however, was skip to the most important things now, not get mired down in wrong, extraneous details. Because he didn't give a shit about George Nicholson or the particulars of what they'd done in some shitty motel. Marjorie would never leave him for George Nicholson or anyone like George Nicholson, and George Nicholson and men like him—high rollers with Hinckleys—didn't throw it all away for unimportant little women like Marjorie. He thought of her nose, red, swollen, smeared with sticky blood dripping onto her green dress. He didn't suppose it could be broken. Noses held up. And, of course, there was a phone in the car. He could simply make a call to the party. He pictured the Nicholsons' great rambling white-shingled house brightly lit beyond the curving drive, the original elms exorbitantly preserved, the footlights, the low-lit clay court where they'd all played, the heated pool, the Henry Moore out on the darkened lawn where you just stumbled onto it. He imagined saying to someone—not George Nicholson—that Marjorie was ill, had thrown up on the side of the road.

The *right* details, though. The right details to ascertain from her were: *Are you sorry?* (he'd forgotten Marjorie had already said she was sorry) and *What does this mean for the future?* These were the details that mattered.

Surprisingly, the raccoon that had been cartwheeled by the pick-up and then lain motionless, a blob in the near-darkness, had come back to life and was now trying to drag itself and its useless hinder parts off of Quaker Bridge Road and onto the grassy verge and into the underbrush that bordered the reservoir.

"Oh, for God's sake," Marjorie said and put her hand over her damaged nose again. She could see the raccoon's struggle and turned her head away.

"Aren't you even sorry?" Steven said.

"Yes," Marjorie said, her nose still covered as if she wasn't thinking about the fact that she was covering it. Probably, he thought, the pain had gone away some. It hadn't been so bad. "I mean no," she said.

He wanted to hit her again then—this time in the ear—but he didn't. He wasn't sure why not. No one would ever know. "Well, which is it?" he said, and felt for the first time completely furious. The thing that made him furious—all his life, the very maddest—was to be put into a situation in which everything he did was wrong, when right was no longer an option. Now felt like one of those situations. "Which is it?" he said again angrily. "Really." He should just take her to the Nicholsons', he thought, swollen nose, bloody lips, all stoppered up, and let her deal with it. Or let her sit out in the car, or else start walking the 11.6 miles home. Maybe George could come out and drive her in his Rover. These were only thoughts, of course. "Which is it?" he said for the third time. He was stuck on these words, on this bit of barren curiosity.

"I was sorry when I told you," Marjorie said, very composed. She lowered her hand from her nose to her lap. One of the little green bows that had been in her hair was now resting on her bare shoulder. "Though not very sorry," she said. "Only sorry because I had to tell you. And now that I've told you and you've hit me in my face and probably broken my nose, I'm not sorry about anything—except that. Though I'm sorry about being married to you, which I'll remedy as soon as I can." She was still not crying. "So *now*, will you as a gesture of whatever good there is in you, get out and go over and do something to help that poor injured creature that those motherfucking rednecks maimed with their motherfucking pick-up truck and then because they're pieces of shit and low forms of degraded humanity, laughed about? Can you do that, Steven? Is that in your range?" She sniffed back hard through her nose, then expelled a short, deep and defeated moan. Her voice seemed more nasal, more Midwestern even, now that her nose was congested.

"I'm sorry I hit you," Steven Reeves said, and opened the car door onto the silent road.

"I know," Marjorie said in an emotionless voice. "And you'll be sorrier."

When he had walked down the empty macadam road in his tan suit to where the raccoon had been struck then bounced over onto the road's edge, there was nothing now there. Only a small circle of dark blood he could just make out on the nubbly road surface and that might've been an oil smudge. No raccoon. The raccoon with its last reserves of savage, unthinking will had found the strength to pull itself off into the bushes to die. Steven peered down into the dark, stalky confinement of scrubs and bramble that separated the road from the reservoir. It was very still there. He thought he heard a rustling in the low brush where a creature might be, getting itself settled into the soft grass and damp earth to go to sleep forever. Someplace out on the lake he heard a young girl's voice, very distinctly laughing. Then a car door closed farther away. Then another sort of door, a screen door, slapped shut. And then a man's voice saying, "Oh no, oh-ho-ho-ho-ho, no." A small white light came on farther back in the trees beyond the reservoir, where he hadn't imagined there was a house. He wondered about how long it would be before his angry feelings stopped mattering to him. He considered briefly why Marjorie would admit this to him now. It seemed so odd.

Then he heard his own car start. The muffled-metal diesel racket of the Mercedes. The headlights came smartly on and disclosed him. Music was instantly loud inside. He turned just in time to see Marjorie's pretty face illuminated, as his own had been, by the salmon dashboard light. He saw the tips of her fingers atop the arc of the steering wheel, heard the surge of the engine. In the woods he noticed a strange glow coming through the trees, something yellow, something out of the low wet earth, a mist, a vapor, something that might be magical. The air smelled sweet now. The peepers stopped peeping. And then that was all.

—2002

TOBIAS WOLFF

Tobias Wolff is an American writer, born in Alabama in 1945. Best known for his short stories and memoirs, he has also written two novels. Wolff's stories belong to the tradition of Maupassant, Joyce, Hemingway, and Chekhov; they are highly crafted, realistic, and focused on the psychological dimensions of character.

In 1949 Wolff's parents separated, and he moved with his mother to Washington State, where they settled first in Seattle and then in the small town of Concrete. As a boy, he lived under the oppression of an abusive stepfather. Wolff's early life is chronicled in his memoir, *This Boy's Life* (1989), a book which received wide critical acclaim; many credited it with helping to revive the genre of memoir in America. *This Boy's Life* was made into a notable film in 1993, starring Robert De Niro and Leonardo DiCaprio.

One of Wolff's earliest creative endeavors was to escape his domestic situation by gaining a scholarship to a Pennsylvania prep school, The Hill School. He won the scholarship by means of forged documents attesting to his academic and athletic prowess. He spent two idyllic years there, before being expelled for his failures in mathematics. After a short period working at sea, he joined the American Army, serving for four years in Vietnam; his second memoir, *In Pharoah's Army* (1994), describes the horror and absurdity of his experiences during that time.

After the war, Wolff attended Oxford University. He graduated in 1975; that same year he published his first work of fiction, *Ugly Rumours*, a novel. His first short story collection, *In the Garden of the North American Martyrs*, (1981) was a critical success, and his novella *The Barracks Thief* (1984) won the PEN/Faulkner award. He has since published numerous short story collections, establishing himself as one of America's preeminent writers of short fiction. Wolff now teaches writing at Stanford University.

Wolff has been cited as a contributor to the "modern renaissance" of the American short story, which critics see as beginning in the 1970s and continuing until the present. Along with his friend Raymond Carver and Richard Ford, Wolff has also been associated with the "dirty realism" school of

American writers who focus on working-class subjects, criminals, alcoholics, and domestic conflict. Wolff rejects such categorizations, saying that his association with Carver was social, not aesthetic, and that the idea of there having been a short-story "renaissance" is inaccurate; he claims instead that there has been an unbroken line of great short stories in America, from Edgar Allan Poe onward. He says "the short story ... is the perfect American form," capturing the nomadic, fragmented experience of modern American life.

In "Powder," the narrator is a boy whose adventure with his father on Christmas Eve crystallizes the moral conflict between his parents. The adventure reveals to the boy the difficulty of knowing what is "right." Is it better to attach oneself to the regulated, civilized world, where one knows what is going to happen next and where one lives responsibly? Or to the world represented by his father, which is exhilarating, without boundaries, and free, but which is "bankrupt of honor" and careless of others? As in many of Wolff's stories, the narrative structure balances these worlds next to each other, leaving the reader to construct meaning and to weigh the moral consequences.

Powder

TOBIAS WOLFF

JUST BEFORE Christmas my father took me skiing at Mount Baker. He'd had to fight for the privilege of my company, because my mother was still angry with him for sneaking me into a nightclub during his last visit, to see Thelonious Monk.[1]

He wouldn't give up. He promised, hand on heart, to take good care of me and have me home for dinner on Christmas Eve, and she relented. But as we were checking out of the lodge that morning it began to snow, and in this snow he observed some rare quality that made it necessary for us to get in one last run. We got in several last runs. He was indifferent to my fretting. Snow whirled around us in bitter, blinding squalls, hissing like sand, and still we skied. As the lift bore us to the peak yet again, my father looked at his watch and said, "Criminy. This'll have to be a fast one."

By now I couldn't see the trail. There was no point in trying. I stuck to him like white on rice and did what he did and somehow made it to the bottom without sailing off a cliff. We returned our skis and my father put chains on the Austin-Healey while I swayed from foot to foot, clapping my mittens and

1 Thelonious Sphere Monk (1917–82) was a famous jazz musician.

wishing I was home. I could see everything. The green tablecloth, the plates with the holly pattern, the red candles waiting to be lit.

We passed a diner on our way out. "You want some soup?" my father asked. I shook my head. "Buck up," he said. "I'll get you there. Right, doctor?"

I was supposed to say, "Right, doctor," but I didn't say anything.

A state trooper waved us down outside the resort. A pair of sawhorses were blocking the road. The trooper came up to our car and bent down to my father's window. His face was bleached by the cold. Snowflakes clung to his eyebrows and to the fur trim of his jacket and cap.

"Don't tell me," my father said.

The trooper told him. The road was closed. It might get cleared, it might not. Storm took everyone by surprise. So much, so fast. Hard to get people moving. Christmas Eve. What can you do.

My father said, "Look. We're talking about five, six inches. I've taken this car through worse than that."

The trooper straightened up. His face was out of sight but I could hear him. "The road is closed."

My father sat with both hands on the wheel, rubbing the wood with his thumbs. He looked at the barricade for a long time. He seemed to be trying to master the idea of it. Then he thanked the trooper, and with a weird, old-maidy show of caution turned the car around. "Your mother will never forgive me for this," he said.

"We should have left before," I said. "Doctor."

He didn't speak to me again until we were in a booth at the diner, waiting for our burgers. "She won't forgive me," he said. "Do you understand? Never."

"I guess," I said, but no guesswork was required; she wouldn't forgive him.

"I can't let that happen." He bent toward me. "I'll tell you what I want. I want us all to be together again. Is that what you want?"

"Yes, sir."

He bumped my chin with his knuckles. "That's all I needed to hear."

When we finished eating he went to the pay phone in the back of the diner, then joined me in the booth again. I figured he'd called my mother, but he didn't give a report. He sipped at his coffee and stared out the window at the empty road. "Come on, come on," he said, though not to me. A little while later he said it again. When the trooper's car went past, lights flashing, he got up and dropped some money on the check. "Okay. Vamanos."[2]

The wind had died. The snow was falling straight down, less of it now and lighter. We drove away from the resort, right up to the barricade. "Move it," my

2 A mispronunciation of *vámonos*, Spanish for "Let's go."

father told me. When I looked at him he said, "What are you waiting for?" I got out and dragged one of the sawhorses aside, then put it back after he drove through. He pushed the door open for me. "Now you're an accomplice," he said. "We go down together." He put the car into gear and gave me a look. "Joke, son."

Down the first long stretch I watched the road behind us, to see if the trooper was on our tail. The barricade vanished. Then there was nothing but snow: snow on the road, snow kicking up from the chains, snow on the trees, snow in the sky; and our trail in the snow. Then I faced forward and had a shock. The lay of the road behind us had been marked by our own tracks, but there were no tracks ahead of us. My father was breaking virgin snow between a line of tall trees. He was humming "Stars Fell on Alabama."[3] I felt snow brush along the floorboards under my feet. To keep my hands from shaking I clamped them between my knees.

My father grunted in a thoughtful way and said, "Don't ever try this yourself."

"I won't."

"That's what you say now, but someday you'll get your license and then you'll think you can do anything. Only you won't be able to do this. You need, I don't know—a certain instinct."

"Maybe I have it."

"You don't. You have your strong points, but not this. I only mention it because I don't want you to get the idea this is something just anybody can do. I'm a great driver. That's not a virtue, okay? It's just a fact, and one you should be aware of. Of course you have to give the old heap some credit, too. There aren't many cars I'd try this with. Listen!"

I did listen. I heard the slap of the chains, the stiff, jerky rasp of the wipers, the purr of the engine. It really did purr. The old heap was almost new. My father couldn't afford it, and kept promising to sell it, but here it was.

I said, "Where do you think that policeman went to?"

"Are you warm enough?" He reached over and cranked up the blower. Then he turned off the wipers. We didn't need them. The clouds had brightened. A few sparse, feathery flakes drifted into our slipstream and were swept away. We left the trees and entered a broad field of snow that ran level for a while and then tilted sharply downward. Orange stakes had been planted at intervals in two parallel lines and my father steered a course between them, though they were far enough apart to leave considerable doubt in my mind as to exactly where the road lay. He was humming again, doing little scat riffs around the melody.

"Okay then. What are my strong points?"

"Don't get me started," he said. "It'd take all day."

---

3 1934 jazz song.

"Oh, right. Name one."

"Easy. You always think ahead."

True. I always thought ahead. I was a boy who kept his clothes on numbered hangers to insure proper rotation. I bothered my teachers for homework assignments far ahead of their due dates so I could draw up schedules. I thought ahead, and that was why I knew that there would be other troopers waiting for us at the end of our ride, if we even got there. What I did not know was that my father would wheedle and plead his way past them—he didn't sing "O Tannenbaum," but just about—and get me home for dinner, buying a little more time before my mother decided to make the split final. I knew we'd get caught; I was resigned to it. And maybe for this reason I stopped moping and began to enjoy myself.

Why not? This was one for the books. Like being in a speedboat, only better. You can't go downhill in a boat. And it was all ours. And it kept coming, the laden trees, the unbroken surface of snow, the sudden white vistas. Here and there I saw hints of the road, ditches, fences, stakes, but not so many that I could have found my way. But then I didn't have to. My father was driving. My father in his forty-eighth year, rumpled, kind, bankrupt of honor, flushed with certainty. He was a great driver. All persuasion, no coercion. Such subtlety at the wheel, such tactful pedalwork. I actually trusted him. And the best was yet to come—switchbacks and hairpins impossible to describe. Except maybe to say this: if you haven't driven fresh powder, you haven't driven.

—1996

TIM O'BRIEN

One of the United States' most provocative writers, Tim O'Brien was born in 1946 in Austin, Minnesota, but lived the majority of his youth in Worthington, Minnesota, which he refers to as the "Turkey Capital of the World." Upon graduating with his B.A. in political science from Macalester College in 1968, he received his draft notice for the war in Vietnam. In a 1990 *New York Times* interview he spoke of the summer prior to his departing for Vietnam: "It was the most terrible summer of my life, worse than being in the war. My conscience kept telling me not to go, but my whole upbringing told me I had to. That horrible summer made me a writer." O'Brien resisted the impulse to either flee to Canada or go to jail (the other options available to men drafted for service at this time), and from February 1969 until March 1970, he served as an infantry foot soldier in Vietnam, an experience that informs much of his work.

On his return from the war, he studied American foreign policy at Harvard's School of Government, and, starting in 1972, interned at the *Washington Post*. He worked for the paper full-time as a national affairs reporter from 1974 to 1975. O'Brien's first book was a memoir entitled *If I Die in a Combat Zone, Box Me Up and Send Me Home* (1973). O'Brien's novels include the novel *Going After Cacciato* (1978), which won the National Book Award for Fiction in 1979, and *In the Lake of the Woods* (1994), winner of the James Fenimore Cooper Prize from the Society of American Historians and chosen best novel of the year by *Time* magazine. Among his other works are *Tomcat in Love* (1998) and *July, July* (2002). He lives in Texas with his sons and teaches at Texas State University.

His fifth book, *The Things They Carried* (1990), a collection of interrelated stories, won France's Prix du Meilleur Livre Etranger and was a finalist for the Pulitzer Prize and the National Book Critics Circle Award. The collection chronicles the experiences of an infantryman in Alpha Company during and after the war in Vietnam. The stories reveal O'Brien's interest in the complex nature of fiction. They feature a character named Tim O'Brien who O'Brien the author insists is not autobiographical. As well, the narratives are often interrupted by "true" stories that are made up, and by similar stories told from different points of view.

While "The Things They Carried" is primarily about the American experience of war in Vietnam, it is also about the nature of story-telling, and the ways in which story-telling can be a means of coping with the unknown.

The Things They Carried

TIM O'BRIEN

FIRST Lieutenant Jimmy Cross carried letters from a girl named Martha, a junior at Mount Sebastian College in New Jersey. They were not love letters, but Lieutenant Cross was hoping, so he kept them folded in plastic at the bottom of his rucksack. In the late afternoon, after a day's march, he would dig his foxhole, wash his hands under a canteen, unwrap the letters, hold them with the tips of his fingers, and spend the last hour of light pretending. He would imagine romantic camping trips into the White Mountains in New Hampshire. He would sometimes taste the envelope flaps, knowing her tongue had been there. More than anything, he wanted Martha to love him as he loved her, but the letters were mostly chatty, elusive on the matter of love. She was a virgin, he was almost sure. She was an English major at Mount Sebastian, and she wrote beautifully about her professors and roommates and midterm exams, about her respect for Chaucer and her great affection for Virginia Woolf. She often quoted lines of poetry; she never mentioned the war, except to say, Jimmy, take care of yourself. The letters weighed 10 ounces. They were signed Love, Martha, but Lieutenant Cross understood that Love was only a way of signing and did not mean what he sometimes pretended it meant. At dusk, he would carefully return the letters to his rucksack. Slowly, a bit distracted, he would get up and move among his men, checking the perimeter, then at full dark he would return to his hole and watch the night and wonder if Martha was a virgin.

The things they carried were largely determined by necessity. Among the necessities or near-necessities were P-38 can openers, pocket knives, heat tabs, wristwatches, dog tags, mosquito repellent, chewing gum, candy, cigarettes, salt tablets, packets of Kool-Aid, lighters, matches, sewing kits, Military Payment Certificates, C rations, and two or three canteens of water. Together, these items weighed between 15 and 20 pounds, depending upon a man's habits or rate of metabolism. Henry Dobbins, who was a big man, carried extra rations; he was especially fond of canned peaches in heavy syrup over pound cake. Dave Jensen, who practiced field hygiene, carried a toothbrush, dental floss, and several hotel-sized bars of soap he'd stolen on R&R in Sydney, Australia. Ted Lavender, who was scared, carried tranquilizers until he was shot in the head outside the village of Than Khe in mid-April. By necessity, and because it was SOP,[1] they all carried steel helmets that weighed 5 pounds including the liner and camouflage cover. They carried the standard fatigue jackets and trousers. Very few carried underwear. On their feet they carried jungle boots—2.1 pounds—and Dave Jensen carried three pairs of socks and a can of Dr. Scholl's foot powder as a precaution against trench foot. Until he was shot, Ted Lavender carried six or seven ounces of premium dope, which for him was a necessity. Mitchell Sanders, the RTO,[2] carried condoms. Norman Bowker carried a diary. Rat Kiley carried comic books. Kiowa, a devout Baptist, carried an illustrated New Testament that had been presented to him by his father, who taught Sunday school in Oklahoma City, Oklahoma. As a hedge against bad times, however, Kiowa also carried his grandmother's distrust of the white man, his grandfather's old hunting hatchet. Necessity dictated. Because the land was mined and booby-trapped, it was SOP for each man to carry a steel-centered, nylon-covered flak jacket, which weighed 6.7 pounds, but which on hot days seemed much heavier. Because you could die so quickly, each man carried at least one large compress bandage, usually in the helmet band for easy access. Because the nights were cold, and because the monsoons were wet, each carried a green plastic poncho that could be used as a raincoat or groundsheet or makeshift tent. With its quilted liner, the poncho weighed almost two pounds, but it was worth every ounce. In April, for instance, when Ted Lavender was shot, they used his poncho to wrap him up, then to carry him across the paddy, then to lift him into the chopper that took him away.

They were called legs or grunts.

To carry something was to hump it, as when Lieutenant Jimmy Cross humped his love for Martha up the hills and through the swamps. In its intransitive form, to hump meant to walk, or to march, but it implied burdens far beyond the intransitive.

Almost everyone humped photographs. In his wallet, Lieutenant Cross carried two photographs of Martha. The first was a Kodacolor snapshot signed Love, though he knew better. She stood against a brick wall. Her eyes were gray and neutral, her lips slightly open as she stared straight-on at the camera. At night, sometimes, Lieutenant Cross wondered who had taken the picture, because he

1 Standard operating procedure.

2 Radio telephone operator.

knew she had boyfriends, because he loved her so much, and because he could see the shadow of the picture-taker spreading out against the brick wall. The second photograph had been clipped from the 1968 Mount Sebastian yearbook. It was an action shot—women's volleyball—and Martha was bent horizontal to the floor, reaching, the palms of her hands in sharp focus, the tongue taut, the expression frank and competitive. There was no visible sweat. She wore white gym shorts. Her legs, he thought, were almost certainly the legs of a virgin, dry and without hair, the left knee cocked and carrying her entire weight, which was just over one hundred pounds. Lieutenant Cross remembered touching that left knee. A dark theater, he remembered, and the movie was *Bonnie and Clyde*, and Martha wore a tweed suit, and during the final scene, when he touched her knee, she turned and looked at him in a sad, sober way that made him pull his hand back, but he would always remember the feel of the tweed skirt and the knee beneath it and the sound of the gunfire that killed Bonnie and Clyde, how embarrassing it was, how slow and oppressive. He remembered kissing her good night at the dorm door. Right then, he thought, he should've done something brave. He should've carried her up the stairs to her room and tied her to the bed and touched that left knee all night long. He should've risked it. Whenever he looked at the photographs, he thought of new things he should've done.

What they carried was partly a function of rank, partly of field specialty.

As a first lieutenant and platoon leader, Jimmy Cross carried a compass, maps, code books, binoculars, and a .45-caliber pistol that weighed 2.9 pounds fully loaded. He carried a strobe light and the responsibility for the lives of his men.

As an RTO, Mitchell Sanders carried the PRC-25 radio, a killer, 26 pounds with its battery.

As a medic, Rat Kiley carried a canvas satchel filled with morphine and plasma and malaria tablets and surgical tape and comic books and all the things a medic must carry, including M&M's for especially bad wounds, for a total weight of nearly 20 pounds.

As a big man, therefore a machine gunner, Henry Dobbins carried the M-60, which weighed 23 pounds unloaded, but which was almost always loaded. In addition, Dobbins carried between 10 and 15 pounds of ammunition draped in belts across his chest and shoulders.

As PFCs[3] or Spec 4s, most of them were common grunts and carried the standard M-16 gas-operated assault rifle. The weapon weighted 7.5 pounds unloaded, 8.2 pounds with its full 20-round magazine. Depending on numerous

3 Privates first class.

factors, such as topography and psychology, the riflemen carried anywhere from 12 to 20 magazines, usually in cloth bandoliers, adding on another 8.4 pounds at minimum, 14 pounds at maximum. When it was available, they also carried M-16 maintenance gear—rods and steel brushes and swabs and tubes of LSA oil—all of which weighed about a pound. Among the grunts, some carried the M-79 grenade launcher, 5.9 pounds unloaded, a reasonably light weapon except for the ammunition, which was heavy. A single round weighed 10 ounces. The typical load was 25 rounds. But Ted Lavender, who was scared, carried 34 rounds when he was shot and killed outside Than Khe, and he went down under an exceptional burden, more than 20 pounds of ammunition, plus the flak jacket and helmet and rations and water and toilet paper and tranquilizers and all the rest, plus the unweighed fear. He was dead weight. There was no twitching or flopping. Kiowa, who saw it happen, said it was like watching a rock fall, or a big sandbag or something—just boom, then down—not like the movies where the dead guy rolls around and does fancy spins and goes ass over teakettle—not like that, Kiowa said, the poor bastard just flat-fuck fell. Boom. Down. Nothing else. It was a bright morning in mid-April. Lieutenant Cross felt the pain. He blamed himself. They stripped off Lavender's canteens and ammo, all the heavy things, and Rat Kiley said the obvious, the guy's dead, and Mitchell Sanders used his radio to report one U.S. KIA[4] and to request a chopper. Then they wrapped Lavender in his poncho. They carried him out to a dry paddy, established security, and sat smoking the dead man's dope until the chopper came. Lieutenant Cross kept to himself. He pictured Martha's smooth young face, thinking he loved her more than anything, more than his men, and now Ted Lavender was dead because he loved her so much and could not stop thinking about her. When the dustoff arrived, they carried Lavender aboard. Afterward they burned Than Khe. They marched until dusk, then dug their holes, and that night Kiowa kept explaining how you had to be there, how fast it was, how the poor guy just dropped like so much concrete. Boom-down, he said. Like cement.

In addition to the three standard weapons—the M-60, M-16, and M-79—they carried whatever presented itself, or whatever seemed appropriate as a means of killing or staying alive. They carried catch-as-catch-can. At various times, in various situations, they carried M-14s and CAR-15s and Swedish Ks and grease guns and captured AK-47s and Chi-Coms and RPGs and Simonov carbines and black market Uzis and .38-caliber Smith & Wesson handguns and 66 mm LAWs[5] and shotguns and silencers and blackjacks and bayonets and C-4

4 Killed in action.

5 A kind of shoulder-fired rocket.

plastic explosives. Lee Strunk carried a slingshot; a weapon of last resort, he called it. Mitchell Sanders carried brass knuckles. Kiowa carried his grandfather's feathered hatchet. Every third or fourth man carried a Claymore antipersonnel mine—3.5 pounds with its firing device. They all carried fragmentation grenades—14 ounces each. They all carried at least one M-18 colored smoke grenade—24 ounces. Some carried CS[6] or tear gas grenades. Some carried white phosphorus grenades. They carried all they could bear, and then some, including a silent awe for the terrible power of the things they carried.

In the first week of April, before Lavender died, Lieutenant Jimmy Cross received a good-luck charm from Martha. It was a simple pebble, an ounce at most. Smooth to the touch, it was a milky white color with flecks of orange and violet, oval-shaped, like a miniature egg. In the accompanying letter, Martha wrote that she had found the pebble on the Jersey shoreline, precisely where the land touched water at high tide, where things came together but also separated. It was this separate-but-together quality, she wrote, that had inspired her to pick up the pebble and to carry it in her breast pocket for several days, where it seemed weightless, and then to send it through the mail, by air, as a token of her truest feelings for him. Lieutenant Cross found this romantic. But he wondered what her truest feelings were, exactly, and what she meant by separate-but-together. He wondered how the tides and waves had come into play on that afternoon along the Jersey shoreline when Martha saw the pebble and bent down to rescue it from geology. He imagined bare feet. Martha was a poet, with the poet's sensibilities, and her feet would be brown and bare, the toenails unpainted, the eyes chilly and somber like the ocean in March, and though it was painful, he wondered who had been with her that afternoon. He imagined a pair of shadows moving along the strip of sand where things came together but also separated. It was phantom jealousy, he knew, but he couldn't help himself. He loved her so much. On the march, through the hot days of early April, he carried the pebble in his mouth, turning it with his tongue, tasting sea salt and moisture. His mind wandered. He had difficulty keeping his attention on the war. On occasion he would yell at his men to spread out the column, to keep their eyes open, but then he would slip away into daydreams, just pretending, walking barefoot along the Jersey shore, with Martha, carrying nothing. He would feel himself rising. Sun and waves and gentle winds, all love and lightness.

What they carried varied by mission.

When a mission took them to the mountains, they carried mosquito netting, machetes, canvas tarps, and extra bug juice.

---

6 Riot-control gas.

If a mission seemed especially hazardous, or if it involved a place they knew to be bad, they carried everything they could. In certain heavily mined AOs,[7] where the land was dense with Toe Poppers and Bouncing Betties, they took turns humping a 28-pound mine detector. With its headphones and big sensing plate, the equipment was a stress on the lower back and shoulders, awkward to handle, often useless because of the shrapnel in the earth, but they carried it anyway, partly for safety, partly for the illusion of safety.

On ambush, or other night missions, they carried peculiar little odds and ends, Kiowa always took along his New Testament and a pair of moccasins for silence. Dave Jensen carried night-sight vitamins high in carotene. Lee Strunk carried his slingshot; ammo, he claimed, would never be a problem. Rat Kiley carried brandy and M&M's candy. Until he was shot, Ted Lavender carried the starlight scope, which weighed 6.3 pounds with its aluminum carrying case. Henry Dobbins carried his girlfriend's pantyhose wrapped around his neck as a comforter. They all carried ghosts. When dark came, they would move out single file across the meadows and paddies to their ambush coordinates, where they would quietly set up the Claymores and lie down and spend the night waiting.

Other missions were more complicated and required special equipment. In mid-April, it was their mission to search out and destroy the elaborate tunnel complexes in the Than Khe area south of Chu Lai. To blow the tunnels, they carried one-pound blocks of pentrite high explosives, four blocks to a man, 68 pounds in all. They carried wiring, detonators, and battery-powered clackers. Dave Jensen carried earplugs. Most often, before blowing the tunnels, they were ordered by higher command to search them, which was considered bad news, but by and large they just shrugged and carried out orders. Because he was a big man, Henry Dobbins was excused from tunnel duty. The others would draw numbers. Before Lavender died there were 17 men in the platoon, and whoever drew the number 17 would strip off his gear and crawl in headfirst with a flashlight and Lieutenant Cross's .45-caliber pistol. The rest of them would fan out as security. They would sit down or kneel, not facing the hole, listening to the ground beneath them, imagining cobwebs and ghosts, whatever was down there—the tunnel walls squeezing in—how the flashlight seemed impossibly heavy in the hand and how it was tunnel vision in the very strictest sense, compression in all ways, even time, and how you had to wiggle in—ass and elbows—a swallowed-up feeling—and how you found yourself worrying about odd things: Will your flashlight go dead? Do rats carry rabies? If you screamed, how far would the sound carry?

---

7 Area of operations.

Would your buddies hear it? Would they have the courage to drag you out? In some respects, though not many, the waiting was worse than the tunnel itself. Imagination was a killer.

On April 16, when Lee Strunk drew the number 17, he laughed and muttered something and went down quickly. The morning was hot and very still. Not good, Kiowa said. He looked at the tunnel opening, then out across a dry paddy toward the village of Than Khe. Nothing moved. No clouds or birds or people. As they waited, the men smoked and drank Kool-Aid, not talking much, feeling sympathy for Lee Strunk but also feeling the luck of the draw. You win some, you lose some, said Mitchell Sanders, and sometimes you settle for a rain check. It was a tired line and no one laughed.

Henry Dobbins ate a tropical chocolate bar. Ted Lavender popped a tranquilizer and went off to pee.

After five minutes, Lieutenant Jimmy Cross moved to the tunnel, leaned down, and examined the darkness. Trouble, he thought—a cave-in maybe. And then suddenly, without willing it, he was thinking about Martha. The stresses and fractures, the quick collapse, the two of them buried alive under all that weight. Dense, crushing love. Kneeling, watching the hole, he tried to concentrate on Lee Strunk and the war, all the dangers, but his love was too much for him, he felt paralyzed, he wanted to sleep inside her lungs and breathe her blood and be smothered. He wanted her to be a virgin and not a virgin, all at once. He wanted to know her. Intimate secrets: Why poetry? Why so sad? Why that grayness in her eyes? Why so alone? Not lonely, just alone—riding her bike across campus or sitting off by herself in the cafeteria—even dancing, she danced alone—and it was the aloneness that filled him with love. He remembered telling her that one evening. How she nodded and looked away. And how, later, when he kissed her, she received the kiss without returning it, her eyes wide open, not afraid, not a virgin's eyes, just flat and uninvolved.

Lieutenant Cross gazed at the tunnel. But he was not there. He was buried with Martha under the white sand at the Jersey shore. They were pressed together, and the pebble in his mouth was her tongue. He was smiling. Vaguely, he was aware of how quiet the day was, the sullen paddies, yet he could not bring himself to worry about matters of security. He was beyond that. He was just a kid at war, in love. He was twenty-four years old. He couldn't help it.

A few moments later Lee Strunk crawled out of the tunnel. He came up grinning, filthy but alive. Lieutenant Cross nodded and closed his eyes while the others clapped Strunk on the back and made jokes about rising from the dead.

Worms, Rat Kiley said. Right out of the grave. Fuckin' zombie.

The men laughed. They all felt great relief.

Spook city, said Mitchell Sanders.

Lee Strunk made a funny ghost sound, a kind of moaning, yet very happy, and right then, when Strunk made that high happy moaning sound, when he went *Ahhooooo*, right then Ted Lavender was shot in the head on his way back from peeing. He lay with his mouth open. The teeth were broken. There was a swollen black bruise under his left eye. The cheekbone was gone. Oh shit, Rat Kiley said, the guy's dead. The guy's dead, he kept saying, which seemed profound—the guy's dead. I mean really.

The things they carried were determined to some extent by superstition. Lieutenant Cross carried his good-luck pebble. Dave Jensen carried a rabbit's foot. Norman Bowker, otherwise a very gentle person, carried a thumb that had been presented to him as a gift by Mitchell Sanders. The thumb was dark brown, rubbery to the touch, and weighted four ounces at most. It had been cut from a VC[8] corpse, a boy of fifteen or sixteen. They'd found him at the bottom of an irrigation ditch, badly burned, flies in his mouth and eyes. The boy wore black shorts and sandals. At the time of his death he had been carrying a pouch of rice, a rifle, and three magazines of ammunition.

You want my opinion, Mitchell Sanders said, there's a definite moral here.

He put his hand on the dead boy's wrist. He was quiet for a time, as if counting a pulse, then he patted the stomach, almost affectionately, and used Kiowa's hunting hatchet to remove the thumb.

Henry Dobbins asked what the moral was.

Moral?

You know. *Moral.*

Sanders wrapped the thumb in toilet paper and handed it across to Norman Bowker. There was no blood. Smiling, he kicked the boy's head, watched the flies scatter, and said, It's like with that old TV show—Paladin. Have gun, will travel.[9]

Henry Dobbins thought about it.

Yeah, well, he finally said. I don't see no moral.

There it *is*, man.

Fuck off.

They carried USO stationery and pencils and pens. They carried Sterno, safety pins, trip flares, signal flares, spools of wire, razor blades, chewing tobacco, liberated joss sticks and statuettes of the smiling Buddha, candles, grease pencils, *The Stars and Stripes*, fingernail clippers, Psy Ops leaflets, bush hats, bolos, and much

8 Viet Cong.

9 *Have Gun, Will Travel* was a television show set in the wild American west. The show's protagonist, a gun-for-hire, was named Paladin.

more. Twice a week, when the resupply choppers came in, they carried hot chow in green mermite cans and large canvas bags filled with iced beer and soda pop. They carried plastic water containers, each with a two-gallon capacity. Mitchell Sanders carried a set of starched tiger fatigues for special occasions. Henry Dobbins carried Black Flag insecticide. Dave Jensen carried empty sandbags that could be filled at night for added protection. Lee Strunk carried tanning lotion. Some things they carried in common. Taking turns, they carried the big PRC-77 scrambler radio, which weighed 30 pounds with its battery. They shared the weight of memory. They took up what others could no longer bear. Often, they carried each other, the wounded or weak. They carried infections. They carried chess sets, basketballs, Vietnamese-English dictionaries, insignia of rank, Bronze Stars and Purple Hearts, plastic cards imprinted with the Code of Conduct. They carried diseases, among them malaria and dysentery. They carried lice and ringworm and leeches and paddy algae and various rots and molds. They carried the land itself—Vietnam, the place, the soil—a powdery orange-red dust that covered their boots and fatigues and faces. They carried the sky. The whole atmosphere, they carried it, the humidity, the monsoons, the stink of fungus and decay, all of it, they carried gravity. They moved like mules. By daylight they took sniper fire, at night they were mortared, but it was not battle, it was just the endless march, village to village, without purpose, nothing won or lost. They marched for the sake of the march. They plodded along slowly, dumbly, leaning forward against the heat, unthinking, all blood and bone, simple grunts, soldiering with their legs, toiling up the hills and down into the paddies and across the rivers and up again and down, just humping, one step and then the next and then another, but no volition, no will, because it was automatic, it was anatomy, and the war was entirely a matter of posture and carriage, the hump was everything, a kind of inertia, a kind of emptiness, a dullness of desire and intellect and conscience and hope and human sensibility. Their principles were in their feet. Their calculations were biological. They had no sense of strategy or mission. They searched the villages without knowing what to look for, not caring, kicking over jars of rice, frisking children and old men, blowing tunnels, sometimes setting fires and sometimes not, then forming up and moving on to the next village, then other villages, where it would always be the same. They carried their own lives. The pressures were enormous. In the heat of early afternoon, they would remove their helmets and flak jackets, walking bare, which was dangerous but which helped ease the strain. They would often discard things along the route of march. Purely for comfort, they would throw away rations, blow their Claymores and grenades, no matter, because by nightfall the resupply choppers would arrive with more of the same, then a day or two later still more, fresh watermelons and crates of ammunition and sunglasses and woolen sweaters—the resources were stunning—sparklers for the Fourth of

July, colored eggs for Easter—it was the great American war chest—the fruits of science, the smokestacks, the canneries, the arsenals at Hartford, the Minnesota forests, the machine shops, the vast fields of corn and wheat—they carried like freight trains; they carried it on their backs and shoulders—and for all the ambiguities of Vietnam, all the mysteries and unknowns, there was at least the single abiding certainty that they would never be at a loss for things to carry.

After the chopper took Lavender away, Lieutenant Jimmy Cross led his men into the village of Than Khe. They burned everything. They shot chickens and dogs, they trashed the village well, they called in artillery and watched the wreckage, then they marched for several hours through the hot afternoon, and then at dusk, while Kiowa explained how Lavender died, Lieutenant Cross found himself trembling.

He tried not to cry. With his entrenching tool, which weighed five pounds, he began digging a hole in the earth.

He felt shame. He hated himself. He had loved Martha more than his men, and as a consequence Lavender was now dead, and this was something he would have to carry like a stone in his stomach for the rest of the war.

All he could do was dig. He used his entrenching tool like an ax, slashing, feeling both love and hate, and then later, when it was full dark, he sat at the bottom of his foxhole and wept. It went on for a long while. In part, he was grieving for Ted Lavender, but mostly it was for Martha, and for himself, because she belonged to another world, which was not quite real, and because she was a junior at Mount Sebastian College in New Jersey, a poet and a virgin and uninvolved, and because he realized she did not love him and never would.

Like cement, Kiowa whispered in the dark. I swear to God—boom, down. Not a word.

I've heard this, said Norman Bowker.

A pisser, you know? Still zipping himself up. Zapped while zipping.

All right, fine. That's enough.

Yeah, but you had to see it, the guy just—

I *heard*, man. Cement. So why not shut the fuck *up*?

Kiowa shook his head sadly and glanced over at the hole where Lieutenant Jimmy Cross sat watching the night. The air was thick and wet. A warm dense fog had settled over the paddies and there was the stillness that precedes rain.

After a time Kiowa sighed.

One thing for sure, he said. The lieutenant's in some deep hurt. I mean that crying jag—the way he was carrying on—it wasn't fake or anything, it was real heavy-duty hurt. The man cares.

Sure, Norman Bowker said.

Say what you want, the man does care.

We all got problems.

Not Lavender.

No, I guess not, Bowker said. Do me a favor, though.

Shut up?

That's a smart Indian. Shut up.

Shrugging, Kiowa pulled off his boots. He wanted to say more, just to lighten up his sleep, but instead he opened his New Testament and arranged it beneath his head as a pillow. The fog made things seem hollow and unattached. He tried not to think about Ted Lavender, but then he was thinking how fast it was, no drama, down and dead, and how it was hard to feel anything except surprise. It seemed unchristian. He wished he could find some great sadness, or even anger, but the emotion wasn't there and he couldn't make it happen. Mostly he felt pleased to be alive. He liked the smell of the New Testament under his cheek, the leather and ink and paper and glue, whatever the chemicals were. He liked hearing the sounds of night. Even his fatigue, it felt fine, the stiff muscles and the prickly awareness of his own body, a floating feeling. He enjoyed not being dead. Lying there, Kiowa admired Lieutenant Jimmy Cross's capacity for grief. He wanted to share the man's pain, he wanted to care as Jimmy Cross cared. And yet when he closed his eyes, all he could think, was Boom-down, and all he could feel was the pleasure of having his boots off and the fog curling in around him and the damp soil and the Bible smells and the plush comfort of night.

After a moment Norman Bowker sat up in the dark.

What the hell, he said. You want to talk, *talk*. Tell it to me.

Forget it.

No, man, go on. One thing I hate, it's a silent Indian.

For the most part they carried themselves with poise, a kind of dignity. Now and then, however, there were times of panic, when they squealed or wanted to squeal but couldn't, when they twitched and made moaning sounds and covered their heads and said Dear Jesus and flopped around on the earth and fired their weapons blindly and cringed and sobbed and begged for the noise to stop and went wild and made stupid promises to themselves and to God and to their mothers and fathers, hoping not to die. In different ways, it happened to all of them. Afterward, when the firing ended, they would blink and peek up. They would touch their bodies, feeling shame, then quickly hiding it. They would force themselves to stand. As if in slow motion, frame by frame, the world would take on the old logic—absolute silence, then the wind, then sunlight, then voices. It was the burden of being alive. Awkwardly, the men would reassemble themselves, first in private, then in groups, becoming soldiers again. They would repair the leaks in their eyes. They would check for casualties, call in dustoffs, light cigarettes, try to smile, clear their throats and spit and begin cleaning their weapons. After a time someone would shake his head and say, No lie, I almost shit my pants, and someone else would laugh, which meant it was bad, yes, but the guy had obviously not shit his pants, it wasn't that bad, and in any case nobody would ever do such a thing and then go ahead and talk about it. They would squint into the dense, oppressive sunlight. For a few moments, perhaps, they would fall silent, lighting a joint and tracking its passage from man to man, inhaling, holding in the humiliation. Scary stuff, one of them might say. But then someone else would grin or flick his eyebrows and say, Roger-dodger, almost cut me a new asshole, *almost*.

There were numerous such poses. Some carried themselves with a sort of wistful resignation, others with pride or stiff soldierly discipline or good humor or macho zeal. They were afraid of dying but they were even more afraid to show it.

They found jokes to tell.

They used a hard vocabulary to contain the terrible softness. *Greased* they'd say. *Offed, lit up, zapped while zipping.* It wasn't cruelty, just stage presence. They were actors. When someone died, it wasn't quite dying, because in a curious way it seemed scripted, and because they had their lines mostly memorized, irony mixed with tragedy, and because they called it by other names, as if to encyst and destroy the reality of death itself. They kicked corpses. They cut off thumbs. They talked grunt lingo. They told stories about Ted Lavender's supply of tranquilizers, how the poor guy didn't feel a thing, how incredibly tranquil he was.

There's a moral here, said Mitchell Sanders.

They were waiting for Lavender's chopper, smoking the dead man's dope.

The moral's pretty obvious, Sanders said, and winked. Stay away from drugs. No joke, they'll ruin your day every time.

Cute, said Henry Dobbins.

Mind blower, get it? Talk about wiggy. Nothing left, just blood and brains.

They made themselves laugh.

There it is, they'd say. Over and over—there it is, my friend, there it is—as if the repetition itself were an act of poise, a balance between crazy and almost crazy, knowing without going, there it is, which meant be cool, let it ride, because Oh yeah, man, you can't change what can't be changed, there it is, there it absolutely and positively and fucking well *is*.

They were tough.

They carried all the emotional baggage of men who might die. Grief, terror, love, longing—these were intangibles, but the intangibles had their own mass and specific gravity, they had tangible weight. They carried shameful memories. They carried the common secret of cowardice barely restrained, the instinct to run or freeze or hide, and in many respects this was the heaviest burden of all, for it could never be put down, it required perfect balance and perfect posture. They carried their reputations. They carried the soldier's greatest fear, which was the fear of blushing. Men killed, and died, because they were embarrassed not to. It was what had brought them to the war in the first place, nothing positive, no dreams of glory or honor, just to avoid the blush of dishonor. They died so as not to die of embarrassment. They crawled into tunnels and walked point and advanced under fire. Each morning, despite the unknowns, they made their legs move. They endured. They kept humping. They did not submit to the obvious alternative, which was simply to close the eyes and fall. So easy, really. Go limp and tumble to the ground and let the muscles unwind and not speak and not budge until your buddies picked you up and lifted you into the chopper that would roar and dip its nose and carry you off to the world. A mere matter of falling, yet no one ever fell. It was not courage, exactly; the object was not valor. Rather, they were too frightened to be cowards.

By and large they carried these things inside, maintaining the masks of composure. They sneered at sick call. They spoke bitterly about guys who had found release by shooting off their own toes or fingers. Pussies, they'd say. Candy-asses. It was fierce, mocking talk, with only a trace of envy or awe, but even so the image played itself out behind their eyes.

They imagined the muzzle against flesh. So easy: squeeze the trigger and blow away a toe. They imagined it. They imagined the quick, sweet pain, then the evacuation to Japan, then a hospital with warm beds and cute geisha nurses.

And they dreamed of freedom birds.

At night, on guard, staring into the dark, they were carried away by jumbo jets. They felt the rush of takeoff. *Gone!* they yelled. And then velocity—wings and engines—a smiling stewardess—but it was more than a plane, it was a real bird, a big sleek silver bird with feathers and talons and high screeching. They were flying. The weights fell off; there was nothing to bear. They laughed and held on tight, feeling the cold slap of wind and altitude, soaring, thinking *It's over, I'm gone!*—they were naked, they were light and free—it was all lightness, bright and fast and buoyant, light as light, a helium buzz in the brain, a giddy bubbling in the lungs as they were taken up over the clouds and the war, beyond duty, beyond gravity and mortification and global entanglements—*Sin loi!*[10] they yelled. *I'm sorry, motherfuckers, but I'm out of it, I'm goofed, I'm on a space cruise, I'm gone!*—and it was a restful, unencumbered sensation, just riding the

10 Vietnamese: "pardon me."

light waves, sailing that big silver freedom bird over the mountains and oceans, over America, over the farms and great sleeping cities and cemeteries and highways and the golden arches of McDonald's, it was flight, a kind of fleeing, a kind of falling, falling higher and higher, spinning off the edge of the earth and beyond the sun and through the vast, silent vacuum where there were no burdens and where everything weighed exactly nothing—*Gone!* they screamed. *I'm sorry but I'm gone!*—and so at night, not quite dreaming, they gave themselves over to lightness, they were carried, they were purely borne.

On the morning after Ted Lavender died, First Lieutenant Jimmy Cross crouched at the bottom of his foxhole and burned Martha's letters. Then he burned the two photographs. There was a steady rain falling, which made it difficult, but he used heat tabs and Sterno to build a small fire, screening it with his body, holding the photographs over the tight blue flame with the tips of his fingers.

He realized it was only a gesture. Stupid, he thought. Sentimental, too, but mostly just stupid.

Lavender was dead. You couldn't burn the blame.

Besides, the letters were in his head. And even now, without photographs, Lieutenant Cross could see Martha playing volleyball in her white gym shorts and yellow T-shirt. He could see her moving in the rain.

When the fire died out, Lieutenant Cross pulled his poncho over his shoulders and ate breakfast from a can.

There was no great mystery, he decided.

In those burned letters Martha had never mentioned the war, except to say, Jimmy, take care of yourself. She wasn't involved. She signed the letters Love, but it wasn't love, and all the fine lines and technicalities did not matter. Virginity was no longer an issue. He hated her. Yes, he did. He hated her. Love, too, but it was a hard, hating kind of love.

The morning came up wet and blurry. Everything seemed part of everything else, the fog and Martha and the deepening rain.

He was a soldier, after all.

Half smiling, Lieutenant Jimmy Cross took out his maps. He shook his head hard, as if to clear it, then bent forward and began planning the day's march. In ten minutes, or maybe twenty, he would rouse the men and they would pack up and head west, where the maps showed the country to be green and inviting. They would do what they had always done. The rain might add some weight, but otherwise it would be one more day layered upon all the other days.

He was realistic about it. There was that new hardness in his stomach. He loved her but he hated her.

No more fantasies, he told himself.

Henceforth, when he thought about Martha, it would be only to think that she belonged elsewhere. He would shut down the daydreams. This was not Mount Sebastian, it was another world, where there were no pretty poems or mid-term exams, a place where men died because of carelessness and gross stupidity. Kiowa was right. Boom-down, and you were dead, never partly dead.

Briefly, in the rain, Lieutenant Cross saw Martha's gray eyes gazing back at him.

He understood.

It was very sad, he thought. The things men carried inside. The things men did or felt they had to do.

He almost nodded at her, but didn't.

Instead he went back to his maps. He was now determined to perform his duties firmly and without negligence. It wouldn't help Lavender, he knew that, but from this point on he would comport himself as an officer. He would dispose of his good-luck pebble. Swallow it, maybe, or use Lee Strunk's slingshot, or just drop it along the trail. On the march he would impose strict field discipline. He would be careful to send out flank security, to prevent straggling or bunching up, to keep his troops moving at the proper pace and at the proper interval. He would insist on clean weapons. He would confiscate the remainder of Lavender's dope. Later in the day, perhaps, he would call the men together and speak to them plainly. He would accept the blame for what had happened to Ted Lavender. He would be a man about it. He would look them in the eyes, keeping his chin level, and he would issue the new SOPs in a calm, impersonal tone of voice, a lieutenant's voice, leaving no room for argument or discussion. Commencing immediately, he'd tell them, they would no longer abandon equipment along the route of march. They would police up their acts. They would get their shit together, and keep it together, and maintain it neatly and in good working order.

He would not tolerate laxity. He would show strength, distancing himself.

Among the men there would be grumbling, of course, and maybe worse, because their days would seem longer and their loads heavier, but Lieutenant Jimmy Cross reminded himself that his obligation was not to be loved but to lead. He would dispense with love; it was not now a factor. And if anyone quarreled or complained, he would simply tighten his lips and arrange his shoulders in the correct command posture. He might give a curt little nod. Or he might not. He might just shrug and say, Carry on, then they would saddle up and form into a column and move out toward the villages west of Than Khe.

—1990

JAMAICA KINCAID

Jamaica Kincaid is the pen name of Elaine Potter Richardson, the daughter of Annie Richardson and Kincaid's stepfather, David Drew (she did not meet her biological father, Roderick Potter, until she was an adult). She was born in 1949 in St. Johns, Antigua, and, until the birth of her three brothers in rapid succession (starting when she was nine years old), she maintained an extremely close relationship with her mother. With the birth of her brothers, however, her parents' attention turned away from Kincaid. Their plans focused on her brothers' future university educations; Kincaid was sent to apprentice with a seamstress. When Kincaid was thirteen, her mother withdrew her from her schooling so that Kincaid could help take care of her brothers and her ailing stepfather. When she was seventeen, Kincaid's parents sent her to the United States to work as an *au pair* in order to help out the family financially. Kincaid would not return to Antigua or see her mother again until almost twenty years later.

In the United States, Kincaid went to work for an Upper East Side New York couple—Kincaid would later draw from this experience for her novel *Lucy*. As Kincaid once stated in an interview, the relationship between her life and what she writes is a complicated mesh. "I write about myself for the most part, and about things that have happened to me. Everything I say is true, and everything I say is not true." After several false starts at other jobs and pursuing courses at various post-secondary institutions, Kincaid eventually began freelance writing for magazines such as *Ms*, *Ingenue*, and *The New Yorker*. In 1973, with her first publication, she changed her name to Jamaica Kincaid: "Part of the reason I changed my name was so that they wouldn't know I was writing. I was afraid I would be laughed at, though it would not have stopped me. Nothing has made me not do what I wanted to do." Many of the stories that appear in *At the Bottom of the River* developed from Kincaid's columns in the "Talk of the Town" section of *The New Yorker*. Kincaid has said that writing for "Talk of the Town" "did two things":

> It showed me how to write, and it allowed me to write in my own voice.... I wrote many very weird "Talk" stories that appeared in *The New Yorker*, very experimental "Talk" stories, and it was from them that I learned how to do the stories in *At the Bottom of the River*.

At the Bottom of the River was published in 1983, went on to win the Morton Dauwen Zabel Award of the American Academy and Institute of Arts and Letters, and was nominated for the PEN/Faulkner Award. Kincaid has published several works since then, including the novels *Annie John* and *Lucy*, and the memoirs *A Small Place* and *My Brother*. She worked at *The New Yorker* as a staff writer from 1976 until 1995; in 1994 she started teaching literature and creative writing part-time at Harvard's African American Studies department.

"Girl" is the first story in the short story collection *At the Bottom of the River*. Kincaid wrote the one-sentence story in 1978 and has said that it was inspired by Elizabeth Bishop's poem "In the Waiting Room." Kincaid writes in the voice of a mother giving a list of impossible instructions to her daughter; as she does so we come to see a fractious relationship between mother and daughter—a motif ubiquitous in Kincaid's work.

Girl

JAMAICA KINCAID

WASH the white clothes on Monday and put them on the stone heap; wash the color clothes on Tuesday and put them on the clothesline to dry; don't walk barehead in the hot sun; cook pumpkin fritters in very hot sweet oil; soak your little cloths right after you take them off; when buying cotton to make yourself a nice blouse, be sure that it doesn't have gum on it, because that way it won't hold up well after a wash; soak salt fish overnight before you cook it; is it true that you sing benna[1] in Sunday school?; always eat your food in such a way that it won't turn someone else's stomach; on Sundays try to walk like a lady and not like the slut you are so bent on becoming; don't sing benna in Sunday school; you mustn't speak to wharf-rat boys, not even to give directions; don't eat fruits on the street—flies will follow you; *but I don't sing benna on Sundays at all and never in Sunday school*; this is how to sew on a button; this is how to make a button-hole for the button you have just sewed on; this is how to hem a dress when you see the hem coming down and so to prevent yourself from

---

1 A type of Calypso music.

looking like the slut I know you are so bent on becoming; this is how you iron your father's khaki shirt so that it doesn't have a crease; this is how you iron your father's khaki pants so that they don't have a crease; this is how you grow okra—far from the house, because okra tree harbors red ants; when you are growing dasheen,[2] make sure it gets plenty of water or else it makes your throat itch when you are eating it; this is how you sweep a corner; this is how you sweep a whole house; this is how you sweep a yard; this is how you smile to someone you don't like too much; this is how you smile to someone you don't like at all; this is how you smile to someone you like completely; this is how you set a table for tea; this is how you set a table for dinner; this is how you set a table for dinner with an important guest; this is how you set a table for lunch; this is how you set a table for breakfast; this is how to behave in the presence of men who don't know you very well, and this way they won't recognize immediately the slut I have warned you against becoming; be sure to wash every day even if it is with your own spit; don't squat down to play marbles—you are not a boy, you know; don't pick people's flowers—you might catch something; don't throw stones at blackbirds, because it might not be a blackbird at all; this is how to make a bread pudding; this is how to make doukona;[3] this is how to make pepper pot;[4] this is how to make a good medicine for a cold; this is how to make a good medicine to throw away a child before it even becomes a child; this is how to catch a fish; this is how to throw back a fish you don't like, and that way something bad won't fall on you; this is how to bully a man; this is how a man bullies you; this is how to love a man, and if this doesn't work there are other ways, and if they don't work don't feel too bad about giving up; this is how to spit up in the air if you feel like it, and this is how to move quick so that it doesn't fall on you; this is how to make ends meet; always squeeze bread to make sure it's fresh; *but what if the baker won't let me feel the bread?*; you mean to say that after all you are really going to be the kind of woman who the baker won't let near the bread?

—1983

2 Another name for taro, a type of edible root plant cultivated in the tropics.

3 Pudding made from plantains, a banana-like fruit.

4 Meat stew.

ROHINTON MISTRY

Rohinton Mistry's early life held little promise of a literary career; he graduated with a degree in Mathematics and Economics from the University of Bombay. Yet Mistry has had a writing life blessed with countless successes. He has won the Commonwealth Prize for Best Book (twice), the Governor General's Award, the Giller Prize, the Kiriyama Pacific Rim Prize, the Royal Society of Literature's Winifred Holtby Prize, the Los Angeles Times Award for Fiction, and the Neustadt International Prize for Literature. His novels have been repeatedly short-listed for the Man Booker Prize and his second novel, *Such a Long Journey*, was made into a critically-acclaimed film of the same name.

Born in 1952 of Parsi parents in Bombay, India, Mistry emigrated to Toronto with his wife in 1975. In Canada, Mistry worked in a bank while studying English and Philosophy part-time at the University of Toronto. Mistry's literary career began in 1983 after he contributed a story to a literary competition and won—he remarked in an interview that the contest was important because, as he says, "I discovered I had talent. I had such a good time telling stories that I want[ed] to keep on doing it." Encouraged by the positive response to his work, Mistry began writing full-time in 1985. His first book, a short story collection entitled *Tales from Firozsha Baag*, appeared in 1987 and was nominated for a Governor General's Award. He followed in 1991 with the novel *Such a Long Journey*, which was short-listed for the Booker Prize, won a Governor General's Award, and won the first of his two Commonwealth Prizes. His next two books, *A Fine Balance* (1995) and *Family Matters* (2002), cemented his reputation, within Canada and around the world. Mistry published his short novel, *The Scream*, in 2008 in support of World Literacy Canada.

"Swimming Lessons" is the final story in *Tales from Firozsha Baag*, a collection of stories detailing the lives of a group of Parsi tenants living in a Bombay apartment building called Firozsha Baag; the collection's interlinked structure and setting have led critic Geoff Hancock to call it "the book as apartment building." The central character throughout the tales is Kersi, a young man of Parsi descent, who eventually goes to live in Canada and is the narrator of "Swimming Lessons." All the other stories in the collection are set in India; this one is set in a suburb of Toronto. The story highlights the narrator's struggle to adapt to the central Canadian suburban environment around him; his "submersion" in the new culture and anxiety around the family he has left behind parallel his attempts to learn how to swim.

Swimming Lessons

ROHINTON MISTRY

THE OLD man's wheelchair is audible today as he creaks by in the hallway: on some days it's just a smooth whirr. Maybe the way he slumps in it, or the way his weight rests has something to do with it. Down to the lobby he goes, and sits there most of the time, talking to people on their way out or in. That's where he first spoke to me a few days ago. I was waiting for the elevator, back from Eaton's with my new pair of swimming-trunks.

"Hullo," he said. I nodded, smiled.

"Beautiful summer day we've got."

"Yes," I said, "it's lovely outside."

He shifted the wheelchair to face me squarely. "How old do you think I am?"

I looked at him blankly, and he said, "Go on, take a guess."

I understood the game; he seemed about seventy-five although the hair was still black, so I said, "Sixty-five?" He made a sound between a chuckle and a wheeze: "I'll be seventy-seven next month." Close enough.

I've heard him ask that question several times since, and everyone plays by the rules. Their faked guesses range from sixty to seventy. They pick a lower number when he's more depressed than usual. He reminds me of Grandpa as he sits on the sofa in the lobby, staring out vacantly at the parking lot. Only difference is, he sits with the stillness of stroke victims, while Grandpa's Parkinson's disease would bounce his thighs and legs and arms all over the place. When he could no longer hold the *Bombay Samachar* steady enough to read, Grandpa took to sitting on the veranda and staring emptily at the traffic passing outside Firozsha Baag. Or waving to anyone who went by in the compound: Rustomji, Nariman Hansotia in his 1932 Mercedes-Benz, the fat ayah[1] Jaakaylee with her shopping-bag, the *kuchrawalli*[2] with her basket and long bamboo broom.

1 Hindi: A maidservant or nursemaid.

2 Hindi: A person employed as a house cleaner.

The Portuguese woman across the hall has told me a little about the old man. She is the communicator for the apartment building. To gather and disseminate information, she takes the liberty of unabashedly throwing open her door when newsworthy events transpire. Not for Portuguese Woman the furtive peerings from thin cracks or spyholes. She reminds me of a character in a movie, *Barefoot in the Park* I think it was, who left empty beer cans by the landing for anyone passing to stumble and give her the signal. But PW does not need beer cans. The gutang-khutang of the elevator opening and closing is enough.

The old man's daughter looks after him. He was living alone till his stroke, which coincided with his youngest daughter's divorce in Vancouver. She returned to him and they moved into this low-rise in Don Mills. PW says the daughter talks to no one in the building but takes good care of her father.

Mummy used to take good care of Grandpa, too, till things became complicated and he was moved to the Parsi[3] General Hospital. Parkinsonism and osteoporosis laid him low. The doctor explained that Grandpa's hip did not break because he fell, but he fell because the hip, gradually growing brittle, snapped on that fatal day. That's what osteoporosis does, hollows out the bones and turns effect into cause. It has an unusually high incidence in the Parsi community, he said, but did not say why. Just one of those mysterious things. We are the chosen people where osteoporosis is concerned. And divorce. The Parsi community has the highest divorce rate in India. It also claims to be the most westernized community in India. Which is the result of the other? Confusion again, of cause and effect.

The hip was put in traction. Single-handed, Mummy struggled valiantly with bedpans and dressings for bedsores which soon appeared like grim spectres on his back. *Mamaiji*,[4] bent double with her weak back, could give no assistance. My help would be enlisted to roll him over on his side while Mummy changed the dressing. But after three months, the doctor pronounced a patch upon Grandpa's lungs, and the male ward of Parsi General swallowed him up. There was no money for a private nursing home. I went to see him once, at Mummy's insistence. She used to say that the blessings of an old person were the most valuable and potent of all, they would last my whole life long. The ward had

3 The Parsis are a small religious community numbering approximately 125,000 in India. They have also settled throughout the world. The Parsis originally fled Iran (ancient Persia) in the seventh century because of religious persecution due to Islamic conquest. Parsis are followers of Zoroaster (or Zarathustra), a prophet born in the sixth or seventh century BCE, and the founder of Zoroastrianism.

4 "-ji" is a Hindi suffix placed after a person's name or title as a mark of respect. In this case the narrator is referring to his grandmother.

rows and rows of beds; the din was enormous, the smells nauseating, and it was just as well that Grandpa passed most of his time in a less than conscious state.

But I should have gone to see him more often. Whenever Grandpa went out, while he still could in the days before parkinsonism, he would bring back pink and white sugar-coated almonds for Percy and me. Every time I remember Grandpa, I remember that; and then I think: I should have gone to see him more often. That's what I also thought when our telephone-owning neighbour, esteemed by all for that reason, sent his son to tell us the hospital had phoned that Grandpa died an hour ago.

The postman rang the doorbell the way he always did, long and continuous; Mother went to open it, wanting to give him a piece of her mind but thought better of it, she did not want to risk the vengeance of postmen, it was so easy for them to destroy letters; workers nowadays thought no end of themselves, strutting around like peacocks, ever since all this Shiv Sena[5] *agitation about Maharashtra*[6] *for Maharashtrians, threatening strikes and Bombay* bundh[7] *all the time, with no respect for the public; bus drivers and conductors were the worst, behaving as if they owned the buses and were doing favours to commuters, pulling the bell before you were in the bus, the driver purposely braking and moving with big jerks to make the standees lose their balance, the conductor so rude if you did not have the right change.*

But when she saw the airmail envelope with a Canadian stamp her face lit up, she said wait to the postman, and went in for a fifty paisa[8] *piece, a little* baksheesh[9] *for you, she told him, then shut the door and kissed the envelope, went in running, saying my son has written, my son has sent a letter, and Father looked up from the newspaper and said, don't get too excited, first read it, you know what kind of letters he writes, a few lines of empty words, I'm fine, hope you are all right, your loving son—that kind of writing I don't call letter-writing.*

Then Mother opened the envelope and took out one small page and began to read silently, and the joy brought to her face by the letter's arrival began to ebb; Father saw it happening and knew he was right, he said read aloud, let me also hear what our son is writing this time, so Mother read: My dear Mummy and Daddy, Last winter was terrible, we had record-breaking low temperatures all through February and March, and the first official day of spring was colder than the first official day of winter had been, but it's getting warmer now. Looks like it will be a

---

5 A right-wing, Hindu political party founded in the 1960s.

6 A state in west Central India of which Mumbai (formerly Bombay) is the capital.

7 A general strike (alternate spelling is *bandh*).

8 A monetary unit of India and Pakistan, worth one hundredth of a rupee.

9 Hindi: Money given as a tip or present.

nice warm summer. You asked about my new apartment. It's small, but not bad at all. This is just a quick note to let you know I'm fine, so you won't worry about me. Hope everything is okay at home.

After Mother put it back in the envelope, Father said everything about his life is locked in silence and secrecy, I still don't understand why he bothered to visit us last year if he had nothing to say; every letter of his has been a quick note so we won't worry—what does he think we worry about, his health, in that country everyone eats well whether they work or not, he should be worrying about us with all the black market and rationing, has he forgotten already how he used to go to the ration-shop and wait in line every week; and what kind of apartment description is that, not bad at all; and if it is a Canadian weather report I need from him, I can go with Nariman Hansotia from A Block to the Cawasji Framji Memorial Library and read all about it, there they get newspapers from all over the world.

The sun is hot today. Two women are sunbathing on the stretch of patchy lawn at the periphery of the parking lot. I can see them clearly from my kitchen. They're wearing bikinis and I'd love to take a closer look. But I have no binoculars. Nor do I have a car to saunter out to and pretend to look under the hood. They're both luscious and gleaming. From time to time they smear lotion over their skin, on the bellies, on the inside of the thighs, on the shoulders. Then one of them gets the other to undo the string of her top and spread some there. She lies on her stomach with the straps undone. I wait. I pray that the heat and haze make her forget, when it's time to turn over, that the straps are undone.

But the sun is not hot enough to work this magic for me. When it's time to come in, she flips over, deftly holding up the cups, and reties the top. They arise, pick up towels, lotions and magazines, and return to the building.

This is my chance to see them closer. I race down the stairs to the lobby. The old man says hullo. "Down again?"

"My mailbox," I mumble.

"It's Saturday," he chortles. For some reason he finds it extremely funny. My eye is on the door leading in from the parking lot.

Through the glass panel I see them approaching. I hurry to the elevator and wait. In the dimly lit lobby I can see their eyes are having trouble adjusting after the bright sun. They don't seem as attractive as they did from the kitchen window. The elevator arrives and I hold it open, inviting them in with what I think is a gallant flourish. Under the fluorescent glare in the elevator I see their wrinkled skin, aging hands, sagging bottoms, varicose veins. The lustrous trick of sun and lotion and distance has ended.

I step out and they continue to the third floor. I have Monday night to look forward to, my first swimming lesson. The high school behind the apartment building is offering, among its usual assortment of macramé and ceramics and pottery classes, a class for non-swimming adults.

The woman at the registration desk is quite friendly. She even gives me the opening to satisfy the compulsion I have about explaining my non-swimming status.

"Are you from India?" she asks. I nod. "I hope you don't mind my asking, but I was curious because an Indian couple, husband and wife, also registered a few minutes ago. Is swimming not encouraged in India?"

"On the contrary," I say. "Most Indians swim like fish. I'm an exception to the rule. My house was five minutes walking distance from Chaupatty beach in Bombay. It's one of the most beautiful beaches in Bombay, or was, before the filth took over. Anyway, even though we lived so close to it, I never learned to swim. It's just one of those things."

"Well," says the woman, "that happens sometimes. Take me, for instance. I never learned to ride a bicycle. It was the mounting that used to scare me, I was afraid of falling." People have lined up behind me. "It's been very nice talking to you," she says, "hope you enjoy the course."

The art of swimming had been trapped between the devil and the deep blue sea. The devil was money, always scarce, and kept the private swimming clubs out of reach; the deep blue sea of Chaupatty beach was grey and murky with garbage, too filthy to swim in. Every so often we would muster our courage and Mummy would take me there to try and teach me. But a few minutes of paddling was all we could endure. Sooner or later something would float up against our legs or thighs or waists, depending on how deep we'd gone in, and we'd be revulsed and stride out to the sand.

Water imagery in my life is recurring. Chaupatty beach, now the high-school swimming pool. The universal symbol of life and regeneration did nothing but frustrate me. Perhaps the swimming pool will overturn that failure.

When images and symbols abound in this manner, sprawling or rolling across the page without guile or artifice, one is prone to say, how obvious, how skilless; symbols, after all, should be still and gentle as dewdrops, tiny, yet shining with a world of meaning. But what happens when, on the page of life itself, one encounters the ever-moving, all-engirdling sprawl of the filthy sea? Dewdrops and oceans both have their rightful places; Nariman Hansotia certainly knew that when he told his stories to the boys of Firozsha Baag.

The sea of Chaupatty was fated to endure the finales of life's everyday functions. It seemed that the dirtier it became, the more crowds it attracted: street urchins and beggars and beachcombers, looking through the junk that washed up. (Or was it the crowds that made it dirtier?—another instance of cause and effect blurring and evading identification.)

Too many religious festivals also used the sea as repository for their finales. Its use should have been rationed, like rice and kerosene. On Ganesh Chaturthi,[10] clay idols of the god Ganesh,[11] adorned with garlands and all manner of finery, were carried in processions to the accompaniment of drums and a variety of wind instruments. The music got more frenzied the closer the procession got to Chaupatty and to the moment of immersion.

Then there was Coconut Day,[12] which was never as popular as Ganesh Chaturthi. From a bystander's viewpoint, coconuts chucked into the sea do not provide as much of a spectacle. We used the sea, too, to deposit the leftovers from Parsi religious ceremonies, things such as flowers, or the ashes of the sacred sandalwood fire, which just could not be dumped with the regular garbage but had to be entrusted to the care of Avan Yazad, the guardian of the sea. And things which were of no use but which no one had the heart to destroy were also given to Avan Yazad. Such as old photographs.

After Grandpa died, some of his things were flung out to sea. It was high tide; we always checked the newspaper when going to perform these disposals; an ebb would mean a long walk in squelchy sand before finding water. Most of the things were probably washed up on shore. But we tried to throw them as far out as possible, then waited a few minutes; if they did not float back right away we would pretend they were in the permanent safekeeping of Avan Yazad, which was a comforting thought. I can't remember everything we sent out to sea, but his brush and comb were in the parcel, his *kusti*,[13] and some Kemadrin pills, which he used to take to keep the parkinsonism under control.

Our paddling sessions stopped for lack of enthusiasm on my part. Mummy wasn't too keen either, because of the filth. But my main concern was the little guttersnipes, like naked fish with little buoyant penises, taunting me with their skills, swimming underwater and emerging unexpectedly all around me, or pretending to masturbate—I think they were too young to achieve ejaculation. It was embarrassing. When I look back, I'm surprised that Mummy and I kept going as long as we did.

I examine the swimming-trunks I bought last week. Surf King, says the label, Made in Canada-Fabriqué Au Canada. I've been learning bits and pieces of French from bilingual labels at the supermarket too. These trunks are extremely sleek and streamlined hipsters, the distance from waistband to pouch tip the

10 A popular Hindu festival celebrating the birthday of Lord Ganesh.

11 The Hindu god of Beginnings and Fighter of Obstacles, represented as having an elephant's head.

12 A day dedicated to the celebration of the coconut's contribution to culture and the economy.

13 A sacred cord worn around the waist by Zoroastrians.

barest minimum. I wonder how everything will stay in place, not that I'm boastful about my endowments. I try them on, and feel that the tip of my member lingers perilously close to the exit. Too close, in fact, to conceal the exigencies of my swimming lesson fantasy: a gorgeous woman in the class for non-swimmers, at whose sight I will be instantly aroused, and she, spying the shape of my desire, will look me straight in the eye with her intentions; she will come home with me, to taste the pleasures of my delectable Asian brown body whose strangeness has intrigued her and unleashed uncontrollable surges of passion inside her throughout the duration of the swimming lesson.

I drop the Eaton's bag and wrapper in the garbage can. The swimming-trunks cost fifteen dollars, same as the fee for the ten weekly lessons. The garbage bag is almost full. I tie it up and take it outside. There is a medicinal smell in the hallway; the old man must have just returned to his apartment.

PW opens her door and says, "Two ladies from the third floor were lying in the sun this morning. In bikinis."

"That's nice," I say, and walk to the incinerator chute. She reminds me of Najamai in Firozsha Baag, except that Najamai employed a bit more subtlety while going about her life's chosen work.

PW withdraws and shuts her door.

Mother had to reply because Father said he did not want to write to his son till his son had something sensible to write to him, his questions had been ignored long enough, and if he wanted to keep his life a secret, fine, he would get no letters from his father.

But after Mother started the letter he went and looked over her shoulder, telling her what to ask him, because if they kept on writing the same questions, maybe he would understand how interested they were in knowing about things over there; Father said go on, ask him what his work is at the insurance company, tell him to take some courses at night school, that's how everyone moves ahead over there, tell him not to be discouraged if his job is just clerical right now, hard work will get him ahead, remind him he is a Zoroastrian: manashni, gavashni, kunashni, *better write the translation also: good thoughts, good words, good deeds—he must have forgotten what it means, and tell him to say prayers and do* kusti[14] *at least twice a day.*

Writing it all down sadly, Mother did not believe he wore his sudra[15] *and* kusti *anymore, she would be very surprised if he remembered any of the prayers; when she had asked him if he needed new* sudras *he said not to take any trouble because the Zoroastrian Society of Ontario imported them from Bombay for their*

14 The short ritual of untying and retying the *kusti*.

15 A sacred shirt worn by Zoroastrians.

members, and this sounded like a story he was making up, but she was leaving it in the hands of God, ten thousand miles away there was nothing she could do but write a letter and hope for the best.

Then she sealed it, and Father wrote the address on it as usual because his writing was much neater than hers, handwriting was important in the address and she did not want the postman in Canada to make any mistake; she took it to the post office herself, it was impossible to trust anyone to mail it ever since the postage rates went up because people just tore off the stamps for their own use and threw away the letter, the only safe way was to hand it over the counter and make the clerk cancel the stamps before your own eyes.

Berthe, the building superintendent, is yelling at her son in the parking lot. He tinkers away with his van. This happens every fine-weathered Sunday. It must be the van that Berthe dislikes because I've seen mother and son together in other quite amicable situations.

Berthe is a big Yugoslavian with high cheekbones. Her nationality was disclosed to me by PW. Berthe speaks a very rough-hewn English, I've overheard her in the lobby scolding tenants for late rents and leaving dirty lint screens in the dryers. It's exciting to listen to her, her words fall like rocks and boulders, and one can never tell where or how the next few will drop. But her Slavic yells at her son are a different matter, the words fly swift and true, well-aimed missiles that never miss. Finally, the son slams down the hood in disgust, wipes his hands on a rag, accompanies mother Berthe inside.

Berthe's husband has a job in a factory. But he loses several days of work every month when he succumbs to the booze, a word Berthe uses often in her Slavic tirades on those days, the only one I can understand, as it clunks down heavily out of the tight-flying formation of Yugoslavian sentences. He lolls around in the lobby, submitting passively to his wife's tongue-lashings. The bags under his bloodshot eyes, his stringy moustache, stubbled chin, dirty hair are so vulnerable to the poison-laden barbs (poison works the same way in any language) emanating from deep within the powerful watermelon bosom. No one's presence can embarrass or dignify her into silence.

No one except the old man who arrives now. "Good morning," he says, and Berthe turns, stops yelling, and smiles. Her husband rises, positions the wheelchair at the favourite angle. The lobby will be peaceful as long as the old man is there.

It was hopeless. My first swimming lesson. The water terrified me. When did that happen, I wonder, I used to love splashing at Chaupatty, carried about by the waves. And this was only a swimming pool. Where did all that terror come from? I'm trying to remember.

Armed with my Surf King I enter the high school and go to the pool area. A sheet with instructions for the new class is pinned to the bulletin board. All students must shower and then assemble at eight by the shallow end. As I enter the showers three young boys, probably from a previous class, emerge. One of them holds his nose. The second begins to hum, under his breath: Paki Paki, smell like curry. The third says to the first two: pretty soon all the water's going to taste of curry. They leave.

It's a mixed class, but the gorgeous woman of my fantasy is missing. I have to settle for another, in a pink one-piece suit, with brown hair and a bit of a stomach. She must be about thirty-five. Plain-looking.

The instructor is called Ron. He gives us a pep talk, sensing some nervousness in the group. We're finally all in the water, in the shallow end. He demonstrates floating on the back, then asks for a volunteer. The pink one-piece suit wades forward. He supports her, tells her to lean back and let her head drop in the water.

She does very well. And as we all regard her floating body, I see what was not visible outside the pool: her bush, curly bits of it, straying out at the pink Spandex V. Tongues of water lapping against her delta, as if caressing it teasingly, make the brown hair come alive in a most tantalizing manner. The crests and troughs of little waves, set off by the movement of our bodies in a circle around her, dutifully irrigate her; the curls alternately wave free inside the crest, then adhere to her wet thighs, beached by the inevitable trough. I could watch this forever, and I wish the floating demonstration would never end.

Next we are shown how to grasp the rail and paddle, face down in the water. Between practising floating and paddling, the hour is almost gone. I have been trying to observe the pink one-piece suit, getting glimpses of her straying pubic hair from various angles. Finally, Ron wants a volunteer for the last demonstration, and I go forward. To my horror he leads the class to the deep end. Fifteen feet of water. It is so blue, and I can see the bottom. He picks up a metal hoop attached to a long wooden stick. He wants me to grasp the hoop, jump in the water, and paddle, while he guides me by the stick. Perfectly safe, he tells me. A demonstration of how paddling propels the body.

It's too late to back out; besides, I'm so terrified I couldn't find the words to do so even if I wanted to. Everything he says I do as if in a trance. I don't remember the moment of jumping. The next thing I know is, I'm swallowing water and floundering, hanging on to the hoop for dear life. Ron draws me to the rails and helps me out. The class applauds.

We disperse and one thought is on my mind: what if I'd lost my grip? Fifteen feet of water under me. I shudder and take deep breaths. This is it. I'm not coming next week. This instructor is an irresponsible person. Or he does not value the lives of non-white immigrants. I remember the three teenagers. Maybe the swimming pool is the hangout of some racist group, bent on eliminating all non-white swimmers, to keep their waters pure and their white sisters unogled.

The elevator takes me upstairs. Then gutang-khutang. PW opens her door as I turn the corridor of medicinal smells. "Berthe was screaming loudly at her husband tonight," she tells me.

"Good for her," I say, and she frowns indignantly at me.

The old man is in the lobby. He's wearing thick wool gloves. He wants to know how the swimming was, must have seen me leaving with my towel yesterday. Not bad, I say.

"I used to swim a lot. Very good for the circulation." He wheezes. "My feet are cold all the time. Cold as ice. Hands too."

Summer is winding down, so I say stupidly, "Yes, it's not so warm any more."

The thought of the next swimming lesson sickens me. But as I comb through the memories of that terrifying Monday, I come upon the straying curls of brown pubic hair. Inexorably drawn by them, I decide to go.

It's a mistake, of course. This time I'm scared even to venture in the shallow end. When everyone has entered the water and I'm the only one outside, I feel a little foolish and slide in.

Instructor Ron says we should start by reviewing the floating technique. I'm in no hurry. I watch the pink one-piece pull the swim-suit down around her cheeks and flip back to achieve perfect flotation. And then reap disappointment. The pink Spandex triangle is perfectly streamlined today, nothing strays, not a trace of fuzz, not one filament, not even a sign of post-depilation irritation. Like the airbrushed parts of glamour magazine models. The barrenness of her impeccably packaged apex is a betrayal. Now she is shorn like the other women in the class. Why did she have to do it?

The weight of this disappointment makes the water less manageable, more lung-penetrating. With trepidation, I float and paddle my way through the remainder of the hour, jerking my head out every two seconds and breathing deeply, to continually shore up a supply of precious, precious air without, at the same time, seeming too anxious and losing my dignity.

I don't attend the remaining classes. After I've missed three, Ron the instructor telephones. I tell him I've had the flu and am still feeling poorly, but I'll try to be there the following week.

He does not call again. My Surf King is relegated to an unused drawer. Total losses: one fantasy plus thirty dollars. And no watery rebirth. The swimming pool, like Chaupatty beach, has produced a stillbirth. But there is a difference. Water means regeneration only if it is pure and cleansing. Chaupatty was filthy, the pool was not. Failure to swim through filth must mean something other than failure of rebirth—failure of symbolic death? Does that equal success of symbolic life? death of a symbolic failure? death of a symbol? What is the equation?

The postman did not bring a letter but a parcel, he was smiling because he knew that every time something came from Canada his baksheesh *was guaranteed, and this time because it was a parcel Mother gave him a whole rupee, she was quite excited, there were so many stickers on it besides the stamps, one for Small Parcel, another Printed Papers, a red sticker saying Insured; she showed it to Father, and opened it, then put both hands on her cheeks, not able to speak because the surprise and happiness was so great, tears came to her eyes and she could not stop smiling, till Father became impatient to know and finally got up and came to the table.*

When he saw it he was surprised and happy too, he began to grin, then hugged Mother saying our son is a writer, and we didn't even know it, he never told us a thing, here we are thinking he is still clerking away at the insurance company, and he has written a book of stories, all these years in school and college he kept his talent hidden, making us think he was just like one of the boys in the Baag, shouting and playing the fool in the compound, and now what a surprise; then Father opened the book and began reading it, heading back to the easy chair, and Mother so excited, still holding his arm, walked with him, saying it was not fair him reading it first, she wanted to read it too, and they agreed that he would read the first story, then give it to her so she could also read it, and they would take turns in that manner.

Mother removed the staples from the padded envelope in which he had mailed the book, and threw them away, then straightened the folded edges of the envelope and put it away safely with the other envelopes and letters she had collected since he left.

The leaves are beginning to fall. The only ones I can identify are maple. The days are dwindling like the leaves. I've started a habit of taking long walks every evening. The old man is in the lobby when I leave, he waves as I go by. By the time I'm back, the lobby is usually empty.

Today I was woken up by a grating sound outside that made my flesh crawl. I went to the window and saw Berthe raking the leaves in the parking lot. Not in the expanse of patchy lawn on the periphery, but in the parking lot proper. She was raking the black tarred surface. I went back to bed and dragged a pillow over my head, not releasing it till noon.

When I return from my walk in the evening, PW, summoned by the elevator's gutang-khutang, says, "Berthe filled six big black garbage bags with leaves today."

"Six bags!" I say. "Wow!"

Since the weather turned cold, Berthe's son does not tinker with his van on Sundays under my window. I'm able to sleep late.

Around eleven, there's a commotion outside. I reach out and switch on the clock radio. It's a sunny day, the window curtains are bright. I get up, curious, and see a black Olds Ninety-Eight in the parking lot, by the entrance to the building. The old man is in his wheelchair, bundled up, with a scarf wound several times round his neck as though to immobilize it, like a surgical collar. His daughter and another man, the car-owner, are helping him from the wheelchair into the front seat, encouraging him with words like: that's it, easy does it, attaboy. From the open door of the lobby, Berthe is shouting encouragement too, but hers is confined to one word: yah, repeated at different levels of pitch and volume, with variations on vowel-length. The stranger could be the old man's son, he has the same jet black hair and piercing eyes.

Maybe the old man is not well, it's an emergency. But I quickly scrap that thought—this isn't Bombay, an ambulance would have arrived. They're probably taking him out for a ride. If he is his son, where has he been all this time, I wonder.

The old man finally settles in the front seat, the wheelchair goes in the trunk, and they're off. The one I think is the son looks up and catches me at the window before I can move away, so I wave, and he waves back.

In the afternoon I take down a load of clothes to the laundry room. Both machines have completed their cycles, the clothes inside are waiting to be transferred to dryers. Should I remove them and place them on top of a dryer, or wait? I decide to wait. After a few minutes, two women arrive, they are in bathrobes, and smoking. It takes me a while to realize that these are the two disappointments who were sunbathing in bikinis last summer.

"You didn't have to wait, you could have removed the clothes and carried on, dear," says one. She has a Scottish accent. It's one of the few I've learned to identify. Like maple leaves.

"Well," I say, "some people might not like strangers touching their clothes."

"You're not a stranger, dear," she says, "you live in this building, we've seen you before."

"Besides, your hands are clean," the other one pipes in. "You can touch my things any time you like."

Horny old cow. I wonder what they've got on under their bathrobes. Not much, I find, as they bend over to place their clothes in the dryers.

"See you soon," they say, and exit, leaving me behind in an erotic wake of smoke and perfume and deep images of cleavages. I start the washers and depart, and when I come back later, the dryers are empty.

PW tells me, "The old man's son took him out for a drive today. He has a big beautiful black car."

I see my chance, and shoot back: "Olds Ninety-Eight."

"What?"

"The car," I explain, "it's an Oldsmobile Ninety-Eight."

She does not like this at all, my giving her information. She is visibly nettled, and retreats with a sour face.

Mother and Father read the first five stories, and she was very sad after reading some of them, she said he must be so unhappy there, all his stories are about Bombay, he remembers every little thing about his childhood, he is thinking about it all the time even though he is ten thousand miles away, my poor son, I think he misses his home and us and everything he left behind, because if he likes it over there why would he not write stories about that, there must be so many new ideas that his new life could give him.

But Father did not agree with this, he said it did not mean that he was unhappy, all writers worked in the same way, they used their memories and experiences and made stories out of them, changing some things, adding some, imagining some, all writers were very good at remembering details of their lives.

Mother said, how can you be sure that he is remembering because he is a writer, or whether he started to write because he is unhappy and thinks of his past, and wants to save it all by making stories of it; and Father said that is not a sensible question, anyway, it is now my turn to read the next story.

The first snow has fallen, and the air is crisp. It's not very deep, about two inches, just right to go for a walk in. I've been told that immigrants from hot countries always enjoy the snow the first year, maybe for a couple of years more, then inevitably the dread sets in, and the approach of winter gets them fretting and moping. On the other hand, if it hadn't been for my conversation with the woman at the swimming registration desk, they might now be saying that India is a nation of non-swimmers.

Berthe is outside, shovelling the snow off the walkway in the parking lot. She has a heavy, wide pusher which she wields expertly.

The old radiators in the apartment alarm me incessantly. They continue to broadcast a series of variations on death throes, and go from hot to cold and cold to hot at will, there's no controlling their temperature. I speak to Berthe about it in the lobby. The old man is there too, his chin seems to have sunk deeper into his chest, and his face is a yellowish grey.

"Nothing, not to worry about anything," says Berthe, dropping rough-hewn chunks of language around me. "Radiator no work, you tell me. You feel cold, you come to me, I keep you warm," and she opens her arms wide, laughing. I step back, and she advances, her breasts preceding her like the gallant prows of two ice-breakers. She looks at the old man to see if he is appreciating the act: "You no feel scared, I keep you safe and warm."

But the old man is staring outside, at the flakes of falling snow. What thoughts is he thinking as he watches them? Of childhood days, perhaps, and snowmen with hats and pipes, and snowball fights, and white Christmases, and Christmas trees? What will I think of, old in this country, when I sit and watch the snow come down? For me, it is already too late for snowmen and snowball fights, and all I will have is thoughts about childhood thoughts and dreams, built around snowscapes and winter-wonderlands on the Christmas cards so popular in Bombay; my snowmen and snowball fights and Christmas trees are in the pages of Enid Blyton's[16] books, dispersed amidst the adventures of the Famous Five, and the Five Find-Outers, and the Secret Seven. My snowflakes are even less forgettable than the old man's, for they never melt.

It finally happened. The heat went. Not the usual intermittent coming and going, but out completely. Stone cold. The radiators are like ice. And so is everything else. There's no hot water. Naturally. It's the hot water that goes through the rads and heats them. Or is it the other way around? Is there no hot water because the rads have stopped circulating it? I don't care, I'm too cold to sort out the cause and effect relationship. Maybe there is no connection at all.

I dress quickly, put on my winter jacket, and go down to the lobby. The elevator is not working because the power is out, so I take the stairs. Several people are gathered, and Berthe has announced that she has telephoned the office, they are sending a man. I go back up the stairs. It's only one floor, the elevator is just a bad habit. Back in Firozsha Baag they were broken most of the time. The stairway enters the corridor outside the old man's apartment, and I think of his cold feet and hands. Poor man, it must be horrible for him without heat.

As I walk down the long hallway, I feel there's something different but can't pin it down. I look at the carpet, the ceiling, the wallpaper: it all seems the same. Maybe it's the freezing cold that imparts a feeling of difference.

PW opens her door: "The old man had another stroke yesterday. They took him to the hospital."

The medicinal smell. That's it. It's not in the hallway any more.

In the stories that he'd read so far Father said that all the Parsi families were poor or middle-class, but that was okay; nor did he mind that the seeds for the stories

---

16 Enid Blyton (1897–1968): a British children's author.

were picked from the sufferings of their own lives; but there should also have been something positive about Parsis, there was so much to be proud of the great Tatas[17] *and their contribution to the steel industry,* or *Sir Dinshaw Petit in the textile industry who made Bombay the Manchester of the East,*[18] or *Dadabhai Naoroji*[19] *in the freedom movement, where he was the first to use the word* swaraj,[20] *and the first to be elected to the British Parliament where he carried on his campaign; he should have found some way to bring some of these wonderful facts into his stories, what would people reading these stories think, those who did not know about Parsis—that the whole community was full of cranky bigoted people; and in reality it was the richest, most advanced and philanthropic community in India, and he did not need to tell his own son that Parsis had a reputation for being generous and family-oriented. And he could have written something also about the historic background, how Parsis came to India from Persia because of Islamic persecution in the seventh century, and were the descendants of Cyrus the Great and the magnificent Persian Empire. He could have made a story of all this, couldn't he?*

Mother said what she liked best was his remembering everything so well, how beautifully he wrote about it all, even the sad things, and though he changed some of it, and used his imagination, there was truth in it.

My hope is, Father said, that there will be some story based on his Canadian experience, that way we will know something about our son's life there, if not through his letters then in his stories; so far they are all about Parsis and Bombay, and the one with a little bit about Toronto, where a man perches on top of the toilet, is shameful and disgusting, although it is funny at times and did make me laugh, I have to admit, but where does he get such an imagination from, what is the point of such a fantasy; and Mother said that she would also enjoy some stories about Toronto and the people there; it puzzles me, she said, why he writes nothing about it, especially since you say that writers use their own experience to make stories out of.

Then Father said this is true, but he is probably not using his Toronto experience because it is too early; what do you mean, too early, asked Mother and Father explained it takes a writer about ten years time after an experience before he is

17 A high-profile Parsi family that developed India's first steel industry.

18 Sir Dinshaw (Manockjee) Petit, 1st Baronet (1823–1901): a Parsi entrepreneur who oversaw the development of Bombay's cotton textile industry and helped lay the foundation for Bombay's commercial prosperity. His contributions to Bombay's economy were so impressive that Bombay earned the title, "Manchester of the East."

19 Dadabhai Naoroji (1825–1917): the first Indian person elected to British parliament (1892). He worked to improve the conditions for people in India and strongly advocated for Indian self-government.

20 Independence (in British India).

able to use it in his writing, it takes that long to be absorbed internally and understood, thought out and thought about, over and over again, he haunts it and it haunts him if it is valuable enough, till the writer is comfortable with it to be able to use it as he wants; but this is only one theory I read somewhere, it may or may not be true.

That means, said Mother, that his childhood in Bombay and our home here is the most valuable thing in his life just now, because he is able to remember it all to write about it, and you were so bitterly saying he is forgetting where he came from; and that may be true, said Father, but that is not what the theory means, according to the theory he is writing of these things because they are far enough in the past for him to deal with objectively, he is able to achieve what critics call artistic distance, without emotions interfering; and what do you mean emotions, said Mother, you are saying he does not feel anything for his characters, how can he write so beautifully about so many sad things without any feelings in his heart?

But before Father could explain more, about beauty and emotion and inspiration and imagination, Mother took the book and said it was her turn now and too much theory she did not want to listen to, it was confusing and did not make as much sense as reading the stories, she would read them her way and Father could read them his.

My books on the windowsill have been damaged. Ice has been forming on the inside ledge, which I did not notice, and melting when the sun shines in. I spread them in a corner of the living room to dry out.

The winter drags on. Berthe wields her snow pusher as expertly as ever, but there are signs of weariness in her performance. Neither husband nor son is ever seen outside with a shovel. Or anywhere else, for that matter. It occurs to me that the son's van is missing, too.

The medicinal smell is in the hall again, I sniff happily and look forward to seeing the old man in the lobby. I go downstairs and peer into the mailbox, see the blue and magenta of an Indian aerogramme with Don Mills, Ontario, Canada in Father's flawless hand through the slot.

I pocket the letter and enter the main lobby. The old man is there, but not in his usual place. He is not looking out through the glass door. His wheelchair is facing a bare wall where the wallpaper is torn in places. As though he is not interested in the outside world any more, having finished with all that, and now it's time to see inside. What does he see inside, I wonder? I go up to him and say hullo. He says hullo without raising his sunken chin. After a few seconds his grey countenance faces me. "How old do you think I am?" His eyes are dull and glazed; he is looking even further inside than I first presumed.

"Well, let's see, you're probably close to sixty-four."

"I'll be seventy-eight next August." But he does not chuckle or wheeze. Instead, he continues softly, "I wish my feet did not feel so cold all the time. And my hands." He lets his chin fall again.

In the elevator I start opening the aerogramme, a tricky business because a crooked tear means lost words. Absorbed in this while emerging, I don't notice PW occupying the centre of the hallway, arms folded across her chest: "They had a big fight. Both of them have left."

I don't immediately understand her agitation. "What ... who?"

"Berthe. Husband and son both left her. Now she is all alone."

Her tone and stance suggest that we should not be standing here talking but do something to bring Berthe's family back. "That's very sad," I say, and go in. I picture father and son in the van, driving away, driving across the snow-covered country, in the dead of winter, away from wife and mother; away to where? how far will they go? Not son's van nor father's booze can take them far enough. And the further they go, the more they'll remember, they can take it from me.

All the stories were read by Father and Mother, and they were sorry when the book was finished, they felt they had come to know their son better now, yet there was much more to know, they wished there were many more stories; and this is what they mean, said Father, when they say that the whole story can never be told, the whole truth can never be known; what do you mean, they say, asked Mother, who they, and Father said writers, poets, philosophers. I don't care what they say, said Mother, my son will write as much or as little as he wants to, and if I can read it I will be happy.

The last story they liked the best of all because it had the most in it about Canada, and now they felt they knew at least a little bit, even if it was a very little bit, about his day-to-day life in his apartment; and Father said if he continues to write about such things he will become popular because I am sure they are interested there in reading about life through the eyes of an immigrant, it provides a different viewpoint; the only danger is if he changes and becomes so much like them that he will write like one of them and lose the important difference.

The bathroom needs cleaning. I open a new can of Ajax and scour the tub. Sloshing with mug from bucket was standard bathing procedure in the bathrooms of Firozsha Baag, so my preference now is always for a shower. I've never used the tub as yet; besides, it would be too much like Chaupatty or the swimming pool, wallowing in my own dirt. Still, it must be cleaned.

When I've finished, I prepare for a shower. But the clean gleaming tub and the nearness of the vernal equinox give me the urge to do something different today. I find the drain plug in the bathroom cabinet and run the bath.

I've spoken so often to the old man, but I don't know his name. I should have asked him the last time I saw him, when his wheelchair was facing the bare wall because he had seen all there was to see outside and it was time to see what was inside. Well, tomorrow. Or better yet, I can look it up in the directory in the lobby. Why didn't I think of that before? It will only have an initial and a last name, but then I can surprise him with: hullo Mr. Wilson, or whatever it is.

The bath is full. Water imagery is recurring in my life: Chaupatty beach, swimming pool, bathtub. I step in and immerse myself up to the neck. It feels good. The hot water loses its opacity when the chlorine, or whatever it is, has cleared. My hair is still dry. I close my eyes, hold my breath, and dunk my head. Fighting the panic, I stay under and count to thirty. I come out, clear my lungs and breathe deeply.

I do it again. This time I open my eyes under water, and stare blindly without seeing, it takes all my will to keep the lids from closing. Then I am slowly able to discern the underwater objects. The drain plug looks different, slightly distorted; there is a hair trapped between the hole and the plug, it waves and dances with the movement of the water. I come up, refresh my lungs, examine quickly the overwater world of the washroom, and go in again. I do it several times, over and over. The world outside the water I have seen a lot of, it is now time to see what is inside.

The spring session for adult non-swimmers will begin in a few days at the high school. I must not forget the registration date.

The dwindled days of winter are now all but forgotten; they have grown and attained a respectable span. I resume my evening walks, it's spring, and a vigorous thaw is on. The snowbanks are melting, the sound of water on its gushing, gurgling journey to the drains is beautiful. I plan to buy a book of trees, so I can identify more than the maple as they begin to bloom.

When I return to the building, I wipe my feet energetically on the mat because some people are entering behind me, and I want to set a good example. Then I go to the board with its little plastic letters and numbers. The old man's apartment is the one on the corner by the stairway, that makes it number 201. I run down the list, come to 201, but there are no little white plastic letters beside it. Just the empty black rectangle with holes where the letters would be squeezed in. That's strange. Well, I can introduce myself to him, then ask his name.

However, the lobby is empty. I take the elevator, exit at the second floor, wait for the gutang-khutang. It does not come: the door closes noiselessly, smoothly. Berthe has been at work, or has made sure someone else has. PW's cue has been lubricated out of existence.

But she must have the ears of a cockroach. She is waiting for me. I whistle my way down the corridor. She fixes me with an accusing look. She waits till I stop whistling, then says: "You know the old man died last night."

I cease groping for my key. She turns to go and I take a step towards her, my hand still in my trouser pocket. "Did you know his name?" I ask, but she leaves without answering.

Then Mother said, the part I like best in the last story is about Grandpa, where he wonders if Grandpa's spirit is really watching him and blessing him, because you know I really told him that, I told him helping an old suffering person who is near death is the most blessed thing to do, because that person will ever after watch over you from heaven, I told him this when he was disgusted with Grandpa's urine-bottle and would not touch it, would not hand it to him even when I was not at home.

Are you sure, said Father, that you really told him this, or you believe you told him because you like the sound of it, you said yourself the other day that he changes and adds and alters things in the stories but he writes it all so beautifully that it seems true, so how can you be sure; this sounds like another theory, said Mother, but I don't care, he says I told him and I believe now I told him, so even if I did not tell him then it does not matter now.

Don't you see, said Father, that you are confusing fiction with facts, fiction does not create facts, fiction can come from facts, it can grow out of facts by compounding, transposing, augmenting, diminishing, or altering them in any way; but you must not confuse cause and effect, you must not confuse what really happened with what the story says happened, you must not loose your grasp on reality, that way madness lies.

Then Mother stopped listening because, as she told Father so often, she was not very fond of theories, and she took out her writing pad and started a letter to her son; Father looked over her shoulder telling her to say how proud they were of him and were waiting for his next book, he also said, leave a little space for me at the end, I want to write a few lines when I put the address on the envelope.

—1987

SANDRA CISNEROS

Born in 1954 as the only daughter in a family of seven children living in the Puerto Rican district of Chicago, Sandra Cisneros readily admits in interviews that her background, gender, and cultural heritage have had a major impact on her writing. Cisneros is part of an important wave of Chicana writers in the United States—Gloria Anzaldúa, Ana Castillo, Denise Chavez, and Cisneros—who first attracted attention in the 1980s by exploring in their work the complexities of race and gender from a specifically Chicana perspective. Cisneros has written one novel, three books of poetry, two short story collections, and a children's book entitled *Hairs/Pelitos*. Her first book of interconnected short stories, *The House on Mango Street* (1984), won the Before Columbus Foundation's Book Award. Her work has received a Lannan Foundation Literary Award, an American Book Award, and fellowships from the National Endowment for the Arts and the MacArthur Foundation.

Cisneros graduated with a B.A. from Loyola University (Chicago) in 1976, and an M.F.A. in Creative Writing from the Iowa Writers Workshop in 1978. She has described her Iowa experience as particularly important:

> My consciousness of growing up, the consciousness of myself, the subjects that I write about, the voice that I write in—I suppose all of that began in Iowa in a seminar class.... I ceased to be ashamed because I realized that I knew something that they [the other students] could never learn at universities. It was all of a sudden that I realized something that I know that I was the authority on.

She began while in Iowa to write the pieces that would make up *The House on Mango Street*. Following her graduate work, she worked at a variety of jobs, including teacher to high-school dropouts, poet-in-the-schools, college recruiter, and arts administrator. She has taught creative writing at the University of California at Berkeley, the University of California at Irvine, and at the University of Michigan in Ann Arbor. She makes her home in the Southwestern United States.

Having grown up with a Spanish-speaking, Mexican father and English-speaking, Mexican-American mother, Cisneros developed an intimate knowledge of the complexities of Chicano culture in the United States and in Mexico. She has described how she feels when she visits Mexico: "like this woman caught in mid-air with my own identity." She regularly includes untranslated Spanish words in her English writing, because "incorporating the Spanish ... allows me to create new expressions in English—to say things in English that have never been said before."

"My Lucy Friend Who Smells Like Corn" is the first story in Cisneros's collection of short stories, *Woman Hollering Creek* (1991). The story is in a section of the book that revolves around the experiences of a group of children and reflects Cisneros's continuing interest in how the inter-mixing of individuals from different cultures and/or backgrounds creates new meanings on the level both of language and of interpersonal relationships.

My Lucy Friend Who Smells Like Corn

SANDRA CISNEROS

LUCY Anguiano, Texas girl who smells like corn, like Frito Bandito chips, like tortillas, something like that warm smell of *nixtamal* or bread the way her head smells when she's leaning close to you over a paper cut-out doll or on the porch when we are squatting over marbles trading this pretty crystal that leaves a blue star on your hand for that giant cat-eye with a grasshopper green spiral in the center like the juice of bugs on the windshield when you drive to the border, like the yellow blood of butterflies.

Have you ever eaten dog food? I have. After crunching like ice, she opens her big mouth to prove it, only a pink tongue rolling around in there like a blind worm, and Janey looking in because she said Show me. But me I like that Lucy corn smell hair and aqua flipflops just like mine that we bought at the Kmart for only 79 cents same time.

I'm going to sit in the sun, don't care if it's a million trillion degrees outside, so my skin can get so dark it's blue where it bends like Lucy's. Her whole family like that. Eyes like knife slits. Lucy and her sisters. Norma, Margarita, Ofelia, Herminia, Nancy, Olivia, Cheli, *y la* Amber Sue.

Screen door with no screen. *Bang!* Little black dog biting his fur. Fat couch on the porch. Some of the windows painted blue, some pink, because her daddy got tired that day or forgot. Mama in the kitchen feeding clothes into the wringer washer and clothes rolling out all stiff and twisted and flat like paper. Lucy got her arm stuck once and had to yell Maaa! and her mama had to put the machine in reverse and then her hand rolled back, the finger black and later, her nail fell off. *But did your arm get flat like the clothes? What happened to your arm? Did they have to pump it with air?* No, only the finger, and she didn't cry neither.

Lean across the porch rail and pin the pink sock of the baby Amber Sue on top of Cheli's flowered T-shirt, and the blue jeans of *la* Ofelia over the inside seam of Olivia's blouse, over the flannel nightgown of Margarita so it don't stretch out, and then you take the work shirts of their daddy and hang them upside down like this, and this way all the clothes don't get so wrinkled and take up less space and you don't waste pins. The girls all wear each other's clothes, except Olivia, who is stingy. There ain't no boys here. Only girls and one father who is never home hardly and one mother who says *Ay! I'm real tired* and so many sisters there's no time to count them.

I'm sitting in the sun even though it's the hottest part of the day, the part that makes the streets dizzy, when the heat makes a little hat on the top of your head and bakes the dust and weed grass and sweat up good, all steamy and smelling like sweet corn.

I want to rub heads and sleep in a bed with little sisters, some at the top and some at the feets. I think it would be fun to sleep with sisters you could yell at one at a time or all together, instead of alone on the fold-out chair in the living room.

When I get home Abuelita[1] will say *Didn't I tell you?* and I'll get it because I was supposed to wear this dress again tomorrow. But first I'm going to jump off an old pissy mattress in the Anguiano yard. I'm going to scratch your mosquito bites, Lucy, so they'll itch you, then put Mercurochrome smiley faces on them. We're going to trade shoes and wear them on our hands. We're going to walk over to Janey Ortiz's house and say *We're never ever going to be your friend again forever!* We're going to run home backwards and we're going to run home frontwards, look twice under the house where the rats hide and I'll stick one foot in there because you dared me, sky so blue and heaven inside those white clouds. I'm going to peel a scab from my knee and eat it, sneeze on the cat, give you three M & M's I've been saving for you since yesterday, comb your hair with my fingers and braid it into teeny-tiny braids real pretty. We're going to wave to a lady we don't know on the bus. Hello! I'm going to somersault on the rail of the front porch even though my *chones* show. And cut paper dolls we draw ourselves, and color in their clothes with crayons, my arm around your neck.

And when we look at each other, our arms gummy from an orange Popsicle we split, we could be sisters, right? We could be, you and me waiting for our teeths to fall and money. You laughing something into my ear that tickles, and me going Ha Ha Ha Ha. Her and me, my Lucy friend who smells like corn.

—1991

1 A Spanish endearment for grandmother; literally, "little grandmother."

LORRIE MOORE

The author of two novels and three short story collections, Marie Lorena Moore (her parents nicknamed her Lorrie) was born in 1957 in Glens Falls, New York, to an insurance executive and an ex-nurse turned housewife. She attended St. Lawrence University, and, while doing her undergraduate work, won the short story contest in *Seventeen* magazine at the age of nineteen. Upon graduation, Moore worked as a paralegal for two years. In 1980 she enrolled in Cornell's M.F.A. program and while there had her short fiction published in a number of magazines, including *Ms*, *Fiction International*, and *StoryQuarterly*. Her first collection of short stories, *Self-Help*, was published in 1985; it is primarily made up of the funny, caustic stories she wrote for her MFA thesis at Cornell. Moore's brand of humour is apparent in the opening line of the story "How to Become a Writer": "First, try to be something, anything, else."

From 1982 to 1984 she worked as a lecturer at Cornell, and in 1984 she began teaching at the University of Wisconsin, where she is currently a full professor and teaches creative writing. Her work has appeared in many periodicals, including *The New Yorker*, *Harper's*, *Granta*, *The Paris Review*, and *Rolling Stone*. Her first novel, *Anagrams*, was published in 1986 and was followed by the short story collection, *Like Life* (1990), the novel *Who Will Run the Frog Hospital?* (1994), and another short story collection, *Birds of America* (1998), which was named by *The New York Times* as one of the Best Books of 1998 and nominated for the National Book Critics' Circle Award. *The Collected Stories* (2008) compilation brought into print three previously unpublished stories, and Moore's 2009 novel, *A Gate at the Stairs,* was a finalist for the PEN/Faulkner Award for Fiction. She has written juvenile fiction (*The Forgotten Helper*, 1987), and edited the anthology *I Know Some Things: Stories About Childhood by Contemporary Writers* (1992). She is the recipient of a John Simon Guggenheim Memorial Foundation Fellowship and a National Endowment for the Arts Fellowship (1989). In 2006, she was welcomed into the prestigious American Society of Arts and Letters.

"You're Ugly, Too" was originally published in *The New Yorker* and is one of the eight stories that comprise *Like Life*. In this story, Moore's characteristic wit while dealing with serious subject matter comes to the fore. Rather than undermining the seriousness of the story, however, the humour highlights the quiet dilemma that the main character Zoë Hendricks faces as she realizes she has reached an impasse in her life.

You're Ugly, Too

LORRIE MOORE

YOU HAD to get out of them occasionally, those Illinois towns with the funny names: Paris, Oblong, Normal. Once, when the Dow Jones dipped two hundred points, a local paper boasted the banner headline "NORMAL MAN MARRIES OBLONG WOMAN." They knew what was important. They did! But you had to get out once in a while, even if it was just across the border to Terre Haute for a movie.

Outside of Paris, in the middle of a large field, was a scatter of brick buildings, a small liberal-arts college by the improbable name of Hilldale-Versailles. Zoë Hendricks had been teaching American history there for three years. She taught "The Revolution and Beyond" to freshmen and sophomores, and every third semester she had the senior seminar for majors, and although her student evaluations had been slipping in the last year and a half—*Professor Hendricks is often late for class and usually arrives with a cup of hot chocolate, which she offers the class sips of*—generally the department of nine men was pleased to have her. They felt she added some needed feminine touch to the corridors—that faint trace of Obsession and sweat, the light, fast clicking of heels. Plus they had had a sex-discrimination suit, and the dean had said, well, it was time.

The situation was not easy for her, they knew. Once, at the start of last semester, she had skipped into her lecture hall singing "Getting to Know You"—all of it. At the request of the dean, the chairman had called her into his office, but did not ask her for an explanation, not really. He asked her how she was and then smiled in an avuncular way. She said, "Fine," and he studied the way she said it, her front teeth catching on the inside of her lower lip. She was almost pretty, but her face showed the strain and ambition of always having been close but not quite. There was too much effort with the eyeliner, and her earrings, worn, no doubt, for the drama her features lacked, were a little frightening, jutting out the sides of her head like antennae.

"I'm going out of my mind," said Zoë to her younger sister, Evan, in Manhattan. *Professor Hendricks seems to know the entire soundtrack to "The King and I." Is this history?* Zoë phoned her every Tuesday.

"You always say that," said Evan, "but then you go on your trips and vacations and then you settle back into things and then you're quiet for a while and then you say you're fine, you're busy, and then after a while you say you're going crazy again, and you start all over." Evan was a part-time food designer for photo shoots. She cooked vegetables in green dye. She propped up beef stew with a bed of marbles and shopped for new kinds of silicone sprays and plastic ice cubes. She thought her life was O.K. She was living with her boyfriend of many years, who was independently wealthy and had an amusing little job in book publishing. They were five years out of college, and they lived in a luxury midtown high rise with a balcony and access to a pool. "It's not the same as having your own pool," Evan was always sighing, as if to let Zoë know that, as with Zoë, there were still things she, Evan, had to do without.

"Illinois. It makes me sarcastic to be here," said Zoë on the phone. She used to insist it was irony, something gently layered and sophisticated, something alien to the Midwest, but her students kept calling it sarcasm, something they felt qualified to recognize, and now she had to agree. It wasn't irony. "What is your perfume?" a student once asked her. "Room freshener," she said. She smiled, but he looked at her, unnerved.

Her students were by and large good midwesterners, spacey with estrogen from large quantities of meat and eggs. They shared their parents' suburban values; their parents had given them things, things, things. They were complacent. They had been purchased. They were armed with a healthy vagueness about anything historical or geographic. They seemed actually to know very little about anything, but they were good-natured about it. "All those states in the East are so tiny and jagged and bunched up," complained one of her undergraduates the week she was lecturing on "The Turning Point of Independence: The Battle at Saratoga." "Professor Hendricks, you're from Delaware originally, right?" the student asked her.

"Maryland," corrected Zoë.

"Aw," he said, waving his hand dismissively. "New England."

Her articles—chapters toward a book called *Hearing the One About: Uses of Humor in the American Presidency*—were generally well received, though they came slowly for her. She liked her pieces to have something from every time of day in them—she didn't trust things written in the morning only—so she reread and rewrote painstakingly. No part of a day—its moods, its light—was allowed to dominate. She hung on to a piece for a year sometimes, revising at all hours, until the entirety of a day had registered there.

The job she'd had before the one at Hilldale-Versailles had been at a small college in New Geneva, Minnesota, Land of the Dying Shopping Mall. Everyone was so blond there that brunettes were often presumed to be from foreign countries. *Just because Professor Hendricks is from Spain doesn't give her the right to be so negative about our country.* There was a general emphasis on cheerfulness. In New Geneva you weren't supposed to be critical or complain. You weren't supposed to notice that the town had overextended and that its shopping malls were raggedy and going under. You were never to say you weren't "fine, thank you—and yourself?" You were supposed to be Heidi. You were supposed to lug goat milk up the hills and not think twice. Heidi did not complain. Heidi did not do things like stand in front of the new IBM photocopier saying, "If this fucking Xerox machine breaks on me one more time, I'm going to slit my wrists."

But now in her second job, in her fourth year of teaching in the Midwest, Zoë was discovering something she never suspected she had: a crusty edge, brittle and pointed. Once she had pampered her students, singing them songs, letting them call her at home even, and ask personal questions, but now she was losing sympathy. They were beginning to seem different. They were beginning to seem demanding and spoiled.

"You act," said one of her senior-seminar students at a scheduled conference, "like your opinion is worth more than everyone else's in the class."

Zoë's eyes widened. "I *am* the teacher," she said. "I do get paid to act like that." She narrowed her gaze at the student, who was wearing a big leather bow in her hair like a cowgirl in a TV ranch show. "I mean, otherwise *everybody* in the class would have little offices and office hours." *Sometimes Professor Hendricks will take up the class's time just talking about movies she's seen.* She stared at the student some more, then added, "I bet you'd like that."

"Maybe I sound whiny to you," said the girl, "but I simply want my history major to mean something."

"Well, there's your problem," said Zoë, and, with a smile, she showed the student to the door. "I like your bow," she said.

Zoë lived for the mail, for the postman—that handsome blue jay—and when she got a real letter with a real full-price stamp from someplace else, she took it to bed with her and read it over and over. She also watched television until all hours and had her set in the bedroom—a bad sign. *Professor Hendricks has said critical things about Fawn Hall, the Catholic religion, and the whole state of Illinois. It is unbelievable.* At Christmastime she gave twenty-dollar tips to the mailman and to Jerry, the only cabbie in town, whom she had gotten to know from all her rides to and from the Terre Haute airport, and who, since he realized such rides were an extravagance, often gave her cut rates.

"I'm flying in to visit you this weekend," announced Zoë.

"I was hoping you would," said Evan. "Charlie and I are having a party for Halloween. It'll be fun."

"I have a costume already. It's a bonehead. It's this thing that looks like a giant bone going through your head."

"Great," said Evan.

"It is, it's great."

"All I have is my moon mask from last year and the year before. I'll probably end up getting married in it."

"Are you and Charlie getting *married*?" Zoë felt slightly alarmed.

"Hmmmmmmnnno, not immediately."

"Don't get married."

"Why?"

"Just not yet. You're too young."

"You're only saying that because you're five years older than I am and *you're* not married."

"*I'm* not married? Oh, my God," said Zoë, "I forgot to get married."

Zoë had been out with three men since she'd come to Hilldale-Versailles. One of them was a man in the municipal bureaucracy who had fixed a parking ticket she'd brought in to protest and then asked her out for coffee. At first, she thought he was amazing—at last, someone who did not want Heidi! But soon she came to realize that all men, deep down, wanted Heidi. Heidi with cleavage. Heidi with outfits. The parking-ticket bureaucrat soon became tired and intermittent. One cool fall day, in his snazzy, impractical convertible, when she asked him what was wrong he said, "You would not be ill served by new clothes, you know." She wore a lot of gray-green corduroy. She had been under the impression that it brought out her eyes, those shy stars. She flicked an ant from her sleeve.

"Did you have to brush that off in the car?" he said, driving. He glanced down at his own pectorals, giving first the left, then the right, a quick survey. He was wearing a tight shirt.

"Excuse me?"

He slowed down at an amber light and frowned. "Couldn't you have picked it up and thrown it outside?"

"The ant? It might have bitten me. I mean, what difference does it make?"

"It might have bitten you! Ha! How ridiculous! Now it's going to lay eggs in my car!"

The second guy was sweeter, lunkier, though not insensitive to certain paintings and songs, but too often, too, things he'd do or say would startle her. Once, in a restaurant, he stole the garnishes off her dinner plate and waited for her to notice. When she didn't, he finally thrust his fist across the table and said, "Look," and when he opened it, there was her parsley sprig and her orange slice crumpled to a wad. Another time, he described to her his recent trip to the Louvre. "And there I was in front of Delacroix's *The Barque of Dante*, and everyone else had wandered off, so I had my own private audience with it, all those agonized shades splayed in every direction, and there's this motion in that painting that starts at the bottom, swirling and building up into the red fabric of Dante's hood, swirling out into the distance, where you see these orange flames—" He was breathless in the telling. She found this touching, and smiled in encouragement. "A painting like that," he said, shaking his head. "It just makes you shit."

"I have to ask you something," said Evan. "I know every woman complains about not meeting men, but really, on my shoots I meet a lot of men. And they're not at all gay, either." She paused. "Not anymore."

"What are you asking?"

The third guy was a political-science professor named Murray Peterson, who liked to go out on double dates with colleagues whose wives he was attracted to. Usually, the wives would consent to flirt with him. Under the table sometimes there was footsie, and once there was even kneesie. Zoë and the husband would be left to their food, staring into their water glasses, chewing like goats. "Oh, Murray," said one wife, who had never finished her master's in physical therapy and wore great clothes. "You know, I know everything about you: your birthday, your license-plate number. I have everything memorized. But then that's the kind of mind I have. Once, at a dinner party, I amazed the host by getting up and saying goodbye to every single person there, first *and* last names."

"I knew a dog who could do that," said Zoë with her mouth full. Murray and the wife looked at her with vexed and rebuking expressions, but the husband seemed suddenly twinkling and amused. Zoë swallowed. "It was a talking Lab, and after about ten minutes of listening to the dinner conversation this dog knew everyone's name. You could say, 'Take this knife to Murray Peterson,' and it would."

"Really," said the wife, frowning, and Murray Peterson never called again.

"Are you seeing anyone?" said Evan. "I'm asking for a particular reason. I'm not just being like Mom."

"I'm seeing my house. I'm tending to it when it wets, when it cries, when it throws up." Zoë had bought a mint-green ranch house near campus, though now she was thinking that maybe she shouldn't have. It was hard to live in a house. She kept wandering in and out of the rooms, wondering where she had put things. She went downstairs into the basement for no reason at all except that it amused her to own a basement. It also amused her to own a tree.

Her parents, in Maryland, had been very pleased that one of their children had at last been able to afford real estate, and when she closed on the house they sent her flowers with a congratulations card. Her mother had even UPS'd a box of old decorating magazines saved over the years—photographs of beautiful rooms her mother used to moon over, since there never had been any money to redecorate. It was like getting her mother's pornography, that box, inheriting her drooled-upon fantasies, the endless wish and tease that had been her life. But to her mother it was a rite of passage that pleased her. "Maybe you will get some ideas from these," she had written. And when Zoë looked at the photographs, at the bold and beautiful living rooms, she was filled with longing. Ideas and ideas of longing.

Right now Zoë's house was rather empty. The previous owner had wallpapered around the furniture, leaving strange gaps and silhouettes on the walls, and Zoë hadn't done much about that yet. She had bought furniture, then taken it back, furnishing and unfurnishing, preparing and shedding, like a womb. She had bought several plain pine chests to use as love seats or boot boxes, but they came to look to her more and more like children's coffins, so she returned them. And she had recently bought an Oriental rug for the living room, with Chinese symbols on it she didn't understand. The salesgirl had kept saying she was sure they meant "Peace" and "Eternal Life," but when Zoë got the rug home she worried. What if they didn't mean "Peace" and "Eternal Life"? What if they meant, say, "Bruce Springsteen"? And the more she thought about it, the more she became convinced she had a rug that said "Bruce Springsteen," and so she returned that, too.

She had also bought a little baroque mirror for the front entryway, which, she had been told by Murray Peterson, would keep away evil spirits. The mirror, however, tended to frighten *her*, startling her with an image of a woman she never recognized. Sometimes she looked puffier and plainer than she remembered. Sometimes shifty and dark. Most times she just looked vague. "You look like someone I know," she had been told twice in the last year by strangers in restaurants in Terre Haute. In fact, sometimes she seemed not to have a look of her own, or any look whatsoever, and it began to amuse her that her students and colleagues were able to recognize her at all. How did they know? When she walked into a room, how did she look so that they knew it was she? Like this? Did she look like this? And so she returned the mirror.

"The reason I'm asking is that I know a man I think you should meet," said Evan. "He's fun. He's straight. He's single. That's all I'm going to say."

"I think I'm too old for fun," said Zoë. She had a dark bristly hair in her chin, and she could feel it now with her finger. Perhaps when you had been without the opposite sex for too long, you began to resemble them. In an act of desperate invention, you began to grow your own. "I just want to come, wear my bonehead, visit with Charlie's tropical fish, ask you about your food shoots."

She thought about all the papers on "Our Constitution: How It Affects Us" she was going to have to correct. She thought about how she was going in for ultrasound tests on Friday because, according to her doctor and her doctor's assistant, she had a large, mysterious growth in her abdomen. Gallbladder, they kept saying. Or ovaries or colon. "You guys practice medicine?" asked Zoë, aloud, after they had left the room. Once, as a girl, she brought her dog to a vet, who had told her, "Well, either your dog has worms or cancer or else it was hit by a car."

She was looking forward to New York.

"Well, whatever. We'll just play it cool. I can't wait to see you, hon. Don't forget your bonehead," said Evan.

"A bonehead you don't forget," said Zoë.

"I suppose," said Evan.

The ultrasound Zoë was keeping a secret, even from Evan. "I feel like I'm dying," Zoë had hinted just once on the phone.

"You're not dying," said Evan, "you're just annoyed."

"Ultrasound," Zoë now said jokingly to the technician who put the cold jelly on her bare stomach. "Does that sound like a really great stereo system or what?"

She had not had anyone make this much fuss over her bare stomach since her boyfriend in graduate school, who had hovered over her whenever she felt ill, waved his arms, pressed his hands upon her navel, and drawled evangelically, "Heal! Heal for thy Baby Jesus' sake!" Zoë would laugh and they would make love, both secretly hoping she would get pregnant. Later they would worry together, and he would sink a cheek to her belly and ask whether she was late, was she late, was she sure, she might be late, and when after two years she had not gotten pregnant they took to quarreling and drifted apart.

"O.K.," said the technician absently.

The monitor was in place, and Zoë's insides came on the screen in all their gray and ribbony hollowness. They were marbled in the finest gradations of black and white, like stone in an old church or a picture of the moon. "Do you suppose," she babbled at the technician, "that the rise in infertility among so many couples in this country is due to completely different species trying to reproduce?" The technician moved the scanner around and took more pictures. On one view in particular, on Zoë's right side, the technician became suddenly alert, the machine he was operating clicking away.

Zoë stared at the screen. "That must be the growth you found there," suggested Zoë.

"I can't tell you anything," said the technician rigidly. "Your doctor will get the radiologist's report this afternoon and will phone you then."

"I'll be out of town," said Zoë.

"I'm sorry," said the technician.

Driving home, Zoë looked in the rearview mirror and decided she looked—well, how would one describe it? A little wan. She thought of the joke about the guy who visits his doctor and the doctor says, "Well, I'm sorry to say you've got six weeks to live."

"I want a second opinion," says the guy. *You act like your opinion is worth more than everyone else's in the class.*

"You want a second opinion? O.K.," says the doctor. "You're ugly, too." She liked that joke. She thought it was terribly, terribly funny.

She took a cab to the airport. Jerry the cabbie was happy to see her.

"Have fun in New York," he said, getting her bag out of the trunk. He liked her, or at least he always acted as if he did. She called him Jare.

"Thanks, Jare."

"You know, I'll tell you a secret: I've never been to New York. I'll tell you two secrets: I've never been on a plane." And he waved at her sadly as she pushed her way in through the terminal door. "Or an escalator!" he shouted.

The trick to flying safely, Zoë always said, was to never buy a discount ticket and to tell yourself you had nothing to live for anyway, so that when the plane crashed it was no big deal. Then, when it didn't crash, when you succeeded in keeping it aloft with your own worthlessness, all you had to do was stagger off, locate your luggage, and, by the time a cab arrived, come up with a persuasive reason to go on living.

"You're here!" shrieked Evan over the doorbell, before she even opened the door. Then she opened it wide. Zoë set her bags on the hall floor and hugged Evan hard. When she was little, Evan had always been affectionate and devoted. Zoë had always taken care of her—advising, reassuring—until recently, when it seemed Evan had started advising and reassuring *her*. It startled Zoë. She suspected it had something to do with her being alone. It made people uncomfortable.

"How *are* you?"

"I threw up on the plane. Besides that, I'm O.K."

"Can I get you something? Here, let me take your suitcase. Sick on the plane. *Eeeyew*."

"It was into one of those sickness bags," said Zoë, just in case Evan thought she'd lost it in the aisle. "I was very quiet."

The apartment was spacious and bright, with a view all the way downtown along the East Side. There was a balcony and sliding glass doors. "I keep forgetting how nice this apartment is. Twenty-first floor, doorman ..." Zoë could work her whole life and never have an apartment like this. So could Evan. It was Charlie's apartment. He and Evan lived in it like two kids in a dorm, beer cans and clothes strewn around. Evan put Zoë's bag away from the mess, over the fish tanks. "I'm so glad you're here," she said. "Now what can I get you?"

Evan made them lunch—soup from a can and saltines.

"I don't know about Charlie," she said after they had finished. "I feel like we've gone all sexless and middle-aged already."

"Hmmmm," said Zoë. She leaned back into Evan's sofa and stared out the window at the dark tops of the buildings. It seemed a little unnatural to live up in the sky like this, like birds that out of some wrong-headed derring-do had nested too high. She nodded toward the lighted fish tanks and giggled. "I feel like a bird," she said, "with my own personal supply of fish."

Evan sighed. "He comes home and just sacks out on the sofa, watching fuzzy football. He's wearing the psychic cold cream and curlers, if you know what I mean."

Zoë sat up, readjusted the sofa cushions. "What's fuzzy football?"

"We haven't gotten cable yet. Everything comes in fuzzy. Charlie just watches it that way."

"Hmm, yeah, that's a little depressing," Zoë said. She looked at her hands. "Especially the part about not having cable."

"This is how he gets into bed at night." Evan stood up to demonstrate. "He whips all his clothes off, and when he gets to his underwear he lets it drop to one ankle. Then he kicks up his leg and flips the underwear in the air and catches it. I, of course, watch from the bed. There's nothing else. There's just that."

"Maybe you should just get it over with and get married."

"Really?"

"Yeah. I mean, you guys probably think living together like this is the best of both worlds, but—" Zoë tried to sound like an older sister; an older sister was supposed to be the parent you could never have, the hip, cool mom. "But I've always found that as soon as you think you've got the best of both worlds"—she thought now of herself, alone in her house, of the toad-faced cicadas that flew around like little men at night and landed on her screens, staring; of the size-fourteen shoes she placed at the doorstep, to scare off intruders; of the ridiculous, inflatable blowup doll someone had told her to keep propped up at the breakfast table—"it can suddenly twist and become the worst of both worlds."

"Really?" Evan was beaming. "Oh, Zoë. I have something to tell you. Charlie and I *are* getting married."

"Really." Zoë felt confused.

"I didn't know how to tell you."

"Yeah, I guess the part about fuzzy football misled me a little."

"I was hoping you'd be my maid of honor," said Evan, waiting. "Aren't you happy for me?"

"Yes," said Zoë, and she began to tell Evan a story about an award-winning violinist at Hilldale-Versailles—how the violinist had come home from a competition in Europe and taken up with a local man who made her go to all his summer softball games, made her cheer for him from the stands, with the wives, until she later killed herself. But when Zoë got halfway through, to the part about cheering at the softball games, she stopped.

"What?" said Evan. "So what happened?"

"Actually, nothing," said Zoë lightly. "She just really got into softball. You should have seen her."

Zoë decided to go to a late afternoon movie, leaving Evan to chores she needed to do before the party—"I have to do them alone, really," she'd said, a little tense after the violinist story. Zoë thought about going to an art museum, but women alone in art museums had to look good. They always did. Chic and serious, moving languidly, with a great handbag. Instead, she walked down through Kips Bay, past an earring boutique called Stick It in Your Ear, past a hair salon called Dorian Gray. That was the funny thing about "beauty," thought Zoë. Look it up in the yellow pages and you found a hundred entries, hostile with wit, cutesy with warning. But look up "truth"—Ha! There was nothing at all.

Zoë thought about Evan getting married. Would Evan turn into Peter Pumpkin Eater's wife? Mrs. Eater? At the wedding, would she make Zoë wear some flouncy lavender dress, identical with the other maids'? Zoë hated uniforms, had even in the first grade refused to join Elf Girls because she didn't want to wear the same dress as everyone else. Now she might have to. But maybe she could distinguish it. Hitch it up on one side with a clothespin. Wear surgical gauze at the waist. Clip to her bodice one of those pins that say in loud letters "Shit Happens."

At the movie—*Death by Number*—she bought strands of red licorice to tug and chew. She took a seat off to one side in the theater. She felt strangely self-conscious sitting alone, and hoped for the place to darken fast. When it did, and the coming attractions came on, she reached inside her purse for her glasses. They were in a Baggie. Her Kleenex was also in a Baggie. So were her pen and her aspirin and her mints. Everything was in Baggies. This was what she'd become: *a woman alone at the movies with everything in a Baggie.*

At the Halloween party, there were about two dozen people. There were people with ape heads and large hairy hands. There was someone dressed as a leprechaun. There was someone dressed as a frozen dinner. Some man had brought his two small daughters: a ballerina and a ballerina's sister, also dressed as a ballerina. There was a gaggle of sexy witches—women dressed entirely in black, beautifully made up and jeweled. "I hate those sexy witches. It's not in the spirit of Halloween," said Evan. Evan had abandoned the moon mask and dolled herself up as hausfrau, in curlers and an apron, a decision she now regretted. Charlie, because he liked fish, because he owned fish and collected fish, had decided to go as a fish. He had fins, and eyes on the sides of his head. "Zoë! How are you! I'm sorry I wasn't here when you first arrived!" He spent the rest of his time chatting up the sexy witches.

"Isn't there something I can help you with here?" Zoë asked her sister. "You've been running yourself ragged." She rubbed her sister's arm, gently, as if she wished they were alone.

"Oh, God, not at all," said Evan, arranging stuffed mushrooms on a plate. The timer went off, and she pulled another sheetful out of the oven. "Actually, you know what you can do?"

"What?" Zoë put on her bonehead.

"Meet Earl. He's the guy I had in mind for you. When he gets here, just talk to him a little. He's nice. He's fun. He's going through a divorce."

"I'll try," Zoë groaned. "O.K.? I'll try." She looked at her watch.

When Earl arrived, he was dressed as a naked woman, steel wool glued strategically to a body stocking, and large rubber breasts protruding like hams.

"Zoë, this is Earl," said Evan.

"Good to meet you," said Earl, circling Evan to shake Zoë's hand. He stared at the top of Zoë's head. "Great bone."

Zoë nodded. "Great tits," she said. She looked past him, out the window at the city thrown glittering up against the sky; people were saying the usual things: how it looked like jewels, like bracelets and necklaces unstrung. You could see the clock of the Con Ed building, the orange-and-gold-capped Empire State, the Chrysler like a rocket ship dreamed up in a depression. Far west you could glimpse Astor Plaza, with its flying white roof like a nun's habit. "There's beer out on the balcony, Earl. Can I get you one?" Zoë asked.

"Sure, uh, I'll come along. Hey, Charlie, how's it going?"

Charlie grinned and whistled. People turned to look. "Hey, Earl," someone called from across the room. "Va-va-va-voom."

They squeezed their way past the other guests, past the apes and the sexy witches. The suction of the sliding door gave way in a whoosh, and Zoë and Earl stepped out onto the balcony, a bonehead and a naked woman, the night air roaring and smoky cool. Another couple were out there, too, murmuring privately. They were not wearing costumes. They smiled at Zoë and Earl. "Hi," said Zoë. She found the plastic-foam cooler, dug in and retrieved two beers.

"Thanks," said Earl. His rubber breasts folded inward, dimpled and dented, as he twisted open the bottle.

"Well," sighed Zoë anxiously. She had to learn not to be afraid of a man, the way, in your childhood, you learned not to be afraid of an earthworm or a bug. Often, when she spoke to men at parties, she rushed things in her mind. As the man politely blathered on, she would fall in love, marry, then find herself in a bitter custody battle with him for the kids and hoping for a reconciliation, so that despite all his betrayals she might no longer despise him, and, in the few minutes remaining, learn, perhaps, what his last name was and what he did for a living, though probably there was already too much history between them. She would nod, blush, turn away.

"Evan tells me you're a history professor. Where do you teach?"

"Just over the Indiana border into Illinois."

He looked a little shocked. "I guess Evan didn't tell me that part."

"She didn't?"

"No."

"Well, that's Evan for you. When we were kids we both had speech impediments."

"That can be tough," said Earl. One of his breasts was hidden behind his drinking arm, but the other shone low and pink, full as a strawberry moon.

"Yes, well, it wasn't a total loss. We used to go to what we called peach pearapy. For about ten years of my life, I had to map out every sentence in my mind, way ahead, before I said it. That was the only way I could get a coherent sentence out."

Earl drank from his beer. "How did you do that? I mean, how did you get through?"

"I told a lot of jokes. Jokes you know the lines to already. You can just say them. I love jokes. Jokes and songs."

Earl smiled. He had on lipstick, a deep shade of red, but it was wearing off from the beer. "What's your favorite joke?"

"Uh, my favorite joke is probably—O.K., all right. This guy goes into a doctor's office, and—"

"I think I know this one," interrupted Earl eagerly. He wanted to tell it himself. "A guy goes into a doctor's office, and the doctor tells him he's got some good news and some bad news—that one, right?"

"I'm not sure," said Zoë. "This might be a different version."

"So the guy says, 'Give me the bad news first,' and the doctor says, 'O.K. You've got three weeks to live.' And the guy cries, 'Three weeks to live! Doctor, what is the good news?' And the doctor says, 'Did you see that secretary out front? I finally fucked her.'"

Zoë frowned.

"That's not the one you were thinking of?"

"No." There was accusation in her voice. "Mine was different."

"Oh," said Earl. He looked away and then back again. "What kind of history do you teach?"

"I teach American, mostly—eighteenth- and nineteenth-century." In graduate school, at bars the pickup line was always, "So what's your century?"

"Occasionally, I teach a special theme course," she added. "Say, 'Humor and Personality in the White House.' That's what my book's on." She thought of something someone once told her about bowerbirds, how they build elaborate structures before mating.

"Your book's on *humor*?"

"Yeah, and, well, when I teach a theme course like that I do all the centuries." *So what's your century?*

"All three of them."

"Pardon?" The breeze glistened her eyes. Traffic revved beneath them. She felt high and puny, like someone lifted into heaven by mistake and then spurned.

"Three. There's only three."

"Well, four, really." She was thinking of Jamestown, and of the Pilgrims coming here with buckles and witch hats to say their prayers.

"I'm a photographer," said Earl. His face was starting to gleam, his rouge smearing in a sunset beneath his eyes.

"Do you like that?"

"Well, actually, I'm starting to feel it's a little dangerous."

"Really?"

"Spending all your time is a dark room with that red light and all those chemicals. There's links with Parkinson's, you know."

"No, I didn't."

"I suppose I should wear rubber gloves, but I don't like to. Unless I'm touching it directly, I don't think of it as real."

"Hmmm," said Zoë. Alarm buzzed mildly through her.

"Sometimes, when I have a cut or something, I feel the sting and think, *Shit*. I wash constantly and just hope. I don't like rubber over the skin like that."

"Really."

"I mean, the physical contact. That's what you want, or why bother?"

"I guess," said Zoë. She wished she could think of a joke, something slow and deliberate with the end in sight. She thought of gorillas, how when they had been kept too long alone in cages they would smack each other in the head instead of mating.

"Are you—in a relationship?" Earl suddenly blurted.

"Now? As we speak?"

"Well, I mean, I'm sure you have a relationship to your *work*." A smile, a little one, nestled in his mouth like an egg. She thought of zoos in parks, how when cities were under siege, during world wars, people ate the animals. "But I mean, with a *man*."

"No, I'm not in a relationship with a *man*." She rubbed her chin with her hand and could feel the one bristly hair there. "But my last relationship was with a very sweet man," she said. She made something up. "From Switzerland. He was a botanist—a weed expert. His name was Jerry. I called him Jare. He was so funny. You'd go to the movies with him and all he would notice was the plants. He would never pay attention to the plot. Once, in a jungle movie, he started rattling off all these Latin names, our loud. It was very exciting for him." She paused, caught her breath. "Eventually, he went back to Europe to, uh, study the edelweiss." She looked at Earl. "Are you involved in a relationship? With a *woman*?"

Earl shifted his weight and the creases in his body stocking changed, splintering outward like something broken. His pubic hair slid over to one hip, like a corsage on a saloon girl. "No," he said, clearing his throat. The steel wool in his underarms was inching down toward his biceps. "I've just gotten out of a marriage that was full of bad dialogue like 'You want more *space*? I'll give you more space!' *Clonk*. Your basic Three Stooges."

Zoë looked at him sympathetically. "I suppose it's hard for love to recover after that."

His eyes lit up. He wanted to talk about love. "But I keep thinking love should be like a tree. You look at trees and they've got bumps and scars from tumors, infestations, what have you, but they're still growing. Despite the bumps and bruises, they're—straight."

"Yeah, well," said Zoë, "where I'm from they're all married or gay. Did you see that movie *Death by Number*?"

Earl looked at her, a little lost. She was getting away from him. "No," he said.

One of his breasts had slipped under his arm, tucked there like a baguette. She kept thinking of trees, of parks, of people in wartime eating the zebras. She felt a stabbing pain in her abdomen.

"Want some hors d'oeuvres?" Evan came pushing through the sliding door. She was smiling, though her curlers were coming out, hanging bedraggled at the ends of her hair like Christmas decorations, like food put out for the birds. She thrust forward a plate of stuffed mushrooms.

"Are you asking for donations or giving them away?" said Earl wittily. He liked Evan, and he put his arm around her.

"You know, I'll be right back," said Zoë.

"Oh," said Evan, looking concerned.

"Right back. I promise."

Zoë hurried inside, across the living room into the bedroom, to the adjoining bath. It was empty; most of the guests were using the half-bath near the kitchen.

She flicked on the light and closed the door. The pain had stopped, and she didn't really have to go to the bathroom, but she stayed there anyway, resting. In the mirror above the sink, she looked haggard beneath her bonehead, violet-grays showing under the skin like a plucked and pocky bird's. She leaned closer, raising her chin a little to find the bristly hair. It was there, at the end of the jaw, sharp and dark as a wire. She opened the medicine cabinet, pawed through it until she found some tweezers. She lifted her head again and poked at her face with the metal tips, grasping and pinching and missing. Outside the door, she could hear two people talking low. They had come into the bedroom and were discussing something. They were sitting on the bed. One of them giggled in a false way. Zoë stabbed again at her chin, and it started to bleed a little. She pulled the skin tight along the jawbone, gripped the tweezers hard around what she hoped was the hair, and tugged. A tiny square of skin came away but the hair remained, blood bright at the root of it. Zoë clenched her teeth. "Come on," she whispered. The couple outside in the bedroom were now telling stories, softly and laughing. There was a bounce and squeak of mattress, and the sound of a chair being moved out of the way. Zoë aimed the tweezers carefully, pinched, then pulled gently, and this time the hair came, too, with a slight twinge of pain, and then a great flood of relief. "Yeah!" breathed Zoë. She grabbed some toilet paper and dabbed at her chin. It came away spotted with blood, and so she tore off some more and pressed hard until it stopped. Then she turned off the light, opened the door, and rejoined the party. "Excuse me," she said to the couple in the bedroom. They were the couple from the balcony, and they looked at her, a bit surprised. They had their arms around each other, and they were eating candy bars.

Earl was still out on the balcony, alone, and Zoë rejoined him there. "Hi," she said.

He turned around and smiled. He had straightened his costume out a bit, though all the secondary sex characteristics seemed slightly doomed, destined to shift and flip and zip around again any moment. "Are you O.K.?" he asked. He had opened another beer and was chugging.

"Oh, yeah. I just had to go to the bathroom." She paused. "Actually, I have been going to a lot of doctors recently."

"What's wrong?" asked Earl.

"Oh, probably nothing. But they're putting me through tests." She sighed. "I've had sonograms. I've had mammograms. Next week I'm going in for a candygram." He looked at her, concerned. "I've had too many gram words," she said.

"Here, I saved you these." He held out a napkin with two stuffed mushroom caps. They were cold and leaving oil marks on the napkin.

"Thanks," said Zoë, and pushed them both in her mouth. "Watch," she said with her mouth full. "With my luck it'll be a gallbladder operation."

Earl made a face. "So your sister's getting married," he said, changing the subject. "Tell me, really, what you think about love."

"*Love*?" Hadn't they done this already? "I don't know." She chewed thoughtfully and swallowed. "All right. I'll tell you what I think about love. Here is a love story. This friend of mine—"

"You've got something on your chin," said Earl, and he reached over to touch it.

"What?" said Zoë, stepping back. She turned her face away and grabbed at her chin. A piece of toilet paper peeled off it, like tape. "It's nothing," she said. "It's just—it's nothing."

Earl stared at her.

"At any rate," she continued, "this friend of mine was this award-winning violinist. She traveled all over Europe and won competitions; she made records, she gave concerts, she got famous. But she had no social life. So one day she threw herself at the feet of this conductor she had a terrible crush on. He picked her up, scolded her gently, and sent her back to her hotel room. After that, she came home from Europe. She went back to her old hometown, stopped playing the violin, and took up with a local boy. This was in Illinois. He took her to some Big Ten bar every night to drink with his buddies from the team. He used to say things like 'Katrina here likes to play the violin,' and then he'd pinch her cheek. When she once suggested that they go home, he said, 'What, you think you're too famous for a place like this? Well, let me tell you something. You may think you're famous, but you're not *famous* famous.' Two famouses. 'No one here's ever heard of you.' Then he went up and bought a round of drinks for everyone but her. She got her coat, went home, and shot a bullet through her head."

Earl was silent.

"That's the end of my love story," said Zoë.

"You're not at all like your sister," said Earl.

"Oh, really," said Zoë. The air had gotten colder, the wind singing minor and thick as a dirge.

"No." He didn't want to talk about love anymore. "You know, you should wear a lot of blue—blue and white—around your face. It would bring out your coloring." He reached an arm out to show her how the blue bracelet he was wearing might look against her skin, but she swatted it away.

"Tell me, Earl. Does the word 'fag' mean anything to you?"

He stepped back, away from her. He shook his head in disbelief. "You know, I just shouldn't try to go out with career women. You're all stricken. A guy can really tell what life has done to you. I do better with women who have part-time jobs."

"Oh, yes?" said Zoë. She had once read an article entitled "Professional Women and the Demographics of Grief." Or, no, it was a poem. *If there were a lake, the moonlight would dance across it in conniptions.* She remembered that line. But perhaps the title was "The Empty House: Aesthetics of Barrenness." Or maybe "Space Gypsies: Girls in Academe." She had forgotten.

Earl turned and leaned on the railing of the balcony. It was getting late. Inside, the party guests were beginning to leave. The sexy witches were already gone. "Live and learn," Earl murmured.

"Live and get dumb," replied Zoë. Beneath them on Lexington there were no cars, just the gold rush of an occasional cab. He leaned hard on his elbows, brooding.

"Look at those few people down there," he said. "They look like bugs. You know how bugs are kept under control? They're sprayed with bug hormones—female bug hormones. The male bugs get so crazy in the presence of this hormone they're screwing everything in sight—trees, rocks, everything but female bugs. Population control. That's what's happening in this country," he said drunkenly. "Hormones sprayed around, and now men are screwing rocks. Rocks!"

In the back, the Magic Marker line on his buttocks spread wide, a sketchy black on pink, like a funnies page. Zoë came up, slow, from behind, and gave him a shove. His arms slipped forward, off the railing, out over the street. Beer spilled out of his bottle, raining twenty stories down to the street.

"Hey, what are you doing!" he said, whipping around. He stood straight and readied, and moved away from the railing, sidestepping Zoë. "What the *hell* are you doing?"

"Just kidding," she said. "I was just kidding." But he gazed at her, appalled and frightened, his Magic Marker buttocks turned away now toward all of downtown, a naked pseudo-woman with a blue bracelet at the wrist, trapped out on a balcony with—with *what*? "Really, I was just kidding!" Zoë shouted. The wind lifted the hair up off her head, skyward in spines behind the bone. If there were a lake, the moonlight would dance across it in conniptions. She smiled at him and wondered how she looked.

—1989

SHERMAN ALEXIE

Sherman Alexie is a Native American writer born in 1966. In 1999 he was named one of the *New Yorker*'s "20 under 40," a list of young writers who "are or will be key to their generation." He grew up on the Spokane Indian reservation in Wellpinit, Washington. At birth, Alexie suffered from hydrocephalus, and he underwent successful surgery at six months of age. This condition left him with a disfigured skull and led to bullying at school. His father, an alcoholic, often left the family for many weeks at a time, and his mother raised her six children, supporting them by the making and selling of quilts.

Alexie survived these early challenges, and his social isolation encouraged an avid interest in reading. He left the reservation and attended high school in Reardon, a town thirty miles away. There he excelled in academics and athletics, particularly basketball, a sport he continues to follow attentively. He won a scholarship to Gonzaga University and began to study medicine, but his studies were interrupted by his own struggles with alcoholism. In 1987 he gave up alcohol and returned to school, this time to Washington State University. He took a poetry class with Alex Kuo, and the experience was transformative. He began to write, and after graduation published two volumes of poems, *I Would Steal Horses* (1992) and *The Business of Fancydancing* (1992). His first volume of short stories, *The Lone Ranger and Tonto Fistfight in Heaven*, was published in 1993 and won the PEN/Hemingway Award for Best First Book of Fiction.

In 1995, Alexie published his first novel, *Reservation Blues*. This was followed by *Indian Killer* in 1996. Both novels are about contemporary Native American experience, exploring themes of despair, helplessness, anger, and redemption. The at-times harsh realism of his stories is tempered by a rebellious, comic voice, and by an ironic humour that contrasts the actuality of Native life with common stereotypes. He says that he avoids writing about Native spirituality, focusing instead on everyday experience: "There are Indian writers who write about things they aren't supposed to. They know. They'll pay for it ... I wouldn't go near that kind of writing. I'd be afraid of the repercussions. I write about a drunk in a bar, or a guy who plays basketball."

Joyce Carol Oates writes that Alexie is "the bad boy among [Native writers], mocking, self-mocking, unpredictable, unassimilable." Alexie continues to write poetry and stories; in recent years he has also written screenplays and performed stand-up comedy.

"Do You Know Where I Am" is a coming-of-age story that was published in the volume *Ten Little Indians* (2003). It is an archetypal tale about the loss of innocence, but, as with all of Alexie's work, he refuses to mythologize, and the story remains realistic and concrete.

Do You Know Where I Am?

SHERMAN ALEXIE

SHARON AND I were college sweethearts at St. Jerome the Second University in Seattle, or, as it is affectionately known, St. Junior's. We met at the first mixer dance of our freshman year and soon discovered we were the only confirmed Native American Roman Catholics within a three-mile radius of campus, so we slept together that inaugural night, in open defiance of Pope Whomever, and kept sleeping together for the next three years. It was primary love: red girl and red boy on white sheets.

Sharon was Apache, and I was Spokane, but we practiced our tribal religions like we practiced Catholicism: We loved all of the ceremonies but thought they were pitiful cries to a disinterested god.

My white mother, Mary, bless her soul, raised me all by herself in Seattle because my Indian daddy, Marvin, died of stomach cancer when I was a baby. I never knew him, but I spent half of every summer on the Spokane Reservation with his mother and father, my grandparents. My mother wanted me to keep in touch with my tribal heritage, but mostly, I read spy novels to my grandfather and shopped garage sales and secondhand stores with my grandmother. I suppose, for many Indians, garage sales and trashy novels are highly traditional and sacred. We all make up our ceremonies as we go along, right? I thought the reservation was ordinary and magical, like a sedate version of Disneyland. All told, I loved to visit but loved my home much more. In Seattle, my mother was a corporate lawyer for old-money companies and sent me to Lakeside Upper School, where I was a schoolmate of Bill Gates and Paul Allen,[1] who have become the new-money kings of the world.

---

1 .Co-founders of Microsoft.

Sharon went to St. Therese's School for Girls. Her parents, Wilson and Pauline, were both architects; they helped build three of the tallest skyscrapers in downtown Seattle. If Zeus[2] ate a few million pounds of glass, steel, and concrete, his offal would look something like those buildings. However fecal, those monstrosities won awards and made Wilson and Pauline very popular and wealthy. They lived in a self-designed home on Lake Washington that was lovely and tasteful in all ways except for its ridiculously turquoise exterior. I don't know whether they painted the house turquoise to honor the sacred stone of the Southwest or if they were being ironic: *Ha! We're Apache Indians from the desert, and this is our big blue house on the water! Deal with it!*

Sharon and I were Native American royalty, the aboriginal prince and princess of western Washington. Sure, we'd been thoroughly defeated by white culture, but dang it, we were conquered and assimilated National Merit Scholars in St. Junior's English honors department.

Sharon and I were in love and happy and young and skinny and beautiful and hyperliterate. We recited Shakespeare monologues as foreplay: *To be or not to be, take off your panties, oh, Horatio, I knew him well, a fellow of infinite jest, I'm going to wear your panties now.* All over campus, we were known as Sharon-and-David-the-Bohemian Indians. We were inseparable. We ate our meals together and fed each other. Risking expulsion for moral violations, we sneaked into each other's dorm rooms at night and made love while our respective roommates covered their heads with pillows. Sharon and I always tried to take the same classes and mourned the other's absence whenever we couldn't. We read the same books and discussed them while we were naked and intertwined. Oh Lord, we were twins conjoined at the brain, heart, and crotch.

I proposed to Sharon on the first day of our senior year, and she accepted, and we planned to secretly elope on the day after our graduation.

In June, the day before graduation, Sharon and I were taking one last walk along the path beside the anonymous creek that ran through the middle of campus. We were saying good-bye to a good place. Overgrown with fern and blackberry thickets, the creek had been left wild and wet.

"'Whose woods these are I think I know,'" I said.

"Robert Frost wrote the poem," said Sharon. We were playing Name the Poet, a game of our own invention.

"'Know' and 'poem,'" I said. "A clumsy rhyme, don't you think?"

"You stink," she said and laughed too loudly. Her joy was always rowdy, rude, and pervasive. I laughed with her and pulled her close to me and pressed my

2 Greek mythology: the god of thunder and ruler of gods.

face into her hair and breathed in her scent. After the first time we'd made love, she'd said, *Now I know what you smell like, and no matter what else happens to us, I'm always going to know what you smell like.*

"Hey," I said as we walked the creek. "How about we climb into the bushes and I get you a little wild and wet?"

We kissed and kissed until she pulled away.

"Do you hear that?" she said.

"What?"

"I think it's a cat. Can you hear it meowing?"

I listened and heard nothing.

"You're imagining things," I said.

"No, it's a cat. I can hear it. It sounds pitiful."

"There must be a hundred cats around here. City cats. They're tough."

"No, it sounds hurt. Listen."

I listened and finally heard the faint feline cry.

"It's down there in the creek somewhere," she said.

We peered over the edge and could barely see the water through the thick and thorny overgrowth.

"I'm sure it's hunting rats or something," I said. "It's okay."

"No, listen to it. It's crying. I think it's stuck."

"What do you want me to do? It's just a dumb-ass cat."

"Can you go find it?"

I looked again at the jungle between that cat and me.

"I'd need a machete to get through there," I said.

"Please," said Sharon.

"I'm going to get all cut up."

"'All in green went my love riding,'" she whispered in that special way, "'on a great horse of gold into the silver dawn.'"

"Cummings wrote the poem, and I'm in love and gone," I said and made my slow way down the creek side. I didn't want to save the cat; I wanted to preserve Sharon's high opinion of me. If she hadn't been there to push me down the slope, I never would have gone after that cat. As it was, I cursed the world as I tripped over ferns and pushed blackberry branches out of the way. I was cut and scraped and threatened by spiders and wasps, all for a dumb cat.

"It's like *Wild Kingdom* down here," I said.

"Do you see him?" she said, more worried about the cat. I could hear the love in her voice. I was jealous of that damn cat!

I stopped and listened. I heard the cry from somewhere close.

"He's right around here," I said.

"Find him," she said, her voice choking with fierce tears.

I leaned over, pushed aside one last fern, and saw him, a black cat trapped in blackberry branches. He was starved, too skinny to be alive, I thought, but his eyes were bright with fear and pain.

"Man," I said. "I think he's been caught in here for a long time."

"Save him, save him."

I reached in, expecting the cat to bite or claw me, but he remained gratefully passive as I tore away the branches and freed him. I lifted and carried him back up the bank. He was dirty and smelly, and I wanted all of this to be over.

"Oh my God," said Sharon as she took him from me. "Oh, he's so sad, so sad." She hugged him, and he accepted it without protest.

"What are we going to do with him?" I asked.

"I don't know."

"We can't keep him," I said. "Let's let him go here. He's free now. He'll be okay."

"What if he gets stuck again?"

"Then it'll be natural selection. Come on, he doesn't have a tag or anything. He's just a stray cat."

"No, he's tame, he's got a home somewhere." She stared the cat in the eyes as if he could tell us his phone number and address.

"Oh, wait, wait," she said. "I remember, in the newspaper, last week or something, there was a lost-cat ad. It said he was black with white heart-shaped fur on his belly."

Sharon had a supernatural memory; she could meet a few dozen new people at a party and rattle off their names two days later. During an English-department party our sophomore year, she recited by memory seventy-three Shakespeare sonnets in a row. It was the most voluminous display of erudition any of us had ever witnessed. Tenured English professors wept. But I was the one who enjoyed the honor and privilege of taking her home that night and making her grunt in repetitive monosyllables.

Beside the creek, Sharon gently turned the cat over, and we both saw the white heart. Without another word, Sharon ran back to her dorm room, and I followed her. She searched for the newspaper in her desk but couldn't find it, and none of her floormates had a copy of the old paper, either, so she ran into the basement and climbed into the Dumpster. I held the cat while she burrowed into the fetid pile of garbage.

"Come on," I said. "You're never going to find it. Maybe you imagined the whole thing. Let's take him to the shelter. They can take care of him."

She ignored me and kept searching. I felt like throwing the cat into the wall.

"This is it," she said and pulled a greasy newspaper out of the mess. She flipped to the classifieds, found the lost-cat ad, and shouted out the phone number. She jumped out of the Dumpster, grabbed the cat, ran back to her room, and quickly dialed.

"Hello," said Sharon over the telephone. "We have your cat. Yes, yes, yes. We found him by the creek. At St. Junior's. We'll bring him right over. What's your address? Oh God, that's really close."

Sharon ran out of the dorm; I ran after her.

"Slow down," I called after her, but she ignored me. Maybe Sharon wasn't a good Apache or Catholic, but she was religious when she found the proper mission.

We sprinted through a residential neighborhood, which may or may not have been a good idea for two brown kids, no matter how high our grade-point averages. But it felt good to run fast, and I dreamed about being a superhero. Fifteen minutes later and out of breath, Sharon knocked on the front door of a small house. An old couple opened the door.

"Lester," shouted the old man and took the cat from Sharon. The old woman hugged the man and the cat. All three cried to one another.

"How'd you find him?" asked the old man, weeping hard now, barely able to talk, but unashamed of his tears. "He's been gone for a month."

"I heard him crying," I said (I lied) and stepped into the doorway. Sharon stood behind me and peered over my shoulder.

"Oh, thank you, bless you," said the old woman.

"I pulled him out of some blackberry thorns," I said. "And then I remembered your ad in the newspaper, and I found the paper in the garbage, and I called you, and here I am."

The old man and woman hugged me, holding the cat between us, all of us celebrating the reunion, while Sharon stood silently by. I think I lied because I wanted to be briefly adored by strangers, to be remembered as a handsome and kind man, a better man, more complete, even saintly. But it was Orwell who wrote that "saints should be always judged guilty until they are proved innocent."[3]

All during this time, Sharon never spoke. I can only guess at her emotions, but I imagine she was shocked and hurt by my disloyalty. Standing in the presence of such obvious commitment between two people and their damn cat, she must have lost faith in me and, more importantly, in herself.

"How can we ever repay you?" asked the old woman.

"Nothing," I said. "We need nothing."

"Here, here," said the old man as he opened his wallet and offered me a twenty.

3 The opening words of George Orwell's essay "Reflections on Gandhi" (1949).

"No, no," I said. "I don't need that. I just wanted to be good, you know?"

He forced the money into my hand; I accepted it.

"You're a good man," said the old woman.

I shook my head, took Sharon's hand, and walked away, leaving those grateful strangers to their beloved pet.

"Why did you do that?" Sharon asked as we walked.

"I needed to," I said. That was the best answer I could give her. It wasn't enough.

"You lied to me, you lied to them, and you took their money," she said. "How could you do that?"

"I don't know," I said.

Sharon broke away from me and ran.

I didn't see her that night as I got ready for graduation, and I didn't see her the next morning.

"Where's Sharon?" asked my mother as she adjusted my cap and gown.

"She's with her parents," I said, which was a true statement, I suppose, but hardly close to the truth.

I went through the ceremony alone; Sharon went through the ceremony alone; we sat ten chairs apart.

The day after graduation, Sharon was still missing. I didn't know where she was. When my mother asked me about her absence, I said she was on a spiritual retreat.

"One month of silence," I said, lying to my mother, to another woman who loved me. "After a big event, like a graduation or birth, the Apaches leave for a month. It's an Apache thing."

"I wish I could do that," she said. "I think everybody should do that. Make it a law. Once a year, everybody has to be silent for a month. We'd all rotate, you know? You have to be quiet during your birth month."

"It's a good idea, Mom, I'm sure it would go over well."

"Sarcasm is a sin, honey."

After another day of unceremonial silence, I assumed Sharon had left me forever, and I finally confessed my fears to my mother.

"Mom," I said. "I love Sharon and I destroyed her."

Was I overreacting to Sharon's overreaction? I'd told such a small lie, had taken credit and reward for such a small act of heroism. But then I wondered if Sharon had always had her doubts about my character, and perhaps had always considered me an undependable braggart. What if she'd been gathering evidence against me all along, and I'd finally committed the last unpardonable crime?

"You have to go find her," my mother said.

"I can't," I said, and it was true and cowardly.

My mother turned away from me and cried while she fixed dinner. Later that night, while she washed dishes and I dried, my mother told me how much she still missed my father.

"He's been gone twenty-two years," she said. "But I can still feel him right here in the room with us. I can still smell him, his hair, his skin."

My mother didn't call my father by name because she wanted the dead to stay dead; I wanted to learn magic and open a twenty-four-hour supermarket that sold resurrection and redemption.

The next morning, Sharon came to see me. I was so grateful for her presence that I leaned against the wall to keep from falling down. My mother hugged Sharon until they both cried. Then Sharon asked my mother to give us some privacy. After my mother left, Sharon took my face in her hands.

"You're a liar," Sharon said. "I'm going to marry a liar."

I didn't want to ask her why she came back. We were so fragile, I worried that one wrong word could completely break us.

For the next twenty-nine years, we lived as wife and husband, as the mother and father of four kids (Sarah, Rachael, Francis, and Joshua) who suddenly grew into adults and became wives and husbands and mothers and fathers. During our long marriage, Sharon and I buried her mother and father and my mother, all of our grandparents, and many of our aunts, uncles, and cousins. I covered high school sports and reviewed movies for the local alternative weekly; an odd pair of beats, I suppose, but I enjoyed the appearance of being odd while living a sedate life. Sharon ran her own coffee shop and wrote lyric odes she never published. We paid our taxes, owned a modest home, and made love an average of three times a week. We didn't have nearly as much money as our parents, and that could be viewed as our failure, but we felt successful. We weren't triumphant, by any means, but we lived a good and simple life, and I often wondered if I deserved it.

All during those years, at every house party, group dinner, family gathering, and company picnic, Sharon told the story of the lost cat.

"My husband, the liar," she always called me. At first, she told the story to hurt me, then she told it out of habit, and then she told it because she'd turned it into a wildly funny and exaggerated adventure: *And then he fell in the creek!* She loved to make people laugh, and so they laughed at my small sins. I wanted the laughter to absolve me, but I'm not sure if that was its purpose. I never asked to be forgiven, and Sharon never offered her forgiveness. We never talked about the lost cat in private; it was our most public secret.

But there were other secrets, of course. Sharon kept most of hers, and I kept most of mine. Those kept secrets were small and ordinary, having to do with broken diets and hidden pornography, and they were of little consequence, but one evening, a decade into our marriage, Sharon confessed to an extramarital affair.

"I don't love him," she said. "It's over now. I only slept with him three times. To be fair, you can ask me three questions about it, and I'll answer them as honestly as possible, and then I don't ever want to talk about it again."

I was hurt by the frankness of her words, by her deal-making, but she cried, and her voice trembled as she spoke, and she'd never been one to feign emotion or cry for dramatic purposes, so I was lost in her contradictions.

"How could you do that to me?" I asked.

"Is that a real question?" she asked. "Or is it rhetorical?"

I panicked. I didn't want to waste my three questions. I wanted to know details, the facts and figures, and not emotional states. But which particular details did I want to know? And which questions would elicit the most information? I needed to be a brutally efficient interrogator. I couldn't believe I was participating in this horrible transaction.

"Listen," I said, "this is ridiculous. Let's talk this out like normal people."

"That's the problem," she said. "Everything is so normal. You didn't used to be normal. I didn't marry normal."

She was a thirty-two-year-old woman with four young kids, and she owned and managed a small business. So she was one of those notorious superwomen. I knew she was always exhausted, but what could I do to help her? I could never tell her she worked too hard, and I certainly couldn't tell her she should spend more time with the kids. I couldn't ask her to choose between her work life and her home life. As a man, I would never be asked to make a similar choice. I spent most Friday and Saturday nights watching other people's children play football, basketball, and volleyball. What kind of father was I? I could best be described as cordially absent on weekends and lovingly distracted on weekdays. What kind of husband was I? Apparently, I was the kind of husband whose wife needed to sleep with at least one other man and an untold number of others who might be waiting in line. There are millions of those clueless husbands, aren't there? Wasn't I yet another cuckolded husband, slightly distinguished by knowing how to self-define with an Old English word? I was eight hundred years old. I was historic, predictable, and planned. I was normal.

"Who is he?" I asked.

"His name is Michael Joyce," she said. "He's a regular at the shop. I've asked him to never come back. He agreed. He's a good man."

I was surprised to discover I wanted to hit my wife. I wanted to punch her in the stomach and make her fall to the floor. I wanted to see her gasping with physical pain. I would never hurt her that way—I hadn't struck another human being since the third grade—but the violent impulse was there, and I was frightened and exhilarated by it. My wife had no idea how dangerous I could be. I felt better knowing I could hurt her far more than she'd hurt me. And then I was revolted. How could I love a person and want to hurt her so much? How could I look at my wife, the mother of my children, and feel only the need for revenge? I paced around the room, ran my fingers roughly through my hair, because I needed to move. I needed to find another space in which to exist. I studied the details of the living room: the antique lamps purchased for full price and the end tables rescued from garage sales and refurbished; the brown leather couch and black leather recliner; the Monet and Kahlo[4] prints on the walls; the bookshelves stuffed with novels and sports histories; and the coffee tables adorned with art books. All of it was tasteful and beautiful and appropriate and hard-earned and useless.

Sharon wore a red blouse and blue jeans. Her feet were bare and needed a pedicure. Once a month, her feet were scrubbed clean and polished by a Vietnamese woman whose name and exact place of business I would never know. Sharon wore a fake pearl necklace her mother had given her for some birthday, and real pearl earrings I'd given her on our fifth anniversary. The fake pearls were prettier than the real ones. I don't know why I noticed her physical details, but it seemed important to take note of all I could. I felt the insistent need to be exact. Since it was laundry day, I knew she'd be wearing her oldest brassiere, and would never initiate lovemaking while wearing it, but would gladly receive my advances after first dashing into the bathroom to quickly remove the tattered bra. How many times had she emerged topless from the bathroom and run laughing toward me? Who keeps accurate count of such wonderful moments? Wouldn't a better husband know that number by heart?

"I'm a bad husband," I said. Why was I apologizing?

She turned away and sat on the couch as far away from me as possible. I kept pacing around the room.

"He's white," she said, volunteering the information, and I was strangely relieved. My emotions were changing and shifting randomly. If I'd been an actor in a musical, I would have broken into song for no apparent reason. I would have tap-danced to the primal 4/4 beat of betrayal. I would have leaped over the couch where she was sitting and rewon her heart with my grace and strength. What a dream life I have, and how instantly I can immerse myself in it! Can you believe I was happy to hear she'd slept with only a white man? I would have been

4 Claude Monet (1840–1926), a French Impressionist painter, and Frida Kahlo (1907–54), a Mexican painter.

tortured to hear she'd slept with another Indian man. Considering her beauty, ambition, and intelligence, I could conceive of an amazing white man or black man who might love her and be loved in return, but I doubted another Indian man of my particular talents existed out there in the world. Call it a potent mix of arrogance and self-hatred, but I was certain I was the one Indian man who was good enough for my Indian wife.

I believed I was being rational, but who can be rational in such a painful situation? Wouldn't my wife and I hold entirely different standards for what made a man good or great? What if she'd slept with a plumber or a construction worker? What if she'd slept with a supermarket graveyard-shift worker or a high school dropout? I couldn't stand the thought of my wife sleeping with a blue-collar man who'd read fewer books than I had. I wanted to believe my wife slept with another man because she needed to be loved in a new way, a more educated and intellectual way, and not because she wanted to hurt me. I didn't understand what I was feeling, and I didn't know what to do, and I couldn't ask her to help me, because that might qualify as my second question and would leave me with only one.

"Don't look at me that way," she said.

"What way?" I asked.

"Like this is inconceivable. Like I'm the Loch Ness Monster."

"I don't know what I'm thinking, feeling, or seeing."

"That's the problem. You've been blind for years."

I sat on the couch beside her. I tried to take her hand, but she pulled it away.

"No," she said. "You don't get to comfort me. And I don't get to comfort you. You have two questions. Ask them."

I was struck with the terrible fear that she'd had sex with Michael Joyce in our house, in our bed.

"Where did it happen?" I asked.

"The first time was in a hotel," she said. "The Westin downtown. A suite. Early. Eight in the morning. I got the kids off to school, opened up the shop. Jody ran the register and Rick made the coffee and Christy waited tables. I told them I had a dentist appointment."

"You told me you had a dentist appointment," I said.

"Yes," she said. "I lied to you directly. I never wanted to do that. I knew I was lying to you indirectly, but I hated to look you in the eyes and lie to you. I hated it."

"The Westin is a decent hotel," I said. Jesus, I sounded like a travel agent.

"The second time was in his car. We parked down on Lake Washington. You were down in Tacoma, covering the football championships."

"I called home that night," I said. "Sara was watching the kids. She said you had an emergency at the shop. The espresso maker was overheating."

"She didn't know I was lying. She thought I was at the shop."

Once or twice a month, I ran the path alongside Lake Washington. I knew I would never run it again. How can I survive this? I thought. How many more of my routines will I have to change? Again I tried to take my wife's hand. This time she let me. We interlaced our fingers. A small moment of intimacy, but enough to keep me from running out of the room and house and fleeing down the street.

"The third time was in his apartment," she said. "In his bed. Lunchtime. I fell asleep with him. I hated that. That's why I ended it. Falling asleep with him felt like the worst thing I could do. I never felt evil until I fell asleep with him."

She leaned over and kissed my forehead. I felt her heat. I didn't want to feel her heat. I didn't want to smell her scent. I didn't want to taste her. And it felt like time squared and cubed and then exploded exponentially. Days and months and years passed before I would find enough stupid courage to ask my third question.

"What did you do with him?"

"What do you mean?" she asked.

"I mean, into which parts of you did he put it?"

She flinched so painfully that I might as well have punched her in her chest. I was briefly happy about that.

"Do you really want to know that?" she asked.

"Yes."

She stood and walked away from me. I assume she was afraid I might really punch her.

"We," she said. "He—I mean, we—did everything."

"Say it exactly."

"I don't want to."

"You have to. It's part of the deal."

"I can't. It hurts too much."

"You don't get to feel as much pain as me. Now say it. Tell me exactly."

She closed her eyes and moaned like some tortured animal, like she was the first animal feeling the first pain. I heard that sound again when she buried her mother and, thirteen months later, her father.

"Tell me," I said. "Exactly."

She couldn't speak. Instead, she pointed at her mouth, her vagina, and her ass. She looked like a pornographic mime. I started laughing. I lay down on the couch and laughed. I couldn't stop laughing. She stared at me like I was crazy. Then she started laughing with me. Softly at first, but soon she had to sit down laughing on the floor so she wouldn't fall down laughing on the floor. She crawled across the floor and climbed onto the couch with me. We held each other and laughed. Then, as suddenly as it started, it stopped. We held each other in the silence.

"If you still love me," she said, "please, please, build me a time machine."

She sounded like a little girl talking to her father. I didn't know what to say. But we lay there together for hours until the kids came home from school and surprised us.

"Mommy and Daddy were doing it!" the four of them chanted and danced around the living room. "Mommy and Daddy were doing it!"

Sharon and I danced with our children. We danced the family dance, three quick spins, two hops, and a scream at the ceiling, and then Sharon and I made dinner, and we ate with our kids and gossiped about their school days and played *Chutes and Ladders* and watched *The Lion King* and made them brush their teeth and wash their faces and forced them into their pajamas and pushed them down the hallways into their beds and read them *Curious George* and *Go, Dog, Go!* and turned off the lights and told them good night and gave them our love, and we sat in the kitchen across from each other and drank coffee and added up our wins and our losses and decided to stay married.

It was Emily Dickinson[5] who wrote, "After great pain, a formal feeling comes." So Sharon and I formally rebuilt our marriage. And it was blue-collar work, exhausting and painful. We didn't argue more often than before, but we did live with longer and greater silences. There were times when both of us wanted to quit, but we always found the strength to get up in the morning and go back to the job. And then, one winter night two years after her confession, after eating a lovely dinner at a waterfront restaurant and slow-dancing in the parking lot while a small group of tourists cheered for us, she read a book in bed while I stood at our bedroom window and stared out into the dark. We were comfortable in the silence. A day or week or month or year before, I would have felt the need to end such a wonderful evening by making love to her, by proving I could share our bed and her body with ghosts. But I felt no such need that night, and I realized we'd completed the rebuilding project, we'd constructed a brand-new marriage, a new home, that sat next to the old marriage and its dusty and shuttered house. Standing at the window, I could almost see our old house out there in the dark, and I missed it. I often thought of it as we continued with our lives.

Suddenly, Sharon and I were forty. For my birthday that year, she and the kids all pitched in together and gave me a T-shirt that read LOST CAT on the front and DO YOU KNOW WHERE I AM? on the back.

I laughed and wore that shirt as pajamas. For two years, Sharon fell asleep next to me wearing that shirt.

---

5 Emily Dickinson (1830–86), an American poet.

"Oh, Lord," I said to Sharon on the day I finally tossed the ragged T-shirt into the trash. "With every new day comes a new monument to our love and pain."

"Who wrote that?" she asked.

"I did."

"It's free verse," she said. "I hate free verse."

We laughed and kissed and made love and read books in bed. We read through years of books, decades of books. There were never enough books for us. Read, partially read, and unread, our books filled the house, stacked on shelves and counters, piled into corners and closets. Our marriage became an eccentric and disorganized library. Whitman in the pantry! The Brontë sisters in the television room! Hardy on the front porch! Dickinson in the laundry room! We kept a battered copy of *Native Son* in the downstairs bathroom so our guests would have something valuable to read![6]

How do you measure a marriage? Three of our children still lived in Seattle and taught high school English, history, and Spanish respectively, while the fourth managed a homeless shelter in Portland, Oregon. Maybe Sharon and I had never loved each other well enough, but our kids were smart and talented and sober. They made less money than we did, as we made less than our parents did. We were going the wrong way on the social-class map! How glorious!

Every Sunday night, we all gathered for dinner (Joshua drove up from Portland with his partner, Aaron, and their son) and told one another the best stories of our weeks. We needed those small ceremonies. Our contentment was always running only slightly ahead of our dissatisfaction.

Was it enough? I don't know. But we knew enough not to ask ourselves too often. We knew to ask ourselves such questions during daylight hours. We fought hard for our happiness, and sometimes we won. Over the years, we won often enough to develop a strong taste for winning.

And then suddenly and mortally, Sharon and I were sixty-six years old.

On her birthday that year, surrounded by her husband, daughters, sons, and six grandkids, Sharon blew out the candles on her cake, closed her eyes, and made some secret wish.

One year later, after chemotherapy, radiation, organic food, acupuncture, and tribal shaman, Sharon lay on her deathbed in Sacred Hope Hospital. Our children had left their children to gather around Sharon, and it was good-bye Rachael! Good-bye Sarah! Good-bye Francis! Good-bye Joshua! She asked our children to give us some privacy. They cried and hugged her and left us alone.

6 Walt Whitman (1818–92), an American poet; Charlotte, Emily, and Anne Brontë, nineteenth-century English novelists and poets; Thomas Hardy (1840–1928), an English novelist and poet; *Native Son*, a 1940 novel by African American novelist Richard Wright.

"I'm going to die soon," Sharon said.

"I know," I said.

"I'm okay with it."

"I'm not. Because I love you so much," I said, "I would fistfight Time to win back your youth."

"You're a liar," she said and smiled, too tired to laugh.

"I lied to you once," I said. "But I haven't lied to you since."

"Is that the truth?"

"Yes," I said.

—2003

EDEN ROBINSON

Eden Robinson's first collection of short stories, *Traplines* (1996), won the United Kingdom's Winifred Holtby Prize for the best first work of fiction in the Commonwealth, and was selected as a *New York Times* Editor's Choice and Notable Book of the Year. This attention, along with the enthusiastic critical reception for her novel *Monkey Beach* (2000)—nominated for Canada's illustrious Giller Prize and the Governor General's Award—has helped establish Eden Robinson as one of Canada's best known female First Nations writers.

Eden Robinson was born on January 19, 1968, the same date, she says, "as Edgar Allan Poe and Dolly Parton.... I am absolutely certain that this affects my writing in some way." She grew up in Haisla territory near Kitamaat Village, British Columbia. She earned her B.F.A. from the University of Victoria, and then moved to Vancouver to pursue work that would give her time to write. She worked for several years at a variety of what she calls "McJobs," including janitor, mail clerk, and napkin ironer, but after she had a short story published in *Prism International* magazine, she enrolled in a master's program at the University of British Columbia. She graduated in 1992 with an MFA in creative writing; the result was the manuscript for *Traplines*, a collection of four short stories. Robinson was also writer-in-residence in the University of Calgary's Markin-Flanagan Distinguished Writer-in-Residence program in 2001-02. Her 2006 novel, *Blood Sports*, is a sequel to a story from *Traplines*, picking up on the lives of the story's characters in five years' time.

Robinson has used her international profile to draw attention to the poor treatment of First Nations people in Canada—and much of her fiction maintains this focus. The short story "Queen of the North," from *Traplines*, follows the blossoming relationship of the main character, Karaoke, with Jimmy Hill. Many reviewers and literary critics have used the term "Northern Gothic" to describe Robinson's work, but this Gothicism is tempered with lightness. In the midst of the violence and sexual exploitation that occurs in "Queen of the North," characters named Pepsi and Cola watch *Star Trek*, and lovers hunt for blueberries; "Queen of the North" defies category.

Queen of the North

EDEN ROBINSON

Frog Song

WHENEVER I see abandoned buildings, I think of our old house in the village, a rickety shack by the swamp where the frogs used to live. It's gone now. The council covered the whole area with rocks and gravel.

In my memory, the sun is setting and the frogs begin to sing. As the light shifts from yellow to orange to red, I walk down the path to the beach. The wind blows in from the channel, making the grass hiss and shiver around my legs. The tide is low and there's a strong rotting smell from the beach. Tree stumps that have been washed down the channel from the logged areas loom ahead—black, twisted silhouettes against the darkening sky.

The seiner coming down the channel is the *Queen of the North*, pale yellow with blue trim, Uncle Josh's boat. I wait on the beach. The water laps my ankles. The sound of the old diesel engine grows louder as the boat gets closer.

Usually I can will myself to move, but sometimes I'm frozen where I stand, waiting for the crew to come ashore.

The only thing my cousin Ronny didn't own was a Barbie Doll speedboat. She had the swimming pool, she had the Barbie-Goes-to-Paris carrying case, but she didn't have the boat. There was one left in Northern Drugs, nestling between the puzzles and the stuffed Garfields, but it cost sixty bucks and we were broke. I knew Ronny was going to get it. She'd already saved twenty bucks out of her allowance. Anyway, she always got everything she wanted because she was an only child and both her parents worked at the aluminum smelter. Mom knew how much I wanted it, but she said it was a toss-up between school supplies and paying bills, or wasting our money on something I'd get sick of in a few weeks.

We had a small Christmas tree. I got socks and underwear and forced a cry of surprise when I opened the package. Uncle Josh came in just as Mom was carving the turkey. He pushed a big box in my direction.

"Go on," Mom said, smiling. "It's for you."

Uncle Josh looked like a young Elvis. He had the soulful brown eyes and the thick black hair. He dressed his long, thin body in clothes with expensive labels—no Sears or Kmart for him. He smiled at me with his perfect pouty lips and bleached white teeth.

"Here you go, sweetheart," Uncle Josh said.

I didn't want it. Whatever it was, I didn't want it. He put it down in front of me. Mom must have wrapped it. She was never any good at wrapping presents. You'd think with two kids and a million Christmases behind her she'd know how to wrap a present.

"Come on, open it," Mom said.

I unwrapped it slowly, my skin crawling. Yes, it was the Barbie Doll speedboat.

My mouth smiled. We all had dinner and I pulled the wishbone with my little sister, Alice. I got the bigger piece and made a wish. Uncle Josh kissed me. Alice sulked. Uncle Josh never got her anything, and later that afternoon she screamed about it. I put the boat in my closet and didn't touch it for days.

Until Ronny came over to play. She was showing off her new set of Barbie-in-the-Ice-Capades clothes. Then I pulled out the speedboat and the look on her face was almost worth it.

My sister hated me for weeks. When I was off at soccer practice, Alice took the boat and threw it in the river. To this day, Alice doesn't know how grateful I was.

There's a dream I have sometimes. Ronny comes to visit. We go down the hallway to my room. She goes in first. I point to the closet and she eagerly opens the door. She thinks I've been lying, that I don't really have a boat. She wants proof.

When she turns to me, she looks horrified, pale and shocked. I laugh, triumphant. I reach in and stop, seeing Uncle Josh's head, arms, and legs squashed inside, severed from the rest of his body. My clothes are soaked dark red with his blood.

"Well, what do you know," I say. "Wishes do come true."

o o o

Me and five chug buddies are in the Tamitik arena, in the girls' locker room under the bleachers. The hockey game is in the third period and the score is tied. The yells and shouting of the fans drown out the girl's screaming. There are four of us against her. It doesn't take long before she's on the floor trying to crawl away. I want to say I'm not part of it, but that's my foot hooking her ankle and tripping her while Ronny takes her down with a blow to the temple. She grunts Her head makes a hollow sound when it bounces off the sink. The lights make us all look green. A cheer explodes from inside the arena. Our team has scored.

The girl's now curled up under the sink and I punch her and kick her and smash her face into the floor.

My cuz Ronny had great connections. She could get hold of almost any drug you wanted. This was during her biker chick phase, when she wore tight leather skirts, teeny weeny tops, and many silver bracelets, rings, and studs. Her parents started coming down really hard on her then. I went over to her house to get high. It was okay to do it there, as long as we sprayed the living room with Lysol and opened the windows before her parents came home.

We toked up and decided to go back to my house to get some munchies. Ronny tagged along when I went up to my bedroom to get the bottle of Visine. There was an envelope on my dresser. Even before I opened it I knew it would be money. I knew who it was from.

I pulled the bills out. Ronny squealed.

"Holy sheep shit, how much is there?"

I spread the fifties out on the dresser. Two hundred and fifty dollars. I could get some flashy clothes or nice earrings with that money, if I could bring myself to touch it. Anything I bought would remind me of him.

"You want to have a party?" I said to Ronny.

"Are you serious?" she said, going bug-eyed.

I gave her the money and said make it happen. She asked who it came from, but she didn't really care. She was already making phone calls.

That weekend we had a house party in town. The house belonged to one of Ronny's biker buddies and was filled with people I knew by sight from school. As the night wore on, they came up and told me what a generous person I was. Yeah, that's me, I thought, Saint Karaoke of Good Times.

I took Ronny aside when she was drunk enough. "Ronny, I got to tell you something."

"What?" she said, blinking too fast, like she had something in her eye.

"You know where I got the money?"

She shook her head, lost her balance, blearily put her hand on my shoulder, and barfed out the window.

As I listened to her heave out her guts, I decided I didn't want to tell her after all. What was the point? She had a big mouth, and anything I told her I might as well stand on a street corner and shout to the world. What I really wanted was to have a good time and forget about the money, and after beating everyone hands down at tequila shots that's exactly what I did.

"Moooo." I copy the two aliens on *Sesame Street* mooing to a telephone. Me and Uncle Josh are watching television together. He smells faintly of the halibut he cooked for dinner. Uncle Josh undoes his pants. "Moo." I keep my eyes on the TV and say nothing as he moves toward me. I'm not a baby like Alice, who runs to Mommy about everything. When it's over he'll have treats for me. It's like when the dentist gives me extra suckers for not crying, not even when it really hurts.

I could have got my scorpion tattoo at The Body Hole, where my friends went. A perfectly groomed beautician would sit me in a black-leather dentist's chair and the tattoo artist would show me the tiny diagram on tracing paper. We'd choose the exact spot on my neck where the scorpion would go, just below the hairline where my hair comes to a point. Techno, maybe some funky remix of Abba, would blare through the speakers as he whirred the tattoo needle's motor.

But Ronny had done her own tattoo, casually standing in front of the bathroom mirror with a short needle and permanent blue ink from a pen. She simply poked the needle in and out, added the ink, and that was that. No fuss, no muss.

So I asked her to do it for me. After all, I thought, if she could brand six marks of Satan on her own breast, she could certainly do my scorpion.

Ronny led me into the kitchen and cleared off a chair. I twisted my hair up into a bun and held it in place. She showed me the needle, then dropped it into a pot of boiling water. She was wearing a crop top and I could see her navel ring, glowing bright gold in the slanting light of the setting sun. She was prone to lifting her shirt in front of complete strangers and telling them she'd pierced herself.

Ronny emptied the water into the sink and lifted the needle in gloved hands. I bent my head and looked down at the floor as she traced the drawing on my skin.

The needle was hot. It hurt more than I expected, a deep ache, a throbbing. I breathed through my mouth. I fought not to cry. I concentrated fiercely on not crying in front of her, and when she finished I lay very still.

"See?" Ronny said. "Nothing to it, you big baby."

When I opened my eyes and raised my head, she held one small mirror to my face and another behind me so I could see her work. I frowned at my reflection. The scorpion looked like a smear.

"It'll look better when the swelling goes down," she said, handing me the two mirrors.

As Ronny went to start the kettle for tea, she looked out the window over the sink. "Star light, star bright, first star—"

I glanced out the window. "That's Venus."

"Like you'd know the difference."

I didn't want to argue. The skin on the back of my neck ached like it was sunburned.

I am singing Janis Joplin songs, my arms wrapped around the karaoke machine. I fend people off with a stolen switchblade. No one can get near until some kid from school has the bright idea of giving me drinks until I pass out.

Someone else videotapes me so my one night as a rock star is recorded forever. She tries to send it to *America's Funniest Home Videos*, but they reject it as unsuitable for family viewing. I remember nothing else about that night after I got my first hit of acid. My real name is Adelaine, but the next day a girl from school sees me coming and yells, "Hey, look, it's Karaoke!"

The morning after my sixteenth birthday I woke up looking down into Jimmy Hill's face. We were squashed together in the backseat of a car and I thought, God, I didn't.

I crawled around and found my shirt and then spent the next half hour vomiting beside the car. I vaguely remembered the night before, leaving the party with Jimmy. I remembered being afraid of bears.

Jimmy stayed passed out in the backseat, naked except for his socks. We were somewhere up in the mountains, just off a logging road. The sky was misty and gray. As I stood up and stretched, the car headlights went out.

Dead battery. That's just fucking perfect, I thought.

I checked the trunk and found an emergency kit. I got out one of those blankets that look like a large sheet of aluminum and wrapped it around myself. I searched the car until I found my jeans. I threw Jimmy's shirt over him. His jeans were hanging off the car's antenna. When I took them down, the antenna wouldn't straighten up.

I sat in the front seat. I had just slept with Jimmy Hill. Christ, he was practically a Boy Scout. I saw his picture in the local newspaper all the time, with these medals for swimming. Other than that, I never really noticed him. We went to different parties.

About midmorning, the sun broke through the mist and streamed to the ground in fingers of light, just like in the movies when God is talking to someone. The sun hit my face and I closed my eyes.

I heard the seat shift and turned. Jimmy smiled at me and I knew why I'd slept with him. He leaned forward and we kissed. His lips were soft and the kiss was gentle. He put his hand on the back of my neck. "You're beautiful."

I thought it was just a line, the polite thing to say after a one-night stand, so I didn't answer.

"Did you get any?" Jimmy said.

"What?" I said.

"Blueberries." He grinned. "Don't you remember?"

I stared at him.

His grin faded. "Do you remember anything?"

I shrugged.

"Well. We left the party, I dunno, around two, I guess. You said you wanted blueberries. We came out here—" He cleared his throat.

"Then we fucked, passed out, and now we're stranded." I finished the sentence. The sun was getting uncomfortable. I took off the emergency blanket. I had no idea what to say next. "Battery's dead."

He swore and leaned over me to try the ignition.

I got out of his way by stepping out of the car. Hastily he put his shirt on, not looking up at me. He had a nice chest, buff and tan. He blushed and I wondered if he had done this before.

"You cool with this?" I said.

He immediately became macho. "Yeah."

I felt really shitty then. God, I thought, he's going to be a bragger.

I went and sat on the hood. It was hot. I was thirsty and had a killer headache. Jimmy got out and sat beside me.

"You know where we are?" Jimmy said.

"Not a fucking clue."

He looked at me and we both started laughing.

"You were navigating last night," he said, nudging me.

"You always listen to pissed women?"

"Yeah," he said, looking sheepish. "Well. You hungry?"

I shook my head. "Thirsty."

Jimmy hopped off the car and came back with a warm Coke from under the driver's seat. We drank it in silence.

"You in any rush to get back?" he asked.

We started laughing again and then went hunting for blueberries. Jimmy found a patch not far from the car and we picked the bushes clean. I'd forgotten how tart wild blueberries are. They're smaller than store-bought berries, but their flavor is much more intense.

"My sister's the wilderness freak," Jimmy said. "She'd be able to get us out of this. Or at least she'd know where we are."

We were perched on a log. "You gotta promise me something."

"What?"

"If I pop off before you, you aren't going to eat me."

"What?"

"I'm serious," I said. "And I'm not eating any bugs."

"If you don't try them, you'll never know what you're missing." Jimmy looked at the road. "You want to pick a direction?"

The thought of trekking down the dusty logging road in the wrong direction held no appeal to me. I must have made a face because Jimmy said, "Me neither."

After the sun set, Jimmy made a fire in front of the car. We put the aluminum blanket under us and lay down. Jimmy pointed at the sky. "That's the Big Dipper."

"Ursa Major," I said. "Mother of all bears. There's Ursa Minor, Cassiopeia ..." I stopped.

"I didn't know you liked astronomy."

"It's pretty nerdy."

He kissed me. "Only if you think it is." He put his arm around me and I put my head on his chest and listened to his heart. It was a nice way to fall asleep.

Jimmy shook me awake. "Car's coming." He pulled me to my feet. "It's my sister."

"Mmm." Blurrily I focused on the road. I could hear birds and, in the distance, the rumble of an engine.

"My sister could find me in hell," he said.

When they dropped me off at home, my mom went ballistic. "Where the hell were you?"

"Out." I stopped at the door. I hadn't expected her to be there when I came in.

Her chest was heaving. I thought she'd start yelling, but she said very calmly, "You've been gone for two days."

You noticed? I didn't say it. I felt ill and I didn't want a fight. "Sorry. Should've called."

I pushed past her, kicked off my shoes, and went upstairs.

Still wearing my smelly jeans and shirt I lay down on the bed. Mom followed me to my room and shook my shoulder.

"Tell me where you've been."

"At Ronny's."

"Don't lie to me. What is wrong with you?"

God. Just get lost. I wondered what she'd do if I came out and said what we both knew. Probably have a heart attack. Or call me a liar.

"You figure it out," I said. "I'm going to sleep." I expected her to give me a lecture or something, but she just left.

Sometimes, when friends were over, she'd point to Alice and say, "This is my good kid." Then she'd point to me and say, "This is my rotten kid, nothing but trouble. She steals, she lies, she sleeps around. She's just no damn good."

Alice knocked on my door later.

"Fuck off," I said.

"You've got a phone call."

"Take a message. I'm sleeping."

Alice opened the door and poked her head in. "You want me to tell Jimmy anything else?"

I scrambled down the hallway and grabbed the receiver. I took a couple of deep breaths so it wouldn't sound like I'd rushed to the phone. "Hi."

"Hi," Jimmy said. "We just replaced the battery on the car. You want to go for a ride?"

"Aren't you grounded?"

He laughed. "So?"

I thought he just wanted to get lucky again, and then I thought, What the hell, at least this time I'll remember it.

"Pick me up in five minutes."

I'm getting my ass kicked by two sisters. They're really good. They hit solidly and back off quickly. I don't even see them coming anymore. I get mad enough to kick out. By sheer luck, the kick connects. One of the sisters shrieks and goes down. She's on the ground, her leg at an odd angle. The other one loses it and swings. The bouncer steps in and the crowd around us boos.

"My cousins'll be at a biker party. You want to go?"

Jimmy looked at me like he wasn't sure if I was serious.

"I'll be good," I said, crossing my heart then holding up my fingers in a scout salute.

"What fun would that be?" he said, revving the car's engine.

I gave him directions. The car roared away from our house, skidding a bit. Jimmy didn't say anything. I found it unnerving. He looked over at me, smiled, then turned back to face the road. I was used to yappy guys, but this was nice. I leaned my head back into the seat. The leather creaked.

Ronny's newest party house didn't look too bad, which could have meant it was going to be dead in there. It's hard to get down and dirty when you're worried you'll stain the carpet. You couldn't hear anything until someone opened the door and the music throbbed out. They did a good job with the soundproofing. We went up the steps just as my cousin Frank came out with some bar buddies.

Jimmy stopped when he saw Frank and I guess I could see why. Frank is on the large side, six-foot-four and scarred up from his days as a hard-core Bruce Lee fan, when he felt compelled to fight Evil in street bars. He looked down at Jimmy.

"Hey, Jimbo," Frank said. "Heard you quit the swim team."

"You betcha," Jimmy said.

"Fucking right!" Frank body-slammed him. He tended to be more enthusiastic than most people could handle, but Jimmy looked okay with it. "More time to party," he said. Now they were going to gossip forever so I went inside.

The place was half-empty. I recognized some people and nodded. They nodded back. The music was too loud for conversation.

"You want a drink?" Frank yelled, touching my arm.

I jumped. He quickly took his hand back. "Where's Jimmy?"

"Ronny gave him a hoot and now he's hacking up his lungs out back." Frank took off his jacket, closed his eyes, and shuffled back and forth. All he knew was the reservation two-step and I wasn't in the mood. I moved toward the porch but Frank grabbed my hand. "You two doing the wild thing?"

"He's all yours," I said.

"Fuck you," Frank called after me.

Jimmy was leaning against the railing, his back toward me, his hands jammed into his pockets. I watched him. His hair was dark and shiny, brushing his shoulders. I liked the way he moved, easily, like he was in no hurry to get anywhere. His eyes were light brown with gold flecks. I knew that in a moment he would turn and smile at me and it would be like stepping into sunlight.

In my dream Jimmy's casting a fishing rod. I'm afraid of getting hooked, so I sit at the bow of the skiff. The ocean is mildly choppy, the sky is hard blue, the air is cool. Jimmy reaches over to kiss me, but now he is soaking wet. His hands and lips are cold, his eyes are sunken and dull. Something moves in his mouth. It isn't his tongue. When I pull away, a crab drops from his lips and Jimmy laughs. "Miss me?"

I feel a scream in my throat but nothing comes out.

"What's the matter?" Jimmy tilts his head. Water runs off his hair and drips into the boat. "Crab got your tongue?"

This one's outside Hanky Panky's. The woman is so totally bigger than me it isn't funny. Still, she doesn't like getting hurt. She's afraid of the pain but can't back down because she started it. She's grabbing my hair, yanking it hard. I pull hers. We get stuck there, bent over, trying to kick each other, neither one of us willing to let go. My friends are laughing their heads off. I'm pissed at that but I'm too sloshed to let go. In the morning my scalp will throb and be so tender I won't be able to comb my hair. At that moment, a bouncer comes over and splits us apart. The woman tries to kick me but kicks him instead and he knocks her down. My friends grab my arm and steer me to the bus stop.

Jimmy and I lay down together on a sleeping bag in a field of fireweed. The forest fire the year before had razed the place and the weeds had only sprouted back up about a month earlier. With the spring sun and just the right sprinkling of rain, they were as tall as sunflowers, as dark pink as prize roses, swaying around us in the night breeze.

Jimmy popped open a bottle of Baby Duck. "May I?" he said, reaching down to untie my sneaker.

"You may," I said.

He carefully lifted the sneaker and poured in some Baby Duck. Then he raised it to my lips and I drank. We lay down, flattening fireweed and knocking over the bottle. Jimmy nibbled my ear. I drew circles in the bend of his arm. Headlights came up fast, then disappeared down the highway. We watched the fireweed shimmer and wave in the wind.

"You're quiet tonight," Jimmy said. "What're you thinking?"

I almost told him then. I wanted to tell him. I wanted someone else to know and not have it locked inside me. I kept starting and then chickening out. What was the point? He'd probably pull away from me in horror, disgusted, revolted.

"I want to ask you something," Jimmy whispered. I closed my eyes, feeling my chest tighten. "You hungry? I've got a monster craving for chicken wings."

Bloody Vancouver

When I got to Aunt Erma's the light in the hallway was going spastic, flickering like a strobe, little bright flashes then darkness so deep I had to feel my way along the wall. I stopped in front of the door, sweating, smelling myself through the thick layer of deodorant. I felt my stomach go queasy and wondered if I was going to throw up after all. I hadn't eaten and was still bleeding heavily.

Aunt Erma lived in east Van in a low-income government housing unit. Light showed under the door. I knocked. I could hear the familiar opening of *Star Trek*, the old version, with the trumpets blaring. I knocked again.

The door swung open and a girl with a purple Mohawk and Cleopatra eye-liner thrust money at me.

"Shit," she said. She looked me up and down, pulling the money back. "Where's the pizza?"

"I'm sorry," I said. "I think I have the wrong house."

"Pizza, pizza, pizza!" teenaged voices inside screamed. Someone was banging the floor in time to the chant.

"You with Cola?" she asked me.

I shook my head. "No. I'm here to see Erma Williamson. Is she in?"

"In? I guess. Mom?" she screamed. "Mom? It's for you!"

A whoop rose up. "Erma and Marley sittin' in a tree, k-i-s-s-i-n-g. First comes lust—"

"Shut up, you social rejects!"

"—then comes humping, then comes a baby after all that bumping!"

"How many times did they boink last night!" a single voice yelled over the laughter.

"Ten!" the voices chorused enthusiastically. "Twenty! Thirty! Forty!"

"Hey! Who's buying the pizza, eh? No respect! I get no respect!"

Aunt Erma came to the door. She didn't look much different from her pictures, except she wasn't wearing her cat-eye glasses.

She stared at me, puzzled. Then she spread open her arms.

"Adelaine, baby! I wasn't expecting you! Hey, come on in and say hi to your cousins. Pepsi! Cola! Look who came by for your birthday!"

She gave me a tight bear hug and I wanted to cry.

Two girls stood at the entrance to the living room, identical right down to their lip rings. They had different colored Mohawks though—one pink, one purple.

"Erica?" I said, peering. I vaguely remembered them as having pigtails and making fun of Mr. Rogers. "Heather?"

"It's Pepsi," the purple Mohawk said. "Not, n-o-t, Erica."

"Oh," I said.

"Cola," the pink-Mohawked girl said, turning around and ignoring me to watch TV.

"What'd you bring us?" Pepsi said matter-of-factly.

"Excuse the fruit of my loins," Aunt Erma said, leading me into the living room and sitting me between two guys who were glued to the TV. "They've temporarily lost their manners. I'm putting it down to hormones and hoping the birth control pills turn them back into normal human beings."

Aunt Erma introduced me to everyone in the room, but their names went in one ear and out the other. I was so relieved just to be there and out of the clinic I couldn't concentrate on much else.

"How is he, Bones?" the guy on my right said, exactly in synch with Captain Kirk on TV. Captain Kirk was standing over McCoy and a prone security guard with large purple circles all over his face.

"He's dead, Jim," the guy on my left said.

"I wanna watch something else," Pepsi said. "This sucks."

She was booed.

"Hey, it's my birthday. I can watch what I want."

"Siddown," Cola said. "You're out-voted."

"You guys have no taste at all. This is crap. I just can't believe you guys are watching this—this cultural pabulum. I—"

A pair of panties hit her in the face. The doorbell rang and the pink-haired girl held the pizza boxes over her head and yelled, "Dinner's ready!"

"Eat in the kitchen," Aunt Erma said. "All of youse. I ain't scraping your cheese out of my carpet."

Everyone left except me and Pepsi. She grabbed the remote control and flipped through a bunch of channels until we arrived at one where an announcer for the World Wrestling Federation screamed that the ref was blind.

"Now this," Pepsi said, "is entertainment."

By the time the party ended, I was snoring on the couch. Pepsi shook my shoulder. She and Cola were watching Bugs Bunny and Tweety.

"If we're bothering you," Cola said. "You can go crash in my room."

"Thanks," I said. I rolled off the couch, grabbed my backpack, and found the bathroom on the second floor. I made it just in time to throw up in the sink. The cramps didn't come back as badly as on the bus, but I took three Extra-Strength Tylenols anyway. My pad had soaked right through and leaked all over my underwear. I put on clean clothes and crashed in one of the beds. I wanted a black hole to open up and suck me out of the universe.

When I woke, I discovered I should have put on a diaper. It looked like something had been hideously murdered on the mattress.

"God," I said just as Pepsi walked in. I snatched up the blanket and tried to cover the mess.

"Man," Pepsi said. "Who are you? Carrie?"

"Freaky," Cola said, coming in behind her. "You okay?"

I nodded. I wished I'd never been born.

Pepsi hit my hand when I touched the sheets. "You're not the only one with killer periods." She pushed me out of the bedroom. In the bathroom she started water going in the tub for me, poured some Mr. Bubble in, and left without saying anything. I stripped off my blood-soaked underwear and hid them in the bottom of the garbage. There would be no saving them. I lay back. The bubbles popped and gradually the water became cool. I was smelly and gross. I scrubbed hard but the smell wouldn't go away.

"You still alive in there?" Pepsi said, opening the door.

I jumped up and whisked the shower curtain shut.

"Jesus, don't you knock?"

"Well, excuuuse me. I brought you a bathrobe. Good thing you finally crawled out of bed. Mom told us to make you eat something before we left. We got Ichiban, Kraft, or hot dogs. You want anything else, you gotta make it yourself. What do you want?"

"Privacy."

"We got Ichiban, Kraft, or hot dogs. What do you want?"

"The noodles," I said, more to get her out than because I was hungry.

She left and I tried to lock the door. It wouldn't lock so I scrubbed myself off quickly. I stopped when I saw the bathwater. It was dark pink with blood.

I crashed on the couch and woke when I heard sirens. I hobbled to the front window in time to see an ambulance pull into the parking lot. The attendants wheeled a man bound to a stretcher across the lot. He was screaming about the eyes in the walls that were watching him, waiting for him to fall asleep so they could come peel his skin from his body.

Aunt Erma, the twins, and I drove to the powwow at the Trout Lake community center in East Vancouver. I was still bleeding a little and felt pretty lousy, but Aunt Erma was doing fundraising for the Helping Hands Society and had asked me to work her bannock booth. I wanted to help her out.

Pepsi had come along just to meet guys, dressed up in her flashiest bracelets and most conservatively ripped jeans. Aunt Erma enlisted her too, when she found out that none of her other volunteers had showed up. Pepsi was disgusted.

Cola got out of working at the booth because she was one of the jingle dancers. Aunt Erma had made her outfit, a form-fitting red dress with silver jingles that flashed and twinkled as she walked. Cola wore a bobbed wig to cover her pink Mohawk. Pepsi bugged her about it, but Cola airily waved good-bye and said, "Have fun."

I hadn't made fry bread in a long time. The first three batches were already mixed. I just added water and kneaded them into shapes roughly the size of a large doughnut, then threw them in the electric frying pan. The oil spattered and crackled and steamed because I'd turned the heat up too high. Pepsi wasn't much better. She burned her first batch and then had to leave so she could watch Cola dance.

"Be right back," she said. She gave me a thumbs-up sign and disappeared into the crowd.

The heat from the frying pan and the sun was fierce. I wished I'd thought to bring an umbrella. One of the organizers gave me her baseball cap. Someone else brought me a glass of water. I wondered how much longer Pepsi was going to be. My arms were starting to hurt.

I flattened six more pieces of bread into shape and threw them in the pan, beyond caring anymore that none of them were symmetrical. I could feel the sun sizzling my forearms, my hands, my neck, my legs. A headache throbbed at the base of my skull.

The people came in swarms, buzzing groups of tourists, conventioneers on a break, families, and assorted browsers. Six women wearing HI! MY NAME IS tags stopped and bought all the fry bread I had. Another hoard came and a line started at my end of the table.

"Last batch!" I shouted to the cashiers. They waved at me.

"What are you making?" someone asked.

I looked up. A middle-aged red-headed man in a business suit stared at me. At the beginning, when we were still feeling spunky, Pepsi and I had had fun with that question. We said, Oh, this is fish-head bread. Or fried beer foam. But bullshitting took energy.

"Fry bread," I said. "This is my last batch."

"Is it good?"

"I don't think you'll find out," I said. "It's all gone."

The man looked at my tray. "There seems to be more than enough. Do I buy it from you?"

"No, the cashier, but you're out of luck, it's all sold." I pointed to the line of people.

"Do you do this for a living?" the man said.

"Volunteer work. Raising money for the Helping Hands," I said.

"Are you Indian then?"

A hundred stupid answers came to my head but like I said, bullshit is work. "Haisla. And you?"

He blinked. "Is that a tribe?"

"Excuse me," I said, taking the fry bread out of the pan and passing it down to the cashier.

The man slapped a twenty-dollar bill on the table. "Make another batch."

"I'm tired," I said.

He put down another twenty.

"You don't understand. I've been doing this since this morning. You could put a million bucks on the table and I wouldn't change my mind."

He put five twenty-dollar bills on the table.

It was all for the Helping Hands, I figured, and he wasn't going to budge. I emptied the flour bag into the bowl. I measured out a handful of baking powder, a few fingers of salt, a thumb of lard. Sweat dribbled over my face, down the tip of my nose, and into the mix as I kneaded the dough until it was very soft but hard to shape. For a hundred bucks I made sure the pieces of fry bread were roughly the same shape.

"You have strong hands," the man said.

"I'm selling fry bread."

"Of course."

I could feel him watching me, was suddenly aware of how far my shirt dipped and how short my cutoffs were. In the heat, they were necessary. I was sweating too much to wear anything more.

"My name is Arnold," he said.

"Pleased to meet you, Arnold," I said. "Scuse me if I don't shake hands. You with the convention?"

"No. I'm here on vacation."

He had teeth so perfect I wondered if they were dentures. No, probably caps. I bet he took exquisite care of his teeth.

We said nothing more until I'd fried the last piece of bread. I handed him the plate and bowed. I expected him to leave then, but he bowed back and said, "Thank you."

"No," I said. "Thank you. The money's going to a good cause. It'll—"

"How should I eat these?" he interrupted me.

With your mouth, asshole. "Put some syrup on them, or jam, or honey. Anything you want."

"Anything?" he said, staring deep into my eyes.

Oh, barf. "Whatever."

I wiped sweat off my forehead with the back of my hand, reached down and unplugged the frying pan. I began to clean up, knowing that he was still standing there, watching.

"What's your name?" he said.

"Suzy," I lied.

"Why're you so pale?"

I didn't answer. He blushed suddenly and cleared his throat. "Would you do me a favor?"

"Depends."

"Would you—" he blushed harder, "shake your hair out of that baseball cap?"

I shrugged, pulled the cap off, and let my hair loose. It hung limply down to my waist. My scalp felt like it was oozing enough oil to cause environmental damage.

"You should keep it down at all times," he said.

"Good-bye, Arnold," I said, picking up the money and starting toward the cashiers. He said something else but I kept on walking until I reached Pepsi.

I heard the buzz of an electric razor. Aunt Erma hated it when Pepsi shaved her head in the bedroom. She came out of her room, crossed the landing, and banged on the door. "In the bathroom!" she shouted. "You want to get hair all over the rug?"

The razor stopped. Pepsi ripped the door open and stomped down the hall. She kicked the bathroom door shut and the buzz started again.

I went into the kitchen and popped myself another Jolt. Sweat trickled down my pits, down my back, ran along my jaw and dripped off my chin.

"Karaoke?" Pepsi said. Then louder. "Hey! Are you deaf?"

"What?" I said.

"Get me my cell phone."

"Why don't you get it?"

"I'm on the can."

"So?" Personally, I hate it when you're talking on the phone with someone and then you hear the toilet flush.

Pepsi banged about in the bathroom and came out with her freshly coiffed Mohawk and her backpack slung over her shoulder. "What's up your butt?" she said.

"Do you want me to leave? Is that it?"

"Do what you want. This place is like an oven," Pepsi said. "Who can deal with this bullshit?" She slammed the front door behind her.

The apartment was quiet now, except for the chirpy weatherman on the TV promising another week of record highs. I moved out to the balcony. The headlights from the traffic cut into my eyes, bright and painful. Cola and Aunt Erma bumped around upstairs, then their bedroom doors squeaked shut and I was alone. I had a severe caffeine buzz. Shaky hands, fluttery heart, mild headache. It was still warm outside, heat rising from the concrete, stored up during the last four weeks of weather straight from hell. I could feel my eyes itching. This was the third night I was having trouble getting to sleep.

Tired and wired. I used to be able to party for days and days. You start to hallucinate badly after the fifth day without sleep. I don't know why, but I used to see leprechauns. These waist-high men would come and sit beside me, smiling with their brown wrinkled faces, brown eyes, brown teeth. When I tried to shoo them away, they'd leap straight up into the air, ten or twelve feet, their green clothes and long red hair flapping around them.

A low, gray haze hung over Vancouver, fuzzing the street lights. Air-quality bulletins on the TV were warning the elderly and those with breathing problems to stay indoors. There were mostly semis on the roads this late. Their engines rumbled down the street, creating minor earthquakes. Pictures trembled on the wall. I took a sip of warm, flat Jolt, let it slide over my tongue, sweet and harsh. It had a metallic twang, which meant I'd drunk too much, my stomach wanted to heave.

I went back inside and started to pack.

Home Again, Home Again, Jiggity-Jig

Jimmy and I lay in the graveyard, on one of my cousin's graves. We should have been creeped out, but we were both tipsy.

"I'm never going to leave the village," Jimmy said. His voice buzzed in my ears.

"Mmm."

"Did you hear me?" Jimmy said.

"Mmm."

"Don't you care?" Jimmy said, sounding like I should.

"This is what we've got, and it's not that bad."

He closed his eyes. "No, it's not bad."

I poured myself some cereal. Mom turned the radio up. She glared at me as if it were my fault the Rice Crispies were loud. I opened my mouth and kept chewing.

The radio announcer had a thick Nisga'a accent. Most of the news was about the latest soccer tournament. I thought, that's northern native broadcasting: sports or bingo.

"Who's this?" I said to Mom. I'd been rummaging through the drawer, hunting for spare change.

"What?"

It was the first thing she'd said to me since I'd come back. I'd heard that she'd cried to practically everyone in the village, saying I'd gone to Vancouver to become a hooker.

I held up a picture of a priest with his hand on a little boy's shoulder. The boy looked happy.

"Oh, that," Mom said. "I forgot I had it. He was Uncle Josh's teacher."

I turned it over. *Dear Joshua*, it read. *How are you? I miss you terribly. Please write. Your friend in Christ, Archibald.*

"Looks like he taught him more than just prayers."

"What are you talking about? Your Uncle Josh was a bright student. They were fond of each other."

"I bet," I said, vaguely remembering that famous priest who got eleven years in jail. He'd molested twenty-three boys while they were in residential school.

Uncle Josh was home from fishing for only two more days. As he was opening my bedroom door, I said, "Father Archibald?"

He stopped. I couldn't see his face because of the way the light was shining through the door. He stayed there a long time.

"I've said my prayers," I said.

He backed away and closed the door.

In the kitchen the next morning he wouldn't look at me. I felt light and giddy, not believing it could end so easily. Before I ate breakfast I closed my eyes and said grace out loud. I had hardly begun when I heard Uncle Josh's chair scrape the floor as he pushed it back.

I opened my eyes. Mom was staring at me. From her expression I knew that she knew. I thought she'd say something then, but we ate breakfast in silence.

"Don't forget your lunch," she said.

She handed me my lunch bag and went up to her bedroom.

I use a recent picture of Uncle Josh that I raided from Mom's album. I paste his face onto the body of Father Archibald and my face onto the boy. The montage looks real enough. Uncle Josh is smiling down at a younger version of me.

My period is vicious this month. I've got clots the size and texture of liver. I put one of them in a Ziploc bag. I put the picture and the bag in a hatbox. I tie it up with a bright red ribbon. I place it on the kitchen table and go upstairs to get a jacket. I think nothing of leaving it there because there's no one else at home. The note inside the box reads, "It was yours so I killed it."

"Yowtz!" Jimmy called out as he opened the front door. He came to my house while I was upstairs getting my jacket. He was going to surprise me and take me to the hot springs. I stopped at the top of the landing. Jimmy was sitting at the kitchen table with the present that I'd meant for Uncle Josh, looking at the note. Without seeing me, he closed the box, neatly folded the note, and walked out the door.

He wouldn't take my calls. After two days, I went over to Jimmy's house, my heart hammering so hard I could feel it in my temples. Michelle answered the door.

"Karaoke!" she said, smiling. Then she frowned. "He's not here. Didn't he tell you?"

"Tell me what?"

"He got the job," Michelle said.

My relief was so strong I almost passed out. "A job."

"I know. I couldn't believe it either. It's hard to believe he's going fishing, he's so spoiled. I think he'll last a week. Thanks for putting in a good word, anyways." She kept talking, kept saying things about the boat.

My tongue stuck in my mouth. My feet felt like two slabs of stone. "So he's on *Queen of the North*?"

"Of course, silly," Michelle said. "We know you pulled strings. How else could Jimmy get on with your uncle?"

The lunchtime buzzer rings as I smash this girl's face. Her front teeth crack. She screams, holding her mouth as blood spurts from her split lips. The other two twist my arms back and hold me still while the fourth one starts smacking my face, girl hits, movie hits. I aim a kick at her crotch. The kids around us cheer enthusiastically. She rams into me and I go down as someone else boots me in the kidneys.

I hide in the bushes near the docks and wait all night. Near sunrise, the crew starts to make their way to the boat. Uncle Josh arrives first, throwing his gear onto the deck, then dragging it inside the cabin. I see Jimmy carrying two heavy bags. As he walks down the gangplank, his footsteps make hollow thumping noises that echo off the mountains. The docks creak, seagulls circle overhead in the soft morning light, and the smell of the beach at low tide is carried on the breeze that ruffles the water. When the seiner's engines start, Jimmy passes his bags to Uncle Josh, then unties the rope and casts off. Uncle Josh holds out his hand, Jimmy takes it and is pulled on board. The boat chugs out of the bay and rounds the point. I come out of the bushes and stand on the dock, watching the *Queen of the North* disappear.

—1996

SHAUN TAN

Shaun Tan is a freelance artist, writer, and director living in Melbourne, Australia. His award-winning picture books use words and illustration to transform the usual narrative landscape; his surreal imagery and dream-like sequences of drawings bring depth and psychological intensity to his spare narratives, which hover on the edges of experience and consciousness.

Born in 1974, Tan grew up in the northern suburbs of Perth, Western Australia, and his drawings still retain qualities of that environment: vast cloudscapes and vistas of land, wasted, hot, and empty, scribbled over with repetitive urban sprawl underneath a sunlit sky. As children he and his brother would take walks to the beach, collecting shells and objects which Tan would then draw. His father, an architect, instilled in him the habits of working with precision and care; he also gave him his first paid job at the age of seven—20 cents for adding a tree to an architectural sketch.

Tan attended a special high school art program, where he had the advantage of being taught by practising artists. He then went to the University of Western Australia and took a degree in English Literature and Fine Arts. He began to draw for money, creating illustrations for magazines, book covers, music posters, flyers, and newsletters. Tan says that his work for science fiction magazines directed his drawings towards certain subjects: time, space, death, history, art, sexuality, and horror, "usually set in some other world (past, future or inter-planetary) than our own."

As Tan began making his own books, he became interested in the interplay between text and image, creating picture books that elude categorization. Books such as *The Rabbits* (1998), *The Red Tree* (2001), *Tales from Outer Suburbia* (2008), and the wordless novel *The Arrival* (2006) are enjoyed by readers of all ages, though Tan is often cited as a writer for children. His mysterious narratives create fables from minimal text interwoven with silent, full-page drawings; the stories are layered and deepened by this technique. Detailed, surreal drawings take the reader into subconscious worlds that contrast with and yet connect to the suburban landscapes where many of these stories begin.

Tan's books have received great critical acclaim, and he has won numerous awards, most recently the prestigious Astrid Lindgren Memorial Award for Children's Literature. In 2011, he won an Oscar as director of *The Lost Thing,* a short animated film based on his 1999 picture book.

"Grandpa's Story," from *Tales from Outer Suburbia*, is a fable about relationship and commitment. The narrator's grandparents embark on an adventure that takes them to otherworldly lands, where, to prepare themselves for marriage, they must complete a series of ritual trials. The lands they visit are "beyond the edge of outer suburbia, past the very last railway line, a treacherous place without logic and comfort." The story shows a way back to a clear, safe, brightly lit world—but a world that can never be looked upon with the same eyes once they return.

Grandpa's Story

SHAUN TAN

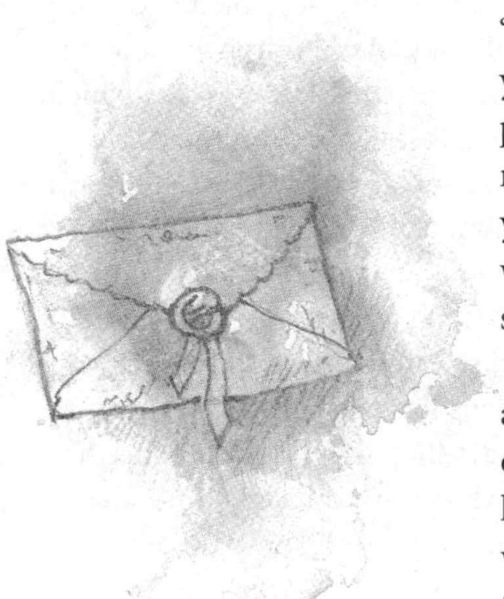

"YOU KNOW that big hill you can see from your bedroom window?" says Grandpa, pointing. "Well, your grandma and I got married on the other side of it, long before you lot came along. Of course, weddings were more complicated in those days, not the short 'n' sweet kind you see today.

"For a start, the bride and groom were sent away before the ceremony, and they were only allowed to have one photo taken upon leaving, and no more until they came back, which might be a long time later. That's why there are so many blank pages in our wedding album—the dark pages we call them. Lucky for us that first picture came out good. Look at the family, all dressed up on the driveway. Look at your grandma there, as though she's just stepped out of a movie. Talk about stylish.

"After the photographer left, we were given a sealed envelope, a compass, and traditional wedding boots—hardy things they were, with steel caps. Each guest told us a special riddle, like a cryptic crossword clue.

We had to listen hard and remember them all, strange instructions that would supposedly make sense later on. We were mad keen to get started and figure it all out, so we didn't hang around. We were off!"

Grandpa is a bit vague at this stage in his story, so it's not clear where they actually went. Somewhere "past the factories and landfills" and "beyond all the signs and roads." When we ask him to show us on a map, he simply shakes his head in an amused way, as if to say "one day you'll know."

He waves aside our further questions and continues: "We weren't allowed to open the envelope until we arrived. Inside was a list of objects we had to find before the end of the day, each corresponding to a clue. This was the Scavenger Hunt, always the most troublesome and feared part of any wedding. Well, we expected to be back home and dressed for the well-rehearsed vows in no time at all—we were young and full of confidence, always in a hurry too. Of course, it was not too long before we ran into trouble, a whole lot of trouble...."

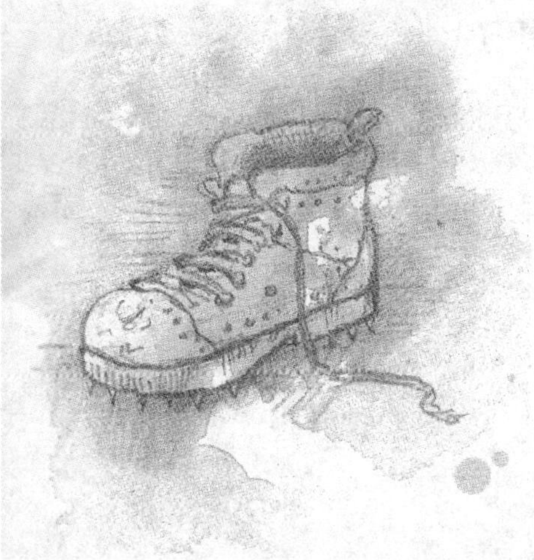

Frustratingly, Grandpa goes off to make a cup of tea at this point. We follow him to the kitchen and press for details. Grandpa just shrugs. "It's hard to explain the terrible things that happened out there. In fact, the more I tell you, the less you will actually understand. Some things in life are like that. You have to find out for yourself....

"They were perilous times. But every setback only made us more determined. Scared? Sure, sometimes, but we had each other. That must be what it's all about, we thought: As long as we stick together, nothing can stop us!

"And true enough, one by one we found those objects on the list. It was hard work, and we had trouble remembering some of the clues. But there was a lot of happiness discovering so many small things in unexpected places. We tied everything to the rear bumper with wedding string in the customary way.

"The sound of that rattling from the back of the car was very satisfying at first, but really started to get on our nerves after hours and hours of driving around. It was late by then, and we had a big problem. A really big problem. You see, the last two objects on our list seemed impossible to find, and I think both of us were beginning to wonder if they even existed. Yet we couldn't return unless we found them. We searched and searched, wracked our brains and did everything we were supposed to. Still nothing.

NADA
NO
CLOSED
NO
NO
VACANCY
NO
NO VACANCY
NO
VACANCY

"We became anxious, desperate, obsessed, driving farther and faster, not thinking about where we were going. Eventually we found ourselves lost in a vast magnetic desert, unable to get a reliable compass bearing. My own old grandpa once spoke of a place all lovers are doomed to visit at least once—maybe this was what he was talking about, I thought. It was terrible!

"The sun was creeping below the horizon. We would never make it back in time for the vows. We'd missed our big moment. Our smiles vanished. We stopped holding hands. And then—*BANG*!—the back tire burst on a pointy rock! Well that was it! Your grandma leapt out, slammed the door furiously, and started blaming me for everything. I leapt out, slammed the door furiously, and started blaming her for everything. We shouted and yelled and carried on, and said a few things we've since lived to regret ... well, you know what it's like when your grandma and I have one of our events.

"Then there was a long and terrible silence, of a kind we had never known before. We refused to even look at each other. It was like all the stones in that desert went down our throats and into our hearts. We wanted to just sink into the ground and stay there forever.

"Of course, as the light faded and the temperature dropped, we soon realized that we would have to do something quick-smart if we were to have any hope of returning to civilization. And we'd have to do it together.

"The spare tire—which we'd never needed before—was somehow rusted into the back of the car; it required the leverage of our combined weight on a crowbar to budge it. With one almighty heave it finally popped free. Our sense of relief was overwhelming. We almost didn't notice something twinkling in the hollow muddy pan of the car's boot. Twinkling just like stars. Well, we rinsed off the mud with the last of the drinking water and still couldn't believe our eyes—two of the most perfect rings you ever saw! If you don't believe me, have a look at this!" Grandpa holds up his hand with a ring on it.

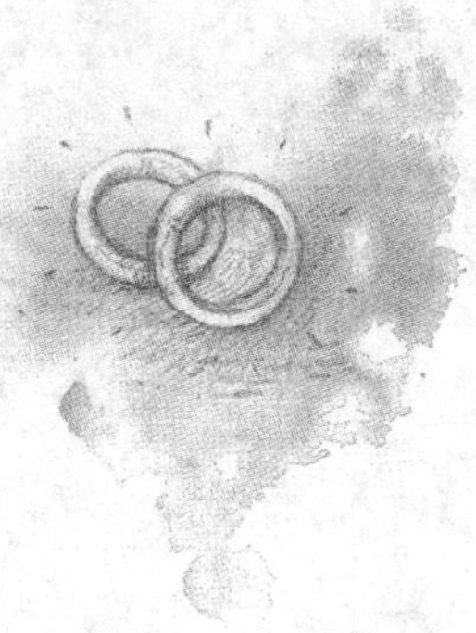

"From that moment on, we picked a random direction and took off at top speed, with a determination that could make any destination turn up on the far side of a bug-plastered windscreen. And sure enough, as we crested that last big hill, we could see all the lights of the outer suburbs unfold before us, streets like old friends, welcoming us home.

"By the time we pulled into the driveway, there was just enough time to shower, dress, exchange our vows, and do all that ceremonial stuff we had rehearsed. It was as if we had been away for only a couple of hours, and everything was normal, with everyone saying congratulations over and over. Your grandma and I kept looking at each other, as though we had just returned from another planet.

"Anyway, that's pretty much it, the story of how we got married, beyond that big hill you can see from the window. Long before you lot came along."

Grandpa shuffles off to the toilet, and then to check on his fruit trees. Admittedly, we are skeptical about everything we've heard, particularly as Grandpa can have a very lively imagination. There is only one thing to do—ask Grandma.

"Well, you know I rarely agree with your grandpa's account of *anything*," she tells us. "But in this case I'll make a rare exception." And she shows us the other ring they found under the spare tire, out in the desert.

—2008

JUST MARRIED

SHEILA HETI

Sheila Heti burst onto the North American literary scene when six of her short stories debuted in Brooklyn writer Dave Eggers's literary quarterly *McSweeney's* in 2000. Heti included those short stories in a collection of thirty stories published under the title *The Middle Stories* in 2001. *The Middle Stories* was published in the US with *McSweeney's* when Heti was twenty-four; since then it has been translated into four languages. In 2005 Heti published her novel *Ticknor*. Her second novel, *How Should a Person Be*? followed in 2010 and made *The New Yorker*'s list of Best Books.

Of Jewish and Hungarian heritage, Heti was born in Toronto in 1976. She studied playwrighting for a year at Montreal's National Theatre School and went on to study art history and philosophy at Trinity College, University of Toronto. Her short fictions are notable for the way in which they transport contemporary malaise to the realm of fable or myth, rendering the banal as extraordinary. In an interview with *McSweeney's*, Heti has described her approach to writing fiction: "Every good story names something. In the way that other languages have words for feelings or experiences for which we don't have equivalent words, a story should be like that word in another language for a feeling or an experience we don't yet have the name for." Her stories have been said to "have an intriguing parable-like quality, yet never offer obvious conclusions."

Heti is known around her native Toronto as the founder of the popular *Trampoline Hall Lecture Series*, a monthly symposium that challenges guest speakers to present on topics they know little about. She is the author of the illustrated children's book *We Need a Horse* (2011) and co-wrote a philosophical handbook entitled *The Chairs Are Where the People Go* (2011) with Misha Glouberman.

"The Raspberry Bush" (from *The Middle Stories*) displays Heti's remarkable ability to "name" the tragedy inherent in the everyday; though the woman in the story apparently cares only about her raspberries, she has a depth that is both appealing and troubling.

The Raspberry Bush

SHEILA HETI

A LITTLE old woman who never stopped smiling walked into her kitchen from her garden. She had been standing in the sun for twenty minutes, tears in her eyes, looking at her beautiful raspberry bush that had died overnight. Instead of perky red raspberries she had found them black and brittle, and they fell to the ground at the slightest touch.

The sun shone through the kitchen window and lit up everything with sparkles of gold as the little old woman who never stopped smiling called up her sister in such a sorrow. Her sister was eighty-eight and lived in California. She said into the phone, "The raspberries are dead."

Her sister replied, "Well, the grandchildren are flunking out of school and Martha is pregnant and Sam is divorcing his wife and his wife is taking up with a gypsy girl. The infant has the flu and she never stops coughing. I was over there the other day and all they talk about is money ever since Tom got fired from the plant. Not to mention that Timothy never stops dating and we all think he has AIDS or gonorrhea or something. The news, I saw it today, told about a hurricane in the Andes which, as you know, is where David and Sue went skiing last week. Everyone here is miserable with grief and worry."

The little old woman listened to her sister, and when she had finished the little old woman who never stopped smiling put down the phone and sat in her kitchen that was dotted with gold.

There was a knock.

"Hello?" called the woman, and she stood up and padded to the door and peeped through the peephole and saw a young man in a delivery cap holding a bouquet of flowers. She opened the door.

"Why," her lips curled up in a smile. "These can't be for me."

"Are you Miss Marcia—"

"No, young man. She's next door." And the little old woman who never stopped smiling closed the door and went to sit at her kitchen table. The day was long; there were eight more hours in it. She had planned to eat the raspberries, one by one, every last one of them. But overnight the bush had died and there wouldn't be raspberries ever again.

The little old woman laid down her head and started to cry. She cried at her table every day, but no one knew it.

—2001

IAN WILLIAMS

Ian Williams is a poet, short story writer, and literature professor. He is the author of *You Know Who You Are* (2010), *Not Anyone's Anything* (2011), and *Personals* (2012). He has been shortlisted for several Canadian literature awards, including the CBC Literary Prizes and the Malahat Long Poem Prize, and he is the winner of the 2012 Danuta Gleed Literary Award. "A radical new voice in Canadian fiction," Williams experiments with space and time, creating a world at once strange and recognizable: one of continual connection and conversation, and one of continual disconnection and isolation.

Williams was born in Trinidad in 1979, and raised and educated in Canada. A precocious student, he moved through high school quickly. As an undergraduate at the University of Toronto, he studied Psychology and English, with the intent of going into medicine. He decided, however, against becoming a doctor and instead pursued his studies in English literature. Though he was writing creatively, he did not take creative writing classes; he preferred to study literature and learn the tricks and formal innovations of earlier masters, particularly those of the Romantic and Modernist periods. Williams describes his writing as "inquisitive about the world, playful with audience, musical and mathematical in form, and lightly muscled in syntax."

Williams studied under the poet George Elliott Clarke and focused his Ph.D. on twentieth-century poetry and theories of voice and tone. He finished his Ph.D. at the age of twenty-five and then took a job as professor of American literature at Fitchburg State University. He is now at Sheridan College, where he continues to teach and write. He has held fellowships and residencies at Vermont Studio Center, Cave Canem, Kimmel Harding Nelson Center for the Arts, and Palazzo Rinaldi in Italy. He was also a scholar at the National Humanities Center Summer Institute for Literary Study.

In the story "Break-In" (from *Not Anyone's Anything*), Williams's experimentation with form involves the radical manipulation of the reader's expectations of narrative time and space: two simultaneous and intersecting plot lines are placed together on the page, and separated by a line. Williams wrote "Break-In" to explore how he could "turn a story into a different physical object." In this instance, the object is a house, with "literal basements ...dual-narratives, semi-detached."

Break-In

IAN WILLIAMS

HOOP planned to get in and out as quickly as possible. Six to eight minutes is all it should take to storm a house. Treat it like a timed shopping spree, like a game show, like a shot clock speeding to 0:00 at the top of the screen. But the back bedroom with its otherworldly girliness threw him, and when he heard the garage door rumbling up, he ran down the stairs, then down one more level (he panicked) into the basement and hid under the stairs. He didn't even see the side entrance.

Late evening, a month into first semester, a guy and his girl walk from school to Phase 2 of The Houses. He leads her to a Siamese house, joined at the cheek. He leads her to the left twin and they enter through the mouth. Inside is a mess of exposed plumbing, wood, and wires. Orange codes are spray-painted on the walls.

He's been in houses like this before, in this situation or nearly.

This house—this whole subdivision—was five stops from Hoop's aging apartment complex. The balconies of his building were streaked with rust. So he was attracted to the new development, and from the back corner seat of the 41 bus, he tracked its progress over the spring like a seed growing in a paper cup. First the land was bulldozed, then mixer trucks planted cement into the patterns of an old civilization, then workers put up wooden walls, then plastic walls, then dark shingles, then various colours of brick. By the end of April some of the houses were almost ready to be occupied. Hoop—not for Hooper, but for his skills balling—and his friend Duane got off the bus early to explore what guys were calling, with bravado, The Houses.

Everyone knew that guys took girls to The Houses to get some, except for the ninth graders, who still preferred the mall for softcore, handholding, closed-mouthed action.

The day Hoop and Duane first explored The Houses, the front door of lot 23L was unlocked. There were beige ceramic tiles in the small front foyer, and a step up to a narrow hallway, then, in walking sequence, powder room, basement door, open-concept kitchen (with breakfast bar), dining and family rooms, and a small raised deck beyond the sliding glass patio doors.

The guy suggests they use the basement to avoid curious homeowners or kids looking for hide-and-seek territory. Those types usually stay on the main floor, or they go upstairs and check out the bedrooms.

"No one ever goes down to the basement," he says. What's there to see? Insulation, concrete floors, a drain, bare bulbs, support beams, maybe a rough-in for a bathroom.

"Look at this," Duane said. He was still at the entrance, one hand on the door, the other on the frame. "All you gotta do is knock and the whole thing'll fly apart."

"What are you talking about?" Hoop walked back to the foyer.

Duane closed the door and turned the lock. "See how this dead-bolt fits in here? The casing—the wood—all around the frame is really thin. The only thing holding it there is these nails. What? Half inch?"

"'Cause of the glass," Hoop said. There were panels on either side of the door, so the lock was barely longer than the door latch.

"Yeah. They can't nail the casing in any more." Duane pulled hard on the locked door and the frame seemed to give. "They best get an alarm up in here."

o o o

At the time *Not at night* At the time *Better in the afternoon when everyone's at work* Hoop had no plans to invade lot 23L *Dress normal—a hoody or a jersey and nobody'll look at you twice* But that little piece of information from Duane *With all the Blacks and Indians in the area you'll just look like somebody's kid* existed for

---

Close to her ear, he says, "We could get our *mmm* on down here" and puckers his lips slightly, cool, touches the brim of his hat.

She knows this is where girls come to let themselves be touched. The fur around her hood dusts her forehead. She's been to The Houses before, not since Phase I though, and then it wasn't with this guy.

Hoop *Who knows his neighbour anymore* like a theory to be proven *Bring a package, ring the doorbell, enter through the door inside the garage* But if it were possible simply to enter a house by kicking down the door *Easy as that* why weren't more houses robbed *Think of the cred, man* or why weren't more people robbing their neighbours?

Bus ride after bus ride *Only bag stuff small enough to fit in a knapsack* the thought swelled in his head *and not too much, laptop, MP3 player, camera* until he finally *If it don't fit you must acquit* finally he

○ ○ ○

tried to get in and out as quickly as possible. Six to eight minutes is enough to take. With seven minutes left, Hoop saw photos over the fireplace. To blue eyes, the girls in separate frames might look like the same girl or twins: each wore two thick plaits like upside down horns on the side of her head, a toothless thick-lipped smile, the same pink sweater though the turtlenecks worn underneath were different. But he could tell that they were not the same girl, not twins either. Just poor, at the time, and wearing hand-me-downs.

He makes a show of opening the basement door for her. She steps down carefully, holding her hair to the sides of her face. Behind her, the guy's arms swish against his bubble vest. This morning he only had style in mind, but during the last two afternoon periods, when he proposed the idea of hanging out after school, the vest turned into something else—padding.

Six left. Hoop saw a glasses case and telephone bill on the arm of the converted patio chair in the family room. The surname on the envelope was Pearson, like the airport.

Five left. Upstairs in the master bedroom, he caught himself, knapsack on one shoulder, in the mirror of the ensuite. On the counter, a bottle of baby oil, a tube of cut-open foundation, and a comb with hair curling in it stared back at him like three guard dogs. He heard for the first time the low growl of the refrigerator downstairs.

Four left. He arrived in the otherworldly back bedroom, the older girl's, wallpapered with posters, carpeted with skirts and dresses left where she stepped out of them. Three left, he didn't know what to take. His bag was still empty. Three left. He heard the 41 pass. Three left. He found an MP3 player with headphones still attached on the bed. Two left. The garage door opened. Two left. He inadvertently ran to the basement. Two left. The car doors closed. There should be two minutes left. He ducked his head under the comforter covering boxes under the stairs. Overtime.

For a gun he had a boxcutter.

o o o

Light slants downward through the small windows on one side of the basement. Flecks of dust turn somersaults in the smoky light. The girl started talking dirty into his ear during third or fourth period, and now she wishes she hadn't. In this hollowed house, its ribs showing like the inside of a cathedral or a half-eaten turkey, she feels both watched and abandoned.

Hoop was already hoping for an inaccurate suspect description, for a neighbour to say, *male black six feet between twenty and twenty-five at least two hundred pounds dark baggy clothes baseball cap with a hood pulled over it.* And that wouldn't be Hoop. He looked eighteen but was fifteen, black yes, tall yes, not wearing what she saw, but an oversized basketball jersey. He was long-necked and his arms had the definition of a woman who curled light weights.

And he was strong, though he didn't look it. Shaking his hand or escaping his headlock, you'd wonder where he stored all that strength. His bones must be made of metal.

o o o

Whatever happened upstairs happened in Hoop's head.

"Some wayward boy do this," the woman said. Her deep voice engorged Hoop's heart with rhythm. *Wayward* was his mother's word.

"Call the police." A teenaged voice.

"Him gone."

"Call the police. Don't touch anything. He could come back. What if he's still here?"

The patio door slid open.

"Let's go upstairs," she says, turning around with her arms folded.

"Hold up, hold up," he says. He takes both her hands in his, unfolds her arms. "Didn't you say you wanted—"

"It's dirty."

"Dirty, huh." He speaks into her lips. "You been talking dirt all day."

"Tasha. Tasha! Stay here."

Pattering, then a child's voice: "I wasn't going anywhere."

"Hello? Somebody break in my house. (From the mother's responses, Hoop could tell what the dispatcher was asking.) I'm at 12 Deerpass Lane. It don't have a number outside, lot 23L. [←Where do you live?] In the kitchen. [←Where are you now?] No, my two girls with me. [←Are you alone?] I don't know. I don't see anybody. The door was open when I come home. [←Is the suspect there?] The front door. [←Which door did you find open?] No, like the inside door from the garage. Him kick it down. [←The front door?] Please send somebody quick, the police. I live at twel—[←The officers will be there any minute.] I didn't look. I don't know. [←Is anything missing?] I think so. We in the kitchen. [←Are you all safe?] Okay. Okay. Mm. Okay. [←Here's what I want you to do ...]."

There's no reason to be afraid of me, Hoop thought downstairs. He was a spider at the heel of a woman. *Three* females. It might be better to get out now, just run, up the stairs, out the front, wave the boxcutter. He could cover his face. When the police came, there'd be no waving the boxcutter. Lord Jesus. Straight to Juvy. And his mother. Lord God.

Isn't anything he says that makes her stay—he could have been on mute—but strobe flashes of him on the court with his wifebeater pulled up behind his neck, and his slow kiss near her locker, thumb on her chin, and girls everywhere razing her with their eyes. This guy was—*real* was the only word, so said his shining bottom lip, his peach breath, and hot hands. She would approach the next few minutes as a job to be done, a vegetable to be eaten.

"Police!" Boots clomped overhead.

"In the kitchen," said the mother, Ms. (there was no man on the mantle) Pearson.

In Hoop's head, and possibly upstairs, the officers were wearing fatigues and Stallone headbands. One of them, Goliath-sized, spoke mechanically into his shoulder-mounted walkie-talkie, which beeped back before emitting a voice hoarse with static. Another officer, shorter, unable to grow facial hair, wearing a too-big uniform, and carrying a bazooka, appeared behind the first like an echo. Goliath told Ms. Pearson and her girls to wait where they were. He told his walkie-talkie, not the family, that he had already searched the first floor, that Echo was proceeding into the basement, and that he would search upstairs.

Echo never seemed to be looking at anything in particular. His gaze darted around as if tracking a housefly. The kind of man who snaps. The soldier cops walked around, touching boxes on their hips or shoulders, and Ms. Pearson stood at a distance inside her house, as if it were the model, open for the public to inspect, to walk on the carpet in dirty shoes. At that moment, Hoop wanted Goliath slain and Echo silenced, for what they had turned her house into.

∘ ∘ ∘

If she feels like it later she might talk to her girls—her real girls—that night. Right now, she doesn't think she'll feel like it.

He, on the other hand, has a breathy re-enactment all set for tomorrow: *She was like* Oh no no, *and I was like Yeas,* No oh, *Yeas,* Noh, *Yeeas,* Oh yeaaas yes!

He only kneads her body for a few minutes. Then it starts to relax.

Every sense shut off except Hoop's hearing. First he heard footsteps descending, each foot a different pitch. The melody made him want to cry. The footsteps belonged to Echo—Echo in his fatigues of a thousand pockets, something deadly in each, bazooka cocked over his shoulder, hand gun held sideways, little red laser searching for Hoop's black forehead.

Then Hoop heard Echo pull a chain. He was so well-covered that he did not notice the light. Or were his eyes closed?

Next rubber across the floor. That was the cold cellar opening. Another chain being pulled. On then off. The door closed.

The feet passed him. The washer opened. The dryer. On the way back to the stairs, the footsteps stopped. The officer knocked some boxes under the stairs with his gun, then again with the bazooka. He was waiting for the thief to screw things up, to sneeze or cough or shuffle. Hoop thought his trembling was seismic. Wasn't he panting? Wasn't his heart drumming? He knew this story from Poe and Lisa Simpson. Now was the time to burst through the boxes, screaming something, throwing his backpack at the feet of the officer, compressing the sides of his head between his hands.

○ ○ ○

His cue comes from her knees, which bounce slowly as if in a pool, then her legs give way. He spits out his gum and kisses her neck, the side of her face. One of her hands slides on the bubble vest beneath her, the other pushes against his shoulder. Something feels sharp, the vest's zipper, maybe a loose nail. She thinks, irrationally and maybe foolishly, but she thinks it all the same: *I don't want to die like this.*

Whatever happened upstairs seemed to happen far away in a smoky, tropical place. Hoop saw them all standing ankle-deep in swampy water.

Goliath got Ms. Pearson's story. She was questioned only for information, as if her fear and sense of violation were extravagances. The girls didn't say anything. They just stood to one side of their mother in descending height, partially obscured by palm fronds. The older one watched the officer drill her mother first with his mouth, then with his eyes, then with something further back in his skull like a low frequency wave.

After each question, Hoop could fill in what Goliath was thinking.

Do you own this home? [←She's probably renting. We should speak to the owners.]

You were all off the premises—[←Dumb down your language, boy.] You were out shopping, you said, when the break-in occurred?

No one saw the suspect. True? [←Black on black crime.]

Goliath studied the woman's hairline. *Unsure*, he wrote, just to write something. He studied the curtains hanging by thumbtacks, the cushions on patio furniture, and wrote *new owners*.

Were these rooms empty before? [←What do you have to steal?]

He backs away suddenly and sits on his heels, fumbling with his zipper now instead of with her. She distracts herself. Where did his hat go? Wasn't he wearing a hat?

He is saying something, but he is on mute again, reaching for his wallet. The sight of it, thick and brown, tips her mind. She looks at the wad of gum on the cement floor.

"Won't hurt."

Echo had been wading in circles around the kitchen, looking for that housefly. After a few moments, he announced his intention (to his walkie-talkie) to search the exterior of the premises.

The patio door opened and closed. Through a nearby basement window, Hoop saw Echo's combat boots walk back and forth. From the attitude of the boots, Hoop guessed Echo was smoking.

He heard, "Not much furniture. Looks like she was robbed before," followed by a rush of air out Echo's nostrils, not a laugh quite. And, most significantly, he heard a smile on the other end of the walkie-talkie.

o o o

When the police left, the upstairs part of the house started to collapse like a deflating air mattress. The conversation was flimsy and tremulous. Tasha didn't have to sleep alone if she didn't want to. The door from the garage needed to be secured until they could change the lock. The thug could come back. The thugs. A gang of them.

A moment after he tears open the package and unrolls the rubber the upstairs door opens. Footsteps patter. A woman's voice, *Too small, this foyer, but look they have a step up to the hallway.* The girl pulls her clothes close to her, straightens up. The guy stops her arm. No sound. *Oh and Kevin look at this kitchen, see I told you the island was necessary, and look looklooklooklook they upgraded the backsplash.*

He heard things being moved. Perhaps the Pearsons were making old-fashioned booby traps. Cans and bottles by the front foyer. A houseplant by the patio door.

Hoop looked at the time on his cell phone. 6:58. He'd been in the basement for hours, and he had hours more to go before the family went to sleep. When they were all in the bedrooms, he'd sneak out. Except for his knees, which had been too sharply bent for too long, he was fairly comfortable under the stairs. Earlier, he had completely removed the comforter from over his head so that his eyes could get adjusted to the dark. But there was nothing to see.

Upstairs, they were watching TV. Drawers and cupboards closed. The music for an entertainment tabloid came on.

"Ready," the mother called over the music. "Tasha, come and eat."

Hoop smelled fried sardines upstairs. He was hungry, and gassy. That was another reason he uncovered his head.

"Did they check the cold room in the basement?" Ms. Pearson asked.

The voices continue upstairs into the bedrooms. In the basement, the guy and the girl look upward, as if listening with their eyes.

When the voices finally leave, the girl says with her palms, *I can't do this. It's too risky.*

"They're gone," he says, but she is already off his vest, brushing shavings from her skirt.

"I don't know. You want me to go down?" The older girl volunteered herself. "Give me a broom or something."

"You don't have to go. Eat." Ms. Pearson sucked her teeth. "I thought I heard—It's the neighbour maybe. They build these houses too close."

"You can use my umbrella," said Tasha.

"Girl, go and sit down!" Ms. Pearson said. "That's your food from this morning."

"I'll check," said the teenaged voice.

The basement light went on. Through the slats in the stairs, Hoop saw her ripple down: one dry bare heel then another, the back of her knee, the fingers of one hand around a yellow and red, Pooh umbrella, the other hand must have been on the banister. She reached the bottom, and, like Echo, walked to the cold room.

"I don't see anything," she shouted up as if checking the hold of a grappling hook.

"Hurry up," a little voice came back.

Ms. Pearson: "Girl, don't make me talk to you again. Sit. Down."

"I said I can't, all right." She starts up the stairs. "Don't follow me right away."

No answer.

"I'll meet you by the site office."

"Whatever."

She squeezes her chin into her neck and looks down on him from the basement stairs. His boxers are showing, as always.

"Whatever," she echoes back.

The upstairs door closed and footsteps ran away from the door of the basement.

Hoop was trying to settle the cover over his head again, but his hand knocked the back of a stair. The sound was enough to alert the girl. She whirled around with the umbrella raised over her head, ready to throw or strike.

"JaniceIwon'thurtanyofyou," Hoop whispered before she could scream or run, before she knew who she was seeing—that wet forehead, those two dark eyes, which were vibrating, barely, like a tuning fork, from fear to fatigue to anger to madness. He was wrapped in her old comforter. He looked like an Old Testament prophet.

Hoop saw the next two hours in a second. His mother's agonized image, the lines from her nose to jaw, her overprocessed hair, the carpet of the eleventh floor hallway, flanked by two soldier cops, Echo's thousand pockets and bazooka, the door opening inward, his mother's heavy bottom lip, one hand on the door. And he could read inside her too. She'd think *don't answer* at the knock. She'd think of herself in church, *God give me strength to raise my child in this country.* And in a few months, in the winter, she

---

Looking through one of the back bedroom windows of an unfinished house, Hoop and Duane, girlfriendless, observe a girl outside crossing tread marks of hardened mud.

Duane looks to see if he'd hit that.

Hoop looks to see if he knows her.

would think of his deviance, his big, expensive feet, while riding the bus between jobs, double-socked, in white no-name sneakers, and she would curse the cold cold winters of this country, and remember her government job in Jamaica, then fall asleep with her head on the window in someone else's grease patch.

Tears came when Hoop blinked. "Please," he said.

o o o

Tasha ran back to the door and opened it when she heard Janice's footsteps approaching the top.

"Did you see the killer?"

"Uh uh."

"I just wasn't sure if they checked," said the mother from the kitchen. "Come eat."

"Girl, you look scared," said Tasha.

o o o

Moments later, a guy emerges from the same house, dusting the front of his vest, looking both ways, putting a thumb to a nostril and sniffing tough-man style, then he picks up a slight limp and exits the site.

Hoop wants to hurt him. Duane wants to check out the house they came from. He puts a fist to his mouth and *whoop whoops*. Starting to limp himself, he walks from the bedroom and says, "That's what I'm talkin' 'bout."

Hoop could no longer hear them, only the zooming sounds of segments changing on the entertainment show. The volume was higher. Janice must have been whispering everything up there, then they'd barricade the basement door, call the cops, then there'd be a loudspeaker and handcuffs and dogs and a helicopter whirring and a camera and *Bad boys, bad boys, whatcha gonna do?*

He started making a deal with God. *Lord, if you, if You, could get me out by some miracle*—How had he known Janice's name? Was that her name? Her name had come so easily to him, though he didn't recall noticing it, unlike the mother's bills on the patio furniture. *God if You, if YOU, could find a way out of this situation for me, then I'll*—Her room, that's where. On the door she had stuck up *Janice's room Keep out!* like a white girl would, Hoop thought, but he had been so distracted by the poster of some glistening, thick-legged, R&B singer, hair blowing like a horse, that he didn't remember the sign.

Then I'll what? Anything you want, Lord Jesus. That's how his mother prayed, every time there was a pause, she would fill up the space with *Lord Jesus*, barely aware that she was saying it.

Hoop made God an offer. But He could refuse. So Hoop started planning his explanations. *It was somebody else's idea. This guy*

Doorbell. There's a security sign on the front glass. That's new.

"Who that could be? Tasha don't open."

"I'm not a baby."

"Tasha I said no."

Tasha opens anyway. Ms. Pearson is flapping her hands dry as she approaches the door.

at school, I heard him talking so I tried it. I wasn't looking for anything, I just wanted to see if I could do it. Play dumb, good. Or *I was curious about how the inside of The Houses looked now that they're finished. There wasn't any car in the driveway. I thought this one hadn't closed yet.* [Didn't you see the shoes and the mat, the furniture?] *Yeah, as soon as I saw all that, the people came and I got scared so I hid.* Better. [What about all the stuff in your bag?] Dang.

The basement door opened again and Janice stepped down to the landing to collect some plastic bags—that's where they kept them, stuffed in a garbage bag, and when she took one more step down from the landing (Hoop could have grabbed her ankle to plead again or just slit her tendon with the boxcutter), she called up with her grappling-hook voice, "I need some air. We should go out."

"So late?"

"It's not late." The plastic bags hissed. "I at least need some air, but I'm not walking around by myself with some crazy in the neighbourhood."

She was at the top of the stairs again, her ankle was out of reach. Light flossed through the crack in the door.

"All right, just now, after Tasha brush she teeth."

"Um," Hoop says. He scratches his nose. He'll have to lie. "I go to Janice's school. She left this behind and I just ..."

"Janice!" her mother shouts.

"You don't have to call her. Here, just give it to—"

"Come inside. She coming. Janice!" Ms. Pearson hurries back to the kitchen, slapping her slippers against the tile.

° ° °

Still Hoop didn't trust her completely. She was evacuating the house so they'd be safe to call the police and dogs, camera, helicopter, *bad boys, bad boys*, etc.

But then footsteps ran down the upper staircase, Tasha protested wearing a coat when Janice didn't have to, chairs were cleared from the entrance, and the front door closed loudly. Hoop waited a few moments in case someone had forgotten her keys or needed to come back to pee. His heart was accelerating again. When the upstairs was still, he came out of hiding, willed his sore knees up the stairs and out the side entrance. He walked to the back of the house, cut across the unfenced back lawns and came out on the main road. Not safe enough. He kept his eyes on the intersection, where the buses travelled more frequently. He pulled the intersection toward him with his eyes because he couldn't run. He had to walk as slowly as anyone watching would expect him to in those jeans and ball shoes.

Hoop steps inside. They've installed bolts on the front door and the one leading to the garage. At the end of the hallway he sees real furniture. Leather.

Janice comes down the stairs. Tasha walks back to the staircase and says *ooh* with her back to Hoop.

He holds out a baseball hat, then he takes his MP3 player from his pocket. "I found it, just now, back by The Houses." He points a thumb over his shoulder.

○ ○ ○

He should have left his stash behind, but his prints were all over everything. Not that he had a record. Pay them back. A thank-you note—just to the girl, Janice.

He wanted to go home directly and go to sleep, but he took the knapsack to Duane's place first, in the apartment building near his. He shook out the booty on Duane's bed, lied and said he found it in Phase 11 of The Houses. Duane photographed everything and put it online. Hoop didn't care for the items either—what, a charger, a small video game, a cheap MP3 player, two brand name baby tees. No laptop, no digital camera.

Only the baby tees didn't sell. Duane and Hoop split the money, unevenly, and spent it on cafeteria lunches, dumping the ones their mothers prepared.

For days, Hoop listened to the news on AM radio, but there was no mention of 23L. Thank God there was worse news. A carjack on the east end, subway evacuations, insurgents overseas. It would be old news after a day anyway, and really nothing worth mentioning was stolen.

It's not mine you best get the hell out of here who do you think you are coming to my mother's house with your broken guilt trying to be all hero acting like you know me you don't know me fool you think you got my back I said you best run before I call the police on your skinny wannabe gangsta self I take you on myself nigga is what Janice would say outside, but not in this house. On this floor.

Hoop had made a deal with God underneath the basement stairs that if He got him out of this one, he'd—it had taken Hoop a while to come up with something sufficiently attractive for God to say *deal*—go to church with his mother again, read the Bible cover to cover, pay back seven times the money. He had specified his end of the deal: to escape wasn't enough, he'd need a guarantee that he would never get caught, specifically that word would never get to his mother. For that, he'd have to throw down more promises. Does the Lord have a price? He'd give up ball. He'd give up balling. He wouldn't ever take a girl to The Houses, wouldn't touch a girl till he was eighteen, till he was married.

I can get you out, the Lord said, but there will always be someone on your back.

You have to guarantee, Lord Jesus.

Then no deal.

Ms. Pearson comes padding back in her slippers. She looks at Janice. She looks at Hoop. Hoop pulls up his pants with one hand and scratches the back of his neck with the other.

"You," she says.

—2011

DEBORAH WILLIS

Deborah Willis is a Canadian short story writer, born in Calgary, Alberta in 1982. In 2009, Willis published her first book of short fiction, *Vanishing and Other Stories*, which was short-listed for the Governor General's Award.

Willis left Calgary to attend the University of Victoria, where she initially studied journalism. She then changed her focus to creative writing, and was taught and inspired by writers Lorna Crozier and Lorna Jackson. Willis has now settled in Victoria, working on her writing in the mornings and as a bookseller in the afternoon and evenings. Her key literary influences are Alice Munro, Anton Chekhov, F. Scott Fitzgerald, and Flannery O'Connor. She states that her reading of popular novels by Elmore Leonard and Stephen King taught her that stories should have a good plot, and it is one of her goals in writing that her work should have "movement and drama." Reading fiction, she says, provides "an imaginative escape from the self and therefore from self-centredness." Although stories may not make us better, reading them is "an essential part of being alive."

Willis began publishing her work in literary magazines, and, after winning a short fiction contest in *Prism* magazine, she was encouraged to publish her first collection of stories. Readers responded with enthusiasm to her emotionally complex narratives. The delicate intricacy of her storytelling brings the experience of the characters to life as they pursue meaning and love in an often fractured and dislocated world. Alice Munro writes that "the emotional range and depth of these stories, the clarity and deftness, is astonishing." This depth is achieved partly through Willis's experimentation with form and point of view: in the collection, she tells stories in the first, second, and third person, sometimes rapidly shifting from narrator to narrator. She allows her readers to consider motives and moral consequences for themselves, offering clear, elegant narratives that disturb the reader's consciousness long after the stories are read.

From *Vanishing and Other Stories*, "The Weather" takes place in the charged and lonely landscape of the Canadian prairie, where a father and daughter live by themselves. The winds and storms that pummel the prairie are mirrored in the emotional lives of the characters as they seek love in different ways. The damage the weather leaves behind is only suggested—as are the parallels that may exist between changes in weather patterns and changes in the patterns of "passion and sweetness and sadness" in human relationships.

The Weather

DEBORAH WILLIS

SHE CAME home with my daughter after school. The neighbour, Jerry, and the guys I hire for haying had left twenty minutes ago, half an hour. I was still in the field, and I saw the two of them walk along the highway: my daughter with her slouch and backpack, and the older girl with neither.

Edith hardly ever brought friends home, not since my wife lived here, so I stopped what I was doing—fixing a yard of fence—and went to meet them on the road. Edith's fifteen, a tough age, so this probably got on her nerves, probably embarrassed her. Her father with a loop of wire hooked on his arm and cutters in his dirty hand. This girl, her friend, obviously came from town. From a house with plastic siding and a lawn.

"Father," Edith said. "This is Rae."

The girl was tall, built like the spindly birch we use as windbreak. She reminded me of girls I knew when I was young, and I didn't like the arch of her back, her cut-off shorts, her weird grey eyes. I didn't like her much at all, and I wouldn't have asked her for dinner if I hadn't noticed the way she breathed. Like she was sucking air along a sandpaper throat, holding it in clogged lungs. Like each inhale was an effort, like it was earned.

The girl offered a quick smile. Gap in her teeth, but she was probably considered pretty, and she probably knew it. "Hi," she said.

It wasn't warm, but the sun glinted off her hair. That's what I remember most: the cool sun, the dropping pressure. Rain was coming, and it was giving me a headache.

° ° °

I introduced them. Father, I said, this is Rae. It was unfortunate, but I couldn't have known.

I met her on the last day of school, when the bus dropped me off near where she walked along the highway. I recognized her even though she was new to the school and two grades above me. I asked if she was lost, and she said she was lost on purpose. She said she likes to go for walks when the air is clear. She also said that her boyfriend's an asshole and when she told him so, he'd opened his car door and left her on the side of the road. She looked angry and like she might have been crying. She asked me, You're Edith, right?

I told her she could come to my place, for a snack or something. I said I was certain my father wouldn't mind. She looked irritated, like I'd ruined her plans. But then she said, Okay. Sure. Thanks.

° ° °

She started coming over nearly every day. Suddenly my daughter was sitting beside that girl in front of the TV, bowls of soggy cereal resting on their knees. Or the two of them would lie in front of the house, moving their towels around the parched grass to follow the sun. They greased themselves in oil, and the girl would wave to Jerry and the guys as they walked by. Edith started wearing her hair down and a borrowed bikini, her body too young for it. Edith, who was usually locked in her room with her books and her mother's old tapes and an attitude. What my wife called "an innate aloofness."

That girl wasn't the kind of friend I'd expected my daughter to make. She wasn't the kind I'd hoped for.

° ° °

That first night, she opened our screen door and strode in like she already knew her way around. This is a cool place, she said.

When we had dinner, she bounced her knees under the table and took huge helpings of potatoes and corn. She'd seen rodeo on television, so she had questions about bull riding and calf roping. At first my father answered with one or two words and he looked shy when he spoke to her. She leaned on the table and kept her eyes on his tanned face, like this was a challenge or a game. I was sure he was a joke to her, someone she'd tell stories about later: a cowboy with greying hair and the top two buttons of his shirt undone. My poor, idiotic father.

By dessert, he became less quiet and seemed to enjoy answering her questions. He told her about branding parties and moose hunting, and when she wanted to know how cattle auctions worked, he asked me to put the kettle on for coffee. Then he told her how loud an auction was and how it smelled like someone had trucked their whole farm into town and dumped it in one building. Which a lot of guys did. He explained feedlots and weights and weaning. He told her about the spring, how busy calving was, but beautiful. He used that word: *beautiful.*

° ° °

I even caught that girl sneaking into our house after Edith had gone to bed. She'd party with other friends—her boyfriends, as far as I could tell, changed with the weather. Then she'd get them to drop her off at our place so her parents didn't meet the guys she was with, didn't smell the beer on her breath. If she saw that I was still up—looking out the window, trying to find something decent on the radio—it never bothered her. She just passed me on her way to Edith's room doing an exaggerated tiptoe, her finger to her lips, as though this was our secret. Which I guess it was, since I never called her mother, though I meant to.

To teach a lesson, a couple of weeks ago, I woke both girls up one morning and forced them to watch the sun rise above the tall grass. Edith came out of her bedroom pissed off, exhausted.

The girl had slept in a pair of my daughter's old pyjamas, and the material was creased, thin as water. "Are you kidding me?" she said.

I kept a straight face, walked them out to the herd, and listened to her teenage whines about dew soaking through her socks. My daughter didn't complain the whole time, so I figured she was seriously angry, seriously humiliated. But then Edith said, "I remember this from when I was a kid. It was my favourite part."

She pointed out the calves who were sickly, or whose mothers wouldn't produce. Then she took the girl's hand and showed her how to lead the calves out of the field and into the loafing pens, walking backwards and letting them suck on her fingers.

One calf suckled the girl's hand and slobbered down her wrist, and another pushed its head against her thigh, looking for milk. "This is the nastiest fucking thing I've ever done," she said when she caught her breath from laughing.

Edith looked at me then as if to say, "City girl." I nodded and gave her a wink. It felt good to see my daughter like that, smiling.

° ° °

Rae carried an inhaler in one back pocket and a pack of cigarettes in the other. She saw the irony of this, but she didn't care. Once, when she gave me a drag off her cigarette, I thought I was dying. My eyes watered and my throat felt like it had been torn.

God, Edith, she said. You're such a baby.

She laughed and passed me her inhaler and I pumped the powder into my mouth. It made me feel the same way I did when I saw her walking up our driveway: light-headed and spinny.

○ ○ ○

Once, she snuck in so late that I was already at the kitchen table. The sun wasn't up yet and the kitchen was dim. She leaned in the doorway, then sat right down across from me. I should have said some adult thing—got mad, got worried—but her clothes were wrinkled, her eyes tired, and I remembered that kind of morning. I got her a mug from the cupboard and took the milk out of the fridge.

"Sugar?"

"Yeah. Please."

When we spoke, we whispered. A little agreement to keep this quiet.

"Don't your parents worry about you?" I sat across from her. "Wonder where you are?"

"No." She stirred four heaping spoons of sugar into her cup. "Not when I tell them I'm at Edith's. They moved me out here so I'd breathe clean air and meet wholesome people like her. So I'd join 4-H."[1]

She poured milk into her cup, holding the jug high so it fell in a thin stream. I looked at her puffy eyes, her blotched skin.

"You look like hell," I said.

"Well, this coffee tastes like hell."

"It should sober you up."

She looked at me, smiled. "Why aren't you married?"

"I am."

She leaned toward me. "That's a story."

"There's no story." I passed her the sugar. "My wife wouldn't stay, and I wouldn't go. That's all."

I sipped my coffee, still too hot, and she slurped from her spoon.

"Nina lives in Victoria now," I said, even though I don't normally like to say her name aloud. "We don't talk much anymore."

"No kidding."

The girl lifted her cup to her lips and blew at the steam. I stirred my coffee, even though it was black.

"It was supposed to be temporary, her leaving," I said. "Nina called from Calgary and said she just needed a couple days away. But then she kept driving." I leaned back in my chair. "Edith really misses her."

The girl nodded, folded her arms on the table, rested her chin. I didn't expect her to say much, but it was nice to sit there with someone. No matter that she was half awake, sleepy-eyed.

---

1 4-H is a youth group focused on building leadership skills and community.

○ ○ ○

Last week we made cinnamon toast, then tried on the clothes my mother had left behind. Neither of us could fit into the tight jeans or the small, high-wedge shoes. But Rae filled out the thin sweaters and the silky, sleeveless tops. She loved the scoop necks, and when she looked in the mirror she said, No wonder your mom left.

She wore one of the shirts—it was pale gold, a shimmery sun-on-wheat—to the dinner table. It was nearly ten at night, but since it was summer, my father had just come in and cooked steak and sweet potatoes. He'd already folded up the cuffs of his sleeves and served himself. He was sitting; Rae was standing. And when he saw the shirt, he looked in her eyes. There was nothing she or I could say. No reason we should have been in his bedroom, rifling in his closet. And no reason we should have found my mom's stuff. No reason he shouldn't have gotten rid of it years ago.

When I saw his face, I thought he might pick up his plate, his fork and knife, his beer, and quietly leave the kitchen. But he just shook his head. And Rae smiled too. It was as though they were sharing a joke. As though they were the only two in the room.

That was it, the only hint I got. Then Rae pulled out a chair and sat down. My father nodded toward the stovetop for us to grab some food, and I got myself a pop. I opened the fridge door and it breathed cold air on my face. Then my father said, just loud enough for us to hear, It fits all right, that's for sure.

○ ○ ○

I poured myself more coffee and the girl drank the sludge in her cup. The house was chilled and she curled up in the kitchen chair, held her knees.

"When did she leave? Your wife?"

The girl was hungover and wanted entertainment, a good story. So I took a breath and told her about the storm. How it had been nearly dinnertime and I'd wanted to head home, but the cattle were acting funny. Whining and lying down, then standing up, being strange.

Once I started telling it, I couldn't stop. I talked about how hot it'd been that day, and how it'd cooled so suddenly the sweat on my shirt made me shiver. Lightning shattered the grey sky every few seconds, and clouds spooled and unspooled themselves. The rain hit hard, but I didn't move from the field. Not even when the funnel cloud dropped and skimmed my neighbour's land. Not until it blew the hip roof off his barn.

Then I climbed into my truck, pulled it over to a bluff of trees, sat and listened. That's what I remember most. The colour—that grey—and the noise. Rain and hail against a metal roof. The wind shot nails and boards past me, hail cracked the front windshield and smashed the side window. Glass landed in my lap, hailstones clattered onto the floor. And then it was over.

The quiet was as hard to take as the storm's noise. I watched the weather spin along the prairie, leaving as fast as it had come. The only sound was water that streaked into the cab, pooling around my boots. The funnel had touched down for less than two minutes. It was nothing. It wouldn't even make the news.

° ° °

The two of us like to imagine my mother's new life. Rae invents episodes that remind me of television soap operas: romantic dates and exotic travel. But from the two times I visited, I know my mother lives in an apartment and works in a college library. What I like to picture are the details. I see her with shorter hair and makeup. I imagine her coming home from work and taking off her coat. Unzipping her high heeled boots and shaking water from an umbrella.

° ° °

When the wind calmed, I climbed from my truck and walked to the house. The front door had been ripped off its hinges and it lay in the front yard, near the saskatoon bushes. Edith stood in the doorway, her arms crossed against the cold. When she saw me, she turned toward the kitchen. Even then, she used that cold tone. "He's here, Mom. He's fine."

In the kitchen, one of the windows was broken and shingles from the neighbour's barn had embedded themselves in the wallpaper. My wife sat at the table and stared at two hailstones that sat like a centrepiece. Maybe she or Edith had picked them up from the yard. Maybe these were the stones that had broken the window. They were as big as my fists.

"You're both all right," I said, and maybe I sounded too rough about it. Maybe I sounded like a businessman checking his stock, a cattleman counting head.

That's when Nina said it: "I hate this place." She pressed her forehead against her hand. "I hate it here, Braden."

I figured it was shock. I figured it would blow over. "Come on now," I said, and started to unbutton my shirt. Water glued it to my chest, and now that I knew my family was safe, my body let itself feel the cold.

"I can't stay here." Her voice was like that moment after the storm, so quiet it spooked me.

The hailstones were soaking into the tablecloth, and I don't know why that made me so angry. I picked them up and threw them out the broken window. Some glass dropped into the sink and Nina flinched.

"I'm going to check the field," I said. My wife didn't answer, so I turned to Edith, put my hand on her shoulder. She looked at me like she hated me. "Stay here," I said. "Keep your mom company."

° ° °

During the storm, my mother pushed me against the kitchen door jamb and held my hands. I could feel the house shake against me, and I remember thinking this must be hard on her. I have my father's bones, my father's flesh, and even at thirteen I was taller than her. She could be wild: she was always dancing to the Rolling Stones in the kitchen, or speeding along the highway. But right then she reminded me of the sick calves my father nursed, the ones he kept in pens and bottle-fed warm, glutinous milk.

I felt the house creak against the wind, and my mother's sweaty hands. Then there was a crack and the front door blew off its hinges. I watched it float and waver in the air, then drop to the grass. My mother squeezed my hands until her knuckles went white. Her face was empty. It was like something my father once described, a blankness he'd seen on some animals. An injured horse determined to stand and survive, or a calf too scared to wail before slaughter.

° ° °

After she finished her first cup, the girl didn't even bother with coffee. Just spooned sugar into her mug, poured milk on top, and ate it like soup. The sun was rising, and Edith was still asleep.

"I should take you home," I said. "You're going to make yourself sick."

"I feel fine."

I didn't want to sound fatherly, because I didn't feel it. Whispering like this, ignoring work and the radio, I didn't feel like me at all.

She reached across the table and tapped my hand. "Show me where you were," she said. "When it hit."

So we left the kitchen. Midsummer, but the grass was crisp with frost, and you could still see the moon through the clouds. I pointed out the silvery birch that blocked some of the wind. Then I took her to the pond where geese land every spring and she picked some water-parsley. I showed her the three hundred head of cattle, the morning air rising out of their big soft nostrils. All the things that charmed my wife, at first. The things Edith used to love too.

When we got to the fence that's separated my property from Jerry's for nearly thirty years, I said, "That's all she wrote. Might as well turn back."

But she squinted and walked forward. She'd seen the lush place where we throw the bones, and the white glint of them.

"It's just the yard," I called out. My wife had always hated it there. The high grass, the smell.

She stopped a few feet away from a bull's rib cage and I stood behind her, back a ways. I watched her neck, her shoulders. Tried to imagine the look on her face. "It's not much to see."

The girl nudged a piece of the bull's torso with her toe.

"I throw them here for the coyotes," I said. "Feed them so they don't bother the herd."

She stepped forward again, her sandalled feet disappearing in the green and yellow grass. She knelt, almost facing me, full of bravery. Then she lifted a cow's skull that was old enough to be picked clean. So heavy it strained her arms.

"I don't take people out here, normally."

She slid her pinkie finger through the bullet hole I'd had to make, can't remember when. Must have been a few years ago, maybe a calving that went wrong.

"Come on. I'll drive you home."

She ran her hand along the forehead. Feeling the rough bone, I guess, against her palm. This is when I figured out she was beautiful. Something about how calm her face was, how curious. She held up the enormous head, looked it right in the hollow eyes.

o o o

She never introduced me, but I'm sure that every one of her boyfriends was an idiot. I called them all by the same name: Kyle. That was the one she was with when I first met her. The one who dropped her off outside my door, some miracle working through him.

How's Kyle? I'd say, and she'd reply, His name is Joel and he's not my boyfriend.

Bullshit.

You're bullshit.

Then she'd smile in a distant way and I'd know her life was made up of endless possibilities, her life was complex and golden. This was while we were flipping through one of her magazines, or while I braided her hair so it would be wavy the next day. I adored her tangled, complicated hair, so many shades of blond and brown all at once.

° ° °

I offered to take her home. "You need some sleep and a shower," I said, and we walked to my truck. We climbed in, and the bench was already warm from the sun. There was still a web of cracks through the windshield, and light splintered through it.

From what I can tell, most city people think it's boring to talk about the weather. But here, it's important. Every morning, Nina and I used to look out the kitchen window to see what was coming: heat, sudden cold, or the possibility of worse. Talking about the weather, you talk about everything that matters—what you want, what you're scared of.

There was a pause—after I turned the key in the ignition, before the diesel engine turned over. The girl and I stared straight ahead, through the cracked glass.

"Beautiful day," she said, and I knew exactly what she meant.

° ° °

Once, I asked her to tell me what it was like.

No way, she said.

Please? Since you've done it uncountable times?

She slapped my face then, but not hard.

Okay, listen. She pressed her forehead against mine and I smelled the nicotine on her breath. It's different every time, she said. Sometimes it's passionate, and sometimes it's sweet, and sometimes it's just sad.

I tried to imagine having direct contact with those: passion and sweetness and sadness.

But I'll tell you one thing, she said. It's not like it is on TV. People don't actually scream like that.

° ° °

I always knew what that girl felt about me, even if I didn't get it. I've known since she came into my kitchen wearing my wife's shirt, and that gold material caught the light from the fixture above the table.

It took me a few seconds to recognize it, to understand what she'd done. To understand that the girl had been in my closet, handling my shirts and pants and belts. Clattering the hangers as she searched through my stuff for the one thing that would catch my eye. The one thing that would make me look at her, look at her different. Then she put it on, knowing exactly what I would feel, exactly how it would hurt. To see that shirt filled out, to see a body move and breathe inside it.

And then one night, so late it was almost morning, she came into my house. She walked up the stairs, through the hall, then opened my door. She stepped into my room.

"Hi," she said.

"Hi."

She sat beside me on the bed and I smelled rain on her, exhaust.

I didn't look at her, just asked, "What are you doing here?"

"I walked over from my place." She whispered. Aware, too, of Edith sleeping down the hall. "I've been thinking about the story you told."

I lay on my back and stared at the ceiling. "You should go home. I'll take you home."

"My parents talk a lot about right and wrong. But I don't believe in that."

And I thought of all of it—my wife, my daughter, the sky's frosts and floods. I looked at her, and she touched my arm. Her hand was cold from the air outside, and I said, "Me neither."

She nodded like she already knew that, and pulled out her ponytail. Her hair hung damp and knotted down her back. Then she unlaced her muddy boots and placed them beside the bed. She unbuttoned her shirt, folded it. Paused, as if thinking it through, then unzipped her dirt-hemmed jeans and slid them from her legs. She stretched herself out and lay beside me. Touched, carefully, the hair on my chest.

She was nervous too. I heard it in her breathing.

o o o

Most nights, she came into my room, then peeled off her T-shirt and jeans. I sat up and watched her do this, squinting through the dark. Then she'd climb into bed, put her arm around me, and say, Shh. Go back to sleep.

Not that night. That night, they thought I was warm in my bed, deaf and dumb. They didn't think the rain woke me. But I heard it. I heard her walk through the house and then I heard her open the wrong door—his, not mine. A mistake, a funny mistake. I expected her to burst into my room, gasping and laughing holy-shit-guess-what-I-just-did.

That night, my bed felt as big and cold as the sky. And if there was one thing I knew, it was that this wouldn't get easier. It would ache for years. That's what I've learned. That's what my father taught me.

o o o

After, we didn't know how to talk to each other. She lay on her back and breathed, air scraping along her throat. I picked up some of her hair, felt its weight, but she wouldn't look at me. The moon shone through the window, and I could see her pale lashes and the pale hair between her legs. She looked skinny. She looked seventeen.

I took a breath, as pained as hers. "Rae—"

"Don't say anything." She stared at the ceiling. She must have been used to these kinds of things being quick and rough—at a party, in the back of a truck. She'd probably never done that before. Been in a bed, beside a man.

She sat up and turned her back to me—embarrassed, now, to be naked. "I should go." She tied up her hair.

"You don't have to." I knew she'd never be in this house again. "You can stay awhile."

She put on her shirt and buttoned it. Then zipped her jeans, buckled her belt. I wanted to touch her arm, take her hand. But she pulled on her socks, laced her boots.

She walked down the stairs and I heard the front door open, then click shut behind her. The same door that flew off its hinges during the storm. The one I replaced with a tarp the next afternoon, the afternoon my wife left. The tarp didn't do much to keep out the cold. I sat at the kitchen table and listened to the wind catch and snap it all day. As I waited for the school bus to pull onto the highway's shoulder. As I wondered what I would tell my daughter, when she came home.

—2009

ACKNOWLEDGEMENTS

"Dead Men's Path," from *Girls at War and Other Stories* by Chinua Achebe. Copyright © 1953, 1972, 1973 by Chinua Achebe; used by permission of The Wylie Agency LLC and Doubleday, a division of Random House, Inc.

"Do You Know Where I Am?" from *Ten Little Indians* by Sherman Alexie, copyright © 2003; used by permission of Grove/Atlantic, Inc.

"Death by Landscape," from *Wilderness Tips* by Margaret Atwood, copyright © 1991 by O.W. Toad Limited. Used by permission of Doubleday, a division of Random House, Inc., McClelland & Stewart Ltd., and the author.

"Sonny's Blues," copyright © 1957 by James Baldwin, was originally published in Partisan Review. Copyright renewed. Collected in *Going to Meet the Man*, published by Vintage Books. Reprinted by arrangement with the James Baldwin Estate.

"Cathedral," from *Cathedral* by Raymond Carver, copyright © 1981, 1982, 1983 by Raymond Carver. Used by permission of Alfred A. Knopf, a division of Random House, Inc.

"My Lucy Friend Who Smells Like Corn," from *Woman Hollering Creek* by Sandra Cisneros, copyright © 1991. Published by Vintage Books, a division of Random House, Inc., and originally in hardcover by Random House, Inc. Used by permission of Susan Bergholz Literary Services, New York, NY and Lamy, NM. All rights reserved.

"A Rose for Emily," from *Collected Stories of William Faulkner* by William Faulkner, copyright © 1930 and renewed 1958 by William Faulkner. Used by permission of Random House, Inc.

"Under the Radar," from *A Multitude of Sins* by Richard Ford, copyright © 2001 by Richard Ford. Used by permission of Alfred A. Knopf, a division of Random House, Inc.

"Hills Like White Elephants," reprinted with the permission of Scribner, a Division of Simon & Schuster, Inc., from *The Short Stories of Ernest Hemingway* by Ernest Hemingway. Copyright © 1927 by Charles Scribner's Sons. Copyright renewed © 1955 by Ernest Hemingway. All rights reserved.

"The Raspberry Bush" by Sheila Heti. House of Anansi Press, 2001. Used with permission of the publisher.

"Girl," from *At the Bottom of the River* by Jamaica Kincaid. Copyright © 1983 by Jamaica Kincaid. Reprinted by permission of Farrar, Straus and Giroux, LLC.

"The Ones Who Walk Away from Omelas," copyright © 1973, 2001 by Ursula K. Le Guin; first appeared in *New Dimensions* 3. From *The Wind's Twelve Quarters*, reprinted by permission of the author and the Virginia Kidd Agency, Inc.

"In the Fall" by Alistair MacLeod. Canada: from *Island: The Collected Stories* by Alistair MacLeod © 2000. Emblem Editions 2001. Ebook edition 2010. Published by McClelland & Stewart Ltd. Used with permission of the author and the publisher. United States: from *Island: Complete Stories* by Alistair MacLeod. Copyright © 2000 by Alistair MacLeod. Used by permission of W.W. Norton & Company, Inc.

"The Lotus Eater," from *65 Short Stories* by Somerset Maugham, published by William Heinemann Ltd., 1976. Used with permission of the W. Somerset Maugham Trust and AP Watt Ltd. on behalf of The Royal Literary Fund.

"Swimming Lessons," from *Tales from Firozsha Baag* by Rohinton Mistry, copyright © 1987. Published by McClelland & Stewart Ltd., 2000. Used with permission of the author and publisher.

"You're Ugly, Too," from *Like Life* by Lorrie Moore, copyright © 1988, 1989, 1990 by Lorrie Moore. Used by permission of Alfred A. Knopf, a division of Random House, Inc.

"Gravel," by Alice Munro. Copyright © 2011 by Alice Munro. Used by permission of the author.

"Miles City, Montana," from *The Progress of Love* by Alice Munro, copyright © 1986 by Alice Munro. Used by permission of Alfred A. Knopf, a division of Random House, Inc., McClelland & Stewart Ltd., and the author.

"The Things They Carried," from *The Things They Carried* by Tim O'Brien, copyright © 1990 by Tim O'Brien. Reprinted by permission of Houghton Mifflin Harcourt Publishing Company. All rights reserved.

GLOSSARY

allegory A story with both a literal meaning and a second, less obvious meaning. This secondary narrative runs parallel to the action of the first (working as an extended **metaphor**) and presents a moral (religious or political) lesson. Characters often represent abstract concepts such as evil, justice, or faith. "The Minister's Black Veil" is an allegorical story about faith, sin, and human nature. See **fable** and **parable**.

allusion A direct or indirect reference in a literary work to a person, place, object, event, or artistic work. This reference is not elaborated upon in the work; rather, its effect depends upon the reader's understanding of the reference. For example, the allusion in "Under the Radar" to James Joyce's novel *Ulysses* (which in turn alludes to Homer's epic, *The Odyssey*) invites the reader to compare the apparently banal life and failing marriage of the story's **protagonist** with the adventures of the hero of the earlier work. (In this case, the reference is also a **parodic** one.) See **intertextuality**, **parody**, and **satire**.

ambiguity An "opening" of language created by the writer that allows for multiple meanings or differing interpretations. In literature, ambiguity may be deliberately employed to enrich meaning; this differs from any unintentional, unwanted ambiguity in non-literary prose.

analepsis See **flashback**.

archetype A **theme**, character, **symbol**, or event that recurs throughout literatures of different ages, cultures, and languages, and is therefore considered to reflect a conventional truth (or, sometimes, a stereotype) or a common human experience. The protagonist's walk along the dangerous path also suggests an archetypical theme (the descent to the underworld).

atmosphere See **tone**.

bathos In literature, an anticlimactic effect brought about by descending from elevated subject matter to the trivial or ordinary.

canon In literature, a collective term for those works that are commonly accepted as possessing authority or importance. In practice, "canonical" texts or authors are those that are discussed most frequently by scholars and taught most frequently in university courses.

characterization The means by which an author develops and presents a character's personality qualities, and distinguishing traits. A character may be established in the story by descriptive commentary or may be developed less directly—for example, through his or her words, actions, thoughts, and interactions with other characters.

chronology The way a story is organized in terms of time. Linear narratives run continuously from one point in time to a later point, while non-linear narratives are non-continuous and may jump forward and backward in time. A flashback, in which a story jumps to a scene previous in time, is an example of non-linearity.

closure The sense of completion evoked at the end of a story when all or most aspects of the major conflicts have been resolved. An example of the resolution of an internal conflict in "The Yellow Wallpaper" is the narrator's "merging" with the woman behind the paper. Not every story has a strong sense of closure.

comedy As a literary term, used originally to denote that class of ancient Greek drama in which the action ends happily. More broadly, the term has been used to describe a wide variety of literary forms of a more-or-less lighthearted character. See also **tragedy**.

conflict Struggles between characters and opposing forces. Conflict can be internal (psychological) or external (conflict with another character, for instance, or with society or nature). The narrator in "The Yellow Wallpaper" experiences an extreme internal conflict. An important element in "The Open Boat" is the (external) conflict between humans and nature.

connotation The implied, often unspoken meaning(s) of a given word or phrase, as distinct from its denotation, or literal meaning.

denotation See **connotation**.

denouement That portion of a narrative which follows a dramatic crisis, in which conflicts are resolved and the narrative is brought to a close. Traditional accounts of narrative structure often posit a triangle or arc, with rising action followed by a crisis and then by a denouement. (Such accounts bear little relation, however, to the ways in which most actual narratives are structured—particularly most twentieth and twenty-first century literary fictions.)

dialogue The words spoken by characters in a story.

diction The author's choice of words. Different types of diction (for example, formal or informal, simple or elaborate, concrete or abstract) produce different effects, and an author may vary diction according to the character, context, or intended purpose of the work. The diction in "My Lucy Friend

Who Smells Like Corn" is distinguished by colloquial language (slang, conversational usage) and helps establish the story's intimate **tone**. The story's seamless incorporation of Spanish words also evokes a particular cultural context.

embedded narrative A story contained within another story.

epiphany In literature, a moment at which matters of significance are suddenly illuminated for a literary character (or for the reader), typically triggered by something small and seemingly of little importance. The term first came into wide currency in connection with the fiction of James Joyce.

exposition In fiction, material that functions to provide information—to fill in background for the reader, to summarize parts of the story that have happened "off-stage," and/or to provide commentary on characters or situations.

fable A short **allegorical** tale that conveys an explicit moral lesson. The characters are often animals or objects with human speech and mannerisms. See **parable**.

fantasy In fiction, a sub-genre characterized by the presence of magical or miraculous elements—usually acknowledged as such by the characters and the narrative voice. In **magic realism**, by contrast, miraculous occurrences tend to be treated by the characters and/or the narrative voice as if they were entirely ordinary. In fantasy (also in contrast to magic realism), the fictional world generally has an internal consistency to it that precludes any sense of absurdity on the part of the reader; and the plot tends to build a strong sense of expectation in the reader.

fiction Imagined or invented narrative. In literature, the term is usually used to refer to prose narratives (such as novels and short stories).

first person narrative Narrative recounted using *I* and *me*. See also **narrative perspective**.

flashback In fiction, the inclusion in the primary thread of a story's narrative of a scene (or scenes) from an earlier point in time. Flashbacks may be used to revisit from a different viewpoint events that have already been recounted in the main thread of narrative; to present material that had been left out in the initial recounting; or to present relevant material from a time before the beginning of the main thread of narrative. The use of flashbacks in fiction is sometimes referred to as **analepsis**.

flashforward The inclusion in the primary thread of a story's narrative of a scene (or scenes) from a later point in time. See also **prolepsis**.

foreshadowing The inclusion of elements in a story that hint at some later development(s) in the same story. For example, in "A Good Man Is Hard to Find," the old family burying ground that the family sees on their drive foreshadows the violence that follows.

form Generally, form refers to the shape and structure of a work, which can be described by referring to (for example) its **genre**, and to the organization of its various components (such as **plot**, **diction**, **characters**, and **style**).

free indirect discourse In prose fiction, commentary in which a seemingly objective and omniscient narrative voice assumes the point of view of one or more characters. When we hear through the third person narrative voice of Jane Austen's *Pride and Prejudice*, for example, that Mr. Darcy "was the proudest, most disagreeable man in the world, and everybody hoped that he would never come there again," the narrative voice has assumed the point of view of "everybody in the community"; we as readers are not meant to take it that Mr. Darcy is indeed the most disagreeable man in the world. Similarly, in the following passage from James Joyce's "The Dead," we are meant to take it as being the view of the character Gabriel that Miss Ivors "had no right to call him a West Briton" and had "tried to make him ridiculous," not to take it as an objective statement of truth on the part of the novel's third-person narrative voice:

> Gabriel tried to banish from his mind all memory of the unpleasant incident with Miss Ivors. Of course the girl or woman, or whatever she was, was an enthusiast but there was a time for all things. Perhaps he ought not to have answered her like that. But she had no right to call him a West Briton before people, even in joke. She had tried to make him ridiculous before people, heckling him and staring at him with her rabbit's eyes.

The inclusion here of phrases such as "he thought that" ("But he thought that she had no right to...") would have the effect of making the narrative perspective more plain to the reader—but it would also make the prose less immediate in its tone, and more wordy.

The term "free indirect discourse" is also sometimes applied to situations in which it may not be entirely clear if the thoughts expressed emanate from the character, the narrator, or some combination of the two.

genre Class or type of literary work. The concept of genre may be used with different levels of generality. At the most general, poetry, drama, and prose fiction are distinguished as separate genres. At a lower level of generality various sub-genres are frequently distinguished, such as (within the genre of prose fiction) the novel, the novella, and the short story; and, at a still lower level of generality, the mystery novel, the detective novel, the novel of manners, and so on.

Gothic In architecture and the visual arts, a term used to describe styles prevalent from the twelfth to the fourteenth centuries, but in literature a term used to describe work with a sinister or grotesque tone that seeks to evoke a sense of terror on the part of the reader or audience. Gothic literature originated as a genre in the eighteenth century with works such as Horace Walpole's *The Castle of Otranto*. To some extent the notion of the medieval itself then carried with it associations of the dark and the grotesque, but from the beginning an element of intentional exaggeration (sometimes verging on self-parody) attached itself to the genre. The Gothic trend of youth culture that began in the late twentieth century is less clearly associated with the medieval, but shares with the various varieties of Gothic literature (from Walpole in the eighteenth century, to Bram Stoker in the early twentieth, to Stephen King and Anne Rice in the late twentieth) a fondness for the sensational and the grotesque, as well as a propensity to self-parody.

"The Cask of Amontillado" is one story in this anthology that incorporates many elements of the Gothic.

grotesque Literature of the grotesque is characterized by a focus on extreme or distorted aspects of human characteristics. (The term can also refer particularly to a character who is odd or disturbing.) This focus can serve to comment on and challenge societal norms. The story "A Good Man Is Hard to Find" employs elements of the grotesque.

imagery Words or phrases about something within the physical world (an action, sight, sound, smell, taste, or touch) that illustrate something about a story's characters, settings, or situations. The imagery of spring (budding trees, rain, singing birds) in "The Story of an Hour" reinforces the suggestions of death and rebirth in the plot and theme.

implied author See **narrator**.

intertextuality The relationships between one literary work and other literary works. **Allusion**, imitation, **parody**, and **satire** are examples of intertextuality.

irony A discrepancy between an apparent reality or statement and its meaning. Three types of irony are verbal irony (in which there is an apparent discrepancy between what is said and what is meant), situational irony (when an event turns out very differently than expected), and dramatic irony (when the reader and sometimes other characters know something that one character does not know). In "Cathedral," the narrator's confession (that he "didn't think much" of his wife's poem, because, he says, "I just don't understand poetry") is a verbal irony. In "The Story of an Hour," the protagonist's reaction to the news of her husband's death is a situational irony. In "The Yellow Wallpaper," the narrator's obsession with the woman behind the paper is a dramatic irony. See also **parody** and **satire**.

magic realism A style of fiction in which miraculous or bizarre things often happen but are treated in a matter-of-fact fashion by the characters and/or the narrative voice. There is often an element of the absurd to magic realist narratives, and they tend not to have any strong plot structure generating expectations in the reader's mind. See also **fantasy**.

melodrama Originally a term used to describe nineteenth-century plays featuring sensational story lines and a crude separation of characters into moral categories, with the pure and virtuous pitted against evil villains. Early melodramas employed background music throughout the action of the play as a means of heightening the emotional response of the audience. By extension, certain sorts of prose fictions or poems are often described as having melodramatic elements.

metafiction Fiction that calls attention to itself as fiction, in an effort to explore the relationships between fiction and reality. Examples of metafictional situations occur when the writing refers to the act of reading or writing, or an author seems to insert him or herself into the story as a character, or an author seems to address the reader directly or interrupt the narrative. In "The Yellow Wallpaper," the fictional situation of the narrator's relationship to her writing has implications for the significance of the story itself, because this suggests the possibility of certain relationships between "The Yellow Wallpaper," its author, and its reader.

metaphor A *figure of speech* (in this case, a trope) in which a comparison is made or identity is asserted between two unrelated things or actions without the use of "like" or "as." The primary subject is known as the *tenor*; to illuminate its nature, the writer links it to wholly different images, ideas, or actions (referred to as the *vehicle*). Unlike a **simile**, which is a direct comparison of two things, a metaphor "fuses" the separate qualities of two things, creating a new idea. For example, in "The Open Boat" the captain speaks to the other men in the boat, "soothing his children." The metaphor likens the relationship between captain and men (the tenor) to that between parent and children (the vehicle). The same idea expressed in a simile would be less concise; in place of "soothing his children" one might write "speaking to his men as if they were his children."

modernism In the history of literature, music, and the visual arts, a movement that began in the early twentieth century, characterized by a thoroughgoing rejection of the then-dominant conventions of literary plotting and characterization, of melody and harmony, and of perspective and other naturalistic forms of visual representation. In literature (as in music and the visual arts), Modernists endeavoured to represent the complexity of what seemed to them to be an increasingly fragmented world by adopting techniques of presenting story material, illuminating character, and employing imagery that emphasized (in the words of Virginia Woolf) "the spasmodic, the obscure, the fragmentary."

motif An idea, image, action, or plot element that recurs throughout a literary work, creating new levels of meaning and strengthening structural coherence. The term is taken from music, where it describes recurring melodies or themes. The recurring focus on blindness in "Cathedral" is suggestive of the narrator's isolation and lack of emotional bearings or direction.

motivation The forces that seem to cause characters to act, or why characters do what they do.

narration The process of storytelling.

narrative perspective In fiction, the point of view from which the story is narrated. A first-person narrative is recounted using *I* and me, whereas a third-person narrative is recounted using *he*, *she*, *they*, and so on. (Second person narratives, in which the story is recounted using *you*, are extremely rare.) When a narrative is written in the third person and the narrative voice evidently "knows" all that is being done and thought, the story is typically described as being recounted by an "omniscient narrator." Third person narratives may also present limited perspectives, however; whether writing in the third person or the first person, authors will sometimes intentionally present narrative perspectives that the reader will have grounds to interpret as unreliable. (See also **free indirect discourse**, **stream of consciousness**.)

narrator The voice (or voices) telling the story. The narrator is distinct from both the author (a real, historical person) and the implied author (whom the reader imagines the author to be). Narrators can be distinguished according to the degree to which they share the reality of the other characters in the story and the extent to which they participate in the action; according to how much information they are privy to (and how much of that information they are willing to share with the reader); and according to whether or not they are perceived by the reader as reliable or unreliable sources of information. See also **narrative perspective**.

omniscient narrator See **narrative perspective**.

parable A brief allegorical story that illustrates a moral or lesson. The term is religious in origin, referring to the stories told by Jesus in the New Testament. Unlike the characters in **fables**, the characters in parables are usually human. "The Raspberry Bush," because of its brevity, structural simplicity, **characterization** (the folktale-like "little old woman"), and lesson in loneliness and sympathy, can be read as a parable.

parody Parody (a type of **satire**) is the imitation of another literary work or style in order to ridicule a target. Parody is recognizable by the extent to which the imitation differs from its original model in a ludicrous way; this difference is achieved by exaggerating or debasing (or otherwise making ridiculous) some aspect of the original. See **intertextuality**, **allusion**, and **satire**.

pathos An appeal to (or the technique of appealing to) the emotions of the reader or listener. In ancient Greece pathos was defined as one of the three methods through which persuasion might be accomplished (the others being **logos**—persuasion through words offering reasoned argument; and **ethos**—persuasion through the presentation of heroic or otherwise ethically admirable characters). In discussing literature the term pathos is most often applied to works (or scenes within works) that arouse feelings of pity or sorrow in the reader or audience through the presentation of narrative material concerning pain, suffering, or loss.

persona The assumed identity or "speaking voice" that a writer projects in a discourse. The term "persona" literally means "mask."

personification A figure of speech in which objects, ideas, or non-human animals are referred to as if they were human (or in which a human figure is created to represent abstract entities such as Wisdom or Peace). An example of personification occurs in "The Open Boat" when the shore is described as "lonely."

plot The organization of story materials within a literary work. The order in which story material is presented; the inclusion of elements that allow or encourage the reader or audience to form expectations as to what is likely to happen; the decision to present story material directly to the reader as part of the narrative or to have it recounted in summary form through exposition—all these are matters of plotting.

"The Story of an Hour" may be used to illustrate the difference between story and plot. It is a story of the aftermath of a railway accident; it is also the story of a marriage. One might have plotted this story material in myriad different ways—showing husband and wife interacting with each other over a more extended period, for example, or narrating the accident directly (rather than having it reported as something that has happened "offstage"), or including material that encouraged the reader to be open to the possibility that the husband may have survived the accident. Instead the story's plot arranges the material so as to focus on only one hour, and on the thoughts and feelings during that hour of only one of the characters.

point of view See **narrative perspective**.

postmodernism In literature and the visual arts, a movement influential in the late twentieth and early twenty-first centuries. In some ways postmodernism represents a reaction to modernism, in others an extension of it. With roots in the work of French philosophers such as Jacques Derrida and Michel Foucault, it is deeply coloured by theory; indeed, it may be said to have begun at the "meta" level of theorizing rather than at the level of practice. It is notoriously resistant to definition—indeed, resistance to fixed definitions is itself a characteristic of postmodernism. Like modernism, postmodernism embraces difficulty and distrusts the simple and straightforward. More broadly, postmodernism is characterized by a rejection of absolute truth or value, of closed systems, of grand unified narratives.

Postmodernist fiction is characterized by a frequently ironic or playful tone in dealing with reality and illusion; by a willingness to combine different styles or forms in a single work (just as in architecture the postmodernist spirit embodies a willingness to borrow from seemingly disparate styles in designing a single structure); and by a highly attuned awareness of the problematized state of the writer, artist, or theorist as observer.

prolepsis Originally a rhetorical term used to refer to the anticipation of possible objections by someone advancing an argument, prolepsis is used in discussions of fiction to refer to elements in a narrative that anticipate the future of the story. The **flashforward** technique of storytelling is often described as a form of prolepsis; the inclusion in a narrative of material that foreshadows future developments is also sometimes treated as a form of prolepsis.

protagonist The central character in a literary work.

realism An approach to literature that endeavours to represent the world in ways that are true to real life. Just as notions of what constitutes "real life" may vary widely, so too has "realism" taken on a variety of meanings. The term "realism" (and later, the term **naturalism**) originated in the nineteenth century to denote literature that eschewed romance and that did not shy away from presenting the grim, unpleasant, and ugly aspects of the real. In the twentieth century **social realism** became a term used to convey very similar notions, while also suggesting that the most important defining conditions of reality are broad social conditions that are susceptible to political forces—and that can be changed by political activism. The term **psychological realism**, on the other hand, refers to fiction that endeavours to portray persuasively the perceptions of one or more individuals. (When the term "realistic" is used to refer to fiction that features plausible and consistent characters, settings, and situations, it is psychological realism that is being drawn attention to.) See also **magic realism**.

satire A literary work designed to make fun of (and, often, seriously criticize) human failings, social evils, and corrupt institutions. See also **parody**.

setting The time, place, and cultural environment in which a story takes place.

simile The comparison of one thing with another, using the words "as" or "like." The story "A Good Man Is Hard to Find," for example, includes the simile "the line of woods gaped like a dark open mouth." See also **metaphor**.

story Narrative material, independent of the manner in which it may be presented or the ways in which the narrative material may be organized. Story is thus distinct from **plot** (see above).

stream of consciousness A narrative technique that conveys the inner workings of a character's mind, in which a character's thoughts, feelings, memories, and impressions are related in an unbroken flow, without concern for **chronology** or coherence. The technique was perhaps most famously employed by James Joyce in *Ulysses* (1922); that novel concludes with a 44-page monologue from the point of view of the character Molly Bloom, which opens in this way:

> yes because he never did a thing like that before as ask to get his breakfast in bed with a couple of eggs since the *City Arms* hotel when he used to be pretending to be laid up with a sick voice doing his highness to make himself interesting to that old faggot Mrs Riordan that he thought he had a great leg of and she never left us a farthing all for masses for herself and her soul greatest miser ever was actually afraid to lay out 4d for her methylated spirit telling me all her ailments she had too much old chat in her about politics and earthquakes and the end of the world let us have a bit of fun first …

Some critics apply the term "stream of consciousness" only to passages such as this one, which are written entirely in the first person. The term is also often used more loosely, though, to refer to any one of (or combination of) a range of techniques that attempt to convey in prose fiction a sense of the progression of thoughts and sensations occurring within a character's mind; extended passages of prose fiction written in **free indirect discourse**, for example, are often described as employing a stream of consciousness technique.

style A distinctive or specific use of language and form.

subtext Implicit or unstated meaning. There is a strong sense of subtext in "Hills Like White Elephants," where much of the story's meaning is suggested by the characters' silence.

symbol Something that represents another thing (an idea, quality, or another object, for example) beyond or in addition to itself. Homer's yellow glove in "A Rose for Emily" (as one example) symbolizes his concern with style.

theme A central idea, unifying principle, or underlying message of a story. A single work may have a number of themes. A predominant theme in "The Open Boat," for example, is nature's indifference to human suffering.

third person narrative A narrative in which there is no *I* or *me* in the story; all the characters are seen "from the outside" as *he*, *she*, or *they*. See also **narrative perspective**.

tone The overall or most dominant impression produced by a work; its **atmosphere** or mood. For example, stories may be bleak, humorous, hopeful, romantic, alienating, wry, or suspenseful in tone.

tragedy In the traditional definition originating from discussions of ancient Greek drama, a serious narrative recounting the downfall of the protagonist. More loosely, the term has been applied to a wide variety of literary forms in which the tone is predominantly a dark one and the narrative does not end happily.

trope Any figure of speech that plays on our understanding of words to extend, alter, or transform "literal" meaning. Common tropes include **metaphor**, **simile**, **personification**, hyperbole, metonymy, oxymoron, and **irony**.

unreliable narrator See **narrative perspective**.

CHRONOLOGY

Publication dates indicate first publication in book form, with exceptions noted.* Please see introductions for more information.

Nathaniel Hawthorne (1804–64)
THE MINISTER'S BLACK VEIL (1836)*

Edgar Allan Poe (1809–49)
THE BLACK CAT (1843)*
THE TELL-TALE HEART (1843)*

Nathaniel Hawthorne
YOUNG GOODMAN BROWN (1846)

Edgar Allan Poe
THE CASK OF AMONTILLADO (1846)*

Herman Melville (1819–91)
BARTLEBY, THE SCRIVENER (1856)

Guy de Maupassant (1850–93)
THE NECKLACE (1884)*

Anton Chekhov (1860–1904)
AN UPHEAVAL (1886)

Charlotte Perkins Gilman (1860–1935)
THE YELLOW WALLPAPER (1892)*

Thomas Hardy (1840–1928)
THE SON'S VETO (1894)

Kate Chopin (1851–1904)
THE STORY OF AN HOUR (1894)*

* *periodical publication*

Stephen Crane (1871–1900)
THE OPEN BOAT (1898)

James Joyce (1882–1941)
THE DEAD (1914)
ARABY (1914)
EVELINE (1914)

Katherine Mansfield (1888–1923)
THE DOLL'S HOUSE (1922)*
THE GARDEN PARTY (1922)*

Ernest Hemingway (1899–1961)
HILLS LIKE WHITE ELEPHANTS (1927)

William Faulkner (1897–1962)
A ROSE FOR EMILY (1930)*

Somerset Maugham (1874–1965)
THE LOTUS EATER (1935)*

Hisaye Yamamoto (1921–2011)
SEVENTEEN SYLLABLES (1949)*

Chinua Achebe (b. 1930)
DEAD MEN'S PATH (1953)

Flannery O'Connor (1925–64)
A GOOD MAN IS HARD TO FIND (1953)

James Baldwin (1924–87)
SONNY'S BLUES (1957)*

Ursula K. Le Guin (b. 1929)
THE ONES WHO WALK AWAY FROM OMELAS (1973)

Alistair MacLeod (b. 1936)
IN THE FALL (1973)*

Raymond Carver (1938–88)
CATHEDRAL (1983)

Jamaica Kincaid (b. 1949)
GIRL (1983)

Alice Munro (b. 1931)
MILES CITY, MONTANA (1986)

Rohinton Mistry (b. 1952)
SWIMMING LESSONS (1987)

Lorrie Moore (b. 1957)
YOU'RE UGLY, TOO (1989)*

Tim O'Brien (b. 1946)
THE THINGS THEY CARRIED (1990)

Margaret Atwood (b. 1939)
DEATH BY LANDSCAPE (1991)

Sandra Cisneros (b. 1954)
MY LUCY FRIEND WHO SMELLS LIKE CORN (1991)

Tobias Wolff (b. 1945)
POWDER (1996)

Eden Robinson (b. 1968)
QUEEN OF THE NORTH (1996)

Gloria Sawai (b. 1932)
MOTHER'S DAY (2001)

Sheila Heti (b. 1976)
THE RASPBERRY BUSH (2001)

Richard Ford (b. 1944)
UNDER THE RADAR (2001)

Sherman Alexie (b. 1966)
DO YOU KNOW WHERE I AM? (2002)*

Shaun Tan (b. 1974)
GRANDPA'S STORY (2008)

Deborah Willis (b. 1982)
THE WEATHER (2009)

Alice Munro (b. 1931)
GRAVEL (2011)*

Ian Williams (b. 1979)
BREAK-IN (2011)

The interior of this book is printed on 30% recycled paper.